The
MX Book
of
New
Sherlock
Holmes
Stories

Part XXXV
"However Improbable . . . ."
(1889-1896)

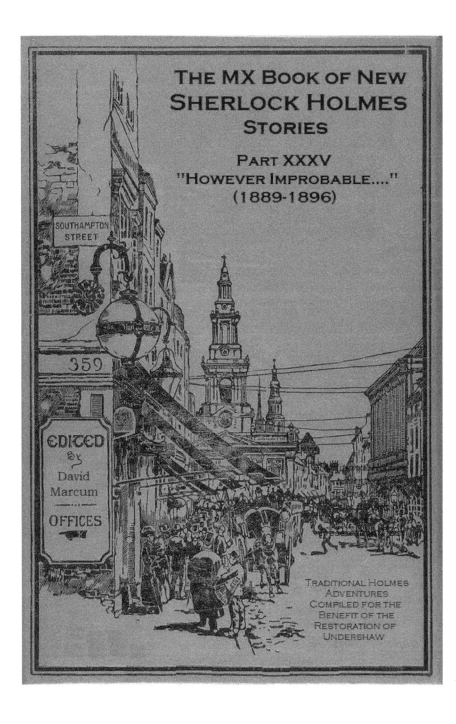

THE MX BOOK OF NEW SHERLOCK HOLMES STORIES

STORIES

PART XXXV
"HOWEVER IMPROBABLE...."
(1889-1896)

SOUTHAMPTON STREET

359

EDITED By David Marcum

OFFICES

TRADITIONAL HOLMES ADVENTURES COMPILED FOR THE BENEFIT OF THE RESTORATION OF UNDERSHAW

ISBN Hardback 978-1-80424-109-7
ISBN Paperback 978-1-80424-110-3
AUK ePub ISBN 978-1-80424-111-0
AUK PDF ISBN 978-1-80424-112-7

Published in the UK by
MX Publishing
335 Princess Park Manor, Royal Drive,
London, N11 3GX
www.mxpublishing.co.uk

David Marcum can be reached at:
thepapersofsherlockholmes@gmail.com

Cover design by Brian Belanger
www.belangerbooks.com and *www.redbubble.com/people/zhahadun*

Internal Illustrations by Sidney Paget

CONTENTS

Forewords

Adventures

(Continued on the next page . . . .)

(Continued on the next page . . . .)

(Continued on the next page . . . .)

These additional Sherlock Holmes adventures
can be found in the previous volumes of
The MX Book of New Sherlock Holmes Stories

(Continued on the next page . . . .)

PART III: 1896-1929

PART IV – 2016 Annual

(Continued on the next page . . . .)

PART V – Christmas Adventures

(Continued on the next page . . . .)

PART VI – 2017 Annual

(Continued on the next page . . . .)

The Unwelcome Client – Keith Hann
The Tempest of Lyme – David Ruffle
The Problem of the Holy Oil – David Marcum
A Scandal in Serbia – Thomas A. Turley
The Curious Case of Mr. Marconi – Jan Edwards
Mr. Holmes and Dr. Watson Learn to Fly – C. Edward Davis
Die Weisse Frau – Tim Symonds
A Case of Mistaken Identity – Daniel D. Victor

PART VII – Eliminate the Impossible: 1880-1891

Foreword – Lee Child
Foreword – Rand B. Lee
Foreword – Michael Cox
Foreword – Roger Johnson
Foreword – Melissa Farnham
Foreword – David Marcum
No Ghosts Need Apply (A Poem) – Jacquelynn Morris
The Melancholy Methodist – Mark Mower
The Curious Case of the Sweated Horse – Jan Edwards
The Adventure of the Second William Wilson – Daniel D. Victor
The Adventure of the Marchindale Stiletto – James Lovegrove
The Case of the Cursed Clock – Gayle Lange Puhl
The Tranquility of the Morning – Mike Hogan
A Ghost from Christmas Past – Thomas A. Turley
The Blank Photograph – James Moffett
The Adventure of A Rat. – Adrian Middleton
The Adventure of Vanaprastha – Hugh Ashton
The Ghost of Lincoln – Geri Schear
The Manor House Ghost – S. Subramanian
The Case of the Unquiet Grave – John Hall
The Adventure of the Mortal Combat – Jayantika Ganguly
The Last Encore of Quentin Carol – S.F. Bennett
The Case of the Petty Curses – Steven Philip Jones
The Tuttman Gallery – Jim French
The Second Life of Jabez Salt – John Linwood Grant
The Mystery of the Scarab Earrings – Thomas Fortenberry
The Adventure of the Haunted Room – Mike Chinn
The Pharaoh's Curse – Robert V. Stapleton
The Vampire of the Lyceum – Charles Veley and Anna Elliott
The Adventure of the Mind's Eye – Shane Simmons

PART VIII – Eliminate the Impossible: 1892-1905

Foreword – Lee Child
Foreword – Rand B. Lee
Foreword – Michael Cox
Foreword – Roger Johnson
Foreword – Melissa Farnham

(Continued on the next page . . . .)

Part IX – 2018 Annual (1879-1895)

(Continued on the next page . . . .)

(Continued on the next page . . . .)

(Continued on the next page . . . .)

PART XIV: 2019 Annual (1891 -1897)

(Continued on the next page . . . .)

(Continued on the next page . . . .)

Part XVII – Whatever Remains . . . Must Be the Truth (1891-1898)

Part XVIII – Whatever Remains . . . Must Be the Truth (1899-1925)

(Continued on the next page . . . .)

The Tollington Ghost – Roger Silverwood
You Only Live Thrice – Robert Stapleton
The Adventure of the Fair Lad – Craig Janacek
The Adventure of the Voodoo Curse – Gareth Tilley
The Cassandra of Providence Place – Paul Hiscock
The Adventure of the House Abandoned – Arthur Hall
The Winterbourne Phantom – M.J. Elliott
The Murderous Mercedes – Harry DeMaio
The Solitary Violinist – Tom Turley
The Cunning Man – Kelvin I. Jones
The Adventure of Khamaat's Curse – Tracy J. Revels
The Adventure of the Weeping Mary – Matthew White
The Unnerved Estate Agent – David Marcum
Death in The House of the Black Madonna – Nick Cardillo
The Case of the Ivy-Covered Tomb – S.F. Bennett

Part XIX: 2020 Annual (1882-1890)

Foreword – John Lescroart
Foreword – Roger Johnson
Foreword – Lizzy Butler
Foreword – Steve Emecz
Foreword – David Marcum
Holmes's Prayer (*A Poem*) – Christopher James
A Case of Paternity – Matthew White
The Raspberry Tart – Roger Riccard
The Mystery of the Elusive Bard – Kevin P. Thornton
The Man in the Maroon Suit – Chris Chan
The Scholar of Silchester Court – Nick Cardillo
The Adventure of the Changed Man – MJH. Simmonds
The Adventure of the Tea-Stained Diamonds – Craig Stephen Copland
The Indigo Impossibility – Will Murray
The Case of the Emerald Knife-Throwers – Ian Ableson
A Game of Skittles – Thomas A. Turley
The Gordon Square Discovery – David Marcum
The Tattooed Rose – Dick Gillman
The Problem at Pentonville Prison – David Friend
The Nautch Night Case – Brenda Seabrooke
The Disappearing Prisoner – Arthur Hall
The Case of the Missing Pipe – James Moffett
The Whitehaven Ransom – Robert Stapleton
The Enlightenment of Newton – Dick Gillman
The Impaled Man – Andrew Bryant
The Mystery of the Elusive Li Shen – Will Murray
The Mahmudabad Result – Andrew Bryant

(Continued on the next page . . . .)

The Adventure of the Matched Set – Peter Coe Verbica
When the Prince First Dined at the Diogenes Club – Sean M. Wright
The Sweetenbury Safe Affair – Tim Gambrell

Part XX: 2020 Annual (1891-1897)
Foreword – John Lescroart
Foreword – Roger Johnson
Foreword – Lizzy Butler
Foreword – Steve Emecz
Foreword – David Marcum
The Sibling (*A Poem*) – Jacquelynn Morris
Blood and Gunpowder – Thomas A. Burns, Jr.
The Atelier of Death – Harry DeMaio
The Adventure of the Beauty Trap – Tracy Revels
A Case of Unfinished Business – Steven Philip Jones
The Case of the S.S. Bokhara – Mark Mower
The Adventure of the American Opera Singer – Deanna Baran
The Keadby Cross – David Marcum
The Adventure at Dead Man's Hole – Stephen Herczeg
The Elusive Mr. Chester – Arthur Hall
The Adventure of Old Black Duffel – Will Murray
The Blood-Spattered Bridge – Gayle Lange Puhl
The Tomorrow Man – S.F. Bennett
The Sweet Science of Bruising – Kevin P. Thornton
The Mystery of Sherlock Holmes – Christopher Todd
The Elusive Mr. Phillimore – Matthew J. Elliott
The Murders in the Maharajah's Railway Carriage – Charles Veley and Anna Elliott
The Ransomed Miracle – I.A. Watson
The Adventure of the Unkind Turn – Robert Perret
The Perplexing X'ing – Sonia Fetherston
The Case of the Short-Sighted Clown – Susan Knight

Part XXI: 2020 Annual (1898-1923)
Foreword – John Lescroart
Foreword – Roger Johnson
Foreword – Lizzy Butler
Foreword – Steve Emecz
Foreword – David Marcum
The Case of the Missing Rhyme (*A Poem*) – Joseph W. Svec III
The Problem of the St. Francis Parish Robbery – R.K. Radek
The Adventure of the Grand Vizier – Arthur Hall
The Mummy's Curse – DJ Tyrer
The Fractured Freemason of Fitzrovia – David L. Leal
The Bleeding Heart – Paula Hammond
The Secret Admirer – Jayantika Ganguly

(Continued on the next page . . . .)

Part XXII: Some More Untold Cases (1877-1887)

(Continued on the next page . . . .)

(Continued on the next page . . . .)

Part XXV: 2021 Annual (1881-1888)

(Continued on the next page . . . .)

(Continued on the next page . . . .)

Part XXVIII: More Christmas Adventures (1869-1888)

(Continued on the next page . . . .)

Part XXIX: More Christmas Adventures (1889-1896)

(Continued on the next page . . . .)

Part XXX: More Christmas Adventures (1897-1928)

(Continued on the next page . . . .)

(Continued on the next page . . . .)

Part XXXIII 2022 Annual (1896-1919)

(Continued on the next page . . . .)

The following contributors appear
in the companion volumes:
Part XXXIV – "However Improbable . . . ." (1878-1888)
Part XXXVI – "However Improbable . . . ." (1897-1919)

The Dramatic Moment of Fate
by David Marcum

"Now is the dramatic moment of fate, Watson, when you hear a step upon the stair which is walking into your life, and you know not whether for good or ill."

– Sherlock Holmes
The Hound of the Baskervilles

In early 2022, we celebrated the 168th birthday of Mr. Sherlock Holmes, (born on January 6th, 1954). We're racing toward his *bicentennial*. That's a true *Good grief!* realization. (And if you think those next thirty-two years to 2054 won't fly by, you're either kidding yourself or still very young. By the time these current volumes see print, we'll almost be celebrating Holmes's *169th*!)

When I was a ten-year-old kid, discovering Mr. Holmes in the mid-1970's, the days of gaslight and hansom cabs were already long gone – but I knew some people who still remembered those days. Just imagine the changes that they lived through. My grandparents were born into the era of horse-drawn vehicles. (My dad's father and mother bought the first automobile ever driven in their small town.) They lived to see the world go from that type of existence to a man landing on the moon. Now, with our own exponential technological advances, we're also seeing changes moving at an even swifter pace. But for many, there's something deep inside that looks backward to different, supposedly simpler, times – and those are farther away with each passing year.

The Holmes Era – essentially the final third of Queen Victoria's reign and the Edwardian era, give or take a few years – conjures up definite images of dark and mysterious London streets and passages, often occluded by rolling fogs. Cabs and carriages carry finely dressed people past pedestrians who could have never afforded a cab ride in their entire lives. There was the rigid formality and ritual for those who *had*, and the scrambling, dangerous, and often short existence of those who *had not* – with all of them living jammed together in the space of just a few square miles.

London's wealthiest sector – the wealthiest sector, in fact, in the whole world – was located within just a few blocks of the City's poorest. These societal extremes must have been mightily confusing. There were

1

expected rules and behaviors that could not be violated. And while the cities pulled all of these conflicting layers tightly together, many rural areas remained just as remote as they had been for centuries. The countryside was dotted here and there with pockets of industry, extending their influence a bit more each year by way of railway tendrils – but only along profitable paths, leaving other vast tracts in isolation.

It was a time when science was revered and pursued by some – academics and gentleman amateurs – while at the same time many embraced superstition and ignorance with enthusiasm and anger by way of mediums and spiritualists. Often it was far too easy for the ignorant to proudly believe that the impossible was possible, consciously choosing to ignore science and knowledge and fact.

And in the midst of this chaos – rich and poor, knowledgeable and willfully ignorant – one clear note began to be noticed, quiet at first, almost beyond hearing, but gradually becoming stronger and more steady, resolving the various discordant tones around it. This note – possibly one could liken it to a steady air on a single Stradivarius string – brought in some small way balance to societal disparity, and light to shadowed and intentional disregard of knowledge.

This resolving influence was Sherlock Holmes.

The human mind is, by nature, drawn to the mysterious, from big questions like what happens after death, to the small, such as what's around that next curve or over that far hill. In the years when Sherlock Holmes was in practice, England was a peculiar stew of modern science and method, along with centuries of acceptance that humans were at the inevitable mercy of an overarching Fate on a grand scale, or mysterious, deadly, and immediate creatures in the shadows right outside the door. Holmes believed that answers could be found – *must be found* – or else mankind, at the bottom of things, had no course but to be blown without choice in whatever direction the fateful wind sent him.

"*No ghosts need apply,*" he famously told Watson in "The Sussex Vampire", refusing to believe in a supernatural explanation for a series of mysterious wounds. This four-word quote is often pulled out and referenced to indicate that Holmes had no use specifically for belief in *ghosts*, but to understand its wider implication, the entire quote must be recalled:

> "*But are we to give serious attention to such things? This agency stands flat-footed upon the ground, and there it must remain. The world is big enough for us. No ghosts need apply.*"

He refers to the *"agency"* – the team of Holmes and Watson – being *"flat-footed"*. Defined by Merriam-Webster, this means *"proceeding in a plodding or unimaginative way"* – or perhaps in a better light, *"in an open and determined manner"*.

Holmes often decries the lack of imagination shown by the Scotland Yarders – they accept the easiest explanation without attempting to see to a deeper layer, or to imagine what might actually have happened. But when Holmes himself shows imagination, it is in a *"flat-footed upon the ground"* way. No ghosts – or any impossibilities for that matter – will be considered, for to do so opens a door that cannot be shut, and the involvement of too many possibilities. If murder suspects include both the likely human candidates and the countless dead who might have involved themselves, then there is no possibility for resolution.

Holmes had no use for the impossible. Why waste time considering something that is *impossible*? Eliminate it, and one will inevitably narrow in upon the true solution, however improbable. In The Canon, he references this method a number of times:

> *"How often have I said to you that when you have eliminated the impossible whatever remains, however improbable, must be the truth?"* and also *"Eliminate all other factors, and the one which remains must be the truth."* – The Sign of Four

> *"It is an old maxim of mine that when you have excluded the impossible, whatever remains, however improbable, must be the truth."* – "The Beryl Coronet"

> *"We must fall back upon the old axiom that when all other contingencies fail, whatever remains, however improbable, must be the truth."* – "The Bruce-Partington Plans"

> *"That process . . . starts upon the supposition that when you have eliminated all which is impossible, then whatever remains, however improbable, must be the truth."* – "The Blanched Soldier"

Too often, because Sherlock Holmes is such a heroic figure, there is the temptation to place him in impossible stories, with situations ranging from absolutely incorrect, where he's living and working in the modern world instead of the correct time period, to having him face actual monsters, serving as a pop-in substitute for Van Helsing or Kolchak the Night Stalker. If a story has these impossible aspects, *then it isn't a*

3

Sherlock Holmes story, but rather a *simulacrum*, with a *faux* Holmes acting out all the Holmes-like parts and making the familiar motions in a situation that would never have actually been a part of Holmes's experience.

Besides the incorrect stories where Holmes is frozen and then thawed in modern times like an amusing duck-out-of-water, or the impossible situations of a modern-day character having absolutely nothing in common with Holmes but a stolen name, there are the efforts to have him battle aliens, vampires, werewolves, and ancient Lovecraftian horrors, and at some point in the story, one is dismayed to find that these turn out to be actual aliens, vampires, werewolves, and ancient Lovecraftian horrors. They might be well written by an author that one respects – but when encountering these, listen for that one clear note, quiet at first, almost beyond hearing, but gradually becoming stronger and more steady. This note has lyrics to resolve the discord:

> *"But are we to give serious attention to such things? This agency stands flat-footed upon the ground, and there it must remain. The world is big enough for us. No ghosts need apply."*

This resolving influence is Sherlock Holmes, and *No ghosts need apply.*

This series of anthologies started because the True Sherlock Holmes was being slowly worn away and diminished. There was a rise of simulacrums – modern Holmes, damaged Holmes, broken Holmes, monster-fighting Holmes. That version was creeping into the public perception of who Holmes truly was like a penumbral shadow sliding across the sun. Too often aspects of these incorrect versions were being included in what were supposed to be representations of the True Holmes, and it was feared that soon the True Holmes would be lost in the umbra.

These volumes have always had the overall basic requirement that the stories *must* present Holmes and Watson as *heroes*, and that the stories can stand alongside the original Canonical efforts that appeared in *The Strand.* It turns out that there was a need for stories like that, as many authors wanted to be part of such an effort, and many readers wanted to experience it. When I first started soliciting stories for these books in early 2015, I truly believed I'd be lucky to get a dozen for a small paperback book. As that year progressed, more and more authors heard about the project and wanted to contribute, and that small beginning led to three simultaneously published hardcover volumes with over sixty stories – Parts I, II and III –

the largest Holmes anthology of its type at that time. We've since surpassed it in a number of ways.

From the beginning, all author royalties have been donated to the Undershaw school for special needs children – called "Stepping Stones" back in 2015 – which is located at one of Sir Arthur Conan Doyle's former homes. As of June 2022, the books – now at 36 massive volumes (with more in preparation) and with over 750 traditional Holmes adventures from over 200 worldwide contributors – have raised over $100,000 for the school. I'm incredibly proud of this achievement, and more thankful than I can ever express for the contributing authors, and also the fans who have bought the books.

But even more important to me is the presentation of adventures reaffirming the True Sherlock Holmes.

After the first three volumes, I actually believed that there would be no more, but within weeks, contributors – both previous and new – wanted to know about being in the *next* set. It didn't take much convincing to keep going, because by then I was quite addicted to people sending me new Holmes adventures nearly every day. The various decisions had already been made regarding the books – sizes, cover style, format, *etcetera* – so it was just a matter of soliciting more stories. That was very successful – so much so that we ended up publishing two sets per year, an *Annual* in the spring, and a themed collection in the fall. These themes have included several sets of Christmas Stories and Untold Cases . . . and seemingly impossible cases that have rational solutions.

When the first set of these was announced, *Eliminate the Impossible* (Parts VII and VIII, 2017), a Sherlockian who only wants to have Holmes facing real monsters, despite Holmes's own words to the contrary, commented on social media at the time that these were "Scooby Doo" books. He was correct – these do have Scooby Doo aspects, where, at the end of the story, Holmes unmasks the supposed monster or ghost to reveal a very-human villain. (One might turn it around to say that *Scooby Doo* was Holmes-like, because in their world – at least for many years until the stories shifted and were ruined when they faced actual supernatural villains – no ghost needed to apply there either.)

There might be ambiguous aspects to the stories in these *Impossible* MX anthologies – maybe there is some unexplained side aspect that might be an actual ghostly encounter – but the solutions absolutely cannot involve real supernatural elements as the solutions – because that's a cheat.

At times, I've had to turn some stories away, as the contributors haven't understood the brief. (Having Holmes, for instance, deduce that he's a character in a fictional story might seem to be a clever idea, but it doesn't fit the scope of these books. Likewise, neither does having him do battle to the death with a real vampire, only to turn and find that Watson is now a vampire too.)

Although a few contributors indicated that they couldn't come up with ideas that fit these requirements, in many other cases it has actually stimulated more clever story ideas. In 2019, the concept was repeated with *Whatever Remains . . . Must Be the Truth* (Parts XVI, XVII, and XVIII). Again, the theme inspired some really brilliant stories from our contributors.

By fall 2021, it was time for me to come up with the idea for the next themed set – because the theme had to be announced in late 2021 to give time for the stories to be submitted by the June 30th, 2022 deadline. Having used all the other pieces of Holmes's famous quote, *However Improbable* was the natural title for this collection:

> *. . . when you have eliminated the impossible whatever remains, however improbable, must be the truth.*

I'm not sure what to do about a similar-themed set a few years down the road. Quite likely I can start using pieces of Holmes's other famed quote from "The Sussex Vampire":

> *"This agency stands flat-footed upon the ground, and there it must remain. The world is big enough for us. No ghosts need apply."*

"Flat-footed Upon the Ground"? Possibly. *"The World is Big Enough for Us"*? No, that sounds too much like a James Bond title. Probably *"No Ghosts Need Apply."* Stay tuned . . . .

When announced, contributions were solicited to receive stories much like the previous sets – primarily cases that seemed supernatural but weren't. But then a fun thing happened: The contributors began to nudge and expand the requirements, opening them up a bit. I received a number of seemingly supernatural-that-aren't cases, but also new stories about seemingly impossible crimes – wherein the impossible was eliminated, leaving the improbable truth. I was thrilled, and it was – as always – great fun to see all the clever impossible situations that the contributors contrived, and how Holmes cut through the tangles to a solution. As expected (and required), he's a hero, and that's what he does.

The beauty of reading Holmes stories – and I read a *lot* of them – is that from their basic underpinnings, they can jump in any direction. The stories in these books have to fit certain givens: Holmes and Watson must act like Canonical Holmes and Watson. The dates in their lives and the history through which they move have to be acknowledged and respected. The contributors can't make any changes like killing major characters. Rather, these characters can be used, but then they have to be put back on the shelf, as good as new, for the next person. After satisfying those basic requirements, every new story is a surprise. It can be a comedy or tragedy, a romance or a technical procedural. It can be narrated by Watson or Holmes or some other person. It can be epic or small, a private affair or something that might lead to global war. It can be set in the city or the country, and in England or on the Continent, or in the United States or Tibet – as long as the time-frame fits with the other events of Our Heroes' lives.

In *The Hound of the Baskervilles*, Holmes states, "*Now is the dramatic moment of fate, Watson, when you hear a step upon the stair which is walking into your life, and you know not whether for good or ill.*" I know of what he speaks. Nearly every day, I receive a new Holmes story in my email inbox, a submission for the MX Anthologies, or one of the other Holmes books that I edit. Each arrives with infinite possibility, and I can't wait to read it and see what previously unimagined adventure is about to entangle The Detective and The Doctor.

When I was a kid, first meeting Mr. Holmes, I soon realized there weren't enough stories about him. Sixty is really a drop in the bucket for The World's Greatest Detective. New stories appeared on a very irregular basis, and I wished so much for so often that I might have more of them. Now, by way of these books and the modern publishing paradigm and the incredibly gifted and generous authors who contribute to this series, my wish has come true.

I'm amazingly lucky to have the opportunity to see these stories first, fresh from the Tin Dispatch Box, and it's always a thrill when the various collections come together and can be released to the wider world. Now, with this new set – Parts XXXIV, XXXV, and XXXVI – there are more Holmes stories than there were before, and that's a very good thing. I hope you enjoy them, and with any luck, we'll be back soon with another round – because there can *never* be enough stories about the traditional Canonical Holmes, whom Watson called, "*the best and the wisest man whom I have ever known.*"

"Of course, I could only stammer out my thanks."
– *The unhappy John Hector McFarlane*, "The Norwood Builder"

As always when one of these collections is finished, I want to thank with all my heart my incredible, patient, brilliant, kind, and beautiful wife of thirty-four years, Rebecca – every day I'm more stunned at how lucky I am than the day before! – and our amazing, funny, creative, and wonderful son, and my friend, Dan. I love you both, and you are everything to me!

With each new set of the MX anthologies, some things get easier, and there are also new challenges. For almost three years, the stresses of real life have been much greater than when this series started. Through all of this, the amazing contributors have once again pulled some amazing works from the Tin Dispatch Box. I'm more grateful than I can express to every contributor who has donated both time and royalties to this ongoing project. I also want to give special recognition to multiple contributors Josh Cerefice Arthur Hall, Tracy Revels, Dan Rowley, Tim Symonds, and Margaret Walsh. Additionally, Ian Dickerson provided not one but two "lost" scripts from the Rathbone and Bruce radio show by Leslie Charteris and Denis Green.

Back in 2015, when the MX anthologies began, I limited each contribution to one item per author, in order to spread the space around more fairly. But some authors are more prolific than that, and rather than be forced to choose between two excellent stories and let one slip away, I began to allow multiple contributions. (This also helped the authors, as their stories, if separated enough from each other chronologically, could appear in different simultaneously published volumes, thereby increasing their own bibliographies.)

I'm so glad to have gotten to know so many of you through this process. It's an undeniable fact that Sherlock Holmes authors are the *best* people!

I wish especially thank the following:

- *Nicholas Rowe* – In 1985, my deerstalker and I were on the front row for the opening-day showing of *Young Sherlock Holmes.* I was a college sophomore and skipped a class that afternoon to be there. (I'm pretty sure that this was the first Holmes film that I ever saw in a theatre.) I'd also bought the novelization, which I started reading that night – waiting until then to be surprised by the film. Although I did have some

8

reservations about a non-Canonical early meeting between Holmes and Watson in their younger days, pre-January 1st, 1881 at Barts, I found the story to be wonderful and exciting, and in particular, Young Holmes was portrayed to perfection by Nicholas Rowe.

Fast forward to 2015, when my deerstalker and I were back in a theater, this time on the opening day of *Mr. Holmes.* Over the previous couple of days I'd re-read the novel upon which it was based, Mitch Cullin's *A Slight Trick of the Mind.* That's a pretty bleak story, and while I give credence over written original versions over film adaptations, in this case I heartily recommend the latter over the former. While I was enjoying how the tone in the film had shifted from the despair of the book to hope, I was also thrilled to find that Nicholas Rowe was back as Holmes – playing a cinematic version that elderly Holmes (played by Ian McKellen) goes to see in a theatre.

I was incredibly surprised when Sherlockian author Paula Hammond put me in touch with Mr. Rowe, and truly amazed when he agreed to write a foreword. Nick, thanks so much for being part of this and your support.

- *Steve Emecz* – From my first association with MX in 2013, I saw that MX (under Steve Emecz's leadership) was *the* fast-rising superstar of the Sherlockian publishing world. Connecting with MX and Steve Emecz was personally an amazing life-changing event for me, as it has been for countless other Sherlockian authors. It has led me to write many more stories, and then to edit books, along with unexpected additional Holmes Pilgrimages to England – none of which might have happened otherwise. By way of my first email with Steve, I've had the chance to make some incredible Sherlockian friends and play in the Holmesian Sandbox in ways that I would have never dreamed possible.

  Through it all, Steve has been one of the most positive and supportive people that I've ever known.

  From the beginning, Steve has let me explore various Sherlockian projects and open up my own personal possibilities in ways that otherwise would have never happened. Thank you, Steve, for every opportunity!

- *Brian Belanger* –I initially became acquainted with him when he took over the duties of creating the covers for MX Books, and I found him to be a great collaborator, and wonderfully creative too. I've worked with him on many projects, with MX and Belanger Books, which he co-founded with his brother Derrick Belanger, also a good friend. Along with MX Publishing, Derrick and Brian have absolutely locked up the Sherlockian publishing field with a vast amount of amazing material. The old dinosaurs must be trembling to see every new and worthy Sherlockian project, one after another after another, that these two companies create. Luckily MX and Belanger Books work closely with one another, and I'm thrilled to be associated with both of them. Many thanks to Brian for all he does for both publishers, and for all he's done for me personally.

- *Roger Johnson* – From his immediate support at the time of the first volumes in this series to the present, I can't imagine Roger not being part of these books. His Sherlockian knowledge is exceptional, as is the work that he does to further the cause of The Master. But even more than that, both Roger and Jean Upton are simply the finest and best of people, and I'm very lucky to know both of them – even though I don't get to see them nearly as often as I'd like – in fact, it's been six years since out last meeting, at the grand opening of the Undershaw school (then called "Stepping Stones"). I look forward to getting back over to the Holmesland sooner rather than later and seeing them, but in the meantime, many thanks for being part of this.

- *Paula Hammond* – Paula has been a regular contributor to these MX anthologies in recent years, and while she wasn't able to send a new adventure for this set, she amazingly "introduced" me to Nicholas Rowe. Paula: Very much appreciated, and thanks for the support and being part of these books!

And finally, last but certainly *not* least, thanks to **Sir Arthur Conan Doyle**: Author, doctor, adventurer, and the Founder of the Sherlockian Feast. Honored, and present in spirit.

As I always note when putting together an anthology of Holmes stories, the effort has been a labor of love. These adventures are just more tiny threads woven into the ongoing Great Holmes Tapestry, continuing to grow and grow, for there can *never* be enough stories about the man whom Watson described as *"the best and wisest . . . whom I have ever known."*

David Marcum
October 2nd,, 2022
143rd Anniversary of
"The Musgrave Ritual"

Questions, comments, or story submissions
may be addressed to David Marcum at

thepapersofsherlockholmes@gmail.com

Foreword
by Nicholas Rowe

I have a confession to make. In life as in fiction, one half of a couple may admit to a past affair simply in order to appease his or her conscience, when best advice might just be for the guilty party to say nothing and carry on without off-loading – Why cause unnecessary hurt? Mine will be a different breed of confession, but I am driven to make it because the secret has been with me for too long now, and I have a sense that I may be among friends here, an unofficial member of a global appreciation Society that worships with varying healthy degrees of dedication at the altar of Arthur Conan Doyle and his creation, Sherlock Holmes.

The fact is that I am a dilettante in this field, or rather an interloper. My "membership" of the club, so full of *bona fide* Sherlock Holmes devotees who have read all there is to read about the Great Detective and who may have gone so far as buying the meerschaum and donning the deerstalker, was thrust on me out of the blue when I was only just out of school. Christopher Columbus (Wait . . . I'm not THAT old . . . I'm talking about the film writer/director) had written a screenplay for Paramount Pictures that imagined Sherlock as a schoolboy, meeting John Watson for the first time, and falling in love with an eccentric inventor's niece. It had the three of them getting involved in an adventure with an Egyptian sect brought to the streets of Victorian London. It was, to all intents and purposes, my first real experience of acting in a film, throwing me in at the deep end playing a character so loved and "'owned" by millions of people . . . and I had only ever read *The Sign of Four*. My knowledge of Holmes and Watson was confined to the brilliant world created by the unbeatable Basil Rathbone (happy to argue about this) and the brilliant Nigel Bruce. At some point I got hold of a clever biography of Holmes and remember a small incident at the Reichenbach Falls . . . but that was it.

Since then I have dallied from time to time with Holmes – a little cameo in Jeffrey Hatcher's *Mr. Holmes*, enjoying Clive Merrison on the radio, watching old re-runs with Jeremy Brett as your man, and of course Benedict Cumberbatch. The eventual success of my first foray (it wasn't an instant hit in the cinema – far from it) made me understand just how robust this character was, and how much appetite there was to see ever more of him. I could have done more research – probably should have done – but (Your Honour), we were all guessing just a little, playing around with characters from a sacred future, but who were for now still in their embryonic form. We perhaps felt we could allow ourselves a little more artistic licence.

So, I have made some excuses, but have I resolved anything?

Maybe . . . As I consider the achievement of David Marcum in compiling a whole new world of Sherlock Holmes stories, hundreds of them, and the bravery and enthusiasm of the many writers who have created them, I tell myself that I just need to relax a little. I am at least in the good company of people who fly the flag for the future of Sherlock Holmes.

Nicholas Rowe
June 2022

"Why, You Are Like a Magician"
by Roger Johnson

Y ou'll remember the incident in "The Adventure of the Beryl Coronet". Sherlock Holmes is gleaning evidence at Fairbank, the house from which the precious diadem has been stolen. When he asks the young mistress of the house, Mary Holder, whether a surreptitious nocturnal visitor is "a man with a wooden leg", her reaction is rather dramatic:

> *Something like fear sprang up in the young lady's expressive black eyes. "Why, you are like a magician," said she. "How do you know that?" She smiled, but there was no answering smile in Holmes's thin, eager face.*

Magicians have proved to be good detectives, of course – in fiction, at any rate. The Great Merlini solves apparently impossible crimes in long and short stories by Clayton Rawson, who was himself a notable magician. On television, there's the equally brilliant Jonathan Creek, who creates the tricks and illusions for an unappreciative egotist named Adam Klaus. Because he knows how these things work, Creek can spot the tell-tale clues that most of us miss. All thirty-two episodes were written by David Renwick, who is otherwise known for his comedies – which shows that you don't have to *be* a magician in order to *think* like a magician.

Members of the Magic Circle are forbidden to reveal their secrets except to *bona fide* students of the art. That, of course, is a restriction that can't apply to the conscientious detective story writer. Derren Brown, David Blaine, or Dynamo don't tell us how they achieve the miraculous, but Clayton Rawson and David Renwick do just that, because a real detective story must have an explanation. The all-time master of the impossible mystery was John Dickson Carr, author, under his own name or as Carter Dickson, of seventy novels and numerous short stories, all devilishly clever and nearly all compulsively readable. It's only fitting that his biography by Douglas G. Greene is called *John Dickson Carr: The Man Who Explained Miracles*.

The "impossible crime" is usually epitomised in the locked-room mystery and its variants, in which a murder or other felony is committed in a space to which no one has access. This was Carr's specialism, but he wasn't the first: Consider Poe's "The Murders in the Rue Morgue", for instance, or that grand Father Brown story "The Dagger With Wings" by

14

G.K. Chesterton. Or – and it's time we introduced Sherlock Holmes – "The Speckled Band".

The apparently impossible becomes even more disturbing in a sinister atmosphere, which is something that all these writers excelled at. There are effective weird touches, for instance, in "The Copper Beeches", "Wisteria Lodge", and "The Blanched Soldier". And this is from Conan Doyle's description of Stoke Moran manor house, the setting for "The Speckled Band":

> *The building was of grey, lichen-blotched stone, with a high central portion and two curving wings, like the claws of a crab, thrown out on each side. In one of these wings the windows were broken and blocked with wooden boards, while the roof was partly caved in, a picture of ruin.*

The supernatural is no more than hinted at in that particular story, but in Sherlock Holmes's most famous case, *The Hound of the Baskervilles*, its presence is almost expected. The same is true of "The Sussex Vampire" – with that title, it would have to be – and "The Devil's Foot". The latter case, which Holmes calls "The Cornish horror", plays out in a landscape that almost outdoes the Dartmoor of *The Hound*:

> *It was a country of rolling moors, lonely and dun-colored, with an occasional church tower to mark the site of some old-world village. In every direction upon these moors there were traces of some vanished race which had passed utterly away, and left as it sole record strange monuments of stone, irregular mounds which contained the burned ashes of the dead, and curious earthworks which hinted at prehistoric strife. The glamour and mystery of the place, with its sinister atmosphere of forgotten nations, appealed to the imagination of my friend, and he spent much of his time in long walks and solitary meditations upon the moor.*

But it's mystery that Holmes loves. Our great detective has no truck with the supernatural. That's as it should be. And that why those stories – and the stories in this book – are so satisfying!

Roger Johnson, BSI, ASH
Commissioning Editor: *The Sherlock Holmes Journal*
June 2022

An Ongoing Legacy
for Sherlock Holmes
by Steve Emecz

Undershaw
Circa 1900

*T*he *MX Book of New Sherlock Holmes Stories* has grown beyond any expectations we could have imagined. We've now raised over $100,000 for Undershaw, a school for children with learning disabilities. The collection has become not only the largest Sherlock Holmes collection in the world, but one of the most respected.

We have received over twenty very positive reviews from *Publishers Weekly*, and in a recent review for someone else's book, *Publishers Weekly* referred to the MX Book in that review which demonstrates how far the collection's influence has grown.

In 2022, we launched The MX Audio Collection, an app which includes some of these stories, alongside exclusive interviews with leading writers and Sherlockians including Lee Child, Jeffrey Hatcher, Nicholas

Meyer, Nancy Springer, Bonnie MacBird, and Otto Penzler. A share of the proceeds also goes to Undershaw. You can find out all about the app here:

https://mxpublishing.com/pages/mx-app

In addition to Undershaw, we also support Happy Life Mission (a baby rescue project in Kenya), The World Food Programme (which won the Nobel Peace Prize in 2020), and *iHeart* (who support mental health in young people).

Our support for our projects is possible through the publishing of Sherlock Holmes books, which we have now been doing for over a decade.

You can find links to all our projects on our website:

https://mxpublishing.com/pages/about-us

I'm sure you will enjoy the fantastic stories in the latest volumes and look forward to many more in the future.

Steve Emecz
September 2022
Twitter: *@mxpublishing*

The Doyle Room at Undershaw
Partially funded through royalties from
The MX Book of New Sherlock Holmes Stories

17

A Word from Undershaw
by Emma West

Undershaw
September 9, 2016
Grand Opening of the Stepping Stones School
(Now *Undershaw*)
(Photograph courtesy of Roger Johnson)

It seems not so long ago I was writing with news from Undershaw, and here we are again with even more achievements to report. The school is now well into our new academic year with an unprecedented number of students on our roll, and we are busy firming up our place as a Centre of Excellence for SEND education, not only in our locality but further afield.

As an example of the positive culture we have at Undershaw, we received the most wonderful feedback from a work experience placement student we hosted recently. Here's what she had to say about our school from the time she spent with us:

> *Coming to Undershaw was a fantastic experience. I really appreciated the opportunity to spend time with your students, and even to take part in some drama improvisation! Your students were articulate, confident, and thoughtful. Sports Day was a real highlight for me – I felt it was inclusion at its best. The range of activities on offer, and the careful thought*

18

that had gone into the design of the day to ensure that every child could enjoy and achieve was inspirational.

Earlier in the summer we took our accolades to new heights when Undershaw was awarded a Gold Award by the Skills Builder Programme. This is a framework which identifies eight vital life skills, such as problem solving, leadership, and listening. When mastered, these skills ensure our students are fully equipped to take their places as economically and socially independent young adults. At Undershaw, we work tirelessly to ensure our students are immersed in every feasible aspect of their academic and character education, both of which furnish them for their rich and dynamic futures, wherever they may lie.

Undershaw is making a mark as a great seat of learning, proven this year with a fantastic set of GCSE, BTEC and Functional Skills results. We are so very proud of the results which are testament to the students' hard work, resilience, and perseverance. The way that they approached the examinations, having had their previous learning and opportunities to practise with mocks disrupted by the pandemic, is remarkable. Our students move on with a great set of qualifications and achieved the school's first ever Distinction grades, but just as important, they have developed their social and communication skills, built their confidence, and have become the most delightful group of young people. We look forward to hearing all about their next steps and their future successes.

I often say we have the best "job" in the world, as we are privileged enough to witness these remarkable students, who may not have had the best experiences in education before they came to us, find and fuel their passion under our tenure and ready themselves to spread their wings. My inbox is awash with emails from alumni telling me of their latest triumphs as they carve out their niche in the world. I will leave you with the sign-off from one alumnus who wrote to me recently and signed off with the words, *"Thanks for the confidence in me"*. That just says it all.

On behalf of all the wonderful students, committed and talented staff, and the families we support, I extend my heartfelt thanks to you all for being by our side. Undershaw would not be the school it is today without the selfless dedication of all at MX Publishing. We are honoured to have such friends in our midst.

Until next time…

Emma West
Headteacher
October 2022

"Undershaw," Hindhead Conan Doyle's House.

Editor's *Caveats*

When these anthologies first began back in 2015, I noted that the authors were from all over the world – and thus, there would be British spelling and American spelling. As I explained then, I didn't want to take the responsibility of changing American spelling to British and vice-versa. I would undoubtedly miss something, leading to inconsistencies, or I'd change something incorrectly.

Some readers are bothered by this, made nervous and irate when encountering American spelling as written by Watson, and in stories set in England. However, here in America, the versions of The Canon that we read have long-ago has their spelling Americanized, so it isn't quite as shocking for us.

Additionally, I offer my apologies up front for any typographical errors that have slipped through. As a print-on-demand publisher, MX does not have squadrons of editors as some readers believe. The business consists of three part-time people who also have busy lives elsewhere – Steve Emecz, Sharon Emecz, and Timi Emecz – so the editing effort largely falls on the contributors. Some readers and consumers out there in the world are unhappy with this – apparently forgetting about all of those self-produced Holmes stories and volumes from decades ago (typed and Xeroxed) with awkward self-published formatting and loads of errors that are now prized as very expensive collector's items.

I'm personally mortified when errors slip through – ironically, there will probably be errors in these *caveats* – and I apologize now, but without a regiment of professional full-time editors looking over my shoulder, this is as good as it gets. Real life is more important than writing and editing – even in such a good cause as promoting the True and Traditional Canonical Holmes – and only so much time can be spent preparing these books before they're released into the wild. I hope that you can look past any errors, small or huge, and simply enjoy these stories, and appreciate the efforts of everyone involved, and the sincere desire to add to The Great Holmes Tapestry.

And in spite of any errors here, there are more Sherlock Holmes stories in the world than there were before, and that's a good thing.

David Marcum
Editor

Sherlock Holmes (1854-1957) was born in Yorkshire, England, on 6 January, 1854. In the mid-1870's, he moved to 24 Montague Street, London, where he established himself as the world's first Consulting Detective. After meeting Dr. John H. Watson in early 1881, he and Watson moved to rooms at 221b Baker Street, where his reputation as the world's greatest detective grew for several decades. He was presumed to have died battling noted criminal Professor James Moriarty on 4 May, 1891, but he returned to London on 5 April, 1894, resuming his consulting practice in Baker Street. Retiring to the Sussex coast near Beachy Head in October 1903, he continued to be associated in various private and government investigations while giving the impression of being a reclusive apiarist. He was very involved in the events encompassing World War I, and to a lesser degree those of World War II. He passed away peacefully upon the cliffs above his Sussex home on his 103rd birthday, 6 January, 1957.

Dr. John Hamish Watson (1852-1929) was born in Stranraer, Scotland on 7 August, 1852. In 1878, he took his Doctor of Medicine Degree from the University of London, and later joined the army as a surgeon. Wounded at the Battle of Maiwand in Afghanistan (27 July, 1880), he returned to London late that same year. On New Year's Day, 1881, he was introduced to Sherlock Holmes in the chemical laboratory at Barts. Agreeing to share rooms with Holmes in Baker Street, Watson became invaluable to Holmes's consulting detective practice. Watson was married and widowed three times, and from the late 1880's onward, in addition to his participation in Holmes's investigations and his medical practice, he chronicled Holmes's adventures, with the assistance of his literary agent, Sir Arthur Conan Doyle, in a series of popular narratives, most of which were first published in *The Strand* magazine. Watson's later years were spent preparing a vast number of his notes of Holmes's cases for future publication. Following a final important investigation with Holmes, Watson contracted pneumonia and passed away on 24 July, 1929.

Photos of Sherlock Holmes and Dr. John H. Watson courtesy of Roger Johnson

The
MX Book
of
New
Sherlock
Holmes
Stories

Part XXXV
"However Improbable . . . ."
(1889-1896)

The Widow of Neptune
by Christopher James

Stay close, Watson, and we will watch the hill,
where each night for a month, the figure
has stood sentinel over the bay. They say
she wears a cloak of seaweed, stitched with
puffin feathers and a clasp of pearl; that she has
knotted her hair with shells and sea glass
and sings a wordless song of the wind and tide.
Down at The Smugglers' Inn they call her
the Widow of Neptune or the Mermaid of Instow.
You've heard how, if you approach her,
she will vanish and leave only a feather of warning.
Do you see her, there, Watson, raising her arms
as a silhouette against the moon? It is a cormorant,
Watson, now let us go inside, before we catch our death.

The Devil of
Dickon's Dike Farm
by Margaret Walsh

It was a chilly, overcast, day in late October 1889, when Mr. Thomas Prosser came to the door of 221b Baker Street. My wife, Mary, was out of town, and I had once again returned to my old rooms – Holmes convivial, and Mrs. Hudson's excellent cooking.

My friend hadn't had a case for several weeks and was possibly more welcoming than Mr. Prosser was expecting, as the man took the offered seat and invitation to partake in a cup of tea with an air of bewilderment.

Over the tea and several of Mrs. Hudson's excellent scones, Mr. Prosser began his tale.

"I have come from Herefordshire to consult you, Mr. Holmes. I own a farm near Eardisley, which is about fifteen miles from Leominster. It's an old place, and my family have owned it for centuries." Mr. Prosser paused and took a sip of tea, followed by a deep breath. "I have to tell you an old tale about the farm. I ask you to be patient. It does have bearing on why I've come to see you."

Holmes waved his hand. "Pray continue. It must be something unusual to bring a sheep farmer all the way from Herefordshire."

Prosser gaped at him. "How did you know that I farmed sheep? I never mentioned it."

"Your coat, whilst of good quality, has several greasy patches upon it suggestive of lanolin, the waxy substance found in the wool of sheep. Additionally, there are several small scraps of untreated wool caught in the lower buttons of your coat."

Prosser smiled for the first time since he had entered our rooms. "You really are a marvel, Mr. Holmes. I feel confident that you will be able to help me."

"Tell us your story," I said, settling myself comfortably in my chair. I record below the tale as told to us by Mr. Prosser:

The Legend of the Devil of Dickon's Dike Farm

The story starts in the twelfth century [he said]. *My ancestor, Richard Prosser, known as "Dickon" to his intimates, built a farm*

35

near to the village of Eardisley, which is close by the town of Leominster.

The farm was in the path of raiders from Wales, and when his sheep were stolen, Dickon swore that he would sell his soul and that of every creature on the farm if the Welsh could be prevented from ruining him.

Lo and behold, the very next day a handsome stranger arrived at the farm and offered to raise an earthen dike around the farm. The man was tall and fair. He looked, so it was said, like one of the Norman lords who had come over with the Conqueror. His price, the man said, was simple: The soul of every man or beast that was in the northern-most field at midnight on any night would belong to the stranger. Much to his wife's anguish, Dickon agreed.

The stranger set to work and the next morning everyone on the farm was amazed to discover that a six-foot high dike had appeared around the farm. The stranger smiled at Dickon and briefly his eyes glowed with flame, as he said, pointing out one particular field, that abutted against the northern edge of the dike: "Remember our bargain," and disappeared, leaving a faint smell of fire and brimstone behind him.

Dickon's wife began to wail, now even more fearful of the bargain her husband had made. Dickon frowned at her. "Hush, wife. Do not be afeard. Just because I made the bargain doesn't mean that I mean to pay it."

"Not pay it?" the goodwife replied, "But how can you ever cheat the Devil himself?"

Dickon smiled, "It will be simplicity itself."

"But how?" cried his wife. "The Devil wants whatever soul is in that field at night."

Dickon replied. "From this night forth, no beasts will remain in that field, nor will anyone dwell in that field. Let the Devil be satisfied with squirrels and hedgehogs, for he will get none of my sheep nor my people."

From that day onwards, that field has been used purely for crops, and the Devil never reaped one soul from the farm.

Prosser finished his story and sat back in his chair.

"Your problem is connected with this field, I assume," Holmes said.

"It is, Mr. Holmes. Two weeks ago, one of my farm hands, Jack Parry was found dead in that very field one morning, dressed only in his night shirt and boots. There was no sign of major injury upon him. Since then, the rest of my workers are reluctant to go anywhere near the field, and I have had several quit. My livelihood is at stake. Please, I beg of you, please come to Devil's Dike Farm and find out what happened to cause Parry's death."

My friend raised an eyebrow. "You don't believe the Devil was taking his payment?"

Prosser snorted. "I am an educated man, Mr. Holmes. I have no time for fairy tales."

Holmes smiled briefly. "A man after my own heart. Tell me, in what state was the body found?"

"Jack Parry lay upon his back. There was no sign of foul play. I attended the inquest in Leominster – but if I am honest, Mr. Holmes, much of what the doctor said went over my head."

Holmes nodded thoughtfully. "Very well then, Mr. Prosser. My good Watson and I shall accompany you back to Herefordshire and see if we cannot send this Devil packing."

It wasn't until we were in the train to Leominster the next morning that I thought to ask Prosser about the field. "You said the field is used only for crops?"

"I did, Dr. Watson."

"What do you grow?"

"I use that field to grow turnips for winter feed for my sheep. Jack Parry was my turnip shepherd."

I blinked at the term. For the moment I had the image of a man with a crook, herding turnips as they rolled along the road.

Prosser saw my confusion. "A turnip shepherd is responsible for tending the fields where turnips are grown," he explained. "He turns the soil, plants them, watches over them, and eventually harvests them. That is why I am so worried. It is harvest time. Only about half of the field has been harvested. If we don't get the rest of the turnips out of the ground, then my sheep will go hungry this winter."

Leominster, pronounced "Lem-stuh" in that wonderful way we British have of not matching spelling to pronunciation, was a charming market town. It was very old, and it had seen much bloodshed, with repeated attacks by first the Vikings and later the Welsh. The town had fallen under the purview of the monks of Reading Abbey at one time. Leominster had one odd claim to fame: It was the last place in England to use a ducking stool on a suspected witch – a poor woman named Jenny Pipes. The ducking had taken place in 1809.

A pony trap was waiting for us at Leominster's railway station, and we undertook the trip to the farm in silence. I was admiring the crisp greenness of our surrounds, while Holmes, as usual, was sunk deep into his own thoughts.

I was impressed with the farm as it came into view. It was dominated by a large, white-washed building with large windows and substantial chimneys that looked to have been built in the sixteenth century. Clustered around the house were various outbuildings. A few chickens scratched happily in the dirt in the yard. I looked northwards. A lone field sat abutted hard up against the dike. It was surrounded by a sturdy fence. To the west side of the fence sat a small building. Only the fact that a scrap of cloth hung at the single window that I could see indicated that it was used as a dwelling rather than for storage.

"Welcome to Dickon's Dike Farm, gentlemen," Thomas Prosser said softly.

Holmes was busily looking around. "That is the field in question?" he asked, gesturing to the northern-most field that I had observed.

"It is, Mr. Holmes."

"Come, Watson, let us take a look."

We climbed, somewhat stiffly, from the trap and walked towards the field. Prosser accompanied us. Several curious farm hands and a well-dressed lady that I took to be Mrs. Prosser came out to watch.

Holmes opened the gate to the field and walked in, stopping just inside. "Where was the body found?"

Prosser took a deep breath and joined us in the field. He walked to what was roughly the centre. "It was about here."

Holmes and I went to join him. I glanced around. We could see the small dwelling place more clearly from here. It was well-kept, with a sturdy wooden door, and appeared to have been recently white-washed. Prosser saw where I was looking. "That was where Jack Parry lived. He liked to be close to the field, in case anyone trespassed."

"Would anyone trespass here?" I asked.

"Thieves mostly. I know turnips sound like an unlikely thing to steal, but animal feed is costly, and the more unscrupulous amongst my neighbours wouldn't hesitate to help themselves if they thought they could get away with it – though they would be more likely to raid the storage shed than the field. The legend is well known in these parts."

I nodded and looked to where Holmes was examining a turnip with great interest.

"Have you never seen a turnip before?" I asked with some amusement.

"This is a most interesting turnip," Holmes replied, tucking the vegetable into the pocket of his Inverness cape.

I briefly wondered what on earth could be interesting about a large turnip with a chunk missing from it. I was, however, used to my friend's quirky ways and accepted that the vegetable must have some relevance to the subject at hand.

Holmes gazed around the field. "Was the gate to the field open or closed when Mr. Parry's body was found?"

"It was open, Mr. Holmes," Prosser replied. "That is what made us think something was wrong. The gate is never left open."

"And that hut was Mr. Parry's residence?" Holmes gestured towards the small dwelling I had noticed earlier.

"It was."

"Excellent!" Holmes turned and walked out of the field, leaving Mr. Prosser and me to follow him.

Holmes turned to our host. "I shall need a copy of the Coroner's Report in regard to the death."

Mr. Prosser scratched his head. "The inquest was held in Leominster. It's a bit late to get a copy now. I shall send a man first thing in the morning."

My friend wasn't happy, but realised that he would have to be content with that.

Prosser's wife, a charming brunette with a care-worn face, welcomed us, and Prosser took us into the house. He showed us into two small but comfortable rooms that overlooked the inner yard of the farm. I could see Parry's hut in the distance. I found myself wondering what exactly had happened that night. I wasn't a man given to fanciful imaginings, but as it grew dark, it seemed to me that the small dwelling and the field beside it took on a sinister aspect. Shuddering slightly, I drew the drapes firmly closed and hurried to ready myself for dinner.

Mrs. Prosser was an excellent cook, though she was ably assisted by several young women. We were served a hearty meal of roast mutton, with potatoes, carrots, and onions. No turnips, which surprised me, until Mrs. Prosser told me that they preferred to keep all their turnips for animal feed. I supposed this made sense, but I do admit to a fondness for turnips. This was followed by a delicious apple and rhubarb pie. Good, solid, country fare.

I was in a much better frame of mind when I retired to sleep.

The next morning, after a breakfast of porridge with honey, several rounds of toast with sweet butter, and some excellent homemade marmalade, Holmes and I joined Mr. Prosser for a tour of the farm. A man had been despatched to Leominster before sunrise, so with luck, Holmes would have a copy of the Coroner's Report before lunch.

I was amazed at the size of the sheep. I had every city man's idea of sheep as being small, cuddly creatures. The beasts that Prosser showed us seemed to be enormous.

"These are Cotswold sheep, Dr. Watson," Prosser said, seeing my bewilderment. "They are one of the largest breeds here in Britain. An adult can weigh between two- and three-hundred pounds."

"That is a hefty weight," I said. "I've played rugby against men who weighed less than that."

"It does make shearing time interesting," Prosser said, "especially as the fleeces can weigh up to twenty-two pounds."

"They are a wool flock then?" I asked.

"They are good for both meat and wool, though I prefer only to send them off for meat as mutton. The wool is too valuable to kill them off as lambs. My flock is well known, and I can easily sell male lambs to other farmers as potential stud stock."

"Fascinating," I said as I watched the sheep grazing contentedly.

"But you can see why I need those turnips harvested before the weather turns."

"I can," I replied. "Animals that size must eat a lot of food." I looked around for Holmes. He was prowling around by Parry's dwelling and walking the line of the fence of the Devil's Field. Prosser followed my gaze.

"I fear your friend isn't a countryman at heart."

"It isn't that, though I admit that he doesn't much care for the rural life. It's just that Holmes came prepared to work and will be restless until he is able to do what he came to do."

"I can understand that. You should talk to my wife. She complains about my prowling around the house every time the weather is too inclement for me to do anything productive."

We walked to join Holmes, and as we were returning to the house, a burly man with a pugnacious expression accosted us. He glared at my friend. "You here to sort out poor old Jack's death?"

"I am."

"You're some sort of famous detective from London?"

"Consulting detective," Holmes replied.

"What does a *consulting* detective know about the Devil?"

"Probably a great deal more than you," Holmes replied calmly, "given the nature of the crimes that we have dealt with over the years." He looked the man dead in the eye. "This death *will* be solved."

The man made a grunting sound and walked away.

Prosser winced. "I am sorry about that. That was Willie Price, my head shepherd. He is a trifle bombastic, but he is a good man and a hard worker."

"And no doubt worried about what happened," I said.

It was early afternoon before Prosser's man returned from Leominster with a copy of the Coroner's Report carefully tucked into his coat.

Holmes took it away to his bedroom to read. He came to find me no more than thirty minutes later and handed me the report. "Tell me what you make of that, my dear doctor."

The report was fairly straight forward, giving Parry's age and general condition at death. There had been no obvious health problems. Cause of death was simply given as *"Heart failure – Cause unknown"*. I looked up at Holmes. "Not exactly helpful. There can be several reasons why the heart stops suddenly. It wasn't a heart attack. There is no sign of damage to the heart. It was most certainly some form of cardiac arrest, but without knowing the cause – "

"Look at the end of the report."

I scanned down to the end as requested and stopped. "'*There were several indentations or cuts upon the deceased's thigh which resembled a cloven hoof.*' What on earth?" I looked up at Holmes in shock. He looked back at me, a glimmer of a smile playing at the edge of his mouth.

"You know what happened," I stated.

"I do."

"Are you going to enlighten Mr. Prosser and his farm hands?"

Holmes frowned. "I talked with a few of the workers this morning, other than the loquacious Mr. Price. They are firmly convinced something diabolical was involved. They're unlikely to be convinced by me."

"Then what – ?"

"Several of them evinced an interest in the Whitechapel Killer."

"The one that the press called 'Jack the Ripper'?"

"Indeed. I understand that they followed the case quite closely – there not being much excitement to be had amongst the sheep and the turnips."

I frowned. "Holmes, I cannot for the life of me see where you're going with this."

"Elementary, my dear Watson. If I cannot convince them of the truth, then I shall have to bring in someone who can."

"Who?"

"I think Dr. George Bagster Phillips fits the bill admirably. After all, he is the doctor who performed the *post mortems* on four of the Whitechapel Killer's victims. His name likely will be familiar to the lads here."

41

"He is also friendly and charming," I observed. "Are you sure he will come?"

"No, I am not," Holmes admitted. "I intend to go into Leominster. I'm hoping that the post office will have a telephone. I shall call Lestrade at Scotland Yard and get him to contact Phillips, who is more likely to respond to an overture from Lestrade, whom he sees more frequently, than one from me."

To my great surprise, when Holmes raised the prospect of going into Leominster to make a telephone call, Prosser told him it was unnecessary to go that far. The police constable in the nearby village of Eardisley had a telephone. Prosser was sure that the man would allow Holmes to make a call to the Yard.

Eardisley was charming, and while Prosser took Holmes to see the constable, I wandered around the village. It was medieval in appearance, with many buildings being the distinctive black-and-white timber-framed buildings that one associates with that time period.

The village church, dedicated to St. Mary Magdalene, was of a more mixed vintage. A churchwarden, seeing me strolling the churchyard, stopped to chat. According to him, the church was built in the twelfth century, though much of what I could see was from much later, including a sixteenth-century tower. The church warden escorted me indoors to see the fine Norman font, which was engraved with fabulous carvings depicting the "*Harrowing of Hell*" – a magnificent feat of workmanship, though not to my personal taste. I did find interesting the fact that church was built by the Baskervilles. I found my mind turning towards Sir Henry Baskerville and the legend of the Hell Hound that plagued his family. I was devoutly hoping that this case would have as prosaic an end.

I heard my name being called and, thanking the churchwarden for his time, hurried out to meet my friend. Holmes was in a good humour.

"I spoke with Lestrade. He is intrigued and promised to go straight to Phillips and lay the case before him."

"Do you think Lestrade will persuade him to come?"

"I have no doubt of it. And I suspect that Lestrade will come himself."

I raised an eyebrow. "Why so?"

"Come, Watson, you know as well as I that Lestrade has a taste for the *outré* and bizarre, though he will not admit it."

I laughed. "That's true enough. When do you think they will arrive?"

"I told him to make sure that Phillips was on board the first train to Leominster in the morning. I've prevailed upon our host to get us there to meet them."

"I would happily go as far as Hereford itself to fetch them, Mr. Holmes," Prosser said, "if it meant that this dreadful death could be cleared up and my farm begin to work again properly."

"Have no fear of that, Mr. Prosser," Holmes assured him. "By this time tomorrow, all will be well."

As we walked back to the cart, I said softly to my friend, "Can you truly make such an assurance?"

"I can. The Devil is no more involved here than he was in the Baskerville case."

"Odd that you should say that," I said. I began to tell my friend about what I had seen in the church.

Holmes listened with every evidence of interest. "Well, my friend, if I were a superstitious man, I would say that that is a good omen."

"But you are not," I said drily, "so you will not."

Holmes smiled slyly but did not reply.

The next morning, Prosser himself drove the pony trap into Leominster to meet the morning train from London. It was no surprise to see that our old friend Lestrade was one of the first to debark from the train, followed by Dr. George Bagster Phillips.

The doctor was well into his fifties, but still spry, with a dour countenance the belied his wit and charm. He had performed the *post mortem* examinations on four of the Whitechapel Killer's victims: Annie Chapman, Liz Stride, Catherine Eddowes, and Mary Jane Kelly, the last performed with the assistance of Dr. Thomas Bond. This work had led to Dr. Phillips becoming a noted name in the newspapers of London – and it seemed, Herefordshire.

Dr. Phillips approached Holmes with his hand outstretched. "It's good to see you again, Mr. Holmes. And you as well, Dr. Watson. Our paths haven't crossed since that investigation of yours at the docks." He was referring to a case that we had investigated during the London Dock Strike the previous August. *

"I was most curious when Lestrade approached me," Dr. Phillips continued. "The case seemed intriguing enough for me to take this little jaunt into the countryside. I am rather looking forward to seeing this Devil's Field. You have the *post mortem* report with you?"

In answer, Holmes withdrew the pages from his pocket and handed them to the man.

We settled ourselves into the trap and as we headed back towards the farm, Dr. Phillips settled in to read the report.

Lestrade and I chatted in a desultory fashion on the comings and goings of various mutual acquaintances. Holmes simply sat and watched

Dr. Phillips. After a while, he looked up. "An interesting read. Have you any idea as to the cause of death, Mr. Holmes?"

"I have." Holmes withdrew the turnip from his pocket and handed it to Dr. Phillips.

Lestrade and I exchanged bewildered looks.

Phillips turned the vegetable around in his hands, then nodded, and handed it back. "I believe that would do it. We shall need to make a bit of a show, of course."

"Of course," Holmes agreed. "If we simply wheel you in and have you pronounce what happened, Mr. Prosser's workers are unlikely to be convinced."

When we arrived, Prosser's farmhands, as well as his wife and their maids, all hastened into the yard when the trap pulled up. Everyone watched eagerly as Holmes escorted Dr. Phillips into the Devil's Field.

The physician examined the ground carefully. Holmes stood beside him, gesturing gracefully as his pointed to Parry's dwelling, to the ground at their feet, and finally to the gate. Dr. Phillips appeared to be asking questions, nodding thoughtfully at Holmes's responses.

The two men left the field and went to Parry's little home. Nothing could be seen until the curtain covering the window that faced the field was twitched aside. Both men could be seen peering out of the window.

Shortly after that, they exited the dwelling and came across to where everyone was gathered. Holmes addressed everyone. "I would like to introduce you all to Dr. George Bagster Phillips, who is the police surgeon for H Division in London. He is well versed in strange deaths."

"I'll say!" A voice called out excitedly. "They don't get much stranger than the Pinchin Street Murder. I read all about that one in the London papers!"

The murder referred to had occurred the previous month, when a legless and headless torso of a woman had been discovered beneath a railway arch in Pinchin Street in Whitechapel. There had been fears that the Ripper had returned, but Dr. Phillips's *post mortem* report had convinced Commissioner James Monro and Detective Inspector Donald Swanson that it wasn't the case.

"Thank you for your welcome," Phillips said. "I have consulted with Mr. Holmes, and I'm in agreement with his findings." He paused. "I shall let Mr. Holmes tell you himself what happened. I'm more used to giving evidence at a Coroner's Inquest, so I fear my recitation of the case might be a little dull."

"I shall tell you the sequence of events," added Holmes, "and then Dr. Phillips will explain exactly what killed Jack Parry."

There was a rustle of anticipation in the audience.

"Jack Parry had readied himself for bed," Holmes began, "but not gone to bed, when he took a last glance out of the window. Parry, I'm given to understand, was a conscientious man who took his duties seriously. Looking out of the window that night, Parry spotted two things: One was the open gate, the other an object moving around in the field. Parry paused only to pull on his boots and then rushed out of his house."

"What did he spot?" Price asked. "The Devil?"

"No, Mr. Price. What Jack Parry saw was a sheep in the field eating one of the turnips. Parry hurried into the field, intent on chasing the sheep out of there. In the dark, he didn't see that there was a second sheep that was lying down in his path. In his haste, Parry tripped over the second sheep and fell heavily, landing with his chest on a large turnip. The sheep took fright, lashing out with its back legs, leaving hoof marks on Parry's legs."

"This is where I come in," said Dr. Phillips. "When Parry crashed to the ground and landed upon the turnip, he did so in such a manner as to cause the vegetable to ram hard against his thorax. The thorax, or chest, contains the heart and lungs. There is a nerve that runs through there that carries signals to the brain. This nerve is called the *vagus nerve*. If this nerve is struck with enough force, then something called *vagal inhibition* occurs, which causes the heart to cease beating instantly. It has been known to happen in fights, where someone is punched with great force in the chest."

"Wouldn't that have caused a bruise?" another man asked.

Dr. Phillips shook his head. "When I said the heart ceases to beat instantly, I meant just that. There is no time for a bruise to form at the point of impact. The heart must be beating for blood to infiltrate the tissues to cause a bruise."

Holmes picked up the thread. "In this instance, the fact that Parry was no doubt running when he tripped over an animal that weighs around two-hundred pounds gave enough impetus that his landing proved to be fatal."

"How do you know there were sheep in the field that night?" Lestrade asked.

Holmes dug into his pocket and pulled out the turnip. He turned it towards us so that we could see the bite marks. "A sheep had clearly been nibbling at this turnip. As the turnips are to be winter fodder, a sheep had no business being in the field. As no animals graze in that field, they could only have entered if the gate had been left open, and out again before morning after they had eaten their fill, leaving no trace – except for a half-gnawed turnip.

"Only two things would have got Parry into that field at night: A thief or a marauding sheep. Given the legend, it was unlikely to be a thief. A thief would wait until the turnips were harvested before attempting theft of the produce. Therefore, the trespasser had to be a sheep."

The men came forward to examine the turnip and to ask Holmes and Dr. Phillips questions. I noticed that one or two even sidled up to Lestrade, delighted to have the chance to talk with the Scotland Yard man.

Price walked up to me after examining the turnip. "It's an odd one, for sure. You're Dr. Watson, aren't you? You wrote that book about the Mormons and the murders? *A Study in Crimson* . . . no . . . *Scarlet*."

"I am, and I did."

"You going to write about this?"

I shook my head. "Perhaps one day. I'm not sure the world is ready for the story of a man killed by a turnip."

Price suddenly laughed. "Well. If you do you could always call it '*Sherlock Holmes and the Devil of Dickon's Dike Farm*'."

I looked to where Holmes and Dr. Phillips were talking now with Prosser and his wife. Phillips was eagerly accepting Mrs. Prosser's invitation to lunch before the return to London. I smiled to myself. "I suppose I could, Mr. Price."

NOTE

This story was inspired by a real death – that of former Member of Parliament, Sir William Payne-Gallwey, who died in 1881 after tripping while out hunting and landing on a turnip.

* See *Sherlock Holmes and the Case of the London Dock Deaths* (MX Publishing, 2021)

The Christmas *Doppelgänger*
by M. J. Elliott

T*his script has never been published in text form, and was initially performed as a radio drama on December 19, 2020. The broadcast was Episode No. 149 of* The Further Adventures of Sherlock Holmes, *one of the recurring series featured on the nationally syndicated* Imagination Theatre. *Founded by Jim French, the company produced over one-thousand multi-series episodes. In addition, Imagination Theatre also recorded the entire Holmes Canon, featured as* The Classic Adventures of Sherlock Holmes, *the only version with all episodes to have been written by the same writer, Matthew J. Elliott, and only the second with the same two actors, John Patrick Lowrie and Lawrence Albert, portraying Holmes and Watson, respectively.*

CHARACTERS:

- SHERLOCK HOLMES
- DR. JOHN H. WATSON
- GREGSON: Scotland Yard Inspector
- FERDINAND CHRISTMAS: 60's. Agreeable enough retiree, burdened with the expectation that he will be more agreeable still
- JOSHUA RETHRIK: 30's, Aspirational middle-class, fighting to keep his situation through constant lying
- DOROTHEA RETHRIK: 30's, Like Joshua, everything she says is carefully phrased, though for different reasons
- ANNOUNCER

SOUND EFFECT: OPENING SEQUENCE: BIG BEN, STREET SOUNDS

ANNOUNCER: *The Further Adventures of Sherlock Holmes.*

MUSIC: *DANSE MACABRE* UP AND UNDER. FADE TO . . . . .

WATSON: Throughout the year 1889, I prided myself upon finding the perfect balance between my marriage, my medical practice, and my shared adventures with Sherlock Holmes. My wife Mary, of course, took precedence over all else, but I flattered myself that I had managed to reserve a certain amount of time for the criminal investigations which I found so fascinating, and which had brought us together in the first place, during the case of *The Sign of Four*. It was not my intention to be away from Mary for very long on the 24th of December, but I had hoped to surprise Holmes with a tin of Balkan Sobranie, an exotic alternative to his usual brand of tobacco. Thus, I advised my wife that I might be at least a few hours, certainly no more than the length of time it would take to smoke a companionable pipe and toast the festive season.

MUSIC: OUT

SOUND EFFECT: A DOOR OPENS, AND WATSON ENTERS

HOLMES: Watson, how very agreeable it is to see you.

WATSON: Good evening, Holmes!

HOLMES: Now come along, we must be going.

WATSON: Going?

HOLMES: To Nightingale Lane. Some haste is required – time is against us, and the police are already present.

WATSON: But I only stopped by wish you the Compliments of the Season!

HOLMES: You can do so in the cab, and at length. I've just received an urgent summons from a former client.

WATSON: You haven't unwrapped your gift yet!

HOLMES: Leave the Sobranie on the fireplace and I shall smoke it later. This really is quite an urgent matter, Doctor – our client has witnessed the murder of one of his neighbours.

WATSON: Oh! And he wishes you to identify the murderer.

HOLMES: No, he knows precisely who the murderer is.

48

SOUND EFFECT: CLOCK TICKS THROUGHOUT

CHRISTMAS: It was me, Dr. Watson! That is – I mean to say – it was *I*! By which I mean myself!

WATSON: So Holmes told me, Mr. – *er* . . . .

CHRISTMAS: Christmas, Doctor – Ferdinand Gascoigne Christmas.

WATSON: Mr. Christmas. But I'm afraid I'm not entirely clear what it is you mean by that. I take it you're not confessing to your neighbour's murder?

CHRISTMAS: Certainly not! What a monstrous notion! Monstrous!

HOLMES: I believe Mr. Christmas is attempting to state that the man he saw earlier this evening bore a strong resemblance to him.

CHRISTMAS: More than that, gentlemen! He looked like me, he dressed like me – he *was* me to the life! Are you familiar with the term *doppelgänger*?

WATSON: Yes, it means "double", doesn't it?

HOLMES: Not quite. A *doppelgänger*, Watson, is the spirit of a still-living person.

WATSON: A spirit, I see. I don't particularly care for ghost stories –

HOLMES: Not even *A Christmas Carol*?

WATSON: As a matter of fact, no. But my understanding of the genre is that one can only become a ghost *after* one has died. How is it possible, then, that Mr. Christmas here saw his own ghost?

CHRISTMAS: One might be dead for a few moments, yes? You've resuscitated patients, haven't you, Doctor?

WATSON: On the battlefield, several.

CHRISTMAS: I believe that something of the sort happened shortly after my birth. Only the actions of a quick-thinking midwife ensured that I might be here, speaking to you today.

SOUND EFFECT: GREGSON APPROACHES

GREGSON: Is this the tale of the ghost again, Mr. Christmas?

HOLMES: Gregson!

CHRISTMAS: You may dismiss such matters out of hand, Inspector, but Mr. Holmes here is a free-thinker!

GREGSON: Often a bit *too* free, to my mind – with his thoughts *and* his opinions.

HOLMES: Both have, I hope you'll admit, been of some use to the Yard over the years. Perhaps they may be so again today.

WATSON: Though I think we would benefit from a somewhat more coherent explanation of this evening's events.

GREGSON: Oh, Dr. Watson, you're here as well? I rather thought you'd be with your wife on Christmas Eve.

WATSON: Yes, I rather thought so as well. But refusing an invitation from Sherlock Holmes, no matter the date, is as futile as trying to stop a charging train by standing on the tracks with one's arms upraised.

GREGSON: My commiserations, Doctor.

WATSON: Mr. Christmas, may I ask you the name of your neighbour, the lady or gentleman –

CHRISTMAS: Gentleman.

WATSON: – *Gentleman* whom you saw murdered this evening?

CHRISTMAS: I'm afraid I've no idea. It's most embarrassing. I've seen him in the street, walking his dog . . . Waved to him, of course, but if I ever heard his name, I've long since forgotten it.

50

GREGSON: Mirkwood. Winston Mirkwood. Haven't ascertained his profession yet.

CHRISTMAS: No, that doesn't sound at all familiar. Perhaps I never heard his name after all. And yet he's lived opposite me these seven years! Shameful of me.

GREGSON: Especially given your reputation for beneficence, if you don't mind me saying so.

CHRISTMAS: My reputation, Inspector, stems solely from my wretched name. I can't help it if I'm called Christmas, but some people wish to view me as the embodiment of the season, which results in my being dragged out of my home every December the twenty-fourth by the Salvation Army, to hand out gifts to the less fortunate.

WATSON: Like a sort of local Father Christmas.

CHRISTMAS: I despise that man, and everything he stands for. Because of him, I'm forced to maintain this beard – not that it's anywhere as grand as the one sported by that irritatingly Saintly personage. At least I'm not expected to gain weight. I'm not sure I'm capable of it.

HOLMES: It pains me to point it out, Mr. Christmas, but you've still yet to comply with Dr. Watson's request for a coherent explanation.

CHRISTMAS: Oh yes! Well, normally, this pampering of the poor goes on long into the evening, but I don't have the strength I once had, and it wasn't even eight o'clock before I felt weary enough to cry off and summon a cab to take me back home to Nightingale Lane. You know, there's something about this time of year that makes drivers quite over-familiar –

GREGSON: The murder, Mr. Christmas.

CHRISTMAS: Yes, yes. Well, I returned to my address just as – What did you say his name was?

WATSON: Winston Mirkwood.

CHRISTMAS: Mirkwood was taking his dog on the last walk of the day. He wished me a Merry – (DOESN'T WANT TO SAY IT) You know

51

... I gave him a wave over my shoulder, and put my key in the door. It was as I opened it that I was knocked to the ground! I looked up and saw myself hurry from my house and bolt across the street, where I collided with Mirkwood! I heard a shot, Mirkwood fell, and I – the other me, that is – vanished into the darkness.

GREGSON: Unfortunately, there are no other persons who claim to have seen two Ferdinand Christmases on Nightingale Lane at the same time.

CHRISTMAS: By the time the shot attracted anyone's attention, my spectre was long gone.

WATSON: You're absolutely insistent that you witnessed your own ghost commit a murder, then?

CHRISTMAS: I have it from Mirkwood's own lips, Doctor!

GREGSON: Oh yes? Was this before or after his murder, then?

CHRISTMAS: In the moments before he succumbed. I rushed over to attend to him, and with his last breath, he said two words . . . "Phantom" and "Ghoul".

GREGSON: His last *two* breaths, then.

HOLMES: It is my understanding, Mr. Christmas, that you wish us to provide Inspector Gregson with sufficient evidence that the person who slew your neighbour in the street was, in fact, this "phantom" or "ghoul".

CHRISTMAS: I appreciate that I'm asking a lot, Mr. Holmes . . . .

HOLMES: I fancy Watson and I are up to the challenge.

WATSON: Is it your intention to charge Mr. Holmes's client with murder, Inspector?

GREGSON: I'm worried that if I did, Doctor, I'd have a riot on my hands. On the other hand, I don't have any other suspects . . . .

WATSON: Mirkwood's body?

GREGSON: Has been taken off to the mortuary. Would you like to do the honours, Dr. Watson?

WATSON: I don't really see that I have any option in the matter.

<u>MUSIC: STING</u>

<u>SOUND EFFECT: INTERIOR OF MOVING CAB</u>

HOLMES: A phantom *and* a ghoul – interesting that the dying man employed both terms, don't you think?

WATSON: Until I'm breathing my last, I can hardly compare my thought processes to his. You didn't tell me about the case you solved for Ferdinand Christmas.

HOLMES: Oh, a very humdrum affair – his sister was convinced that she was responsible for the suicide of her fiancé. I proved beyond a shadow of a doubt that he he'd been poisoned by his secret wife in Chiswick. (PRONOUNCED: *CHISSICK*) Not at all worthy of your time or consideration, Doctor.

WATSON: Unlike this case?

HOLMES: I consider it my Christmas gift to you. How can you possibly resist a seasonal ghost who has, for reasons best known to himself, taken to murdering random dog-walkers?

WATSON: A pair of slippers would have been just as welcome.

HOLMES: Slippers will eventually show signs of wear. Memories of the macabre remain forever fresh.

WATSON: I take it you're not subscribing to this theory of the *doppelgänger*? It may be the time of year for miracles, but they're traditionally of a more benevolent nature, are they not?

HOLMES: How old would you say Ferdinand Christmas is, Watson?

WATSON: In his early sixties, perhaps?

HOLMES: Then his ghost has walked this Earth for sixty years without apparently being noticed before now, and only recently discovered the address of its corporeal self?

WATSON: Speaking of corporeal, this *doppelgänger* was certainly solid enough to wield a gun and shoot Winston Mirkwood with it.

HOLMES: There are certainly a good many contradictions to untangle before the night is out.

WATSON: *And* before Christmas Day arrives, which shouldn't be too onerous a task. The case seems clear as day to me.

HOLMES: Enlighten me, my dear Watson.

WATSON: Plainly, Christmas did not see his own ghost, but rather, someone dressed up to look like him.

HOLMES: I concur.

WATSON: Splendid!

HOLMES: But to what end?

WATSON: If I had to guess –

HOLMES: I would strongly advise against it.

WATSON: I should say that this disguised individual intended to rob Christmas's home, carefully selecting an evening he knew the owner would be out.

HOLMES: Intriguing.

WATSON: Unfortunately, Christmas returned home unexpectedly. The burglar fled and bumped into Mirkwood, whom he killed while escaping.

HOLMES: It shows a greater degree of ingenuity than the average house-breaker possesses.

WATSON: But you'll agree that my explanation fits all the facts.

HOLMES: It would doubtless satisfy Inspector Gregson.

WATSON: That doesn't sound like a whole-hearted endorsement.

HOLMES: Ferdinand Christmas is a retired tobacconist. He lives modestly, and possesses no valuable items.

WATSON: So far as he's aware. He might well have something valuable in his possession without realising it. You admit it's possible?

HOLMES: Possible. But why the gun?

WATSON: Eh?

HOLMES: You say the criminal selected the precise time he knew Christmas would be out of the house? Then why go to the trouble of carrying a weapon?

WATSON: A precautionary measure, in case something went wrong. Which it did.

HOLMES: Then why go to such lengths at all? Why not simply barge into the house at any time and hold Christmas at gunpoint?

WATSON: I suppose you have an explanation.

HOLMES: No. I have seven. It remains to be seen which of them, if any, is correct.

WATSON: But the thief undeniably targeted Christmas's home for a specific purpose. Hence the disguise.

HOLMES: Of that, there can be no doubt.

WATSON: Christmas isn't a tall fellow. *You* certainly couldn't impersonate him convincingly, Holmes.

HOLMES: I'm uncertain whether that's meant as an observation or a challenge.

SOUND EFFECT: OUT

HOLMES: Your thoughts, Doctor?

WATSON: I have a good many – very few of them about this chap. The bullet struck the sixth rib on the right side, sending fragments into the aorta, causing it to rupture.

HOLMES: Would there have been enough time for Mirkwood to make the unusual statement Ferdinand Christmas claims to have heard?

WATSON: Barely.

HOLMES: You've noticed his hair, I take it?

WATSON: Dyed black, obviously. Vanity, I expect.

HOLMES: We can deduce something more than that, I believe.

SOUND EFFECT: GREGSON WALKS IN

GREGSON: (APPROACHING) I see you started without me, gentlemen.

WATSON: Almost finished, as it happens, Inspector.

GREGSON: (INTRIGUED) Hmm . . . .

HOLMES: Something the matter, Gregson?

GREGSON: Not sure. For a moment there, he looked familiar. I've only seen him under street-lamps before now.

WATSON: What was it you were about to say, Holmes?

HOLMES: The marks on Mirkwood's palm indicate that he persistently held his dog's lead in his right hand.

WATSON: Ergo, he was right-handed.

HOLMES: Typically, a right-handed man parts his hair on the left. Mirkwood parted his on the right. However. If we rearrange it . . . .

WATSON: It was covering a rather a nasty scar. I wonder what made it.

GREGSON: Barber's blade, held by his brother. They fought like Cain and Abel, those two.

HOLMES: You recognise him at last, then?

GREGSON: I do, Mr. Holmes – Chester Crackenthorpe, a member of the Hooper Street Gang.

WATSON: *Former* member.

GREGSON: Long before his death, Doctor. Must be . . . oh, nearly fifteen years ago. The gang was run by a fellow called Pinky Fenton. He was quite an ambitious character. (TO HOLMES) What's that fellow you've got a bee in your bonnet about, Holmes? That Professor?

WATSON: What professor?

GREGSON: Anyway, Pinky fancied himself a bit like the Professor, convinced if he could pull off one big crime, he'd be king of the criminals. Then, he got his chance.

HOLMES: How so?

GREGSON: You might not be aware of this, but once a year, the Bank of England destroys all of their old banknotes –

HOLMES: – In a blaze at a secret location. Last year, for instance, the notes were burned on Wanstead Common.

GREGSON: I suppose Lestrade told you, did he? Obviously, it has to be done in secret, and also the police are present at all times. Pinky's sister . . . Well, she "ingratiated" herself with one of the officers, if you get my meaning.

WATSON: I think we all get your meaning, Inspector. She discovered from him where the notes were to be incinerated.

HOLMES: And where her brother and his gang might steal them.

GREGSON: The stakes were big, but Pinky didn't care how many coppers had to die, just so long as he got his hands on that money. But that was too great a risk for Crackenthorpe's nerves. He came to me, and told me Pinky's entire plan. On the night the notes were supposed to be burned, we had an armed contingent in wait for Pinky and his lads. It was a bit of a bloodbath, as it turned out.

WATSON: The leader, Pinky – did he survive?

GREGSON: He did not, Doctor. There were few left alive to arrest, in the end. As for Chester Crackenthorpe, I lost track of him – until this evening.

HOLMES: The reason for the disguise becomes clear, then – the killer broke into the home of Ferdinand Christmas, then lay in wait until Crackenthorpe, now going by the name Mirkwood, was due to walk his dog. Seeing someone he believed to be a neighbour, he would suspect nothing until the fatal shot had been fired.

WATSON: Then . . . Mirkwood-*alias*-Crackenthorpe was the target the entire time?

GREGSON: You're only just now reaching that conclusion, are you, gentlemen?

WATSON: It's very easy to say that you'd made your mind up on that point once Mr. Holmes has apprised you of the facts, Inspector.

GREGSON: I would have you know, Doctor, that I've already placed a man under arrest for the charge of killing Mirkwood.

HOLMES: Oh?

GREGSON: I would have mentioned it sooner, but I was momentarily distracted by the discovery that Mirkwood and Crackenthorpe are the same person – not that it has any bearing on the case.

HOLMES: You're quite certain of that, are you, Gregson?

GREGSON: One of the officers posted on Nightingale Lane heard the sound of glass smashing at the back of Mirkwood's house. He discovered this fellow let himself in through the kitchen window, in order to retrieve a threatening letter.

WATSON: A letter addressed to Mirkwood, or else you wouldn't be in any doubt as to which of the fellow's identities he was targeting.

GREGSON: You know, he's really come along with you as his tutor, Mr. Holmes.

HOLMES: What is the name of the gentlemen presently in your custody?

GREGSON: Rethrik. Joshua Rethrik.

WATSON: Has he confessed to the murder?

GREGSON: I expect him to do so before Christmas Day arrives.

WATSON: For the sake of my marriage, I certainly hope so. (TO HOLMES) Well, Holmes, it seems as though the affair of Ferdinand Christmas's *doppelgänger* has become quite mundane. I should probably be on my way.

SOUND EFFECT: HE SETS A MEDICAL INSTRUMENT DOWN

HOLMES: My dear Watson, don't you wish to be present at Gregson's interrogation of Joshua Rethrik?

WATSON: Is that really necessary?

HOLMES: I think we would do well to study the inspector's methods. This has been a humbling experience, and a reminder that one is never too old to learn. (TO GREGSON) That is . . . if you have no objections, Gregson?

GREGSON: After such an admission, Mr. Holmes, how could I object? I would never have thought you capable of such humility.

HOLMES: Perhaps that will not be the only surprise you'll experience tonight.

GREGSON: So . . . why don't you make this easier for all of us, son, and tell us you did it?

RETHRIK: I *did* do it.

GREGSON: Listen, I don't appreciate that kind of – What?

RETHRIK: I did it. I killed Winston Mirkwood.

WATSON: (SLIGHTLY OFF-MICROPHONE) What about Chester Crackenthorpe?

RETHRIK: I don't know who that is.

GREGSON: You see, Holmes? Nothing to do with it at all. As I said.

HOLMES: (SLIGHTLY OFF-MICROPHONE) So it would appear. Would you mind asking Mr. Rethrik to stand up, Inspector?

GREGSON: I'm not done with my interrogation yet. (TO RETHRIK) Why did you shoot him?

RETHRIK: I think my letter makes that clear.

GREGSON: The letter * says you've had enough of being blackmailed. Beyond a few lines about your wife's irreproachable character, it doesn't actually give any details.

SOUND EFFECT: * GREGSON RAISES THE LETTER

RETHRIK: I don't understand why you need them. I've told you I killed him. Surely that should be enough.

GREGSON: You've confessed here and now. I don't want you recanting the moment you stand up in court, and I've got nothing else to base my charge on!

RETHRIK: (A LONG SIGH) He was blackmailing me.

60

GREGSON: I know that. We *all* know that! Why?

RETHRIK: My wife . . . I love Dorothea very much, but she has a sickness – of the mind. A compulsion to steal. Over the years, I've done much to prevent word of it from ever getting out.

WATSON: (SLIGHTLY OFF-MICROPHONE) You could always have sought treatment for her.

RETHRIK: Not without word getting out! My position may not be influential, but discretion is of the utmost importance in what I do.

HOLMES: (SLIGHTLY OFF- MICROPHONE) What is it that you do, Mr. Rethrik?

RETHRIK: I'm an attendant at the Houses of Parliament. My reputation has to be spotless.

HOLMES: (SLIGHTLY OFF-MICROPHONE) Unlike the reputations of most politicians.

GREGSON: This is an interrogation, Mr. Holmes, not an issue of *Punch*. (TO RETHRIK) What exactly did Winston Mirkwood know about your wife?

RETHRIK: (WHO'S MAKING THIS UP AS HE GOES) He . . . uh . . . I was led to believe that he had signed accounts from individuals who had seen Dorothea taking items from Gamages Emporium. I wasn't allowed to see them, but I couldn't risk that they should find their way into the hands of the police. So . . . I formed a plan. I disguised myself as one of his neighbours, a man named Christmas. I broke into his house.

HOLMES: (SLIGHTLY OFF-MICROPHONE) How?

RETHRIK: W-what?

HOLMES: (SLIGHTLY OFF-MICROPHONE) How did you break into his house?

RETHRIK: I just did. That part doesn't really matter, does it? While I was waiting, this Christmas fellow came back, earlier than I expected. I

61

ran out into the street, knocked him over and practically collided with Mirkwood. Next thing I knew, the gun was in my hand, and – and I shot him.

GREGSON: Just as I pictured it. Too often, my colleagues overlook the importance of imagination in detective work, but that's where most crimes are solved, you see – up here.

RETHRIK: I'm not done.

GREGSON: Oh, please, pour your heart out, Mr. Rethrik – it only makes my job easier.

RETHRIK: If Christmas hadn't returned when he did, I would've searched for the papers after killing Mirkwood. Only I didn't have the chance, and I had to come back later.

GREGSON: Right! I believe that covers everything. Thank you for being so cooperative. I only wish you could've seen sense before you decided to take a man's life. (TO HOLMES) There isn't anything else is there, gentlemen?

HOLMES: Just one thing, Inspector.

GREGSON: Oh, yes. (TO RETHRIK) Would you mind standing up, just to appease Mr. Holmes here?

SOUND EFFECT: RETHRIK PUSHES BACK HIS CHAIR

HOLMES: Yes. Your story, Mr. Rethrik, lacks only the virtue of truth.

RETHRIK: I beg your pardon?

HOLMES: How tall are you?

RETHRIK: Six-foot-one.

HOLMES: Six-foot-one. (TO WATSON) Watson, how tall would you estimate Ferdinand Christmas to be?

WATSON: Five-foot-five, I should say.

HOLMES: Scarcely a convincing *doppelgänger*.

GREGSON: But . . . well . . . .

HOLMES: Gregson, you have made a mistake, and an egregious one. I only hope there's still time to correct it.

<u>MUSIC: STING</u>

<u>SOUND EFFECT: A FIRE BLAZES AWAY. DOROTHEA USES A POKER ON THE BLAZE. OUTSIDE, A FIST HAMMERS AT THE DOOR</u>

GREGSON: (BEHIND THE DOOR) Mrs. Rethrik! Mrs. Rethrik!

<u>SOUND EFFECT: HAMMERS ON THE DOOR AGAIN</u>

GREGSON: (BEHIND THE DOOR) Scotland Yard, Mrs. Rethrik! If you don't open the door this minute, we shall be obliged to knock it down!

WATSON: (BEHIND THE DOOR) Do you really care so little about your husband, Mrs. Rethrik?

DOROTHEA: (A LONG SIGH)

<u>SOUND EFFECT: SHE DROPS THE POKER, WALKS TO THE DOOR, OPENS IT</u>

HOLMES: Very wise, Madam. (TO GREGSON) Gregson, the fire!

<u>SOUND EFFECT: GREGSON HURRIES OVER TO THE FIRE WHILE HOLMES AND WATSON ENTER AT A REGULAR PACE</u>

DOROTHEA: My opening the door is not an invitation to barge in.

GREGSON: There's still a few – Ow! Bits of the disguise left unburned. Not enough, though!

HOLMES: Forgive us for not introducing ourselves, Mrs. Rethrik. I am Sherlock Holmes. This is Dr. Watson, and the gentleman burning his fingers extracting portions of burned clothing from your fireplace is Inspector Tobias Gregson.

DOROTHEA: I opened the door only because you mentioned my husband and intimated that he might be in some difficulty. I insist that you explain yourselves.

GREGSON: You've doubtless realised that your husband is presently in custody, Madam.

DOROTHEA: I cannot imagine why. Please be aware, Mr. Holmes, it's only because I recognise your image from press that I don't scream for my neighbours to come in here and expel you all.

WATSON: That would hardly do, Mrs. Rethrik. You'll forgive me for saying so, but you appear more outraged than shocked at the news that your husband is facing a charge of murder.

DOROTHEA: I'm not sure I can forgive a word that any of you have said, Dr. Watson. And no one mentioned murder. What is all this talk?

GREGSON: Joshua Rethrik has confessed to the killing of one Winston Mirkwood. Have you heard of that gentlemen?

DOROTHEA: What if I should refuse to answer?

GREGSON: Then I should say you've already given us your answer, Madam.

HOLMES: Do you have any idea of the reason he gave us for wishing Mirkwood dead?

DOROTHEA: I'm sure I couldn't say. But I demand to be taken to him.

GREGSON: I'm certain that can be arranged.

HOLMES: Perhaps I should explain that, as part of his plan to kill Crackenthorpe, your husband claims he disguised himself as a Mr. Ferdinand Christmas, a disguise that now burns in your fireplace. Did you do so at his instruction?

DOROTHEA: It's my understanding that a wife cannot provide testimony against her husband.

GREGSON: Interesting that you should know that, Mrs. Rethrik.

HOLMES: More interesting still that you didn't bother to ask me who Crackenthorpe might be, since you knew full well that Mirkwood once went by that name, when a member of the Hooper Street Gang.

DOROTHEA: (QUIETLY) What?

HOLMES: Joshua Rethrik lied in order to protect you, his wife. He could never have posed as Ferdinand Christmas, since he's entirely too tall. *You*, however, might do so quite convincingly.

DOROTHEA: I refuse to say anything more until I've spoken to my husband.

HOLMES: That will be entirely unnecessary. The story of what occurred tonight is plain for all to see. Two members of Pinky Fenton's gang evaded capture fifteen years ago – Chester Crackenthorpe, who sold his friends out to the police, and Pinky's sister, who so ably charmed one of the officers tasked with overseeing the destruction of the used bank notes. Both began new lives, but neither strayed too far from London. It was your great misfortune that Crackenthorpe, now going by the name Mirkwood, happened to discover that you were now Dorothea Rethrik.

DOROTHEA: (IT'S ALL COMING OUT, SO HER PROTEST ISN'T PARTICULARLY STRONG) Lies. All of it.

HOLMES: Thus began the blackmail, Mirkwood having far less to lose than you should if the truth came out. It was you, not Joshua, who formulated the plan to pose as Christmas at a time he would be away from his home, and lay in wait for Mirkwood.

WATSON: As a former criminal, you'd know how to pick a lock, and enter a house without leaving a trace.

HOLMES: I don't imagine you'd be prepared to tell us precisely how your husband came to know of the murder? Perhaps you confessed to him, perhaps he saw you in your Ferdinand Christmas disguise, which would undoubtedly be stained with blood. But the fact that he sent a threatening letter to Mirkwood without your knowledge meant that he had to retrieve it, immediately.

WATSON: Less artfully than you managed it, however. He was forced to break a window, which attracted the attention of a constable.

GREGSON: That explains why he was so reluctant to tell us how he broke in the Christmas's home – because he *couldn't* tell us.

WATSON: Bravo, Inspector! You've really come along with Holmes as your tutor.

HOLMES: Without your confession, Mrs. Rethrik, Joshua will undoubtedly hang. The destruction of your disguise means there's no evidence to exonerate him. Are you still the same hard-hearted woman you once were, that you would allow your husband to face the consequences of *your* crime?

DOROTHEA: (AFTER A LONG PAUSE, HER COCKNEY ACCENT NOW APPARENT) Damn Chester Crackenthorpe! Even dead, he ruins everything for me.

GREGSON: Is that a confession, Mrs. Rethrik?

DOROTHEA: It's whatever you want it to be, Copper. Joshua's a good man, he's just not very bright. Sooner or later, I was gonna get what's coming to me, but he doesn't deserve that. Just my bleedin' luck.

HOLMES: I fear no luck was had by anyone this Christmas. Fifteen years ago, you set in motion a plan that resulted in many deaths – Your crimes have finally caught up with you.

MUSIC: BRIDGE

SOUND EFFECT: CAB INTERIOR

WATSON: A shabby finish to a shabby business.

HOLMES: Joshua Rethrik's story of his wife's kleptomania was, of course, an exaggeration, but an understandable one, based as it was on her natural criminal tendencies. He was obliged to tell us that the blackmail concerned his wife, since the threatening letter he was attempting to retrieve mentioned her.

WATSON: We do foolish things for love, don't we?

HOLMES: I'm sure I wouldn't know. Of course, Ferdinand Christmas chose to imagine that Mirkwood's last words were "phantom" and "ghoul". In fact, what the dying man actually said was –

WATSON: (INTERRUPTING) "Fenton", the name of the leader of the Hooper Street Gang. And instead of "ghoul", what Mirkwood actually said was "girl" – the *Fenton* girl.

HOLMES: Gregson was right, Watson, you really are coming along. I sense that all's not well with you.

WATSON: Am I so transparent?

HOLMES: Only to the trained observer.

WATSON: This has hardly been a joyous affair, has it, Holmes?

HOLMES: Justice knows no joy, Doctor.

WATSON: I was thinking of Joshua Rethrik – wondering whether I would have acted differently, were I in his shoes.

HOLMES: Once he learned his wife's true identity, this moment became inevitable.

WATSON: A rather harsh assessment.

HOLMES: I have done things in many areas of my life which I believed were for the greater good, but which have taken some unfortunate victim along the way. I take no pleasure in it. In fact, I regret persuading you to join me on this particular adventure.

WATSON: If I've learned anything from tonight, it's to appreciate what one has while one may. If it's all the same to you, Holmes, I'd rather not join you at Baker Street for a drink. I'd prefer to be with Mary.

HOLMES: Which is precisely why I told the cabbie to drop you off first. Merry Christmas, Watson.

WATSON: Merry Christmas, Holmes.

SOUND EFFECT: OUT

MUSIC: *DANSE MACABRE*

The Terror of
Asgard Tower
by Paul D. Gilbert

As I sat in my parlour in the pale sunlight of a late summer morning, I realised how badly I had been missing my wife since she took an extended visit. Although not uncommon during the warmer months, my practice had been worryingly slack of late and the morning papers, with which I had concluded my breakfast, were bereft of anything worthy of interest or note.

As a result, my thoughts had turned more and more towards my former lodgings at 221b Baker Street and, of course, my friend and long-time associate, Mr. Sherlock Holmes.

This reminiscing of mine had been accompanied by pangs of guilt, for I felt certain that throughout our acquaintance, never before had I neglected paying him a visit for so long a period of time. Not that this circumstance should have been attributed to me alone, for I had been keeping a keen interest in his career throughout this time, courtesy of the many newspaper reports of his recent triumphs abroad. Nevertheless, I had made no great effort in going round to congratulate him, so engrossed had I been in the novelty of married life. I resolved there and then to put matters to right.

Consequently, when our maid announced Holmes's arrival at my door at that very moment, my great surprise and pleasure can be easily understood. I rushed up to greet him before the maid even had a chance to show him in, and I ushered him to my table in an exuberant display of hospitality. I had the maid to bring us some coffee and Holmes took to his chair, with some diffident amusement on his face.

"So, friend Watson," Holmes said with a sardonic smile, "it seems that married life has turned you into quite the host."

I offered him my tobacco and, as we filled our pipes, I noticed him studying me closely.

"I see that Mrs. Watson is taking an extended trip away," he observed, "and that your surgery has been exceptionally quiet of late."

My raised eyebrow of curiosity was all the prompting that my friend had needed.

"Oh, I'm certain that had your wife's return been imminent," Holmes explained, "you wouldn't be using your coffee cup for an ashtray, nor would your morning papers be strewn about the room in such disarray. I have yet to hear of a doctor's surgery that begins its day at so late an hour, and your shave is clearly two days overdue."

"I cannot deny that you are correct on both counts, and that my wife's return isn't due for another three days."

"Ha! So you wouldn't be adverse to an overnight stay close to the town of Haslemere, in Surrey?"

"I should be delighted!" I exclaimed with all sincerity.

"Then you should waste very little time in preparing your overnight bag. A cab awaits us outside and our train departs in less than an hour."

I had been so thrilled at the thought of the chase once more that I hadn't the time to feel aggrieved at Holmes's presumption. Consequently, Holmes had barely an opportunity to become impatient and agitated for I joined him in the cab even before he had finished instructing the driver. Holmes glanced across at me a couple of times as we rattled along the street, and he seemed glad to have my company.

"So the journey begins once more." He smiled excitedly.

However, he wouldn't be drawn upon the reason for this impromptu trip until we were safely aboard our train to Haslemere. Unfortunately, there had been no express available from Waterloo that day, so the forty-three-mile journey would have seemed an age under normal circumstances.

This extra time allowed Holmes the opportunity to outline, in great detail, the events that had led him to my door that morning. As a result, the journey positively flew by.

"What do you know of The Devil's Punchbowl?" Holmes asked me abruptly.

"I am afraid to say, very little," I offered. "I recall from a previous trip that it is an area of great natural beauty and interest and that there is a legend of some sort that recalls a cataclysmic battle between the Devil and the great Norse God, Thor. The resulting upheaval of the surrounding terrain created the huge indentation that has subsequently been so dramatically named."

"Excellent, although I'll warrant the recent dramatic events that have so drawn my attention are every bit as remarkable as those ancient tales of yore. In retrospect, I must admit that there is a certain atmosphere of intrigue and mystery about the place that would have inspired those epic legends. Do you recall a young detective, Sergeant Stokes?"

"Well, of course I do. Was he not the officer in charge of the investigation into the missing tea merchant, Connor Donahue?"

"Indeed he was, but since then he has gone on to bigger and better things, and he has made inspector at a very young age. It was he that first brought the current mystery to my attention, and we are making this journey at his behest."

"Hmm, so it must indeed be a baffling matter – murder?"

"So it would appear at first glance, although as you know I will never formulate an opinion until I'm absolutely certain of my data. The facts, as I understand them, are these . . . ."

At this juncture, Holmes paused to light a cigarette. He then leant towards me, with his forearms resting on his knees, and he dropped his voice as if we were conversing within a crowded carriage.

"Brook Tavernier, the controversial philosopher and author of ill repute, has been found dead. He was discovered upon The Tower of Asgard, the name bestowed upon his estate, which is located upon the rim of The Devil's Punchbowl in Surrey. It is a messy affair, for the majority of his face has been shot away by a small-bore shotgun at close range." I was amazed at the placidity of my friend's tone as he recounted so horrific an end.

"How awful!" I exclaimed. "I know that some of his ideas and writings are controversial," I protested, "and indeed considered to be heretical in some circles, but to meet with such a ghastly demise for expressing those views is simply grotesque."

"Indeed it would be, if that is the reason for his murder, but to speculate as to the motive at this stage is detrimental to the process of attaining the truth.

"The Tower of Asgard was built in the eighteenth century in the Neo-Gothic style and, although neither he nor his family had a hand in its construction, Tavernier took great pride in the fact that its summit is the highest point in all of Southern England. Indeed, when the weather is favourable and with a good set of binoculars, it is just possible to view the face of the Elizabeth Tower housing Big Ben from such a vantage point.

"I bring these facts to your attention, not merely to satisfy your boundless enthusiasm for such trivia, but also because of their potential relevance to the matter at hand. You see, not only did Inspector Stokes bring the murder to my attention in his wire, but he made mention of the strange sightings that some of the locals have been reporting recently."

"Sightings, you say?" I asked with an air of amused curiosity. "What kind of sightings?"

"You must understand that Mr. Tavernier had become something of an eccentric recluse in recent years, and the only permanent member of staff that he retains is Carrington, who doubles as both his butler and valet. His cook, maid, and groundsman all return home at the end of their day's work, but Tavernier is never seen. According to Carrington, Tavernier's latest tome is a speculative piece regarding the existence and nature of the

Devil himself. In itself, that isn't so hard to accept when you consider the legends that are associated with the surrounding area. However, Tavernier has carried his research to bizarre extremes and has taken to dressing in a dark red costume, replete with horns, atop of his tower when there is a full moon. This unnatural silhouette has generated all kinds of rumours and speculations amongst the simple local folk and only Carrington knows the full and horrific effect that Tavernier's research has had on his mind."

"Good Lord, surely these people cannot believe that the Devil is truly abroad in those parts?"

Holmes nodded emphatically.

"None of them have ever seen nor met Tavernier, nor do they have any notion as to the nature of his work. All they know is what they see, and it is just possible that one of them has taken matters into their own hands. In their minds, the Devil has finally been slain!"

"Have any witnesses come forward?"

This time Holmes shook his head.

"Carrington had been alerted to this tragedy at a quarter-past midnight by the unmistakable sound of shotgun fire close by. He pulled on his dressing gown and, aided by the powerful light of a full moon, he made his way towards the sound, which led him to The Tower. He climbed to the summit where he found his master in the state that I have previously described. In shock, he chose to wait with the body. As soon as the groundsman arrived in the morning, he was despatched by Carrington to fetch the police. All the while, he remained with his master, who was lying in a pool of his own blood and in full costume, exactly where he had fallen."

By now our train had pulled into Haslemere Station, and before long a horse and trap was transporting us through some of the most spectacular countryside that it was possible to imagine. It would be easy to suppose that nothing could have been further from our minds than any thoughts of the Devil and the evil that had been wrought in his name.

The rooms that Holmes had arranged for us were within a charming inn, situated but a short drive from Tavernier's home, Asgard's Tower. Not surprisingly, I could see The Tower from the window of my room, and once I had unpacked and enjoyed a leisurely aperitif with our charming landlord, Holmes joined me for a surprisingly good lunch. Throughout the meal, my friend wouldn't be drawn further upon the matter at hand, and I had to accept that no further enlightenment would be forthcoming prior to Inspector Stokes's prearranged arrival. Nevertheless, my friend's frustration at having to wait until then, was obvious to a trained observer.

The inspector arrived promptly, and after he had joined us for a quick cup of coffee, Stokes drove us towards Asgard's Tower in a small cart and at a surprisingly leisurely pace. The lack of urgency was soon easily explained and much to my friend's obvious annoyance. In fact, even as we climbed aboard the cart, I could sense some uneasiness within the young detective. To his credit, Stokes soon clarified the situation, even before we had begun the gentle ascent towards the summit of The Bowl's rim.

"Mr. Holmes, although I wouldn't even consider depriving you of a visit to the location of the crime, nor of enjoying the incredible views afforded by The Tower, I should mention at the outset that the mystery of the death of Mr. Tavernier has already been solved, and as recently as this morning."

The infuriation upon Holmes's face was discernible even from the briefest of glances. He ground his teeth and began to tap the side of the cart with a pent-up resentment.

"Of course, I would have notified you sooner," Stokes explained apologetically, "but the new evidence only came to light today, after I knew that you were already traveling."

"That is very gracious of you, Inspector." Holmes growled sarcastically as he lit a cigarette. "Pray tell of the nature of this evidence."

Stokes had been ready to ask the driver to stop and return us to our lodgings, but Holmes ordered the man to continue.

"It would be shameful to come all of this way without experiencing the views from The Tower. Now pray tell of the nature of this evidence of yours." I smiled when I considered Holmes's customary dislike of the countryside and how oblivious he was to such surroundings as a rule.

"It appears to be quite a simple matter, actually. As I mentioned in my extensive wire to you, many of the locals have become convinced of the presence of the Devil in our community, and one of them did indeed take the matter into his or her own hands.

"Mrs. Granville, the wife of the local blacksmith, arrived at the station this morning to report her husband missing. After he failed to arrive home from work two evenings ago, she had assumed that he had gone to visit his brother who occupies a small cottage on the far side of the rim. However, when Granville remained absent on the second day, she despatched their young son to the home of her brother-in-law, who told the boy that he hadn't seen his brother in weeks.

"His wife then explained that of all of the townsfolk who had voiced concern at the nature of Tavernier's work, her husband had been the most animated and aggressive in his condemnation of Tavernier and the strange goings on at Asgard's Tower. 'The man should be hounded out of the county!' Granville had cried on more than one occasion. Now I know that this is all rumour and hearsay, Mr. Holmes, but you should also know that the shotgun which Granville kept above his fireplace has also gone missing."

Holmes finally roused himself from his malaise of disappointment and shot the inspector a brief glance of interest.

"Well, that is certainly most damning, wouldn't you say?" I suggested.

"Circumstantial, Watson, circumstantial, but it does seem as if our journey may not have been a complete waste of time, after all."

"Oh, come along" I proposed. "The gun of a type used in the killing has disappeared and its owner is clearly afraid of returning home. This is a man, don't forget, who has more than once condemned the victim for his demonic behaviour, and he does have a reputation for aggressive tendencies. Surely it isn't beyond the bounds of probability that the perpetrator of this awful crime is the missing blacksmith?"

Holmes emitted a barely discernable grunt, which told me that he was at least considering that possibility. Nevertheless, I knew that he wouldn't be completely satisfied until he had inspected the scene in the minutest of detail.

Although doubtless of great historical interest, the house itself was considerably smaller than one might have expected and had been fashioned from an unremarkable, dark grey stone. However, it was the spectacular tower of Asgard that had understandably drawn our attention. The edifice reared up into the sky in a manner that conjured up visions of the Biblical Tower of Babel, and the owner of such an edifice might easily imagine himself as the lord of all that he surveyed.

We were met at the base of the steps by a tall, elegant gentleman who could have been none other than Carrington the butler. He was smartly bedecked in the customary black suit of such a servant, but there had been something aloof in his manner that told of his resentment at having to occupy such a servile position.

"Good day, Inspector. I take it that you and these gentlemen intend to examine The Tower once again, rather than pursuing the man responsible for the death of my master?" Carrington asked haughtily.

"These gentlemen are Mr. Sherlock Holmes and Dr. Watson, and they have kindly travelled down from London to aid me in my inquiry. My men are currently searching the length and breadth of the county in pursuit of the refugee Granville and yes, that is our intention – if you have no objection?" Stokes retorted sarcastically.

Carrington bowed compliantly and stood to one side that we might have access to the never-ending spiral staircase that led to the summit of

Asgard's Tower. Carrington made to follow us up the stairs, but Holmes bade him remain at their base.

"As you wish sir, although I can assure you that there is nothing more to be learnt up there."

"Nevertheless, I am rather prone to drawing my own conclusions, thank you. By the way," Holmes asked as he was about to begin the ascent, "were there any other indications of the tragedy that was about to ensure, prior to the sound of the shotgun fire?"

Carrington shook his head emphatically.

"Although my room is located on the far side of the house, I am certain that I would have heard some noise had there been any. The night had been eerily still and quiet."

"Thank you, Carrington," Holmes called out as he began to race up the narrow, red-brick staircase.

Then he slowly retraced his steps, as if something had suddenly occurred to him. He whispered a few words to the young detective before Stokes went down to join Carrington at the foot of the stairs. Holmes then bade me to follow him, but at a distance.

Initially, Holmes had moved up the stairs at an urgent pace, but as we neared the top of The Tower he slowed down to a crawl and began to analyse the upper steps with his glass. He continued thus until we had reached the upper level, and there he shifted his focus towards the wall that bounded the far side of the turret. Once he had completed his examination and returned his glass to its pocket, he turned towards me with a gravity etched into his features, the like of which I had seldom seen before.

"Watson, did you come with your loaded army revolver?" he asked anxiously.

"My overnight bag wouldn't have been satisfactorily packed without it."

"Then draw it now and race down the stairs to the aid of Inspector Stokes, for I fear that he is in grave need of your assistance."

Not for a second did I question the reasons for Holmes's request, and I bounded down the stairs with my weapon drawn. I could hear Holmes careening down after me, but I didn't look back. At The Tower's base I was confronted with a sight that I hadn't even considered possible: The butler Carrington had drawn a knife and he was standing there with the blade pressed hard against the neck of the young inspector, his eyes ablaze with the fire of a violent maniac!

This sight had brought me up short and I paused for Holmes's instruction before I raised and levelled my gun.

"Can you make out his shoulder?" Holmes asked calmly.

I nodded my confirmation.

"Then bring him down." Holmes ordered, not doubting my ability to do so for an instant.

I did his bidding and my bullet crashed into and completely shattered Carrington's shoulder. With a cry that echoed around The Tower, Carrington let the knife fall from his hand and he collapsed to the ground clutching his bloody and awful wound. Allaying his shock and fear, Stokes bent down for the knife, and he stood over his would-be assassin whilst clutching the blade most threateningly.

By now, Holmes had joined us at the base of The Tower.

"Apply your cuffs, Inspector, and hand me the knife." Holmes held out his hand and, once Stokes had willingly obliged, my friend led us towards the grey stone house. We paused in the drawing room, but only for the time that it took us to pour a nerve-steadying glass of whisky. We then proceeded to the gun room, where Holmes lit a cigarette before undertaking a meticulous examination of the various weapons that the room contained.

In the complete absence of any staff, I went in search of a clean sheet or two, in which I intended to wrap the butler's wound. On more than one occasion, as I turned a dark and eerily silent corner, I shuddered in horror at the sight of so many paintings that depicted Satan and his minions. Dark and menacing images of every conceivable form of torture and the frantic horrified faces of the many victims told of the sick mind that had put together such an appalling collection.

I tended and bound Carrington's wound with a clean sheet, although a surgeon would be needed at some point. The wounded man was now able to recline in a degree of comfort, Holmes proceeded to outline the rationale for all that had just occurred.

"Gentlemen, we have sitting here before us a dangerously deluded and desperate man. Having secluded himself for nigh on twenty years and then immersed himself in the Devil and all of his demonic works, he only needed to take a very short step before he passed through the very portal of evil with which he had become so obsessed." There wasn't even an indication of exaggeration nor of the dramatic as Holmes made this bizarre pronouncement. He merely stated it as a matter of fact.

Inspector Stokes seemed to mirror my own look of bemusement and Holmes soon recognised the fact that not everyone shared his profound understanding of the situation. He genuinely seemed to think that no further explanation was necessary.

"Oh, is the matter still not clear to you?" Holmes asked, without even attempting to disguise his amusement. "This creature, sitting here before us, is none other than *Brooks Tavernier himself – disguised as the butler!*" Holmes declared, much to the consternation of Inspector Stokes.

"That is impossible, Mr. Holmes," Stokes quietly replied. "Tavernier remains currently reside upon a slab in the local mortuary."

"Can you really be so certain of that, Inspector? After all, was it not yourself, in your most excellent and detailed report, who informed me that the shotgun wound had obliterated at least half of the dead man's face?"

"Those are the facts sir, yes, but the dead man was also dressed in the bizarre garb with which Tavernier had recently become associated. What other conclusion could either I or the coroner have reached?"

"Let me propose an alternative interpretation of events: I first became drawn to my conclusions when I observed how ill-fitting Carrington's suit was. A man in his position would never accept a pair of trousers that hang a good inch above his shoes, nor would his master. Yet see how large a gap there is on these and the distance between Tavernier's wrists and cuff."

We followed Holmes's lead and couldn't deny those inconsistencies.

"Surely one could also say that it is indicative of nothing more sinister than poor tailoring." I proposed.

"Of course it could, if that were the only anomaly. From there, seeing the rest of his disguise was obvious. My examination of the steps told an entirely different story to the one offered. After I allowed for the presence of the Good Inspector and two of his officers who removed the body, I could only account for two other sets of prints. A light covering of moss, which had accumulated over the years, made my readings quite easy to interpret. I can assure you that there had been nobody else present there, so the supposed threat presented by the gun-wielding blacksmith was nothing less than pure fabrication."

"Are you saying that Granville, the missing blacksmith, was never here?" Stokes asked.

"He never was, and his absence from home must be attributed to another activity as to which I have no clue." Holmes paused for a moment to light a cigarette and he handed over to Stokes the shotgun that he had been examining.

"Do you notice a covering of dust that has accumulated over a long period of unemployment and neglect?" Holmes asked.

"No, Mr. Holmes, I must admit that I do not."

"Yet, if you were to examine every other weapon in the room, you would discover that most-telling layer of dust. You see, Inspector," Holmes declared triumphantly, "this shotgun has been used most recently, a fact that can be further attested to by the residue of gun powder present at the tip of the barrels."

Stokes turned angrily toward the man masquerading as the deceased butler. Just then we all observed a dramatic and horrific alteration in Tavernier's countenance. He rolled his eyeballs to the upward limit of their sockets and his lips contorted into the grimace of a feral beast. Indeed, he had become the very embodiment of the entity with whom he had become so obsessed.

"That fool Carrington continually interfered with my research!" Tavernier growled suddenly. "That night, he refused to believe that a number of the local townsfolk were approaching The Tower with violent intent towards me. I could see a small group of men climbing towards the summit of The Punchbowl, each of them armed with a shotgun. That idiot even tried to hold me back as I strode back up the stairs of The Tower armed with a weapon of my own.

"He followed me to the top of The Tower and, as I took my aim, Carrington rushed towards me and tried to snatch the gun from my grasp. Naturally I released both barrels immediately, and he fell to the floor clutching at his destroyed face, crying out like a rabid dog as he died. I grabbed two more shells from my pocket, but as I turned my attention towards the approaching men, I realised with dismay that they had completely and inexplicably disappeared from view!

"Once my presence of mind had returned to me, I realised that Carrington's wounds had presented me with the opportunity for subterfuge that Mr. Holmes has previously described. I changed clothes with him, disguised myself – we weren't dissimilar – and then waited all night with the body, but the attack never came."

"You would doubtless have succeeded had it not been for his skills and intervention." Stokes admitted ruefully.

Then as if on cue, one of Stokes' officers entered the room and whispered briefly in his ear before retreating.

"Gentlemen, you might be interested to know that Mr. Granville has now returned home, together with his gun. It seems as if he and his friends enjoyed one drink too many on the night before a proposed hunting trip. They became hopelessly lost and returned home, with their tails between their legs, without a single shot having been fired.

"Thank you, Mr. Holmes," Stokes declared bashfully. "You have without doubt saved me from abject humiliation and also prevented a heinous crime from remaining unpunished."

"Not at all," Holmes smiled. "I'm certain that with a little discretion on our part, your blossoming reputation will remain untarnished."

"That is most gracious of you . . . ." Stokes suddenly noticed that Tavernier was muttering irrationally to himself.

"Heinous crime you say? Surely an act of self-defence is not a crime!"

Without warning, the deluded man suddenly jumped up out of his chair and made a dash for the door, while shrieking declarations of his innocence as he ran. We were slow to react to his manic behaviour and, by the time that we had reached the door, Tavernier was well on his way towards his beloved tower. To my surprise and horror, Holmes held me back for a moment and he allowed the man to make good his escape.

Just then, Tavernier's true intention dawned on me, and I redoubled my efforts at catching up with Stokes and the crazed fugitive. Despite his wound, Tavernier was far surer of his footing than either of us, and he arrived at the top of The Tower before we were even halfway up. Although he was out of our view, a final blood curdling cry told us that he had already taken the ultimate act of self-preservation.

The result of Tavernier's leap had been as bloody as it had been inevitable, and I was left with the unfathomable conclusion that Holmes's callousness had allowed Tavernier the opportunity to take his own life. Then again, upon further reflection, perhaps his had been an act of great mercy.

"You see, Watson," Holmes remarked as we joined Stokes at his cart, "it's impossible for a man to make a pact with the Devil and remain unscathed. Inevitably, one will always become just another of his minions."

The Well-lit Séance
by David Marcum

"You are considering a holiday?" asked Sherlock Holmes as he attempted to light the somewhat-dried dottles left over from his previous day's pipes. "Is Mary in on the planning, or will it be a surprise?"

"At this point, it's only the vaguest thought of my own," I said with a smile. "Of course, you watched as my gaze wandered from my old desk which has become rather buried under your own books and papers, and thence to the bookcase, specifically the gazetteers there on the second shelf, and finally to the cabinet used to store your impressive collection of Ordinance Maps. No doubt my expression became unfocused at that point as I pictured various pleasant locations, and I recall that I touched my wedding ring."

"That, and the fact that yesterday you mentioned that Mary's health has been somewhat off of late, and that you had prescribed a change." He tossed his match into the fire and sat down across from me with a smile. "Sometimes it isn't so much sharp observations and deductions as simply interest in a friend's plans. Do you have anywhere in mind?"

I related my ideas for a few possible sites, but I was a bit limited in my choices due to the fact that it was October – not always the best month for making a journey. However, winter would soon follow, and if we didn't go now, we might be forced to wait until spring.

I had dropped into Baker Street that Sunday morning in order to meet with Holmes and Inspector Peter Jones regarding any remaining details that needed to be discussed concerning our activities the night before in the vaults of the Coburg branch of the City and Suburban Bank. It had been a most remarkable affair resulting in the arrest of John Clay, a man that Holmes considered was the fourth smartest in London. His plan to tunnel into the bank had been bold, and the distraction he'd devised leading up to it, tricking the poor man who owned the shop at the other end of the tunnel into leaving every day to copy the encyclopedia while the tunnel was being dug, was audacious – but one would never think of Clay as smart based upon the way he acted after his arrest. He devolved into a ranting foul-mouthed jackanapes who had to be restrained by four constables before he could be locked into the police van.

"The Professor will be upset," Holmes had murmured as the criminal was driven away.

But that was yesterday, and for now the escalating game that Holmes was playing with London's criminal element was paused for a moment. Over coffee, Holmes and I debated the strengths and weaknesses of various holiday locations until the doorbell rang. In moments Inspector Jones had joined us and, over a pleasant breakfast prepared by Mrs. Hudson, we elaborated on the facts that led to the previous night's events.

"It's an airtight case, thank the Lord," said Jones, wiping his mouth. "Clay's argument that he was just a bystander is absurd, considering that he was the one who first pushed up the vault floor before the eyewitnesses – each of us waiting in the vault – and even his mates behind him in the tunnel have turned on him. And yet, with Royal blood in him, and considering the fools who regularly sit on juries, it's very possible he still might get off. I want to sew this one up good and proper."

Jones made no mention of Professor Moriarty, Clay's shadowy master, and neither did Holmes nor I – Jones because he may or may not have known of the Professor at that point in time, and Holmes and I because we still didn't completely know whom we could trust, even on the official force.

We talked for a few more minutes, about attempted bank robbery and other cases, and a bit of gossip regarding the other Scotland Yard inspectors. Our visitor could only shake his head when the conversation turned to the Yard's *other* Inspector Jones, Athelney. "Bless him," said Peter Jones, "his heart's in the right place, and there's no one braver – you know most of all, Mr. Holmes, with what he was willing to do to his own reputation and career during the Ripper mess to save The Crown – but if the rest of us didn't keep him on the rails . . . . And if I see the two of us confused in the newspapers one more time – !" He tipped up his cup and finished his coffee. "It's enough to drive a man to drink!" He stood up with a grin. "I know you wrote about Athelney in that book earlier this year, Doctor – the one about the Sholto murder. Should you ever record me in one of your tales, please promise to be a bit more kind!"

I nodded. "I simply record the facts, Inspector. You have nothing to fear."

Then, with a nod and thanking us for our help, and for bringing the matter to him – he'd long coveted the capture John Clay – he departed. We heard him pass Mrs. Hudson on the landing, thanking her for breakfast, and then the good lady entered, bringing Holmes a note before gathering the breakfast dishes.

"It was hand delivered by a nice-looking fellow," she explained while Holmes examined the envelope. "Tall, well-dressed. About thirty, I'd say. He had a watch fob with the initials '*R.B.*', and his fingernails were clean."

81

"Thank you, Mrs. Hudson," said Holmes, who had by this point read the letter and passed it to me.

As Mrs. Hudson departed and pulled the door shut behind her, I said with a smile, "She is becoming more observant. Your methods are rubbing off on all of us."

By that time we had moved back to our chairs beside the fireplace, and Holmes was relighting his pipe. He gestured with the stem toward me, saying, "Then tell me what *you* observe."

I examined the letter, noting that it was expensive paper with a matching envelope. "The address in Mayfair indicates wealth. The writing, both on the envelope and on the single sheet, were made by a right-handed man using a pen with a nib in good condition and expensive ink. There was no sign of hesitation or emotional distress – the lines were firm and clear, running evenly from left to right. It is signed *Richard Birlsthorpe*. An interesting name," I added. "And his father, Giles Birlsthorpe – Surely that must be the same fellow responsible for Birlsthorpe's Gargling Oil, and all those other patent medicines produced by that company."

"And the letter?" prodded Holmes. "Can you make anything from the limited contents?"

I read it again:

Mr. Holmes,

> *Please forgive my intrusion on a Sunday. I have a family problem related to my father, Giles Birlsthorpe, which is mounting by the day, and after the events of last night, my mind is made up that I must do something about it. When I get a notion, I can't rest until it's settled.*

> *If possible, may I visit you on Monday to explain my situation? A reply to the provided address will serve to fix the appointment time.*

Very best,
Richard Birlsthorpe

I replaced the folded sheet into the envelope and again pondered the address – Hill Street, just west of Berkeley Square. "Nothing but the obvious – that it concerns something related to his father, an ongoing situation that escalated last night."

As I spoke, Holmes rose and walked around his chair to the shelf of ponderous commonplace books to the left of the fireplace. Pulling out a volume near the middle, he carried it over to the dining table. I rose and followed.

I could see that he had chosen the volume for "*P*", which I could only assume stood for "*Patent Medicine*" rather than "*Birlsthorpe*". His filing system was definitely something of his own devising, but I had come to have a limited understanding of it during the years I'd known him, and at times I could even make use of the books on my own.

"Books" is too generous a term, I suppose. They were great scrapbooks, filled with newspaper clippings that Holmes found of interest related to people, places, and things which might be of use to him. Often he saw connections and patterns, sometimes running back and forth across years, and his documentation of these had been useful on more occasions than I could count. In addition to the various clippings, there were countless loose items tucked into the pages – theatre tickets and pamphlets, more than one type of feather, and occasionally envelopes filled with soil samples. Once I'd opened one of the volumes to find a small vial of blood tucked inside, which started to fall when freed. I barely caught it, and my admonition about putting something so fragile in such a place seemed to have found root, because as far as I knew, Holmes never again stored objects of that sort in such an unlikely location.

"Hmm," he said, reading the biography of Giles Birlsthorpe. "Born September 1818 – he turned seventy-two last month. Married late, had one son, Richard, born 1859. Mrs. Hudson was nearly right about his age. The wife died five years ago. The father is famous, as you recognized, for the invention and marketing of a number of patent medicines, starting with his Gargling Oil in the 1860's. Before that, he'd had a tedious job working for a London chemist in Shoe Lane. He started selling his Oil on his own time, and within a year, he'd earned enough to turn around and buy the his employer's shop. After that, success followed success as he came up with more and more of his medicines: Birlsthorpe's Bitters for Seasickness, Birlsthorpe's Black Draught, a purgative full of saline, and – most curious – Birlsthorpe's Eclectric Tonic, to regulate the body's inner electricity. *Eclectric* . . . ?"

"And the son?" I asked. "Do you have any notes related to him?"

Holmes shut the book with a disappointed look. "Nothing beyond his date of birth as part of his father's narrative." He shelved the volume and turned to look at me. "Would you be interested in hearing his story? If so, what time should I have him arrive?"

"I would, and four o'clock, if that's acceptable. Monday's are always busier – catching up after the weekend."

Holmes nodded and indicated that he would make the appointment by return note. After a few more minutes, I left. Walking home to

Paddington, I considered what I knew of Birlsthorpe's *faux* medicines, and realized that it wasn't much, except that I would never prescribe them, and whenever a patient told me about using them, I quickly recommended something else. From what I'd heard, they were harmless – unlike some others like Fowler's Solution, full of arsenic, that were sold as a treat-all for many illnesses which they could never cure, including some forms of cancer. Then there was Godfrey's Cordial, full of laudanum and often called "Mother's Friend" because it was prescribed to quiet cranky children. But too often it was overused, and children died.

I had never heard anything bad about Birlsthorpe's potions – except that those who used them wasted their money, bottle after bottle – funds that could have been better-spent elsewhere.

I reached my own doorstep with quite a bit of curiosity as to what Richard Birlsthorpe might have to tell us on the morrow. Possibly his father had become involved in some unsavory or dishonest business deal.

It turned out that I couldn't have been more wrong, and it was nothing that I could have imagined. But that was usually the case.

"What do you know of the human aura?" asked the man sitting in the basket chair. I could see that Holmes was, for once, in the dark. He glanced at me, and I nodded that I'd heard of it.

"There is a belief," I explained, " – *not* shared by the majority of the medical field – that all living things produce an energy field." I wondered how this related to the sales of bogus medications. "Based on the field's strengths, its ebbs-and-flows, and even its coloring if one can see it, the state of the organism's health and well-being can be determined. If this field shows signs of darkness, for instance, the patient is in a condition of spiritual and electric illness, and should be treated accordingly."

"From your tone," said our visitor, "I gather you don't put much stock in it."

"It's claptrap," I replied with certainty. "Ineffable twaddle."

"Quite right," Richard Birlsthorpe nodded vigorously. "I agree entirely, Doctor, and thank you for your honesty." Then he looked toward Holmes. "My father, however, is a convert to this . . . this '*ineffable twaddle*'. He believes in it, and is well on his way to becoming a missionary for it. He's even managed to get a few legitimate medical men interested. It's bad enough he made his fortune selling quack remedies and nostrums to the gullible. Now he's trying to read other people's 'atmospheres'. He thinks he has the 'gift', and it's because he's under the influence of someone – a fraud – that I want you to investigate."

Truly, this was not what I expected, and I could tell that Holmes was caught afoot as well. As I'd discussed the affair with Mary the night

84

before, I'd convinced myself that the Birlsthorpe son was seeking a consultation about some prosaic matter – never anticipating that it concerned human auras. And yet, I thought that once the peculiar trappings of this nonsense were stripped away, the idea was really no different than other forms of patent medicine.

Once again, I couldn't have been more wrong.

When I'd arrived at 221 Baker Street on Monday afternoon, Richard Birlsthorpe was stepping down from a cab. He was handsome and carried himself with confidence. He paid the cabbie, and then took a moment to look up and engage the man in conversation, asking if the fellow was married or had children. When the cabbie affirmed both, Birlsthorpe gave him something extra, causing the cabbie's eyes to widen. He expressed enthusiastic thanks before moving on.

I had introduced myself and said that I'd be joining him and Holmes, if that was all right. He'd heard of me, and indicated that he had no objections at all. Then I rang the bell, rather than using the key that I still retained. Mrs. Hudson nodded to me with a smile and said that Holmes was upstairs, and that she'd be right up with tea. I led Birlsthorpe up to 221b and introduced him to Holmes, and thus there was no chance for a comparing of notes before refreshments were served and the man began his narrative.

"This fraudulent person," said Holmes. "What can you tell us about him?"

"He is my father's secretary. Clayton Kenneth Pounds. He's about fifty – from up north somewhere. My father . . . he is a difficult man. He always has been, but particularly so for the last five years. It has become more and more difficult for him to retain a secretary. Father is seventy-two, but he refuses to retire, or to hand over the reins to his managers, each of whom are more-than-competent to continue running the business.

"After his last secretary quit, having put up with far more abuse than should be expected, Pounds interviewed and obtained the job. He's unmarried, and I don't know much about him. He's close-mouthed, and has never responded to my efforts to find out more about his private life. I've considered hiring a detective before, just to discover out more of his past, but I never followed through. However, recently the man's influence on my father has become more and more fixed, and it's he that's encouraging my father to pursue his interest in these 'atmospheres' and 'auras' that supposedly linger around the human body like a colored cloud."

"Is he encouraging your father toward questionable business dealings?" I asked, thinking that my theory might still be verified.

"Probably. But what finally drove me to take action is the séances."

I had been perched forward on my chair, but this caused me to settle back. I glanced toward Holmes, and there was a glint of interest in his eyes.

"Tell us more," he said.

Birlsthorpe nodded. "Last March, when the previous secretary quit, interviews were held to replace him. Pounds was hired, and from what I've seen of his resume, there was nothing about him that was any more or less qualified than the other applicants. As my father runs through secretaries like others wear out socks, the interview process has become rather standardized.

"As I said, Pounds is a taciturn man, and my efforts to get to know him have been for naught. I like people, and take an interest in them, but Pounds seems to have a wall around him. Not just with me – I understand that some people are private, and others just don't get along, but Pounds makes no effort to create any connections with any of the rest of my father's staff. In fact, the only person that seems to have that connection is my father himself.

"While I no longer live in the Mayfair house, I'm a regular visitor, and I have certain duties within the company that require that I visit my father daily. Through these visits, I've seen Pounds begin to have greater and greater influence, setting himself up as something of a gatekeeper around my father. This is only made easier as my father gets older and becomes more feeble and dependent – although he would never admit it, as he believes he's just as strong and capable as he was twenty years ago.

"My father's successes have been documented, but he found his calling, such as it is, before I was born, so I don't know what he was like then. However, by the time I was in my teens, I could see that he truly believed that his brews, elixirs, and philters were fully efficacious in dealing with people's ills. He becomes quite contrary if someone gives any indications that they are merely colored water and flavored tonics with no actual benefit, other than that which the patient convinces themselves to believe – the *placebo* effect, I believe it's called, Doctor."

I nodded.

"At least our products don't injure or kill people. Father has never been one of those who believe that a small dose of poison has benefits – since there are too many people who think that if a little is good, more must be better, and they take greater and greater doses of some of our competitor's products, with the result being a permanent injury or death." He glanced at me. "You know the ones of which I speak."

"I do," I said. "Fowler's, of course. And then there are Dr. Rush's Bilious Pills and Godbold's Vegetable Balsam, both containing mercury. Someday they will be illegal."

86

"And don't forget Soliman's Water and Swaim's Panacea – also dispensing medicinal mercury by way of the shelves of every chemist in the nation." He shook his head. "It's enough to disgust you with human nature."

"All very interesting," interrupted Holmes. "But what of the séances?"

"Right. About six weeks ago, Pounds showed my father something new – lenses that apparently allow the wearer to see the 'atmospheres' surrounding a person. My father was quite enthusiastic about it, and couldn't wait to show me on my next visit. I must admit that it was a curious sensation. Pounds had found a set of leather goggles – he was quite vague as to where – which had dark-tinted lenses, rather like what one sees on eyeglasses worn by the blind. The goggles fit tightly around one's head, and then . . . and then, when looking at a person, one can see an outline around them, as if they are lit from behind by a bright light – rather like how the moon looks during a solar eclipse. I've only tried it twice, and to be honest, the experience is quite unpleasant, although Father insists it becomes easier with practice. It made my eyes burn and water."

"And did you see the different colors?" I asked with interest, thinking that this in fact might be a diagnostic tool, different from the useless "medicines" bottled by the elder Birlsthorpe.

"I'm not sure," replied the son. "I . . . I may have, but as I said, looking through the looking through the lenses hurt my eyes, and I wouldn't trust what I saw."

He looked at Holmes. "I can see that you're getting impatient to hear about the séances. They aren't that, precisely – not the same mumbo-jumbo that the spiritualists usually display. My father doesn't summon ghosts or attempt to transmit messages back and forth from the dead. There are no knockings on the table or floating phantasms. Rather, he gathers a small group and, using the goggles, he makes readings about them, and their conditions. He started by simply commenting on their atmospheres, and whether someone looked healthy or unwell. But lately, with Pounds' encouragement, he's been delving deeper, claiming that he can see details of their everyday lives – their relationships, and their jobs, and their financial situations. He claims that as he uses the goggles more and more, he becomes attuned their waves and vibrations – and that everything he's said has been confirmed to be correct. He first talked of making them into a product that we might sell along with the medicines, but now – enjoying the attention he's receiving, I suppose – he wants to keep having his 'counseling sessions', as he calls them, and he selfishly wants to be the only one who has such a power."

"And Pounds is encouraging this."

"He absolutely is!" said Birlsthorpe, suddenly pounding his fist on the arm of the basket chair. "I have no idea why, except that it makes him even more trusted by my father. He's saying what my father wants to hear, while any reasonable word to the contrary that I provide is only driving a wedge between us."

"Which do you want?" asked Holmes. "For Pounds to be investigated, and exposed if he's some sort of confidence man? Or do you want the truth about the goggles and the séances?"

Birlsthorpe looked to each of us. "Both, I suppose. Whichever one is necessary to free my father from this man's influence, and also to prevent whatever is going to happen in relation to the goggles. Public embarrassment? A lawsuit? I have no idea where this is headed."

"Tell me the truth, Mr. Birlsthorpe," said Holmes, sitting up straighter and setting aside his pipe. "Are you concerned that the increasing divide between you and your father might lead to you losing your inheritance?"

Birlsthorpe looked a bit nonplussed, but he showed no signs of anger. Holmes continued.

"After receiving your message yesterday, I did a bit of research. I found that, as expected, you are your father's only heir, and that you expect to receive a sizable inheritance upon his death. His financial dealings are of interest in various quarters, as it's hoped that the business will remain stable after his passing. You are not the only one concerned about the influence of this man, Pounds, but you *are* the one who stands to lose considerably should the secretary obtain full control over your father."

Birlsthorpe nodded, showing no anger or irritation as I might have expected at Holmes's statement. "I do want to make sure that I receive what's coming to me. But it isn't greed, Mr. Holmes. It's responsibility.

"My father married late, and I was born when he was already in middle age. He was already the man who built up his business from nothing. But my mother was a good soul who saw the good that was still in him, and she was a wonderful influence on him while she lived. He realized it and appreciated it. But then she died, and in his loneliness, he has slipped back into the rather ruthless fellow that apparently he once was.

"I am ashamed of how my father has taken advantage of those who needed better help than they received, and how that part of him seems to be on the ascent once again. I love him, for all his vexations, and I will miss him, but when he's gone – when I'm in control – I intend to use the money for good."

"That may cause as much consternation in various boardrooms as if Pounds were to gain control," said Holmes. "I take it you don't plan to continue producing and marketing your company's ineffectual products?"

"I do not. I plan to pivot to items of proven and beneficial value." He leaned forward. "You say that there is concern about the direction of the company – and how my father is being manipulated?"

"There is – but I heard no mention of these atmospheric readings as part of the vague distress. That . . . intrigues me." Then Holmes nodded. "I will take your case. When is the next . . . *séance*, as you called it?"

"Tomorrow night. Pounds is now running several of them a week. The one on Saturday night was the most outrageous yet – at least that I've seen. I don't go to every one of them, and I certainly have the sense when I'm there that I'm not a welcome visitor, but I haven't been obnoxious when I attend, so my father allows me to stay. I simply sit and watch . . . and wonder what's going on. In this last case, there were eight people present besides my father, Pounds, and myself, and father gave very specific advice to six of them – quit your job, for instance, or your wife has deceived you. He told another that the child he thinks of as his own son belongs to another. Regardless of whether these 'atmospheres' exist around a person, there's no way he could *see* that kind of information – and no reason that he should be sharing it, true or not. Pounds has convinced him of his own skill and authority, and it's only going to get worse. It must be stopped."

"Can you arrange to have Dr. Watson invited to the event tomorrow night?"

I didn't react at this inclusion in his plans without Holmes first verifying that I might have other commitments, but I too was intrigued, and if I had been otherwise obligated, I would have attempted to free myself in order to attend the meeting. Birlsthorpe drummed his fingers on the chair arm for a moment and then said, "I can. It will be a bit difficult, but father won't deny it – especially if it seems as if I'm coming around to his side." He looked at me. "Number 4, Hill Street, in Mayfair. Eight o'clock. I'll meet you outside five minutes or so beforehand."

I nodded. "Perhaps I should attend under an alias?"

"Do you have something in mind?"

"Perhaps . . . Dr. Jabez Roylott?"

Birlsthorpe frowned, and Holmes interjected. "Possibly something that doesn't sound like a circus ringmaster, Watson."

"Campbell, then," I replied. "James Campbell."

"Excellent," replied the client. Then he looked at Holmes. "Do you need anything else from me?"

"I think not. There is plenty of time between now and then for me to set further inquiries into motion."

We rose and shook hands, and then Birlsthorpe departed. After we heard the downstairs door shut, I turned back to Holmes. "Circus ringmaster?"

He laughed in that peculiar silent way of his. "You must admit that 'Jabez Roylott' is a bit over the top."

I nodded, laughing as well. "Is there any assistance that I can provide before tomorrow night?"

"I think not. Discovering Pounds' background should be routine, and I have some thoughts about the séance. I believe that while you're in attendance at the main performance, I'll see what I can determine backstage."

"I'm not sure what you hope to find," I said. "It sounds as if the usual bogus séance tricks aren't used – no tooting horns or ectoplasm. Birlsthorpe's father doesn't even pretend to be possessed by a five-thousand-year-old Pharaoh."

Holmes nodded. "In addition to researching Pounds, I'll see what I can found out about the household. When researching the Birlsthorpes *père et fils*, I learned that the old man has very few servants. In fact, since Pounds has come to work for him, the number has dropped to a maid, a cook, and an old man-of-work who carries out odd jobs."

"Funny that the son didn't mention that – another example of Pounds isolating the father."

"He told us the gist of the story. Perhaps he simply neglected to think of it. In any case, it means that the house will be that much easier to visit tomorrow night during the performance."

"What do you expect to find?"

"I have no idea – but I'm confident that I'll find something!"

The next morning, I completed my rounds near Covent Garden and, having some time before I needed to return for office hours, I decided to do some further research of my own. I hailed a cab, instructing the driver to cross the river and carry me to St. Thomas' Hospital, directly across from the Palace of Westminster. Big Ben was just striking eleven at the top of the great clock tower when I went inside, asking to speak with Dr. Walter John Kilner, who I had found mentioned in several journals the previous night while researching the curious question of atmospheres and auras.

I had met him a few times before, but we were not close friends. On the first occasion, I was eating lunch with my friend Doyle, always rather too impressionable and credulous when faced with pseudo-science, when he spotted Kilner at a nearby table. He introduced us, stating that Kilner was the medical electrician at St. Thomas, and was in charge of electrotherapy, delivering measured charges of current to the body to treat various ills. Barts, where I had been associated, had been involved in medico-electrical research since the mid-eighteenth century, but it was never an area that I had bothered to examine – or to which I had given much credence.

Kilner was an average looking fellow, thick dark hair parted in the middle over a wide forehead. He had straight brows across expressionless watchful eyes, and a mouth that seemed wider than it actually was as his face narrowed toward his chin. He never seemed to smile, and in spite of Doyle's typical jovial efforts on the day that I was introduced, the man didn't make any interested response.

I probably wouldn't have bothered with talking to him at all, except in my limited researches the night before, his was a name that I recognized, and he was in London.

I was led to a basement laboratory where Kilner's office was located. I couldn't put my finger on it, but there was a feeling there that I didn't like – the same as one finds when touring the torture rooms of old castles. There is something about the old buildings that have absorbed terrible human suffering, wherein they have their own atmospheres and auras. Holmes has scoffed at this when I've mentioned it to him, but at times when we've visited such places, and he hasn't realized that I was watching, I can see that he is aware of such things too.

Kilner was welcoming enough when I knocked on his office door, and willing to take a few minutes to answer my questions. I explained that I was involved in an investigation as to whether humans could produce atmospheres that couldn't be seen by the human eye, and also a new lens device that I'd heard of that was used to observe them.

"No," he said, "I'm unaware of any such thing, or atmospheres such as you describe, but that doesn't mean that they don't exist. I take it that you have the layman's knowledge of electricity," he added.

"I believe that I do. I understand current, and how voltaic batteries and generators work. The principles of circuitry – "

"Yes, yes," he interrupted impatiently. "Well, the body generates electricity too. A very small amount, certainly, but it's there none-the-less. The heart, for instance, has an electrical current, and so does the brain. One can see the effects that electricity in different levels has on tissue. Large amounts, such as a lightning strike, can burn the flesh, or superheat the water inside the body so suddenly that it explodes. But smaller controlled amounts of electricity can do amazing things. We're only in the early stages of understanding it, you realize – regulating heart-beats, stopping seizures, using shocks to treat insanity or discourage deviant behavior. But we progress daily. Who is to say that we will find next? Ritter discovered ultraviolet light nearly a hundred years ago. He only did so by seeing how some unknown factor was discoloring silver chloride. Perhaps the body does emit its own fields. It would explain a great deal, wouldn't it? Those who scoff at human beings' *spiritual sides* – that there is such a thing as a *soul* – might acknowledge such a thing as an electric aura, generated by the body during life, and then – after death . . . ?"

He rattled on for quite a bit longer, talking about conservation of energy and showing more enthusiasm than I'd seen from him on any previous meeting. His professional focus was something that provided him great joy. Yet, I quickly began to realize that Kilner had very little to offer that would be useful to me, so I gradually disengaged myself with thanks. He rose from behind his desk, offering his hand. "Please tell me what you learn. What you have suggested is fascinating. It opens up all sorts of possibilities for treatment . . . ."

Outside, I was glad that I hadn't specifically mentioned Birlsthorpe, as Kilner would likely be calling on him by day's end. In hindsight, I wondered at the wisdom of my visit. Now that Kilner was aware of the concept, it might lead him to further investigate it, wasting his time on a dead-end path. On the other hand, possibly there was something to it after all. Kilner's explanations about the electrical nature of the body were enough to realize that we really know very little indeed.

I found a cab and returned to Paddington in time for office hours, but too late for a proper lunch.

At five-minutes-to-eight that night, I stepped from my cab at the corner of Hill Street and Berkeley Square, and then walked the short distance west to Number 4. Waiting on the street was our client, dressed in a conservative dark suit. He offered his hand. "Dr. *Campbell* – so good of you to join me." He emphasized the name, as if to make sure that I'd noticed he remembered. "They're expecting us."

I looked both ways but no one was nearby. "Was there any difficulty in making the arrangements?"

He shook his head. "My father didn't care. He's so convinced by his own powers that the idea of another stranger stopping by is of no concern. Pounds was quite tight-lipped about it, but what could he do?"

"Have you heard from Holmes?" I whispered. "Did he give any indication of his plans – how he intends to enter the house?"

"I spoke with him this afternoon and let him know the best way to obtain access, and how to stay out of the way of the remaining servants. He seems very capable, doesn't he?" He nodded toward the door. "Come inside. They'll start soon."

It was a handsome house, but I was rather surprised that it wasn't larger. Surely the elder Birlsthorpe could have afforded something much grander in scale. It was a corner property, four stories plus a basement that could be accessed by an areaway, and an attic, as indicated by dormer windows. Curiously, the entire right side of the building and the ground floor of the left were painted white, but the upper three stories on the left were of red brick. It gave the place a most conflicted appearance, as if one type of house had sprouted out of another.

Birlsthorpe appeared to read my thoughts and stopped on the stop step. "My father originally lived in a much finer house, closer to Hyde Park, but when he married my mother, she insisted that something more modest was proper, and he agreed. She was a very beneficial influence on him, and it's truly a tragedy that she passed." Then he knocked, and almost immediately the door opened. A tall shadowed man saw us and then stepped aside for us to pass.

"Master Richard," he said, as if he were addressing a school-boy instead of a man in his early thirties, "you're nearly late." Then the man looked at me, measuring up and down to see what I presented. Apparently he wasn't impressed.

"This is Pounds," said Richard Birlsthorpe. "My father's secretary." He shed his coat and handed it, along with his hat, to the man as if he were just another servant – an intentional diminution to put him in his place, I was sure. I handed him my outer garments as well – Why should I undo our client's efforts?

"We'll go in now," said Birlsthorpe, giving the man no further attention. I followed down a darkened hallway, and then left into a well-lit parlor.

It was tastefully furnished with a few small tables here and there, supporting vases or bowls. I suspected that this was the lingering influence of the dead wife and mother. I noticed them only for instant, however, as my gaze was drawn to the center of the room, where a large round table rested underneath a bright electric chandelier of the type that one occasionally saw in finer homes. The table was surrounded by chairs – seven of them. Four were already filled, and one was soon taken by Pounds, who quickly sat down next to an elderly man who projected an air of authority.

"Richard," the man grumbled, "you were almost late. I would have had Pounds lock the door. The readings cannot be disturbed. You know that! This is your friend?"

"That's right," said Birlsthorpe as he directed me to one of the two remaining empty chairs, directly across from his father. I sat at

Birlsthorpe's right and took a moment to look at the other members of our party.

Across the table was Giles Birlsthorpe, with what could only be the atmosphere-reading goggles lying before him. To his right was Pounds, and then – between the secretary and Richard Birlsthorpe – was an elderly bird-like woman who was watching the father and son with great interest, her gaze darting back and forth as if she expected some sort of lightning storm to spring up between them.

"You're Doctor Campbell," declared the old man. "Where do you practice?"

"Barts," I replied. "I consult on trauma cases."

"Hmm," he replied. "I'll bet you have a story or two. I can't wait to see *your* atmosphere." Then he gestured to the woman.

"This is Mrs. Emmaline Calvert. A widow. She's been here before." She nodded at me, and I could see as the light shifted that she was in her sixties. Her small frame had initially given the impression that she was younger.

"And these two," continued the elder Birlsthorpe, nodding his head to his left, "are John Reynolds and Vaughn Taylor." He referred to the two men that sat between him and me, both in their thirties, and lounging back with the same shared attitudes that they were tolerating a foolish elder in the hopes of picking up some useful scrap along the way – even if it was just an amusing anecdote for later use at their club.

Giles Birlsthorpe lifted a blue-veined hand gnarled and knobbed by arthritis and laid it on the goggles. "Let's begin." He grasped the strap awkwardly and lifted the device toward his head. Pounds rose and stepped behind him, helping to place the strap in the correct place and seat the lenses before the old man's eyes. I risked a glance at Richard Birlsthorpe, and could see the pain in his expression at his father's feeble condition, and also a hint of anger at the involvement of the secretary, Clayton Kenneth Pounds.

As I watched, I wished that I knew what Holmes was up to. I'd meant to go by Baker Street during the late afternoon and see what he'd learned, but an emergency call had prevented that. In fact, I'd been lucky to get free in time to attend this gathering. Was Holmes already in the building? And what did he hope to accomplish after he arrived? If there were no typical séance tricks, there was no one to catch upstairs or in the cellar, manipulating objects that might be mistaken for ghostly manifestations. Apparently Giles Birlsthorpe simply wore his goggles and made comments about his guests – all very trite, except for the bizarre nature in which the comments were generated.

There was no effort made to dim the light, as I had seen so often before at spiritual séances. It was often explained that the bright lights scared away the ghosts – when in fact it made it too easy for the participants to see wires or assistants dressed all in black moving behind the chairs, reaching in to shift objects or touch things. No, these proceedings were well-illuminated.

With the goggles in place, Pounds returned to his seat, looking expectantly at the old man. He in turn looked around the table, one after another, silent for several minutes. Then:

"You all have atmospheres. That's good. I'd hate to meet someone who didn't!" He laughed – the first such emotion I'd heard from him – and it was actually engaging, as if this might be a pleasant fellow after all. He looked foolish, however. The goggles were a great leather piece that completely covered his face from forehead to lower cheeks. A raised section of darker leather was spliced in to arch over his nose, and his white hair stuck out over the top, tousled and uncombed, giving him a look of madness. The lenses themselves were great greasy-looking black circles, held in place by additional circles of leather trimmed in the same shape, and apparently riveted to affix them on either side of the nose piece. It was a solid construction, and it wouldn't be falling apart anytime soon.

I wasn't surprised when I was Giles Birlsthorpe's first subject.

"Campbell," he said. "Good atmosphere – Red. That's energetic and well-grounded. You have hints of green – that means you're social – and some yellow as well. The means you're creative. The edges are straight – no jagged places that would indicate emotional turmoil, or dark intruding spots trailing from out cancer or other illnesses." He nodded. "I'm glad my son brought you. He does well to have such friends. Come back again. As I'm able to make subsequent readings about a person, I can tell more about them. It will be useful for you – you'll be glad you did."

Then his attention turned to the others at the table. Next was Mrs. Calvert. He asked her if what he'd told her about her son's financial secret had turned out to be true.

"It was!" she exclaimed, bursting into motion like a beater-flushed pheasant. Her hands and arms flapped as she enthusiastically sat up and chirped for several minutes about all that Birlsthorpe had told her, and how every bit of it had been correct. Meanwhile, the man in the goggles just watched her and nodded sagely, unsurprised at everything she listed.

Then Birlsthorpe turned to the two men beside him. "Reynolds, you've been gambling again. I see that you lost several hundred – no, just over a *thousand* pounds at the tables last night."

Reynolds suddenly looked sheepish and dropped his gaze. "That's true," he mumbled. "It's all right though. I'll make it back tonight." He looked back up. "What do you see? Am I showing any orange? Will this be a good night?"

Birlsthorpe nodded, the light glinting off the round black lenses. "Absolutely. In fact, if you can beg or borrow some more funds, take them with you. You're set to win tonight – and big!"

Reynolds nodded and sat back, satisfied. Then Vaughn Taylor perked up, knowing that his turn was next.

Birlsthorpe watched him for several silent minutes, and the mood around the table, which had been rather charged following the announcement of Reynolds' impending good luck, began to feel rather grim.

"You didn't follow my advice," was the elder Birlsthorpe's declaration, and Taylor grimaced.

"I . . . I couldn't. She wouldn't have listened."

"She's your *mother*, man!" Birlsthorpe's expression was neutral, the goggles revealing nothing, his voice was angry. "Her atmosphere is still intruding upon yours. I can see it there, edging in toward your own heart – and unless you do something, she will die within a fortnight! Do you understand what I'm telling you? Do you?"

"I . . . I do. I'll do my best. But if she won't listen – "

"She must! I have been given this gift – to help. To *heal*! But how can I do so when you refuse to listen?" Then he reached up and pulled the goggles from his head, tossing them aside in disgust. "It's too much," he muttered. Then, louder, "We're done for tonight. I can't see such suffering and know that nothing will be done to prevent it. Don't you know that I can see when you're lying, Taylor? It might as well be tattooed on your forehead! You have no spine to stand up to your mother, and without treatment she will die."

He turned in his seat. "Help me to bed, Pounds. I'm done here."

And without another word, he stood and shambled from the room. He seemed to stumble for a moment before finding which direction he wished to go. The secretary stood as well, looked around at each of us for a few seconds, his expression turning speculative as it passed over me, and with the hint of a frown at Robert Birlsthorpe. For the others he had no expression at all. Then he followed his employer into the hall, and in a moment I heard them both ascending the stairs.

The rest of us stood, encompassed by an awkward silence. Then, without any additional conversation, we all went outside, pulling the front door shut behind us.

I was surprised that our client hadn't remained behind to check on his father, but perhaps he felt that it was better to stay with me. We stood outside the door as the two men walked off together to the west and into

96

the October darkness, while the little woman continued down Hill Street back to Berkeley Square, no doubt to find a cab. When they were gone, Birlsthorpe whispered, "Mr. Holmes said that he'd meet us here."

And in fact, it was just seconds later that he did so, appearing from around the corner to the mews. It was too dark to see his face, but his silhouette – his notable Inverness and fore-and-aft cap – made his identity quite obvious. He gestured to us. "Hurry – if we don't lose her, we may have this affair settled within the hour."

I was used to Holmes's unexplained commands, and thankfully, Birlsthorpe didn't question him, but instead joined us as we moved along Hill Street toward the better-lit Square a few hundred feet away. As we approached it, Holmes held up his hand and we paused. Then he darted ahead and looked to the south. Then, with a gesture, he hurried us forward.

"She has found a hansom. Hurry – summon that growler before we lose her!"

The driver was quick to act, understanding Holmes's instructions to follow the hansom without letting us be seen. Then, when we were in motion, he settled back with an explanation.

"Her name is Annie Henderson – Annie Sweet, they call her, because her of supposed kindly disposition."

"You know her then?"

"I know of her – and what I know convinces me that her involvement is all we need to know about this charade. Now we just need specific details."

"Did you find anything when you searched the house?" I asked.

Holmes nodded his head. "To be honest, I didn't really expect too, but the opportunity couldn't be ignored. Thank you for your information, Mr. Birlsthorpe. I was able to enter and move about exactly as you predicted, without encountering anyone or being seen. Of course, there was nothing to find in relation to a typical supernatural séance, so I didn't bother. Instead, I looked through your father's papers – and more specifically, the secretary's papers, as well as his bedroom. What I found was most instructive."

Birlsthorpe gestured with a hand, rather impatiently, for Holmes to continue.

"It seems," said Holmes, "that Mr. Pounds is accumulating a little trove of documents, all signed by your father, which are steadily giving him more and more power within your father's business, and in some cases, more and more bits of ownership as well. There are powers of attorney, deed and property transfers, and outright financial payments – quite substantial in size. Additionally, there are instances where your father has even signed over the rights to patents for his different medications."

Birlsthorpe was speechless. Then – "I knew that Pounds was up to something, but I had no idea what, or to the extreme that he's carried it. He's managed to completely worm his way into my father's confidence and do all of this in the little time that he's been employed?"

"Much less time than that, in fact. The dates on the various documents are no older than five weeks."

"Just after he began wearing the goggles," I said. "But what's the connection?"

"I suspect, from the research that I was able to carry out today, that he's being systematically blinded, and as Pounds accelerates his schemes, he's having your father sign papers that he cannot see, based on the misplaced trust he has in his secretary."

"Blinded?" cried his son. "How?"

"When he stood tonight," I said, "to leave the room, your father appeared to stumble, and to correct his course before heading straight to the door. Diminishing sight might explain that."

"It's the goggles," said Holmes. "I managed to reach Doyle on the telephone. He is an optic surgeon of our acquaintance," he added for Birlsthorpe's benefit. "When I described the goggles, he said that they might be coated with various dyes that would give the illusion of an aura or atmosphere when light passes through them. The best dyes for this purpose would be coal-tar derivatives, which – when placed that close to the eyes, and for longer and longer extended periods – would produce a quite-deleterious and cumulative effect."

Birlsthorpe's mouth became a tight line. "If we weren't going to find out more about what's been occurring, I'd stop the cab right now and go back to the house, and beat that man within an inch of his life."

As we'd talked, our route had taken us south and east, and we were then crossing the Lambeth Bridge. The night had cooled, and the river was flat and dark. The reflections from the gaslights were still – there was no chop or ripple upon the water. Then we were on the other side, moving slower down Old Paradise Street. A couple of turns to the south, and the hansom before us in the distance turned into Hamish Street. We reached the corner as it stopped halfway down, and the small lady disembarked, tossing up a coin to the cabbie.

Holmes knocked on the ceiling of our cab and we stopped as well. He told the driver to wait, and then we three set off down the street toward Annie Henderson – introduced to me not so long before as Emmaline Calvert, a widow.

She heard our footsteps and turned, suddenly tense. I couldn't blame her, and I felt ashamed – three men hurrying toward a single woman on a dark street. It wasn't so long since the Rippers had roamed the lanes of the capital. "Mrs. Calvert," I called, attempting to calm her.

She leaned forward, peering toward us. Her expression lightened. "Why, it's Mr. Birlsthorpe and his friend, the doctor." She straightened and a warmth came into her voice. Then she saw the third member of our party, and his distinctive garb. Her voice faltered and hardened. She no longer sounded very sweet. "And – I know you, Mr. Sherlock Holmes." Her tone was now flat and toneless.

"I expect so, Annie," said the detective. "Now what's to be? Will you answer our questions here, or at the Station?"

She sagged as if a string had been cut. "Here, I suppose. I've done nothing wrong." She looked over her shoulder. "Do you want to come inside?"

"No need. This will take five minutes, I think."

"That's right, it will," she agreed. "I was just doing a favor, you see, and earning a little bit besides."

"Who hired you?" asked Holmes.

"Mr. Pounds – the secretary. All I had to do was show up and agree with whatever the old man said, and remember it so that when he asked me about it the next time, I could agree again, as if whatever he claimed was correct."

"To make him think he had magical powers?" prodded Holmes. "That he could see auras, or give accurate advice and predict the future?"

"That's right. Whatever he said, I was supposed to act like he was right."

"I don't understand," said Richard Birlsthorpe.

"It's something of a reverse confidence game," I said, comprehending what was going on. "Pounds convinced your father to try the goggles – coated in something that causes an 'aura' in bright light. He wants your father to wear them more and more so that the coating will blind him."

"Blind him?" asked Annie Henderson. "I didn't know that anyone was supposed to be hurt! I thought that it was just to fool some of the other people who came to the little parties."

"I suspect that the others there were all also playing the same game," I said, and Holmes interjected, nodding.

"The goggles were making him go blind. Pounds hired people like you, Annie, and no doubt the other two men at the table tonight, along with others, to do what you were doing. They simply had to show up and let their atmospheres be read. Your father, Mr. Birlsthorpe, would then make announcements about what he thought he saw, and everyone would always happily agree. As his confidence grew in his abilities, he would make more statements and predictions, ever bolder, and whatever it was – a financial matter, a wager, a sick relative – the attendees simply agreed, further giving Birlsthorpe the belief that he has powers – and making him more and addicted to the wearing of the injurious goggles – and also becoming more and more dependent on his secretary, who had first directed him toward this miraculous 'gift'."

"You were listening from the hallway tonight," I said. "After you finished your search."

Holmes nodded, adding, "That's how I recognized Annie here, and knew that we had the opportunity to follow her and find out what her involvement was in all of this." He looked at her. "The other two men – John Reynolds and Vaughn Taylor. Of course they were hired by Pounds as well."

She nodded. "I don't know Reynolds, but Taylor is really Seth Peters. He'll do whatever you ask, if the money's right."

"I believe we'll find that every one of those who have sought readings will have been paid by the secretary to agree with whatever comments are thrown their way. Watson's invitation must have left Pounds nonplussed – here was a man who wasn't in on the game." He looked at the son. "Fortunately for Pounds, your father was cautious in his initial readings about a stranger. Have there been any other outsiders at these parties?"

"None that I know of for sure. I haven't been to every séance, but Dr. Watson is certainly the only outsider that I've brought."

"I believe that's right," added Annie Henderson. "I've known some of the others that have attended, and had the feeling that the ones I hadn't met before were also in on what was happening. And this man that you call Pounds? His true name is Willard Gables of Stepney. I've known him forever. I realized that when he was hired as a rich man's secretary, he must be up to something. A man like him couldn't simply accept his good fortune and make an honest go of it. His type has to turn it nasty." She turned to look at the younger Birlsthorpe. "I'm sorry, sir. I had no idea that your father was being injured. He seems a good sort." Then, back to Holmes. "I suppose that I have to make a statement to the police."

Holmes nodded, and within moments we were back in the four-wheeler, crossing the bridge and traveling alongside the river to the new building where Scotland Yard had recently relocated.

Our friend Inspector MacDonald was on duty, and he quickly understood what had occurred. Birlsthorpe swore out a complaint, and then we, along with several constables, were headed back to Mayfair.

Birlsthorpe unlocked the front door and allowed the policemen to enter quietly. He then led them upstairs, but after indicating where Pounds could be found, he went a different direction, to his father's room in order to explain what was happening, even as the secretary was being dragged from his bed and so downstairs.

Holmes and I stood in the hall, about midway between the two bedrooms. From Pounds' room we heard muffled noises, and then angry bellows. Then the secretary was being pulled from the room and into the hall, fighting the two burly officers gripping him on either side and looking ridiculous in his nightshirt and uncombed hair. When they reached the bottom of the steps and he saw Annie Henderson standing there, all the fight went out of him. He understood then that his scheme was undone.

Holmes stepped into the parlor and then returned, carrying the curious goggles. He glanced at the man in custody, getting his first good look at him before handing the device to MacDonald. "For the Black Museum, Mr. Mac," he stated. "Not quite as sinister as Jack's letter from Hell, but rather memorable nonetheless."

It was then that Richard Birlsthorpe assisted his father downstairs. The old man pulled his arm loose and stepped in front of Pounds, looking up at him while his mouth worked, as if he were chewing his rage into something manageable.

"I trusted you," was finally all the he could mutter. He raised a feeble arm as if to strike the secretary, but his son stepped forward, gently taking and lowering his wrist, and putting his other arm around his father's shoulders before turning him away.

"That's it, then," said MacDonald. "Belk, go upstairs and get this man some clothes. He can change at the Yard." Then he looked at us. "Will you join us – to go over the finer points?"

"Certainly," replied Holmes. "But there's no need for Watson to stay out any later. He has calls to make in the morning."

MacDonald nodded. "Still, I may stop around tomorrow, Doctor, if that's satisfactory, in order to confirm a few points."

I nodded. Then, with a general shuffling, everyone moved toward the door. I saw that Annie Henderson was also glumly now in the custody of a constable. I glanced over my shoulder to where Richard Birlsthorpe was explaining things again to the wizened man before him.

Mary was waiting up when I arrived home, and made for a most fascinated and attentive audience as I related the events of the supposed séance and subsequent journey across the city to obtain the true facts from Annie Henderson. Two days later she remained with curious interest as we entertained Dr. Kilner, who had stopped by at my invitation to hear more about the curious goggles. I understand that he was initially skeptical, but as the years passed, he ended up devoting a great deal of time and energy into his explorations of the mysterious auras and atmospheres that supposedly surround the human body.

Clayton Kenneth Pounds, more properly known as Willard Gables of Stepney, lost all interest in the topic on the night of his arrest. After a stretch in prison, I understand that he relocated to Australia, where I'm sure that a man with his dark and stunted character quickly found new ways to cause trouble.

Richard Birlsthorpe, on the other hand, was able to generate a great deal of good from the affair of the blinding goggles, convincing his father, who had thankfully suffered no permanent damage to his eyes, to evince a much more generous and charitable spirit before his passing a few years later. The secretary's plan, in a round-about way, had accomplished some good after all.

The Adventure of the Deadly Illness
by Dan Rowley and Don Baxter

Perhaps this wasn't a very splendid idea after all. I stood across the street from my intended destination, hesitating as memories overcame my earlier determination. My friend, Sherlock Holmes, had been dead for two years, done in by that arch-fiend Moriarty. And my beloved Mary had recently passed away just a few months ago. Shivering as much from the memories as from the unexpected spring chill, I reached inside my overcoat and retrieved the telegram that had brought me here. Perhaps that would renew my will.

Watson.

Have a problem with a patient. Would like to consult. I have a splendid idea of how you might assist. I'll be in London tomorrow. Meet me at five at Criterion Bar.

Newdegate

Sam Newdegate and I had met at Netley in 1878 for Army Surgeon training. Although we'd stayed in touch, primarily when he had occasion to travel from his home in Hounslow to London, we hadn't seen each other in well over a year.

While I was rereading the message, a hand lightly rested on my shoulder. It was Newdegate, a short, slim man about my age, with a receding hairline and no facial hair. "Watson, so capital to see you! I'd hoped you would come. Actually, I knew you couldn't resist a somewhat cryptic message. Let us leave this cold and repair to the bar. Have you been here before?"

"Yes, it's where I ran into Stamford, a dresser under me at Barts, who introduced me to Sherlock Holmes."

"I heard that he died. And Mary as well. I'm so sorry for your loss."

"Thank you. And it's good to see you as well. I agree that the bar should be more pleasant than out here in the street."

We made our way across, passed under the awning, walked through the entryway, and entered the main room. Little seemed to have changed since I had last been there – the gilded ceiling, the sparkling mirrors, the long bar with a vase of flowers at one end, the individual intimate tables. I forced myself to focus on the reason for being there today, rather than that long ago, fateful meeting with Stamford.

We settled ourselves at one of the tables, and Newdegate went to the bar and returned with two whisky-and-sodas. We spent several minutes catching each other up on events that had transpired since we'd last met, as old acquaintances will do.

"Well, Watson, let me explain why I asked to see you. It concerns a patient of mine – the owner of Hounslow Manor: Jules Armand."

"I don't know how much assistance I can render, as you are every bit as good a physician as I have known."

"It's only partly your medical expertise upon which I wish to call. Perhaps even more important is your association with Sherlock Holmes."

"Whatever do you mean?"

"There's a mystery here, and I'm hoping your familiarity with Holmes's methods can help me solve it. Allow me to explain in more detail.

"Jules Armand is a Provençal, born and bred in Marseille. His father was in shipping, and when Jules came of age, he expanded and started an import-export business for his own account. He moved to London about twenty years ago, and has grown the business quite remarkably. He focuses primarily on materials such as hemp, cotton, and jute. And he has more recently branched out into lubricants of various kinds. He has mainly industrial customers, but the recent expansion of the Royal Navy has been much to his benefit, as they have a number of uses for his products.

"About six years ago, he purchased Hounslow Manor as a country retreat. That's when he became my patient – at times where he and his family aren't here in London. Up until a month or so ago, he was very hale and hearty. But then he started to have rather serious problems."

"What are the symptoms?"

"He has lost weight and is often fatigued and drowsy. Periodically he suffers from elevated temperature, accompanied by perspiration, gastric pain, and weakness. Despite the fevers, his complexion becomes more pale with each passing day. And most recently his urine at times has a darkened hue."

"Good Heavens, do you suspect poison? Those symptoms sound remarkably like arsenic poisoning."

"That was my first thought – but I haven't been able to collect any samples to conduct a Marsh Test. The man is quite stubborn about some things. I consulted my treatises, however, and he doesn't have some of the other arsenic symptoms, such as vomiting or white bands on his

104

fingernails. I understand based on my reading that every case doesn't manifest all the symptoms, so my inclination is to believe arsenic is involved, just as you suggested. But the real puzzle for me is that I cannot determine how the poison is being administered."

"How so?"

"When I first suspected poison several weeks ago, I instructed him only to consume what all the other members of the household eat and drink, and have all of it brought to the table in common serving dishes, so that everyone eats from the same food. I advised the same with any drink – that is, that he only imbibe from a bottle or pitcher that is serving others."

"Did that help in any way?"

"No. If anything he is weaker than when he started on my recommended regimen. He conducts business from the manor and has stopped going to London. If trips to the City are necessary, his son or partner make them. I've given him a full physical examination to ensure there are no puncture marks from injections, on the chance that someone is using a syringe while he sleeps, as unlikely as that seems. There are no such marks."

"And what of this 'splendid idea' of yours as to how I can be of assistance?"

"My thought is this: What if you come to stay at the manor for a few days so that you can observe things and at the same time treat him. Hopefully, you learned enough from Holmes to be able to deduce how and why arsenic is being administered. What do you think? Will you help me?"

"I haven't quite made up my mind. Do you think you can convince Armand of this scheme of yours?"

"I believe so. He trusts me, and I can tell him I would like to have a colleague there full time for a few days to make more detailed observations. We can have you use an assumed name, just in case anyone in the house has read any of your stories."

"I could go by Doctor James." I said it without thinking. Mary had occasionally called me "James", rather than "John", so I suspect that was the reason it came so quickly to mind.

"Wonderful idea. Do you have any other questions?"

"Who are the members of the household?"

"In addition to Armand, there is Marie, his second wife. She is a bit younger and from Paris. His son from the first marriage, François, works for his father. Come to think of it, I believe his mother was Norman. Apparently Armand prefers women from the north rather than his native Provence.

"That is the family proper. Also living there while Armand has ceased commuting to London is Jacque Belfort, his business partner. He's from the Alsace region, and consequently has connections in that area to complement Armand's in the Mediterranean. Finally, Armand has an English private secretary by the name of Arthur Moffett."

"And what about servants?"

"There's a butler and two maids. And – oh yes – the cook. Armand fancies himself as quite the gourmet. There is a constant influx of new chefs, as he prefers to call them, so that he can try new cuisines. The newest one is an Italian, but I cannot recall his name.

"Please help me, Watson. I'm at my wits end. I will not presume to call on our friendship, but rather appeal to your sense of justice and duty that I came to know so well in the Service. I can think of nowhere else to turn, and if we don't do this, I fear Armand will perish. He can be a rather difficult person at times, but he is a diligent man who actually is helping our naval program. No one deserves such an agonizing death."

As he looked at me anxiously, I thought for a few moments. After Mary's passing, I was in the process of selling my Paddington home and practice and of negotiating to repurchase my old Kensington practice in order to spend more time on my writing. I did have some time on my hands, which only tended to increase the *ennui* which had cursed me since the loss of Mary and Holmes. Truth be told, I missed the thrill of the adventures that Holmes and I had shared, a sensation I had come to believe I would never experience again. And then of course there was the consideration that an apparently innocent man might meet his doom at the hand of another, something neither Holmes nor I could tolerate.

"I believe you are correct that an attempt should be made to save this poor man. And I could use something more stimulating than my current activities, so I'll do it. You can let me know in the morning if your stratagem has worked."

"Very well, Doctor 'James'. I'll notify you when all is arranged." With that, he left. I decided to dine in the adjacent Brasserie before returning to my empty abode. Although the meal of lamb, spring potatoes, and new carrots, washed down with claret, was good, my appetite wasn't up to full enjoyment. When I returned to my rooms, I spent some time examining a few books related to poisons. I concentrated on passages related to arsenic, as it seemed the most likely medium, given Newdegate's description. With such thoughts swirling in my brain, I retired for the night.

The next morning, as I was finishing my after-breakfast coffee, a telegram arrived from Newdegate, indicating everything had been arranged. I packed a bag, bundled into my overcoat to ward off the cold, and set out for the station to catch the train to Hounslow. Sitting in the car and looking for as-yet non-existent signs of spring in the countryside as we left London, I took the opportunity to muse on Holmes's methods and how I might put them to use.

His first step always consisted of collecting the evidence. He often chided me for seeing but not observing. I had come to realize that meant approaching the evidence without preconceptions or theories that impeded looking at all the evidence available with a clear and open mind. The second stage was to deduce what the evidence was telling us, again without bias or some fanciful theory. Finally, one makes sense of the evidence and deductions as a whole, doing away with explanations that simply aren't possible. One would then arrive at a conclusion that rests solely on fact and deduction warranted by those facts, not speculation. I only hoped I could live up to such rigor as my friend's pursuits exemplified.

Arriving at the Hounslow station, I located a growler and instructed the driver to take me to the manor. We arrived shortly at a charming Jacobean building with three dormers and a cornice between the top two floors. It was surrounded by a pleasant park and gardens with a small lake off to the side.

After thanking and paying the driver, I went to the front door and rang the bell. It was answered by a tall, thin man dressed in a black morning coat. "I am Doctor James," I announced. "I'm here to see Monsieur Armand. I believe he's expecting me."

He indicated I should follow him and led me through the entry hall toward the back of the manor. On the right was a large door, which he opened and bowed for me to enter. This obviously had been a library, but was converted to an office or study. By the windows looking out at the lake was an enormous ornately carved desk. Behind it in a large leather chair sat a man in his mid-fifties. Obviously once robust, he showed signs of recent weight loss. His clothes were a little more than a size too large, and his pale, bald head with a fringe of grey hair glistened with perspiration.

"Thank you, Charles. That will be all for now. Doctor James, I presume." We shook hands and he resumed his seat, pointing to a chair across from him. "James, I'm not sure what you hope to accomplish, but I trust Newdegate, so we might as well try whatever you two have in mind."

"Thank you, sir. Let us start with how you're feeling today. I notice you are perspiring. Do you feel feverish?"

"Not at the moment, but I feel weak. I just completed my toilet and came down here. I fear the exertion has tired me considerably."

"Did you have nothing for a mid-day meal?"

"I stayed in my dressing gown this morning. I have a small work area in my bedroom. Arthur, my secretary, worked with me there. We each had a bowl of bean soup from the same serving piece, as Newdegate instructed.

We also consumed water from the same pitcher. Although Newdegate hasn't said so, I know he thinks something is being put in my food or drink. The idea is preposterous, but to humor him we serve everything *en famile* now."

"Have you had more cramps?"

"Yes, I woke during the night with them. It took me several hours to go back to sleep."

"Do you eat or drink anything during the day or evening other than at meal times?"

"If I feel the need, I make some tea and perhaps a biscuit. I fix it myself out in the kitchen and use food that is in jars from which we all eat. To be truthful, James, this eating routine is driving me to distraction. I recently hired a new chef at some expense. He has been limited in what he can prepare, as some of the household don't share my tastes. We have compromised by experimenting with some peasant fare from the Mediterranean, such as the bean soup we had for lunch."

"I see. Might I ask what are the sleeping arrangements for the other inhabitants?"

"My bedroom is at the front of the house on the right. My wife sleeps in the room adjacent to that, in the back of the house. It's inconvenient because there is no connection between the two, but I decided it would allow her more peaceful evenings if she moved there, given my waking in pain at times. Also, I sleep with the windows open this time of year because I find the air most invigorating, but Marie does not. My son and my partner sleep across the hall. Moffett has a room on the second floor across from where we will put you."

"Do you have asthma or take any medications?"

"No. Now I have some more work to finish. Is there anything else?"

"Thank you. I believe that will be all."

"Fine. Dinner is at eight. The men normally gather for a drink at seven in the drawing room. It's in the front of the house on the opposite side. Charles will show you to your room. I hope you don't mind the second floor." He rang a small bell and the butler reappeared.

"Charles, show Doctor James to his room. Use the one across the hall from Moffett."

As we retraced our steps to the stairway at the entrance, I decided to engage the butler in a bit of conversation. "I say, Charles, I noticed the beautiful gardens when I arrived. I have a garden, of course, though not as elaborate as these, but I have a dreadful rodent problem. How do you deal with that?"

"That, sir, is not my bailiwick. We have a gardener who comes three times a week. I believe he has found arsenic to be most effective."

"Interesting. I will have to look into that."

We had reached the door to my bedroom. It opened into a comfortable room with a four-poster bed, a chair and table, and a washstand. Best of all was a large fireplace that already had a comfortable fire going. I placed my bag on the floor and arranged my things on the washstand and in the wardrobe. After a short rest, I freshened myself and dressed for dinner.

Going back downstairs to the front hall, I located the drawing room as indicated, very typical with comfortable chairs and sofas scattered about, a nice fire, and a large sideboard with a variety of beverages on it. I didn't see Armand, but as soon as I entered a tall man of about thirty came over to me. Clearly English, he was ruggedly handsome with broad shoulders and wavy hair.

"Hello, Doctor James. I'm Arthur Moffett, Monsieur Armand's private secretary. We serve ourselves. May I get you a sherry? Hope you like sweet, as that's all they have here." He went over to the sideboard and returned with my drink. "Let me introduce the others."

We went over to a tall, rather stocky young man with black hair and a rather full face. He looked to be in his mid- to late-twenties. "This is François Armand, the son and heir apparent. He helps out with the business."

At that moment a short wiry man entered the room. He wore glasses and had heavily pomaded black hair parted in the middle. François had a slight grimace upon seeing him. He said, "And this is *pater*'s business partner, Jacque Belfort."

For the next three-quarters-of-an-hour, we made small talk of no consequence, or so it seemed to me. I couldn't help wondering if Holmes could have gleaned something from the banal conversation of this entourage. Thankfully, Charles came in to announce dinner was ready. We all exited and went into the dining room immediately adjacent. It was quite large, and clearly at some point it had served as a more-formal dining area. François muttered to me, "They used to have so called 'state' dinners in here. Father quite loves to know he dines where statesmen used to settle great affairs."

At that, Armand entered the room with a most striking woman on his arm. She was petite with a perfectly proportioned face and raven black hair. She couldn't have been a year over twenty-five. François seemed again about to comment, but didn't have the chance as Armand came over to introduce me to his wife, Marie. "So nice to meet, Doctor. Please excuse – my English isn't so good."

"Do not think anything of it, Madame. Your charms quite overcome any linguistic matter." I walked over to the head of the table. "This place setting is remarkable. Might I be so presumptuous as to look at it more closely." At her nod, I leaned over and examined the china, cutlery, and stemware. "Absolutely exquisite. Your taste is quite admirable. It quite complements the decoration of the room – particularly the wallpaper." She smiled. "Jules does indulge me so. Before we moved in, we repainted and replaced all the wallpaper. So much easier when the house is empty, *c'est non*?" Still smiling, she beckoned us to take our seats.

I watched carefully as the preliminary courses were served: A consume, and a light salad. Everyone was served from the same dishes, but Arnaud hardly touched his food. He seemed rather tired. François glared at everyone, Belfort was lost in thought, and it seemed to me Moffett was taking some interest in Marie, with whom he was having an animated conversation. Armand made desultory attempts to engage me, and I tried to reciprocate without losing sight of the others.

Armand perked up when Charles entered with a steaming casserole. "Ah, James, I don't know if you have ever had cassoulet. This is like my mother made." Charles ladled out the thick mix of beans, duck, and cured meats. Although I hadn't partaken of this before, I must admit it was quite savory.

After eating about half his dish, Armand wiped his lips and placed his napkin on the table, presumably a signal he was done. "Charles, I must complement Giacomo. Please ask him to come in here."

Charles left and returned with a dark-complected man of about forty, obviously an Italian with thick curly black hair. "Giacomo, this was magnificent. Did you prepare it as we discussed?"

"Yes, Signor. I cut back on the gelatin as you suggested, and it still came out thickened and crispy. And, as we agreed, I used fresh beans to enhance the flavors of the meat. I'm very pleased you enjoyed, and pray that everyone else did as well." There were smiles and nods around the table, some more enthusiastic than others.

"Well, I'm going to retire. You all may stay for cheese, brandy, and cigars. Marie, I'm sure you don't want to stay for that. Would you prefer to read for a bit?"

"Yes, Jules. I will go to the library and see you in the morning."

We all stood as they left and then sat back down for some delightful Stilton, brandy, and Cubans. Although Moffett invited me to the drawing room for another drink, I declined, explaining I was tired and wanted to read a bit before bed.

The next morning, I came down for breakfast in the same dining room we had used last night. Before entering, I hesitated out in the hall as I heard a very loud voice inside. I could only hear parts of one side of the conversation, if one could call it that. ". . . Intolerable . . . will not stand for it . . . of age . . . your antiquated views . . . ." Suddenly, François burst

110

from the dining room, very red in the face. He didn't notice me as he stormed up the staircase. I waited a few minutes before entering, so as not to embarrass whomever had been the recipient of the tirade.

Upon coming through the door, I discovered that Armand was the only occupant. He seemed unperturbed by his son's actions. After greeting me, he rang for Charles, who promptly appeared with that usual efficiency of an English butler. "James, I'm only going to have some toast and coffee this morning, but you may have whatever you desire."

"Many thanks. Charles, I will have some eggs and a rasher of bacon, along with toast and coffee." Charles left and I turned to Armand. "And how was your night?"

"Miserable, if I am honest. The blasted cramps returned."

"How do you feel right now?"

"Tired and a bit feverish."

I went over and placed my hand on his forehead, which confirmed he felt a bit warm. In spite of that, he still was pale rather than flushed.

Resuming my seat, Charles and one of the maids entered with the food. I noted that the coffee was in a pot and the toast was on a rack, so that we both were consuming the same things as far as that was concerned. While eating we discussed current politics. I asked his opinion about Gladstone and the Liberals, who had been able to unseat the Conservatives late the previous year, and whether that would have any impact on naval and other defense expansion. He felt not, and expressed the notion that it was too late to turn back the expansion, given that it was already several years underway.

Once Armand had finished, he indicated he had a meeting with Belfort and needed to prepare. I told him to call on me if he felt worse. He seemed more haggard than yesterday, but that could have been the result of lack of sleep and the slight fever.

I had another cup of coffee and perused the morning paper. Contented for the moment, I decided to take a walk outside in the back garden. I went through the door into the hallway leading to the kitchen. Charles was sitting in a cubicle working on what appeared to be household records. I inquired whether they kept coats about, for it still was rather chilly and what I had brought with me wasn't warm enough. He led me to a cupboard and helped me select a nice, warm hunting jacket. I went outside for an invigorating stroll. The gardens were precisely laid out. Although it was too cold for flowers to bloom, the meticulously manicured shrubbery were delightful.

As I passed the French doors leading into Armand's office, I couldn't help but glance inside. Armand was calmly seated behind his massive desk, but Belfort was walked back and forth, wildly gesticulating in an agitated manner. I couldn't hear what he was saying, but could discern, or as Holmes would say "*Observe!*" – that this was an argument of some sort. Before they could notice me, and uncomfortable eavesdropping, I turned back toward the garden and proceeded until I came across a small shed. Outside it stood a wizened creature in coveralls, battered cap, and a mud-spattered coat. I greeted him, and he explained he was the gardener and went by the name Martin.

"I'm pleased to meet you, Martin. I was asking Charles yesterday about rodent control. He informed me you swear by arsenic."

"Aye, 'tis nothing better for the varmints. Come, let me show ye." We entered the shed, where he proceeded to point out to me the materials he used in his various battles. I thanked him, and was about to leave when he spied a shelf full of empty jars. "What do you think I use these for?" he asked.

Clearly proud and eager to show off, he continued, "Kind of me own invention. I use 'em to start seedlings. Even have them thoroughly washed in boiling water to make sure nothin' hurts the plant."

"Quite ingenious. May I look some more?"

"Go right ahead. I best get back to me chores, but take yer time."

After a few more minutes in the shed, I left and went back to the house. As I returned the jacket to the cupboard, I realized it was time for lunch, so I made a quick trip to my room to wash up before returning to the dining room.

Armand didn't join us for lunch that day and, upon inquiry, Charles informed me that he and Moffett were working in the office, as they did most days. After we were done with a cold collation, I went up to the front bedroom and knocked. That was answered with, "Enter."

When I came in, Armand and Moffett were working at a table by the window. Next to each of their work spaces was a soup bowl, Armand's partially full. "I came in to check on you."

"Moffett, go down and fetch the papers related to the Portsmouth Navy Yard order." After Moffett's departure, he looked at me. "My cramps have been off-and-on since I saw you at breakfast. And I feel rather warm. Please excuse me for a moment."

While he stepped away, I went over to look at his lunch bowl. He returned shortly.

"Well, I need to get back to work."

"All right. I will check on you later today. May I impose on you to inspect your bedroom later this afternoon?"

"Yes. I will be going down to the office in about an hour. You may do it then. But whatever for? I frankly don't understand what you are doing, other than checking on me periodically. Is any of this accomplishing a thing?"

"I merely want to have a better feeling for your accommodations when these nightly cramps occur. I'm making progress and have some thoughts, but I'm not quite ready to share them with you. I ask that you bear with me a bit longer. Thank you for your understanding." He scowled but said nothing, returning his attention to the papers before him. Taking my leave, I went up to my bedroom to make some notes. In an hour, I proceeded back downstairs to Armand's bedroom. I spent some time examining all its contents – perhaps not as thoroughly as Holmes, but I did my best. Finished, I returned to my own room.

The rest of the afternoon was uneventful. I checked on Armand at about five. He and Giacomo were discussing how to prepare the main course for dinner, apparently some sort of macaroni dish with lightly spiced beans. The main point of contention appeared to be how much mustard and oil should be used. While they talked, I inspected the shelves and was delighted to find a copy of *The Influence of Sea Power Upon History*. I had heard of this work by the American Mahan published just a few years earlier, and understood it had a fairly global readership. I decided to look it over once I was done talking to Armand.

Giacomo left, and I inquired after Armand's health. He looked weary. His face was lined, apparently from tension. He explained that he had slight abdominal discomfort and the fever hadn't left him. I went up to my room and retrieved some bicarbonate of soda from my grip, which I mixed with tap water and took it back to him. I waited until he finished to ensure no one added anything to the glass in my absence. I reminded him to call if he needed me, and went to the drawing room to look over Mahan's volume.

Shortly before returning to my room to dress for the evening, I stopped and knocked on Armand's bedroom door and entered. He looked at me and said, "Good grief, man, what is it now?"

"Good evening. I've decided to take the first train to London in the morning. I believe it will only require one day, and I can be back the first thing the next morning. I would ask that you stay in your bedroom all day tomorrow. Tell the household you are feeling the need for some rest and quiet. When you feel hungry, go down to the kitchen and select fruit at random, or slice some bread from a loaf. I would also ask that tomorrow you only eat that and drink water from the faucet in there. If someone questions you about the food, tell them you don't feel very hungry and that it's easier to look to yourself as to what might satisfy the little appetite you have."

113

He shook his head but reluctantly agreed to my request. "This is the last impertinence I will tolerate. If Newdegate hadn't vouched for you, you may believe me that I would not comply." Assuring him again I had a plan, I quickly left and went downstairs.

Drinks and dinner were the same as the night before. Everyone ate and drank from common receptacles, and I carefully watched to make sure that no one slipped anything to Armand. He again left us once he had eaten the main dish, as did his wife. After brandy and cigars, Moffett asked if I would care to join him for a cordial in the drawing room. Realizing this was an opportunity to ask some questions, I readily assented.

We settled ourselves by the fire with our drinks and, after some pleasantries, I broached what I had come for. "If you will pardon me, I wanted to ask a few questions. As Monsieur Armand's physician, I need to ascertain whether there is anything emotionally disturbing him that could cause or exacerbate his symptoms."

"Ask away – although I will warn you, he is the most phlegmatic man I've ever encountered. I doubt anything could bother him enough to cause a physical reaction."

"Let me start with his relationship with his son. This morning when I came down for breakfast, I couldn't help but overhear François rather heatedly saying something to his father. I don't know what it was about, but wondered if that could be an upsetting issue."

He chuckled. "Not for Armand. François believes he has fallen in love with the local vicar's daughter. She is only eighteen, and of course her father has no real money to speak of. Armand has other plans. He wants François to marry someone from France that comes from a family with a substantial fortune. A rich girl from England might do as well, but I believe he has in mind the daughter of one of his business associates. According to what François tells me, she is older than he is, and there are good reasons why she hasn't found a suitor, despite her father's wealth. But of course, Armand controls the purse strings, and even could disinherit François. He is quite capable of such ruthlessness."

"I see. I'm afraid I also caught a glimpse of Armand and Belfort arguing about something as I was walking in the garden this morning and passed the French doors into the office. Again, I couldn't hear what was going on."

"Armand has the upper hand there as well, so I don't see how it could bother him in the slightest, let alone in a physical manifestation. You see, Armand and Belfort aren't equal partners. Armand controls the partnership and takes the lion's share of the profits. My guess is that what you saw is one more scene in an ongoing drama. Belfort believes they should diversify their customer base more widely. He feels they are too tied to the

114

current naval expansion here in England, which he believes isn't sustainable. Armand disagrees and, as I indicated, he makes the decisions at the end of the day. And he holds the whip hand. He has the right to buy out Belfort under a formula that vastly favors him by undervaluing Belfort's share."

"How are the shares treated if one of the partners dies?"

"That dissolves the partnership, and the valuation formula no longer applies. As Madame Armand and François are completely uninterested in the business, I imagine that even if they kept their share Belfort would have an easier go of it. You aren't suggesting – "

"By no means. I'm simply attempting to determine any possible impact on my patient's health. As you note, it seems unlikely any of this would bother Armand enough to make him sick – certainly not with the symptoms he shows."

With that we chatted about mundane matters for a while, until Moffett indicated he wanted to retire, as he and Armand had business to tend to in the morning. I decided to sit by the fire for a while and have another cigar. I don't know how many pipes Holmes would need for this matter, but I knew I needed some time to think.

With a start I realized it was after midnight and that I had nearly fallen asleep. I went out to the hall and started slowly up the stairs, as it was fairly dark. I hesitated before going onto the first floor landing, because I thought I heard a noise. Peering over the top stair, I saw Moffett leaving the back bedroom and using the servants' stairs to ascend to the second floor. I waited a few minutes before going on up to my room and turning in for the night.

The next morning, I had Charles take me to the station to catch the earliest train to London. Fortunately, my mission only required one day, although a rather long one. The next morning a companion and I boarded the train bound for Hounslow. I had trouble concentrating on the newspaper I held, for my nerves were on edge. While I was fairly certain I had the answer, I still would have taken comfort by having Holmes rather than my companion accompanying me. We arrived at Hounslow and took a cab to the manor.

Without knocking, we entered the front door. I whispered, "You know the plan. Follow me but stay out of sight until I give the word."

We proceeded, and I went through the doorway. We made our way unobserved through the quiet house to a closed door at the rear. There, leaving my companion behind, I entered. The perpetrator looked up and said, "What can I do for you, Doctor?"

"Let us not waste time. I know you have been poisoning Monsieur Armand. I also have divined how and why you're doing it."

The perpetrator cried out, "You will not live to tell the tale!" and then he lunged at me. I was prepared. I pulled out my service revolver and used the butt to knock the malefactor to the ground, shouting, "Now!"

My companion rushed in and quickly placed handcuffs on the perpetrator, who clearly looked like wanting another go at me.

"Your reaction confirms that I'm right. This is Inspector Lestrade of Scotland Yard. He will stay with you while I go up and talk to Monsieur Armand." With that, I left and went to Armand's bedroom. Upon knocking, I heard him bade me enter. He was alone

"James, I'm glad you're back so that we put an end to this foolishness. Have you found out the source of my ailments?"

"Yes, but first I should clarify that my real name is Doctor John Watson."

"What in blazes!" His face ran through a number of emotions in mere seconds. "Have you been in my home under false pretenses?"

"I fear it was a necessary deception, concocted by me and my friend, Doctor Newdegate. I was associated with the late Sherlock Holmes. Newdegate asked me to come both for my medical expertise and due to my familiarity with Holmes's methods. We didn't want anyone here to know the dual purpose of my sojourn. I beg your pardon and forgiveness, as I've found out what's been happening."

"You have? Please explain all this to me immediately."

"I would be glad to. For your peace of mind, be assured that the perpetrator is now in the custody of a Scotland Yard inspector.

"First we start with motive: Who would want to make you sick, a sickness that eventually would have led to your demise? I learned, unfortunately for you, that nearly everyone of your family, business and personal, might have reason to wish you dead. Before you start to object, allow me to lay out the facts. Your son is angry that you will not allow him to marry as he wishes. You may even have threatened to disinherit him."

"How on earth do you know that?"

"My sources are irrelevant. As my friend Holmes would say, please allow the facts to speak for themselves. Your business partner is greatly dissatisfied with the amount of business you are allocating to the Royal Navy. You again may have used a heavy-handed threat to force him out at less than a full price. As I understand it, that wouldn't happen if you were to die." Armand sullenly shrugged, which I took it to mean silent consent as to both François and Belfort.

"Finally – a most delicate matter, but one that I feel it my duty to mention: It seems to me that your wife and Moffett have become infatuated with each other."

Before he could express the words of anger or denial that rose to his lips, I raised my voice and continued, talking over him until he was quiet. "Delicacy prohibits me from going further than that. Suffice it to say a young wife being attracted to a person more her own age often leads to tragedy for the older spouse. So we have four people, any one of whom had what they might deem sufficient reason to want you out of the way.

"Let us turn to the means of the plot that might have been used, in that this might reveal the perpetrator's identity. Newdegate and I both initially conceived this was arsenic poisoning. You have many of the normal symptoms such as drowsiness, fever, pale complexion, weakness, and abdominal pain. Moreover, your gardener uses arsenic for pest control, so there is a plentiful supply in his shed at the back of the garden.

"That led me to ponder the method of delivery. It was in this regard that Holmes's methods were of the utmost use to me. There are four possible means of administering arsenic: Ingestion, inhalation, injection, and absorption through the skin. I looked at each of these to eliminate the ones that weren't possible in your situation.

"First, ingestion is the most common method of poisoners. Newdegate's precautions about food and drink in the manor would seem to rule that out. I observed closely, and at no time were you the only one who drank or ate a particular thing. You may recall that our first evening here I complimented Madame Armand on the table setting. I was actually inspecting your place setting to ensure no one had coated any of it with arsenic. All of it – china, silver, and stemware – was glistening and sparkling. Had anyone dusted or otherwise coated any of it with arsenic, it would have left a dull sheen, which wasn't there.

"As to inhalation, I quickly ruled out any gaseous substance containing arsenic. If that had been attempted in any of the rooms outside your bedroom, others would have become sick. Your bedroom also seems an unlikely place for several reasons. You sleep with the windows open, which would dissipate any such gas. And you and Moffett work here in the mornings, but he shows no symptoms. Another inhalation source could be wallpaper paste, which often contains arsenic. But upon my inquiry, your wife confirmed that you had redecorated everything after you purchased the manor, so that, if there were arsenic in the wallpaper that was all put up at the same time, presumably using the same paste, again you wouldn't be the only one afflicted.

"Another source of either ingestion or inhalation could be medicine, because some medications, such as Fowler's Solution for asthma, may contain arsenic. Yet you indicated you don't take any medications.

"Newdegate informed me that he examined you thoroughly, and there were no signs of injection. So ingestion, inhalation, and injection did seem

117

to be a viable method of delivery of arsenic. As far as method went, I hadn't yet decided how it was done.

"That was when I went to London to do some further sleuthing. When I was in the gardener's shed, he showed me some jars that he uses for seedlings. Based on his description, I realized they were nearly sterile. When he left me alone, I took the opportunity to obtain several of them. When I was here in your room that afternoon, I took the liberty of snipping pieces of your wardrobe, towels, and bed clothing, along with samples of tooth powder, cologne, shaving soap, and talcum from your water closet, to determine if contact with any of those were the method of delivery by absorption through your skin. Earlier, when you and Moffett were out of the room, I also took some of your leftover soup just to double check my hypothesis about ingestion.

"I don't have Sherlock Holmes's chemical abilities, so my first stop in London was an old friend who runs a laboratory. You are probably unaware that there is a simple test for arsenic invented by a German named Reinsch some fifty years ago. One places some copper foil and the test sample in a test tube and heats it. If there is arsenic present in the sample, the foil will show white crystals. Our quick test confirmed there was no arsenic present in any of the samples I had collected. I had begun to suspect something other than arsenic was being used, and this confirmed those suspicions.

"I next went to see Holmes's brother Mycroft, who has many and varied connections within the Government. I explained that I'd found your seemingly inordinate interest in naval matters worth further thought. You've persisted in selling to the Royal Navy over the objections of your partner and to the possible detriment of your business. And your interest goes beyond that, as you have a copy of Mahan's book and a number of other treatises on naval matters in your office – more than the simple sale of lubricants and fibers would warrant. Something struck me as out of kilter in all this.

"Mycroft told me I was correct to suspect something. He explained that, since the Naval Expansion Act of 1889 here in England and the ousting of Bismarck from the German chancellery in 1890, German foreign policy has vacillated between aligning with Britain or Russia. Consequently, it has increased its espionage in both countries, primarily focused on military matters.

"Mycroft very reluctantly admitted that you have been under observation for quite a while. You were recruited by the Germans to spy on the Royal Navy, given that your constant contact and level of supplies would be a valuable source of information. But you have been playing a double game, passing information back to the British Government and feeding the Germans false information. I assume that, as a Frenchman, you would prefer England over Germany. There is no need to bluster. I have the facts."

He sighed. "You are correct. We have some German customers through Belfort's contacts. One of them introduced me to a member of German Military Intelligence. He offered me money to pass him information on British naval expansion. He reasoned that I could determine such information from the volume of my sales and conversations with naval procurement officials about projected future demand. But I hate the Germans, after what they did to us in the 1870 war, especially when they humiliated us at the siege of Paris and stole Alsace Lorraine. So I approached one of my British naval customers, and he put me in contact with an intelligence officer. We agreed I would supply the Germans with false information, as your Mycroft Holmes correctly informed you."

"Unfortunately for you, Holmes told me that his sources have believed for some time that the Germans have discovered your duplicity. Thus, it's likely that the attempt on your life was at the behest of the Germans.

"But how was the perpetrator accomplishing this? The poison wasn't arsenic, and the method of delivery was difficult to fathom. My next stop was the extensive library of the Royal College of Physicians. After several hours of searching and with the assistance of the excellent research staff, I found my answer in an issue of *The Lancet*. It contained a *précis* of research done by an Italian named Male-Bertolo in 1886. He had found that certain males of Mediterranean ancestry could sicken and die when exposed to a certain substance. The symptoms are remarkably like arsenic poisoning – abdominal pain, paleness, fever, fatigue, and so forth. You are the only person in the household of such descent. Your wife is Parisian, your son part-Norman, Belfort Alsatian, and Moffett English. Therefore, you would be the only one affected. So I had my answer as to motive and means."

Armand was ashen. "What substance might that be?"

"Fava beans."

"But that means – "

"Giacomo is the culprit. I noticed that he used such beans in at least one dish a day. Everyone but you could safely eat it. He played on your vanity as a self-proclaimed gourmet, and even involved you in the planning of the very dishes that would lead to your demise. He may also have known that tea can exacerbate the effects of the beans, and was pleased when you brewed your own.

"Giacomo was under surveillance by the British Naval intelligence Department for some time, but they lost him at about the time he came to work for you. He will be taken by the Yard's man and be dealt with appropriately.

"According to Mycroft Holmes, Giacomo is from northern Italy and has relatives in the portions of Italy possessed by the Austrians. They used that leverage to force him to work for them. From time to time, the Austrians loaned him to their German allies. Because Giacomo has worked as a cook while so engaged in spying, I believe he learned of the deadly effects of fava beans on people of Mediterranean descent. Or perhaps he learned it through folklore growing up. In any event, he probably tried the beans on you when first planted as your chef. To his delight, he found you are susceptible to the deleterious effect of the beans."

"You are correct. One of the first dishes he made for me was a bean salad with onion and carrot, dressed with olive oil. Now that you explain this, I do recall feeling queasy after that. I even mentioned to Giacomo to check that the oil wasn't rancid."

"Of course, your usefulness to the British intelligence service is at an end. I don't know how you will guard against further attempts, if any, by the Germans. Perhaps you can speak to the person who handled you in your double role. As for the issues here in your household, that is up to you. While not in my medical purview, I might suggest some frank conversations and perhaps changes of behavior."

"James – er, *Watson* – this is all quite extraordinary. In spite of the upsetting news which you've shared about my household, I must thank you for finding the root of my ailment. Still, I must say that your amazing recital has left me a bit dumbfounded."

I smiled. "My dear late friend likely would have told you it was 'Elementary'. I cannot claim such powers as he. It is I who must thank you, however. This adventure has restored to me a feeling that I feared had been lost forever."

Doctor Watson's
Baffled Colleague
by Sean M. Wright
and DeForeest B. Wright, III

READERS PLEASE NOTE: A large envelope was recovered from the double-drawer of an old rolltop desk in 1977. Within was found a completed manuscript of a novel, (later published in 1979 as Enter the Lion). *Another large manila envelope contained some partial manuscripts, apparently abandoned attempts at novelization, along with notes outlining those narratives. In company with these were found other memoranda and carbon copies of several letters. All were discovered to be the work of Mr. Mycroft Holmes. One letter in particular is of more than casual interest to Holmesian devotees, concerning an event which took place while Sherlock Holmes was thought to have died.*

Diogenes Club
20 October, 1894

Dear Doctor Watson,

Your letter, delivered to me here at the Club, formed the final course, so to speak, of an enjoyable dinner of roasted chicken, steamed Brussels sprouts smothered in Béarnaise Sauce, and creamy mashed potatoes. To this was paired a luscious, and no less buttery, chardonnay.

Herr Yosep Schmidt, our club's chef for barely two years, continues to delight our palettes. He recently introduced for the dessert course a confection popular amongst his Dutch relations living in the mid-Atlantic area of the United States. It is a pie but, unlike most of our own varieties, the crust is quite short, light and flakey, filled with thin slices of pumpkin and apple, layered one over the other, the top dusted with cinnamon and nutmeg.

Your letter thus finds me in an expansive mood.

Should I suspect your request to know more about the period from 1891 to 1894 and the part I played in Sherlock's absence during those three years is prompted by a desire to replenish your stock of sensational stories for *The Strand*? If so, I cannot begrudge you your oft-stated desire to share examples of my brother's singular gift for solving difficulties – especially seeing how thoroughly your charming and homely sketches demonstrating Sherlock's wit and industry were anticipated by an enthusiastic readership.

I therefore regret being unable to assist you in this regard. Diplomatic considerations constrain me from sharing details of my brother's sojourning through Persia, Tibet, Arabia, and especially his audience with the Khalifa at Khartoum. These must, at present, remain the exclusive possession of Her Majesty's Foreign Office.

Still, I am obliged to find a way of thanking you for the superlative snuff and the box of fine *habanos* with which you gifted me. [1] My brother's return allows me to more fully acquaint you with certain details relating to the incident which left Doctor Jasper Anstruther so utterly baffled. I still insist that my part in clearing up the affair was quite negligible, little more than calling the bluff of an *agent provocateur*.

It was my intention to offer this explanation upon my brother's return from his self-imposed exile, but I did not wish to trespass on your grief at the time of your own sadness and loss. [2] Time has been a tonic, I see, and, now that you have resumed your old rooms in Baker Street, I am glad to give fuller clarity to the case.

You'll recall, my dear Doctor, that you sent your colleague to the club to consult me, but I was not there. Having no duties in Whitehall that afternoon, I decided myself to forego my normal schedule: Entering the Diogenes at precisely a quarter-before-five to dine. Lingering over the newspapers while enjoying a good cigar, I allow the quiet to aid my digestion. At twenty minutes past the hour of eight, I always depart the club, cross the street, and enter my own front door.

To my deep chagrin I have learned to suspend my routine on the fifth of November to escape being accosted by swarms of high-spirited children roaming the city, carrying buffoonish effigies of Guy Fawkes and Pope Leo hanging on poles, and gaily insisting, "Penny for the Guy, sir! Penny for the Guy!"

Having had an audience with the late frank, outspoken Cardinal Manning, I pondered whether would he might still share the same fate as Cardinal Vaughan surely will. [3] The tradesmen join in the clamour selling bangers, eels, chestnuts, and other comestibles as, to the cheers of the throng, the bonfires are touched off and the effigies burnt. *Panis et circensis, per omnia secula seculorum.* [4]

Re-reading the previous paragraph, I sound like a sour, old cynic, do I not? In truth, I've not entirely forgotten the frivolities of youth. I encourage Mrs. Crosse, or the maid, or the tweenie to deal with the youngsters' raucous merriment by gifting them with pennies taken from the pile I leave each year on the side table in the foyer. [5]

In her continuing quest to keep me apprised of all things Catholic, Mrs. Crosse had arranged the newspaper on my luncheon tray, so I could not fail to notice a story about the Oratorian Order of priests and brothers. It regarded completion of the façade over the south door of their church in Brompton. Construction had begun two years earlier and was nearing completion.

Consternation had arisen within their ranks after it was announced that the statue of St. John the Baptist appearing in the original design of the promising young architect (and recent convert), Herbert Gribble, had been supplanted by a statue of the Virgin. The reporter found it worthy of note to identify both devices as Gribble's work. A final decision was expected within the fortnight. It seemed a tempest in a Holy Water stoup to me.

The rest of my afternoon was taken up reading about the high-minded, conscientious Queen Anne. The biography was somewhat less than accurate, based as it was, on the Duchess of Marlborough's malicious memoirs. [6]

It was near tea-time when the front doorbell rang. The setting sun cast long shadows across the floor. Surely it was too early for the urchins to begin making their rounds?

In the event, Florinda, the tweenie, brought a calling card on her salver announcing my visitor to be a Doctor Jasper Anstruther. Wondering how I might assist a medical professional, Doctor Johnson's gentle wisdom came to mind: *"Curiosity is, in great and generous minds, the first passion and the last."* I instructed Florinda to let the gentleman know that I was in.

Rising from my chair. I watched the doctor in the foyer remove hat, overcoat, and gloves. A tall, well-formed gentleman, Doctor Jasper Anstruther walked with a slight stoop, leaning heavily on a silver-headed walking stick. His brilliantined hair was severely-cut and prematurely greying.

The doctor's well-tailored clothing, gleaming silk hat, and chamois gloves of the finest make, not to mention his boots, the best found in Bond Street, proclaimed him a physician catering exclusively to the carriage trade. Milords and ladies, the landed gentry, men of property – these were the patients who met within the confines of his consulting room.

No expectant fathers pounded on his door hours before sunrise. He would never be called on to cross town in a mad dash to dose a Kensington doxy or patch up a fumbling Whitechapel cutpurse.

In treating ailments afflicting the affluent, Doctor Anstruther was less concerned with leeching black eyes than with preaching the benefits of banting. [7] Any broken bones he set came from patients playing cricket or leaping a tennis net. In short, he treated gout, never scurvy.

Behind his silver-rimmed *pince-nez* was a friendly, open face. Have you noticed, my dear doctor, how the puffiness surrounding your friend's watery blue eyes offsets his obvious intelligence with an air of dissipation? He seems anemic. Has he a kidney disease?

Doctor Anstruther offered his hand and begged my pardon in a friendly yet distracted manner. He told me he had first gone to the Club but was directed to find me at home.

Asking me to forgive his intrusion upon my time, he then explained that having spoken to his "professional neighbor in Paddington," you – my dear Doctor Watson about an odd situation having taken place the day before which was preying on his mind. [8] You, in turn, having "great confidence" in my abilities, suggested he seek my help.

I told Doctor Anstruther that my contact with you was irregular, but I was aware of how highly esteemed you were by my late brother, and I would do what I could to be of some help. [9]

I rang for the maid and informed Nora that there would be another for tea.

"I hope I can live up to Doctor Watson's expectations," I said. "Allow me to point out that you were previously in Her Majesty's Navy – I would suggest as a commissioned officer?"

"Indeed, that is so!" Doctor Anstruther admitted, a note of astonishment in his voice. "How could you know?"

"The tip of an anchor tattoo appears on your wrist, just below your shirt-cuff. Your demeanor suggests that of an officer. And you have clipped your moustache with precise military fastidiousness."

The doctor's brow knotted. "Could not a decent barber have done as well?"

"Too be sure," I agreed, "Yet, despite pomading your hair, it is obvious that it could stand a cutting. A good barber would never have allowed you to leave his establishment without attending to both your tonsorial needs."

"Well, sir," said Anstruther with a dry snort, "that's putting your brains to good work. Very well, I'm convinced that you're the man who can solve my problem."

At the sight of his obvious prosperity, I recalled, dear doctor, our chat in the Stanger's Room – telling me how impressed you had been by Sherlock's inference that you had the more lucrative practice since your steps were worn down three inches more than your neighbor's. After meeting Doctor Anstruther, I realized my brother's deduction was so much

124

twaddle. [10] Despite his oft-stated warnings to the contrary, Sherlock occasionally falls victim to making bricks without clay.

Getting back to my visitor, I waved him into the barrel chair opposite my own and asked him to tell me his tale.

"Since our practices adjoin each other," the doctor explained, "we alternate as each other's occasional *locum*. [11] An incident I found quite baffling occurred this week as I sat in my consulting room."

Nora returned with tea and cakes. As she poured, the doctor reached into the breast pocket of his frockcoat and took out a small Bible bound in soft, pebbled, black leather. Between its pages was a small white envelope. He handed me both.

I inspected the envelope. In an almost illegible scrawl was written the word "*Doctor*" above the Paddington address. The same hand had printed the following words:

> *From the sole of the foot even unto the head there is no soundness in it; But wounds, and bruises, and putrefying sores: They have not been closed, neither bound up, neither mollified with ointment.*

> *Isaiah I:VI*

The envelope was of ordinary bond. The address and message had been written with a double broad nib by a person using his off-hand. The Biblical citation was written on a page of yellow, lined paper torn from a pad, such as used by solicitors. Holding up the paper to the light, I noticed two circular marks, presumably left by a pair of pint glasses set down on the pad before the message was written, indicating the likelihood of its being written in a pub.

"How came you by the Bible and message?" I asked.

He cleared his throat, "Well, yesterday morning one of those Roman chaps – a priest, you know – made a call at my practice. He gave his name as Father Genesius O'Toole, belonging to the Oratorian Order."

I immediately recalled the story from the morning paper.

"Truly? That's certainly of interest."

I rose from my chair, crossed the room to sit at my heavy oaken desk, and opened its rolltop reaching for a sheet of foolscap and a pen.

"Pardon me, but I should like to take down your description of this man."

"He is, I would say, about twenty-five years," recalled the doctor, "a shortish young man, perhaps five-feet, six-inches in height. He had close-set blue eyes, a round head, with straight, light-brown hair brushed down over his forehead.

"May I ask the reason for his visit, if it is not a breach of ethics?"

The doctor shrugged. "Oh, I can't see any harm in it. Said he'd felt done in for several weeks and hoped I might suggest a good tonic to bring him back up to snuff for all his religious duties."

"Can you describe his attire?"

"Well, let's see," Doctor Anstruther began after taking a sip of tea. "He wore a black low-crowned hat with a circular brim. He also wore one of those long black gowns with a fringed sash around the middle into which he had thrust this very Bible, which he wore on his hip."

"I believe the gowns are called *soutanes*," I interjected as I started writing on a second piece of paper. "You examined him, of course. What else was he wearing?"

"He wore a pair of black trousers and a white shirt with that backward-style collar Roman clergymen prefer. I noticed that his shoes were a little down at the heel, if that is of any help."

"And your diagnosis?"

"Oh, definitely anemic," he said, picking up his plate with two small tea cakes on it. "Told him to get out in the sun more. See if he could arrange to eat more red meat and liver. I prescribed ferrous sulphate tablets of 5.02 grains," he added before taking a bite of cake. "To be taken twice per day."

Looking up from my desk and turning round to Doctor Anstruther, I asked, "Getting back to this message: Did he hand it to you when he paid?"

The doctor's brows knotted again.

"Well, that is the odd part. As he was dressing, I wrote out a prescription and handed it to him. I then made out a receipt for two pounds, telling him I was remitting one pound since he was a man of the cloth. Having rebuttoned his, ah, *soutane*, he looked up and said, 'Gold or silver have I none, but such as I have I will give thee.' [12]

"So saying, he drew his Bible from his sash, flung it at me, and bolted out of my consulting room and into the street. I attempted to give chase, but he was a good fifteen years younger than me, and my legs aren't the best, anyway. By the time I reached my front door, he had vanished. Not knowing what else to do, I burst out with a hearty laugh and yelled after him, 'Pon my word, sir, this is the first time some blighter has used the Testament for the purpose of avoiding a payment!'

"Returning to my inner chamber I retrieved the Bible, discovered the unsealed envelope still within, opened it, and read the citation from Isaiah. This is what I told Doctor Watson and why I am now here."

I considered his story for a moment.

"Your practice is close by Saint Mary's Hospital in Praed Street, I believe?"

"Yes, quite close."

"You acted as *locum* for Doctor Watson this week, I dare say."

"Why, yes, on Monday and Tuesday."

"This is Thursday and Mister O'Toole visited you on Wednesday."

"Father O'Toole you mean."

"Mister," said I. "The man you describe was not a priest, Roman or otherwise."

He blinked three times, rubbed his eyes, and said, "Forgive me Mr. Holmes, but I – I saw the *soutane*."

"Oh, I have no doubt of that," I said. "but alas, certain anomalies within your strange but detailed narrative leave no doubt that this man took advantage of your unfamiliarity with Catholic customs and practices for his own purposes.

"He very likely read the same article I did about the Oratorian Order finishing up a church. But real Oratorians do not wear the Roman collar. They wear a soft, *revers* collar over the black tops of their *soutanes*. That was the first anomaly.

"The second was that they do not carry small Bibles in their sashes. Their Latin prayerbooks, called *breviaries*, resemble Bibles to the untrained eye, but they contain daily readings and chants: Psalms, prayers, parts of the Gospel, and tales about various saints which all priests are bounden to chant or read at certain hours.

"And the third anomaly is that even if they did carry Bibles, they certainly would *not* carry the Anglican Authorized Version. Catholics have their own English translation, you know. The Authorized Version is forbidden for Catholics to read, having been put on *The Index* long ago."
[13]

Looking again at the quote from Isaiah, it seemed that might be a connection.

"On Monday or Tuesday, while acting for Dr. Watson, had you a patient seeking a cure for with an open wound, running sore, or some skin disease? Perhaps something on the order of *tinea pedis*? [14] Something which the patient claimed to have suffered from for a period of time?"

"Why, yes, I did!" my visitor exclaimed after a moment's recollection. "A pretty though tartish young woman, perhaps five-feet-two-inches tall, with curling, blonde hair, very blue eyes, a short nose and freckles. Her breath, however, was extremely odiferous. The name she gave, I believe, was Henrietta Jenkins."

"Excellent! Thank you for the description." I nodded, adding the particulars to my note. "Now, tell me what occurred during her call."

I examined her feet and wrote a prescription for an ointment which she disparaged, saying she had used it before to no avail. She then removed a one-pound note from within her blouse, slapped it on the desk, then flounced out of the office."

I put the sheets upon which I had been writing in an envelope. Ringing for Florinda, I gave her with a five-pound note, bidding her take the message to the corner telegraph office to be sent to the address on the front.

"Well, Doctor," said I, "this Miss Jenkins is working with the O'Toole creature.. Since you were acting for your neighbor, first the woman, then the man, believed you were actually Doctor Watson.

"Meeting in a nearby pub, Jenkins told O'Toole what had happened in your office. They seem to have some knowledge of Scripture and found the text from Isaiah concerning putrefying sores being left unalleviated by ointment as fitting the situation, As you had prescribed the same ointment other doctors had without success, the two thought up this prank as an extravagant Guy Fawkes Day charade with O'Toole playing a sham priest. The ruse was concocted simply to taunt you."

Doctor Anstruther considered my explanation a moment or two then gave a short laugh. "Why, yes, that must be the answer. As you explain it, all the puzzle pieces fall into place."

Finishing his cup of tea, my visitor stood up and, taking my hand, was most effusive in his thanks. Waiving away his offer to pay for my time, I let him know I found his tale a pleasant diversion of an afternoon. He graciously invited me to stop by his practice should I ever have some medical need.

Collecting his habiliments, Dr. Anstruther walked out the door and into the crowded streets as the frolicking and merriment of Guy Fawkes Night commenced.

This is where the tale ended originally, Doctor Watson, and I dare say that you and Doctor Anstruther shared some laughter over the Biblical scorn for poor doctoring. In fact, the situation was not quite finished at this point.

The citation from Isaiah was certainly aimed at you, Doctor, but it had nothing at all to do with disease – it was a deadly threat.

With Sherlock supposed to be dead, the Government's hands were tied in some respects. In my story, I tell of sending Florinda, my tweenie, to the telegraph office. The telegram she sent for me, concerning Doctor Anstruther's descriptions of his two visitors, was sent to the Home Secretary.

You recall I mentioned the marks of two pints of beer being set on the paper containing the quote from Isaiah? With your and Anstruther's medical practices so near Saint Mary's Hospital in Praed Street, I suggested the Home Secretary wire the Commissioner of Police. with instructions to send two of his men to the Fountains Abbey pub, also in Praed Street. They were to be on the lookout for O'Toole and Jenkins. The day had not ended before the two were apprehended and detained by Scotland Yard.

A telegram from Inspector Athelney Jones identified the young man and woman as "for hire" to anyone with the money to pay for burglary, smash and grab, and other minor crimes. They have yet to be caught in the act, but have been seen in the vicinity where a crime has occurred.

I was unable to explain at that time, Doctor, but Colonel Sebastian Moran, Mr. Moriarty's lieutenant, had been spying on your movements, having taken it into his head that you knew where my brother was concealing himself. I believe he came to this conclusion when your accounts of Sherlock's cases began appearing in *Strand Magazine* two months after my brother's disappearance and reported death. [15]

A custom has grown up among some of London's criminal gangs to send veiled threats to each other using curses, imprecations, and maledictions found in Holy Writ. Moran paid the Jenkins woman to come to your office with a real medical complaint. That done, O'Toole, in the guise of a priest, was sent with the threat culled from Isaiah. Moran's intent was to threaten you so that, when he confronted you demanding to know of Sherlock place of concealment, you would comply without putting yourself or your good wife in danger.

Unfortunately for the Colonel, Jenkins and O'Toole bungled it. You, Doctor Watson, were gone and they mistook Doctor Anstruther, who obviously never identified himself as acting as your *locum,* for you.

Since you had no idea that Sherlock was alive, let alone where he was travelling, this persecution had to be brought to a quick end. I thus fought fire with fire, so to speak, by using O'Toole's Bible to convey to Moran a message from the Foreign Office, not mentioning myself at all.

The way I sent my message was to use a double-broad nib to write a series of Biblical citations from Genesis, in order, in an envelope marked *Moran.* The words I wanted Moran to read I had underlined with pinpricks thus:

Genesis 19:17: *stay*
Genesis 2:10: *out of*
Genesis 2:23: *my*
Genesis 3:24: *way*

Genesis 13:9: *or*
Genesis 2:9: *evil*
Genesis 2:18: *will*
Genesis 42:4: *befall*
Genesis 3:11: *thee*

Scotland Yard returned the Bible to O'Toole with directions to give it and the envelope to Colonel Moran, and make no mistake about it.

The old hunter understood the threat, and that it was backed up with the might of Her Majesty's Government. He left you alone from then on. He was unable to trace Sherlock until that fateful night earlier this year, when you and my brother were able to bag him as he attempted to shoot my brother.

I hope, my friend, that the true details of the problem which baffled Doctor Anstruther may somehow find their way into your adventures.

And now, the calendar shows that, come three weeks, the strains of *"Remember, remember, the fifth of November, Gunpowder Treason and Plot!"* shall again be heard across London.

We have come full circle. And I shall again keep to my rooms. Yet I shall continue to regard you, Doctor Watson,

With sincere best wishes,
Mycroft Holmes

NOTES

1. Non-cigar aficionados will want to know that "*habano*" refers to the dark-colored leaves cut from the top of tobacco plants. These are used to wrap the filler tobacco in cigars, imparting a strong, slightly sweet, flavor.

2. "*In some manner he had learned of my own sad bereavement, and his sympathy was shown in his manner rather than in his words.*" and "*Work is the best antidote to sorrow, my dear Watson.*" (From "The Empty House".) We see that Sherlock Holmes's source for this knowledge was very likely Mycroft. This sadness is often taken to be the death of Watson's wife, the former Mary Morstan, heroine of *The Sign of Four*.

3. Henry Edward Cardinal Manning (1808-1892), along with Herbert Alfred Cardinal Vaughan (1832-1903), were successive Archbishops of Westminster following the reestablishment of the Catholic hierarchy in England by Blessed Pius IX in 1850. Nicholas Cardinal Wiseman was the first to hold the office, dying in 1865, succeeded by Manning. The Catholic hierarchy begun by St. Augustine of Canterbury in 597 ended when Queen Mary died (1558). The reestablishment was not popular. The attitude taken by *The Times* (14 October, 1850), labeling the site in London for the archbishopric as either a "*clumsy joke*" or else "*one of the grossest acts of folly and impertinence which the Court of Rome has ventured to commit since The Crown and the people of England threw off its yoke,*" reflected the feelings of many in England.

4. Mycroft's Latin lament is translated "*Bread and circuses, world without end*" (literally, "*through all ages of ages*" – sometimes rendered as the more banal phrase, "*forever and ever*").

5. The merriment of Guy Fawkes Night is similar to the U.S. celebration of Halloween as observed in former times, as a boisterous festival for children without the month-long assault of candy adverts. The annual event in England celebrates the failed Gunpowder Plot of 1605. A group of English Catholics, tired of persecution and the loss of basic human rights, hoped to assassinate Protestant King James I and substitute a Catholic monarch in his place. On November 5th, Guy Fawkes was arrested while guarding a great pile of explosives ready to be touched off beneath the House of Lords as soon as the King arrived.

6. Anne, younger daughter of James II and last reigning monarch of the House of Stewart in 1702, followed the joint monarchy of William and Mary. An assiduous ruler, Anne was, by the Acts of Union (1707), the first to reign over the kingdoms of England, Scotland, and Ireland united as a single sovereign entity known as Great Britain. The Duchess of Marlborough was Sarah Churchill, one of Sir Winston's forebears. She had been Anne's closest friend. They fell out over policy. Until the mid-twentieth century, Sarah's spiteful memoirs have colored opinions of Queen Anne among less critical historians.

7. *Banting*: William Banting (1796-1878) wrote a booklet detailing the first known low-carb, high-fat diet. He eliminated all grains, granular sugar,

131

vegetable and seed oils, and grains, specifically wheat. His booklet became so popular that "banting" became another word for dieting.

8. In "The Boscombe Valley Mystery", the now-married Watson, invited to join one of Holmes' investigations, hesitates, citing a long list of patients to be seen. "*Oh, Anstruther would do your work for you*," says Watson's wife, the former Mary Morstan.

9. Watson's short accounts of the Holmes adventures began appearing in the pages of *The Strand Magazine* in June 1891, garnering great acclaim after a very short time.

10. Holmes's deduction about Watson's practice by looking at his front steps, was included by the doctor in the opening of "The Stockbroker's Clerk".

11. The seasoned Sherlockian likely will not need to know the definition. For others, *locum tenens* is a Latin phrase meaning, "*to hold the place of*". In other words, a professional who is called on, for a generally short length of time, to take the place of another in the same profession, used especially regarding a doctor or a clergyman. Watson's wife's remark about Dr. Anstruther has already been noted: In "The Stockbroker's Clerk", Watson declares, "*I do my neighbor's when he goes. He is always ready to work off the debt.*" And when Holmes asks for his friend's company in "The Final Problem", Watson replies, "*The practice is quiet,*" said I, "*and I have an accommodating neighbor.*"

12. Acts 3:6. Simon Peter's reply to a lame beggar seeking alms before raising him up and bidding him walk, the Apostle's first miraculous cure following the Ascension of Jesus.

13. *The Index of Forbidden Books* (*Index Librorum Prohibitorum* in Latin) began informally with Pope Gelasius I, c. 496, who recommended some books to Catholics and forbade to read others that he found malignantly harmful to their faith and morality. During The Council of Trent (1545-1563) the first printed *Index* was published in 1559 by the Sacred Congregation of the Roman Inquisition (precursor to the Sacred Congregation for the Doctrine of the Faith). The Authorized "King James" Version was on *The Index* – not due its translation, but because of its pernicious footnotes attacking, denying, mocking, and even misstating aspects of Catholic belief.

14. *Tinea pedis*: The medical terminology for "*Athlete's foot*".

15. Sherlock Holmes and Professor Moriarty fought in May 1891. The following July, the first of Dr. Watson's short accounts appeared, "A Scandal in Bohemia".

The Case of the
Deity's Disappearance
by Jane Rubino

Upon the conclusion of the Adair matter, and the arrest of the infamous Colonel Moran, Sherlock Holmes had pressed me to return to my old lodgings, and, as I received an unexpected – and very handsome – offer for my practice, and preferred companionship to solitude, within a few weeks of his own return, I found myself installed at Baker Street once more.

One morning, not long after I had resumed my old address, an item in *The Times* caught my eye. "Holmes!" said I, "Here is a curious bit of business, and it involves two of our old friends from Dartmoor – Doctor Mortimer and old Frankland."

"What? Has Frankland once again dragged the Good Doctor before a magistrate for exhuming some prehistoric skull without notifying its next of kin?"

"It is more than a skull this time," I replied, and read the item aloud:

> *A dispute of some consequence has arisen between two of Dartmoor's well-known residents over a remarkable discovery in an ancient barrow upon the property of Foulmire, a farm owned by Mr. Robert Underwood.*
>
> *The grounds of Foulmire have long been an object of interest to both amateur and professional archaeologists for the barrows upon its northernmost border. In the past, these mounds have yielded little worthy of interest, but weeks of heavy rains had so eroded one of them as to expose a white, somewhat rounded protrusion, which Mr. Underwood first took for a portion of skeleton.*
>
> *Unwilling to risk harm to what might be an object of historic significance, the farmer immediately communicated his discovery to Doctor James Mortimer, an enthusiast in the early history of the region, and secretary of The Dartmoor Preservation Society. Doctor Mortimer examined the site and determined that the object was not bone, but rather sandstone, and it appeared to be the forehead and crown of a large*

carving of some sort, the greater portion lying deep within the barrow.

Doctor Mortimer immediately commenced an excavation of the site and was able to expose a sizeable stone figure, just above five feet in length, of a male form, bound with cords and lying prone upon a bed of three rocks. The sculptor's effort to work an expression of impudence upon the visage, and the manner in which the figure had been posed, suggested to Doctor Mortimer that it was an image of the Norse god Loki and that it could therefore be no prehistoric relic, as are often found upon the moors, but a rare specimen of the early Middle Age.

"There is some record of the Norsemen in our part of the world," stated Doctor Mortimer, "but to date, there has been no material discovery of such import. The historical significance of this finding cannot be understated, and one can only imagine what other such relics our district may yield!"

Unfortunately, Doctor Mortimer's delight at the discovery was short-lived, for it soon came to light that, in his eagerness to bring up the object, he and the few farm laborers he had engaged to assist him, hadn't observed that the barrow lay across the boundary (albeit unmarked) which separates Foulmire from the grounds of Lafter Hall, the residence of Mr. Alastair Frankland.

Indeed, only the head and shoulders of this relic were within the bounds of Foulmire, while the greater part lay squarely upon Mr. Frankland's property, and when that gentleman – who is well known in the district for his legal affrays – learned of the exploit, he immediately claimed all right to the relic and threatened to bring a charge of trespass against both Doctor Mortimer and Mr. Underwood.

"If I recall my folklore aright," Holmes said, as I laid aside my paper, "Loki was said to be a trickster. His *metier* was stirring up discord. I don't believe that he could have fixed upon two opponents better suited to his penchant for mischief."

"Surely you don't attribute this dispute to some mythical deity?"

"Not to a deity, only to debris. Our fair realm is littered with the residue of our ancient visitors and this object, no doubt, is the long-abandoned remnant of some primitive altar or shrine. Well, well, the matter will go before a magistrate, I daresay, and if the fellow has any sense, he will apply Solomon's guile to the dispute and order the object severed at the boundary line, with each party taking his portion. A pretty little *contretemps,* but not the sort that is likely to find its way to our door."

This he said with some bitterness. Following the resolution of Ronald Adair's murder, Holmes had expected to resume his profession at its former pace, and yet, though his return had been celebrated by all of England, its aftermath had produced only two or three minor cases, none which had offered any features of interest or called upon the full measure of his singular gifts. With each passing day, the strain of inactivity became more acute, and each pull of the bell would set off a "Surely it must be a client, Watson!" – only to end in a bitter curse when it proved not to be the case.

One morning, a few weeks after *The Times* item caught my notice, the bell was pulled with particular urgency, followed by an animated exchange with our landlady below and then a rapid footfall upon the stair. "A client!" Holmes cried, rubbing his hands together gleefully, and a client it was, though I daresay neither Holmes nor I could have predicted that the client would be the very subject of that *Times* article: Doctor James Mortimer.

Little of the tall, stooping figure, or the keen, peering countenance had changed. His expression, however, was not one of absent-minded benevolence, but of extreme anxiety.

"Mr. Holmes!" our visitor cried, without ceremony. "You must come at once! He is gone! Vanished!"

"My dear Doctor Mortimer!" Holmes greeted. "Why, it wasn't long ago that I told Doctor Watson we might soon find you at our door! What hour is it – just after ten? You must have left Dartmoor before dawn. Your boots," he added, answering the doctor's puzzled look. "That accumulation of West Country mud suggests that you set out in rather wet and dirty terrain, and the fact that you now deposit its caked and dried residue upon our good landlady's carpet tells me that some three or four hours have passed since."

"Yes – the special left Exeter before six this morning. But I forget myself," he added, and wrung Holmes hand. "How stunned we all were in our parts when we heard news of your return. I am so very glad to see you!"

"Glad, I think, that my skull, which you once so coveted, isn't disintegrating somewhere below Reichenbach Falls?"

"It would be a grievous loss," said the doctor with a solemnity that provoked a laugh from both Holmes and myself.

"Well, you mustn't abandon hope. But now, tell us who has vanished and where we must go at once?"

135

"To Paddington! It is Loki! He has disappeared!"

"The sandstone carving unearthed from a farmland barrow?"

"You know of it, then?"

Holmes nodded. "There was some dispute over possession, was there not, between yourself and the quarrelsome Mr. Frankland?"

"Yes – the wretch! It is true that in our zeal to exhume the piece, we may have trespassed, but is no allowance to be made for the claims of history? And now it has vanished! Into thin air – or a cloud of smoke, to be precise. The police have been summoned, but I insisted upon bringing you in as well. You must come, I beg you, for I am at my wits' end!"

"My dear Doctor Mortimer, calm yourself. If I am to be of service, you must favor me with a few details first." Holmes waved the doctor into a chair. "You tell me that this stone figure has vanished? The reports state that it is above five feet in length. That an object which must weigh several hundred pounds might be stolen is highly improbable, but that it should vanish altogether is impossible."

"Unless it is the work of this prankster god." I said this in jest, and yet the doctor's sober nod suggested that he hadn't ruled out the possibility.

"Come now!" Holmes admonished. "The disappearance of so material an object can no more be the work of a mischievous deity than Sir Henry's persecution was the work of a phantom Hell-hound."

"That does very well for the sitting room," lamented the doctor, his spindly fingers playing at the buttons on his frock coat, "but you didn't see what I saw, and then what I did *not* see. And I can think of no explanation that reconciles the two other than an unnatural one."

Holmes sat and leaned back in his chair, his fingertips pressed together in the old, familiar pose. "Then begin with what you *did* see, from the time the object first appeared. On a moorland farm, was it not?"

"Foulmire. Over the years, the moors have given us a great many tokens of the past, but the barrows at the border of Foulmire have rarely been explored. It is grazing ground for Mr. Underwood's Exmoors, and the rams do not always take kindly to interlopers. The weather has been unusually wet, and between the melting snows and heavy rains, a few of the barrows were worn down, and it was at one of them where Mr. Underwood spied the portion of the carving. When he summoned me, I confess I was so overcome with excitement that I immediately enlisted Mr. Underwood and a few of his stout laborers, and together we dug 'round the object, then fashioned a harness and brought it up and laid it next to the mound. Other than some wear upon the base at the corners, it is remarkably well-preserved for a specimen that must be five-hundred years old, at least."

136

"If it is genuine."

"Oh, there is no doubt of that, none whatsoever. I wired Mr. Wollaston Franks – or rather, Sir Augustus, I must say, as he was knighted some weeks ago. He is Keeper of Antiquities at the British Museum and a foremost expert on the subject. He came down from London straight away to examine the work and will vouch for its authenticity. He agrees, as well, that the figure's age and its pose confirm that it is the likeness of the Norse god, Loki. If you recall the legend, Loki was a rogue and a trickster, and as punishment for one of his many acts of mischief, he was bound upon three rocks with the entrails of his own son."

'You say that you exhumed the piece and then called upon this expert to examine it. Why did Mr. Frankland not immediately intervene?"

"As chance would have it, he was here in London at the time."

"Some matter of business, I take it?"

"No, pleasure. You wouldn't think it of the old crank, but his love of the arts even exceeds his fondness for litigation, and when he doesn't squander a favorable award on his next grievance, he treats himself to a round of London's theatres and galleries. He is especially fond of the opera. His late wife was said to be musical. Some mention was made of a benefit performance of *Lohengrin*, I believe. At any rate, art and Wagner did nothing to sweeten his temper, for when he returned and saw what had been done, there was a great row. He accused us of trespass and destruction of his property and vowed that he would have us all before the magistrate. Poor Sir Augustus attempted to plead with the old malcontent, but he wouldn't listen to reason, and so we were at stalemate until the matter was brought to court."

"And what was the outcome?"

"Frankland argued that Mr. Underwood had known right well where the boundary line lay, and by allowing his laborers and myself to violate it, he ought to be ordered to forfeit his share of the discovery. The magistrate wasn't prepared to go so far,. He ordered that Mr. Underwood and I pay a small fine for trespass, but as to entitlement to the relic itself, he stated that he couldn't rule on that until he had made a more thorough study of the issue. Frankland didn't wait upon the law, but took matters into his own hands."

"How, pray?"

"That very night, he harnessed his end of the statue to a pair of cart horses and towed the entire piece onto his property. I daresay, if it were it not for the drag marks upon the ground from the boundary line to his stable, he would have set down its disappearance to Loki's mischief."

"He made off with it?" I asked. "What does he intend to do with it?"

137

The doctor ran a shaking hand over his brow. "He has made up his mind that every grief and misfortune our district has suffered over the years – from his wife's demise to Sir Charles' death to Sir Henry's ordeal to Miss Frankland's – Mrs. Lyons' – estrangement from her husband, to the time that a band of moorland vagrants made off with a pair of Mr. Underwood's prize ewes – must all be set down to Loki's mischief – that it hadn't been buried deep enough in the ground to offset the blight upon our district, and that if we are to have any peace, the relic must be dragged to the Grimpen Mire and sunk."

"Great Heavens!" I cried.

"In that case, I think the mystery of its disappearance is easily resolved," said Holmes. "You must simply follow the drag marks from Frankland's stable to the mire."

"It didn't vanish from his stable, Mr. Holmes, but from the special that Sir Augustus had hired to transport it to London this morning!"

"Indeed! Frankland was persuaded to surrender it, then? How did that come about?"

"That was Sir Augustus' doing. He took it upon himself to make a thorough search of deeds and titles and discovered that the boundary line in question had been established no more than seventy or eighty years ago, and that prior tenure had shifted about a good deal. He then called upon Frankland and declared that at our next appointment with the magistrate, he would maintain that if the relic was five-hundred years old, its ownership must be fixed according to the titles and boundaries of the era, which might well place it entirely within the borders of Foulmire."

"A frail argument," remarked Holmes. "And one that wasn't without risk. Records of those ancient boundaries might have gone against your antiquities' expert."

"Perhaps, but it was enough to rattle the old fellow. Frankland well knows how capricious the law could be in matters of property, for he himself had successfully sued for a public right of way to be opened straight through Sir Robert Middleton's private park, and for Fernworthy Commons to be closed off to the public. When he asked Sir Augustus how much time the museum would want to fit up an area for the relic's exhibition, we took that to mean that he had surrendered his claim."

"Did he say as much?"

"Not in so many words, but he did suggest that the relic remain in his stable for those two weeks – where it might be protected from the elements, he said."

"Two weeks!" Holmes snorted his disdain. "It wouldn't take two hours to have the relic dragged to the mire and sunk."

"I confess to some anxiety on that score, but just after Frankland and Sir Augustus seemed to come to terms, the old man ran up to London. I assumed that he meant to seek out some advocate or records that would support his claim."

"Did it not occur to him that, in his absence, you and Sir Augustus might break into his stable and make off with the prize?"

Holmes said it in jest, but Mortimer's sheepish expression suggested that such a scheme had, indeed, occurred to him. "Frankland left his groundsmen to keep a sharp watch over the place and, even if we could work out a plan to make off with it, we had not time, because Frankland was only gone for the night. He was back at Lafter Hall on Sunday morning."

"And for the next fortnight until the relic was to be transported to the museum. How did Frankland conduct himself?"

"Well, I saw little of him, but when we did meet, he was surprisingly civil – even merry in his cantankerous fashion. Sir Augustus meanwhile hired a local carpenter to put together a crate suitable for transporting the relic. This was delivered to Lafter Hall yesterday evening – and this morning, Sir Augustus and I were to retrieve the artifact and transport it to Exeter, where Sir Augustus had arranged for a special to convey us and the relic to London."

"And this morning – did all go as planned?"

"Yes. When we arrived, we saw the crate lying just outside the stable, and Frankland's groundsmen were carrying out the relic. They set it in the crate. The old miser even supplied straw and paper wadding for them to cushion it against the jostling of the train."

"You said that you left Exeter before six this morning so this must have been quite early – scarcely past dawn. You're certain that what you saw Frankland's men lay in the crate was this artifact?"

"Quite certain. True, we stood some feet off while Frankland's men laid it in the crate and swaddled it with paper and straw, but even in early half-light, Sir Augustus and I recognized the object that I had taken up from the barrow only weeks before. Such a unique piece could not be mistaken for a Michelangelo, or one of Lord Elgin's marbles."

"And you transported the relic to Exeter without incident?"

"Yes. Frankland's men got the crate onto our wagonette, and one of them sat behind to steady it while Frankland followed in his dogcart with the others, so that they might carry it to the railway car. At Exeter, the special was waiting, and we were able to depart as soon as the crate was placed aboard, since Sir Augustus had arranged with the traffic manager well in advance for the line to be cleared."

"How many were in your party?"

"Five all together. Sir Augustus and myself, the engineer and stoker, and a guard provided by the railway."

"How many carriages in the special?"

"Four. The engine followed by a vacant carriage – "

"To dampen the oscillation."

"Yes. The third was divided into a first-class compartment at the fore, second class at the rear, with a smoking compartment between, and the last carriage was the brake van where the crate had been stored."

"The engineer and stoker were in the engine carriage, of course, and the second was vacant, and you and Sir Augustus were seated in first class at the fore of the third carriage, I presume. And the guard?

"In second class."

"Not in the brake van with the relic?"

Mortimer shook his head. "It wasn't deemed necessary. The van was quite secure, and it would have been an uncomfortable for a passenger to spend above three hours in a bare compartment that had neither seats nor windows."

"There were no windows, you say? There were doors on either end, I gather."

"Yes. The door at the rear of the van opened inward, but it was secured on the inside with a stout cross-bar. Both the bar and the mounts were solid iron. It would take a battering ram to knock through it from the outside. The door at the front was padlocked on the outside and the railway guard kept the only key."

"And the second-class compartment would be just forward of the brake van. Could the guard see it from where he sat?"

"There was a small window in the rear door of his compartment. Certainly he could see the last carriage if he cared to look out. But Mr. Holmes, once we set out, a thief would have to hop on to the coupling between the cars, force the padlock, and then make off with a sandstone carving three or four times his own weight! And all while the train kept to a speed of fifty miles an hour! It isn't humanly possible!"

"Let us concentrate what *was* humanly possible. Is it possible that, before you set out, someone concealed himself in the brake van, or in the vacant carriage?"

"No. The brake van was utterly bare. Sir Augustus, the guard and I all entered it and watched as Frankland's men set the crate down and after they departed, we made certain that the rear door was barred, and then Sir Augustus and I watched as Briggs – the guard – padlocked the other door. And as for the carriage behind the engine: Had anyone been inside, someone would have to pass through our carriage to get to the brake van."

Holmes was silent for a few moments. "How many groundsmen?"

140

Mortimer blinked. "I beg your pardon?"

"Frankland's groundsmen who laid the relic in the crate and carried the object to the guard's van. How many were there?"

"Why . . . four."

Holmes lifted his brows. "So many?"

"Many? I had some concern that four were too few for the task, but they were stout, robust fellows, and they managed well enough."

"No," Holmes protested. "What I mean to ask was whether Lafter Hall requires four groundsmen. The property wasn't extensive, as I recall."

"Well, I call them groundsmen, but they are general laborers, on license from Princetown, who are useful to the old fellow in other ways. Old Frankland's mind is still as sharp as ever, but he is too frail to do all that must be done to keep up the property, and there are always a few stout fellows who have seen enough of the inside of a cell and aren't opposed to labor if it will keep them out of it."

"Quite so. Now to be clear: Five people boarded the train at Exeter, with the cargo securely locked in the last of four carriages, and the journey proceeded without incident."

"Entirely without incident until the very end."

"And pray, what happened at the very end?"

"Briggs states that when we were perhaps a half-mile or so from the platform at Paddington, he heard a banging or hammering from the guard's van."

"The train would have reduced its speed as it approached the station. Could that sound have been the knocking from the wheels as the brakes were applied?"

"No, Briggs swears that the sound came from the guard's van. He opened the door to his compartment and, with the train slowing though still in motion, he stepped across the coupler and unlocked the door to the van – " Mortimer ran his hand over his brow. "He was immediately blinded by a thick cloud of smoke and was forced to retreat. He stumbled into his compartment and pulled the communication cord and we came to a halt not a hundred feet from the platform, close enough for the waiting passengers to witness our plight and take up a cry of 'Fire!' Sir Augustus and I raced through the carriage and saw that Briggs had just thrown open the rear door of the carriage so that the smoke might dissipate. It was then that we saw that the crate's lid had been thrown open, and – but for the piles of straw and wadding – it was empty! Loki had vanished! A railway worker who had heard the cries and seen the smoke climbed in to see if he might be of use, and Sir Augustus had him to summon the police, while I have come for you. I beg you, Mr. Holmes!"

Holmes pushed himself up from his chair. "Well, well, it is a pretty problem, and I think I can spare what remains of the morning to look into it. What do you say, Watson? I don't believe there is anything pressing."

"Nothing that cannot be put off," I said, holding back a smile.

Holmes quickly pocketed his cigarette case and reached for his old gray travelling cloak and cloth cap, and within a few moments we three set out.

"Tell me, Doctor," said I as we rattled toward Paddington Station, "if old Frankland is as fond of the arts as you say, is it not strange that he threw off his daughter when she married an artist?"

"To be frank, I have come to understand that the situation wasn't quite as I had first represented to you, but I had no intimate knowledge of the situation. Miss Frankland's marriage to Lyons, and their separation, had already occurred before I came to the area. After my own marriage, you see, I didn't settle in Dartmoor straight off. Instead, I remained in town, and I took on assignments as a *locum* in the hope that one of these appointments might lead to a consulting practice. It was in this role that I happened to attend Sir Charles Baskerville when his own London specialist was abroad, and he was rather pleased with my services and urged me to apply for the post of Medical Officer at Grimpen, and so, with no prospects forthcoming in London, my wife and I moved to Dartmoor. Society in the country is very different that in town, and of course I was quite preoccupied with acquainting myself with my new post. I saw very little of Mrs. Lyons and nothing at all of her husband, and so did not, I regret to say, always distinguish gossip from truth."

"And, pray, what was the truth?" asked Holmes.

"It seems that Lyons had come to Dartmoor to sketch the moors and happened to stray into Frankland's property. He ran out to confront the trespasser but then caught sight of Lyons' sketch-book, and admired his work, and they fell into conversation. Frankland found Lyons to be a clever, learned sort, and an invitation to dine was followed by an invitation for the young artist lodge at Lafter Hall for the duration of his visit. Miss Frankland had been keeping house for her father since her mother's death, and eligible suitors for a handsome, educated woman weren't plentiful, which may explain why she and Lyons were drawn to one another, and to such a degree that, without seeking Frankland's consent, they ran off and eloped. Frankland was gravely disappointed. He liked Lyons well enough, but the young artist could scarcely earn his own keep, much less support a wife. Still, he resigned himself to the match, and even gave them the funds to take a handsome set of rooms at Coombe Tracey for a wedding present.

"Unfortunately, it appears that Lyons' devotion was divided between his bride and his art, and not always in equal measures. When he was at

Coombe Tracey, he would shut himself up in one of the rooms to sculpt or sketch or paint, and then he would fly off to submit his work to some art competition or gallery in London or the Continent, abandoning his young wife for months at a time. It didn't help matters between father and daughter that Frankland abetted Lyons' endeavors. Perhaps Frankland thought that in promoting his son-in-law's ambitions, he was helping the young man to the sort of success that would allow him to better provide for his wife, but I daresay she felt that she had been deserted by her husband and was resentful of her father for taking Lyons' part. The situation was made more painful – for Lyons at least – because he wasn't without gifts.

"But," Mortimer shrugged his shoulders, "the arts are a fickle trade – or rather, success in them is in the hands of a fickle public, and inevitably, Lyons returned from his excursions poorer than when he had set out, and at last he left and said he would send for her when he had the means to do so." Mortimer sighed. "I have had to settle for far less than that consulting practice in town of my old dreams, and so I must feel for the man. I hear that he has been reduced to turning out cover illustrations for yellow-back novels and producing decorations for the stage, while she provides a modest living for herself on the pittance left in trust by her mother and what small income she earns with her typewriting. "

"It is easy to see why the situation left her such easy prey for a blackguard like Stapleton," I said.

"And I have no doubt that Stapleton," Holmes observed, "once in possession of the lady's ear and the lady's affection, did all he could to cast her husband in the worst light and to encourage her estrangement from her father."

"Sadly, yes. Father, daughter, husband – all are at fault to some degree, and all too stubborn to make amends. After so many years, I don't think anything can reconcile them."

Our arrival at Paddington cut short this unhappy tale, and Holmes and I followed Mortimer along the platform, through a gauntlet of irritable passengers whose travel had been disrupted by the occurrence. At the far end of the platform, Inspector Lestrade was addressing the occupants of the special. I made out the engine driver and stoker, and concluded that the tall fellow with the official bearing was Briggs, the railway guard, and that elderly gentleman in a traveling cloak was Sir Augustus Wollaston Frank.

"Mr. Holmes!" Lestrade greeted. "It's a puzzler – but just the sort of case you used to fancy. I have kept everyone – "

"And I must ask you to keep them a bit longer," Holmes interrupted. "First, I would like to examine the guard's van. The crate hasn't been moved, I trust?"

"Everything is what Mister Briggs – " He gave a nod to the guard. " – met with when he unlocked the van."

With a signal for me to follow, Holmes made for the brake van. He first examined the door and then stepped into the vacant and windowless carriage that still bore the residue of smoke. Holmes went to examine the rear door that had been left open to air the carriage. "Set the bar into its mounts, Watson," he said, and sprang from the van as I did so. A moment later, I heard him endeavor to force the door from the outside, but without success. "It is as Mortimer said," he said, as he climbed back into the van. "No one could have got through the rear door from outside."

"And the other was padlocked on the outside and the guard saw no evidence that it had been tampered with when he went to unlock it."

"Hmm." Holmes then turned his attention to the long crate that lay in the middle of the car. It was constructed of wooden slats with a hinged lid that had been thrown open, exposing the mounds of wadding that had cushioned the artifact. Holmes squatted down and began to root through piles of straw and shredded paper and pasteboard scraps. "An odd sort of packaging material," he muttered as he drew up a stiff, pulpy square of cardboard.

"I suppose Frankland used whatever he had at hand."

"Note that it is not burnt, Watson – not even scorched. Straw, paper, pasteboard – those would have gone up in seconds, no matter how well sealed this carriage may have been."

Holmes tossed the wadding back into the crate and sprang down from the carriage and approached Lestrade and the passengers. "You say," Holmes addressed the railway guard, "that you unlocked the door because you heard a sound?"

"I did, sir. A loud knock or thump."

"As you were nearing the station?"

"Yes, sir."

"And you're certain it came from within the van?"

"Dead certain."

"And yet, there was no one in the van when they set out, and no one could have got in after," Lestrade said, grimly. "It's a puzzler, all right."

Holmes nodded. "When you heard a knock, the train had slowed and you were able to step across the coupler and unlock the van's door. You were immediately overcome with smoke, so you retreated to your compartment to pull the cord. You left the door to the brake van open?"

"Yes, sir. It would have been foolish to take time to lock it up again."

"And in fact, the train was drawing up to the platform. You heard a cry of 'Fire!' from the platform, but you don't say that you saw flames."

Briggs frowned. "No, sir, I did not. Only smoke."

144

"A railway worker boarded to see if his assistance was needed?"

"Yes, sir."

"What was this accommodating fellow's name?"

Briggs frowned and shook his head. "That I cannot tell you."

"His appearance? How was he dressed?"

Briggs shrugged his shoulders. "A common navvy. Rough trousers, a waistcoat, shirt-sleeves, and a good layer of soot." He thought for a moment. "Well-spoken for one of the class."

Holmes seemed to ponder the man's words for a few moments and then, in one of his startling shifts from grave introspection to action, he turned on his heel and dashed to the end of the platform, sprang down, and began to walk alongside the tracks, his gaze trained on the ground. When he had got about fifty feet from the special, I heard him cry out, "A-ha!" and snatch something from the side of the tracks before proceeding onward, disappearing from view when the track came to a curve.

"What the devil is he about?" Lestrade asked. "He doesn't hope to find your great stone statue lying at the side of the rails."

Not a moment later, we heard Holmes shout, "Halloa!" and race toward us, his coat flying behind him like a sail. Lestrade and I had to help him onto the platform, for he was clutching an object in each hand. "Tell me – what do you make of this?" He held up a long, stout cylinder.

Lestrade took it and turned it around in his palm. "A plumber's rocket," he said.

"And a good-sized one. There is no fire without smoke, as the old expression goes. There may, however, be smoke without fire."

"But Mr. Holmes," Sir Augustus protested, "The brake van was absolutely empty before the crate was brought in. If an object of this size had been lying about, it wouldn't have escaped our notice."

"Unless it was *inside* the crate."

"But we watched Frankland's men lay the relic in the crate and bundle paper and straw around it. Of course, I suppose that one of them might have slipped it in among a large wad of the material."

"Material similar to this?" Holmes held up the object in his other hand, a curved, dun-colored scrap of pasteboard. "I found it lying upon the track, some fifty yards beyond the plumber's rocket."

"There were scraps of cardboard like this inside the crate," I said.

"Does it not strike you that it is unlike typical cardboard?"

"May I, Mr. Holmes?" Sir Augustus took the scrap and examined it. "I have seen material similar to this – a sort of composite. Sir William Flowers, who is curator of the natural history exhibits, had been experimenting with a sort of *papier-mâché* that might be used to fashion replicas of large mammals. Marine mammals, whales and such – the sort

145

of creatures that aren't easily obtained for exhibit, or that a taxidermist might find too daunting."

"Yes," Holmes muttered, absently, "Doctor Mortimer, you stated that Frankland ran up to London to seek counsel or records that might support his claim. And that he left in the afternoon and returned on the following morning."

"He had likely been advised that his standing was weak, or that his claim would be too costly to defend."

"But you said that he returned on a *Sunday* morning. What offices, or legal agencies could he have hoped to access on a Saturday?"

"I never thought – "

"A shocking habit. And when he returned, you state that his conduct was unexpectedly cooperative and civil. Even merry."

Mortimer nodded. "I saw little of him at all, but yes, he was cordial, in his fashion."

"Might it have been the opera that sweetened his temper? Perhaps he ran up to London not for legal counsel, but for another performance of – What was it, you said? *Lohengrin*? As I recall, the reviews were excellent – " Holmes broke off, abruptly and hummed a few bars from the piece, his expression taking on the dreamlike introspection that I had so often seen in the old days, but never since his return.

I saw our party glance at one another, as if to express – or repress – their doubts regarding the state of Holmes's faculties. Holmes surveyed their uneasy glances and grinned. "I think, Sir Augustus, it would be best if you sent a note around to the museum and informed them that they must not expect to see the promised relic today."

Sir Augustus groaned and nodded.

"Tomorrow will have to do."

"What – tomorrow? Do you know where it is, then?"

"Well, let us say, I know where it is not," replied Holmes. "And I have every expectation that I may restore it to you, but only if you all follow my instructions. You, Sir Augustus, must arrange for a special to depart for Exeter within the hour. You and Doctor Mortimer – and you, Mr. Briggs – have had a very long journey this morning, and I am sorry that I must ask you to turn around and journey back again. And if you would be so good, Lestrade, as to wire the authorities at Dartmoor and have Frankland apprehended – if he is at his home, they may detain him there. You will want to accompany us and see this little problem through, I trust, so Watson, arrange for us to be conveyed from the station to Lafter Hall. A wagonette will do for the seven in our party."

"But – we are only six," protested Mortimer.

"No, there is one more. I go to collect him now. I will not be gone above an hour, and we must be ready to set out as soon as I return."

With that, Holmes strode quickly through the crowds milling upon the platform and vanished.

"Doctor Watson," Mortimer said as we watched my friend's tall form disappear from view, "has Mr. Holmes been quite right since his return?"

"Right as rain."

Doctor Mortimer gave me a dubious look, and I wondered – and not without some amusement – whether he were pondering how far a decline in my friend's health might hasten the availability of his skull.

A full hour passed, in which time a special – the very same carriages, in fact, that has carried the party to London – had been secured, and waited only on our orders to depart. At last, we saw Holmes hurrying along the platform, a companion at his heels. This man was perhaps under forty, of middle height, with handsome, refined features though his attire, and the battered leather satchel slung over one shoulder, were more common to a member of the working class.

"Ah! Here we are!" Holmes said. "Introductions may wait until we depart. Let us take the smoking compartment. It can best accommodate seven, and I am in need of a cigarette."

"You, sir – " Briggs addressed my friend's companion as we settled into our seats. "I know you! You were the navvy who heard our cry of 'Fire' and came to offer aid!"

"It might be more accurate to say that this gentleman set off the cry of 'Fire!'" said Holmes. "Allow me to introduce you to Mr. Richard Lyons, Mr. Frankland's son-in-law. And I have you, Sir Augustus, and you, Doctor Mortimer, to thank for raising the possibility of his involvement in the matter."

"But . . ." Doctor Mortimer blinked, "I have never met Mr. Lyons."

"Nor have I," said Sir Augustus.

"No, but I daresay you are familiar with his work. Sir Augustus, when I showed you that scrap of pasteboard, you said that it was similar to a material that a one of your colleagues had employed to fashion replicas for natural history exhibits. It occurred to me that there might be other applications – theatrical props, for example. In fact, it the material had been used quite recently for that purpose – at the benefit performance of *Lohengrin* that Mr. Frankland attended – the reviews were universally positive, as I recall, with the design and set pieces singled out for particular praise – the great swan for the swan boat was said to be a large as a man, unlike anything ever before seen. You generally don't see the terms 'unparalleled' and 'lifelike' lavished upon the props unless they are truly exceptional. Your work, Mr. Lyons."

147

"It has been a living," Lyons said with a sigh. "Not the one I wished for."

"When Frankland ran up to London, he didn't go to seek proof of his claim to the relic. It was to bring Mr. Lyons to Dartmoor so that he might make a reproduction of it."

"A reproduction!" cried Sir Augustus. "For what purpose?"

"To convince you that what you carried to London this morning was the genuine article."

I looked at their expressions of open-mouthed astonishment. I daresay I wore the same expression on my own face.

"You must understand," Lyons said, "I did it only for Laura's sake – the price that Frankland said he might get for that block of sandstone will allow her to live the sort of life that I could not provide."

"Why – " sputtered Mortimer. "He has no intention of selling it!"

Holmes sighed. "It seems, Mr. Lyons, that you, too, were deceived. No doubt Frankland was convinced that, artist that you are, you wouldn't take part in the destruction of a priceless artifact, and so he told you that he intended to sell it."

"Destruction!"

Doctor Mortimer repeated what he had told us, and Lyons' face went ashen with shock. "That old fox!" he groaned. "That mad old fox!"

Lestrade scratched his head. "I confess I am in the dark, Mr. Holmes. If what these gentlemen brought up to London was a pasteboard copy, then where is the relic?"

"Where it has been for some weeks, Lestrade, and where it was when our friends set off for London this morning – in the stable at Lafter Hall."

"But – even if you are correct, and the object that Doctor Mortimer and I saw placed in the crate this morning was a replica – I must say, Mr. Lyons, it was an extraordinary piece of work if that is the case! Where is this replica now? We saw it placed in the crate, we followed the crate to the special and watched as it was it locked in the brake van – and there it remained until we had nearly reached our destination when Mr. Briggs unlocked carriage door and found nothing in the crate but a pile of paper and straw!"

"And what of the smoke?" Lestrade demanded. "And that plumber's rocket tossed at the side of the tracks?"

Holmes held up his hand. "I must ask you to possess your souls in patience. It would be best to hold off a recital of the events until we may have them corroborated by the gentleman who set them in motion."

With that, Holmes turned his attention to the window, and settled into one of those tight-lipped spells that could be so trying to those around him.

For the whole course of the long journey, Holmes silent except for an occasional "Ha!" when something along the tracks caught his eye.

Mr. Lyons, at least, was better prepared for the ordeal than we. In his pouch he carried a large sketch book and a box of pencils, and we whiled away the time sketching likenesses of all of us – and very good ones, too. Holmes would never concede that I knew anything of art, but I think I knew enough to see that Lyons' work was as fine as what I'd seen hanging in many London galleries.

Only once did the fellow look up from his sketch-book, having drawn a likeness of Frankland that gave his features a more youthful and considerably more amiable cast. "He wasn't always the contrary man he is today, you know. Laura once told me that he had once been quite affable, that he had been very well-liked when his wife was alive, and has been bitterly lonely since her death."

"Perhaps he would be less lonely if he didn't drag his neighbors into court over trifles," declared Mortimer.

"Perhaps he wouldn't turn to the courts if some other form of society were offered to him," replied Lyons. "Tell me, Doctor, how often do you or any of your neighbors call at Lafter Hall just to see how the Frankland gets on? When have you invited him to tea or put him up for a membership in the Dartmoor Preservation Society?"

Lyons' words called up a scene from the Baskerville matter – how I had encountered the Frankland idling at his gate that opened upon the high road, how pleased he had been to see a passer-by, and how he had pressed me to stop for a glass of wine. What I had taken for irksome curiosity may have been nothing more than loneliness.

"Of course, I may be prejudiced where Mr. Frankland is concerned," Lyons added, in a more moderate tone. "He took an interest in my ambitions and gave me encouragement when I met with nothing but rejection elsewhere."

At the station, a large wagonette, pulled by a sturdy pair of cobs, was waiting for us, and Holmes himself took the reins. In twenty minutes, we were at the high road that passed Lafter Hall. A constable stood at the garden gate, and we could see beyond the house where another had been posted at the stable.

"The object is in the stable," said the constable when we had alighted. "They say it is a work of art, but all I see is a hideous block of stone. As for Frankland, you will find him in the library and in no good humor."

In the library, we found Frankland pacing about as he castigated his two custodians, another constable and a lady who I recognized: Mrs. Lyons. The years had been surprisingly kind to her, removing those traces of coarseness and indelicacy that I had observed upon our first meeting,

149

and leaving in their place a long-suffering serenity, though she was anything but serene when she turned on our party and spied her estranged spouse.

"Richard! What have you to do with this? What sort of impossible scheme has my father brought you into now?"

"It was a joke!" declared Frankland. "A practical joke! And so, Mr. Holmes, you return to our part of the world – and just when we had all got used to having you dead."

"I'm sorry, Laura," said Lyons. "You didn't play fair with me, sir! You said that you meant to sell the artifact! I would have had no part in this if I thought you were going to destroy it."

"I think a full recital of the facts would be the best way to atone for the part you played," said Holmes. "I believe that I can reconstruct the episode fairly well, Mr. Lyons, and you and Mr. Frankland may correct me where I go astray."

"So you have it all worked out, have you?" muttered Frankland.

"I believe so. You returned from one of your visits to town, Mr. Frankland, to find that Doctor Mortimer had unearthed a rare relic which lay across the boundary line that separates your property from that of your neighbor. This was no flint or fossil or prehistoric skull, but an idol to which you attributed many years' worth of mischief and misfortune, and you were convinced that peace couldn't be restored unless the idol was cast into the Grimpen Mire. Personally, I should think that a god who could stir up discord from a barrow might do as much from a bog, but you had made up your mind to take possession of it and arrange to dispose of it. The latter object was difficult, since your property and stable were being closely watched by Doctor Mortimer and Sir Augustus and the local constabulary."

"Busybodies!" cried Frankland.

"As I said, you wanted opportunity, but you are something of a trickster yourself. You allowed Doctor Mortimer and Sir Augustus to think that you had reconciled yourself to surrendering the relic. You gave every appearance of resignation and were even merry, in your fashion, and I daresay your conduct caused Sir Augustus to be more forthcoming regarding the arrangements for transporting the relic: A special with few passengers and the crated relic that would travel in a brake van. All you needed to do was to convince Sir Augustus and Doctor Mortimer that what they conducted to London was the original and not the counterfeit that you commissioned from your son-in-law. Your groundsmen were very cooperative, though I think they may have violated the terms of their leave. In any case, they packed the imitation in the crate and lifted it onto the

150

brake van where it would be locked away until the party arrived in London."

"Mr. Holmes," said Sir Augustus, "it is true that in the half-light of dawn, and with only a brief glimpse of the relic before it was laid in the crate and covered up with wadding, Doctor Mortimer and I believed that what we saw was genuine – not only because it was an extraordinary reproduction. Quite unlike anything I have ever seen, sir," he added, with a nod to Lyons, "but because we watched four strong men carry the counterfeit relic from the stable, lay it in the crate, and then lifted the crate onto the brake van."

"And I daresay they made a very good show of it. Of course, what they carried was somewhat heavier than a *papier-mâché* capsule, they also had to bear the weight of what lay inside."

"Inside!"

"Think of the dimensions of the relic. It was said to be above five feet in length and must be at least three or four feet in circumference at its widest points. A man – provided he isn't a very tall or bulky fellow – might easily fit within the replica – "

"Impossible!" cried Sir Augustus.

"Ambitious, not impossible," said Holmes. "But, of course, Mr. Frankland might not be able to discard the genuine relic before the reproduction arrived in London – and once the fraud *was* discovered, it would be assumed that the original was still in his possession, and Sir Augustus would immediately arrange for the authorities in Dartmoor to take custody of it until he could retrieve it. What if, however, the object in the crate vanished – vanished in a cloud of smoke and from a locked carriage? There would be no reason to suppose that what had disappeared was anything but the actual relic, and no explanation for its disappearance but the work of its mischievous subject. After all, Doctor Mortimer, when you brought the case to me, you were not as reluctant as a man of science should be to attribute the object's disappearance to a supernatural agency."

"I could think of nothing else that would account for it."

"Once the crate was locked away, and the special was in motion, you, Mr. Lyons, worked your way free. I daresay a simple palette knife would do for cutting your way out of a *papier-mâché* exoskeleton. You threw open the crate's lid and set about cutting up the counterfeit Loki. Some bits of it we found in the crate, and as for the bulk of it, you unbarred the rear door and tossed it along the tracks where it would be taken for just so much refuse. I made note of a number of those pasteboard scraps on our journey to Exeter."

"And the business of the plumber's rocket?" Lestrade asked.

151

"That Mr. Lyons also carried with him, to create a diversion that would facilitate his escape. It would be an interesting bit of alchemy to reach Paddington and find that Loki had vanished and left an artist in his place, but it would not do. The slowing of the train would alert Lyons that the special had neared Paddington and that is when Mr. Briggs heard a knocking sound from the van. That, of course, was you, Mr. Lyons, pounding on the door to attract the attention of someone in the next carriage. As soon as he heard the key in the padlock, he set off the plumber's rocket, directing it at you, Briggs, so that you would be blinded and driven back to pull the cord, which allowed Lyons to exit the open door, jump onto the tracks, dispose of the plumber's rocket, and then hurry toward the platform where he had the impudence to ask if he might be of use before returning to his lodgings near the theatre. My own researches directed me toward an artist, and one who might have designed a replica from material similar to that which I found at the site of the disappearance, which – thanks to your information, Doctor Mortimer – suggested Mr. Frankland's son-in-law as the likely agent. The theatre manager furnished me with his address, and together we returned to the station. I think there is nothing I've left out – except," Holmes added, thoughtfully, "I seem to recall that one of the quirks of this trickster god was that as disposed as he was to make mischief, he was just as quick to repent and set matters right."

"When matters can be set right," Lyons said in a low voice.

"Sometimes reconciliation calls for a human agency," said Holmes.

"I am not certain that Holmes meant for his remark to produce the response that it did, but at any rate," Doctor Mortimer said, "Mr. Frankland, I have been thinking for some time that I would like to put up your name for membership in the Dartmoor Preservation Society. We are not always very formal – sometimes it is just a pint at The Three Crowns and a bit of gossip – but where we have differences on points of local history, you, as one of our oldest residents, might advise us as to where we go wrong."

Frankland scowled, as if to consider the proposal. "I suppose I might have an evening or two to spare."

"And now, we will excuse ourselves," said Holmes. "Lestrade, Watson, and I return to London. Will you come, Mr. Lyons?"

Lyons looked at his wife. "I think perhaps I will stay. There is a matter I would like to try to set right."

"Then good day to you."

Mortimer walked us to the wagonette. "The Dartmoor Preservation Society!" he groaned. "What have I done?"

"I think," replied Holmes, "you have rescued us both from sinking into the dull mire of routine existence."

152

The Tragedy of
Mr. Ernest Bidmead
by Arthur Hall

As my readers will surely be aware by now, my friend Mr. Sherlock Holmes would never admit the existence of the supernatural. Indeed, his first response when confronted by a problem that seemingly involved such aspects was always to strive to prove that the explanation was within the bounds of normal experience. In almost every instance he was successful, though there were some where I remained unconvinced. One of these I have recorded elsewhere as "The Adventure of the Moonlit Shadow", but there were others. The following tale is one of these.

"My dear fellow, you look distinctly ill," Holmes said to me at breakfast one day in early summer. "Since my return to London, I have observed that you have become pale and, unless I am mistaken, that your nerves are troubling you."

I ate the last of my toast, with much-reduced appetite. "I do apologise. I confess that the strain of Mary's passing, although now over a year ago, and your more recent unexpected reappearance, have worn me down. Also, Mrs. Hudson has commented recently that I'm suffering from overwork. Perhaps she is correct."

"I'm certain that she is," he smiled across the table, "and I have already acted to remedy the situation. Here is the reply to my enquiry."

He placed before me a letter from a Mrs. Winter, who I had a vague recollection he had once mentioned while relating an old case. The lady wrote from her home, a boarding-house in a village situated a few miles from Truro.

"She expects us for a holiday!" I exclaimed.

"Is that agreeable to you?"

I nodded, in a sudden rush of enthusiasm.

"A seat is reserved for you in a first-class smoker in the early train on Saturday," Holmes added.

"For me? Am I travelling alone?"

A frown appeared, momentarily altering his pleasant expression. "The road to securing the conviction of Mr. Percival Strike has been a long one, but I'm now able to prove that he leads a double life. He is a respectable manager of the London and Provinces Commercial Bank by day, and the head of a gang who guarantee the demise of anyone you choose by night. In disguise I visited them, to be told that the identity of the victim and the required sum would ensure the disappearance of anyone who is a source of annoyance to me. Really, having gained information about their activities, I cannot allow them to continue."

"So you wish to follow this to the end. If I agree to journey to Cornwall, when may I expect you?"

"Whenever the first train leaving the capital arrives in Truro – after the guilty verdict. I would estimate Wednesday."

I considered for a moment. Lately I had become impatient and prone to an unnatural tiredness. I had been summoned in the early hours more frequently than usual to deliver babies or attend to sudden emergencies. My encounters with Holmes had been few and brief, as he was fully taken up with the Strike case, and I had missed his company. And, yes, I was weary.

"I'm grateful to you," I said as a feeling of pleasant relief swept over me. "It will be good to walk again along the cliffs of the Cornish coast."

So it was that I found myself outside a house of solid stone, with suitcase in hand. The warm air against my face was a welcome change from the London atmosphere and the smell of the sea, although I was some little distance from it, had filled my nostrils since I boarded the trap at the station.

Mrs. Winter was a jolly, middle-aged woman. She was welcoming, obliging, and, I was soon to discover, a cook to rival Mrs. Hudson. It crossed my mind that I might be able to learn something of her past connection with Holmes as we became more familiar with each other, but I dismissed the notion. If he wished me to know, he would tell me when he was ready.

I settled myself in the small but very clean room she provided. It was by now late afternoon, and I felt the need of a short nap before changing for dinner. The dining room, with starched white tablecloths and gleaming cutlery much in evidence, looked down from the back of the house. During our introductory conversation, Mrs. Winter had poured tea from a china pot and explained that she was able to run this establishment alone, since it catered for only three guests at a time. There were of course rooms reserved for Holmes and myself, and that remaining was currently occupied by Mr. Bidmead, whom I would meet at dinner.

The gentleman who sat opposite me to partake of Mrs. Winter's roast beef was tall and thin with a magnificent handlebar moustache. I noticed as he entered the room that he had a pronounced limp which he eventually explained in a north country accent as, "A souvenir of Afghanistan, as are your wounds. I curse the day that those savages learned about firearms."

He proved to be a most interesting conversationalist. I was amazed at the extent of his knowledge of a wide variety of subjects, and at his passion for places of historical interest.

"I seek them out all the time," he told me over breakfast the next morning. "Since my wife passed away, I'm rarely at home. When I read or hear of some former manor house or castle, I'm keen to see it and explore. It has become my reason for living, you might say."

"A very consuming pastime, I would imagine," I remarked as I passed him the butter dish.

"Immersing myself in the history of these places has been an enormous help in filling my time and my thoughts. Last week I visited an old manor house near the outskirts of Birmingham, where King Charles the Second hid from Cromwell's men. It was a fascinating place."

"Are you here to explore similar houses in Cornwall?" I enquired.

"I am. I'll wager that you haven't realised that we are at this moment sitting within two miles of a wonderful example. Goosemoor Grange has lain derelict since the last owner died without heirs, some years ago. No one goes near the place now. You'd think it was haunted."

"But is it?" Not a serious question, I reflected. Holmes would hardly have approved.

Mr. Bidmead laughed. "I've heard of that sort of thing, but never come across it. The strangest thing was when I climbed the battlements of a castle in Wales. The smell of roasting meat was thick in the air, although no cooking had taken place there for centuries."

"Strange indeed," I commented.

As Mrs. Winter brought our tea, I could see that he was giving some notion his consideration, so I wasn't altogether surprised when he put down his empty cup and made a request.

"I'll tell you what," he said as if the idea had just occurred to him. "I'm going to Goosemoor Grange this morning. I can't walk the distance because this leg won't carry me that far, but Mrs. Winters has told me that I can hire a mount from the fellow at the inn down by the crossroads. What do you say to coming with me? You seemed interested in my adventures, and I know for a fact that there are two horses for hire at The Cornish Lad. We'll have a drink there when we take the horses back. What d'you think?"

I toyed with his proposition for a moment, before realising that the weariness that had contributed to my presence here still weighed upon me like a stone. A short walk among the tree-lined lanes before dinner, and an hour or two of sleep afterwards seemed more appealing, I decided.

155

"I would like that very much," I replied then, "but not today. I've had rather a rough time of it lately, but I'll probably be fit for tomorrow, if you are agreeable."

Disappointment clouded his face for an instant, but quickly faded.

"Capital! I'll go alone today – there's more than enough to see during a single visit – and reserve horses for tomorrow."

"I'll look forward to it," I said politely.

He set off shortly afterwards, and I settled myself on the bench among the wisteria and abundance of poppies in the tiny front garden. I immersed myself in the contents of the local newspaper, and was disturbed only twice before dinner: First by Mr. Bidmead as he rode by after collecting his mount – he waved and shouted to ask if I'd changed my mind about accompanying him – and then, about mid-morning, by Mrs. Winter who brought me coffee and biscuits.

I found the faint breeze soothing. The sun was high but the air not excessively warm, and the morning passed quickly. Luncheon was curried pork, hotter than that to which I am accustomed, but very welcome. Mr. Bidmead didn't appear, and I mentioned this to Mrs. Winter.

"Oh, I wouldn't be concerned, Doctor," she replied. "He's most likely absorbed in something or other at Goosemoor Grange. It wouldn't be the first time."

Having witnessed Mr. Bidmead's enthusiasm, this didn't surprise me. I had already deduced that this wasn't his first visit here.

"If he returns before dinner, he'll be unlucky though," she added. "I'm visiting my aunt this afternoon. If you see him, would you mind telling him that I've left some cold cuts for him in the kitchen?"

"Not in the least," I smiled.

A local man arrived in a cart soon after to collect her. Now alone, I felt an enormous tiredness, no doubt encouraged by my relaxed nerves and the most pleasant surroundings. I considered returning to my morning haunt, but decided instead to retire to my room for an hour or two so as to avoid being disturbed by passing carts or coaches, few as these had been.

I took off my shoes and coat before lying full-length upon the bed. The book I had brought with me, a stirring sea story by R. H. Dana, Jr. I quickly grew heavy in my hands. I have no recollection of putting it aside before sleep took me.

Sunlight still streamed faintly through the drawn curtains when I was forced from my slumber. I shook my head to clear it from the remaining drowsiness and fumbled with my pocket-watch.

I had slept for a little more than two hours.

But what had woken me so suddenly? I had a faint impression in my head, as if a terrible cry had driven me from sleep. A dream, surely? But

156

no, it came again. I heard my name, shouted in near-hysteria, and now came the heavy footfalls of someone rushing up the stairs. I had half-risen, intending to investigate, but I had hardly regained my feet when the door burst open.

Mr. Bidmead stood there, his clothes in disarray and his tie askew. I saw at once that he was covered in grey dust that had discoloured his face and adhered itself to his clothes and moustache. He trembled like a man with the ague and his expression was full of alarm. As I stood aghast, he struggled to speak.

"What is it, man?" I enquired urgently. "What has happened to you?"

He made several attempts to reply, then seemed to collect himself.

"Doctor Watson," he gasped. "You must help me. Come to the house. It was awful."

I at once put on my shoes and coat and picked up my medical bag, before asking, "Is it an accident?" Then again, "What has happened?"

At that, his expression changed to that of someone who has forgotten something. "But I must get back," he said in a strange and breathless voice. "I haven't long to stay away."

He turned then, to descend the stairs at a frantic pace. I was vaguely conscious of wondering how he could do this when handicapped by his leg injury, but I paid the notion no attention. I followed, expecting to ride double on his horse, but neither he nor the animal was anywhere to be seen as I reached the roadside.

I wondered at this for but a moment, for I have long known that men do strange things in times of great excitement. There was nothing else for it, I saw, but to walk or run the two miles to Goosemoor Grange as best I could.

As it turned out, Mr. Bidmead had over-estimated the distance. By my reckoning I had run and walked alternately for under a mile-and-a-half before I arrived, breathless and overheated, to find a square Tudor mansion of two storeys. It was a wide structure of grey local stone, surrounded by a tiny courtyard leading directly from the road.

I stood for a moment, regaining my breathing. Outside the remains of the walls, a small but dense wood of tall elms flourished, and beyond it a lake was visible. A strange sound came to my ears, puzzling me until I realized that it was the cackling of many geese, no doubt the reason for the name of the house.

I saw that Mr. Bidmead's horse was tethered to a bush, and was busily grazing on the grass beneath it. Strangely, the animal didn't appear to have been ridden recently – it wasn't lathered or breathing heavily.

The courtyard showed signs of much neglect. Weeds stood tall between the stones and the walls had crumbled in several places. The

157

metal-studded door hung crookedly, but as I approached I saw that it was ajar sufficiently to admit me. I entered into a hallway where rusted armour lay abandoned upon the floor and leaned at odd angles against the dark wooden panelling. Weapons, shields, and the remains of portraits littered the cracked and discoloured tiles. Doors with enormous hinges stood to either side, but I ignored these and strode ahead, through the open entrance that confronted me.

The swirling dust that filled the room was no less dense that the fogs that obscure the capital in winter. I tied a handkerchief across my nose and mouth in an attempt to stem the violent coughing that suddenly racked my body. When I had regained some control of myself, I proceeded cautiously into the semi-darkness, which was relieved only by what light could penetrate the tall and almost opaque windows somewhere beyond the thick clouds. My footsteps echoed upon the floorboards, and from high above I heard the objections to my presence by birds who must have nested in the damaged roof. I waved my arms to dispel the dust, and succeeded to a small extent.

At once the cause of the dust and Mr. Bidmead's terror was apparent. The great curved staircase to the upper floor had collapsed, leaving the internal structure sagging and threatening to fall also. Bannisters and balustrading were scattered before me, among piles of splintered planks.

I wiped my eyes and peered into the wreckage. Clearly, it was recent and the cause of the dust. I called to Mr. Bidmead several times, but no answer was forthcoming and I wondered if, in his excited state, he had either somehow lost his way or taken refuge in the roadside trees to rest.

Then, to my horror, I saw that a bloodied arm projected from the debris. I dropped my medical bag and set to, pulling madly at the heavy remnants of carved woodwork and brass rails. A few minutes of this brought me to the point of exhaustion, and the thought came to me that Holmes had been right about my condition. A huge lump of stone or plaster lay atop the body and, try as I might, I couldn't move it.

I suffered a moment of complete despair before the sounds of footfalls echoed from without, and a figure emerged from the shadows. Then another pair of hands were with mine in frenzied assistance, and the obstruction was rolled away. The face beneath was revealed, dead and staring distantly, as my heart lurched.

It was Bidmead!

My entire body was as if frozen, the shock was profound. I felt as if I couldn't move, as a hand took my arm and guided me to my feet.

"Leave, my son. He is beyond your help. I will tend him now."

I realised then that my new companion was a priest. I staggered, coughing once more, from the room and out into the open air. By the time

158

my breathing had become normal, the curate, an extremely thin, narrow-faced man, emerged.

"I am Father Whiteacre," he explained when his own breathing had steadied. 'I was passing, returning to St. Margaret's after visiting a parishioner, when I perceived your plight. You are visibly upset, but you must calm yourself, my son. When you are feeling better, I think it best that you should take that poor fellow's horse and ride to inform the authorities. I will remain with him until they arrive."

I couldn't get the image of Bidmead's dead face out of my mind, and so it was some little time before I was able to set off. But the mare handled easily, and I continued along the road past Mrs. Winter's house until I found myself approaching a village green surrounded by a cluster of busy shops.

The Cornish Lad was a large and very old inn, disproportionately built and with blackened beams. I slowed the horse and rode beneath the arch to the stables beyond, where a lad who displayed alarm at my appearance took the reins. I staggered into the building, where the sympathetic proprietor sat me in an upright chair, gave me brandy, and prevailed upon a customer to fetch the local constable.

Sergeant Pengelli was fat and red-faced, but he quickly took stock of the situation and, after making notes, issued instructions and set off on his bicycle to relieve Father Whiteacre at Goosemore Manor. I felt drained and exhausted, but I forced myself to my feet, feeling rather embarrassed because, by now, the eyes of many locals were upon me as if I were a curiosity or an exhibit in a museum. I thanked those who had assisted me and staggered from the inn.

The walk back to Mrs. Winter's house seemed an endless trek. On arrival, I collapsed onto the bench in front of the building. Presently the good lady returned, and it was my unpleasant task to relate to her the events of the afternoon and the fate of Mr. Bidmead. The way her happy face changed to one of distress touched my heart because it was I whose words caused the transformation, and I did what I could to comfort her. Her resilience surprised me, however, for after I had bathed and changed my clothing, she was able to serve a late dinner of a most acceptable cottage pie with no difference to her appearance, save the slight quiver of her lips and the evident unshed tears.

By breakfast the next morning, she had apparently made a valiant effort to recover herself, though she noticeably avoided the subject of her deceased guest and had become rather pale. When she brought my mid-morning refreshment to where I had once again settled myself upon her front-garden bench, it was accompanied by a telegram. As she left me I tore open the yellow envelope, leaving my coffee untouched in my eagerness for word from my friend.

I was not disappointed.

> *All is complete here.*
> *Will arrive by the mid-day train.*

> *Holmes*

I felt immediate relief that I would soon be sharing my strange experience of yesterday with him. The more I thought about those happenings, the less I could believe them. How could I have followed so closely behind Bidmead, only to find that he was buried in the ruins of a collapsed staircase in the hall of Goosemoor Manor? How was such a thing possible? As a medical man, I had automatically taken note of his condition, which was that of a man already dead for an estimated two hours! I was a loss to imagine how even Holmes could explain such contradictory facts, but of one thing I was absolutely certain: He would entertain no suggestion of supernatural or unearthly influence. Most probably, there were aspects here which I had overlooked, or were ignorant of – elements which, once revealed, would place everything in a rational and easily comprehendible light. If anyone could untangle this web, it was Sherlock Holmes!

I had explained my friend's imminent arrival to Mrs. Winter, and she had agreed to delay luncheon accordingly. I again sat at the front of the house, inhaling the fragrance from the blooms around me, until the commotion of a cart pulled by a frisky horse caused me to lower my newspaper.

The cart came to rest near the gate and my friend alighted. The driver handed over a worn suitcase before receiving his due plus a smiling word of thanks and turning the cart around to retrace its journey. Holmes's thin form stood tall and erect, dressed in his grey tweed suit surmounted by the ear-flapped travelling cap that he had worn on so many of our adventures together.

"Watson!" He shook my hand as if we hadn't seen each other for years, but then his smile faded slightly. He had read in my face, as I knew he would, that something was amiss.

"I'm truly glad to see you, Holmes."

"But what is it?" His expression lightened again. "Has Mrs. Winter not been treating you well?"

I shook my head. "That good lady has been faultless, but she is now in a sorrowful state because of the death yesterday of her other guest. As

160

you have doubtlessly observed, this has affected me also. The circumstances were, to say the least of it, extraordinary, and I would value your opinion as to what actually occurred." I made an effort to stem the torrent of words which were tumbling from my mouth far too quickly, for I realised then that he looked tired and was certain to be hungry. "But come – I have already delayed you too much. Luncheon awaits us."

We entered the house where a rather subdued Mrs. Winter welcomed Holmes, mentioning a previous encounter of which I had no knowledge. When he had inspected his room and deposited his luggage, he joined me in the dining room where our hostess produced a fish pie that would, he remarked, rival that of Mrs. Hudson. When we had eaten our fill, he pushed away his empty tea-cup and regarded me across the table.

"I'm exceedingly sorry that this short holiday hasn't had the beneficial effect upon you that I intended," he said, as his calm grey eyes searched my face. "When we have finished here, I suggest that we adjourn to your room or mine, or outside in the sunshine if you prefer, so that you can explain to me the events that have caused you and Mrs. Winters such distress. I am of course at your disposal to assist you in any way that I can."

"My profound thanks to you." It then occurred to me that I hadn't yet enquired as to his activities since I left London. "But what of the forthcoming trial of the murder gang that you described?"

He shrugged. "About that, there is little to tell. It took the combined skills of both Lestrade and Gregson, but they were able to keep from each other's throats long enough to make the arrests. Strike, the organiser of the gang, was determined to avoid capture. He threw himself from a high window in the bank where he was employed, into the path of a heavy dray. I regret that I was unable to be there in time to prevent this."

I nodded. "But your efforts were rewarded. The residents of the capital can sleep easier in their beds."

"For now. There will of course be others."

"Who will doubtless be dealt with." We rose together. "If you are agreeable to an afternoon stroll, perhaps we could wander in the direction of Goosemoor Grange?"

Holmes indicated his agreement, lighting his old briar as we set off. We saw but two riders as we neared the house, neither of whom acknowledged us. Rather, they galloped past with fixed expressions, and neither were familiar to me.

By the time we reached the decrepit forecourt I had related all that had occurred the previous day. He had listened in silence, making no comment as he exhaled clouds of fragrant smoke.

"A strange account indeed," he remarked as we stood before the crumbling gateposts, "but thus far it isn't without explanation. Come, Watson. I'm curious to see this place."

We entered the house with caution, as I had done before. I saw at once that some of the armour and other objects that littered the floor had been displaced, probably by the attendants who had removed the body later. Holmes's eyes were everywhere, his view enhanced because the dust had now settled.

The inner room was a battleground. The collapse of the staircase had wreaked more damage than I had been able to see before. Some of the wood, bricks, and plaster had been removed from the pile in order to extract poor Bidmead, and Holmes noticed blood in several places despite the poor light.

He stood for some moments, deep in thought.

"There is nothing to be learned here, I think," he said then, "that would enhance your account. For once, I can see no sinister element. This unfortunate fellow met his end at the hands of Father Time, one might say, since it was age that weakened the staircase."

How like him, I reflected, to seek indications of criminal involvement first.

"But, Holmes, as I explained – Bidmead summoned me from Mrs. Winter's house. I saw him as clearly as I see you, yet he lay here dead when I arrived."

He nodded slowly, returning his empty pipe to his pocket. "I understand, but there is something else that puzzles me more."

"How could that be?" I asked as we picked our way around the debris and emerged into the sunlight. "What else is there?"

He stood erect for a moment, perhaps listening to the cacophony from the distant lake. The geese were in fine form today.

"Come, let us make our way back," he placed a hand on my arm, "for I perceive that the atmosphere of this place upsets you still."

We had walked no more than a hundred yards when I enquired again. "Holmes, kindly be so good as to tell me what perplexes you."

"The priest that arrived to assist you."

"Father Whiteacre?"

"Indeed. How did he know what was occurring within the house?"

I remained silent, attempting to recover the memory of my own actions as I discovered Bidmead. Yes, I was quite certain.

"I cannot explain that. That I made no sound, I am sure. The clouds of dust were choking."

"As I imagined, but we will leave that for the present. You're anxious to learn how Mr. Bidmead could have returned to Mrs. Winter's house, and yet have been dead a while by the time you arrived at Goosemoor Grange, are you not?"

"I can conceive of no answer."

His voice took on a gentle tone, and I was warned. "My dear fellow, there can be but one explanation. I feel it will distress you but I must impress upon you that I have seen it before, in others as well as in yourself, and it is known to be a passing thing that peace will dispel."

"Holmes, what is it that you refer to? Am I ill? Did I imagine this?"

"You will recall," he said after a short silence, "that shortly after my return to London, you experienced a period of excessive tiredness. You appeared to have difficulty in fending off sleep both at breakfast and during dinner. For weeks you retired much earlier than is your usual custom – is that not so?"

"It is," I confirmed. "But failing to diagnose the cause, I consulted my colleague, Doctor Elias Baldwin, who is renowned for his use of extracts from foreign plants to cure such conditions. After a course of one of his concoctions, I was restored."

"He attributed your condition to nervous strain?"

"Considerable overwork, he said, coupled with residual grief from the loss of Mary."

"As I suspected at the time, although I was careful to make no mention of it. As a doctor, you were clearly embarrassed to be so afflicted. I venture to suggest that one of your symptoms was of experiencing hallucinations."

I ceased to walk, turning to face him as he also became still. "That is so. I could have sworn that I saw John Clay several times, watching our lodgings. Do you believe that this condition has recurred?"

"Lately, you have again worked excessively – more so than I have known before. Consider several facts that support my statement: When you set out to follow Mr. Bidmead from Mrs. Winter's house, he had already disappeared, yet the horse showed no sign that it had been ridden recently. He couldn't have made the journey on foot because of his injured leg, which was strangely absent at that time. The body, you have stated, had already been dead for some time when you found it. There are other factors, but do you see, Watson, the impossibility of the situation otherwise?"

He paused, perhaps to allow me to consider, "However, I believe the solution to your difficulties to be in our own hands. The Striker affair is over, and there are no urgent matters to command my attention for at least three weeks. I suggest a further respite, perhaps a short sea voyage, as a cure for your shattered nerves and my need to put my thoughts in order. What do you say?"

My head was spinning, and I knew in my heart that my friend was correct in his observations and that I had known it myself and denied it for some time.

I was about to agree to his proposal, which I knew was at some cost to himself since he loathed to leave the capital, when I chanced to glance behind us. In the distance a figure had appeared, unsteadily riding a bicycle. It approached rapidly, as I realised that Holmes still awaited my answer.

"Holmes, if we can put this aside for a moment – did you not wonder at the priest's sudden appearance yesterday?"

He nodded, with a slightly disappointed air. "Indeed. I had intended to interview him on that subject."

"That may be unnecessary. He is here now."

We turned to see Father Whiteacre come to rest with a squeal of brakes that were in need of some oil.

"Doctor Watson," he gasped as he strived to regain his breath, "I was bound for Mrs. Winter's house to see if you had recovered from your ordeal of yesterday." He paused and glanced at Holmes. "But I haven't had the pleasure of making your friend's acquaintance."

I made the introduction and the priest's narrow face lit up.

"Of course I have heard of you, my good sir! The accounts of your work are astounding."

Holmes smiled politely. "Thank you, Father, but it is to Watson here who repeatedly over-dramatized trivial incidents, that the credit must go for any literary success."

"They are extraordinary tales, nevertheless."

"There is something Mr. Holmes would like to ask, if he may," I interrupted then.

Father Whiteacre's face was suddenly wreathed in a broad smile, and it occurred to me that he might be expecting Holmes's question to be of a religious nature.

His eyes twinkled as he looked at my friend expectantly. "What is it, my son?"

"First, I would like to express my gratitude for your assistance to my friend at Goosemoor Grange at such a perilous time," Holmes began tactfully.

"My work in the service of the Lord summons me to wherever there is a need, Mr. Holmes."

"Of that I am certain, but I confess to some confusion regarding the event."

The priest's smile was replaced by an expression of incomprehension. "Indeed? How is that, may I ask?"

"I'm puzzled as to how you knew of Watson's plight, since you could have seen no indication of it from the road, and he swears that he didn't cry out."

For some moments, Father Whiteacre went completely still. No sound, save that of cattle in a distant field, reached our ears until he spoke again in a curiously awed voice.

"Gentlemen, you have set me a question that I'm at a loss to answer. I was passing Goosemoor Grange and noticed the horse tethered outside, but that isn't unusual since from time to time inquisitive souls choose to enter the place as a form of entertainment. There was a notice warning of the dangerous condition of the house affixed to the gateposts, but it has long disappeared – I suspect to be used as firewood. No, what attracted me was the echoing voice calling loudly and repeatedly: 'Help me! Help me!' It reminded me, I suppose, of St. Paul on the road to Damascus, and I found its urgency compelling. I now recall wondering, when we spoke later, how the normal voice of Doctor Watson could be so different, but I confess to have forgotten the contradiction since then."

"Can you describe the quality of the voice that summoned you? How, pray, was it different?"

The priest considered. "It was, I believe, the *accent* that differed. Prior to my appointment here, I ministered to a parish in the County of Durham, and so I'm familiar with the speech of the people there. Have you, Doctor Watson, lived in that area also?"

"Never," I replied, feeling increasingly disquieted. "The other person must have been outside, for I was alone in the building until you joined me."

"Then it is a mystery, since I saw no one either, but a harmless and, as it turned out, beneficial one. The Lord does indeed work in mysterious ways." He pulled a battered pocket-watch from his waistcoat and glanced at it briefly. "But now that I have established that there have been no permanent effects to you, Doctor Watson, I must continue on my daily round. Mrs. Trehearne, at the age of ninety-two, has recently accepted the faith, and I'm anxious to impart as much of the Scriptures as I am able to her." He mounted his bicycle and struggled to attain his balance. "Good day to you, gentlemen. I'm sure that we will meet again before your holiday is over, God willing."

With that, and a final wave, he pedalled away.

"Holmes," I said as the black-garbed figure disappeared into the distance, "I'm aware that you have no belief in anything that isn't down-to-earth and rational, but there is something very odd indeed, here."

"Something more? Clearly, the priest was summoned by someone calling. As it wasn't yourself, it has to have been someone who remained unnoticed."

"But Bidmead was from the north of England! His accent was pronounced to the extent that I sometimes had difficulty in understanding his words."

He raised his eyebrows and regarded me with a kindly expression. "I see that you are determined to attach an unreal quality to this incident, Watson. Perhaps I can allay your fears and confusion, so that we can enjoy the remainder of our time here. Let us retrace our steps to Goosemoor Grange, and see what can be learned."

When we stood before the house once more, Holmes gestured that we should be still and not speak. The fragrance of the wild flowers that grew along the roadside and the edges of the tiny courtyard was pleasant, and the slight breeze that had been present since my arrival in Cornwall felt warm against my face.

"Listen, Watson," said my friend. "Do you not now realise what it was that the priest must have heard?"

I shook my head. "I hear only the sighing of the wind through the trees and the confused babble of the geese on the lake."

"That is all there is to hear. Apply a little imagination, and listen again. Think of the late Mr. Bidmead's voice, in as much as you remember it after such a short acquaintance. I shall be surprised if you cannot detect a resemblance to human tones in the noise that surrounds us now."

I did as he asked for several minutes. As always, he was correct.

"I suppose, if one is inclined to be imaginative, that almost any voice could be heard."

"Such an observation has been made before now, as I have recently read. These birds are also reputed to be better sentinels than are dogs. Their curious cries, especially when excited, are often mistaken for those of people in distress. I would speculate that our friend the priest saw the horse in the courtyard and, having a fertile imagination like yourself, heard the birds and became convinced that he was needed to assist with the difficulties of someone within the house. So you can see, Watson, how easily explained these so-called 'mystic' experiences often are. Come along and let us stroll into the village and allow ourselves a pint of good ale at the inn that you mentioned, before returning to Mr. Winter's house for what I'm certain will be an excellent dinner."

I conceded, and we conducted ourselves as Holmes had suggested. Later, after a rich lamb stew followed by a glass of vintage port that Mrs. Winter insisted we should consume as we sat smoking in her sitting room,

Holmes elaborated as to the concluding events of the Strike affair that had occupied him for so long.

He was never again to mention the fate of Mr. Ernest Bidmead, and appeared confident that his explanation of the affair covered its every aspect and would bear scrutiny.

As for me, having actually witnessed all that occurred at the time of the poor man's demise, I will never be certain.

The Adventure of the
Buried Bride
by Tracy J. Revels

"It is good to see you again, Maxwell," Holmes said as he ushered our visitor into our rooms at Baker Street. I knew the handsome young man, with the build of a star rugby player, as the police inspector for the charming village of Marbleton. Like so many men who were beginning their careers in detective work, Horace Maxwell was an avid follower of Holmes's adventures, and had stopped by more than once to discuss a difficult problem. I was glad to rise and shake his hand, as he was a youth with a keen mind and a lively sense of humor. Holmes dropped into his armchair as Maxwell and I exchanged pleasantries. "Besides the fact that you are now married, have come into a small inheritance, and have spent a brief holiday on the Cornish coast, what other details would you like to share with us?" my friend asked.

Maxwell chuckled as he took a seat. "You'll not draw me into your magic so easily, Mr. Holmes – though it still amazes me how quickly it all comes to you. Every aspect is correct, and I suppose you gleamed it all from my ring, my new suit, and the chapped skin on my face. I hope my case might be solved so easily."

"Ah, so what troubles you?"

"Visions of a ghost."

Holmes lifted an eyebrow. "This agency does not deal in the supernatural – you are well aware of that."

Maxwell's cheeks colored and he nodded briskly. "Of course. And I don't wish to waste your time. I wouldn't bring it before you except . . . these *visions* are questioning my ability as an investigator. If I don't clear this matter up, the village may lose confidence in me, and I am already beginning to doubt myself."

The young man's words moved Holmes, and he asked Maxwell to continue.

"Have you heard of Reginald Chambers, the Sea Devil?"

"An eighteenth-century pirate, was he not?"

"Yes. He was the great-grandfather of the current Captain Albert Chambers. The Sea Devil turned privateer in the end and avoided hanging in chains. His loot allowed his descendants to purchase the ancient manor

168

of Windwood and live quite comfortably, though Captain Chambers' father squandered much of it. The son, realizing his reduced prospects, followed his ancestor to the sea."

Holmes nodded. "Yes, and I recall that this Captain Chambers had a career in the Royal Navy, and was rising rapidly in that service until there was an incident. Do help yourself to a cigar, Maxwell."

The inspector stood and lit one, leaning back against our mantel. "Please allow me to provide more details, as they affect the business I need to put before you. Captain Chambers didn't go down with his ship, and rumors reached the Admiralty that it was his negligence which cost Her Majesty a fine vessel and twenty lives. Nothing was proven, but he resigned under a cloud and returned to his manor near Marbleton at the age of forty, with a foul temper and a battered body. His left leg was shattered in the explosion, leaving him crippled, and his right arm was burned and withered.

"Chambers lived a miserable, solitary life. He quickly gained a reputation as a contentious neighbor and an unforgiving master. Only the most desperate domestics would accept service with him, as – to give just one example – he became notorious for hurling plates at their heads when meals displeased him. Yet he would walk around the village with a great yellow diamond known as The Eye of the Siren attached to his cravat, as if daring anyone to doubt his importance.

"Then the miracle occurred – the Sea Devil fell in love with an angel. Miss Clarice Stiller was an exceptionally beautiful young woman who arrived in the village with an artist named Hans Martin. She was like a creature from a fairy story, with long copper hair, skin like milk, and a way of dressing as a peasant girl from the past. The captain saw her wandering across his fields one morning and stormed out with the intention of abusing a trespasser. Instead, he conceived a great passion for her. If he had still been upon the waves, he no doubt would have seized her and carried her off like a buccaneer, but for once he seemed to recall where he was, and so began to court her earnestly and honestly."

"One moment," Holmes interrupted. "What was the relationship between the girl and the artist?"

"They claimed to be distant cousins. However, on the eve of the girl's wedding, Martin slipped away on the last train from town with the air of a jilted lover. Shall I continue?"

Holmes shifted in his chair. "Only if this story is more than an insipid romance."

Maxwell shook his head. "It is possible murder."

Holmes rubbed his hands together. "Then the tale grows more intriguing. Proceed."

169

"Captain Chambers and his lady had been married less than a month when the troubles began. They started when the lady's elderly mother arrived with the expectation that she would live at Windwood. The captain begrudgingly obliged the old woman, but the servants reported loud rows. Then, not three months into their marriage, Mrs. Chambers was found dead in the millpond upon the property."

"It was your investigation?" I asked.

"Yes, Doctor Watson. Naturally, I suspected the husband, but he had an alibi, as he was in London when the girl drowned in the reedy water. There were no signs of violence upon her body, no marks of strangulation or struggle. Keller, the butler, informed me that the girl often walked alone, and a broken railing on the bridge across the pond suggested that she might have leaned against rotten wood, which gave way beneath her. However . . . ."

"You believed it was self-destruction," Holmes said.

"I did – Heaven knows the girl could have been driven to it, caught between a cruel mate and a demanding mother. But as there was no suicide note, her death was ruled an accident. Captain Chambers seemed truly distraught at his loss. He gave his wife the most elaborate funeral the community had ever witnessed. And he did something so remarkable at her service that it is still talked about in the village. Immediately before the coffin was closed in the church, he rose from his seat and removed The Eye of the Siren from his chest. With a loud announcement that he had lost all that was precious to him, he slipped the diamond into the dead woman's hands. He then stayed by her coffin until it was placed on a bier inside the family mausoleum on the property and locked away forever.

"And now, Mr. Holmes – I come to why I am seeking your help. The buried bride is reaching out, demanding justice for her murder."

The next morning found us travelling from Paddington Station to Marbleton. Holmes and I had risen long before the sun, and I had enjoyed very little sleep, for Inspector Maxwell's revelations had captured my imagination.

It seemed that just a week before, around the first month anniversary of Clarice Chambers' death, the girl's elderly mother – who remained a resident at Windwood – had begun to dream that her daughter was appearing beside her bed, clad in dripping garments and begging her mother to find the truth behind her tragic demise. The ghostly figure blamed her husband for her death and pleaded that her coffin be opened. These dreams so disturbed the lady that she brought her fears to Inspector Maxwell. Not being a superstitious man, the inspector was ready to dismiss the vision as utter nonsense. However, at the same time, Hans

Martin had returned to the village and was causing trouble. Deep his cups, the artist lingered at the local pub, accusing Captain Chambers of murder, and threatening to go and deliver justice himself if no new inquiry was launched.

"I've had words with him," Maxwell assured us, "and told him that if he kept up such foolish prattle, he'd end up sued for slander, if not beaten senseless by the captain himself. I'd hoped to encourage him to leave the village, but he refuses to go, and just three days ago I found him at the edge of the captain's property, staring at the mausoleum. It would all be nothing than a bother, but yesterday Captain Chambers himself roared into my office and flung down the elegant portrait he had commissioned of his late wife, one which had graced the mantel of his dining hall. Something astonishing had happened to it, and the captain's pride and honor were offended. I will show it to you if you come and help me sort out this most painful affair."

We were pulling into the station at that very moment. I glanced down at my friend's feet, where a small carpetbag rested.

"You have brought your chemicals?" I asked. Holmes roused himself from one of his dreamy introspections.

"Indeed not. Why do you think I would require them?"

"Because of the portrait. Inspector Maxwell said it was weeping blood. As I recall from our very first meeting, the Sherlock Holmes Test can be utilized, long after the fact, to determine whether a substance was hemoglobin or some other dark fluid."

My friend favored me with an amused look. "And why would it matter whether the painting was defaced with paint or actual blood? We know that ghosts don't exist – we don't admit them as criminals or as victims into our reality. Therefore, whether the painting was marred with blood from the kitchen, or paint from a work shed, or merely red ink from the study, is irrelevant. True, it would be intriguing to conduct my delicate test on a new surface, but as it will have no bearing on the case, I see no reason to transport my philosophical instruments out of London."

"Then what is in your bag?"

"Tools for a different kind of work."

Inspector Maxwell met us at the train, the relief clear on his face.

"Thank you for coming, Mr. Holmes, Doctor. This may be nothing, yet I cannot escape the feeling that my professional career might hinge upon it."

Holmes patted the young man's shoulder. "It may also resolve another matter that has bothered me for some time. You have the photograph I asked for?"

171

"Yes, and the painting is also in my office. And I have another surprise for you as well!"

The inspector's quarters were small and shared space with the lone cell, where a single prisoner was snoring upon a bench. He was a thin, sharp-faced, auburn-haired man of about twenty-five or so years, much disheveled and reeking of gin.

"That is Hans Martin. Our constable arrested him late last night. He was drunk and disorderly, shouting obscenities in the street, all of them against Captain Chambers. Locking him up was as much for his protection as for his disturbance of the peace." Maxwell picked up a tin cup to bang against the bars, but Holmes halted him, indicating Martin shouldn't be disturbed.

My friend stepped forward and carefully observed the slack face of the prisoner. I looked as well but discovered nothing more than a sad young man who was throwing away his life. His clothes were second-hand and ill-fitting, his hair was drooping to his shoulders, and his russet beard was untrimmed. Holmes crouched down and made a special study of his shoes.

"Let me look at the picture before we awaken the gentleman."

Maxwell opened his desk and drew out a photograph of an elderly woman. Her face was thin and delicate, her dark eyes were piercing, but the entire composition was spoiled by the shape of her nose, which appeared to have been broken and twisted noticeably to the right. Holmes passed it to me, then nodded for the inspector to remove the drape from a large picture which hung on the opposite wall.

The portrait showed a woman of great beauty, wearing a simple white gown and sitting in an armchair with her long red-brown tresses flung carelessly about her shoulders. It had been painted by an artist of only meager talent, for while it illuminated the young lady's fair appearance, it gave little hint into her soul, making her something of a lovely but ultimately meaningless enigma.

One was drawn immediately, however, to the startling distortion in the picture – the large droplets of blood which poured from the subject's eyes, obscuring their color, and marring the purity of her face. Below, across the bottom of the picture, the same red substance spelled out "*find the truth*".

Holmes stepped closer to study the writing with his lens.

A hideous wail erupted from behind us. The prisoner was on his feet and flailing his arms through the bars.

"Clarice! Clarice my darling! How could he have done this to you?"

Inspector Maxwell barked for him to be silent, but Holmes waved his hand and redirected his attention to the shrieking youth.

172

"What was the late lady to you, sir? And do not insult my intelligence by claiming that she was your cousin."

The man took a quivering step backward and raked a nervous hand through his tangled hair.

"She was my muse, my inspiration. I haven't been able to hold a brush without trembling since that murderous fiend stole her from me!"

"Ah," Holmes said, "that does clarify a great deal. You were her lover."

"You make that sound vile and sinful. Yes, I was her lover, and the pact we made to each other was more sacred than any offered up in a church. But as I had no money, we couldn't marry until my art was sold. It was her mother who pressured her to accept Chambers as a husband, instead of waiting for my talent to be recognized."

"So the girl threw you over," Maxwell said.

"No, she swore to me that she might give him her body, but never her heart. I begged her not to go through with it, but the old lady was ill and demanding to be cared for. Clarice sacrificed herself to the brute for her mother's sake. But she never loved him!"

Maxwell clearly had no patience for the man. "You slipped out like a thief in the night – you didn't even pay your rent!"

"What else could I do? She was going to marry that monster. I couldn't bear to watch."

"I am more interested in why you returned," Holmes said. "Why are you back now, a month after her demise?"

"Because I have dreams," the prisoner answered, his hands gripping the bars. "Clarice comes to me. She stands before me in her sopping gown, weeds tangled in her hair, and she begs me to avenge her. She tells me the brute killed her, and that we need only open her tomb to find the truth."

"You will find that impossible," Holmes said. "Captain Chambers is even now making the preparations to have her coffin moved. You will no longer be able to haunt his manor and mope around her mausoleum, for his wife will soon rest in a secret place."

I began to open my mouth but at the last second snapped it shut. I caught the edge of Maxwell's sleeve. He turned sharply as if disgusted and gave me a quick nod. Neither of us knew what Holmes was up to, but it behooved us to play along.

"Inspector," Holmes said, "your prisoner seems to have sobered considerably. Perhaps you should release him."

With a stern warning against further public intoxication, Maxwell opened the cell and handed Martin his jacket. The man stomped out without a civil word.

"Shall we follow him?" Maxwell asked.

"It would be pointless to do so," Holmes said. "Let us go to Windwood."

A half-hour later, we were being welcomed into the manor house. Windwood was an ancient home, much cobbled together, with jutting wings that spoke to at least four different periods of architecture. It lacked any charm in its grey stones, crumbling bricks, and rotting wood. A vicious, drooling mastiff raised up from the steps and kept us at bay until the butler called him off. Keller, a tall and gray-haired man, mournful in the face, and with an air of dignity befitting an Oxford don, guided us into a hallway lined with ancestral portraits.

"Captain Chambers is out riding, sirs, but I feel certain Mrs. Stiller will receive you."

"In the dining room, if you don't mind," Holmes said.

If the butler found this an odd request, he gave no indication. As we entered the dining hall, Holmes's keen gaze went immediately to the mantel, and the spot high on the wall where a painting had clearly been snatched down, leaving dangling strings behind.

"What a large fireplace," Holmes said. "Tudor, I suppose?"

Keller shook his head. "We believe it dates to the late 1300's and was part of the original interior of the house. My dear little mistress found it wonderfully antique and charming."

The man's tone warbled, as if he were fighting back tears. "You were much attached to her," Holmes noted.

"Yes, sir. Her death has left me shaken by things so unforeseen."

"And you also dream of her?"

The man's face turned ashen. "I wish I could, sir. Despite the horror such a vision might entail, I find I long to see her more and more . . . her kindness, her goodness to us all . . . Our loss has never known relief."

"Perhaps we can give her the justice she seeks. Do bring her mother to us, Keller."

The butler exited the room. The moment the door closed, Holmes sprang into action.

"Watson, how tall would you say this fireplace is?"

"Some seven or eight feet," I said. "It could easily roast all three of us at once!"

"Now there's a pleasant thought! For the lady's picture to be hung above it, one would need a ladder or . . . ." Holmes began to hurry about the room. He gave a sharp cry when he reached the chair at the head of the table. He knelt to examine something in it.

"They're coming," Maxwell hissed, having moved to stand by the door. Holmes popped up like a jack-in-the-box, smoothed his hair, and leisurely strolled back to my side. The butler bowed in Mrs. Stiller.

She had been described to us as an elderly woman in need of physical care, but she wasn't as old as the photograph of her had suggested. Though her face was thin, her wrinkles were few, and she moved with an agility that was uncommon for anyone above the age of fifty. Her hair, however, was as white as snow, and the mourning garb that she wore added an air of decay and fragility. She sank into one of the chairs with a groan.

"The inspector told me he hoped you would come. Please, Mr. Holmes, you must convince him that even if he doesn't believe in ghostly visitations, he must have some respect for a mother's intuition. My daughter was *murdered* by that fiend! You are a man of science, I am told – surely science is clever enough that if my daughter's body was examined by an expert, it wouldn't be too late to find evidence of the crime and the criminal."

Holmes spoke gently, but I who knew him well heard the razor beneath the velvet. "Mrs. Stiller, how can you remain here at Windwood if you suspect your son-in-law of such a dastardly act?"

"I have nowhere else to go!" she wailed. "Clarice was my only child. My husband died some years ago and left us deeply in debt. I sold everything I had until there was nothing left, and I was turned out of my home. Where else shall I go? There is nothing but a workhouse to take me in. I would die of shame!"

"But do you not fear for your life in this place?"

She pulled a handkerchief from her sleeve. "Yes, but . . . I don't speak of it to *him*! Keller is the only one I confided in, and he advised me to take my dreams to the police. Oh, it required all my nerve to tell the inspector what I have been seeing. The captain doesn't know my suspicions and you must not tell him." She wrung her hands together. "He has been decent, if not truly loving, toward me, and if I am in error – if mine are only an old woman's nightmares – I will fall to my knees and beg his forgiveness. Then he may throw me in the street if he pleases! Only . . . I must know! I must know for my poor girl's sake!"

Holmes leaned on the chair. "One final question: What brought on the quarrels between your daughter and the captain?"

The old woman exploded into tears, necessitating that Keller be dispatched to fetch her a glass of water. She struggled to compose herself.

"It was all my fault, sir. Clarice had been a naughty girl. She ran away from home when she was just sixteen and took up with a series of sinful men who made her promises but gave her nothing. That so-called artist was the last. I brow-beat her with letters when I learned that a wealthy man was courting her. I thought I knew best – was I not proof that security is better than love? But Clarice had no idea how to be a good wife, or tend to a home, or manage the servants. I tried to correct her, and when I did, he grew angry with me, and she defended me and . . . Oh, what a misery! May God forgive me."

"Did she truly love the artist?"

"Love? Bah, what a silly word!"

Holmes looked toward Keller, who was almost invisible in the shadows, his face a mask.

"Yet some people clearly loved *her*. That will be enough, Madam. I would suggest that you reach out to the charity of the church, or to whatever distant family you still possess. To get to the truth of this matter, we must lay our case before Captain Chambers."

"You cannot!" the woman cried.

"I fear we must. Now, if you will excuse us?"

Keller assisted the hysterical lady from the room. Maxwell regarded my friend with a scowl.

"That was cruel, Mr. Holmes."

"It was necessary," he answered. "Trust me when I say we should waste no sympathy on the lady. Did you not notice a connection?"

"To what?"

"Ah, it eludes you, but soon it will be clear. I hear a clatter in the halls. It can only be the master returning."

Indeed, a minute later the infamous Captain Chambers was standing there, turning the full fury of his black eyes upon us. Despite his crippled leg and damaged arm, he was still a formidable presence, clad in his riding attire with a hunting crop in his clenched left hand.

"So you are the London tattlers!" he sneered. "Maxwell, are you not sufficient to root out this foolishness beneath my roof? I know it must have been one of the servants who ruined her picture. By God, I could beat it out of them!"

"Captain Chambers, let me assure you that Mr. Holmes is a specialist who – "

"Will you make the raven-haired local perfumer your next bride?" Holmes asked, out of the blue.

All the bluster abruptly went out of the man. He deflated as rapidly as a popped balloon and dropped nerveless into the chair the old woman had just abandoned. His eyes went wide. He struggled to speak. His voice at last emerged as a timid whisper.

"You . . . you have my attention, sir."

"Excellent," Holmes said, "I shall require very little of your time for an interview, but if you wish to have this matter resolved before it leads to scandal, you will obey me when I give you orders. Is that clear?"

The man nodded, sweat suddenly dripping down his wide brow.

"Why did you quarrel with your late wife?"

He hung his head. "Many reasons . . . Her mother is a vicious, nosey old cat who wanted to command my household. I have lived alone too long to accept a female as my commander. When I threatened her with the heave-ho, Clarice erupted in tears. And there was the man – that *artist*. I feared Clarice might still abandon me – flee to him, for she spoke of him a great deal, and in a loving way. And . . . sir, I am a wicked old sailor. I was even jealous of the servants, who all adored her. Keller, that old fool, wrote her poetry! I simply couldn't bear it, and I lashed out at her when the fault lay with myself. I don't believe she fell from the bridge . . . I believe she jumped, to get away from her sorrows."

Holmes took the opposite chair and asked for my notepad and pencil. He began to scribble furiously.

"This is what you must do, Captain. Leave Windwood, return to the village, and begin planning to have your wife's coffin moved from the mausoleum tomorrow. Offer tempting rewards to workmen and drivers. Go to the pub afterward, quench your thirst, and make sure that every loiterer hears your intention to have your wife removed from your property."

"But I am planning no such thing."

"Yes, you are, and you will do it," Holmes said, ripping off the sheet of paper and handing it to him. "An English village has a thousand ears and twice as many mouths. Your intention to change your wife's burial spot should be buzzing by Vespers."

"But where am I taking her to be interred?"

"I will tell you later. Until then, say only that you fear her eternal slumber may be disturbed. And be certain to take care of the last thing that I have written on this paper. Am I clear?"

The man nodded miserably and limped away at Holmes's dismissive gesture. My friend looked back to us.

"There is just time for some refreshments, I think."

"Mr. Holmes," Maxwell said, "how in Heaven's name did you know about Miss Evette, the perfumer? I don't believe I shared that bit of village gossip."

Holmes smirked. "I didn't know her name, but the captain didn't acquire several long, black, glossy hairs upon his lapel, a smudge of rogue upon his cheek, or the heady aromas of vanilla and sandalwood from a brisk gallop across his fields now, did he?"

177

Later that day, just as the sun was sinking, we made our way back to Windwood, climbing out of our carriage a quarter-mile from the property.

"A bit of a walk will do us good, after such a hearty repast," Holmes said. "Maxwell, I have great admiration for your patience. It took Watson some years to learn that when I play my cards closely, it is with a reason, and not purely to be mischievous."

The young inspector nodded. "I confess it has driven me to distraction, but I suspected you didn't wish your business discussed in the village. I shall take your comment about 'ears' and 'mouths' to heart," he chuckled. "But surely no one can overhear us here. What is your purpose in sending the captain on such a strange errand?"

Holmes's tone was lightly tinged with impatience. "Even if you don't hunt, you understand the principle of flushing the game, I presume? It was important that our culprit believe the lady's body would be moved tomorrow. There is no more time to wait, and he must strike tonight."

"But . . . I thought this case was about the possibility that the captain murdered his lady."

"No, no, Maxwell. That was merely the screen. Our criminal has no interest in her death. His goal is much more material."

"I still fail to understand."

"You will see it all very soon – but until then I must beg a favor." We had reached the outskirts of the manor's grounds. Holmes pointed to the house with his cane, and then drew an invisible line from it to the large marble mausoleum, which stood between the house and the millpond. "Our sinner is grateful that clouds are forming. What he must do requires him to hurry across this open ground to the sepulcher. And what I must do requires you to wait here, Maxwell, and look the other way . . . for I must break the law in the name of justice."

Maxwell's gaze lowered to the bag that Holmes carried. "You are going to burgle a tomb?"

"All for a worthy cause. And I promise you, the late lady's corpse shall not be disrespected." Holmes directed his protégé toward a row of trees. "Hide there and keep watch. You will see our villain before the daylight – likely before midnight. Give him a few moments and come with alacrity if you hear a cry. Is that clear?"

This wasn't the assignment he preferred, but the inspector nodded and, with great agility, quickly scaled one of the trees and perched among its branches. Holmes signaled for me to follow him. We leapt over a stone fence and dashed to the mausoleum, a marble temple of surprising size, complete with a pair of large brass doors. Holmes opened his bag and selected from a set of polished tools.

178

"I could have asked Captain Chambers to provide us with the key, but I feared he might give the game away with some untoward comment. Ah – there we are – the dead aren't terribly secure."

Holmes pushed the door open. We had a pair of dark lanterns with us, provided by the inspector. By their light, we made a detailed inspection of the tomb. It was almost perfectly square and lined with slots in which a half-dozen coffins, some of rotting wood, others of lead, were stored. A stone bier stood in the center of the room, with a mahogany coffin atop it. Holmes directed his light onto the lid. The silver plate read *Mrs. Clarice Chambers – A Perfect Pearl*, along with her dates of birth and death. Holmes directed my attention to the side of the box. Short marks scared the wood, as if the coffin had been scratched at by an animal.

"Good Lord! Who would do such a thing?"

"We are about to find out, I believe. Take a place in that corner, and I shall stand in this one. We should be far enough from the door not to be immediately spotted. You have your revolver? Excellent."

"Holmes," I hissed, "who is coming?"

He held up a hand. Someone was rattling at the door, as if attempting the same burglary that Holmes had performed. I leapt back into my assigned corner, as Holmes took up his position.

There was a clank of metal, and suddenly the door was pushed open. I perceived two hooded figures in the space.

"Are you certain?" a male voice hissed.

"Yes. We dare wait no longer! We will be on the train tonight before anyone misses us." This voice was female, and far more forceful than its male counterpart. "How like the minx to keep it for herself, even in death! Well – get to it!"

The man stepped forward with a crowbar. Before I could react, he wedged it under the lid and grunted with effort. There was the sharp sound of wood popping, then my friend's commanding shout.

"Have you no respect for your 'lover'?"

I opened my lamp, immediately blinding Hans Martin. He was so startled that he dropped his tool onto his foot and started yowling in pain. The woman behind him gave a cry and gathered up her skirts to bolt.

"Will you leave your son to hang?" Holmes called.

The woman froze. Slowly, she raised her hands above her head, and twisted to face us.

"You don't understand," she whined, as Holmes tossed me a pair of handcuffs to bind the young man. "We are only trying to find justice for Clarice! That monster who murdered her is going to move her body and then – "

"That game is over, Mrs. Stiller. Oh, should I say – *Madam Trinket?*"

179

The woman once again whirled to flee, but Holmes easily caught her by her cloak, hauling her back inside before summoning the inspector. I thrust the young man against a wall, and Holmes made the woman sit beside him. All pretense vanished – never had I viewed a pair of guiltier faces. Holmes chuckled softly.

"I had an advantage, Watson – I saw immediately the resemblance between the young man, the old lady, and the dead woman. I matched their family traits with my knowledge of crime. Scotland Yard will tell you many tales of the Trinket Gang, as they call themselves. A mother with a broken nose, a dim-witted son, and a lovely young daughter – our American cousins have coined the term 'confidence men' to describe their ilk, though here it applies to the fair sex as well. The Trinkets have adopted many disguises and personalities to defraud wealthy individuals, but their specialty, the thing that has made them the bane of the Yard, is their skill at stealing jewels. The marriage and the residency of the aged mother was an act aimed at acquiring some legendary loot."

"You can go to Hell!" the man snapped.

"Hush, you idiot!" the woman shrieked.

"You would do well to listen to your mother," Holmes chuckled. "But as we wait upon the official forces, let me tell my friend Watson what you planned. The marriage was unsuccessful in getting you what you most wanted – The Eye of the Siren, the massive yellow diamond plundered by the Sea Devil. Something went wrong. Perhaps Clarice fell in love with her husband and didn't wish to rob him. In your greedy eyes, she grew selfish and disobedient. Tell me, Madam Trinket, where were you when she drowned?"

The woman shrank into herself. "You can never prove such a thing."

"Oh, but it's true," the young man said, "Mother killed her! Clarice refused to steal the diamond and run away with us. My sister liked being the lady of a big manor. She didn't want to pull jobs anymore!"

The woman whirled, her long fingers crabbing towards the boy's face. I was able to pull her back, just as Inspector Maxwell joined us inside the tomb. Holmes quickly relayed our adventure, while I struggled with the woman. It took all my strength to prevent the harridan from clawing out her own son's eyes.

"Watson, will you assist the inspector with transporting his prisoners?" Holmes asked. "I suspect a complete confession may be coming from this young man, one that may serve the Queen's Justice well, and help to hang a despicable, unnatural woman."

"Of course," I said, "but aren't you coming also?"

Holmes shook his head. He picked up the crowbar and looked toward the violated coffin. "This drama isn't finished. Don't worry, Watson, I am in no danger. I will see you at the station in the morning."

True to his word, Holmes met us on the platform just moments before the London train arrived. He bid Inspector Maxwell goodbye, commending him for such a career-making capture. When we were at last in our compartment, I studied my friend closely. He had clearly not slept, and his skin was drawn tight against his bones.

"Good Heavens, Holmes, what happened?"

"Let me tell it all together," my friend said. "When Maxwell gave us his story, I was intrigued by the characters, for the Trinket Gang had been missing for almost a year and this sounded very much like their *modus operandi*. I was certain I knew my criminals and their game."

"But what really happened to the daughter?"

"We are in the land of speculation, but this is a working theory that I believe the lackluster son will confirm. Furious that the girl wouldn't cooperate with their scheme, the mother shoved her off the bridge and left her to drown, no doubt thinking it would be easier to find a way to steal the diamond once the contentious conspirator was removed. She was thwarted when the stone was unexpectedly buried with her daughter. She corresponded with her son, demanding his return and participation in creating suspicion about the captain. Both mother and son aren't only of the 'confidence' school – they are also gifted performers of sleight of hand. My belief is that the mother was planning to demand to be present at the exhumation, where she would stage a moment of supreme emotion, 'fainting' over her daughter's corpse and swapping out the real stone for a paste replica. It has all been done before, Watson. There was a similar case in Sacramento in '74, and one in Nantes in '82, where coffins were opened and unsavory types made off with valuable grave goods."

"What an evil pair! But why did they not attempt to break into the lady's coffin earlier?"

"For a simple reason that you saw without observing – the captain keeps an especially vicious mastiff on the property, a dog that is loosed every night. The Trinkets couldn't avoid it or eliminate it without drawing attention upon themselves! My final instruction, scribbled on your paper, was for the captain to make a point to his household that the dog had taken ill and he would be confining it to its kennel that evening, in preparation for a veterinary visit in the morning. This, along with the announcement that the lady's coffin would be moved to a secret place, was enough to compel our criminals to act."

"Well, I am certainly glad we didn't have that dog snapping at our heels," I chuckled. "But . . . why did you remain in the tomb?"

"Because there was another thread to be grasped until the skein unraveled. Madam Trinket didn't mention the defaced picture or her daughter's 'bleeding' eyes. Why not? Surely it would have bolstered her supernatural case if she had created it. She didn't even react to its absence in the dining hall, the way a truly grief-stricken and ghost-haunted mother would. Already, I had noticed that the picture couldn't have been easily reached by an individual of ordinary height, or even a tall man. You recall my inspection of the chairs? In the velvet seat of one, I found the clear impression of square-toed boots, such as Keller was wearing. I had begun a mental inventory of the footwear of all our gentlemen, and Keller was the only square-toed aficionado. Of course, the impression might have been made when Keller fetched it down for his enraged master, but surely in that capacity his dignity would have made a ladder the booster of choice, rather than a chair,. He would have only used the chair in secret, if the defacing occurred in the middle of the night."

Holmes leaned back, his gaze drifting to the window.

"And there was more – Do you recall Keller's words about his late mistress?"

"He seemed genuinely grieved – though he expressed himself in a very stilted style."

"Indeed, for in his misery he was quoting ancient poetry. I recognized the translation of lines from *Pearl*, a medieval elegy. He was clearly an educated man, and a creative one. Do you recall the captain's complaint that Keller wrote poetry for the girl? Creative minds run in many directions. Mrs. Stiller told him of her dreams. Though she was seeking an ignorant ally, her words inspired him to deface the portrait, which hung in a place his master would see, turning it into a supernatural accusation. It seems that he, too, didn't accept his master's innocence in his mistress's demise.

"And then – the scratches on the coffin lid. Someone had made a previous attempt to open the lid but failed. Why? If the butler desired the diamond, he of all people would have had the best opportunity to burgle the tomb and leave no one the wiser. If those marks were made by Keller, what stopped him? Now he, as well as the others, knew there were plans to move the body. I deduced that he too would come to the mausoleum.

"I had only another hour to wait, and this time the sound I heard was a key being inserted into the lock. The moon had emerged, and from my angle I watched as Keller's long form entered the tomb. I had closed the damaged lid, and I held my peace until I saw him fumble clumsily about it. Then I opened my lantern and confronted him.

182

"What a sad wreck he was, Watson, He sank immediately to the ground and began to weep. I was firm but not strident, for I hoped he would confess the truth to me and perhaps there would be no need to trouble either Inspector Maxwell or Captain Chambers.

"Keller told me that Miss Clarice was truly a divine creature, and that in the short days before her mother arrived, her essence had changed the captain, made him a better man. Keller is a former schoolmaster who fell upon hard times and went into service late in life. He loves poetry, especially the most antique of English verses. He created several poems and sonnets inspired by the captain's lady, for while her brother only pretended her to be a muse, to Keller she was a real one.

"Then came her dreadful death, which left him nearly mad with grief, yet in his role as household *major domo*, he was expected to maintain his composure and dignity. Something possessed him to make a grand romantic gesture for the woman he described as 'a perfect pearl' in mimicry of his favorite poem – a description so powerful and apt that her husband had it engraved on her coffin plate. Keller took all the verses he had composed for her, made a copy of them, and then – on the night she lay in repose at home – Keller secreted the manuscript in the lining of her coffin. He planned to send the duplicates of the verses to a publisher and have them printed in her honor.

"Imagine then, his distress, when he returned from the funeral and found that a careless housemaid had flung the copy of his poems into the fire! He tried desperately to rewrite them from memory. You, as an author, know how frustrating that task is. In the end, Keller felt he couldn't recreate them, and therefore could not honor his beloved mistress.

"Just over two weeks ago, he chained the dog and came to the tomb to take away the pages – only to be overcome with grief and nerves. That accounts for the clumsy scratches on the coffin. Not long afterward, Mrs. Stiller took him into her confidence about her dreams. Though it pained him to do so, he daubed red paint on the portrait to anger the master, for he knew Captain Chambers was sensitive about his honor and would perhaps demand an exhumation to clear his name of any supernatural accusation. Keller's clumsy plan was to beg for the return of the papers at the exhumation, even though the revelation would certainly cost him his position. Upon learning that his hopes for the coffin to be legally opened were dashed, he worked up the courage for one last attempt at recovering his manuscript."

I shook off my astonishment. "What did you do?"

"For a moment it was difficult to decide. The man was misguided, yet his love was the lady was pure – he would have been a much better parent to her than her devilish mother. No disrespect was intended, and if the act remained between us, no one need know of it. He told me where the papers were placed. I asked him to wait outside.

"What frail beings we are, Watson. How delicate is our clay. The lady had been deceased only a short time, yet already her mortal remains were a thing of horror. I retrieved the manuscript from beneath the satin and returned it to Keller, who promised to leave Windwood at once, and never speak of what we had done. The coffin was closed, the lady left to her rest. I told Captain Chambers that the nefarious Trinket Gang had attacked the coffin, but no significant damage had been done, and he need not remove his late wife's body unless he chose. He was most grateful to have the matter closed – and, as I noted, he will soon move on to another spouse, hopefully one without criminal connections.

"Oh, and a final thing."

Holmes reached into his coat pocket and pulled out a handkerchief, opening it in his palm. Inside was a large yellow diamond.

"Holmes!" I shouted. My friend looked up at me with a mischievous grin.

"Do you think I have stooped to grave robbing? No, Watson – but once it suggests itself, I am unable to resist the need to confirm a theory. I never believed Captain Chambers put the actual Eye of the Siren within his dead wife's hands. It is worth almost as much as the Stuart Sapphire, and he would be a fool to part with it, when the sale of such a gem could restore his fortune. However, a wildly romantic gesture might win him female admirers. His hasty marriage to Miss Stiller, a woman he barely knew, speaks of loneliness and rejection. If the community saw him as more than just a reincarnation of the 'Sea Devil', his life might change. This is a paste replica – the true Eye of the Siren is locked in the captain's chest."

"You are certain?"

"I placed this on his desk, as I told him of the Trinket Gang's machinations. He confirmed my speculation that it was worthless, then he insisted I take it with me. What a strange *memento mori*."

I toyed with the false diamond. "Do you believe Clarice Stiller was a wicked girl?"

"I believe some things are beyond our poor ability to discern. Mrs. Chambers, *née* Stiller, was for a time a wanted criminal, but perhaps she repented and changed into a loving wife and a kind mistress – the paste diamond miraculously transformed into a perfect pearl." Holmes folded his arms and slowly closed his eyes, speaking with soft reverence.

"May she rest in peace, her true nature known but to God."

Soldier of Fortune
by Geri Schear

Mycroft Holmes seldom ventured beyond his usual sphere: His office, the Diogenes Club in Pall Mall, and his rooms. That evening in July 1894, he arrived without either warning or ceremony and sat down by the fire. I offered to leave but Holmes himself demurred. He and his brother had no private matters to discuss, and if there was a case in the offing, well then, I should stay to hear all the details.

"A peculiar situation has arisen, Sherlock," Mr. Holmes said. "One that cries out for your, ah, unusual talents. A woman who lives in Battersea makes a living telling fortunes – "

Sherlock Holmes snorted. "Oh, come, Mycroft," he protested.

"Hear me out, brother dear. Her name – the name she practices her, ah, *craft* under – is Jezebel Fortuna."

At that, Holmes and I both dissolved in laughter. The stern expression on Mycroft Holmes's face only made us worse, I'm afraid.

"This is a serious matter," Mycroft said. "Perhaps I should return when you are both able to contain your humour."

With an obvious effort, my friend managed to force a serious mien on his face. "I apologise," he said. "I assure you, you have my full attention."

I swallowed my chuckles and hid my smile behind the coffee cup. Unconvinced, Mycroft Holmes continued. "We believe her real name is Jenny Grady. We think she is Scottish, but she may well be Irish. The problem is this: A senior officer in Her Majesty's Army has become enthralled by this woman. She now has total sway over him, to the point where he will not make a decision without her guidance. What's more, many of her prognostications seem to come true – or at least the general has convinced himself that they do."

"General?" Sherlock Holmes asked.

"Lang."

"Not Albert Bartholomew Lang!"

"I am afraid so, Sherlock."

My friend whistled. "Why, his entry runs seven pages in the Who's Who. Much of the success of the Zulu Campaign was his alone. He is considered the greatest military mind of the century, almost certainly in line for a Field Marshal post."

"An adviser to the government on all military matters," I added. "I would have thought a man of his integrity would be above such silliness as fortune telling. I did hear, however . . . ." I trailed off, wondering if saying more would betray a friend's trust.

"Whatever it is, my dear fellow," Sherlock Holmes said, "I urge you to tell us. It may be of considerable importance."

"I agree. Doctor, you may be assured we will treat everything you tell us in the greatest confidence."

"Well, I know someone who is close to the general. I should rather not identify him unless it becomes necessary. But what I was told was the general's young son, his only child, died a few months ago from typhus. Since then, he and his wife have been in deep despair. The wife began to try to reach the child via séances. At first, the general decried such attempts, but then one day his wife returned home strangely calm."

"Someone claimed to have contacted the son," Sherlock Holmes said with a snort.

"Quite the contrary. She had been urged to see a particular fortune teller – I can only assume it is the same woman – and she urged Mrs. Lang to stop these efforts. She said the so-called mediums were charlatans, and the boy was at peace. Oddly, Mrs. Lang seemed assured by the woman's words."

"Thank you, Doctor," Mycroft Holmes said. "I knew about the boy's death, but I hadn't heard the rest of that story."

"Very helpful, Watson," Holmes said. "Do you know any more?"

"Not really, only that the general seemed greatly relieved by the change in his wife's demeanour and her apparent acceptance of their son's death. Mind you, it is several weeks since I spoke with . . . the person who shared this with me. No doubt much has happened in the meantime."

"No doubt," Holmes replied. "Mycroft, what is it you want me to do?"

"Investigate this woman. See what you can find out about her and her accomplices, and what she is telling the general. Most importantly, find out who is behind this nonsense."

"I assume you already have a number of suspects?" Holmes asked.

"The list is too great to mention. Any military power who bears us a grudge, or who hopes to thrash us in a conflict. In short, any foreign power who would benefit by our weakness, be it real or imagined."

"And of course, anyone with any sort of personal animus against the general himself," Sherlock Holmes said. "The list may be almost interminable."

"Indeed. And I'm afraid I have no information that would suggest any particular culprit."

We all fell silent, mulling over the situation. As a former soldier, I had no illusions about the hatred of our foes. The general was someone I had long admired, believing him to be a man of honour and possessed of a deep sense of duty. That he might have so insidious an enemy distressed me.

Mycroft Holmes's voice interrupted my reverie. "Over the past three weeks, Lang has objected to two proposals designed to fund the building of new and innovative weapons, weapons he had a hand in designing. Overnight, he seems to have turned into a pacifist. If the country follows his ideology, it could lead to utter ruin. His opinion is highly regarded, as you both know. He has the backing of the Queen herself, and the public adores him."

For a short time after Mycroft left, Holmes and I sat in silence. I turned my attention to the newspaper, and for a while was able to enjoy the peace and quiet. Of course, with a man like Sherlock Holmes as a flatmate, I should have realised that my serenity wouldn't last.

When next I looked up, I saw that he was buttoning up his coat. As he reached for his hat, he said, "When are you going to see Miller?"

I lowered the paper and stared at him. "What makes you think Miller was my confidant to the general's behaviour?"

He smiled as he leaned against the mantel. "Three weeks ago, you mentioned you'd spent the evening playing cards with Miller. You spoke of him being a good man from the Fifth Northumberland Fusiliers. I just looked up General Lang's entry in the *Who's Who* and a number of recent articles in the newspapers. There were several mentions of his aide-de-camp, Major Miller from your old squad. The deduction wasn't a difficult one."

"Holmes, I know you are discreet, but please don't mention Barn Owl to anyone else."

"Barn Owl?"

"That's what we used to call him. His first name is Barney, and with his thick glasses . . . Well, you know soldiers."

"Quite," he said in an unimpressed tone. "You may be assured, good fellow, that I shall not breathe a word of his involvement to anyone. But if I may return to my original question: When are you going to see him?"

"I shall go to the club this evening. He usually attends on Friday night. Where are you off to? A call on this fortune teller woman?"

"That is where I'm heading now. I'm planning to watch her from a distance, at least initially."

"Do you need me to accompany you? She may be dangerous."

He chuckled. "Have no fear, my dear Watson. I have no intention of encountering her. I just want to get the lay of the land, as it were. Good luck with Miller."

Fortunately for me, Barn Owl arrived at the club about an hour after I did. We sat at our usual table and played a couple of hands. I could see he was distracted, and I beat him easily.

"Sorry," he said, rising from the table. "I'm afraid my mind isn't on it tonight."

I persuaded him without any difficulty to join me for a drink. We found a quiet table in the corner and after we chinked glasses and took our first gulp, I said, "You seem out of sorts this evening, Barn Owl. Anything I can help with?"

"Oh, Johnny," he said, "if only you could."

"Would it help to talk about it?"

He took another gulp and studied me for several interminable seconds. "You remember I told you how worried I was about the general?" he said. "I know people might say he's my CO and nothing more, but there's no one I admire more. He's the most decent, brave, and honest man I've ever met. To see him . . . ." He hesitated and sipped another mouthful of his drink before saying, "I say, Johnny, you won't reveal what I'm about to tell you to anyone, will you? His trust is very important to me. I'd hate for him to think I've betrayed that."

"Not without your permission, Barn Owl. You have my word."

That seemed to satisfy him for he continued, "He's changed over the past few weeks. He's still a kind and decent man, but some of the things he's been doing, and the decisions he's been making are, well, bewildering, to say the least."

"Can you give me an example?"

"There are too many to choose from, but here's one. About a month ago, he came to me, very agitated – that in itself was unusual, as you know – and he asked me to place a bet on a horse for him at Newmarket."

"A horse! Why, I never heard that the general was a betting man."

"He isn't. That is, he never has been. Indeed, when he handed me the hundred pounds, he admitted he'd never placed a bet in his life, but he had been urged in the strongest terms that he should do so now."

"A hundred pounds! How astonishing!"

"What was astonishing was that the horse won. A three-year-old filly who had never raced before, at least not that I know of. There were very few bets on her as you can imagine, being untried, but won she did, making the general richer by several thousand pounds."

188

"Good Heavens! Do you think it was that fortune teller you told me about who passed on this information?"

"The general said it was. When I returned with his winnings, he stared at it in utter surprise. 'I told her I was sceptical of fortune telling,' said he, 'and she said that she would prove herself. She told me to place the bet. I did so with no great expectation, but you see yourself the result.' At that, he handed me five-hundred pounds."

I almost spluttered my scotch onto the table. "How much?" I asked.

"I know, I was stunned. 'You're a fine young man, Barney,' he said, 'and I don't express my appreciation often enough. I want you to invest in something of value – buy a house and settle down. There's more if you need it.'"

"My word."

"That was just the beginning. After that, things seemed to happen every other day. Take this morning . . . ."

He took another sip of his drink and wiped his mouth with the back of his hand. Then he said, "We were in the carriage on our way to Westminster when suddenly the general shouted to the driver to take a different route. At that moment, we heard a loud noise that startled the horses. For a minute, I thought we were all in mortal danger, but fortunately the driver managed to regain control, and no one was hurt. Once things settled down again, the general told me that Miss Fortuna had warned him of this just the day before."

"Coincidence?" I said, though I confess I was as bewildered as he.

"I don't know. These things shake me up, Johnny, but they're nothing to the changes I've seen in the way the general behaves. This witch has been telling him all sorts, and it's got so he won't make a move without her. He's second-guessing the weapons he, himself, designed. He's doubting things he believed in with his whole heart. I don't know what to do or how to help him."

"That's awful. Barn Owl, this is too important to keep to yourself. Let me talk to Sherlock Holmes about it."

My friend hesitated. "I don't know, Johnny," he said. "It feels like I'm being disloyal to the general. Even telling you is hard for me, and that's saying something. How could I doubt the man who saved my life?"

"That was a long time ago. I am very grateful for your trust and your friendship. I hope that you will trust me when I say that Holmes is discretion itself. Perhaps he can investigate this woman and show the general how he is being swindled. You do believe this woman is a fake, don't you?"

He hesitated again. "Yes," he said slowly. "I suppose that I do, it's just . . . How does she do it, Johnny?"

189

"I've no idea, but I have no doubt that Holmes is the man to find out."

The great bells of Bow chimed eleven just as I let myself into 221b. As I often did when I heard the sound, I softly hummed the *Oranges and Lemons* tune so beloved by children. Thanks to an excellent scotch, and Barn Owl finally agreeing that I may reveal his tales to Holmes, I was in good spirits.

The empty coat-peg told me that my flatmate hadn't yet returned, and since I was tired after a long day, I went straight to bed. I fell asleep immediately and have no idea what time Holmes came in, but he joined me at the breakfast table the following morning looking as sharp and alert as ever.

"Ah, Watson," he said. "How did you get on last night?"

"Pretty well. Barn Owl reluctantly gave me his permission to tell you about his experiences with the general and this fortune teller." I went on to tell him about the horse race.

"And this was intended to prove that she was legitimate?" Holmes shook his head. "Interesting."

"How the devil could she have known the outcome?" I asked.

He shook his head. "You're asking the wrong question. The real puzzle is why a man of sense would put £100 on a horse when he has no great faith in the outcome."

"Yes. That is odd, and it isn't all," I said, and went on to describe the event of the startled horses.

"What caused the noise?" he asked when I had finished.

"Ah, I do not know. Lots of noise in London."

He frowned. "And no one actually came to any harm?"

"Well, no, but they might have."

"What was the point of a warning if there was no actual danger?"

I was about to argue the point, to say it was only the skill of the driver that saved them, but I realised that was Holmes's point.

"How did you get on?" I asked, changing the subject.

He poured himself a cup of coffee and took a sip before replying. "I went to Battersea, to our fortune teller's neighbourhood, and visited the local drinking establishment. It didn't take much to persuade the locals to talk about her."

"I can imagine," I said, smiling. "Fortune tellers always tend to be viewed with suspicion."

"Except, in this case, the woman – I just cannot make myself call her Miss Fortuna – seems to be as well thought of as anyone of her ilk could wish. She is pleasant to her neighbours, keeps a clean house, pays her bills

190

promptly. She has, besides, treated illnesses, and even warned against some visitors who were up to no good."

"So they weren't quite as hostile as you expected?"

"No, indeed. That isn't to say they embrace her whole-heartedly. Many of them remain suspicious of her. She isn't from the area, after all. They call her a gypsy, though I doubt she actually is one. I believe Mycroft was correct when he said that she seems to be a Scot or Irish."

"Did you see her, talk to her?"

"No, but I kept watch on her house and on the people who visited her. A motley crew they were, I must say. A bishop, an unfaithful lady, and a fellow who works for Lord Cecily. All of them arrived after midnight, which is suspicious in itself."

"You recognised all these people by sight?" I said, already suspecting the answer.

"The bishop, I did. Bishop Palmer – he was in all the newspapers a few months ago. That business with the ambassador's wife."

"Oh, yes, I remember."

"And the lady, while I didn't recognise her, I can find her easily enough. She's very obviously the wife of a junior minister. The hour at which she made her visit, and the furtive look she wore made her infidelity as unmistakable as a lightning strike. As to the third, no, I didn't recognise him, but I accidentally borrowed his wallet when I bumped into him."

"Accidentally," I said with a snort.

He chuckled. "I shall return it to him this morning, have no fear."

"Do you think he has something to do with the general's apparent change in behaviour? Either the one who hired Fortuna, or one of her accomplices?"

"It is too soon to speculate. Mycroft's people have been keeping watch for two weeks and have already ruled out her visitors thus far. Of course, her accomplices may seem perfectly unremarkable at first glance. Consider that incident on the road yesterday. Somebody arranged for that noise to happen at that moment."

"What about the person who hired her?" he asked. "They would be wealthy, wouldn't they? A person of influence?"

"The probability is high if they are motivated by personal animus. It would have to be someone who moves in similar circles to the general. However, if they are in the employ of a foreign power, they may fall into the category of the easily overlooked. We may rule out no one.

"I believe the woman meets with her paymaster and, probably, her associates, in some very circumspect manner. Exchanging notes in newspapers, for instance. I may have to search her premises for the information."

191

"But surely, if you just watch her – "

"Mycroft has had men watch her for two weeks. Good and reliable men. They have discovered nothing. Time isn't on our side. The general is due to appear before the government committee in less than a week."

I had planned to spend the morning working on my papers, but as the day had dawned bright and sunny, and Holmes was going to return the purloined wallet, I agreed to accompany him. As we walked, I reminisced about my military days and how I'd met young Barn Owl.

"His eyesight is poor," I said, "and he wears thick glasses. They, in conjunction with his name, Barney Outland, gave rise to his nickname. His eyesight caused him to take a nasty tumble during some minor skirmish and he suffered some troubling injuries. I managed to get him to safety and had him back on his feet in a few weeks. He's a very clever and pleasant chap, and we remained friends. He was only a lowly captain like myself back then."

"And his devotion to the general? Is there a story behind that?"

"The general inspires devotion and loyalty. He's the sort of man who leads by example, with extraordinary courage and compassion for his soldiers.

"Because Barn Owl tended to be a bit accident prone – more because of his eyesight than any carelessness, I should say – the general one day said, 'Captain Outland, you are going to get yourself – or worse, *me* – killed. There's only one thing for it: I shall have to promote you to major and make you my *aide-de-camp*. Poor old Jock has had it, I'm afraid.'

"Jock had been the general's aide for two years, but he had never been the same after a bullet shattered his humerus. The general wanted to send him home right after the medics patched him up, but Jock wasn't having it. He continued to do his duties – well, he tried, but he really wasn't up to it. Eventually, he had to admit defeat. Jock went home and Barn Owl took over and never looked back. I must say, the general seemed very happy with him, too. For all that he could be a bit of a duffer on the battlefield, Barn Owl has a first-rate education and is exceedingly well-informed on a wide range of subjects. He plays chess, too, which Jock didn't. That was very much in his favour.

"When the general was sent home to take up a post here in London, he brought Barn Owl with him. Since then, my friend has become invaluable. I venture to say he and the general have become good friends."

Holmes listened quietly as we walked along the Strand towards Holborn. "And there's no doubt of his devotion to the general?"

"Not the slightest. He's as honourable and loyal a man as you could hope for."

Whether because of the bright sunshine or for some other reason, even Londoners seemed in rare, good spirits. As we hurried along, I asked, "What do you know of this fellow whose wallet you, ah, *found*?"

An odd expression crossed Holmes's face. He held a long index finger to his lips, then said softly, "His name is Howard H. Howard."

"Howard H. Howard?" I said.

Then with mirth that couldn't be contained, he added, "The third!"

At that point, we both succumbed to loud chortles. It took me a few minutes to gather my sense of propriety. "Poor fellow!" I managed, and then we both began to laugh again.

When we had recovered from our jocularity, Holmes went on. "Young Mr. Howard has been employed by Lord Cecily for almost ten years. He keeps a low profile. I haven't learned much of consequence about him. He appears to be one of those fellows who is a nonentity, visible only when he stands in the light cast by his employer. I do know that he is married and has two children. He lives modestly, although he seems reasonably comfortable, thanks to a generous inheritance from his father."

"Howard H. Howard the second," I said.

"Quite. Our Mr. Howard was educated in Cambridge and has a degree in history. He wrote his thesis on the dissolution of the monasteries. Ah, we're here."

The house was an elegant Georgian building, one of a dozen or so in a small square. A park of sorts sat in the centre. Though summer all over the city, this park seemed limited in colour. The trees and grass were in verdant bloom, but there were no flowers to be seen. A shame. I enjoy seeing a splash of natural colour amid the unrelenting greyness of London.

The door was answered by a footman, and he showed us into the library. A few minutes later, a dull fellow in an ill-fitting and unflattering grey suit joined us.

"Mr. Sherlock Holmes?" he asked looking from one of us to the other.

"I am he," Holmes replied. Then, with an admirably straight face said, "You are Mr, ah, Howard Howard?"

"The same, sir. How may I help you?"

"Someone happened upon your wallet last night, and it found its way to me. I have come to return it."

"Oh, my!" the fellow said, taking the slender leather item. "I thought it lost forever. Thank you, Mr. Holmes."

With some difficulty I managed to keep my face straight. Holmes, to do him credit, had the grace to look somewhat embarrassed. "You should make sure everything is there," he said.

Mr. Howard Howard did as Holmes suggested. He smiled, changing his entire bearing from a dull, officious looking fellow to a much kinder and genial man.

"All here," he said, "down to the last farthing. It's nice to know there are still some honest people in the world."

"Uh, quite," Holmes replied. Only the pink tips of his ears revealed his embarrassment. "You really must be careful, a man with your responsibilities. Battersea isn't a safe area, particularly at night."

"Battersea?" Howard said. "I wouldn't be seen in such a place. I can only imagine that the person who found it lied about where it was retrieved, perhaps for some nefarious reason of their own."

"Indeed?" Holmes's voice was icy.

"Why should someone lie?" I said.

"I think it would be wise if you were to tell me the truth, Mr. Howard," Holmes continued. "Or perhaps I should take up the matter with Lord Cecily?"

"No! Please, Mr. Holmes, I beg you! No, I will tell you the truth."

Holmes and I sat on the elegant but uncomfortable settee. Howard took the seat that faced us.

"I am married with two children, a boy of ten and a girl of six," said he. "We were very happy until a few weeks ago. Then I discovered that my wife's brother Linus has been amassing debts. He owes a substantial sum of money to some very unsavoury people. Linus fled the country, and the villain to whom he owes these sums has come after my wife. Mr. Holmes, he is threatening her. He will hurt her if I don't pay him. We are desperate, as you may imagine. A friend of my wife's told her about a fortune teller in Battersea. She has a talent for seeing the future. I went there last night to consult with her."

"Was she helpful?"

"I thought she was . . . That is, she seemed very comforting and sympathetic. She said no doubt the situation would be resolved soon, and I shouldn't worry about it."

Holmes and I shared a sceptical glance.

"But that could mean anything," I said. "Did she say how it would resolved? And would it be to your satisfaction?"

"Ah, no, only that everything would be all right."

Suddenly Howard seemed less certain, and his face contracted into a tangle of worry-lines.

"I see," Holmes said. "How much does your employer know about this?"

"Nothing. Oh, Heavens no, nothing! He would be horrified. I cannot imagine he would be willing to keep me in his employ if he knew. Please, Mr. Holmes, I implore you, don't tell him!"

Holmes was silent for a moment, looking pensive. At last, he looked up at the unfortunate fellow.

"Write down the name of the man who has been threatening you, where I may find him, and how much your brother-in-law owes him."

Howard did so and handed the paper to Holmes with a shaking hand.

"Ah, this bounder," Holmes said. "That is an extraordinary sum of money, Mr. Howard. Do you know how your brother-in-law came to amass such an extraordinary debt?"

"Cards. He played cards. I know it sounds improbable, but that is what this villain told me."

"I have no difficulty believing it. I am familiar with the fellow in question. You may cease to worry, Mr. Howard. I shall take care of him. And unlike Lady Fortuna, I can guarantee the outcome."

"You will? Oh, thank you, Mr. Holmes. I cannot tell you what a weight that is off my mind."

"I would like a truthful answer to one last question: What do you know about General Lang?"

"General Lang? Only what I have read in the newspapers."

"You have never met him?"

"No, sadly not. He seems a remarkable man."

Howard Howard looked bewildered and I, for one, had no difficulty believing him.

It was difficult to keep pace with Holmes when he marched up the street in high dudgeon. "Well, that didn't go as I planned," he stormed. "You may put me down as a duffer, Watson. I utterly misread this situation."

"You believe him, then?"

"I do. Do you?"

"Yes, I found him highly credible. Despite the silly name, he seems a decent and unassuming sort of fellow. I say, Holmes: You don't suppose his middle initial '*H*' stands for '*Howard*' too?"

He managed an amused snort and then, to my relief, hailed a hansom.

"So that leaves the bishop and the lady," I said.

"Or none of the above. I shall drop you off at Baker Street, then see if Mycroft has any new information."

"Isn't it possible that the woman genuinely possesses some skill in terms of precognition."

Holmes snorted. "Do be serious, Watson."

"You're the one who always says that once you've eliminated the impossible, whatever remains, no matter how improbable, must be the truth."

"I'm glad to see you've been paying attention. I've said it once. Perhaps twice. In any case, this situation falls under the improbable category. No, there must be another explanation."

Back at Baker Street, I resumed work on my notes while Holmes went on to visit his brother. He returned a little over two hours later, as irritable as a hungry wolf.

"I gather your meeting shed no new light on the situation?" I said.

"Nothing. The only thing I have accomplished thus far is to put the fear of God in Devon Mulholland."

"Who?"

"The villain who has been threatening the Howard family. I have had some dealings with him before. He is as detestable a creature as you could ever meet. He knows to keep well away from me. I have, again, put the fear of the Almighty into him and he shall trouble the Howards no more."

"You are sure of that?"

"There is no question. I know enough about this fellow's organisation to put the lot of them away for the rest of their lives. He will do as he's told."

"But why don't you just have the lot arrested, if they're so bad?"

"Because they have, on occasion, proven useful. Sometimes, Watson, it is helpful to set a villain against another villain. It's a dangerous game and they don't like it, but it can be useful. Mulholland, for all his unpleasant characteristics, has a great fondness for children. He's a father himself, and I've seen him take a beating rather than let harm befall a child. All it took in this instance was to remind him that Howard has two children of his own. Well, that and some reminders of my power."

"But you learned nothing new from your brother?"

"No."

I returned to my writing, and Holmes flopped down in his chair and lit a cigarette. All was serene for ten or so minutes. Then he shot up and paced like a caged beast. Up and down, up and down. I was on the point of remonstrating with him when he suddenly returned to his seat again.

The peace didn't last long. Just as I managed to once more become absorbed in my writing, he suddenly shot up again.

"For pity sake, Holmes – ! " I began.

"It is no use. I shall have to enter the lion's den."

"Excuse me?"

"That Jezebel woman. I need to get into her house and take a look around. The more cautious approach isn't going to work."

"You mean break in?"

"Not necessarily. If I can find an open door or window, it's only entering. You need do nothing but provide the distraction."

"I don't like it."

"It doesn't have to be dangerous or even difficult. I'll get the Irregulars to help. You merely need to keep her occupied."

Before I could reply there was a knock at the door. I was surprised, as it was ten o'clock. I was no less surprised when Holmes opened it to admit Howard H. Howard (the third).

"Mr. Howard," Holmes said. "Please take a seat. What may I do for you?"

"You've already done it, Mr. Holmes. That hooligan, Mulholland, has been to see me and has said there was a mistake and I owe him nothing. He even apologised and returned the money I had already given him! He said he never would have troubled me if he'd known I was a friend of yours."

"That is excellent news, Mr. Howard. I am delighted to hear it."

"One good turn deserves another, Mr. Holmes, and though I can never repay you for your kindness, I hope I may be able to help you a little.

"After my money troubles were solved, I got to thinking about General Lang. As I said, I have never met the man, but my employer, Lord Cecily, knows him well enough."

Holmes looked at the man with hawk-like intensity. "I hope you didn't mention my involvement – "

"Not a word, Mr. Holmes. A man in my position must be the very soul of discretion. All I did was to casually mention to His Lordship that the general was on the cover of this evening's newspaper."

"Your employer knows who it is who wishes to destroy the general? Is it, by chance, Sir Neville Powell?"

"Oh, so you already know. I had hoped to save you some work."

"I merely surmised, and your confirmation is of more importance than I can say. What, precisely, did Lord Cecily tell you?"

"He said that the general was a fine fellow, one of the best, but, 'He'd better watch his back or Powell will bring him down.'"

"What grievance would the shadow minister have against the general?" I asked.

Howard replied, "I asked His Lordship what he meant, and he said that Powell wanted to chair the committee overseeing the Irish Land Law act. He owns several large estates in Ireland, and Lord Cecily reckons he wanted to feather his own pocket."

197

"What happened?" I asked.

"The committee post went to Jack Barber on the general's recommendation. According to my employer, Powell vowed to destroy the general, saying he has too much power. He evidently said a few days ago that it wouldn't take much to reveal him as a fool, and then all his recommendations would be for naught."

"Well, well, well," Holmes said. "I am indebted to you, Mr. Howard. Please keep this information to yourself."

"You have my word, Mr. Holmes." He took out his wallet and said, "Pray, tell me, how much do I owe you?"

"Not a farthing, Mr. Howard. Your information is payment enough. Good luck to you. If ever I can be of service again, I pray you will let me know."

After Howard left, I said, "How did you know it was Powell, Holmes?"

He chuckled. "It was thanks to that tale of your friend Major Miller about the horse race. It was won by a filly called Trébuchet."

"And Powell owns her!" I exclaimed.

"Who else could know for sure what the outcome would be?"

"It was a risk. After all, one of the other horses might easily have beaten her."

"Knowing what I do about Powell, I suspect he took steps to ensure that any real competition would be . . . *slowed*."

"You mean . . . Good Heavens! The blighter! To handicap an innocent animal for such an ugly cause."

"Nothing I have heard about that fellow endears him to me. A more bloody-minded villain you'd be hard to find. Even Mulholland, vicious though he is, has more integrity. I am very much obliged to our friend with the foolish name."

I yawned and stretched. "Yes, indeed. And I am grateful that we don't have to break into that fortune teller's house."

"Whyever should you think so?" he asked. "We still need to learn who her associates are. No, no, we must proceed as planned. I thought we might adopt a similar device as when we inveigled our way into Miss Adler's home, except this time, you shall be the hapless visitor."

"You me to dress as a clergyman and pretend to faint? I don't know, Holmes."

"You will do splendidly, and there's no need for you to don a disguise. While you distract her, I shall see if I can find any clues to her accomplices."

"Do I have to start a fire, too?"

"There was never a real fire in Miss Adler's home and, no, you don't. You don't even have to act like a minister. Just act a little disoriented, addled. Keep her busy, and I shall handle the rest."

As I continued to hesitate, he added, "Come, think of the honourable gentleman who stands to lose everything if this woman isn't stopped. Do it for your friend, Barn Owl. Do it for England!"

And so, a little after eleven o'clock that night, Holmes and I found ourselves in a dark and insalubrious street in Battersea. Sounds of bawdy songs drifted from the public house, carried on the stench of beer and tobacco.

"That's her house over there," Holmes said, pointing. "The one on the end with the tall bushes. Everything is in place. All you have to do is cross the road and act alarmed when the coach rushes towards you."

"Coach – what?"

"Count to thirty after I leave you, just to make sure I have a head start. Then wander out into the street. You were lost in thought and didn't see the coach coming. Here is some dye for your face, it makes an excellent alternative to blood. The Irregulars will call the lady to help. Then all you need do is act confused and in pain. Good luck."

"Wait – !" But he was already gone.

I huddled in the shadows, taking care to avoid the street light. With considerable trepidation, I counted to thirty, as directed. Then, gathering all my courage I stepped out into the street.

In hindsight, the coach missed me by some distance, but in that moment, the thunder of hooves and the rattle of the carriage as it sped up the cobbles towards me seemed deafening. When I collapsed in a heap on the pavement, there was no need for acting. I was truly distressed.

Out of nowhere, a group of people surrounded me. Suddenly I became aware of someone holding a glass of water to my lips. I shook, spilling half the contents. Then, as I returned the glass, I looked into a pair of extraordinary amber eyes, as slanted as a cat's.

"There now," she said. "Is that better?"

"I . . . I don't know," I stammered.

"Come now, let's get you inside and you can rest awhile."

With her hand on my arm, I stumbled into the house. She led me to the small sitting room and helped me to sit on the sofa.

"Ach, you're as white as the *banshee*," she said, her accent as musical as a harp. She insisted that I lie down.

"There now," she said. "How about a glass of wine? It will help to settle you."

"Thank you," I said. "I'm sorry to give you so much trouble."

She went to the small bookcase in the corner and I heard the sound of liquid being poured. A moment later she handed me a glass of red wine.

I took a sip and found it surprisingly tasty. I thanked her.

"A little brew of my own concoction," she said, then laughed. "'Tis a jest. Poteen I can make, but I wouldn't have a notion how to make wine. Enjoy it. It'll help steady you."

I did as she said and felt myself relax.

The dimly lit room full of books and plants and pictures that I couldn't clearly see felt surprisingly relaxing. The fortune teller adjusted the small cushion under my head and covered me with a red rug.

"Close your eyes for a few minutes," she said. "That's better. Just breathe and feel your strength return."

I felt, rather than saw, her sit beside me "We may as well have a little fun while you're recovering. Here, give me your left hand."

"Whatever for?"

"So I can tell you your fortune."

"I don't believe in that . . . sort of thing," I said.

"Oh, come, it's just a bit of craic, like. Entertainment."

I let her take my hand. She had an air about her, a magnetic energy that only the wealthy or powerful seem to possess – though Holmes, too, has it in abundance.

"Interesting," she said as she examined my palm. "You are a man of deep loyalty, committed to the welfare of your fellow man. You are intelligent and very kind, qualities that aren't always appreciated by those around you. There is a man here, he is very tall, lean, and – What's the word? – *mercurial*. That's it. As changeable as an Irish summer." She laughed. "You enjoy the horses, playing billiards, and have recently become interested in matters of government." The tawny eyes met mine and seemed to bore through me. I managed to nod, though I still felt light-headed and lethargic. I wondered how long I had been there. Had I given Holmes enough time to conduct his search? The effect of the near-accident had undoubtedly affected me more than I had realised.

Over the next few minutes, she lay out every detail of my life before me. The deepest secrets of my childhood, the anguish of my war-time experiences that I had told no one, and even the most confidential of cases Holmes and I had worked together.

At last, she said, "You seem to be feeling better, Doctor?"

I suddenly realised that I did feel better. All the doubts and forebodings I that seemed to have weighed upon me had somehow drifted away. Then I said, "Doctor?"

"I told you that you were a healer and you said you were a doctor, remember?"

"Oh, that's right."

A moment later, I was at the door. Precipitously, a cab arrived, and the fortune teller told the driver, "Look after my friend, Mister. Take him back to Baker Street."

I sank back in my seat. I felt most peculiar, relaxed, peaceful, and yet unsettled. It wasn't until we were outside Baker Street that I began to shake off my stupor. I climbed unsteadily out of the cab and stood looking up at 221b. I suddenly wondered how I had arrived here.

The cabby climbed down and stood before me, a look of concern in his familiar eyes. Again, it took me a moment to realise what was happening. "Holmes?" I said.

He lay a silencing finger on his lips and nodded at someone who had come up behind me.

"Thank you, Mr. Barkus," Holmes said, and handed the fellow a banknote. "I am much obliged to you."

"Any time, Mr. 'Olmes," said the cabby. "Good evening' to you, and to you, Dr. Watson." He then climbed up into the driver's seat and drove away.

Taking me gently by the arm, Holmes led me up the steps and into the house. Moments later, sitting by the fire, I found myself sipping a cup of very strong coffee.

"Holmes?" I said.

"I am so deeply sorry, my good fellow. It was an unforgiveable error. I should never have persuaded you take such a risk. The fault is entirely mine. I should never forgive myself if you came to harm."

"I was just startled by the sudden appearance of the carriage. I wasn't hurt."

He shook his head, "Oh, Watson, you haven't yet grasped the truth. But then, how could you?"

He seemed to be talking more nonsense than usual, and I was having difficulty understanding him. I rose to my rather unsteady feet and said, "Do you mind if we continue this conversation in the morning? I find myself exhausted after the events of the day."

For a moment he seemed uncertain but at last he nodded. "That's fine. Are you all right going upstairs? Do you need help?"

"I've been climbing stairs since I was a wee laddie, thank you. I can manage perfectly well."

Holmes was already at the breakfast table when I came down the following morning.

"How are you feeling, Watson?" he asked with an unaccustomed tone of concern.

201

"I'm well, thank you. I slept very soundly."

"Excellent." He continued to study me as I filled my plate with toast, eggs, sausages, and all the rest of Mrs. Hudson's splendid breakfast.

Feeling somewhat snappish, I said, "Is there something on my nose? I cannot imagine why else you are staring at me in that unsettling manner."

"There seems no lasting damage," he observed, as he refilled his coffee cup. "I confess, I was concerned."

"Damage? What the deuce are you talking about? The carriage didn't actually hit me, you know. I admit I was a bit shaken after the event, but I am perfectly well."

"Oh, my dear Watson, I am relieved to hear you say so, even in such waspish tones, but it isn't the carriage that troubles me. It is the potion that that contemptable woman put in your wine."

"Potion?" I was suddenly far less sure of myself. "You must be mistaken."

"I assure you, I am not. I overheard the entire conversation. Yes, you may well look troubled. A few minutes after you drank the wine, she began to subject you to a series of questions. You forgot all your usual discretion and told her everything she wanted to know: Your name, the general's case. Mycroft."

"Oh, my God!"

"The fault is mine, my good fellow. I failed to anticipate the possibility that she was relying not on associates or, at least, not entirely, but on hypnosis."

"Hypnosis! Oh, Heavens, Holmes, did she hypnotise me to perform some heinous act?"

"No, no, only to answer her questions. I'm afraid she knows all about your friend Barn Owl, though."

"Oh, no! Why didn't you stop her, Holmes?"

"Do not worry, my friend. As soon as I was sure you were safe, I arranged for her to be arrested. I'm going to Scotland Yard to interview her as soon as you finish your breakfast."

I instantly set down my knife and fork. "Come along, then. Let's go!"

In the cab, Holmes explained that he had gone to see his brother once he was sure I was safe in my bed.

"Mycroft has already seen to the arrest of Sir Neville Powell."

"They surely cannot send a knight of the realm to prison?"

"It's hardly without precedent. However, in this case I suspect he will be urged to retire for the good of his health."

"Urged?"

"In the strongest terms. And then placed under house arrest."

"And Miss Fortuna?"

"Miss Grady, you mean. A spell in prison, I suspect, but first we shall give our Jezebel a taste of her own medicine."

To my surprise, Mycroft Holmes met us at Scotland Yard. He inquired after my health. I assured him I was perfectly well.

"I am relieved to hear it, Doctor. If it is any comfort at all, you have done your country a fine service. Now, shall we meet this woman, Sherlock?"

We followed a young constable through the meandering corridors and stairways that took us down into the dreary bowels of the building and the cells they held. Lestrade met us and said, "She's a fierce little kitten that one. Nearly scratched the eyes out of one of my sergeants."

"Do we have everything set up?"

"Yes, Mr. Holmes, just as instructed."

We entered the interrogation room – an intimidating place with a high ceiling, pale green walls, and a flickering gaslight. The cold seemed to get into my very bones, and I pulled my coat tighter around me.

Three chairs lined behind the long wooden table. On the opposite side stood one alone, the one the prisoner would occupy. I sat in the middle of the three chairs, with the Holmes brothers flanking me. A jug of water and an enamel mug sat before us, both connected to the table by a sturdy chain.

"On no account drink the water," Holmes said softly.

Moments later, the fortune teller was brought in. Wearing a plain worsted prison dress, her hands and legs in manacles, she was a very different creature from the beauty of the previous night. Her hair was a mass of wild tangles, and her eyes flashed in fury.

"You!" she cried to Sherlock Holmes. "I know you! Mr. Interference and nosey-parker! You ought to be strung up, you should!"

"Calm yourself," Mycroft boomed in a terrifying voice, and the young woman fell instantly silent.

"We already know about your plot to destroy General Lang's reputation. Your only hope of leniency is to tell us the truth. The whole truth."

"Like I'd talk to the like of you," she sneered.

"Come, Miss Fortuna," I said gently. "For your own sake, will you not speak with us? Surely you do not owe allegiance to the people who hired you."

"You," she snarled. "This is how you repay my kindness."

"I really am trying to help you."

"Oh, sure you are. Make yourself useful and give me some water. Haven't had a drop or a bite since last night, thanks to Mr. Plod, here."

She nodded over her shoulder at Lestrade, who stood at silent alert.

With a nod from Holmes, I poured her a full cup of water and handed it to her.

"Do you need help?" I asked.

"I can manage," she snapped. Manage she did, though the chains rattled against the table as she drank.

We remained in silence and soon she set the empty cup down on the table before her.

"You feel better now," Holmes said.

"I feel better now," she agreed, her voice flat.

"What's your real name?"

"Jenny . . . Jenny Grady."

"How did you first meet the general?"

"Bloke comes to see me – says 'e's Sir Neville Powell. Snooty chap, but 'e 'ad deep pockets. Said 'e 'ad a score to settle. Tells me about some general and 'is missus who had lost a nipper and were all boo-hooing. Neville says 'e knows some woman who were a friend of the general's missus and would persuade 'er to come and see me. I do me work, and she's so impressed that the general would soon follow. Worked like a charm, it did."

The lilting Irish brogue had all but vanished, leaving coarse Cockney in its wake.

"And what were you to do with the general?" Holmes continued.

"Plant some ideas in 'is 'ead, make 'im feel like a, whatsit, a pacifist. Not 'ard. Course, I 'ad ter give 'im some reminders of my powers," she grinned maliciously, "so 'e'd never doubt a thing I said."

"For instance?"

"For instance, Powell gave me some inside track on a horse, and I persuaded the general to bet on it. Won a bloomin' fortune, 'e did, and gave me a big chunk of the winnings, too, which were mighty decent. I told 'im all sorts. The general, I mean. Tried to give 'im one weird prediction a week to come true. Bert 'elped. And 'course, I made 'im believe that anything out of the way that 'appened, I 'ad predicted it."

Over the next two hours she regaled us with various tales of her exploits and her assault on the senses of the general. She named her accomplices and Lestrade immediately sent out his men to bring them in.

Before he dismissed her, Holmes told her she would forget everything I had told her the night before. He also made her forget any secrets revealed by the general or any other innocent. When she was led back to her cell, humming to herself, Mycroft Holmes said, "All this over jealousy and greed."

The door to the room was left open and I started when the general himself joined us. Instantly, I stood at attention.

"You heard?" Mycroft said.

"Every word. What a bloody fool I've been. Thank you, Mr. Holmes, for sending for me. I doubt I'd have believed it if I hadn't heard the words from her own mouth."

"Hardly your fault, sir," Holmes said. "There was a very clever conspiracy against you. Fortunately, you are surrounded by loyal friends who took steps to protect you."

The general shook his head, and I could see the anguish more in the set of his shoulders than on his face.

"There's no real harm done," I said. "This assault on your character was stopped before it took root."

"I know you, don't I?" he said. "It's Watson, isn't it?"

"Yes, General. Watson, John H., formerly of the Fifth Northumberland Fusiliers."

"That's right. Dr. Watson." He shook my hand. I felt deeply moved. He motioned for me to sit down, and he followed suit, taking the seat vacated by the erstwhile fortune teller.

"How did you get her to talk?" he asked.

Holmes nodded towards the water jug. "Chloral Hydrate taken from her own supply. She kept the bottle by the wine carafe and put two drops into your glass when you visited her. She did the same to Watson and, I suspect, to anyone she thought might have information that might profit her."

"And Powell was behind it? What a corrupt and wicked thing to do. Oh, Lord, my poor wife . . . ."

"There's no need to tell her, surely?" I said. "For all the wickedness Jenny Grady has done, at least she was able to lend comfort to your wife. Nothing can be served by taking that away from her."

"The doctor is perfectly correct," Mycroft Holmes said. "None of this will be made public. There is no reason for your wife to know anything about it."

"I do not keep secrets from my wife unless they are matters of state or national defence. Besides, she must be told why I am resigning."

"Resigning!" I cried. "But, General, you cannot! Why, it would accomplish nothing other than to further Powell's ends."

"I have betrayed my oath. Who knows what I have told that woman while I was under her influence?"

"Come, sir," Holmes said, "your integrity does you much credit, but Watson is correct. Your resignation would serve no one but this country's enemies. Besides, all memory of your conversations with her have been erased.

"General, consider: A fellow like Powell isn't content merely with seeing you humiliated. He wants to get rich for his efforts. It is surely not unlikely that he has entered some sort of agreement with a foreign power to get you out of the way."

This was something I hadn't thought of.

"My brother is quite correct," Mycroft Holmes added. "If you resign, our enemies win."

"Oh, Heavens – I objected to the production of the K-111 and the MP-17. What was I thinking?"

"Tell the committee there was a spy attempting to infiltrate the committee. You wanted to buy time to wheedle him out."

The general nodded at Holmes's words, and everything proceeded just as planned.

Much of what then followed remains protected by the Official Secrets Act of 1889. I can say, though, that in the end, General Lang was persuaded to retain his position. Jenny Grady agreed to subject Sir Neville Powell to her particular brand of fortune telling, and while I may not divulge the details of his revelations, I can say that several countries with hostile intentions towards the Empire were exposed as his paymasters. What became of him thereafter I cannot say.

Jenny Grady and her accomplices served short prison sentences and then vanished.

All that remains of note is that Sherlock Holmes, his brother Mycroft, and I were granted the extraordinary privilege of military honours for our efforts. About five months later, Barn Owl brought fine Havana cigars for Holmes and me to celebrate that he was engaged to be married, and that the General and Mrs. Lang were expecting twins. She thereafter had two healthy boys. The family continues to thrive.

The Mystery of the
Murderous Ghost
by Susan Knight

"Dr. Watson! Dr. Watson!"

I knew that voice. My heart sank. However, I could hardly pretend to be deaf, common courtesy requiring me to turn with a smile on my face.

"Miss Pyne!" I exclaimed. "What a pleasant surprise! Whatever brings you to the Regent's Park?" For the woman had been a neighbour of Mary's and mine in Paddington, some distance from where we now found ourselves.

She returned my smile with a twisted one of her own that did nothing to enhance her thin, yellow face.

"Like yourself, I suppose, Doctor. Enjoying the clement weather."

It was indeed a fine day in early spring, bright but with an invigorating nip in the air. I had decided to escape from Baker Street, where, for he had nothing else to do, and no new case to investigate, Holmes was furiously playing some discordant piece of modern music – Russian, I think – on his Stradivarius, or when he gave up on that, slumping back in his armchair with a dark frown, puffing his vile pipe fumes into an already-stuffy room.

The park, up to that moment, had lifted my spirits, along with the spears of daffodils I could discern rising from the earth, fat buds ready to burst open on the cherry trees, young leaves about to uncurl. Truly spring is a glorious season, casting off the gloom of winter and giving rise to hopes and expectations for the future. It had been difficult for me near the anniversary of losing my beloved Mary, and then – unable to bear living any longer in the house where, for but a too brief time, we had been so happy together – returning bereft to Baker Street and Holmes. Yet on this March day nature's balm had proved even more soothing than the understanding sympathy I received from Mrs. Hudson. Precious little of the same, I might add, from Holmes himself, though, since I wasn't expecting any, I could hardly be disappointed at my friend's lack of empathy. How could he, whose heart had never been given to another, share my feelings of loss?

But now the lightened mood that had descended on me evaporated like a morning mist.

"Dear Dr. Watson." The woman hurried forward, her sharp little face avid. "I cannot tell you how very, very sorry I was to hear about poor Mary. I can only hope she was peaceful at the end – that she didn't suffer too terribly much."

I thought of my wife in her last hours, fighting for each breath, and myself unable to do anything more for her except to hold her hand and tell her that I loved her. I wasn't about to discuss this with my present interlocutor, however.

"It is kind of you to ask," I replied. "Yes, it was very peaceful."

"Thank the Lord for that," she said. "You know what a very dear friend I was to Mary. I was distraught not to be able to attend the funeral. I only learnt about it, you know, when it was quite over."

"According to my late wife's wishes, it was a very private affair."

"Yes, but surely she'd have wished her dearest friends to be there."

The pain was too much. Overcome with emotion, I prepared to walk on, courtesy be d----d. This woman, Eliza Pyne, despite what she claimed, was no great friend to Mary, who spoke of her as a busybody of the worst kind, always pleased to spread scandalous and usually unfounded gossip. I had no desire to prolong the conversation. However, I was not to be permitted to get away so easily.

"You poor, poor man!" Miss Pyne continued, actually catching hold of my sleeve. "But you know, you must believe Mary isn't truly gone. She will always be with you."

I nodded. "I will never forget her."

Again I tried to shake her off but the woman was as tenacious as a dog with a bone. Short of physical violence, I couldn't detach her.

"Ah, yes," she continued. "But you are in need of more solace than memories alone can provide, Doctor." Her darting eyes were bright. "And it just so happens that I know where you can get it." Her voice held a triumphant note. "This chance meeting of ours was assuredly meant to be."

I had a sudden dark suspicion that perhaps there was no chance at all in this meeting. Eliza Pyne might expect that, living so near, I would be in the habit of taking a turn in this park of all places. Was it possible that she had been lying in wait for me? Surely not. Yet it was a disturbing coincidence.

"Dr. Watson," she went on. "I must tell you that I have recently met with a truly amazing woman. She has great powers, you know – Signora Alma Contini. Well, you have no doubt already heard of her, for she is proving to be a great sensation in London."

No, I replied, I hadn't heard of the lady.

"That's a great pity. And it surprises me. Her name should be shouted from the rooftops." Her voice sank to a hoarse whisper. "She is able, you see, to communicate with those who have . . . *gone before.*"

"Oh, you mean a medium. Miss Pyne, I hardly think – "

"Stop right there, Doctor. I know what you're thinking, a rational man like yourself. I was sceptical too before my dear friend, Miss Wraggs – you no doubt know her, another great friend of your Mary's . . . ." I shook my head. "Well now, I am most astonished at that, Doctor. I should have thought – Sally Wraggs rings no bells?" I shook my head again. "No matter. Dear Sally induced me to attend a séance with la Signora – against my better judgment, I must say, for I am an even more rational being than yourself, you know. However, I went and was completely won over. The woman has powers over and beyond any other medium I have ever consulted. Here, take this." She thrust a leaflet into my hand, crudely depicting the image of a woman with penetrating eyes and Medusa-like curls, ghostly forms wreathed in ectoplasm peering over her shoulder. Inscribed upon it were the words "*Signora Alma Contini speaks with The Dead every Friday at eight o'clock at the Scriveners' Hall, Chelsea.*"

I started to explain that I had no wish to try and summon my late wife from whatever realms she now inhabited. Heaven, I had to assume, given Mary's goodness.

The woman refused to give up.

"Just promise one thing: That you'll attend a séance as an observer, and make up your mind then. What harm in that?"

I was tempted to tell Miss Pyne that I found a lot of harm in such activities. I abhorred them and fully believed that those who practised them were nothing more than quacks and charlatans, preying on the susceptible and needy. However, I simply demurred again, a little more forcefully, though still, I trust, within the bounds of politeness.

"Well," she said at last, more coldly, "I have to confess I am quite taken aback, Dr. Watson. I rather understood your feelings for your wife to be stronger. I imagined you, like Orpheus, would have travelled even to the Underworld itself to catch a glimpse of her again."

With that riposte, she turned on her heel and walked away from me, leaving me my mouth open. Orpheus, indeed! Wherever had that come from? I couldn't even be offended. It was too ludicrous.

I continued my walk around the lake, trying to distract myself from the unpleasantness of the recent encounter, and paused to watch three small children who were feeding the ducks, laughing delightedly and jumping up and down each time one of the birds made off with some crumbs. It was a pretty sight, yet I couldn't but recall how my dear wife and I had planned to have children – a whole tribe of them, as Mary used

209

to say smiling. A fury rose in me then at Eliza Pyne's suggestion that I hadn't loved enough. I sat down to compose myself and try to shake off the meddlesome woman's remarks, the way the ducks were shaking water off their backs.

"What's this?" Sherlock Holmes was lifting the leaflet I had carelessly cast on the table. "Notice of a séance! Watson, have you become credulous in your old age?"

I explained about my encounter in the park.

"You see!" he replied, shaking his head. "As I have often tried to tell you, it is dangerous to indulge in unnecessary exercise. And yet . . . ." He peered more closely at the paper. "Alma Contini. I have come across that name quite recently in some connection." He paused to think and then clicked his fingers. "I think I have it."

He rummaged through a pile of newspapers until he found what he wanted, an illustrated publication entitled *Il Secolo XIX*. He turned the pages, scanning each with eagle eyes.

"Here," he said finally, thrusting the paper towards me. "Read that."

"You are joking of course," I replied. "It's in Italian."

"A-ha, yes. You have not yet mastered that mellifluous tongue. Ah well, let me translate." He took the paper back.

> *Mysterious occurrence at séance* [he read]. *On Tuesday last in the crypt of the Abbey of St. Carlo Borromeo, during a séance conducted by Signora Alma Contini, a young girl, Guilia Molinaro aged sixteen, fell unconscious, the near-victim of a murderous ghost who threatened her with Hell, fire, and damnation. In resonant tones . . . .*

Holmes looked up at me. "*Toni risonante,* mark you, Watson." He read on.

> *In resonant tones, the imperturbable Signora Contini ordered the ghost to be gone, thereby it is believed, since the thing dematerialised immediately, saving young Guilia's life.*

"Good Heavens! How melodramatic!"

"Indeed. But, wait, it gets even better:

> *When she regained consciousness, Guilia spoke of being dragged by a multitude of ferocious demons towards a dark tunnel – the entry as she understood, to the Kingdom of*

210

Hades. Despairing that all was lost, she then heard faintly at first but in crescendo, *the resonant tones* (Mark those tones again, Watson!) *of Signora Contini. Whereupon the demons ran howling from her and she returned to the land of the living, swearing to mend her ways and live a purer life. The powers of Signora Contini are truly amazing, a witness said later. She saved not only Guilia's life, but also her soul.*

Holmes put down the paper and looked at me, a smile playing over his lips.

"Well," he said, "after all that, are you still telling me you have no interest in making the lady's acquaintance?"

"Even less than before," I replied. "I have no interest whatsoever in involving myself with the Dark Arts."

"The Dark Arts indeed. A telling phrase. Well, let us see. Every Friday. So the next session with the resonant Signora will take place in three days' time. I should like very much for you to be there."

I laughed. "For *me* to be there? I don't think so. Go yourself if it interests you so much."

"It's true I am bored to death just now, with no juicy case to interest me. Indeed, while you were gone, I had a visit from some wretched woman who actually wanted me to find her chambermaid. The girl has made off with the family silver. How unutterably tedious!"

"She should contact the police."

"That's what I told her, but there's more to it. The family the silver belongs to is that of her husband, and as yet he knows nothing of the theft. She fears he will blame her. An angry and violent type of a man, by the sound of it. Discretion is what she wants and is willing to pay for. I have sent her to Rayfield."

Joshua Rayfield was a young man and admirer of Holmes who had just set himself up in the private investigation business.

"He will be glad of the work," I said.

"Yes, indeed. Though I doubt he's up to it. Well, no matter. However, you asked just now why I wouldn't attend the séance myself. A naïve question, Watson, if I might say so. That I, probably the most rational being in the whole world, should be seen consulting a medium! I should never live it down. You, as a widower, however, have the best excuse in the world."

I rose up, mortally offended.

"Holmes, if you think I would stoop to exploit my grief over Mary's death for your idle amusement, then you are an even colder fish than I took you for! How can you even suggest such a thing?"

211

He had the grace to look chastened.

"My dear fellow," he replied, "I had no such motive. It wouldn't be for my amusement, I assure you. Not at all. No, I have a feeling there is more to this Signora Contini and her activities than meets the eye."

"A feeling? You are generally not inclined to follow your feelings." If you even have any, I thought, still angry with him. "Unless, of course, there is evidence to back them up."

Holmes tapped the newspaper.

"This story intrigues me. One might imagine the lady would use it to advertise herself and her powers." He picked up the leaflet I had been given by Eliza Pyne, "But she does not. Hardly anyone in London has heard of her. Why is that? Are you not intrigued, too?"

"If I go," I said, already hating myself for giving in, "it will be as an observer pure and simple. I shall not let Mary come into it at all."

Holmes actually shook my hand.

"Capital, Watson!" he said. "Capital!"

The Scriveners" Hall was a surprisingly dingy building, at least from the outside, set in an unprepossessing street that bordered rather on the working class district of Fulham than the prosperous Chelsea of the given address. I was surprised, the Scriveners" Guild being a worthy and prestigious organisation.

The interior of the building, at least, bore out my preconceptions. The entrance hall was handsomely appointed, with a marble floor inlaid with the crest of the guild, and banners bearing the same hung from fine oak-beamed rafters.

I was accosted by an ancient with an alarmingly dark-red complexion – a sure symptom of Bright's Disease – in some sort of frogged uniform, complete with breeches and gaiters. I took him to be the gatekeeper.

"Your business, sir," he asked briskly, though politely enough.

"I am here to attend the séance," I replied.

At that, he frowned and muttered something, directing me to a room at the rear of the hall with a door that stood slightly ajar.

"In there," he said.

I tapped on the door, waited a moment and, hearing nothing, entered.

The place was dimly lit, its gloom only relieved by a few guttering candles, but I soon discerned a crowd of people seated in rows before a stage. A woman approached me, modestly dressed in black, a large silver crucifix around her neck. Was this Signora Contini? If so, she looked nothing like her printed image, with her smooth, prematurely grey hair and pale complexion and eyes.

When I asked, the woman laughed lightly.

"Good Heavens, no," she said. "The Signora is preparing herself. Mentally, you understand. I am Miss Violet Beynon, her humble assistant. But you are most welcome, sir. Please take a seat."

She tried to usher me to the front, but I slipped into a chair at the rear.

"As you please. I wonder," and she produced a notepad, "if I might take your name." She smiled. "Unless, of course, you prefer anonymity."

"Not at all," I replied, and identified myself. But when she asked for my address, I hesitated, reluctant to reveal as much. "Paddington," I said, which wasn't exactly a lie for my old house was still my property, though now rented out.

While sitting waiting for the show to begin, I took care to observe as much as possible, knowing I would be thoroughly quizzed by Holmes on my return. The low stage in front of us was screened off by a black curtain. The walls of the room were panelled in dark wood, topped by dusty-looking plaster mouldings depicting the accoutrements of the scriveners' trade: Quill pens, ink wells, open tomes, and the like. An unlit chandelier hung above us. The place was cold and smelt musty. It was all rather dispiriting, and I wished I hadn't come.

A few more shadowy people had entered after myself, to be greeted in the same way by Miss Beynon. By then I estimated that about forty people were in the room, most of them identifiably female by their bonnets. We waited on, some of the ladies starting to fidget and murmur.

Abruptly and without warning, the black curtain slid back. The whole audience, including myself, gasped, for now revealed in an intense shaft of light, a tiny woman sat huddled on a chair, her head down, arms crossed over her breast, hands lightly resting on her shoulders. From that attitude, I reckoned, she surely couldn't have drawn the curtain herself, and yet who else could have done it? No other person was near, the assistant standing behind us. And whence came that light where previously there had been none?

Now, slowly, the woman raised her head. I caught my breath. Before me was perhaps the most beautiful woman I had ever seen, delicately featured with skin of a porcelain whiteness, jet black curls piled high on her head. For some time she stared out at us, motionless and silent. At last she stood up, extending her arms above her head and then letting them fall in a graceful gesture of welcome, the sleeves of her loose black robe, falling back at first almost to her shoulders and then down, to cover her lowered hands. It was a piece of impeccable stagecraft.

Holmes was to remark as I later described the scene that I had quite clearly become so besotted by the woman that my account of the séance was less than useless.

213

"Can you never be trusted not to have your head turned by a pretty face?" he asked, exasperated.

I was annoyed with him, reckoning I had given a fair description of what had happened. Signora Contini was beautiful, so why should I not say so? Of course, I had no belief in the woman's channelling of the voices of those who had passed over, as she described them. In fact, it had turned out to be an unremarkable, even disappointing evening from the point of view of spiritualist manifestations, of which there were none. No ectoplasm. No poltergeists, Yet there was no doubt in my mind that Signora Contini was a consummate professional, and even perhaps worked some good by bringing comfort to those she singled out. I could mention in particular a mother whose only son had recently died of consumption. Young Bertie told his mother, through the Signora, that he dwelt in a delightful garden of eternal summer, at peace, surrounded by the splashing of water, sweetly-aromatic flowers, and the song of birds.

"All a bit general," Holmes said, when I recounted the same to him later. "I could have invented something better than that."

"Yes, but then Bertie asked his mother if she remembered the Paradise Gardens at Littlehampton, which they had visited together years before, and she said she did, clapping her hands with joy. Well, it's just like that here, he told her. Now, how could the Signora have known such details, Holmes? The boy's name. And then Littlehampton of all places! I ask you that?"

"Beware, Watson. You are in danger of falling into the bottomless pit of credulity. If Signora Contini was aware that the woman was likely to be present, she would have investigated her in advance. That's how these quacks operate. I should expect to learn that the mother had attended a previous séance and, like you, had given her name and address."

"I didn't give my address."

Holmes made an impatient gesture. "No, but the mother probably did."

"I don't deny absolutely that trickery is involved. I just can't see how it works."

"It's elementary," he replied. "Ask any magician. In fact, I imagine I could do as well myself if I could be bothered to try." He threw back his head, revealing his noble profile. "Yes, indeed. It might be quite amusing. What do you think, Watson? The Great . . . ." He clicked his fingers. "The Great *Cialatano*, perhaps." He turned back to me. "In any event, I trust you will respond to the lady's invitation."

For, at the end of the séance, after the Signora had disappeared again behind her curtain and we were all making our way out, dropping our

214

monetary contributions into a tray positioned for that purpose by the door, Violet Beynon had hurried up to me.

"The Signora particularly requests that you attend a more intimate meeting, Doctor," she had whispered. "A private séance with just a few chosen ones. She senses that you have experienced a loss and wishes to help you."

How the woman had even known I was present, sitting as I had so far from the stage was one mystery, and why she should have singled me out from all the others there present was another.

I had mumbled something non-committal, being torn. On the one hand, I had no desire to cheapen my grief over Mary with conjuring tricks. On the other, I admit the beautiful Signora intrigued me. When Violet Beynon pressed a note into my hand, inscribed in a flowing hand, it turned out to contain a date, time, and an address in Hampstead.

"You must come," she had said. "The Signora wishes it, you know."

It was almost an order and, despite myself, I had nodded.

Now Holmes rubbed his hands together.

"I might have expected as much," he remarked.

"Really?"

"Indeed, Watson. Your status and evident prosperity make you an attractive catch."

The population of London had been congratulating itself prematurely on the advent of spring, since, on the night that I set out for Hampstead, an icy wind was blasting the hill, howling through trees and causing them to hurl their still bare branches towards the Heavens as if pleading for mercy. Only a few hardy souls had ventured out, and those I saw looked barely human, scurrying by, bundled up and bent against the elements. By the heath, a fox crossed my path, stopped and turned and looked at me, its eyes flashing in the trembling glimmer of a street lamp. I shivered with a sense of foreboding.

Once again I wondered how Holmes had managed to talk me into such an enterprise. Even the prospect of again seeing the Signora could hardly make up for the ordeal of such a journey. If I were a superstitious man, I might even have thought that nature was conspiring to prevent my arrival, that the wind was crying, "Go back! Go back!" Or perhaps it is only writing this after the event that I imagine such a thing.

Worse was to come, however, for I soon realised that I was hopelessly lost, and now there was none but shadows to ask the way. The warren of dark little streets offered no guide. I must have been walking in circles, for again I found myself on the edge of the heath, its lumpy bushes darker against the dark like lurking hunchbacks. I turned away, and then nearly cried out in shock, for right behind me loomed an apparition in the shape of an old tramp, his hand stretched out.

"For pity, sir, on such a wild night."

His voice, though low and coarse, reassured me that this, after all, was no creature spun of mist but one of flesh and blood. My cold fingers fished a coin from my pocket and, as I gave it to him, I asked the way to Steeple Street.

It seemed I must have given rather more than I intended, for his gratitude was such that he insisted on conducting me to the steps of the very house that I sought, a tall building in a narrow street of similar edifices. When I looked back to thank him, he was nowhere to be seen. My sense of foreboding returned. I hammered on the door.

"A bad night and no mistake." Suddenly everything became normal again as the door opened on a bright hallway. The woman who greeted me was a homely body with a mob cap perched on grey curls, and a wide smile over her broad face. "You'll be here for the meeting, sir?"

I told her that I was. The housekeeper, I thought.

"This way then."

She bustled ahead, soon showing me into a well-lit and thankfully warm room with nothing sinister about it, just the usual appurtenances of any well-appointed parlour: A thick Persian carpet surmounted by several armchairs and a chaise longue, all most tastefully upholstered in dark green velvet, a fine marble fireplace within which embers yet glowed. A glass-fronted cabinet displayed a collection of china figurines – sentimental shepherds and shepherdesses, a boy in a sailor suit, crinolined ladies, a gallant in a three-cornered hat. A grandfather clock stood against one wall, an upright piano, sheet music open upon it, against another. Above all were hanging portraits in heavy gilt frames of worthy but rather grim gentlemen and ladies, perhaps the earlier denizens of the house. The only somewhat out-of-place feature was a large and highly polished round mahogany table in the centre of the room, around which eleven upright chairs were set, on which several persons were already seated.

If the wind continued to howl outside, in here we were unaware of it, protected as we were by heavy drapes that hung over the windows.

I had feared to be late but from the number of empty chairs, it seemed that not all were yet present. Of the Signora there was again no sign. However, her assistant stepped forward to greet me.

"I am delighted you have come, Doctor," she said. "Alma will be so pleased."

Just then I heard a squawk from one of those already seated. One of the women twisted herself round in her chair and fixed me with a quizzical eye.

"Dr. Watson! And you claimed not to be interested in such things!"

That rasping voice again! I might have expected Eliza Pyne to be one of the chosen. She made me sit next to her, something I could hardly refuse. Wedged in on her other side was a woman of grisly aspect and astounding girth, whom she introduced as Sally Wraggs, the other supposedly dear friend of my late wife's. The unfortunate woman's moon face was disfigured with a number of hairy warts, and several chins hung over her massive bosom.

"But of course you already know each other," Miss Pyne asserted.

I could truthfully say that I had never met the lady before, since, once seen, such a personage would only with great difficulty be forgotten. In any case, Miss Wraggs confirmed it.

"No, Lizzie," she said in a strangely high-pitched and somewhat childish voice, "I have to say I've never had the pleasure."

"Well now, I am astounded to hear that," Eliza Pyne retorted. "I could have sworn you and the Doctor here were acquainted. The recital in the town hall. Hubert Parry, you know."

"Alas," I replied, recalling the event. "I missed that concert. I had to attend a patient that night. In the end, Mary went with her cousin."

Miss Pyne shook her head and sniffed as if doubting my word and that of her friend over her own convictions.

More people were now arriving, including a fragile young girl who was shown to the seat beside me. I smiled at her but she looked away nervously. Perhaps, I thought, it was her first séance.

Now with only two seats remaining empty, including a throne-like one directly across from me, no doubt for the medium herself, Miss Beynon started to prepare the room. She placed a screen in front of the fire and extinguished the lights until only one candle remained, that in the middle of the table. The sudden gloom blotted out everything that had made the room familiar. All that could be seen outside our circle were flickering shadows. All that could be heard was the steady ticking of the grandfather clock, and soon enough Miss Beynon dealt with that as well, opening its front panel and halting the motion of the big brass pendulum.

Once again, most of the visitors here were women. Apart from myself, the male sex was represented only by a stout man of advanced middle age, dressed in tweeds, with a large walrus moustache and thinning hair, who looked to be more at home striding across the heath with a large dog than dabbling in the occult. In addition, a youth sat hunched in his chair as if hoping to disappear into it. This individual was skeletally thin and phthisic-looking, purple shadows under his eyes, lank hair long over his collar. A poet or some such, perhaps, dying for love of the Signora.

Silence hung uneasily over us until Eliza Pyne, unable to restrain herself, made some remark *sotto voce* to her neighbour. At which, Miss Wraggs started to shake with laughter, setting the whole table, against which her enormous bosom was pressed, trembling and vibrating. A cold "*Shh!*" from Miss Beynon soon brought the pair to order again, apart from a couple of quickly repressed final snorts.

The Signora clearly liked to keep people waiting – I suppose to increase the nervous susceptibility of her audience – but at last she entered, or most exactly floated in, all in black as before, wearing a loose garment that revealed nothing of her form, a mantilla over her head and face. She arrayed herself upon her throne – Miss Beynon taking the empty chair beside her, to her left – and stayed thus for a while, presumably regarding us all, though exactly where her gaze was directed couldn't be told through the black lace. Finally, raising her arms – this time encased in long, tightly-cuffed sleeves, so that we were sadly not vouchsafed a view of those slender limbs – she lifted the veil from her face, revealed now as lovely as ever, with, it struck me, the mature beauty that comes to some women in their middle years. She had to be forty at least, and yet seemed to be without age, youthful and ancient at the same time, like a Greek statue. (How Holmes would laugh at such a notion. I often thank my lucky stars that he isn't able to read my mind. At least, not completely.)

Signora Contini now informed us in that charmingly low-pitched Italian accent of hers that she would endeavour to summon her spirit guide, a Roman slave from the eastern Empire named Puerus. Miss Pyne helpfully whispered to me that such guides – mostly of ancient and exotic origin – are common among mediums.

"Now," the Signora said, frowning at Miss Pyne, "please take the hands of the persons on each side of you, and, no matter what happens, hold tight not to break the circle. Do not forget. This is very important for all our safeties."

For my part, I was happy to keep hold of the cold little hand of the young girl to my left, though less pleased at having to grasp the damp paw of Eliza Pyne.

At a signal from the Signora, Miss Beynon blew out the candle and we were instantly blanketed in a total and unnerving blackness, until a faint gleam from the partially screened fire restored some shape to the room and particularly illuminated the white face of the Signora. I wondered indeed if she had anointed her face with some sort of luminous cream to enhance the effect.

Several times she called on Puerus, and at first there was no response. Then, at last, a boyish voice, quite unlike that of the Signora, replied that he was indeed present. A shiver of anticipation rippled through our circle.

218

"Have you any messages for anyone here?" That was Miss Beynon speaking.

Yes, it seemed, speaking through the Signora, that Puerus had messages – just like, I couldn't help thinking, some sort of astral telegraph boy.

The first was to an elderly woman, Mrs. Grace Herbert, from her late husband, Horace. He told her not to trust the man with one leg.

It sounded an unlikely piece of advice, but Mrs. Herbert squealed.

"That's Alfred!" she cried. "He's talking about Alfred Smith! Oh dear oh dear oh dear! But Alfred is always so kind and helpful."

"He is after your money," Puerus said flatly. "Have nothing more to do with him."

There were a few other similar and rather trivial sounding messages to others in the circle. Miss Wraggs, for instance, was chided by her mother for forgetting to keep the aspidistra watered, to which Sally replied in her childish voice, "Sorry, mama." Once again, I wondered what the devil I was doing there.

Then Puerus said, "*M . . . M . . .* there's an *M* here with an urgent wish to contact the living."

Eliza Pyne squeezed my hand, but I said nothing.

"*M* . . . a lady . . . she suffered much. Who recognises her?"

I frowned and clamped my teeth together. Eliza Pyne made nudging motions with her elbow but I refused to respond. I just hoped she wouldn't answer on my behalf.

"No one wants M?" The call sounded plaintive.

Then the stout gentleman said, "I suppose it could be my maid Molly, who died from a kick in the head from my horse, Arion. A beauty, but such a nervous beast, you know." Presumably referring to the horse. "Well," he continued, "if the silly goose would go into the stable yard, she was asking for trouble. However, what urgent message she could have for me, I can't think."

Maybe to care more for humans than for beasts, I thought.

But no, it wasn't the unfortunate Molly. Puerus finally gave up and moved on. I let out a deep breath. Forgive me, Mary, I thought.

"A man – a father, I think – wishes to warn his daughter," Puerus said. I felt the cold little hand of my neighbour tremble in mine.

Suddenly, shockingly, another voice, a hoarse and brutal male voice shouted out, "*It is too late, Annette, to repent your evil ways! Too late! You have shown yourself heartless and must in punishment lose your heart! Hell has opened its doors wide for you. Prepare to meet your doom!*"

Immediately, Hell broke loose quite literally. A cacophony of false notes crashed from the piano, the grandfather clock started chiming,

219

objects flew about the room in all directions, the fire flared up behind its screen, casting writhing shadows, then died down as quickly. A portrait fell with a heavy thud. But far worse than all, a horribly decayed face, as of one long in the tomb, loomed huge and ghastly through the murk above us, only to swoop down upon the girl at my side. She uttered a long-drawn out shriek and then collapsed head foremost on to the table in front of her. Some of the women started to scream, Eliza Pyne among them, gripping my hand as though her life depended on it.

"Stop!" It was the Signora, in her own voice again, in what were undoubtedly resonant tones. "Stop this at once. Begone foul fiend!"

A sudden silence and a thickening of the darkness. Then, at last, someone lit a candle, revealing the table to be strewn with broken china ornaments, the now headless gallant in front of me. Amidst all this, the girl still lay prone, I still holding her limp hand in mine, though the circle must already have been broken by whomever lit the candle – someone I soon recognised as Violet Beynon hurried round to us. To give her space, I relinquished my hold on the girl's hand, and the assistant bent over her, trying to rouse her.

"What has happened?" the Signora called over to us. "Is the child all right?"

Miss Beynon looked across at me, horror on her face, and almost imperceptibly shook her head.

"You tell me, Doctor," she said in a shaky voice, moving aside.

I felt for a pulse in the girl's neck. There was none. I gently lifted her head. Her eyes were wide and staring, staring but unable to see anything ever again.

"She is dead!" I said finally.

The moment of horrified silence was broken by a mighty scream from the Signora, who leapt up and rushed over to us. The mantilla fell from her head and her black hair streamed loose about her shoulders.

"No! it cannot be!" she cried, and held the poor corpse to her. "You are wrong, Doctor, cruelly wrong. There is life here yet. Her heart still beats."

She pulled the girl back and tore open her dress as if to prove it. Eliza Pyne, leaning over my shoulder, shrieked out and pointed.

"Look! The hand of the ghost." Indeed, bloody imprints of clutching fingers were branded on the ivory skin over the left breast. "The ghost snatched out her heart. Like he said he would!"

Could the foolish woman not hold her tongue!

The assembly gasped. As for the Signora, she fainted away into my arms.

A murderous ghost! It was absurd – and yet I could honestly attest that no living person had approached the girl before she collapsed. The circle had remained unbroken, I holding the girl's hand on one side and the surely blameless Mrs. Herbert the other. Indeed, the poor old lady was quite overcome, as were the other females present, particularly the wretched pair to my right, while the phthisical young man moaned and trembled as if about to have a fit.

The rational mind says that ghosts don't kill people. Sometimes, it is true, people die of shock, though not usually healthy young girls. But what of the marks on her breast? Oh, how I wished Holmes were present to tell me what to think!

Meantime Violet Beynon was taking care of the Signora, now conscious again but paler than ever, while the stout man seemed to think it incumbent upon himself to take control of the situation.

"A bad business," he said, shaking his head. "The police will have to be notified, of course."

"What! So that they can arrest a ghost, I suppose," Eliza Pyne put in tartly.

"And we must call an ambulance," I said.

"Isn't it a little late for that, Doctor?" Eliza again.

"The poor child will have to go to the morgue to be examined further," I said gently. "Does anyone know who she is?" I looked at Miss Beynon.

"She just gave her name as Annette de la Roche," she replied. "Of Paris."

"Oh, a Frenchie!" exclaimed Miss Pyne, as if that explained everything.

"That is most unfortunate," I said. "What is to be done?"

"The police will no doubt accomplish what's necessary, ambulance and all, without further help from us," the stout gentleman said, glaring at me as if I questioned his better knowledge.

"Well, now," Inspector Lestrade was chuckling a while later. "This is the last place I should have expected to find you, Dr. Watson. Is your esteemed colleague present, too?"

"He is not."

"Not yet, eh? I don't suppose he'll be able to keep away from a case like this." He laughed. "They're all telling me a ghost did it."

We were ensconced in the small study off the main hall that Lestrade had taken over for his interviews. It was a pleasant, book-lined den, with a handsome roll-top desk. I should, under other circumstances, be pleased to pass time there.

221

"Now I've always taken you for a reasonable man, Doctor," Lestrade continued. "Perhaps you can describe what happened here tonight in terms that don't include supernatural killers."

I shook my head.

"I have been trying," I replied, "to make sense of it all, but I'm sorry to say that the evidence indeed points to the ghost." Lestrade was about to interrupt. "Let me explain. We were all sitting in circle, holding each other's hands . . . ."

Lestrade consulted his notes. "Yes. In the dark."

"In the semi-dark. It was possible to make out shapes. I had on one side of me Miss Pyne and on the other, the unfortunate victim. Not only can I be absolutely certain that we kept hold of each other throughout, but also that no one approached the girl until the ghost swooped down on her and she collapsed."

"You'd swear to that, Doctor."

"I would. However, I shall be most interested in the results of the autopsy. Then it will be clear if the girl died of shock – not an impossibility. The experience was, even for me, a frightening one, and perhaps the poor child had a weak heart. But, of course, I should also like to know whether there is evidence of some human involvement."

"We all would. I can't see my superiors being too happy if I told them I'm to arrest a ghost." He again turned to his notebook. "But perhaps just now you could take me through the events of the entire evening as you recall them."

I did so, in the knowledge that Holmes's training had sharpened my powers of observation to a creditable extent. At least, Lestrade seemed satisfied, making the odd note and nodding frequently while I spoke, confirming that my account tallied with that of the others. At last I reached the climax.

"Less sensational on the whole than that provided by certain of the ladies," Lestrade remarked. "And doubtless more accurate for that. But what do you make of this business of pianos playing by themselves, stopped clocks chiming, and china flying about the place? I have to say it sounds very peculiar. Very peculiar indeed."

"Nothing more than a clever magician could engineer, Inspector."

The new voice belonged to Holmes. I'm not sure who was the more astounded at his sudden entry, Lestrade or myself.

"Apologies for my intrusion," he added.

"I thought you said he wasn't here." Lestrade regarded me accusingly.

"He wasn't."

"No, I just happened to be in the neighbourhood," Holmes said airily, "and observed the commotion outside this premises. Hey ho! said I to myself. Isn't that where Watson is attending a séance?"

Happened to be in the neighbourhood, indeed! I regarded him suspiciously, but his face revealed nothing.

"The housekeeper, Mrs. McDuffin, kindly let me in, when I told her who I was. She has of course heard of me." Spoken with a degree of smugness. "Since I'm here," he went on. "Perhaps I might be permitted to have a look at the location of the – Can we even call it a crime if the suspected perpetrator is . . . er . . . *disembodied*?"

Lestrade frowned. "I'd like to say no," he said. "I'd like that very much. But this one's a puzzler, and no mistake." He sighed. "Perhaps you can see things in that room, Mr. Holmes, that have escaped the rest of us mere mortals."

"Show me the way," Holmes replied.

In the hall we were accosted by Miss Beynon, who addressed herself to Lestrade.

"Inspector," she said. "The Signora's in a most dreadful state. Can she not go to her room?"

It was Holmes who answered.

"In a little while, after I have spoken to her, Madam.

She looked at him queerly but, since Lestrade didn't contradict him, nodded her acquiescence.

"This is the Signora's assistant, Miss Beynon," I explained to Holmes, who regarded her keenly. I had mentioned her to him before.

We then made our way to the parlour. It was empty of all but poor Annette – now laid out on the chaise longue and covered with a shawl – as well as two burly constables, the rest of the company having decamped to the breakfast room.

"No, no, no," Holmes said. "This will not do. Lestrade, please ask your fellows to leave. They are trampling all over the scene with their big flat feet, destroying evidence as they go."

Lestrade sniffed his displeasure at being thus ordered, but duly instructed the constables to withdraw. Holmes then commenced his investigation, getting down on to his knees to examine, painstakingly and most particularly, the floor around the table. Meanwhile, he questioned me. Who sat where? I reconstructed the space as well as I could remember.

"Ah! So the victim was next to you there, Watson. The Signora directly opposite. Good."

He rose to his feet. If he had found anything, he didn't share the intelligence.

"What was the precise sequence of events?" he asked. "For instance, how long after Signora Contini dismissed the ghost was the death discovered?"

I closed my eyes to prompt my memory. "The ghostly head swooped. The girl collapsed. The Signora spoke. Then silence . . . ."

"Excuse me, Watson. Did the other manifestations – the music, the clock, the poltergeists – did they continue throughout while the ghost made those threats?"

"No. They had stopped. I think. Well now, it was definitely silent after."

He sighed. "Thank you. How long was this silence before anyone moved?"

I was about to say no time at all, but that wasn't correct. "Some moments," I said at last.

Holmes shook his head and tut-tutted. "Moments! How many? Think Watson."

"Not long, but maybe half-a-minute."

"Half-a-minute is long enough."

"Someone lit a candle. The one on the table."

"I see. And then you say the assistant – "

"Miss Beynon, yes. She came round to see what was wrong with the girl."

"On your side or the other?"

"On my side. I had to shift my chair back. Miss Beynon soon realised something was terribly wrong and asked me to confirm her worst fears."

"And then and only then the Signora started to scream."

"Everyone started to scream. Well, all the ladies."

Holmes picked up the headless china gallant, still lying on the table in front of my seat. It seemed to amuse him. The he moved to the chaise longue and gently lifted the shawl from the girl's body.

"A pretty child," he said, with more emotion than I had heard him express for a long time. "So where is the mark of the hand?"

I lifted the torn dress from the girl's breast. The ghastly red imprint still corrupted the white flesh. Lestrade shuddered.

"Hmm," Holmes said. "If it were blood it would have turned black by now." To my horror, he drew a dampened finger across the mark and lifted it to his nose. He sniffed and then tasted it. "No taste or smell. Cochineal, unless I'm very much mistaken" he pronounced.

"*Cochi*-what?" asked Lestrade.

"A red dye derived from insects."

"I don't understand," I said.

"Come now, Watson. It is surely simple enough. Remember the Italian newspaper article. This is quite certainly another trick employed by the delightful Signora to fool the credulous."

"A trick that went badly wrong, then."

"Well, that depends on your point of view. The ghost no doubt thought it turned out perfectly."

I disliked his levity. "But you don't believe in ghosts."

"Of course not. For one thing, if the girl is French and her wicked father the same, why did he speak English?"

"How did you know that?"

"Because you, Watson, who speak nothing but English, told me what he said. Maybe he even spoke English with an Italian accent, eh?"

He smiled at me archly.

For his part, Lestrade had been looking more and more puzzled.

"What newspaper article are you talking about?" he asked. "Don't tell me this has happened before?"

Holmes had then to explain his earlier discovery.

Lestrade scratched his head. "All most peculiar. So what do you make of it then, Mr. Holmes?"

"Clearly the masquerade was part of the show put on by the Signora, without intending, we may assume, the girl's death. She was assuredly to have been saved in the nick of time, as on the previous occasion, with the Signora as the heroine of the hour, and worthies like Watson here as witnesses. All present would then make a sizable donation to the lady, and spread the word of her powers. But someone had other ideas. The question is, why should this surely blameless child fall victim?"

"Unless indeed she died of fright."

"Unlikely if she was in on the trick, as she must have been."

"Well, I can only repeat that no one came near her." I threw up my hands. "I give up. It's an impossible murder."

"Hardly impossible," Holmes replied drily, "since we have the plain evidence before us that it indeed took place. Tell me everything again, Watson. Leave out nothing. Not a single nuance. And then I should like to meet the rest of the company."

As we made our way to the breakfast room, we met the housekeeper coming away with an empty tray. She had clearly been providing tea, or perhaps something stronger, to the shaken company.

"Ah," Holmes said. "The very woman. Please tell me, Mrs. McDuffin, does the Signora own this house?"

"God bless you, no sir. It belongs to Mrs. Grace. Mrs. Herbert, that is. Didn't she invite the Signora to visit her here after attending one of her séances, the first time the Signora was over from Italy, just after Mr.

Horace passed on. Now she stays whenever she's in town." Mrs. McDuffin shook her head. "We've never had nothing like his happen before, sir. That poor little girl . . . ." She sighed deeply. "I can only thank God Mr. Horace isn't here to see what them spirits have done to his lovely parlour. All Mrs. Grace's lovely ornaments broke. I told her no good would come of it, but would she listen? Not to say that the Signora isn't a nice enough lady. It's the rest of them."

"The rest of them?"

"The ghosts, sir. In my opinion," and she tossed her head with its little mob cap on top of it, "the dead should be left rest in their graves, where they belong."

"Amen to that," said Holmes piously. I threw him a suspicious glance.

"Mrs. Herbert," Holmes whispered to me as Mrs. McDuffin withdrew. "Wasn't that the person sitting on the other side of Annette?"

I nodded.

As we entered the room, all eyes turned towards us. Many of the ladies had been weeping, none more loudly than Miss Pyne and Miss Wraggs – their faces red and blotchy. None more desolately than the Signora, with Violet Beynon sitting beside her, holding her hand.

"When will we be allowed to go home, Inspector?" the stout gentleman asked irascibly, consulting his fob watch. "It's getting very late. And," looking at my companion, "who the devil is this fellow?"

"Well, if it isn't Sherlock Holmes," exclaimed Eliza Pyne. There was a gasp of surprise, or perhaps dismay, from somewhere. "Oh, Mr. Holmes, please tell me we aren't all about to be murdered by that horrid ghost."

"No, no," Holmes said. "You're safe enough."

"How can you be so sure?" It was Sally Wraggs who spoke in that baby voice of hers. She put a hand to her stupendous bosom. "My heart's still thumping at the memory of that awful apparition."

"We will get to that in a moment," Holmes said. "But first I should like to commiserate with the Signora upon the death of her daughter."

More gasps. Signora Contini, however, regarded Holmes, her lovely dark eyes glistening wet with tears.

"How did you know?" she said.

So it was true.

"Come now, Signora," he replied. "You can't do the same trick over and over and expect no one to figure what is going on." He turned to the assembled company. "I regret to inform you that you have all been fooled tonight, fooled by two very clever people. Excuse me, Madame. I think you are left-handed."

Signora Contini nodded, puzzled, whereupon Holmes caught hold of her right arm and, loosening the cuff, pulled something from the sleeve. A balloon. He held it up. Flattened and shrivelled, it was yet recognisable as the same ghastly face that had loomed over us.

"You see," he said to Eliza Pyne. "You aren't likely to be at risk from this deflated fellow."

An indignant, nay angry, rumble spread through the company. The Signora shrank back in her chair.

"Fear not, Signora," Holmes smiled at her. "I shan't ask you to reveal what other devices are concealed beneath that flowing garment of yours."

"I won't believe it," said old Mrs. Herbert. "All those things flying about. The piano. The clock. That couldn't be faked."

"Sleight of hand," Holmes replied. "And an elaborate system of wires and small explosives. I have already found certain suggestive traces beside the Signora's chair. It's quite simple, you know. Any magician worth his salt could explain it better than I, and even reproduce the effects. I imagine the Signora and her assistant were granted free access to the parlour before the event."

"Oh yes," Mrs. Herbert agreed. "In fact, Mrs. McDuffin was rather put out." She looked across at the Signora. "How could you, Alma? I trusted you! And all my lovely ornaments – smashed!" She pressed a lacy handkerchief to her face.

"Your stupid ornaments! Is that all you care about? A few trashy trinkets." The Signora leapt to her feet in a sudden Latin fury. "What about my daughter! It was you, wasn't it! You killed my daughter! You envious old woman! Grace Herbert!"

"I – " Mrs. Herbert fell back in her chair, amazed. "Alma, whatever are you saying?"

"It must be either you or the Doctor here. Only one of you two could have done it."

Now everyone turned to me with hostile eyes, even Mrs. Herbert. I felt most uncomfortable

Holmes stepped forward.

"I can answer for my friend and colleague, Dr. Watson," he said. "He is entirely blameless. As for Mrs. Herbert," he regarded that lady for a few moments, "I'm convinced that she too had nothing to do with it."

"Then who, Mr. Private Detective?" the stout gentleman demanded. "If you're so clever, you tell us. Who committed this impossible crime?"

Holmes smiled charmingly at him, and shook a finger at him.

"Improbable, not impossible," he said. "If you will kindly hold your horses, sir, I am about to explain." He sat himself on a convenient chair, leaned forward, and built the fingers of his two hands into a steeple. "First of all, we have to ask ourselves what motive could there be for such a killing. Young Annette or . . . What was her real name? Guilia?"

227

"Guilietta," said the Signora, with emotion. "My lovely girl. *Bellissima ragazza.*"

"Hmm," Eliza Pyne grumbled, "so even the name is fake!"

"What had Giulietta done to deserve her fate?" Holmes continued, ignoring the interruption. "Yes, she had taken part in some dubious trickery, but surely that was no good reason. So maybe the question should be not what had she done, but who she is."

"And how did you find that out, might I ask?" Lestrade was clearly put out that he wasn't privy to Holmes's reasoning.

"After seeing the article in the Italian newspaper, I simply did some further investigations, and soon discovered that the Signora was blessed with a daughter, now aged about sixteen."

The lady nodded.

"We are famous in Italy," she said.

Infamous more like, I thought.

"I can see," the stout gentleman remarked, "how, on discovering the fraud, someone might have borne a grudge. Of course I can't speak for anyone else, but I personally was prepared to make a sizable donation for the privilege of attending a séance held by the renowned Signora Contini." A murmur of agreement spread through the company, while the speaker glared at the lady. "Yes, indeed, I think we were all prepared to pay over the odds. Now, I don't say that, even in the heat of the moment, finding himself – or herself – duped in the way Mr. Holmes has explained, someone would have been angry enough to commit murder, but even if they were, surely she – " He pointed at Signora Contini. " – would be the proper victim."

"You are correct," Holmes said. "But isn't she a victim, too? The Signora has lost perhaps the only person in this world who means anything to her. Isn't that right, Miss Beynon?"

That lady, taken aback at being suddenly addressed, mumbled, "Yes, I suppose so."

"How long have you been in the Signora's employ?" he continued.

"Oh, just a few weeks. Since she arrived in England."

I was surprised, having thought the association far more established than that.

"And before?"

"Before that what?"

"What did you do? Worked in a pharmacy, perhaps. Alongside your husband?"

Her eyes were wide. She didn't contradict him. The rest of us waited, all agog.

Holmes continued. "Have you always believed in spiritualism, Madam?"

"No!" The reply burst out perhaps a little more forcefully than Miss Beynon intended.

"Mothers," said Holmes. "What they will not do for their children. Isn't that right?"

The room was hushed in expectation. No one could imagine what was coming next.

"You too have a daughter, I believe. Or rather, you *had* a daughter."

In Afghanistan, I once saw a snake hypnotise a pika. The little creature stood frozen in its tracks until the snake pounced and swallowed it whole. That was a little like what I was witnessing here. Miss Beynon too was staring, immobilised, at Holmes.

"My daughter . . ." she murmured at last.

"What was her name?" He spoke gently.

"Lilian."

"And tell us, please, how did Lilian die?"

Violet Beynon rose up, suddenly full of fire. "How did she die? She killed herself." She glared at us all. "She killed herself after attending a séance." She turned on Signora Contini, who shrank back further into her chair. "Remember the last time you were in England? You claimed to have made contact with Lilian's betrothed, Frank, who had been killed fighting in South Africa." Miss Beynon laughed, a chilling sound. "Frank 'told' Lilian that he was in a beautiful garden where he would await her until they could be reunited for all eternity. It's part of Alma's regular patter, you know."

"Designed to bring comfort, Violet," the Signora murmured. "No harm meant at all. The opposite."

"Yes, but you see – Lilian *believed* it. She believed that if she killed herself, she would be reunited with her beloved and spend eternity with him in a paradise garden. So she came home and took poison."

"Oh, my God, Violet! I am so sorry."

"The Signora took away your daughter," Holmes asked, still gently, "so you decided that you would take away hers. Isn't that right?"

Miss Beynon fingered her crucifix. "An eye for an eye. A tooth for a tooth. A daughter for a daughter. Let her suffer as I have suffered. I bided my time." She looked triumphantly at the Signora. "Using my maiden name, Alma, I persuaded you to employ me. But I don't think you even remembered poor Lilian."

The company looked at Miss Beynon aghast. She actually seemed proud of what she had done.

"The question still remains, how she pulled it off." Lestrade said. "You haven't told us that, Mr. Holmes."

"Oh, that's the simplest of all, Inspector. The girl had already applied the bloody handprints to give the appearance that her mother's claims were true. After the girl pretended to collapse, Miss Beynon hurried round as planned, apparently to see what was the matter with her. What did you do?" He turned back to the assistant. "Prick her with a rapid-acting poison? I saw a tiny mark on her neck."

Miss Beynon said nothing.

"Or maybe you gave her a draught of something before the séance? You remarked on how cold she was, Watson." He turned back to the woman. "No matter. The autopsy will tell us what we need to know."

It was over. The spring storm had passed and we were back in Baker Street enjoying a warming cup of Mrs. Hudson's excellent Smoking Bishop.

"How did you uncover all that so quickly, Holmes?" I asked.

"Having nothing better to do, I amused myself with some basic research into the Signora and her entourage. Of course, I had no idea then that it would end in tragedy."

"But Miss Beynon seemed a sound woman, devoted to her employer. I should never have suspected her. In unmasking her, you yourself looked to possess some psychic powers."

"Nothing of the sort. I reasoned that since both you and Mrs. Herbert could be ruled out as murderers – along, of course, with the vengeful ghost – there was only one other person with an opportunity to kill the girl and that was Violet Beynon. I then simply employed the basic trick of the quack medium's trade. You deduce one small thing and then get the subject to tell you the rest, without them realising they are doing it."

"But what small thing did you deduce?"

"I spotted the faint mark of a wedding ring on the finger of her left hand. That sounded an alarm at once. Why would Violet Beynon wish to pass herself off as unmarried? Most women of her years like to be thought of as wives or at least as widows, some spinsters even wearing their mother's wedding band to give that impression. Clearly then she wished to pass herself off as something that she was not."

"But how did you know about her daughter?"

"I take it you didn't notice the brooch pinned to her blouse?"

"I only saw the crucifix."

"Well, of course that was another clue to Miss Beynon's creed, since the Christian Church abhors meddling with the paranormal the way mediums do. You must have noticed the vigorous way in which she dismissed spiritualism." I nodded. "But back to the brooch – a mourning brooch. It contained a curl of blonde hair, cut from the tresses of a child or young woman. A daughter, I surmised, quite recently deceased. Miss Beynon told us the rest herself."

"I am still amazed that you happened to turn up at Steeple Street at all, Holmes."

"Oh, I had one of those feelings, Watson, of which you think me incapable. A feeling, based of course on my researches, that something was up. In fact, I visited earlier in the day and had a most interesting chat with the inestimable Mrs. McDuffin. As a result of what she told me, I was determined not to miss the fun. As you so nearly did."

"I?"

"Thank goodness for the old tramp who set you to rights. By the way, Watson, here's your sovereign. Absurdly generous, I might say."

I sat, open-mouthed, while he tossed the coin back to me.

Mycroft's Ghost
by The Davies Brothers

The funeral was a quiet affair, befitting a man of simple needs. The Prime Minister was present, of course. For all their occasional disagreements, the premier was well aware of just how much he owed the man whose coffin lay upon the altar of that famous church. Members of the cabinet were there too, as were a select few civil servants. Of his family, only one was in attendance in the cavernous nave of St. Martin-in-the-Fields: Mr. Sherlock Holmes.

The vicar rather mumbled through his sermon, an oratory at odds with the colourful life of the man he was attempting to memorialise, for Mycroft Holmes was in many ways as curious a character as his younger brother – a brother who was making no attempt to hide his displeasure at the dull and rather generic tribute.

"Come, Watson," my friend snapped at last, even as the vicar hadn't finished listing the departments and colleagues with whom Mycroft had shared his talents during a distinguished career as "special adviser" to the government. I did as my companion requested, allowing that he wasn't of sound mind in that moment. I felt compelled to nod my apologies to the other mourners, few as they were, as I followed Holmes down the aisle to the back of the church.

"Holmes, are you quite well?" I asked when we were outside.

"Mycroft would never countenance expending my precious energy on sentimentality," he replied flatly.

"He was your family," I implored. In fact, as far as I was aware, Mycroft had been the very last of his family. "It is natural to mourn."

But Holmes appeared not to hear as he strode down Pall Mall, in the direction of his late brother's rooms. I rushed after him, catching up as he climbed the steps to Mycroft's flat.

Holmes unlocked the lacquered oak door and entered the hallway. I followed, aware that I was a mere onlooker, so engrossed was my friend in his own thoughts. In the tastefully appointed passage, he looked left and right, surveying the walls, the carpet, the ceiling. He ducked into a room and I followed. I felt a responsibility in that moment, as his friend but more especially as his physician, to stay with him and ensure that he did nothing rash.

This room belied the more refined exterior and hallway. Its position in the flat suggested a sitting room, as did the fireplace and high ceiling, but its appearance was closer to that of an archive or the unkempt library of a small law firm.

"He didn't allow anyone in here," Holmes said. "Not even his housekeeper."

It was almost ascetic in its simplicity – just a solitary armchair in front of the hearth, and every wall obscured by overflowing bookshelves. Mycroft had spent most of his time at work, of course, and he had passed his leisure hours at the Diogenes Club, so it shouldn't have come as a surprise to find such Spartan living quarters. However, I felt a pang of sympathy for a man who had spent so many years in these lonely circumstances. I wondered if, perhaps, Mycroft's younger brother might have lived similarly if I weren't there to force him to keep a semblance of normality in his daily routines.

Holmes pulled some papers from a shelf and rifled through them, searching frantically.

"What is it?" I asked.

"There must be something," he murmured, to himself rather than to me.

"Holmes," I said softly, "I think you need to rest."

"Some clue," he continued. "Some . . . ." Rather than finish his sentence, he pulled a thick file from another shelf, its loose contents tumbling out and falling to the dusty floor. He barely looked at these papers before grabbing another pile of documents, then another. This was the first time I had ever seen Holmes like this – not the analytical sleuthhound, but a whirlwind of frenetic energy without method or purpose. I confess to feeling frightened for his sanity.

"Holmes," I said, but he didn't respond. I tried again, more sharply. "*Holmes!*"

My companion stopped and looked at me. I held his gaze for some seconds until, at last, he slumped down on that well-worn armchair, defeated. He stared at the high ceiling and the wrought-iron chandelier, which, I realised with horror, was the place where poor Mycroft had hanged himself.

"It does not . . . ." Holmes muttered, then stopped. I was about to console him when he began again. "It doesn't correspond with anything we know about him. It simply does not . . . tally."

I kneeled next to the chair and patted his arm. "These things rarely do," I said, keen to soothe him, and equally anxious to get him away from that gloomy place. "Let us return to Baker Street."

The following days were quiet ones. Holmes refused to receive guests, and he spent much of his time in his own bedroom, even requesting that Mrs. Hudson leave his meals at his door. My attempts to coax him into our shared sitting room were met with firm refusal.

Between medical consultations, I did my utmost to discover what I could about the events leading to Mycroft Holmes's death. I was desperate to find some explanation or, at the very least, a crumb of comfort for my dear friend who had been so terribly affected by his brother's loss. As Holmes had said, Mycroft's suicide simply didn't tally with all we knew about him – the shrewd logician, the mastermind of so many government plans, whose analytical brain had helped us avoid war with at least two Continental powers.

Besides Whitehall, which I imagined a closed shop to a mere physician such as I, the only other place that Mycroft used to visit was his club. The problem was that, in keeping with his reclusive existence, he had founded the Diogenes Club to serve, as Holmes had once put it, "the most unsociable and unclubbable men in town". These were qualities not conducive to my need for answers. However, with home life now so quiet, I took a short detour to visit their rooms on Pall Mall each evening after I had completed my work duties. Over the following days, I made my acquaintance with Huntley, the suitably taciturn doorman. Initially, he was dismissive of my approaches, but, on learning that we were fellow veterans of Afghanistan, he softened slightly, and I persuaded him to let me inside. Huntley allowed me to sit for an hour in the Stranger's Room, the only part of the club in which conversation was permitted, while he enquired discreetly whether any member would be willing to talk to me. In that cosy little parlour, I perused the papers and partook of their excellent brandy, but on the first two occasions I left disappointed. Then, exactly a week after the funeral, the creak of the door interrupted the silence.

A tall, remarkably thin gentleman entered. His head was completely bald, reflecting the light off his smooth scalp. His chin was long and pointed, and he stroked it constantly as he approached the armchair to my right. I was unsure whether he was here to see me as he ignored my smile of greeting. He took the day's *Times* from a side table, sat down, and began to read. He cleared his throat, his face hidden by the pages of the newspaper, then spoke. It was a low, gruff voice, rasping slightly, and I judged that he wasn't accustomed to using it often.

"A friend of Mycroft's."

I was taken off-guard, surprised by his utterance and unsure whether it was a statement or question.

"Yes," I said. "Well, I was acquainted with him. I'm really a friend of his brother's."

"Sherlock Holmes. Interesting chap." He lowered the newspaper and looked at me with bright, inquisitive eyes. His voice was smoother now, as if his vocal cords were warming up. "Mycroft spoke highly of him."

"At the club?"

"Of course not. He'd have had to blackball himself." He chuckled at the idea. "The name's Smythe, I'm – " He stuttered and corrected himself, his face serious again. "I *was* a colleague of Mycroft's, in Whitehall."

I introduced myself and explained to him about Holmes's melancholy. "I just wish I could find out more about Mycroft's last days. I hoped that perhaps I could help his brother begin to understand."

"Huntley tells me you were in the Berkshires," Smythe said. "Maiwand?"

I nodded, rather perplexed by his unorthodox line of conversation, and discomfited by mention of that wretched place.

"Royal Engineers," he said. "Terrible business."

As with my exchanges with the doorman, it is a peculiarity among military men that a mere word or two can convey so much – the camaraderie, the honour, the pain. I could feel my old injury throbbing at these thoughts, but my reverie was soon interrupted.

"Mycroft wasn't a man prone to sentiment, but he was fond of Lord Stanley-Johns."

"Lord Stanley – ?"

Smythe lowered *The Times*, and turned his head towards me. "You must have read the papers. Last month – Hyde Park."

"Ah, yes," I said, reminded now of the crime. Stanley-Johns had been the Foreign Secretary until his untimely death. On a Sunday afternoon stroll with his wife, he had been targeted by a pickpocket, a boy no older than twelve or thirteen. When Stanley-Johns attempted to apprehend him, the boy slashed at his arm with a knife. It was the desperate, unthinking act of a street urchin who simply wanted to escape a night in the cells. By terrible chance, however, the blade sliced along the ulnar artery, and poor Stanley-Johns died within minutes from the wound.

"A great loss to us all," Smythe said, shaking his head. "Mycroft and he were close – well, as close as Mycroft ever got to anyone. I believe that he even had dinner on occasion with Stanley-Johns' family. For a man of his habits, that was . . . ." Smythe trailed off, but I understood. Mycroft was a man of such entrenched routine, that he rarely ventured anywhere but his flat, his office, and this club – all within a few hundred yards of each other. Even his funeral had been at the end of the street! For him to be intimate enough with a person to visit his home was, indeed, surprising.

"Mycroft was under a great strain, I believe," Smythe continued. "Not only personally, of course. In his position, Stanley-Johns had been central

235

to a great many communications with our friends abroad – and even those not so friendly."

I noticed that Smythe was growing more verbose by the minute, and I sensed that, despite belonging to such an unusual club, he was glad of the opportunity to talk.

"You mean that his death had national ramifications?"

"International!" Smythe corrected. "Stanley-Johns was in the middle of rather sticky negotiations with . . . Well, it would be remiss of me to offer any more details, but let's say that he would return from meetings at one particular embassy with the unmistakable whiff of caviar on his breath."

Inwardly, I chuckled at the man's utter lack of discretion, all the more amusing given his initial reticence to speak to me.

"And Mycroft was tasked with continuing those negotiations, you believe?"

"Yes. Well . . . ." He looked around the empty room, suddenly conscious of having said too much. "Mycroft's role was a singular one, as you know. While there are ministers and under-secretaries responsible for specific branches of government, it was Mycroft's job to consider all aspects of a situation, especially in times of crisis. Stanley-Johns' death was a personal tragedy for Mycroft, but there was also the rather delicate matter of . . . ." He whispered these last words: "A missing ring."

"A ring?"

"An engagement ring, to be precise. It belonged to a prominent member of the royal family of . . . one of our European neighbours. She had lost it while staying at Claridge's. Thankfully, it was found by one of our agents before the matter became public."

"Then why was it not returned to her?"

"Because she wasn't supposed to be in the hotel. She wasn't even supposed to be in the country!" Smythe licked his lips and stroked that long chin of his lasciviously. "And she wasn't with her fiancé. She was with one of the more dashing members of our own royal . . . ." He gave a little cough here, unwilling to complete the sentence, even though it was clear that he was relishing the opportunity to discuss the scandal.

I struggled to contain my shock. "You mean – "

He laughed slightly, a surprisingly high-pitched, girlish giggle. "As you can imagine, it was in the interests of all parties to return the ring to the lady as soon as possible, but it needed to be done very carefully."

"Surely it was a simple transaction. A small package."

"One doesn't just post a diamond ring worth thousands of pounds to a royal palace at the other end of the Continent."

"Then through diplomatic channels."

"We couldn't risk anyone knowing of the lady's indiscretion. There are some in that country who would leap upon evidence of such a scandal – some even within their own government. Revolution is in the air over there, and . . . ."

I digested this information. It would indeed be a delicate problem, and one that Mycroft would have been perfectly suited to solve.

Smythe continued. "Mycroft entrusted Stanley-Johns with holding the ring in safekeeping. It was thought prudent to keep it away from official government channels. Plausible deniability, and all that."

"And it was stolen by that boy in Hyde Park?"

"No, Stanley-Johns would never have been so careless as to keep it upon his person. It was taken a few days later, from the safe in his London apartments."

"Why was it still there?"

"Because only a handful of people knew of its existence, let alone its location." Smythe sighed. "Mycroft deemed it as secure there as anywhere else. Stanley-Johns had apparently built a secret hiding place in his home, which wasn't known even to the servants. Mycroft sent a couple of our best men to keep an eye on the house, of course, and Lady Stanley-Johns was under strict instructions not to allow anyone unfamiliar inside."

"She was aware of the contents of her late husband's safe?" I asked. "She knew of the ring?"

"No, no, no. But she did know that the safe contained important documents, so she would never have . . . ." He smiled wistfully. "She's a fine, honourable woman."

"So I take it that the ring disappeared?"

"I'm afraid so. Once Mycroft had established a safe means through which to return the ring, he went to the Stanley-Johns residence in order to retrieve it personally. Lady Stanley-Johns showed him to the safe, but it was empty." Smythe gave a little gasp, enjoying the drama of his story. "Mycroft searched frantically, of course, and he interrogated the lady thoroughly, but she was a trusted friend, completely honest and loyal. She swore that nobody knew of the secret hiding place, nor the code to the safe. And she swore that no one had entered the house, apart from a handful of well-wishers, all of whom she trusted implicitly."

"Quite the mystery," I said.

Smythe's eyes grew misty. "The incident rather hit poor Mycroft for six. Never had I seen him so bereft. It was as if, for the very first time, he had discovered a terrible truth." He paused again, as if unable to countenance what he was saying: "Mycroft Holmes was . . . *fallible*."

I was all too aware of that weakness in both Holmes brothers. Each had complete confidence in his own ability, and in almost all instances that confidence was justified. There is a danger, however, in such conceit, for the realisation of an error is that much more devastating. For Mycroft, it seemed, it had been too much to bear.

I took a cab back to Baker Street, anxious to relay to Holmes all that I had learned. I hoped that, at the very least, Smythe's story would help my friend begin to understand his brother's terrible final act. I hoped, too, that the mystery of Stanley-Johns' safe might just fire up his mental faculties and bring him out of his funk, for there was still a missing ring to be traced, a thief to apprehend, and possibly even a civil war to prevent.

To my surprise, I found Holmes on the landing, shaved and dressed, and putting on his hat.

"Holmes," I exclaimed, "I'm glad to see you up."

He gave me a rather distant nod of greeting. I noticed that his skin was greyer, his eyes retreated even more deeply into that hawk-like face of his.

"I am going to pay a visit to Mycroft's rooms," he said. My heart sank, for I feared that he would only fall further into melancholy if he were to return to the place of his brother's suicide.

"But, Holmes. I have just spoken to one of Mycroft's old colleagues. It seems that he was at the heart of a difficult situation. Perhaps you could unknot the mystery if – "

Holmes didn't look at me as he spoke. "My practice is closed," he said. I didn't know how final this statement was, and, I am ashamed to say, I was too scared to ask for clarification. If Sherlock Holmes were to relinquish his role as our city's greatest consulting detective, then I feared that he would relinquish his very purpose for living.

"It is time for me to go," he said, standing. "I have an appointment at Mycroft's and I don't wish to be late."

"I insist on joining you," I said firmly.

Holmes shrugged, and I followed him out of our flat and into the very same brougham that had just brought me from Pall Mall.

"Who are we meeting?" I asked in the cab.

Holmes seemed to consider for a few seconds, and I was rather hurt by his secretive attitude. I had become accustomed to accompanying him on his various adventures, and he was rarely so circumspect when discussing them with me.

"Madelina Grace," he said in a low voice, then turned his head to look out of the window. The golden shimmer of twilight silhouetted Holmes so I couldn't see his facial expression clearly, but I judged that he was waiting for my response.

"Grace," I muttered, searching the corners of my mind for the familiar name. When it came to me, I understood Holmes's reticence. "Madelina Grace – the *spiritualist*?"

The fashion for séances had swept through London in recent months, and Madelina Grace had gained renown as one of its eminent practitioners. While previously it had been considered a music hall frivolity – and, indeed, Miss Grace had begun her career on the stage – these supernatural visitations had lately become commonplace, even in the higher echelons of society. But for Sherlock Holmes to employ the services of a spiritualist! The man for whom the only truth was irrefutable fact. It was preposterous.

"Holmes," I said, barely suppressing my surprise, "surely you don't believe in such things. Why, you've told me yourself that – "

"I am aware of my previous statements," he snapped back. "I never discounted all possibility of the supernatural. Simply, I am yet to be convinced."

I didn't press him on the matter. It was distressing, however, to witness such a *volte-face* from my friend. Why, he had even mocked me at times for my more romantic attitude to the unexplained. Now here he was, looking to a medium for comfort, hoping to make contact with the brother who had hanged himself. For the first time since we had met, I felt pity for Holmes.

"Miss Grace comes well recommended?" I asked, attempting to sound neutral.

"She helped Eric Grisham after his wife passed."

Grisham lived in Baker Street, just a few doors down from 221. He was an amiable fellow, a solicitor whom Holmes had assisted after a recent burglary at his home. I remembered that Grisham's wife had succumbed to cancer a few months prior, which is why he was so devastated by the theft of her portrait. Thankfully, Holmes had managed to track the painting down to a Highbury auction house of dubious morals and return it to its rightful owner.

"Miss Grace seems well regarded among Grisham's circle," Holmes explained. "And he said that he felt a closeness to his wife during the séance that couldn't be refuted. Miss Grace knew things about the late Mrs. Grisham that could never have been learned elsewhere."

"I see," I said, keen to choose my words carefully. "You believe she may be able to make contact with . . . *the other side*?"

"Consider it an experiment," Holmes said, perhaps trying to justify his actions to himself rather than to me. "If she can open up the channels of communication between Mycroft and myself, of all people, then that is the greatest proof of her gift."

It was difficult to argue with Holmes's logic. My fear, of course, was that Miss Grace would *not* be able to bring Mycroft back – and this would have an even more devastating effect upon my friend.

It was dark by the time we reached Mycroft's Pall Mall apartment. The place was unnervingly quiet, and Holmes told me that the housekeeper had left to stay with her sister's family. "We have the place to ourselves. Come, we must prepare."

As we entered the dining room, I was relieved to see that it was clean and well-furnished, quite unlike the rather depressing chamber where Mycroft had died. We carried four wooden chairs through to that shabby lounge-cum-library and arranged them in a circle around a card table that we had retrieved from the drawing room.

"Who are the chairs for?" I asked.

"You, me, Miss Grace."

"And the fourth? Is someone else joining us?"

He paused, bashful, his voice low. "And Mycroft."

"Mycroft?"

"Those are Miss Grace's instructions," he said, picking up some of the papers that he had scattered on our previous visit, and keen not to catch my eye.

The doorbell rang and Holmes went to let Madelina Grace inside. I looked around the room and shivered. If the lady was able to bring back the deceased, then all I knew about life and death was about to be altered permanently. If she was a charlatan, however, then my friend was likely to sink deeper into his malaise. Smythe's words ran through my mind of how Mycroft hadn't recovered from his terrible discovery – that he was, indeed, fallible.

"No, no, no," Madelina Grace said as I stood to greet her. "This won't do at all." Her accent was refined, with the merest hint of a West Country twang. She didn't match my image of a medium at all. She was a handsome woman, no older than thirty, with thick dark hair sweeping down her back. Her dress was a deep blue, elegant but unfussy, and her eyes had a frankness that I hadn't expected. She carried a large cloth bag which she placed upon one of the chairs. From this bag, she pulled out a thick scarlet tablecloth, which she threw over the card table. Then she retrieved six long red candles on brass stands. She placed these about the room and lit them, then she turned off the gaslights. She looked at the open curtains and snorted.

"There must be no outside influences," she said as she pulled the curtains tightly closed, shutting out the muted glare of the streetlamps. "There are no servants in the house?"

240

"The housekeeper has been sent away, as promised," Holmes said.

"Excellent. The lines of celestial communication are brittle, and we don't wish them disturbed."

Lit only by candles, the room felt oppressively murky, even sadder than it had in the cold daylight after Mycroft's funeral. I couldn't prevent myself from looking up at the chandelier. It appeared to move now – an optical illusion created by the six dancing flames.

"No," she said, to herself rather than to us. She looked around the dark room. "This isn't conducive to . . . ." She opened the door and stepped back out into the hallway.

"Mycroft," she called. "Mycroft!" I looked at Holmes, but he remained impassive as we heard Madelina Grace pace up and down the hallway, repeating the name of his late brother, before re-entering the room.

"Yes," she said, "I sense his approach." She smiled knowingly, then nodded to us to sit down.

Holmes took the chair nearest the door, and I sat to his right. Miss Grace was next to me in that circle, leaving an empty chair between her and Holmes. She pulled her bag off this remaining seat and placed it on the floor. She looked at the empty chair a moment, then at the candles.

I glanced at Holmes, and I noticed an eyebrow cocked. I was relieved that he was as bemused as I was in that moment. Miss Grace stood up and busied herself adjusting the placement of the candles.

"This room," she said in a hushed voice. "It is where Mycroft spent most of his time?"

"When at home, yes," said Holmes.

"And it is where he passed over to the other side?"

"Yes," Holmes said quietly. I noticed his eyes flash upwards at the chandelier.

"Very well," she nodded, satisfied that the candles were positioned correctly. "We shall begin."

Miss Grace sat down again and took a deep breath. She closed her eyes and reached her hands out. I took her left hand, while Holmes had to reach out across the empty chair in order to take her right.

"That's it," she said kindly. "This way we will connect with Mycroft, *through* Mycroft. Now, close your eyes, gentlemen, and let us breathe together."

I saw Holmes do as she asked, then I followed suit. Following her rhythm, I inhaled and exhaled deeply and attempted to empty my mind of cynical thoughts. I owed it to my dear friend to at least show respect for this ritual as Madelina Grace began her incantations.

In the darkness, the candlelight shimmering through my eyelids, I felt a strange calm. Miss Grace's voice was deep and soothing, almost hypnotic as she muttered in a haunting monotone. The warmth of the room added to my drowsiness as my mind began to drift, my misgivings and suspicions melting away.

Suddenly, I heard the scrape of a chair moving on the wooden floor. Instinctively, I opened an eye, and I could swear that I saw the empty seat moving of its own accord.

"Close your eyes," Miss Grace chided me softly, and I complied at once. She returned to her whispered chant, gripping my hand tightly as her voice drifted away into silence.

I dared not open my eyes again, yet I felt certain that something bizarre was happening, a ghostly fog sweeping through the room and through my brain.

The door! It opened, then slammed shut!

I couldn't help it. My eyelids parted, and I saw that Miss Grace's stare was upon me. Her eyes seemed to be glazed over, though, looking not at me but *through* me. Then she looked up, at the ceiling and the iron chandelier.

"Mycroft Holmes!" she called. "Mycroft, I know you are there!"

Holmes had opened his eyes too, our hands still linked to hers.

"Mycroft! Your brother and his friend are here." She breathed deeply through her nose, her nostrils flaring with passion. "Yes! Yes! Come to me, Mycroft, follow my voice."

From above us, there was a loud thud.

"Yes, Mycroft," she said, a weird smile on her lips. "You are safe with us. We shall not harm you. Sherlock is here. He wishes to speak to you."

There was another heavy thud, and the chandelier shook slightly.

"I understand," Miss Grace called out. "It is painful for you, here at the scene of your passing."

Holmes's eyes were wide, just as uncertain as I was.

"You wish to speak?" She waited for a response. After a few seconds, there were two bangs from the chandelier. "Two knocks for yes. I understand. One knock for no."

A pause, then two thuds again.

"Yes. Is there anything you wish to tell Sherlock?"

Bang, bang. *Yes.*

"Sherlock," she said kindly. "What do you want to ask your brother? He is with us, but his voice is weak. He hasn't yet completed the metamorphosis to his phantom self."

"Mycroft," Holmes gasped, his voice dry. "I need to know that it is you." He looked to Miss Grace, who nodded. Then he turned his attention above, to the chandelier. "How many trees were in our garden when we grew up?"

Bang! Bang!

Holmes's expression remained blank.

A third bang shuddered through the house, even louder.

Holmes's lips parted, moved by this cosmic connection.

"Three trees," Miss Grace cried out. Then her voice became hushed, croaking. "Three trees, Sherlock. How we liked to climb them!"

Holmes and I looked at her, stunned. His expression softened. "Yes, Mycroft, we did, we did."

Two more gentle thuds emanated from the ceiling.

My pulse was racing, but I still felt uneasy. Surely, this wasn't happening. Surely, Mycroft Holmes hadn't returned from the dead.

"Remember mother scolding us when we got our best clothes dirty." It was Miss Grace again, her eyes rolled back in her head. Her voice was distant, quiet, as she channelled Mycroft. We leaned forward to hear her.

"She made us wash our garments ourselves," Holmes added. "But you would always help me, of course, big brother." He glanced at Miss Grace, and I fancied that perhaps he was testing her.

"No!" Mycroft's voice said firmly through Miss Grace. "No!"

"That is correct, Mycroft," Holmes replied with a wistful smile. It seemed that our medium had passed his test. "You are right. You would pay me a ha'penny to clean yours too."

"Yes, I remember, Sherlock," Miss Grace rasped, her eyes still rolled back. "Sherlock . . . ."

"Why did you do it, Mycroft?" Holmes's face was serious, looking at the empty chair. "Tell me why."

The weird voice came again from Madelina Grace, hoarse and low as if from deep inside. "The answer is in my papers."

"What papers?"

It pained me to see Holmes so helpless, so desperate for answers. I was accustomed to him being in possession of all the solutions, but here he was like a frightened child, searching for comfort.

"My personal papers . . . ." That strange voice said again. "My most precious belongings."

"Your attaché case?"

"Yes." Miss Grace paused then sucked in some air, her eyes still distant. "Is it safe?"

"Do not fear," said Holmes. "I deposited it in your security box, at the bank. All of your documents are quite secure."

243

"No!" said the voice emanating from the spiritualist. "You must move it. They will find it!"

Holmes was worried. "What do you mean? Who?"

"Move it!"

"Mycroft," Holmes implored. "Who is after your papers?"

"So many secrets . . . *Danger!*"

"Don't worry, Mycroft."

"Not the bank!" Miss Grace's expression was panicked now. The empty chair fell suddenly, and I couldn't contain a gasp. The lady's face was contorted now, in terrible pain. "Not the bank! They have contacts there!"

Holmes was anxious to calm her – or, more correctly, to calm Mycroft.

"Don't fear, my dear brother!"

"Move it!"

"I will move it then," Holmes said quickly. "I will give it to your government colleagues."

Another thud from above us. *No.*

"I don't understand," Holmes protested.

"Not the office!" Miss Grace screeched. "It's too dangerous."

"Where, then, Mycroft? Where shall I keep it?"

He looked to Miss Grace, hoping for a response. She was squirming on her chair, in agony, like she was trying to strain loose from invisible bonds.

"Keep it somewhere close," she gasped. "Trust no one . . . Trust no one."

"I will," Holmes said.

A last scream came from Miss Grace's throat, before it cut out completely. Her entire body went limp then crumpled to the floor.

"Good God!" I called as I went to help her.

Holmes shot up from his chair. He ran to the window, flinging open the curtains then unlatching the window. The candles flickered as the chill evening breeze swept through the room. He stayed there a second, staring into the night, as if in a trance. He raised a finger to the windowpane and traced a small circle.

"Holmes!" I blurted. "Get her some water."

This roused Holmes from his strange state. He shook his head, like waking from a bad dream, and dashed out of the room.

I cradled Madelina Grace's head and whispered. "Miss Grace, are you quite alright?"

Holmes returned with a glass of water in one hand and a bottle of whisky in the other. I placed the water to the lady's lips and she sipped lightly. Her eyes flickered open.

"Miss Grace. Can you hear me?"

She looked around the room and I nodded to Holmes, who flicked a gaslight into life then extinguished the candles. He grimaced as some of the hot red wax dripped on his fingers.

"What happened?" the lady asked groggily.

"You are safe," I said. "Do you know where you are?"

"Mycroft!" she yelped. "He was . . . *with us*?"

"Yes, Miss Grace. He was here," said Holmes.

"I don't remember." She shook her head briskly, struggling to think. "What did he say?"

Holmes and I helped Madelina Grace off the hardwood floor and into the threadbare armchair. She gulped for air, then took the glass of whisky that Holmes had poured and downed it in one gulp.

"It isn't important what he said," Holmes replied at last. "It's only important that you brought him back to us."

Miss Grace smiled at this. "The great void was wide this evening," she said. "Such a long way to travel. We should try again soon. I sense that Mycroft has more to say."

Holmes smiled wistfully as Miss Grace collected her belongings and left.

In the cab home, I attempted to converse with Holmes, but he was deep in thought again. It was only when we were close to Baker Street that he spoke.

"Watson, you wanted to tell me something this evening, before we went to Mycroft's."

"Well, yes," I said, surprised. It seemed such a long time now since my talk with Smythe, but I relayed what the civil servant had told me at the Diogenes Club. "It may be," I concluded carefully, "that Mycroft felt responsible for the ring's disappearance."

"This is a most interesting development," muttered Holmes, before returning to his introspection. He stared out of the window, rubbing the dried red candlewax between his fingers.

"Good night," he said as we entered our flat, and he went into his room at once.

I had hoped that, at the very least, the séance might have brought Holmes some succour – or perhaps my news from Smythe might have fired up his analytical instincts. On the contrary, over the following days, Holmes was as distant as he had been immediately after Mycroft's death.

He remained in his room, apart from an occasional evening walk, his depressed demeanour amplified by his unshaven face and shabby clothing – as if he had given up on presenting even a façade of basic civility. He refused my requests to join him, insisting that he wished to be alone with his thoughts.

Then, on the Saturday evening, he entered the living room as I read the newspaper.

"Watson, would you care to join me tonight?"

"Of course," I said, happily. "In what?"

"In another séance."

I couldn't hide my disappointment. I was worried that this new-found interest in the occult may have been developing into an unhealthy obsession.

"At Mycroft's?" I asked, hesitantly.

"No," Holmes said. "Here."

I was uneasy at the prospect, and not only out of concern for my friend. For all my initial cynicism, our experience on Pall Mall had rather shaken me. Through our many battles against some of the most villainous men in the country, I always felt that I could equal any of them in a violent struggle. But when facing forces of the supernatural, we are all utterly disempowered. I couldn't neglect my friend, though, and I was glad, at least, that he wished me by his side in this strange endeavour.

"Certainly, I will help in any way I can."

"Splendid!" There was a spark of energy in Holmes now. He clapped his hands together and began preparing the lounge just as we had at Mycroft's: Four chairs around a card table, and six long candles dotted about the room. "It seems only fair to provide our own candles this time," he said.

When satisfied that everything was ready, Holmes checked his watch. As I was pouring us some brandy, the bell rang, and Holmes spoke. "Would you mind? Mrs. Hudson is out for the evening."

I let Miss Grace inside and went to help her with her bag. Instead, she handed her heavy fur coat to me without a word, as if I were the maid. She looked around the hallway, motioning me to be quiet. She peered upstairs and took a deep breath, taking in her surroundings.

"Yes," she said with an enigmatic smile. "Yes. I sense that Mycroft is much nearer. He must have cared deeply for his brother."

I led her up to the sitting room, where Holmes welcomed her warmly. Miss Grace held him close, and I was surprised to see my friend allow such intimacy.

"You are in much pain," she said as she stepped away, her eyes fixed on his face. "Mycroft knows this. We will try to contact him more directly this evening."

Holmes nodded, and at last I understood what had made me feel so discombobulated by the arrival of Miss Grace into our lives. Holmes was allowing another person to lead him, to tell him what to do. There was something pathetic, almost childlike in his manner, as if he were a little boy appealing for his teacher's approval. Through my work I am no stranger to grief, of course, and I have often seen it induce this infantilising effect. My mind drifted back to Afghanistan, where the most common scream of the dying soldier was, "Mother!"

"I hope that you're satisfied with our preparations," Holmes said, motioning to the table, the chairs, the candles, all positioned with great care.

Miss Grace gave a barely perceptible start.

"No!"

"I'm sorry, Miss Grace," Holmes said.

"The candles – ?"

"I placed them just as you did at Mycroft's."

"But they haven't been purified." As she said this, she retrieved her own long red candles from her bag. "These were blessed by a medicine man from the deserts of Jalisco." She put her candles in place, lighting them one by one. Holmes said nothing, content to demur to her every demand.

Miss Grace threw her thick red cloth over the table, and we all sat in the same positions as before. We linked hands, then she closed her eyes and took in a deep breath. Holmes and I followed her lead, and I immediately felt that soothing sensation again, as my heart slowed and my body tingled with expectation.

The lady broke from her low chant to call out. "Mycroft Holmes! Mycroft, are you there?"

Just like at the Pall Mall flat, there were two heavy bangs from somewhere in the house. *Yes.*

My eyes opened.

"Mycroft," called Holmes.

"Sherlock, no," she said urgently. "We must wait until he is ready."

But Holmes was too anxious to wait. "Mycroft, was it the missing ring that drove you to despair?"

Two knocks.

"Yes," Miss Grace said, her eyes becoming misty, and her voice deeper, more masculine. "The ring."

"Do you have any idea who took it?" Holmes asked.

Knock, knock.

"You do? Who?"

There was a long silence. Then Mycroft spoke through Miss Grace, her voice turning disarmingly deep and hoarse. "My colleague – "

"Your colleague? Who?"

There was a pause, then the spiritualist finally whispered in Mycroft's voice: "Smith."

"Smythe!" I blurted, unable to restrain myself.

Miss Grace's body spasmed grotesquely. "Smythe!" she seethed. "That traitor!" There were more thuds from the walls and the ceiling. The ghost – and there was no other word for it now – was becoming wilder, frenzied, trying to break through the great divide, back to our physical realm.

My mind raced, terrified by the violence of Mycroft's spirit and desperate to make sense of this revelation. I tried to deduce why Smythe would have talked so openly to me at the Diogenes. Surely it would be in his interest to distance himself from Mycroft's death entirely – Unless, of course, his plan was to deliberately mislead me. I cursed myself for my gullibility. He would have been certain that Holmes would be on the case soon enough, and he knew that I would talk to my companion. So Smythe had been using me to set Holmes on the wrong trail!

Madelina Grace yelled, louder and more hysterical, her eyes still distant. Beneath her terrible screams, the bangs and scrapes continued, as if the whole house were coming alive. She writhed in her seat, ever more violently, and I was compelled to hold her for fear that she may injure herself. Holmes sat motionless, stunned, perhaps, by this revelation of betrayal within the corridors of Whitehall.

Finally, Miss Grace stopped screaming. Her breathing levelled and her spasms ceased. She was limp now, slumped back in her chair like a ragdoll.

The terrible noises from the ceiling ceased too. The silence felt almost as stifling as the mad terror of seconds earlier.

Madelina Grace looked up at me, and her eyes flickered with recognition, revived from her catatonia.

"Mycroft has passed back to the spirit realm," she said through short, quick breaths, her voice her own again.

I nodded and helped her to sit upright. I noticed that Holmes was snuffing out the candles, his back to us. I fancied that he needed some time to gather his thoughts. He opened the window to let some air inside, placing his hand on the glass again, just as he had at Mycroft's flat. Then he poured our guest some water.

248

The cool night air was a welcome tonic, and I felt my heartbeat return to its normal speed.

Then my blood ran cold.

Footsteps!

Yes, it was definitely the sound of footsteps, heavy and slow, coming down the stairs. Yet there was no one else at home. Mrs. Hudson had gone out for the evening.

The steps were distant at first, then closer.

Louder and louder.

"Holmes!" I gasped, but he remained unmoved.

The door handle began to turn!

We were all frozen, unable to move or speak. For a few seconds, the world stood still.

Finally, the door creaked open.

A man entered the room.

In my many exploits with Sherlock Holmes, I'm not sure that I had ever felt as stunned as I did in that moment.

Standing before us in the doorway, just a few feet away from me, was a ghost –

The spectral form of Mycroft Holmes!

I believe that I may have yelped with shock, but that was nothing to the reaction of Madelina Grace, who gave a shrill scream quite unlike those deeper, guttural cries of moments prior.

"No!" Her eyes were wide with horror. "It can't be! You're – You're *dead!*"

Mycroft's apparition gave a wry smile. "I thought that was rather the point."

At that, Madelina Grace fainted.

By the time that the spiritualist came round, she had been joined on the sofa by her accomplice, a man whom Mycroft had dragged downstairs with him – a wiry, pinch-faced fellow dressed in a black leotard, such as might be worn by the circus acrobat. He snarled and writhed, but Mycroft had bound his hands tightly with rope and stuffed a handkerchief in his mouth.

"Now, Miss Grace," Holmes said, not without kindness. "You see that the game is up, so your best course of action is to explain all. If you play fair with us, then we will strive to be fair with you and your nimble-footed friend here."

Madelina Grace merely snorted haughtily.

"Very well," Holmes said. "In that case, Mycroft and I will relay what we know, and you may feel free to correct us on any point of error."

I poured some scotch for the Holmes brothers and myself, feeling a chill from the open window. "Do you mind if I close the window, Holmes?"

"In a few minutes," he said. "When the peyote fumes have quite subsided."

Miss Grace and her companion started at this.

"I am correct?" said Holmes, evidently pleased with himself. "It is definitely from the cactus family. I found traces of it in your candles during our last encounter." I remembered back at Pall Mall, when some of the candlewax had burned Holmes's fingers. "Peyote is found in the deserts of Mexico, I understand. Highly hallucinogenic when digested, but still potent even when breathed in. I presume that it helps your clients become more receptive to your little tricks, Miss Grace."

I sat down with the two Holmeses at the card table and handed them the whisky. Madelina Grace and her partner remained silent spectators on the low sofa. On the table was the black leather satchel that Mycroft had been holding when he had appeared so dramatically at our door, a bag that he had retrieved in the struggle upstairs with the burglar.

"Watson," Sherlock Holmes said. "I apologise for my strange behaviour in recent days."

"And I apologise for my death," added Mycroft drily.

"You both made a fool of me!" I blasted. "Why on earth did you not confide in me in the first place?"

"It had to be utterly convincing," Mycroft shrugged, "for all parties."

"But why the ruse at all?" I asked, unsatisfied by his explanation.

Holmes looked to his brother, who nodded.

"I believe it is safe to share the story just between these walls," said Mycroft. He motioned to the couple on the sofa. "And those two already know enough." He took a metal case from his pocket and offered me a cigar. He snipped the ends off as he began his tale. "It all began with the death of Stanley-Johns then the disappearance of the ring. I take it that Smythe told you – "

"Yes. Smythe," I confirmed, lighting my cigar. "And now I hear that he betrayed you."

"He did nothing of the sort," Mycroft laughed.

"She said that he – "

"She said that "Smith" took the ring," said Holmes. "The most common name in London. Then you corrected her."

"Yes, because . . . ." I felt my face redden as the truth dawned on me. I had fallen for the most elementary trick. Miss Grace hadn't told me the name. Rather, I had told her!

"All that Smythe said was true," Mycroft explained. "I'll have to have words with him about his lack of discretion. That infernal ring could have caused civil war in the errant princess's home country, and considerable embarrassment to our own Royal Family. However, Lord Stanley-Johns' death was, I believe, a terrible accident. The agents of revolution wouldn't rely upon a child to carry out their crimes. They are far more clinical than that."

"So what happened to the ring?" I asked. "It was in Stanley-Johns' safe, was it not?"

"It was," Mycroft said, and the mischievous twinkle in his eye had disappeared. "That was my gravest error. I shouldn't have left it there. Lady Stanley-Johns is an intelligent woman, but she was in mourning. Those in grief are prone to acts of desperation."

"Such as employing a medium to try to bring their loved one back," I said.

"Precisely," said Mycroft. "Among the trusted well-wishers she permitted into her home, she also invited Miss Grace. She only told me afterwards, unfortunately, when it was too late." Mycroft sighed and shook his head self-reproachfully. "The poor woman is beside herself."

His brother continued the story. "Mycroft told me about the ring disappearing after a séance, and I remembered the case of our neighbour, Eric Grisham. He too had employed a medium after his wife had passed away, and he too was the victim of a robbery soon afterwards. Some discreet enquiries suggested a pattern: Wherever Madelina Grace goes, a theft soon follows."

"Then why not arrest her at once? If it were of national importance . . . ."

"Because we had no proof of any wrongdoing," Mycroft said, "and any arrest would lead only to denials. We needed indisputable evidence of a crime. Unfortunately, as these two only prey upon the bereaved, then we also needed a death."

Mycroft gave a little bow to our captives. Both Holmes brothers had clearly enjoyed their little game.

"Was the funeral really necessary?" I asked. "The Prime Minister was there!"

"It needed to appear completely authentic," explained Mycroft. "Miss Grace clearly does her research, so everything had to seem real – the death notice, the obituaries, the funeral itself. Any hint that I was not actually dead, and the game was up for us."

"Did the Prime Minister know the truth?"

"Good Lord! Absolutely not. He's even more indiscreet than Smythe!"

251

Sherlock Holmes laughed. "You will have some explaining to do at the office on Monday, Mycroft." Then he trained his detective's gaze trained upon our captive spiritualist.

"You use your position to gain information from the mourners, Miss Grace, and you try to manipulate them to do your bidding, just as you tried with me. You insisted I retrieve Mycroft's private papers from the bank and keep them close to me, in my bedroom. This would make it ever so much easier for your friend here to find them upstairs as we were distracted by your performance down here."

"There is one thing," I said. "Did she know just how important that ring was, in Stanley-Johns' house?"

Miss Grace shook her head.

"It seems that our medium is a mere opportunist," Sherlock Holmes said. "The ring would have been a welcome surprise, I fancy. But anyone would have known that Stanley-Johns' safe held a great many secrets, and would be worth a large sum of money to the right bidder."

"As would my own papers," Mycroft added, with a touch of conceit.

"How does she do it?" I asked.

"She establishes trust to convince the victim that their loved one is speaking through her," Holmes explained. "It is just a matter of suggestion. The number of trees in our childhood garden, for example."

I remembered how the "ghost" had knocked three times for three trees. "How could she ever have known?" I asked.

"She did not. It is a simple music hall trick. Knock once, then wait. Then again and again, until the victim's expression alters. And there you have your answer! Am I right, Miss Grace?" Her eyes conveyed the fact that he was, indeed, correct.

"There were actually twelve trees in our garden," Holmes added with a grin. "But that would have taken much too long, and your friend here might have grown tired."

The man in the leotard spat an epithet through his gag. Holmes sighed.

I was replaying the previous séance in my mind. "But she knew about you climbing those trees when you were children, and dirtying your clothes."

"What young boys haven't climbed a tree in their garden?" Holmes said in response. "She posited the idea, and as soon as I concurred, she added small details and studied my reactions to confirm or deny them. Any mistake, of course, could be blamed on the weak signal across the astral plain, or some such nonsense." He emitted an empty laugh. "Once she has gained a victim's trust, then it is an easy task to elicit information – about their most treasured possession, for example: The whereabouts of a hidden safe, or its combination." On this last word, he looked accusingly at the lady, whose eyes remained fixed on her feet.

"It's obscene," I said, imagining the suffering the crime must cause its victims.

Holmes remained impassive as he spoke to our two captives. "I take it your insistence on closing the curtains was the signal for your friend to scale the wall and climb into an upstairs window." Holmes looked at the gentleman sitting next to Madelina Grace and nodded. "Dezzy Conway, if I'm not mistaken."

The man's eyes widened with shock.

"Yes," continued Holmes. "I have admired your work from afar, Mr. Conway, and I was hoping that our paths would cross soon. The theft of Grisham's portrait on this very street, of course. Then the Letts robbery, and that unfortunate incident at the British Museum this April. They each had the mark of a burglar possessed of theatrical training – the disguises, the sleight of hand, the subterfuge."

Dezzy Conway groaned through his gag, his eyes revealing the question he wished to ask.

"How did I know it was you?" Holmes said coolly. "Simple deduction. On suspecting a showman of those crimes, I perused the programme of every theatre and circus in London, acquainting myself with the acrobats and tumblers. I could discount anyone performing on the night of a robbery, until my list of names dwindled down to one. Those burglaries all occurred on nights when you were *not* on the list of players. Then, when I realised in Pall Mall that Miss Grace was using a fleet-footed accomplice, I made further enquiries and discovered that in her music hall days, Miss Grace had often shared the bill with Dezzy Conway, the Human Spider! What's more, in my casual conversations with various stagehands in the guise of a workman for hire – "

"Your night-time walks!" I chuckled, remembering Holmes's haggard appearance on those few occasions when he left our flat in recent days.

"There is a great camaraderie among the backstage workers in the music hall district," Holmes said. "I discovered that Dezzy Conway had recently become engaged to none other than Madelina Grace. Congratulations to you both."

Conway's shoulders slumped, utterly defeated. Our prisoners' morose demeanours betrayed their guilt entirely. Holmes continued.

"And what better time than during a séance for someone to go clattering about a house without being apprehended. In fact, it only adds to the supernatural ambience." Holmes blew a ring of smoke into the air, evidently satisfied with his deductions.

"But he would knock 'yes' or 'no'," I recalled. "How did he know when?" Conway would have been upstairs both at Pall Mall and here, the ceiling and oakwood floorboards separating him from us.

"When Miss Grace was so insistent on closing the windows and curtains at Mycroft's flat, I became suspicious. You'll remember when she fainted that I took the chance to open the window immediately. That was because I suspected some narcotic in those candles, but it's also when I saw a small circle on the glass."

Mycroft reached into that black bag on the table, and he pulled out an item that I recognised immediately: A doctor's stethoscope. The only difference from the one that I carried on my rounds was its extraordinarily long tube.

"He was listening through it when I caught him upstairs, the tube hanging out of the window," said Mycroft.

Holmes held the other end of the tube. "And this is what made the suction mark on the windowpane – both at Mycroft's and here this evening." He examined the bell of the stethoscope in his fingers, surrounded by a round rubber sucker. "He would attach it to the glass downstairs on his way up, enabling him to listen – helped, no doubt, by Miss Grace raising her voice at certain moments. Once I saw the mark at Pall Mall, I knew that Miss Grace had an accomplice upstairs. Her wish to hold another séance gave Mycroft and me the opportunity to act."

"The poor fellow got quite a shock when I emerged from a wardrobe, Sherlock," Mycroft said, amused by the recollection.

Now that it was explained to me, Grace and Conway's scheme seemed so rudimentary, yet I had to admit that it was remarkably effective. To Lord Stanley-Johns' widow it must have had an even stronger influence, her judgement diminished by grief. My own bitter experience of loss told me just how vulnerable she must have been in that moment. A clever plan, then, but utterly wicked in the way that it preyed upon people at their most desperate.

Mycroft's expression hardened. He stood in front of the two captives, his great frame dwarfing them.

"Do you still have the ring?" he asked.

Madelina Grace stayed quiet, unable to meet his gaze, but Conway mumbled something through the handkerchief. Mycroft pulled the sodden square of silk out of his mouth.

"We've still got it!" he blurted desperately. "We haven't sold it yet."

"Take me to it at once," Mycroft said.

The pair nodded meekly, and Mycroft went to the window. He signalled to someone in the street and, within seconds, two large men entered the room, handcuffed the prisoners, and took them to a windowless carriage outside. Mycroft followed with a nod of gratitude to his brother.

Alone with Holmes, I struggled to meet his gaze. I was still stung by his lack of trust in me. I had worried so much about his mental state, but in return I had been hoodwinked.

"You are disappointed in me," said Holmes, once we had tidied away the card table and dining chairs.

I snorted my annoyance as I sat on the sofa and picked up my book. I was in no mood for conversation.

"I really am sorry," Holmes was contrite. "The most difficult part of this entire game was deceiving you."

"It was beneath you," I said, opening the novel.

"My dear Watson," Holmes said. "Evidently it was not. But it would have been beneath *you* to participate willingly in such a deception. I knew that you were too honest to play along convincingly. It was selfish of me, I know, but I wanted you alongside me on this adventure. The only way I could do that was to make you truly believe that I was pining for my brother."

"Your little act at Pall Mall – I feared for your sanity. I thought that . . . ." I couldn't finish, so upset was I by his behaviour.

Even Holmes was lost for words in that moment, an awkward silence enveloping the room.

My eyes were fixed upon the pages of the book, although my mind paid little heed to the words. I was thinking about what Holmes had said. He was right, I had to concede: I would never have been able to sustain such a deception over two evenings with Madelina Grace, regardless of the justifications. By duping me as Holmes had, then I was able to act as if I truly were taken in by the woman's trickery, emboldening her to continue her appalling charade.

"Pour me another Scotch," I said tersely. Holmes did as I requested, then he sat down in his armchair and emitted a plaintive sigh. He took his violin from its dusty case and, for the first time in weeks, he began to play.

I ventured a look at my friend now. The fire from the hearth was reflected in his keen eyes, and I noticed that the colour had returned to his cheeks. His shoulders seemed broader, and his movements more certain than they had been for days.

This evening, Mycroft Holmes had come back from the dead.

So, too, had his younger brother.

The Terror of
Trowbridge Wood
by Josh Cerefice

"'*Wolf-man Sighted in Wiltshire Town*,'" I read aloud across the breakfast table, shaking my head in incredulity. "Now I've heard it all!"

"Evidently the press hasn't lost its propensity for the sensational," replied my friend, Sherlock Holmes, in between mouthfuls of boiled egg. "Alas, it is fiction, not fact, that sells newspapers these days."

Before I had a chance to reply, Mrs. Hudson announced the arrival of a visitor. He was a slim, dark-haired man of about twenty-and-five with a navy-blue frock coat covering his slender shoulders, and an expression of weary despair hewn upon his haggard face. It didn't take a person of Holmes's Delphic insight to discern that our guest was in a state of considerable disquietude.

"I apologize for disturbing your breakfast, gentlemen," said he, "but I've come here on account of a most grave matter."

Holmes laid down his knife and fork. "We have just finished our meals anyway," he said, rising from the dining table and inviting our guest to take a seat by the fire. My friend then occupied the chair opposite him and regarded the gentleman with a look of attentive curiosity. "Now, this 'grave matter' of which you speak – no doubt you're referring to your father's death. That's the reason why you've travelled all the way here from Trowbridge, isn't it, Mr. Villiers?"

A look of puzzled astonishment passed over the man's face. "But I've never met you before, Mr. Holmes! How can you possibly know all this about me?"

"It's really quite simple," Holmes explained. "In your left breast pocket is a folded-up train ticket, upon which I can make out the words '*From Trow to Padd*' above the material of your jacket. "'*Padd*' must be Paddington Station, for London is your destination. As for '*Trow*', the departure and arrival times printed on the top-left corner of the paper tell me that your passage was precisely an hour-and-fifty-two minutes, a length of time which corresponds to the distance between here and Trowbridge. Therefore, I judged it likely that you'd hailed from there."

"And my name?"

"You bear a striking resemblance to Harold Villiers, the wealthy industrialist whose face has adorned the pages of *The Times* by virtue of

256

his recent death." He pointed at the man's sleeves. "What's more, your cufflinks are inscribed with the initials '*J.V.*', which served to substantiate my theory."

"You are correct on all scores, Mr. Holmes," he said, clearly impressed by my friend's powers of ratiocination. "My name is James Villiers, the son of the man of whom you've just spoken, and whose murder has caused me to call upon you this morning."

"I'm sorry for your loss," I offered. "I know all too well what it's like to lose a loved one."

Villiers gave a grateful nod.

Holmes, however, was more concerned with facts than feelings. "Fortunately, the morning columns have already provided me with the most salient details of the case," he said, picking up the paper from the table beside him and reading thusly:

> *At eight o'clock on Sunday night, the body of a man was discovered by a pair of local ramblers in a woodland on the outskirts of Trowbridge. Police shortly arrived at the scene and identified the victim as textile tycoon, Mr. Harold Villiers. A murder investigation has since been launched by the Trowbridge Police, though the officer in charge, Inspector Forrester, has refused to divulge any further details until an arrest has been made.*

Holmes folded the paper and replaced it on the table. "Given your presence here, it would appear that the investigation hasn't yet borne fruit."

Villiers shook his head. "It hasn't stopped the local gossip-mongers from wagging their tongues, though," he said, looking rather vexed by it all.

"Usually, in the absence of answers, rumours are all the rifer," Holmes said sagely. "Incidentally, what is the nature of this tittle-tattle?"

"From what I've overheard, most of it relates to this . . . *wolf-man.*"

"That's curious – I was just reading about that before you arrived," I said. "It's a local legend, I understand?"

Villiers nodded. "According to the tales, it has the body of a man and the face of a wolf and roams the local woods," he said. "The newspapers have dubbed it *The Terror of Trowbridge Wood.*"

"I'm a man of science, not superstition," Holmes declared. "As such, I firmly believe that whomever is responsible for your father's murder isn't half, but wholly, human." He folded his legs. "Speaking of which, did your

257

father have any enemies at all? Anyone who would wish him harm? Think hard, Mr. Villiers. This could be crucial."

"Not that I'm aware of," he said after a pensive pause. "My father was respected by everyone who knew him – in business and life."

"Is that so?"

"I realize it isn't much to go on . . . ."

"Admittedly, I'll need more data than that if I'm to find your father's killer."

"You'll help me then?"

Holmes nodded. "I have nothing else presently occupying my time, so I'll be happy to offer my assistance."

"Thank you, Mr. Holmes," he said with a grateful bow of the head.

Holmes rose to his feet. "Watson and I will accompany you on the next train to Trowbridge. You go ahead. We'll meet you at Paddington at one-thirty. Oh, and I almost forgot!" He fetched a pen and paper from the desk and passed it to Villiers. "I'll need the address of the police station so I can wire ahead to inform Inspector Forrester of our arrival." Villiers scribbled it down and handed the note back to Holmes. "Thank you. We shall see you shortly.

When our client had gone, Holmes turned to me and said, "We ought to pack a case of spare clothes, Watson – there's no telling how long we'll be away. Oh, and bring your revolver. I have a feeling you'll need it."

After a scenic train journey through the beautiful Wiltshire countryside – the verdant river valleys and cloudless periwinkle skies were a welcome change from the dimly-lit alleyways and deadly pea-soupers of London – we arrived at our destination shortly before half-past-three. It was on the platform that we parted company with Villiers. Despite Holmes's further questions, he hadn't provided any useful information during the journey down from London. As we separated, we promised to keep him informed of any news relating to the investigation. Then we hailed a brougham into Trowbridge, where we booked a room for the night at a quiet little taphouse. It was there that we deposited our luggage before heading across town to the local police station, an unassuming, red-bricked building which looked more like a luxury abode than a bastion of law and order.

"We're here to see Inspector Forrester," said my friend to a surly-faced desk sergeant who was busy scribbling away. "I'm Sherlock Holmes, and this is my friend and associate, Doctor Watson."

The sedulous sergeant stopped writing and lifted his head. "Have you made an appointment?"

"I wired ahead this morning to inform the inspector of our arrival."

258

He began riffling through some documents, doubtless searching for Holmes's telegram. Then, seemingly satisfied that we weren't imposters, he said, "Down the hall, up the stairs, second door on the left."

Leaving the sergeant to his clerical duties, we followed his directions until we came to the office of "*Inspector N. Forrester*", whose name was etched upon the frosted glass. Holmes knocked, and a booming voice from the other side of the door bade us to enter. Crossing the threshold, we stepped into a spacious, wood-panelled room lined with bureaus and bookshelves on which piles of papers were perilously perched. In the centre of the room, hunched over a mahogany escritoire in front of a sash window that looked out upon the rooftops of Trowbridge, sat a large lion of a man in his mid-thirties with a mane of sandy hair, a round, ruddy face, and a walrus moustache.

"Ah! Mr. Holmes, Doctor Watson! Good afternoon to you," he said, leaning across the desk to proffer a chubby hand. "Your journey here was a pleasant one, I trust? Ah, splendid! I'm glad to hear it." He waved us into a pair of straight-backed chairs. "Before we begin, I'd like to thank you once again for coming. I don't usually consult with members of the public, but I couldn't well turn down the opportunity to work alongside the great Sherlock Holmes now, could I?"

"I certainly hope I can be a useful ally," said my friend.

"Of that I have no doubt! Now, to business." He ran a finger through his moustache. "As you're probably already aware, on Sunday evening – around eight-thirty – the body of Harold Villiers was discovered in the wood near the Pendleforth Estate by a Mr. and Mrs. Mulvahill, who chanced upon the corpse while they were enjoying an evening stroll. The area isn't too difficult to reach, as there is something of a clearing there, and it's occasionally used by picnickers, although this was a bit late in the day for that. We're not sure why Villiers was there. His son hadn't seen him in several days, and his staff, consisting of just a man and wife, said he kept his own hours and didn't keep them informed of his schedule. We think that he may have arranged to meet someone there."

"Has the coroner's report been completed?" asked Holmes.

Forrester nodded. "Mr. Villiers perished at approximately seven o'clock on Sunday evening."

"I see," said my friend. "And are there any suspects at present?"

"There's the son," replied Forrester. "By all accounts, he stands to inherit a large sum of his father's fortune."

"Why, though, would he solicit Holmes's help if he was guilty?" I asked.

"It'd certainly be a risky plot," Forrester conceded. "Nonetheless, we mustn't discount him just yet."

259

"I agree," agreed Holmes. "And what about the couple who raised the alarm?"

"The Mulvahills. A neighbour saw them in their garden at seven – at the time of the murder."

"We can tentatively eliminate them from our list of suspects for now," Holmes said, "although we may revisit them if someone more likely isn't found. I understand from the newspaper that Villiers was married, but he and his wife are estranged, but still residing together. Have you spoken to her yet?"

"Other than notifying her about the murder on Sunday night," answered Forrester, "and having her identify the body, no I haven't. When I went back on Monday morning, the housekeeper told me that she'd left town very early to stay with her sister in Torquay. I've verified that she did go there, and also which train she used, but it still seems a bit suspicious to me."

"Indeed, it is," agreed Holmes. "Is there anything else we should know, Inspector?"

"As a matter of fact, there is." He reached into a drawer and pulled out a series of photographs, which he then lay flat on the desk in front of us. "These were taken at the location of the crime," he said, pointing to the first. "I felt that it was important to have the scene recorded."

"Excellent," murmured Holmes, rising to examine the images. I joined him.

"Good God!" I exclaimed, upon seeing the disfigured corpse of the elder Villiers sprawled out upon the blood-stained mud. "His face . . . it looks like a piece of butcher's meat!"

"Given the severity of the victim's facial injuries," Holmes surmised, "I'd surmise that a blunt, heavy object was used to strike the face several times with considerable force – but also something with an edge to it."

Forrester nodded in confirmation. "My men found a garden spade near the body while they were searching the area. It was covered in blood. It would account for both types of wounds."

Holmes then turned his attention to the second photograph, which depicted a trail of footprints in the mud. Forrester pointed to a white strip laid upon the ground near the prints. "My tape measure," he said. "The stride between each print is two-feet, nine-inches."

Holmes glanced up at him, impressed. "Good thinking, Inspector. Without a relative scale, determining the stride simply from photographs would have been impossible. It's clear that these footprints belong to a man of lofty stature with substantive stride length, which, incidentally, is comparable to my own – " He picked up a third photograph, with a close view of the footprint. " – and who walks with an uneven gait," He said it with the proficiency of a professor translating Mesopotamian cuneiform. "See here how the right foot has created a deeper impression than the left?" Forrester nodded. "It suggests that a greater amount of weight was borne on that leg, thereby explaining their lopsided bearing. Incidentally, there are some features of interest in the prints themselves that make them easily identifiable. See the unique shape of the sole, and these cracks and wear marks here and here?"

"Your reputation isn't unfounded, Mr. Holmes."

He waved the compliment away. "It's the simple application of reason, Inspector. Nothing more."

"The prints . . . Could they be the killer's, perhaps?"

"Given their proximity to the body, I believe it's a possibility." Holmes then began studying the final photographs. "Ah! More prints, I see!"

"We found these ones behind a tree about a thirty yards or so from the victim's body."

"Notice the size and shape of the feet?" Holmes said, hovering a finger over the photograph. "Also a man's, but different from the others – and quite a bit bigger."

"A witness?"

"Possibly," Holmes said, sliding the photographs across the table. Once Forrester had replaced them in the drawer, the conversation turned to the so-called "Terror of Trowbridge Wood".

"According to Mr. Villiers the younger," my friend said, "many of the townsfolk believe that his father was savaged by the wild beast."

"The people of Trowbridge have rather fertile imaginations," Forrester said. "It's all utter hogwash, of course. The story has been around for a while, obviously – something made up by the newspapers. Nothing but a local legend created to attract tourists to the town. The superintendent has even sent the occasional search party out to look for the damned thing! We're busy enough as it is, and he has us hunting down a creature that doesn't even exist! And then, when this murder occurred two days ago, the newspapers immediately attributed it to the beast."

"I don't suppose the hundred-pound reward provided by the local newspaper has helped matters either," I said, alluding to the "*Killer Wolf-Man!*" posters I had seen when we passed through the town. "I imagine that your office has been flooded with all manner of bogus reports during the past couple of days."

"You wouldn't believe how tall some of the tales are! In fact, just this morning, the local grocer walked into the station, claiming that the wolf-man has been stealing tinned food from his shop for months, and demanding that I do something about it." He heaved a weary sigh. "Some people will say almost anything to get their hands on the reward money, even if it means wasting valuable police time."

Holmes was eager to return to the matter at hand. "Was the victim carrying any personal effects?"

Forrester drew our attention to a small, velvet-lined box on the right-hand side of the table. "This was the only article we found about his person," he said, taking out a brown leather wallet.

"May I have a look?"

"Of course."

Holmes picked up the wallet. "Italian leather, not inexpensive, showing signs of age. It appears that Mr. Villiers, a man of considerable means, also had frugal habits. What's inside, I wonder?" He opened it up. "A business card for Trowbridge Textiles bearing the names *Harold Villiers and Charles Pendleforth, Owners.*" He turned to Forrester. "Didn't you say that Villiers's body was discovered near the Pendleforth Estate?" The inspector nodded. "And according to this, Pendleforth was the co-owner of the company," he said, slipping the card back into the wallet. "It may not be merely a coincidence."

"Do you think that Pendleforth could be involved?"

"We mustn't leap to conclusions before we have all the necessary data," Holmes advised. "However, I find it interesting that Villiers was murdered near the home of the man who happens to have been his business associate."

"The same thought occurred to me as well."

"Have you spoken to Pendleforth yet?"

"I went to see him yesterday, but he was out of town."

"We shall pay him a visit later today then," Holmes resolved. "What else, Inspector."

He reached back into the lined box and produced a silver wristwatch. "This was found on the ground near the body," he said, handing Holmes the timepiece. "Although it may have been dropped earlier by someone else, that seems to be too coincidental. Have a look."

Holmes inspected the object. "Despite a few scratches on the face, it's in adequate condition." He turned it over. "Hmm . . . The owner of this must have had expensive taste and, given its design, could belong to either a man or woman. You say it was found near the body? Was it Villiers's, I wonder?"

Forrester shook his head. "The man's son said his father never wore a watch, and there was no evidence on his wrist to contradict that. It's possible that it belonged to the killer and fell from his or her wrist when dealing the fatal blow." My friend handed the item back to the inspector, who put it away.

"Did a search of the dead man's home reveal anything of value?"

"At the time, I only made a cursory examination, but I saw nothing of immediate importance. For instance, there was no note fixing an appointment to meet in the wood where Villiers was murdered." Forrester crossed his arms. "What do you propose we do now, Mr. Holmes?"

"As I've said, we'll call upon Pendleforth, but later this afternoon. Before we do that, I should like to speak to the victim's wife. That'll be a good place to start, I think."

"An excellent idea," said Forrester. "Just before you arrived, I was informed that Mrs. Villiers has returned to Trowbridge."

Shortly afterwards, Holmes, the inspector and I were in the parlour of Georgina Villiers, a petite, freckle-faced woman in her early forties who didn't appear the least bit aggrieved by her husband's passing. On the contrary – she was a woman scorned.

"I suppose you're wondering why I'm not playing the part of the weeping widow?" she asked, and I noticed that she wasn't dressed in the customary mourning attire.

"It did cross my mind," replied Forrester, sipping on a cup of tea.

"Months ago," she explained, "I discovered that Harold had been spending time with ladies of the night – his trips to London weren't solely limited to 'business', it transpired – and I've been petitioning for a divorce ever since," she explained. "Frustratingly, however, the courts rejected it on the grounds of insufficient evidence."

"In a curious way, then, your husband's death has unshackled you from an unhappy marriage," Holmes said, finishing her thought.

"You could say that, yes."

"We spoke to James Villiers. He indicated that his father was respected by all, in every aspect of his life."

The woman shook her head. "My step-son is naïve, and in spite of living in the same town, he and his father really didn't have much to do with one another. Oh, they were cordial, but James is a teacher, and I believe that Harold was disappointed when his son didn't follow him into business. Harold's first wife died when James was a boy, and by the time I married Harold five years ago, they were already living their own lives. It's no wonder that James has an idealized version of his father. I can assure you that it wasn't accurate."

The inspector began his enquiries. "Where were you at seven o'clock on Sunday evening, Mrs. Villiers?"

"I was here," she attested. "Is that when he was killed?"

"Can anyone testify to that?" countered the inspector, ignoring her question.

There was a protracted pause before she shook her head. "You aren't suggesting that I murdered my husband, are you, Inspector?"

"I'm simply establishing the facts."

"I hated Harold for what he did to me," she admitted. "But I didn't kill him, I assure you."

"You left town after the murder," said Forrester, his tone now rather accusatory. "When we informed you of your husband's death on Sunday night, you were told that we would be back on Monday to speak with you further. However, when I arrived, I was told by your housekeeper that you'd gone that morning to stay with your sister. Why was that?"

"Because when I notified her about Harold's death, she insisted that I shouldn't be alone, and she came and collected me the next morning. But today, I decided that I needed to be here after all. I just arrived home an hour ago."

"What do you inherit under your husband's will?" asked Holmes, changing the subject.

The woman frowned. "Nothing. When I began to explore divorce proceedings, he changed his will so that James receives everything, except for certain parts of his business, which are tied up with his partner."

Forrester moved on. "What time did your husband leave the house Sunday evening?"

Mrs. Villiers furrowed her brow, trying to recollect. "I think it was about half-past-six."

"And did he say where he was going?"

She shook her head. "He was probably seeing another one of his harlots, I imagine," she said bitterly. "He could do what he liked, for all I cared. Our marriage was over a long time ago. I simply had nowhere else to go." She glanced around. "It remains to be seen whether James will do anything to help me, once he learns the truth about his father."

Holmes stood up. "Well, thank you for your time, Mrs. Villiers. I would offer my condolences, but I suspect that your husband's death is less of a loss to you than it is a gain."

"You aren't wrong there," she said, and as we left, I thought, in spite of her precarious situation, that I saw the ghost of a smile growing upon her lips.

Following a pleasant journey along twisting country tracks and emerald-green pastures, our carriage soon rolled to a stop outside Pendleforth Manor, an impressive gothic building with long lancet windows and tall crenelated towers. Behind it stretched acres of dense woodland.

264

"Back so soon, Inspector?" said the grey-haired butler. "And you've brought guests along with you this time, I see."

"Yes, Watkins. Allow me to introduce Sherlock Holmes and Doctor Watson," Forrester said. "They're assisting me with the investigation."

The old man gave a stiff bow. "Well, I sincerely hope you catch the cursed creature soon," he said. "The maid is scared out of her wits and is having nightmares about it." He rubbed his red-rimmed eyes. "I can't get a wink of sleep for all her screaming."

"Tell her she need not worry," said my friend. "'The Terror' is no more real than her nightmares."

Forrester suddenly remembered the reason for our visit. "Is Mr. Pendleforth around?"

"You'll be pleased to know that you haven't wasted another journey, Inspector. He returned home earlier this afternoon."

"Ah, good! May we speak to him?"

"I don't see why not, though I'll just make sure he isn't otherwise occupied. Wait here a moment, please." Retreating into the hallway, he reappeared moments later. "He says he can spare you five minutes."

So saying, he conducted us through a series of gloomy passageways until we eventually found ourselves in a small, crimson-carpeted study, the most notable features of which were an oil painting of two square-jawed young men – from their striking resemblance, I supposed they were brothers – and an old writing table, behind which there sat a middle-aged man with a pate of salt-and-pepper hair and a Van Dyke beard. Although he had changed greatly, I could see that he was the shorter of the two men in the painting. As we entered, he was peering absorbedly at a sheet of paper through a pair of golden *pince-nez* and was so enraptured by his reading that he didn't appear to be aware of our presence until the butler announced us.

"Thank you, Watkins," he said to the old man.

The butler bowed reverentially. "Very good, sir."

Once he'd dismissed the servant, Pendleforth stood up and shuffled over to a side table, where he poured himself a sherry – pointedly not inviting us to join him. Then, returning to his chair, he sat and asked, "To what do I owe the pleasure, gentlemen?"

"We're here concerning the death of your late business partner," said Inspector Forrester as we folded ourselves, uninvited, into tastefully worn leather chairs before the table. "As you've surely heard, two evenings ago, his body was discovered in the wood bordering this estate."

"Yes, I've heard the tragic news," he said sombrely.

Forrester forged ahead with his enquiries. "You've just returned home. May I ask where you've been?"

"Manchester. I left early Monday morning." Pendleforth smiled.

"And you didn't hear of your partner's death before you left?"

"I did not. I left quite early. And," he added, "apparently no one from the police thought to notify me."

Forrester frowned. "Being Mr. Villiers' business associate, you must have known him rather well, I presume?"

"Yes, I suppose that I did."

"And what were your memories of the man?"

"He was a fine fellow whom I respected greatly," Pendleforth eulogised.

"Did you and he ever have your differences?"

"We ran a business together, Inspector," he answered, as though it were an inane question. "It wouldn't be normal if we didn't."

"What were the nature of these disagreements?"

"I sometimes felt as though Harold wasn't fully devoted to the company, that's all. For the last couple of years, he's seemed to be more interested in squandering his money on strumpets and drink than investing his time into running the business. But then again, he always did put pleasure before profit."

"Did the business suffer as a result?"

Pendleforth nodded. "Revenues began to fall, and our employees were beginning to leave in droves. We've recently been in dire straits, to put it mildly, and the business has suddenly been on the cusp of being dissolved. In the end, I wanted to buy Harold out and run it alone, but despite my persistent appeals, he refused to relinquish his share. As stubborn as an ox, he was."

It was Holmes's turn to ask a question. "And how has his death affected the business now? Although it's only been two days since the murder, I would imagine that it's still in an equally precarious position?"

Pendleforth shook his head. "Now there is hope. When Harold and I signed our partnership contract, we included a clause which allowed the surviving partner to take sole ownership of the company should one of us end up in the grave."

"Which means that you now own one-hundred-percent of the business?"

"That's correct, yes."

"In a peculiar way, then, I suppose you could say that Mr. Villiers's death will perhaps leave Trowbridge Textiles in a better state than if he was alive. It's a rather tragic irony, don't you think?"

"I haven't thought of it in such terms," he said, leaning back and stroking his beard, "but yes, with Harold out of the way, there's a chance

266

that the company can become successful once again. I know that may sound harsh, but it's the truth."

During the time that Forrester had been questioning Pendleforth, Holmes had risen to his feet, wandering the room, looking at the bottles on the side table, the books upon the shelves, and the view of the forest from the large window. Then, apparently deciding to advance the questioning more directly, he asked, "Where were you at seven o'clock on Sunday evening, Mr. Pendleforth?"

Pendleforth had been watching Holmes's explorations with mixed amusement and irritation. "If my memory serves me correctly," he answered, while Holmes returned to sit across from him, "I was here, in my study, going over some paperwork." Pendleforth shifted in his seat. "Why do you ask?"

"Because that is when Mr. Villiers was brutally murdered."

This seemed to displease our host. He sat up, asking, "What are you insinuating, Mr. Holmes?"

"I'm merely inquiring – that's all."

"As I've already told you," he said tersely, "I was here. You can ask Watkins if you don't believe me."

Holmes flashed a propitiatory smile. "Oh, I'm sure that won't be necessary."

This, however, didn't seem to mollify the man. "Instead of accusing me, shouldn't you be out there, searching for The Terror?" He gestured to the mountain of papers on his desk. "Now if you don't mind, gentlemen, I have been away for two days, and have business to which I must attend."

"Yes, we can see that you're a busy man," said Holmes, rising to his feet. "Thank you for your time, Mr. Pendleforth."

Abruptly dismissed by our host, we left the study without so much as a handshake and retraced our steps back through the house until we reached the entrance hall, where we were shown out by Watkins the butler.

"Before we go," said Holmes as we hovered on the threshold, "may I ask you a quick question?"

Watkins nodded. "But of course."

"Where was your master at seven o'clock on Sunday?"

"From what I recall, he was in his study."

"You're sure of this?"

He nodded. "He locked the door at around half-past-six and said he didn't wish to be disturbed."

"But you didn't actually enter the room at any point between half-past-six and seven?"

"No . . . I did not."

"And when did you next see him?"

267

"Around eight, I suppose. He was going upstairs. I believe that he was getting ready for his trip the next morning."

"Thank you," said Holmes. "You've been most helpful."

No sooner had the butler bade us farewell and closed the door than Holmes led us toward the back of the house, staying close to the building so that we might not be seen from the windows above us.

"Has it rained since Sunday?" he asked, to which Forrester replied that there had been rains on Saturday, but none since.

"Excellent," said Holmes softly. "Saturday's rain wet the ground for the footprints to show, and since they won't have washed away.

By that time we were at the rear of the building, on the lawn just outside Pendleforth's study. Holmes raised a finger to indicate silence, and then he cast around for a moment before spotting something that interested him. With a gesture, he set off in a line toward the nearby woods. Once we were in the trees and couldn't be seen from the house, he stopped and spoke.

"There was a line of footprints in the grass, leading from the study window to here." He pointed to the dirt trail, where the marks were easily observed. "These are identical to the ones shown in your photograph, found near the body. They must belong to the same person."

"Why don't we test that theory and see where these prints go?" Forrester suggested.

"You've read my mind, Inspector."

At several points along the way, the trail faded into shallow streams and crossed rocky areas where the footprints vanished, but through sheer perseverance, and by casting along in the general direction in which we'd already been traveling, we were able to pick up the trail once again. Eventually, after negotiating thick foliage and meandering our way along muddy tracks, we found ourselves in a clearing surrounded by a coppice of oaks where, according to Forrester, Villiers had met his grisly end.

Forrester gestured toward where a larger trail entered the clearing on the far side. "Just along there is the road. That's where the public enters to walk these woods, or to have picnics here." He gestured to the where the prints stopped. "It appears that you were right, Mr. Holmes. This is the spot where the victim's body had been discovered on Sunday evening."

"I seldom err in my judgement, Inspector," Holmes said as he wandered around the copse.

"I wonder that there wasn't another set of footprints leading back the way that we came."

"Possibly the murderer was interrupted," speculated Forrester, "and chose to depart in a different direction."

"A-ha!" interrupted Holmes. "What have we here?" Having seen all that he wanted where the body was found, he had ranged to the trees around the perimeter of the clearing. Now he was at the edge of the trees, where he announced, "*Another* set of footprints!"

"That's right, Mr. Holmes," answered Forrester. "Those are the second set that were in the photographs."

"And did you follow them as well?"

"I tried, but I lost them soon after leaving the clearing."

"Then perhaps I'll have better luck." And then, without warning, he bounded off, leaving the inspector and me struggling to keep pace with his long, loping strides as we set upon yet another trail. At times, Holmes also seemed to lose the way, stopping regularly to look this way and that before energetically resuming. Finally, after almost ten minutes – by which point, my legs were smarting and my heart drumming – we emerged into another clearing where, much to my relief, the footprints suddenly ended. We found ourselves alongside a rock bluff, twenty or thirty feet high. There was an indentation at the base, not really a cave, but enough to provide shelter from the elements. There were several folded blankets pushed to the rear, apparently used as bedding.

"It appears that your grocery shop thief was real all along, Inspector," Holmes said, gesturing to a small mound of empty food tins lying on the ground beside the smouldering remains an old fire. Then, he knelt down and began examining the embers. "Still warm," he observed. "Whoever was here must have left mere moments before we arrived. He probably heard us coming."

"It's possible that he witnessed the crime," I said softly. "Should we wait for him to come back?" I asked, wondering if I should draw my revolver.

Holmes shook his head, murmuring, "I doubt if he will – he's probably watching us right now. Besides which," he added, glancing at his pocket watch, "the light will soon be fading, and it wouldn't be wise to make our return journey through the woods under the cover of darkness."

"In that case, we had better make haste," I said, turning on my heel and beginning to head back whence we'd come. The inspector followed closely behind, but rather inexplicably, despite his insistence for expeditiousness, Holmes crouched on the ground beside the remains of the fire for several a moment catching up with us. What he'd been doing, I wasn't sure, but I thought better than to question it, and instead focused my efforts to retrace our steps back through the wood to the clearing.

Soon enough, the sun had begun to sink behind the tips of the trees, shrouding the place in purple shadow. As the light faded, so too did my fortitude, and I found my thoughts inexorably returning to the night-time terror which was reputed to roam the wood. Was it lurking in the gloom of the trees even now, hunting for its next victim?

Those fears grew further when, not far from the clearing where the body had been found, we heard the snap of a twig nearby. "Did you hear that?" I asked my friend, finding myself frozen to the spot and drawing the revolver in my jacket pocket.

"I think it came from that direction," Holmes said, pointing west toward the setting sun.

Careful not to make a noise, we tiptoed tentatively toward the sound. As we drew nearer, two voices came into earshot from behind a cluster of trees.

"All right . . . Not much longer now," said the first. "We've almost got it."

"This is intolerable!" replied the second. "I've been standing here for ages."

It was then that we approached close enough for the owners of the voices to come into view. One of them was dressed in a tweed suit and had his head buried under a black cloth, peering fixedly through the lens of a camera, which was mounted on a tripod. The second figure was standing motionless, his clothes torn and tattered, and his wolf-like face contorted into a soundless snarl as he held his hands aloft, as though about to pounce upon his would-be prey.

"Perfect . . . hold that position," said Tweed Suit. "Just a few more minutes now . . . ."

Werewolf Man, however, had clearly had enough. He pulled off his black wig, threw it in the mud, and stomped off, mumbling obscenities under his breath.

"Bert . . . don't go!" Tweed Suit called after him. "We haven't finished yet – "

"It seems that you need to keep a tighter leash on your pet," said Holmes, causing the man to swivel around with a start.

"Good God!" he said, clutching his chest. "You nearly frightened the life out of me!"

"By the looks of it, you are the one trying to scare people witless."

He shrugged. "I'm just sniffing out a good story, that's all."

"And you are – ?"

"Simeon Lynch of *The Trowbridge Tribune*," he said, straightening his bow tie. "I must admit, I didn't expect to see anyone else here. With all the rumours flying around, most people are giving this place a wide berth."

"Fortunately, we don't believe in lycanthropes."

"What are you doing here then?"

"We're investigating the murder of Mr. Villiers," answered Forrester, "who was killed here two nights ago."

Lynch gave a sorrowful shake of the head. "It's such a tragedy, isn't it?"

"You speak as though you knew him."

"Only a professional basis."

"How so?"

"When he bought the shares to Trowbridge Textiles," he said, "I reported on the story and interviewed him about it. I also spoke to his business partner."

"Mr. Pendleforth?" I asked.

He nodded. "I could tell that he was the one who was more invested in the company. Said that he'd waited all his life for such an opportunity, and that woe betide anyone who stood in the way of his success."

"Did he now?" Holmes said, a thoughtful expression etched upon his aquiline face. "Well, we'll leave you to find your wolf-man." He jabbed a thumb over his shoulder. "I think he went that way."

We reached the road and then made our way around to Pendleforth Manor, where we retrieved our carriage. Forrester drove us back into Trowbridge, and we agreed to meet in the morning. Feeling fatigued from all the walking, I was relieved to return to the comfortable surroundings of The White Swan. As I sat beside the coal fire, enjoying a delicious dinner of Devizes Pie with homemade chips – which, according to the gregarious landlord, was "gurt lush" – I couldn't help but overhear the idle gossip in which many of my fellow patrons were eagerly engaged, most of which pertained to "The Terror of Trowbridge Wood".

"I hear the creature does tear his victims limb from limb with his bare hands," said a hatchet-faced man at the table beside us, "and that he does have claws as sharp as knives. "Makes ye hairs stand on end just thinking on it, don't 'e?"

"'Tint savvy to be venturing near that Pendleforth place, that's for sure," replied his portly friend. "Ye heard what did happen to that Villiers kiddie, didn't ye?" He shook his head in incredulity. "Bleeding turball, 'twas."

"He isn't the first, and he won't be the last."

"What do ye mean?"

Hatchet Face leaned over the table in a conspiratorial manner. "You'll recall that Charlie Pendleforth had a brother, but no one has seen neither hide nor hair of him in almost a year."

"Ye think the beast killed him too?"

"Aye, that's exactly what I think, Ted."

271

Suddenly, a familiar voice chimed in. "It seems that Lynch isn't the only person looking to make a quick shilling from all the rumours," Holmes said as he sat down nearby, alluding to the bottle of Werewolf Whisky sitting on the table in front of me.

"He and others like him are certainly part of the reason why people are so petrified," I said, shaking my head disapprovingly. "He should be ashamed of himself."

"Such men don't care for morality, only money. Speaking of which, Villiers's death has no doubt lined the pockets of several people, Pendleforth being chief among them."

"Do you that he killed him?"

Holmes nodded. "He is certainly the most likely suspect, for obvious reasons."

I considered for a moment. "If Pendleforth is to be believed, Villiers's profligate lifestyle was having a detrimental effect upon Trowbridge Textiles, potentially resulting in its dissolution if things continued in the same vein. As Lynch told us, it wasn't within Pendleforth's character to countenance such a failure. His repeated attempts to convince Villiers to sell his shares were to no avail, however, so possibly he decided to resort to more drastic measures in order to get him out of the picture."

"And now, with his partner removed from the board, Pendleforth can assume sole ownership of the company and has set about repairing the damage," said Holmes, taking my thought to its natural terminus. "It's quite the coincidence, wouldn't you agree?"

I nodded.

"The footprints from the house to the scene of the murder are certainly damning," I said. "Is there anything else that points towards his guilt?"

"His dubious alibi, for one thing."

"Yes – supposedly in his study for the entire evening."

"Exactly, Watson. However, as you heard, his butler didn't enter see him from when he entered the room at six-thirty until eight, when Pendleforth was observed climbing the steps. As such, no one can confidently vouch for his whereabouts between those times."

"How, though, did he lure Villiers into the wood?"

"Although a physical message may exist, to be found after a better search, it's more likely that Pendleforth would have simply made a verbal agreement with Villiers to meet in the woods – for if he was planning a murder, he wouldn't have wanted a record of it in writing."

"It's a plausible theory," I conceded, "but it isn't exactly conclusive proof, is it?"

"No, but the footprints we discovered at the scene of the murder are," he said, sipping on his beer. "You may recall that they belonged to a man with a slight limp," he reminded me. "Earlier today, you will have noticed that when Pendleforth walked over to the side table to pour himself a sherry, he exhibited both of those characteristics. Furthermore, as you know, the trail of prints we followed into the wood originated on the patch of grass immediately outside his study – beginning where he would have clambered out of the window after making sure that he'd be undisturbed. In addition, there's also the silver wristwatch the police found near the body."

"You think that was Pendleforth's?"

He nodded. "It could be. While he was talking to us, I observed a faint untanned outline upon his wrist where such an object would have resided."

"Incriminating as all this is, will it be sufficient for Forrester to make an arrest?"

"It may be enough to hold Pendleforth in custody for a while, but I'll need more evidence if I'm to prove his guilt." He rose to his feet. "And tonight, if my plan works, I may just have it," he said, taking a final draught of ale before leaving me alone to ponder the import of this cryptic comment.

I started to ask what his plan was, and if I might assist, but he raised a hand. "Get your sleep, Watson. This is something that I can manage alone. With any luck, this will provide a quick solution. However, if what I hope doesn't occur, then we're back to the point where every person in Trowbridge is a suspect, for in truth we haven't yet eliminated anyone."

Later that evening I was in my room, preparing to turn in for the night, when I suddenly heard soft footsteps outside the door. I remember thinking it strange for someone to be passing in the hallway at such an unsocial hour – the mantel clock read half-past-ten – and I wondered who it could be, for there were only two guest rooms in the tavern, both of which were occupied by my friend and me. My curiosity getting the better of me, I darkened my lamp and silently cracked open the door, peeking out to observe a tall, dark-coated figure lurking in the hallway. In the dim light, I couldn't see his or her face, for it was hidden under a broad-brimmed hat and concealed behind a bandana. I found his furtive manner to be exceedingly suspicious, however, and my misgivings multiplied when I realized that this person was standing outside Holmes's room.

Quickly fetching my revolver from the bedside table, I hastened into the hallway, only to find, quite bewilderingly, that the stranger was no longer there. Fearing that he had somehow gained access to my friend's room while I had turned my back, my trepidation grew when I saw that the door was slightly ajar. Clutching my Webley, I gently pushed against the panel with my shoulder, wondering what awaited me on the other side of the threshold.

I entered the room to find myself staring at a man whose face was entirely covered in thick, black hair – like that of a wolf! Though his demeanour was far from threatening, instinct compelled me to train my revolver upon him.

"You have no need for that," said Holmes, who I realized was standing by the bed. "I believe that we're in the company of an ally, not an enemy." I warily lowered my weapon. "Watson, allow me to introduce you to Robert Pendleforth, the brother of the gentleman we met earlier today, and the man who saw Villiers being murdered on Sunday evening. Before you arrived," he said in answer to my quizzical look, "he had just introduced himself and confirmed that he indeed witnessed the heinous crime."

"I'm sorry about that," I said reluctantly, pocketing my revolver. "I thought you were a . . . Well, I'm not sure what I thought really."

"There's no need to mince your words," he said. "I know what I look like."

In truth, his appearance was dreadful. In addition to the fact that his entire face and hands were covered with thick black hair, his clothing was terribly worn, in some places nearly falling apart, and in truth, he carried about him an animalistic odor, as if it had been many months since he or the clothing had been washed.

There was an uncomfortable silence. Mercifully, Holmes was there to break it. "I'm grateful for your coming here tonight, Mr. Pendleforth. I realize that it wasn't without its risks."

"It seems that every wall in town has my face upon it," he replied, appearing vaguely amused by the notion. His voice was rough, as if he didn't use it very often. "Fortunately," he smiled, lighting his otherwise hideous features, "I usually travel *incognito*."

"Most prudent." Holmes said, waving his guest into a chair beside the window – thankfully open, I noticed. "Now, tell us what you saw the other night and omit nothing in your account. Even the most trivial of details could prove crucial at the forthcoming inquest."

"I'll endeavour to be as thorough as possible. Toward that end, I shall begin by relating my own story, which will provide some context for the events that followed."

"Very well," Holmes acquiesced. "Recount your narrative in its entirety."

And so Robert Pendleforth proceeded to share his tragic tale. "Though it may be difficult to believe," he began after a moment's pause, "I haven't always looked like this."

"We know," I interrupted. "It's you in the painting in your brother's study," I explained. "When the two of you were younger."

He nodded. "That's right. I was once an ordinary man, living an ordinary life. Then, a year ago, everything suddenly changed: At first, the signs were subtle and amounted to nothing more than a few more hairs in the bottom of the bathing tub. Shortly, however, the signs became increasingly obvious, and I knew that something was terribly wrong. Eventually, I would gaze into a mirror and scarcely recognize the man staring back at me." He hung his head in despair. "Within mere months, I had turned from a man into the monster you see before you.

"During that dark and distressing period of my life, I struggled to understand what was happening to my body, and even many of the doctors who called upon me at the time – all of whom I had sworn to secrecy – were unable to fathom the strange medical mystery. Desperate for answers, my then-wife and I decided to take a trip to Eindhoven, where we'd arranged to meet the pre-eminent dermatologist, Dr. Van Liezen. After conducting several tests, he confirmed his initial diagnosis: That I was suffering from an extreme form of *hypertrichosis*, or 'Werewolf Syndrome', as it's more commonly known – a disorder, he informed me, that can cause excessive hair growth all over the body, and for which there is no known cure.

"As time went by, my condition worsened, and no sooner would I shave than the hideous hair would grow back. I began to withdraw from society and live the life of a recluse, too ashamed to step outside my door for fear of the ridicule I would inevitably receive. The illness was also beginning to take a toll on my marriage. My wife and I began quarrelling more frequently, and though she never expressed it in as many words, I knew, from the way she shrank at my touch, that she was repulsed by what I had become. In the end, we petitioned for divorce, and after it was approved by the court, I moved away and went to live in secrecy with my brother in our late father's country manor.

"Although he reluctantly agreed to the arrangement out of a sense of fraternal duty, from the minute I crossed the threshold it was made clear that that my presence there was a tremendous inconvenience to him, and that I was to live as a recluse there as well. He secretly fixed rooms for me in an unused part of the house, and nailed boards over the windows so that there would be no signs of light showing at night. None of the servants – except for the butler, old Watkins, knew that I was there. Each day, either my brother or Watkins would arrange to sneak food to me, and no one ever suspected that I was there.

"I sometimes felt that my brothers conditions were extreme, but at the same time, I was despondent over my lost life, and willing to put up with my new existence.

"Things went on this way for a while, but then my brother's resentment of me began to be more obvious, and my disruptive influence upon his life became even more evident when he later blamed me for having to abandon a business venture of his, suggesting it was impossible to pursue such an enterprise while he was caring for his ailing brother. This made no sense to me, but that didn't matter, as this resentment soon turned into paranoia, and I found that he began looking upon me as his prisoner, locking the doors and forbidding me from leaving the estate, lest my terrible secret should ever come to light."

"That's barbaric!" I said, wondering how someone could be capable of such cruelty.

"In truth, I hadn't tried to leave even once, but when I found the doors locked, getting away became something of an obsession.

"Soon," continued Pendleforth, "my miserable existence plunged me into a state of profound malaise, and any hope of freedom seemed to erode with each passing day. In the end, however, my fortitude prevailed over my fears, and I managed to break out of my gilded cage. One evening Watkins forgot to lock the door after bringing my food, and so I fled the house and into the nearby woods, where I have since lived a primitive life amongst the trees, far from my brother's reach. Or so I thought . . . ."

"You have spent the entire time living in that rock shelter?" I asked.

He nodded. "It was terrible – particularly as my escape occurred in the winter and on some nights I nearly froze to death."

"And," added Holmes, "you were watching us today, weren't you?"
Pendleforth nodded.

"You saw your brother again two nights ago, didn't you?" Holmes asked.

"I was walking through the woods and collecting some wood for my fire," explained Robert Pendleforth, "when I spied a man standing beside an old oak – it must have been Villiers, although I'd never met him. From the way he kept checking his pocket watch, appeared to be waiting for someone. Moments later, from behind a tree on the far side of the clearing, there appeared a second man, carrying what looked like a garden spade. He crept forward in silence, closer and closer to the first man, who was looking in the wrong direction. The next thing I knew, the second man had reached the first, and there was by a blood-curdling crack, followed by a deathly silence. As I watched in horror, not quite believing what I'd just

276

seen, the second man then began to assault the first with the spade, hitting him with the flat side and then stabbing down with the sharp end. At that moment, my foot snapped a branch underfoot, immediately causing the killer to turn his head in my direction. For a few long seconds, the shock kept me rooted to the spot, unable to move as I stared into the cold, unblinking eyes of my brother.

"Realizing that I was in mortal danger, I quickly turned on my heels and ran to my camp as fast as my legs would carry me, where I spent the rest of the evening by the fire, trying to make sense of what had happened. I knew that my brother had a ruthless streak – that was something I had experienced first-hand – but never did I imagine that he would be capable of killing a man in cold blood."

"Did you consider going to the authorities?" I asked.

Pendleforth shook his head. "I knew they would pay little heed to what I told them. After all, I thought, who would believe a monster like me?"

"And yet, here you are."

"I had a change of heart," he said with a shrug. "No longer could I just sit idly by while my brother walked free. At first, I thought that Mr. Holmes's invitation might be a trap, but I considered it a risk worth taking."

"I'm glad my message had the desired effect," Holmes responded.

"Invitation?" I asked, and then I recalled the moment my friend had remained crouched beside the campfire as the inspector and I had gone on ahead. "So that's what you were doing!"

"Before I departed the camp," my friend explained, "I used a twig to scribble a short message in the mud, asking the recipient to meet me here at half-past-ten. I knew it was likely that whoever read it might possess information pertaining to Villiers' murder." He turned to Pendleforth. "And given what you've just divulged, my hunch proved to be correct."

Pendleforth looked puzzled. "There's still something I don't understand, Mr. Holmes: How did you know I was there when Villiers was killed?"

"It was quite simple" he expounded. "In addition to the killer's footprints, the police also discovered another pair, which led us to infer that someone else had been present at the time of Villiers's death. When we followed them, they ended up taking us to your camp."

"I see," said Robert Pendleforth. "And now I suppose you want me to stand up in a courtroom full of people and tell a judge and jury what I saw?"

Holmes nodded. "I realize it won't be easy for you, but your brother needs to be punished for what he's done – both to you and Villiers. With my evidence and your testimony, his innocence will be untenable."

"Very well," Pendleforth said after a moment's deliberation. "I'm prepared to do whatever it takes to see Charles get his comeuppance." He stood, roused by his own resolve. "For weeks, he made me a prisoner. Soon, I shall return the favour."

After making arrangements to meet in the morning, Robert Pendleforth departed. When he'd gone, I asked, "Can you be certain that he won't flee right now, never to be seen again?"

"No," said Holmes simply, "but we shall take him at his word."

A thought occurred to me. "Is it possible that Robert Pendleforth is framing his brother? After all, he could have sent a message to Villiers, using Charles's name, asking for a meeting in the woods, and then he could have used a pair of his brother's shoes to leave the footprints from the manor to the scene of the murder. This could be an elaborate plot to get Charles out of the way, executed for murder, so that Robert can inherit the manor, as well as Charles's shares of the business."

Holmes shook his head. "Robert's feet are much larger than Charles's – even if he could have stolen a pair of Charles's shoes, he could never have worn them to leave the footprints. One can wear larger shoes, but one can't fit into smaller shoes. Besides, such a clue was a bit too subtle. It's doubtful that the local police could have been counted on to find the trail of footprints leading from the house to the wooded clearing."

I nodded, realizing that I couldn't recall the sizes of either of the Pendleforth brothers' feet.

Leaving Holmes settling in to smoke his pipe, probably all night, I returned to my room and tried to get some sleep. I drifted off thinking about the Wolf Man of Trowbridge, huddled around the fire at the base of a rock outcropping, and wondering if he would be present in the morning as promised.

The next morning, Holmes and I returned to Pendleforth Manor, along with Inspector Forrester, and we were once again welcomed at the door by Watkins, the butler, who, judging by his bleary-eyed expression, still appeared to be suffering from his sleeping woes.

"Good morning, gentlemen," he said. "I hope that the investigation is going well."

"I'm pleased to report that it's reaching its conclusion," said my friend. "Soon, the monster responsible will be brought to justice, and that frightened maid of yours will no longer be keeping you awake at night."

"I'm relieved to hear it," he replied. "Now, what can I do for you?"

"Is your master in?" Forrester said. "We still have a few more questions to ask him, I'm afraid."

"Yes, he's still shackled to his desk." He went to see if we would be admitted, and the returned to show us through to the study where, for the second time in as many days, we were greeted by Charles Pendleforth.

"Well, well, well!" he said with sarcastic false cheer. "If it isn't Mr. Holmes and his two lapdogs!" Apparently he was still bristling at my friend's insinuations the previous day. "And what crime are you going to accuse me of this time?"

"Only the murder of Mr. Villiers," replied Holmes with a smile.

Pendleforth stood abruptly and puffed his cheeks. "Must you persist with this fiction?" he snarled. "It's all becoming rather tiresome."

"You can plead your innocence all you like," said Forrester, "but we know you killed him."

"And what reason could I possibly have for doing such a thing?" the businessman challenged.

"It's quite simple, really," my friend averred. "You knew that Trowbridge Textiles wouldn't survive much longer if Villiers's imprudent ways continued to go unchecked. You tried to persuade him to hand over his share of the business numerous times, but your protests fell on deaf ears. And so, with no other choice, and feeling desperate, you decided to murder him, knowing that, as per your contract, you would become the sole owner of the company and would be in a better position to rebuild it."

Pendleforth blinked. "That's your reason? That's meaningless. The man's wife had more reason to kill him than me. Have you spoken to her?"

Holmes began to wander the room, looking here and there as he had the day before.

"I was here the entire evening," Pendleforth continued, holding his arms akimbo in a gesture of innocence and trying to catch Holmes's attention.

"That's what you wanted everyone to believe," said Holmes, stopping by the window.

"I beg your pardon?"

"At half-past-six, you locked the door and asked not to be disturbed, making your butler think that you were in the room the entire evening," Holmes explained. "Unbeknownst to the old man, however, you climbed out of the window, took to the woods which border this estate, and waited patiently for Villiers to arrive at the pre-arranged spot at seven o'clock. You then killed him with the garden spade – but you were forced to leave it behind when you realized, perhaps, that there was a witness to your crime. You then returned to your study without being seen, giving Watkins

279

the impression that you'd been in there the whole time – in fact, until he saw you going upstairs at eight o'clock."

Pendleforth barked an incredulous laugh. "That's nothing but conjecture, Mr. Holmes!"

"On the contrary," my friend gainsaid. "We have irrefutable evidence to prove it."

"What evidence?"

"First, we discovered a set of footprints at the location of the crime, which belonged to a tall person with an uneven gait. Yesterday, I observed how you walked with a slight limp. Therefore, I knew there was a possibility that the footmarks found near the victim's body were yours."

"You can't surely be suggesting that I'm the only man to suffer from such an injury?"

"Indeed not," Holmes granted. "Though it isn't a common affliction, either."

"Come, come, Mr. Holmes. It's hardly unequivocal proof, is it? Someone could be framing me."

"Oh, but there's more." Holmes nodded to Forrester, who rummaged in his jacket pocket and pulled out the wristwatch. "This was found near Villiers's body," explained the inspector. "I believe it belongs to you," he said, gesturing at the faint untanned outline on Pendleforth's right wrist. "It must have been loose and fell from your arm when you administered the *coup de grâce*."

"You think that will stand up in court? I lost my watch a week ago."

"So this is your watch?" asked Holmes?"

"Yes, but – " Then Pendleforth seemed to sense a trap. "I mean, it looks like my watch. It could belong to anyone. You're more deluded than I thought."

"Perhaps by itself, the watch isn't enough evidence, or even the limping footprints. But then there's the fact that the same footprints that we found in the forest lead from just outside this window – " He gestured to it. " – and the same footprint is here in the dust on the sill from where you climbed out – while you were supposedly in here from six-thirty to eight, working undisturbed." He took a step toward Pendleforth's table. "It was seeing the footprints in the window dust – which certainly match your shoes – that first gave me the idea to look outside under the window for corresponding prints where you had climbed out. From there it was easy enough to connect you with the site of the murder."

As Pendleforth tried to formulate a response, Holmes relentlessly continued. "But I suspect that the judge won't be quite-so-willing to ignore all of this evidence when it's considered in court alongside your brother's testimony."

"Robert?" Pendleforth mumbled, a sudden trace of fear flickering in his eyes. "You've spoken to him? Impossible!"

Holmes nodded. "He was a variable you hadn't factored into your plan, but it initially seemed to work to your advantage, as the mutilated corpse looked like the work of The Terror. Suddenly the newspapers were full of stories about the monster, and your brother was the perfect scapegoat. You simply had to let things take their course. Should he be found and interrogated, his story would be discounted because people were already willing to believe that he was a guilty. Unfortunately for you, however, I was able to see through the deception and lure him out of the shadows."

"He won't testify – not while he's the most wanted man in Wiltshire!"

"I wouldn't be so sure, Mr. Pendleforth," said Holmes. "Given the abominable way in which you treated him, I think he'll do almost anything to see you get your just deserts – especially as *your* guilt will prove *his* innocence. In fact, he's already told us that he intends to stand up in the witness box to testify against you."

"Is that so?"

"Yes, it is."

"Then where is he? I think you're bluffing!"

"No, he isn't," said a voice from the doorway, which had opened to reveal the missing brother, standing tall and impressive, despite his ragged clothing and hirsute features. "Hello Charles," he said coolly. "It's been a long time."

Pendleforth was staring at his brother with his mouth agape. "Robert!" he stammered when he had finally managed to move close it again. "How – how did you get in?"

"Watkins. He was glad to see me, I think."

"I . . . don't know what to say. How – how are you?"

Robert laughed at the absurd question. "How am I? How am I? For weeks, you kept me locked in this house like a wild animal, until I had to flee and live like a wild man. Then I hear that you were going to let the public convict me of a murder *you* committed. And now," he scoffed, "you have the audacity to ask how *I* am. How am I, indeed!"

"I'm sorry, Robert," said Charles, stepping back and sinking into his chair. "If I could go back and change what I did . . . ."

"I don't want your contrition, nor do I need it," Robert snapped. "It's too late for that . . . much too late."

Having been firmly put in his place, Charles Pendleforth decided to address the most important matter of all. "I'm led to believe that you intend to testify against me in court," he said. "Is that true?" Robert nodded, and

Charles continued. "It will do you no good!" Charles snapped. "I've changed my will – you'll get nothing!"

Seeing the look of disgust cross Robert's face, Charles added, "After the suffering I've put you through, I imagine you'll derive a great deal of satisfaction by sending me to the noose, won't you?"

"I'd be lying if I said that I won't, Charles, but I realize now that this is about much more than petty revenge. This is about justice."

Sensing defeat, Pendleforth decided to resort to truly desperate measures. He stood up and walked to the side of the room. Holmes, Forrester, and I were each alerted, and both the inspector and I removed guns from our pockets. But Charles Pendleforth simply pulled open the door to his already-open safe and drew out a thick wad of bank-notes. When he sat back down at his table, he began dividing them into four equal shares and placing them on the table in front of him. "There's ten-thousand pounds for each of you," he said, "enough to make you very rich men. If you agree to say no more about the matter – that nothing goes further than this room – then it's all yours."

"Put your money away, Mr. Pendleforth," snapped Holmes. "You're just making it worse for yourself."

"Get him out of my sight!" instructed Robert Pendleforth, even more indignant than before. "Or I may not be accountable for my actions."

The sandy-haired inspector took this as his cue to step forward. "Mr. Pendleforth, I'm placing you under arrest for the murder of Harold Villiers – and now for attempted bribery as well," he added, clapping the irons in place. "If you'd like to accompany me to the station, please."

"I'm grateful for everything you've done, Mr. Holmes," said our client, James Villiers, as we stood outside the Trowbridge court almost two months later. "Though it won't bring my father back, knowing that his killer will be punished has afforded me a small measure of comfort."

"You're very welcome," replied my friend. "It's heartening to know that we've been of some help."

He shook our hands. "Farewell gentlemen – and thank you once again."

Once we'd bidden goodbye to our client, I turned to Holmes and said, "I've known many villains in my time, but Charles Pendleforth is certainly among the worst."

"Monsters do not always have sharp teeth and long claws, Watson," he said. "Sometimes, they look no different from you or me."

"He even had the gall to try and blame his brother for it all," I said, sickened by the man's sanctimony.

282

"The way Pendleforth saw it, having Trowbridge Textiles succeed was worth any cost." He paused. "In the end, that desperation proved to be his undoing."

"Talking of the 'other' Pendleforth, what he did today showed a great deal of courage," I said, recalling the gasps of horror when Robert Pendleforth had stepped up to the witness stand. "He's more of a man than his brother ever was."

"I quite agree."

"What will become of him now, I wonder?"

"It's difficult to know," Holmes said as we climbed down the steps. "Though he's no longer considered a public menace, I very much doubt he'll be favourably welcomed by the people of Trowbridge, who will continue to look upon him as a pariah. The truth may finally be out, but legends live long in the memory."

He raised his hand to a passing hansom. "Alas, in many people's minds, Robert Pendleforth will forever be known as 'The Terror of Trowbridge Wood'."

The Fantastical Vision of
Randolph Sitwell
by Mark Mower

It was in the latter part of June 1895 that I presented to my good friend Sherlock Holmes a most singular case which I now have the pleasure of setting before my readers. It was a little after nine o'clock that particular morning – a bright, sunny day, which looked set to continue the run of exceptionally warm weather we had been experiencing in London for much of the early summer. I sat at the table of our Baker Street apartment trying to read the newspapers, but my inability to concentrate had not been lost on my ever-vigilant colleague.

"I note that you are distracted, if not a little agitated, Watson," said he, leaning forward and placing his coffee cup down on the table beside the armchair. "Your jaw is set hard, and the fidgeting of your legs has been excessive even by your standards. Is it something with which I could assist?"

To that point, I hadn't considered unburdening myself to my friend the detective on what was essentially a medical matter. But in the moment, I realised that he might indeed have some insight into the case which was troubling me.

"You may remember my esteemed colleague Dr. Philip Everett," I began, noting that Holmes was already giving me his full attention.

"Yes. Short chap, originally from Gloucester, whom you have known since medical school. Specialises in cases of mental disorder, I seem to remember."

I was a little taken aback, for I had but once introduced Holmes to the fellow at a charity auction in Marylebone only a few weeks after we had first begun to lodge at 221b. "Yes, that's the man. Fine surgeon and a brilliant psychiatrist. He has built an enviable client list from his small practice in Kensington."

"And yet he has recently asked you to provide a second opinion on one of his more challenging cases," replied Holmes, clearly eager to get to the nub of the issue at hand.

"Indeed. But how did you know that?" I asked incredulously.

"You might remember that I left here late yesterday afternoon to travel to Pimlico where I'm currently assisting Inspector Lestrade with a poisoning case. Just before I left the house, a telegram arrived. Mrs.

Hudson took delivery of it, indicating that I need not dally, for the missive was addressed to you. It is rare for you to receive telegrams at home and, when you do, they are invariably from your medical colleagues or patients.

"When I returned just after nine o'clock last night, I noted that your medical bag was in the downstairs hallway, indicating that you had been called out on a medical matter during my absence. I surmised that this had been prompted by the earlier telegram. Ordinarily, you carry the bag upstairs, placing it below the coat stand. That you didn't do so last night hinted at your preoccupation with that same medical matter. And for the rest of the evening, you were cordial but reflective, reinforcing that notion.

"This morning your introspection has continued – something that occurs habitually when you are concerned or perplexed by a case. And the mention of Dr. Everett's name prompts me to conclude that it was he who contacted you yesterday with this very thorny problem – one which has baffled him. Am I correct?"

I couldn't deny the accuracy of his hypothesis. "Yes, he asked me to sit in on a consultation with one of his long-standing patients, a Mr. Randolph Sitwell, who was once a talented young barrister."

Holmes interjected once more while reaching for his pipe. "I see. And what was the nature of the malady affecting Mr. Sitwell?"

"He has quite a history, but I will furnish you with a summary of the pertinent facts which led Everett to request my assistance. A little over three years ago, Sitwell was in demand as one of the brightest and most able criminal barristers of his generation. Still in his late twenties, he had never lost a case in court and his career appeared to be gold-plated. Yet all that was to change when he was assaulted one evening while crossing Westminster Bridge. There was no great conspiracy involved – he had simply been the victim of a commonplace street robbery by a man wielding a heavy cosh. But the concussion which resulted had a lasting impact on both his speech and memory, forcing him to step back from his legal career for a period of about a year. In that time, his physical health improved, but the longer-term mental scars have continued to haunt him."

Ever attuned to the linguistic nuances of any verbal information presented to him, Holmes smiled wryly and interposed. "I sense that your choice of words may have been most deliberate. You used the words *haunt him* when, ordinarily, I might have expected you to use a term such as 'affect him'. Or am I overstating this?"

"In this case, you are not," said I. "Sitwell was referred to Dr. Everett by his own physician. He began to see Everett on a regular basis, sometimes two or three times a week depending on the nature of his anxieties. Alongside periods of sleeplessness and depression, he claimed to be having troubling visions at night, seeing things that could only be explained by the mania which gripped him from time to time. These visions were focused on one anxiety in particular – namely, that he was about to be attacked by flying creatures. All too often he would wake from his irregular slumber to see what he thought were bats circling the ceiling of his bedroom.

"Everett worked methodically to ascertain the underlying cause of these night terrors. Through patient enquiry, he discovered that when Sitwell was six years old and at boarding school, he had been aroused from his sleep one night to find a pipistrelle bat climbing up the blanket of his bed towards his face. His screams and violent reaction ensured that all the pupils in the dormitory were alerted to the intruder. But when the bat had been caught and released through the open window from which it had gained access, the young lad was taunted mercilessly – a pattern that was to continue for some months."

Holmes reflected on this while drawing on the churchwarden. "So having established the likely root cause, was Sitwell able to cure him of these unwanted visions?"

"Yes, by and large. With some carefully prescribed drugs and his psychiatric interventions, Everett was able to get Sitwell back into a regular sleep pattern which helped to reduce both the number and severity of the nightmares afflicting the barrister. And yet, two weeks ago, with the conclusion of a particularly lengthy and demanding court case, Sitwell had something of a relapse and returned to Everett's consulting room saying that the visions had begun once more. Everett prescribed a change of scenery and, with the help of two of the barrister's close friends, Sitwell was encouraged to embark on a walking holiday in Scotland.

"The three travelled up to Dunbartonshire and booked into a small country hotel close to the village of Cardross, on the north side of the Firth of Clyde. The fresh Scottish air and vigorous exercise had an immediate impact on the troubled patient, who slept soundly for the first three nights of their adventure and claimed to be full of energy and enthusiasm. Sadly, this was not to last, for on the fourth day something occurred which brought about an immediate and fateful collapse in Sitwell's physical and mental state. His friends had no option but to cancel their planned excursions and return to London, where Sitwell was once again placed under Everett's supervision. Alongside the reoccurring visions, the young man has also admitted to having suicidal thoughts."

"Hence Everett's request for a second opinion on the case?"

"Yes. While the matter falls well outside of my professional domain, Everett knows that he can trust me to give him an honest opinion. He simply wanted me to hear what Sitwell had to say, for the patient is adamant about the truth and reality of what he says he has experienced. In

286

short, Sitwell claims that while in Scotland he was attacked by a gigantic spectral bat which rendered him unconscious, and no amount of talk or therapy can convince him otherwise. Everett is at a loss to know how he can continue to treat his patient given this impasse."

"I see," said Holmes, clearly intrigued by the nature of the narrative. "Are you able to elaborate a little more on the account given to you by Sitwell?"

"Certainly. I arrived at Everett's consulting room shortly after six o'clock. Prior to Sitwell's arrival on the half-hour, Everett shared with me much of the background you have already heard. He said that the patient had consented to my sitting in on their session and readily agreed to recount his experience in Cardross.

"Randolph Sitwell is a tall, thin, fellow with something of a stoop. He seemed relaxed enough when seated in the consulting chair, but his tousled, sandy-coloured, hair and slightly unkempt appearance, testified to his current fragility. He spoke confidently enough and began by telling me why he had chosen to travel up to Scotland. Apparently, he had always wanted to visit the land of his ancestors, for the Sitwell family had resided in Dunbartonshire for well over three-hundred years. He was born in London and, not being much of a traveller, had rarely ventured outside the capital.

"The three men fell into a regular pattern during their stay. Rising early for breakfast, they would head out on a walking route chosen the evening before. This included visits to local landmarks and luncheon, teas, and ales at specially selected taverns. They would consistently return to the hotel in time for an evening meal at around eight o'clock. However, on the fourth day, this pattern was disrupted.

"They had chosen to hike around the hills overlooking the Firth of Clyde. The weather was good, and the day had gone well, so much so that Sitwell was considerably upbeat. A little after seven o'clock, he announced that he was keen to find the rural farmhouse which had been home to his family for countless generations. His friends were a little lukewarm to the idea, particularly as one had begun to suffer leg cramps. In the event, it was agreed that they would return to the hotel, while Sitwell retained one of the maps they were carrying to enable him to navigate his way around.

"The excursion proved successful, for within half-an-hour the barrister had located the farmhouse. Tentatively knocking on the door of the sizeable property, he was delighted to find that the present occupants were only too happy to invite him in when learning that he was a Sitwell. They knew much about the history of the property and, having offered him a glass of single malt and something to eat, regaled him with numerous tales about his illustrious forebears. Mindful of his colleagues back at the hotel, Sitwell stayed for as long as he felt it polite to do so, before thanking his hosts and setting off once more across the hills.

"By now the time was beyond nine o'clock. The day was drawing in and Sitwell realised that it was likely to be dark by the time he reached the hotel. In his haste to find the right route, he misread the map and, approaching a signpost to a '*Wallacetown Farm*', realised that he was someway off course. To adjust for the error, he began to descend a steep hill.

"The sky had taken on a most unusual colour, the approaching sunset casting vibrant shades of red and pink across the vista. Sitwell was unnerved by the predominantly scarlet hue which reminded him of blood. A light mist had also begun to descend across the lower reaches of the hill as he stumbled onwards. At this point, he had begun to approach a small hedgerow which ran across the hill for almost thirty feet. He realised that he would have to walk around this, but was momentarily transfixed by the bushes which were covered in a thick sheet of cobwebs above which now sat a thin veil of fog.

"There had been little by way of sound in the few moments preceding this, but Sitwell was now aware of what sounded like a loud flapping noise behind and above him. As he turned quickly to look upwards, he was greeted by the sight of a huge black bat descending towards him at speed, its twelve-to-fourteen-foot wingspan and wriggling body looking like a phantom from Hell. As he took in the full horror of the vision before him, the creature struck the top of his head, sending him backwards onto the grassy slope of the hill.

"He was momentarily dazed, but roused himself quickly from the ground, fearful that the spectral bat might return. Holding his aching head, he began to make his way along the hedge line, listening and watching for any signs of the attacker. Continuing then a little further down the hill, he had by this time reached a path he recognised as one leading to the hotel. A short while later he could see the lights of the establishment and wasted no time in jogging towards the safety of the building.

"Sitwell's friends were disturbed to hear what he had to say and did their best to hide their natural scepticism. Seeing the clearly visible bruising to his temple, they were inclined to believe that a blow to the head had brought about some form of hallucination. What had really caused the injury they had no way of knowing."

Holmes had listened to all of this with some intensity. I had imagined that he might be scornful of the whole affair, but he showed no signs of it. "The physical injury is important, Watson. As it was seen by his friends, it confirms that something tangible struck him. Did anything else occur that night?"

"No. Sitwell later refused to go to his room and sat downstairs in the lounge bar of the hotel growing increasingly hysterical. His friends had no option but to sit with him, explaining to the bewildered night porter that Sitwell was unwell and would be returning to London the following day. When they did return to the capital, their first call was to Everett, who took charge of the uncommunicative barrister."

"I take it that Everett has had some success in rehabilitating his patient?"

"Yes. Sitwell is now sleeping more soundly and has had fewer manic episodes, but the admission of suicidal thoughts is extremely worrying."

Holmes nodded and then asked, "Having heard what Sitwell had to say, what did you conclude?"

I took a few moments to reply, realising that my answer might surprise him. "I have to say that I remain unsure what to make of Sitwell's account. We talked for some time after he had relayed the story. I found him to be both open and credible. He showed no signs of hysteria, and his conversation was both calm and rational. After Sitwell had left us, Everett asked me the very same question you have just posed. I felt unable to answer him in that moment and agreed to give him my thoughts after a period of reflection. It was a stalling tactic on my part. If I were pushed to give an honest opinion, I would say that I believed Sitwell's account. I have little doubt that he saw something which terrified him. The question is whether that vision was real or one that was induced by a chemical imbalance in the brain or some other psychological disfunction."

Holmes smiled enigmatically. "How plausible is it, that a large supernatural *chiropteran* could descend from a blood-red sky into swirling mists and giant cobwebs to attack an innocent hill walker? Unlikely, I would suggest. Yet, that is the vision which has been presented, however improbable. Fortuitously, there are one or two points in the narrative which strike me as suggestive, so I'm confident that we are likely to find a more straightforward explanation."

So saying, he leapt from the armchair and proceeded to tap out the remains of his pipe in the empty grate before placing the churchwarden back on the mantelpiece.

"Then you are willing to look into the matter?" I ventured.

"Of course. I will start immediately with a trip to the Natural History Museum."

I was delighted to hear this but expressed an immediate concern. "I cannot join you, I'm afraid. I have four patients to see today and have arranged to call in on Dr. Everett at three o'clock this afternoon to give him my thoughts on the Sitwell case."

Holmes chuckled as he crossed the room towards the coat stand. "No need to worry, my friend. I'm confident that I can begin to unpick some of this very quickly. If it suits your purposes, I could meet you at Everett's practice a little before three."

This was more than I could have hoped for. A short while later he was gone and I prepared for my first house call of the day. Stepping outside, it was already busy in Baker Street, and it took me a good five minutes to hail a cab to my destination. But with the warmth of the sun on my face and the thought that Holmes was on the case, my disposition felt altogether much brighter.

The hours dragged that particular day. My calls proved to be straightforward in nature and by one-thirty I had returned to Baker Street. It was just as well, for Mrs. Hudson had taken delivery of a telegram from Holmes addressed to me. It read simply: *Ensure Sitwell is at meeting for three – SH*. I quickly arranged for a telegram to be sent to Dr. Everett to facilitate this.

I set off on foot for Kensington shortly after two-thirty. Arriving at the Russell Road practice, I was delighted to see that Holmes was already lingering on the pavement outside the premises. He greeted me with a knowing smile. "I trust that your day has been every bit as productive as mine. And how was Mr. Aspall's rheumatoid arthritis?"

I had no idea how he knew that Aspall had been on my list of calls but had no time to quiz him on the matter, for at that moment Randolph Sitwell arrived in a hansom cab and I had to hastily introduce him to my colleague. Sitwell seemed delighted to meet the detective whose career he said he had been following, "with very great interest."

With the four of us assembled in Dr. Everett's spacious consulting room and the pleasantries completed, it was Holmes who took the lead.

"Gentlemen. I hope you will forgive me for inviting myself along today and requesting that Mr. Sitwell join us. And I trust that Watson and I haven't crossed any ethical boundaries in discussing Mr. Sitwell's case outside of this consulting room, but, given the nature of the mysterious event which occurred in Scotland earlier this month, I felt obliged to do all that I could to bring some relief to Mr. Sitwell and to find an explanation for what really happened."

I could see that Everett was a little bewildered by Holmes's opening gambit, but Sitwell had no hesitation in voicing his appreciation. "Mr. Holmes. I had already expressed to Dr. Everett my hopes that he could get to the bottom of this matter using whatever methods he deemed necessary.

That he has wisely chosen to enlist the services of both yourself and Dr. Watson is a great comfort to me. I would welcome any thoughts or observations you are able to offer."

Luckily, Dr. Everett didn't seem inclined to admit that he had no idea the detective had been consulted on the matter. He merely added, "I am in your hands, Mr. Holmes. Like my client, I would be delighted if you could shed any light on this affair."

Holmes thanked them both. I had no doubt that he had something positive to share with us but hoped it would be sufficient to satisfy both Sitwell and Everett. In the event, I wasn't disappointed.

"At the risk of seeming insensitive to you, Mr. Sitwell, I will be honest in sharing what I had already said to Dr. Watson: Namely, that the idea of a large supernatural *chiropteran* descending from a blood-red sky into swirling mists and giant cobwebs to attack you seemed implausible. But by focusing on the individual elements which made up that vision, it is far easier to understand how they combined to make you believe that some grand and ghostly scheme was in operation.

"Let us start with the scenic backdrop. The sun is setting on a remote Scottish hillside, and you are presented with a sky the likes of which you have rarely seen. You admitted to Dr. Watson that you are no traveller and have seldom ventured outside London. The canvas before you was possibly the broadest panorama you have ever witnessed, and the colours must have seemed overwhelming. I did wonder if the deep red hues you observed were the result of a lunar eclipse which can produce a 'blood moon' effect, but a quick telegram to an expert at the Royal Observatory in Greenwich confirmed that the last full lunar eclipse was on the eleventh of March.

"The setting sun can illuminate the sky with tints from the full colour spectrum, including the dark crimson hues which put you in mind of blood. If we then add to that the perfectly natural phenomenon of low-lying mist, we can begin to understand how this scenic backdrop was beginning to exacerbate some of your anxieties on an evening when you were both alone and seeking to find a familiar route back to your hotel. And of course, it is at this point that you see the thick sheet of cobwebs adorning the hedgerow like some supernatural barrier preventing your passage.

"I was convinced that there would again be a perfectly logical and natural explanation for this. My knowledge of flora and fauna is good, but by no means extensive, so first thing this morning, I visited a friend at the Natural History Museum to ascertain whether there could be any natural explanation for what you saw. Professor Harold Fenton is an expert botanist and entomologist. Fortunately, he is also one of the country's leading academics in the field of *lepidoptery* – the study of moths and butterflies. When I described the hedgerow and the scale of the 'cobwebs', he had no hesitation in saying that it was the work of the larvae of the Ermine Moth. These can sometimes form huge communal webs on trees and hedgerows from May to June to provide protection for the caterpillars which feed on the leaves of the plants affected."

Dr. Everett responded excitedly. "Yes, I've heard of that! It certainly helps to explain part of what Mr. Sitwell saw. But what possible explanation could there be for a giant bat?"

"Well, let us now consider this aerial attacker. The bruising on Mr. Sitwell's head was witnessed by his two friends at the hotel. As a result, the attack couldn't have been a figment of his imagination. However implausible, I had to rule out the possibility that a giant bat species might exist in the hills overlooking the Firth of Clyde. When I put it to him, Professor Fenton was adamant that such a bat doesn't exist. He said that the noctule bat is generally regarded as the largest in Britain. It has a wingspan of up to sixteen inches. The largest bat in the world is the giant golden-crowned flying fox, whose wingspan is considerably larger at up to 5.6 feet. However, this fruit-eating bat is only found on the islands of the Philippines, and is, in any case, too small to be our attacker.

"Fenton then suggested that I visit the British Museum to speak to a Dr. Simon Tremaine, who is an expert in the developing science of aerodynamics. Fenton said that Tremaine had spent many years studying the flight patterns of all sorts of large flying creatures, so might be able to help.

"It didn't take me long to travel across to the Museum and locate Dr. Tremaine. He was pleased to assist. At first, he looked a little puzzled when I asked if he knew of any flying creature in Britain with a wingspan of twelve to fourteen feet. But when I then explained the nature of the sighting in the Cardross area of Dunbartonshire, his face lit up. He gave me the name of a lecturer at the University of Glasgow, whom he said could solve the riddle of the phantom flyer.

"Armed with this new information, I wired a man called Percy Sinclair Pilcher. Our subsequent exchange of telegrams was most illuminating and should help to put this matter to rest. You see, Pilcher is a lecturer at the University and another expert in aerodynamics. But outside of his academic studies, he builds flying machines, and I'm certain that it was one of these you saw that fateful night. From the start, I had my suspicions that some human element might be behind this but needed to eliminate all the other possibilities."

Randolph Sitwell looked momentarily confused, but then smiled gently. "A flying machine, you say? I've heard of such contraptions, but

292

this had no hot air balloon or propulsion of any kind. It looked exactly like a giant bat."

"And therein lies the greatest irony," said Holmes. "That day, Pilcher had been testing the latest of a long line of aircraft he has been constructing in the Cardross area. The particular model he was flying is called the *Bat*. The craft has no way of propelling itself. It essentially glides in the air. Pilcher had taken it to the top of the hill that you were descending. When at the top, he had run a short way down the hill to enable the *Bat* to be launched into the air. The sound you heard wasn't the flapping of its wings, but the wind catching the fabric of the craft which is fixed onto a bamboo framework.

"Pilcher had no idea that you were descending the hill. With the fading light, this was to be his last flight of the day. As he reached you, you were momentarily hidden by the thin veil of mist. And by the time he did see you it was too late, for his feet caught the top of your head. You see, his body was suspended below the framework to enable him to steer the aircraft by shifting his weight. To you, this looked like the moving body of a bat.

"Having narrowly avoided crashing into the hedgerow, he landed the *Bat* safely a little further down the hill. He then unstrapped himself and made his way back up the hill to look for you, but by that time you had fled, fearing a return of the phantom flyer."

"Incredible!" said I.

"Unbelievable," said Dr. Everett.

"Well, in this case, Doctor, it is wholly believable," replied Holmes. "Mr. Sitwell can rest assured that what he saw that night wasn't a ghostly bat, but an experimental aircraft. Mr. Pilcher has asked me to pass on his sincere apologies for causing you such distress."

Sitwell beamed for the first time. "I really don't know how to thank you, Mr. Holmes. Your reputation is justly deserved. I still think it will take some time for me to come to terms with all that I have experienced, but this should help me to move on with the continuing assistance of Dr. Everett."

A short while later Holmes and I returned to Baker Street. As we smoked and reflected on the fantastical vision of Randolph Sitwell, Holmes made a rare admission. "Fortune smiled on me today, Watson. I was optimistic that I could unpick one or two of the threads of this case quite quickly, but I couldn't have foreseen how fortuitous my visit to Professor Fenton would be. Had he not suggested the name of Dr. Tremaine at the British Museum, I believe it would have taken me some considerable time to link all of this to Percy Pilcher. The science of deduction rarely depends on luck, but in this case it has proved to be a decisive factor!"

NOTE:

Percy Sinclair Pilcher continued to make experimental aircraft in the years after this. His most famous glider – or "soaring machine" as he termed it – was the *Hawk,* which in 1897 set a world record-breaking flight distance of over eight-hundred feet. In 1899, he hoped to complete a test flight in his newly built triplane, which was powered by a four horse-power combustion engine. A number of onlookers and potential investors were invited to the launch, which was due to take place in a field near Stanford Hall in Leicestershire. However, a couple of days prior to this, the engine crankshaft on the aircraft broke. Rather than disappoint his guests, Pilcher decided to fly the *Hawk* instead. While mid-air at a height of around thirty feet, the tail of the bamboo framework snapped, sending the glider and its pilot plummeting to the ground. Pilcher died two days later from his injuries. He is remembered as one of Britain's early aviation pioneers. – JHW

The Adventure of the Paternal Ghost
by Arthur Hall

It is well known to readers of my accounts of the extraordinary cases of my friend, Mr. Sherlock Holmes, that he preferred, and indeed conducted, some of his most memorable investigations into problems of an unusual or singular nature. Before now, I have committed many of these to paper so that those who have interest might appreciate the deductive genius of the man who was, at that time, London's only consulting detective. My following recollections will illustrate this further.

Holmes's jubilant mood at breakfast one fine spring morning did not surprise me. Over the previous few days, he had seen the successful conclusion of the Market Street scandal, the affair of Mrs. Juliette Kerr, and the thwarting of the attempted ruination of Mr. Percy Fellingham.

"You really have succeeded to a remarkable extent," I remarked, although he hadn't mentioned his triumphs.

"I would believe that you had taken to reading my mind, were I not aware that my facial expression had betrayed my thoughts. But you are correct. I'm pleased immensely by the outcome of our activities."

"I contributed little enough, but I hope I was of some small assistance."

"Nonsense, my dear fellow. You were instrumental in at least two instances to my arriving at the correct conclusion in the most trying of circumstances. You cannot imagine how many times I've asked myself where I would be without my Boswell."

I felt my face begin to flush with both embarrassment and pride. "You are most kind."

Before he could say anything more, our landlady knocked and entered to ask if we required more coffee and to clear away our empty plates. We both declined and she left us, carrying a laden tray. Moments later the doorbell rang and, after a short conversation below, Mrs. Hudson reappeared to usher a rather bewildered man of about forty years into our presence.

"Mr. Cedric Topham, to see Mr. Holmes," she announced, before closing the door softly as she left.

Our visitor paused, glancing from Holmes to myself. In this brief interval, I decided to use my friend's methods to scrutinise the fellow and see what information I could glean.

He was a tall man, though not so tall as Holmes, in his middle years and dressed in a fashionable morning-coat. His face had a lop-sided appearance, an effect which I quickly realised was produced because his hair was combed in such a way as to be piled to one side of his head. His expression struck me as glum and his voice, when first he spoke, held a note of grief – or fear.

"Good morning, gentlemen," he began uncertainly. "Which of you, pray, is Mr. Sherlock Holmes?"

Holmes was before him in two strides, extending his hand and dismissing the man's dilemma.

"It is me that you seek. Allow me to introduce Doctor John Watson. His assistance in my work has been invaluable, and you may be assured that he is the soul of discretion."

"I'm indebted to you for granting me an interview without an appointment."

"You have, in fact, called at an opportune time. I have no cases requiring my immediate attention." He guided Mr. Topham to the hearth. "But I see that something is indeed troubling you. Allow me to take your hat and coat, and then take the basket chair, so that we can see what can be done."

When we all three were settled, Holmes enquired if the young man would like tea.

"Thank you, no, Mr. Holmes. I'm not inclined to eat or drink at all just now. My burden of worry is so great that I feel no desire to do so."

"I wouldn't recommend such a course," said I. "Lack of nourishment can have nothing but a detrimental effect, regardless of your present circumstances."

Holmes nodded his agreement. "Pray elaborate, and we will assist you in any way we can."

"I'm not sure that anyone can help. Scotland Yard would probably think me mad."

"They are not noted for their imagination. Continue, please."

Our client swallowed heavily. "I'm being haunted – hounded – by a ghost."

I expected my friend to immediately assure our client that, based on much experience, he had formed the impression that no such things existed, and so it surprised me when his expression remained unaltered.

"Is this apparition of someone with whom you were acquainted?"

"It is that of my father."

Holmes and I glanced briefly at each other, and I wondered if he could be thinking, as I was, that this was a situation that we hadn't before encountered.

For a moment or two there was silence, except for the faint noise of our landlady rattling crockery in the kitchen downstairs, and that of the hooves of passing horses along Baker Street.

"It would be best, I think, if you were to begin at the beginning," Holmes said then. "Kindly be as specific as you can, even to the smallest detail."

Mr. Topham hesitated, obviously with some embarrassment.

"It is normal, thankfully, that parents should love their offspring," he began, "but in our house the opposite was true. I can recall no instance when my father favoured me with a smile, much less a kind word. Unlike him, my mother wasn't cruel, but rather indifferent, and I have long since formed the opinion that I entered this world unbidden."

"I'm exceedingly sorry to learn this," I interrupted, earning myself an immediate scowl pf impatience from Holmes.

"My father seemed always to be irritated by any number of things, my presence among them, as I grew from a child to a man. Gradually his disposition became worse, as he was consumed on occasion by violent rages that worsened year by year. About six months ago, these became both more frequent and more intense, to the point where I was obliged to forcibly restrain him to protect my mother."

"It came about that he injured her?" Holmes asked.

"Indeed. I returned home one day – I should mention that I'm unmarried and live still in my parents' home for convenience sake – to find her covered in blood. My father stood over her with a fire-iron, raving like the madman he had become. A neighbour, alarmed by the screams and calls for help, had summoned a constable, who arrived minutes after me. Together we disarmed my father, and he was put in handcuffs. As he was being led away, he screamed at me hysterically, threatening to kill me when he was released."

"Did he, in fact, attempt this?" Holmes enquired seriously.

"He couldn't, because he was committed to an asylum by the local court. This didn't surprise me, since my mother died from her injuries not long after his arrest. Some weeks later, news was brought to me that he too had passed from pneumonia, doubtless contracted in the place of his detention. I spoke at length with the bearer of these tidings and learned that the body had already been buried for fear of contagion. I asked the messenger whether my father had mentioned me as his end approached, and the man's hesitant reply is with me still. My father said he looked forward to seeing me in Hell."

"A dreadful story," I acknowledged. "You have my sympathy, sir."

Mr. Topham expressed his thanks as Holmes seemed to be considering the matter.

"You have said that your father's ghost has appeared to you. Kindly tell us how that came about."

"It must be four weeks ago – I must apologise for my inaccuracy, my mind has been in turmoil – since I appealed to my employer, who is a kindly man, for a few days of rest. He was aware of the effect that the death of my parents has had upon me, and allowed me three days without pay. I decided that a long walk would help to clear my head, and so the first day found me ambling beside the Serpentine. Eventually I sat upon a bench, occupying myself with nothing more than watching the sunlight play upon the surface of the water, when I chanced to glance towards the opposite bank where a group of elderly people appeared to be listening to a lecture from a man who made much use of gestures to illustrate his talk. Standing alone and a short way apart from the group was a man who seemed to be staring in my direction. I was shocked, and racked with disbelief when I saw that it was my father! A dizzy spell overcame me briefly, but immediately it passed. I got to my feet and made off towards where I could cross to the other bank. When I arrived at the spot the lecture was continuing, but of my father there was no sign. I imagined that he'd retreated into the nearby trees and left the scene from there."

Holmes leaned his thin body forward in his chair. "Why are you so certain that this man was your father? From such a distance, wouldn't recognition be difficult?"

"I'm blessed with long-sightedness," Mr. Topham struggled with the recollection, "but even so I couldn't see his features clearly. It was more his stance, the way he held himself, and his general appearance that convinced me."

"You identified this man as a ghost, but was there any reason that he couldn't have simply resembled your father? After all, those who claim to have seen such apparitions invariably describe their form as transparent, and the encounters as taking place at night."

"No, Mr. Holmes, he looked to be as solid as you or me. However, that isn't the end of it. The following day, I discovered a piece of tattered parchment on the floor of my hallway. It hadn't arrived by post since there was neither envelope nor stamp upon it. I've brought it for your inspection."

With that, he reached into the pocket of his morning-coat and withdrew a discoloured fragment of paper. My friend took it and examined it with his lens.

298

"This paper isn't ancient. It has simply been made to appear so by the application of heat. The message reads:

the madness that engulfed me awaits you also. your time is short.

"Is this in your father's hand, Mr. Topham?"

Our client nodded. "I've seen no example of it for many years, but to the best of my recollection, it is. Also, he was never much of a scholar. You will have noticed the absence of capital letters."

"Indeed. An unusual ghost who writes letters, wouldn't you say?"

"I suppose my assumption was fanciful."

"It was exactly the conclusion you were intended to reach. Has anything else occurred?"

"Subsequently, there were two more letters."

Again, he took them from his pocket and passed them to Holmes, who examined them as he had the first.

"Their intent is the same: '*you cannot escape your fate*' and '*your destiny is in your own hands*'. The content seems to suggest that you should contemplate suicide. Evidently, the object of all this is your demise. Who would benefit from that?"

"There is no one." He looked perplexed at the notion. "I have no friends and few remaining relatives."

"And there has been nothing more?"

"There has. Since the letters, I have been accosted by a man who I remember from my youth. He was once our greengrocer, and was apparently unaware of my father's death, which he said couldn't be, as he had recently seen him in Paddington High Street. When I insisted that my father had passed on, he gave me a peculiar look and excused himself."

"Did this man elaborate, or converse with 'your father'?"

"No, he saw him on the edge of a crowd, on the opposite side of the street."

"From a distance, as you did?"

"It must have been."

Holmes folded his hands in his lap, but I saw by the glitter in his grey eyes that he had become interested.

"What action did you take then?"

Our client fell silent for a moment. "I needed, you understand, to know the truth of this. I acted in a way of which I'm not proud, and that I wouldn't normally consider."

"You had your father's body exhumed?"

"I did," he said in a dull voice, "but not legally. I know how long it takes for the wheels of the law to turn, so I resorted to the only other way there was."

"Grave robbers?"

He hung his head. "Two of them. We went to St. Michael's Churchyard, late one night. They must have been experienced, for they made short work of it."

"What did you discover?" I asked then.

"I jumped down into the opened grave and prised the lid from the coffin myself. It was empty!"

"Someone has put themselves to a great deal of trouble to convince you that your father has risen from the grave," said Holmes. "But that notion is easily disproved. Before you return to Paddington, your singing, and your employment as a gentleman's barber, I would be grateful if you would inform us as to anything more which you consider might be helpful to our investigation. In particular, anything of your father's history."

Mr. Topham appeared astonished. "Mr. Holmes, I'm aware that I mentioned that my father was supposedly seen in Paddington, but I didn't state that I reside there. Neither did I mention my profession, nor the fact that I'm a gifted tenor. You amaze me, sir."

"There is really no mystery about it." A quick smile passed across Holmes's face. "When I see affixed to your morning-coat a button bearing an insignia that I recognise, that of the Paddington Hairdressers Choral Society, and then notice marks of the habitual use of scissors on your thumb and forefinger, what else am I to conclude? As you will now realise, it was simplicity itself."

"As you explain it, yes, but I would never have thought of such things."

"It is my business to do so."

"Of course. As to my father, I've already explained his rejection of me. That is why, having no parental guidance, I had to find my own place in the world. Our local barber, who both my father and I patronised, kindly took me on as an apprentice. I progressed, and have been a partner in his establishment for about three years." He paused, realising perhaps that he had digressed. "I recall that I asked my father several times, over the years, about his occupation. My mother, it seemed, had always been kept in ignorance of it. My father's only reply to such an enquiry was a vague reference to a government post of some secrecy, which was also offered as an explanation for his frequent long absences from home."

I underlined this in my notebook, in which I had been recording the essence of the conversation throughout, knowing that Holmes might wish to refer to it later.

"Did your family ever experience financial difficulty?" he asked.

Our visitor shook his head. "Not that I recall. I cannot say with certainty that my father's income was sufficient, though. I once overheard a conversation between my parents, during which it was mentioned that my uncle, Mr. Albert Topham, was a contributor to our household. This didn't surprise me, since I knew already that our house was given to us by him."

"He is a man of some means, then?"

"I don't believe he was at the time when he invited us to live with him, during my childhood. Like myself he was unmarried, and after a few years became determined to make his fortune in the South African gold fields. He left us, with the provision that we should pay a modest rent during his absence. Subsequently he informed us that he had transferred the deed of the lease to my father. I also discovered that he sent a goodly sum regularly to assist in our maintenance. I regret to say that we have heard nothing from him for some time, so that I had begun to wonder if, as he has mentioned occasionally in past letters, he might at last be coming home."

"Most interesting," Holmes acknowledged. "Mr. Topham, it will greatly assist us if you can provide a likeness of your father. A photographic portrait, perhaps?"

"I regret that I cannot, for the only image of him that I know of is the portrait that hangs in the hallway of what is now my home. It seemed a strange variation of his usual character when he sat for it, and I wondered if it was commissioned because he wished, out of envy, his image to be displayed alongside that of his brother."

"A possibility, of course," Holmes nodded. "If it is convenient, Doctor Watson and I will now accompany you to your residence, where we can view these portraits. It is of paramount importance that we are able to recognise this 'ghost', should we encounter him."

"But certainly. You are both most welcome."

A cab was procured without difficulty. I said little during the journey, but Holmes and Mr. Topham conducted a conversation that mostly consisted of our client's account of the further indifferences of his father and his jealousy of his brother's success. It seemed to me that Mr. Albert Topham's generosity had passed largely unnoticed by his brother.

I took to gazing out at the passing scene, although the monotone of our client's voice was still clearly audible to me. I watched St. Mary's Hospital pass by, and Paddington Green Police Station of considerable reputation. Our driver turned into a tree-lined lane before we reached the High Street, and we soon found ourselves confronted by tall iron gates standing open. In the paved courtyard, I asked as we alighted that the cab should wait for us.

The house was smaller than I expected from Mr. Topham's description. It was a square structure of grey stone that had crumbled in places, without wings or extension. We were met by an attractive young girl in the uniform of a maid, and our client explained that, apart from the elderly cook, she was his only servant. As we had refused refreshments, he led us immediately to a low oak-beamed passage where three portraits were displayed. We stood back to obtain a better view, and I saw that Holmes was examining them carefully.

He stood before a picture of a grim-faced man, dark-haired and with eyes that appeared, even on canvas, as rather empty.

"The plaque reads '*Mr. Jeremiah Topham*'," he said to our client. "He was your father, I presume?"

"He was. It is an excellent likeness."

"And the other, in the frame decorated with gold leaf?"

"My uncle, Albert, who, to the best of my knowledge, still resides in the Transvaal."

The image was that of a heavier man with a jovial expression. The resemblance to our client and his father was nevertheless evident.

Holmes moved a few feet along the passage to where a smaller frame held the painted countenance of a man with some similarities to the others.

"Another uncle?" I asked.

"That is my nephew, Mr. Benjamin Stokehouse," Mr. Topham said. "He is the son of my elder sister. Sadly, both she and her husband succumbed to a local influenza epidemic a number of years ago."

"But Mr. Stokehouse still lives?" Holmes enquired.

"Indeed he does, although he too is often ill and prone to chest infections. He was fortunate in that his investments enabled him to retire quite early. For most of his life, he has suffered from severe bronchitis."

"Does he live in London?"

"He does as far as I'm aware, since I see little of him. It will not surprise you to learn that he and my father disagreed about many things, which is probably why he is almost a stranger to me." He looked at Holmes with some surprise. "Surely he cannot be connected to your investigation?"

"You will recall at the outset that I mentioned the importance of even minor details."

"Of course. Somewhere in my study I have his Notting Hill address. Please step this way, gentlemen, and I will find it for you."

We left shortly afterwards. During our return to Baker Street, Holmes requested our driver to stop once so that a telegram could be despatched.

"To Lestrade?" I asked as he resumed his seat upon reappearing from the Post Office.

"To Mycroft," he corrected me. "But now, a luncheon of Mrs. Hudson's trout awaits us, I think."

Holmes ate with unusual enthusiasm, though his preoccupation with the new enquiry was evident. He refused dessert as he often did, leaping to his feet the moment our coffee cups were empty.

"I will be with you in an instant," I said, rising from the table.

"There is no need to inconvenience yourself. I don't anticipate that I shall be away for long. Should Mrs. Hudson be out, pray be so good as to receive Mycroft's reply for me. It may arrive before my return."

I barely had time to reply in the affirmative before he had seized his hat and coat and departed. It occurred to me then that I had once more allowed my unread medical journals to accumulate, so I settled myself in my chair and began to read. No more than two hours had passed, however, before I heard my friend's familiar tread upon the stairs. He shouted a greeting as he entered and poured two glasses of port from the decanter immediately after shedding his outer garments.

"Have we heard from my brother?" he asked as he lowered himself into his chair.

I took a sip and placed my glass upon a side-table. "Not as yet. Your mood suggests that your afternoon was successful."

"It was, though I perceive from your tone that you are slightly aggrieved that I didn't request your company. The lady whom I consulted is wary of another presence when acting as my informant, so it was for the best that I saw her alone. All that I learned wasn't unexpected."

"Who is she?"

"You have heard me speak of her before now. She's an actress currently performing at the Lyceum with Henry Irving – Miss Gloriana Roland."

"I recall your previous mentions of her. But what was your purpose in visiting her today?"

His reply was delayed as he took a long draught of his drink. I heard the shouts of a newspaper-seller from somewhere along Baker Street, announcing the mid-day edition.

"My purpose was the same as that of sending a wire to Mycroft: I'm trying to separate the truth of Mr. Jeremiah Topham from his lies. Miss Roland, though a successful actress, is something of a busybody, and is aware of all that occurs within the theatrical profession in the capital. She is certain that no one of her acquaintance has been hired to impersonate a dead man, or to equip another to do so."

303

"So we are seeking someone who has learned his skills, if he has any, elsewhere." I smiled in anticipation of Holmes's response to what I was about to say next. "Unless of course, we are at last involved in the pursuit of a genuine ghost."

He scowled, predictably. "You are aware of my opinions and deductions on that score. It did, however, occur to me at once that our client might be completely unaware of his father having an identical twin brother." He considered for a moment. "It is unlikely, but I will ask this of Mr. Benjamin Stokehouse, who I intend to interview soon. As a member of the family, he is sure to know the answer."

Before I could reply, the doorbell rang and we heard our landlady at the front door. Minutes later, a yellow envelope was in Holmes's hands.

He extracted the form and glanced at it briefly. "It is as I suspected. Mr. Jeremiah Topham is unknown in Whitehall."

"Then what was his occupation? How can his absences be truly explained?

"That we will doubtless discover shortly."

He would say no more of the subject, but took up his violin to play a mournful tune that suddenly erupted into a fast pace and then a shrill crescendo. I suspected it to be his own composition, and when I looked up from my reading, it was to see that his eyes were closed and his face held an expression of rapturous delight, as if the strains were a comfort to his soul.

Dinner was one of Mrs. Hudson's steak-and-mushroom pies. I ate mine with relish but, not unexpectedly, Holmes merely sampled his portion before toying with the remains. He requested that our landlady provide an extra pot of coffee, which he consumed before I had begun mine. As we repaired to our armchairs, he was already contemplating the steps we should take to bring about a conclusion to this puzzling case, and I had resigned myself to an evening of little conversation between long silences, when the peal of the doorbell brought him out of his thoughts.

"Are you expecting anyone?" I asked.

He wore the look of a man emerging from a deep sleep. "I have no appointments."

"It could be an emergency. Fortunately, I've re-stocked my medical bag." I rose and peered through the window, as we heard the front door open.

"It is another telegram. The boy has just left. A new client, perhaps?"

"We will know in a moment. Mrs. Hudson is on her way."

With that he got to his feet and took the envelope from her at our sitting room door. By the time he resumed his seat, the form was open and he read it without expression, before passing it to me.

Mr. Holmes,

Help me. He attempted to take my life.

Topham

Holmes now wore a furious look, but his anger was against himself.

"I should have foreseen this. How many times have I emphasised the danger of making assumptions? Yet I assumed that this 'ghost' would go no further than attempting to terrify our client by his random appearances." He stood up quickly. "Bah! I would have expected more of an amateur."

Within moments we were outside and at the street. Holmes promised our cab driver an extra half-sovereign if he could get us to Paddington quickly, and so we found ourselves before Mr. Topham's door before the light began to fade.

Holmes raised his stick, but the door opened immediately.

"Mr. Holmes, Doctor Watson! Thank God!" Our client stood aside unsteadily to allow us to enter. I saw that his face was skinned along one side, with blood still seeping onto his collar. His clothes were torn, and his hand badly bruised. He limped slightly as he led us to a comfortable sitting room with new furniture. He didn't forget his manners.

"First, can I offer you gentlemen something? The cook is still here. It was she who went to send the telegram."

Holmes brushed the kind suggestion aside. "No, thank you, Mr. Topham. Doctor Watson will attend to your injuries, as you relate the circumstances in which you came by them."

At that, I took bandages and ointment from my medical bag and began treating him. It was soon apparent that the smeared blood worsened the appearance of the wounds. The cook, a pleasant middle-aged lady called Mrs. Cranmore, supplied hot water and towels. Despite Holmes's request, my patient said little during my ministrations so that I concluded that he had suffered a severe shock. I resolved to leave an adequate amount of laudanum with him on our departure.

"Has the pain lessened?" I enquired when I had dressed the last of his wounds.

"Yes, thank you, Doctor," he replied in a shaky voice. "I'm a little unsteady, but I believe that I've come to no serious harm."

"Nevertheless," I handed him the medication, "you must not exert yourself for the next few days and should take this regularly. Your facial abrasions should heal quickly. They aren't serious."

"Are you able, now, to explain to us?" Holmes enquired with some impatience.

Mr. Topham nodded. "There is very little to it. My maid reported that, as she left here at the end of her duties, a man began to follow her. She immediately retraced her steps and advised me of her fear, whereupon I accompanied her to her home."

"Did you, yourself, notice any pursuit as you walked with her?"

"There was none, I'm certain of it. She lives with her parents in a cottage near the station, less than a quarter-of-a-mile distant, and we hardly saw a soul. In fact, she apologised as we arrived, saying that she must have imagined the incident, and that she was sorry to have caused me so much trouble. I saw her safely inside and returned."

"Has the girl mentioned similar incidents, previously?"

"Never, but she is of a nervous disposition, and I confess that I believed her fears were imaginary. I thought it would do no harm to accompany her to dispel her anxiety."

"Most commendable," I murmured.

"I had walked almost halfway back, to a place where two lanes meet to form a crossroads, when a cart appeared. It was driven at a fast pace, and as it overtook me and swerved into my path. I was knocked off my feet and landed in a thorn bush, where I received these injuries. By the time I disentangled myself, the cart was disappearing among the trees along the lane ahead – but I had already seen the driver's face."

"It was the man that you have identified as your father's ghost, of course," Holmes concluded.

"I'm quite certain of it. He wore a wide-brimmed hat, but I'm in no doubt."

"Further proof, if any were necessary, that it is a man we are dealing with."

Our client shook his head. "Yet the coffin was empty, and the resemblance was clear to me. What does this mean, Mr. Holmes?"

"Simply that you are being persecuted for reasons as yet unknown to us." My friend spent a moment in consideration. "If you're feeling somewhat recovered, Doctor Watson and I will leave you now. On our way back to Baker Street, I'll telegraph Inspector Lestrade of Scotland Yard, requesting that he assign a constable to remain outside your home until tomorrow, when I expect to have brought these events to their conclusion. I suggest that you ensure that all the doors and windows of this house are locked until the officer arrives. I also recommend a glass of brandy, to still your nerves and cause your trembling to cease."

He glanced at me for a sign of approval, which I gave, before remembering, "Is Mrs. Cranmore on the premises still?"

"She will have left by now. Her husband invariably arrives to collect her."

"Excellent. Goodnight then, Mr. Topham. I would be obliged if you would visit us at Baker Street at, say, four o'clock tomorrow afternoon, if that is convenient. I will confirm this by wire."

Appearing somewhat bemused, our client assented, and we left.

There was little conversation between us in the hansom, as Holmes had lapsed into a silent reverie. It was now late evening and, as we resettled ourselves in our armchairs, I knew that he would wish to retire soon, since he had inferred that there was work to be done on the morrow. He had, I recalled, twice suggested that this affair would be over soon.

"Holmes," I began as we filled our last pipes of the day, "how can you be sure that Mr. Topham's problem will be solved so quickly?"

He blew out a cloud of aromatic smoke and leaned back in his chair. "Consider: Our client's father, Mr. Jeremiah Topham is deceased – I'm in no doubt of that – and his uncle, Mr. Albert Topham, still resides in South Africa."

"So we are given to understand."

"Then who else is related to our client, and therefore is likely to be able to tell us more?"

"Mr. Topham mentioned a nephew," I said after a moment's recollection.

"He did indeed. Mr. Benjamin Stokehouse, who lives in Notting Hill. If the truth of this business is as I suspect, then he will provide us with confirmation in the morning."

Holmes's irritation as I consumed my breakfast was evident. He had taken no more than two cups of coffee, refusing anything more substantial as he often did when the end of a case was in sight.

"I do think that you could eat a little faster without inviting indigestion," he scowled.

"Have a care. I will be finished in a moment."

I gulped down the last of my coffee and rose, to find my hat and coat immediately thrust at me. A few minutes later we halted a passing cab and Holmes shouted our destination to the driver.

In Notting Hill, we left the hansom in a quiet street of terraced houses. The residence of Mr. Benjamin Stokehouse proved to be elderly, bearing signs of much repair.

The door opened to reveal a thick-set man, evidently intending to leave the premises since he was about to put on his hat.

"Mr. Benjamin Stokehouse?" Holmes asked.

"I am, sir," the man's difficulty in breathing was immediately obvious. "Who are you, and to what do I owe this pleasure?"

"My name is Sherlock Holmes, and this is my associate, Doctor John Watson. I am a consulting detective, investigating some curious incidents involving Mr. Jeremiah Topham."

Mr. Stokehouse stared at us blankly, then nodded. "Yes, I believe I've heard of you. But, Mr. Holmes, I fear that you have had a wasted journey. You see, my grandfather, scoundrel that he was, died several months ago. Tell me sir, if it isn't breaking a confidence to do so, who it is who is so unaware of this as to hire you."

"My client is Mr. Cedric Topham."

"Cedric? Why, I haven't seen my uncle for many a year. We aren't a family who are close. In fact, I discovered my grandfather's death through a third party." He ceased speaking abruptly, to succumb to a fit of coughing. When it had subsided, he turned back to us. "What is troubling him?"

"He claims that he is being haunted."

"A joke, surely." He laughed, with some effort, briefly. "I don't remember him as being so fanciful."

"He has seen his father since the burial."

"Ridiculous! Have I not just stated that the man is dead?" Mr. Stokehouse removed his hat as he retreated over the threshold. "Come in, sirs. Clearly there is something amiss here, and it is probably as well to discuss it."

Shortly afterwards, we found ourselves in a sitting room panelled in dark wood. We refused our host's offer of sherry and seated ourselves in worn but comfortable chairs.

"Your uncle is quite certain that he has seen his father several times," Holmes repeated. "He was concerned enough to cause the grave to be opened, only to find the coffin empty."

Mr. Stokehouse struggled noisily to breathe. "If this were some sort of trick, I can see no purpose in it. However, I wouldn't put such a scheme out of the question. My grandfather, as my mother often stated, was an absolute blackguard who thought nothing of beating her and his wife for the least of reasons. Uncle Cedric, I understand, didn't fare well either."

"No indeed. Shortly before he died, your grandfather cursed your uncle."

"That is no surprise to me. I was appalled at his treatment of my grandmother. My father had long held the suspicion that there was another woman, possibly a lady of the night, involved."

"Certainly our client described his father's long absences from home," I remembered.

308

"There were many." With difficulty, he attempted to breathe evenly. "I'm striving to recollect more of my grandfather that might explain his apparent resurrection, but the fact is that he was estranged from me for a number of years." His thoughtful expression cleared suddenly. "There is one man who may be able to assist you. I recall my mother mentioning him several times. He is my grandfather's solicitor, whose name, if my memory serves me, is Mr. Bradwood Kitterly."

Holmes's face lit up immediately, but Mr. Stokehouse appeared not to notice. He continued to relate several more minor incidents of his grandfather's misdeeds towards members of the family before we took our leave.

"I'll wager that the name of that solicitor had some significance for you," I said, watching Holmes's face as he raised his stick to summon a cab.

"You improve constantly, Watson. Mr. Kitterly and I are certainly known to each other. He has the distinction of obtaining the release of scores of blackguards and scoundrels from their rightful imprisonment by exploiting contradictions in our ill-conceived laws. His other methods include the production of false witnesses, and possibly the blackmail of those who would otherwise furnish truthful testimony. There are few methods of deceit unknown and yet-to-be practised by him, I think."

"I'm astounded that you or Scotland Yard haven't caused him to be disbarred, at the very least."

"Ah, but he is clever. One day he will make an error sufficient for Gregson, Lestrade, or myself to pounce upon, and the wheels of justice will turn more smoothly afterwards."

We ate a scant luncheon at a coffee house on the outskirts of Kensington. The premises of Mr. Bradwood Kitterly, Holmes confided, were a short walk away. So it was that less than ten minutes had passed before we found ourselves before a stone-faced middle-aged woman who sat before a typewriting machine in a tiny office.

"Is Mr. Kitterly expecting either of you gentlemen?" she asked in response to Holmes's request.

"That I would doubt. Kindly present my card to your employer."

She took it from where he had placed it on her desk and made her inspection. "You are a consulting detective?" she retorted, with a disapproving glare.

"That is my profession."

She hesitated for so long that I became convinced that she would find a reason to dismiss us, but then she glanced at the door at the back of the room and nodded. "Very well, I will see whether Mr. Kitterly has time."

309

She rose and turned abruptly to strut away and knock at the door. After a moment, a faint voice bade her enter the room beyond.

"Impertinent woman," I commented.

Holmes smiled. "She is exactly the sort that I would have expected Mr. Kitterly to employ. I would be surprised indeed to learn that she knows the true nature of his business."

"He is so shrewd, then, to be able to deceive his secretary?"

"Much more so. His respectable appearance is vital to his activities."

She reappeared in the doorway frowning, possibly because her employer's decision was unexpected.

"Mr. Kitterly will see you now, gentlemen," she announced in a regretful tone.

Holmes granted her an undeserved smile as we passed, and she closed the door behind us. We were now in a room at least twice the size of the other, lined with leather-bound books on both sides. Behind the well-polished desk sat a small man wearing a grey coat over a white shirt with a wing collar. His appearance was mild, even benign, but his eyes held the look of a cunning fox.

"Ah, Mr. Sherlock Holmes and Doctor Watson." His voice was perfectly calm, but the welcoming smile had the artificial quality of that of a horse-racing tout. "We have crossed swords before, but never actually met."

He didn't rise or offer his hand, instead gesturing that we should take the chairs at the front of the desk. We did so and he smiled wistfully, while waiting for Holmes to explain himself.

"You are indeed known to me," my friend confirmed. "On three occasions you have deflected the arm of the law from justly punishing those whom my investigations have exposed. I'm aware of your activities, sir, as you are aware of mine."

Mr. Kitterly's expression didn't alter. "Come, come now, Mr. Holmes. Our system of law isn't perfect. There are bound to be instances when innocent men, and sometimes women, become entangled in crime simply because they are unfortunate enough to be nearby when such acts are committed. I consider it my duty to help these luckless souls, for justice, as you know, is always depicted as a statue wearing a blindfold."

"A fact of which you have invariably taken advantage," Holmes replied dryly.

Perhaps I imagined it, but I thought that the smile had narrowed.

"Much as I would be delighted to discuss such matters with you gentlemen for the remainder of the afternoon," he replied, "my curiosity compels me to enquire the reason for your presence here. Please be brief, as there are currently many demands upon my time."

"We are here to ask how you arranged for the father of my client, Mr. Cedric Topham, to appear to return from the grave. I have assured him of a rational explanation, but he is quite distressed, nevertheless."

The smile narrowed further. "I'm neither a surgeon nor a magician, Mr. Holmes. Mr. Jeremiah Topham was a client and friend for many years. I attended his funeral and, always in my experience, the dead remain so."

"Except when they *seem* to return, of course. How did you achieve such a deception?"

"I really cannot – "

"I should emphasise," Holmes interrupted, "that needless further investigation would prove most irksome to me. Delay in settling this matter would doubtless result in a review of my files, and who knows what forgotten uncompleted affairs I may discover? For example, the three instances that I mentioned – The Calderware Swindle, the Mossington Land Scandal, and the Unfortunate Investments of Mr. Fergus Dooley – have never, in the eyes of Scotland Yard, been satisfactorily concluded. Until now, I've withheld the essence of these crimes for my own reasons, but they are weighing with increasing heaviness upon my conscience."

Mr. Kitterly, suddenly in obvious discomfort, shifted his chair. "I would have nothing to fear from such disclosures, naturally. I had no inkling that these events remain unfinished. Nevertheless, I do see your difficulty in the case of Mr. Topham and, coincidentally, I was presented with a most curious proposition in connection with his father. I will explain it to you in detail, and you will surely see that I have broken no law . . . ."

"He is as deceitful as any man I have encountered," I remarked a short while later as we searched for a cab.

Holmes nodded. "He knows that nothing as yet can be proved against him, although he all but admitted the hiring of someone to falsify the handwriting of our client's father. However, it is now within my grasp to bring this affair to a satisfactory conclusion. As you see, a hansom has just deposited its fare near the corner. If we are quick, we will procure it before that rather stout gentleman who has emerged from the tailor's shop and then, after a pause to despatch telegrams to Lestrade and our client, it will convey us back to our lodgings. I will be surprised if all hasn't become clear by the time Mrs. Hudson is ready to serve our dinner."

As it was, we had been in our rooms long enough for our landlady to serve tea before clearing away the cups when our visitors arrived within a few minutes of each other. Inspector Lestrade was accompanied by a man who, I saw at once, bore a striking resemblance to the portrait of Mr. Jeremiah Topham that was displayed at our client's house in Paddington.

The "ghost", as Holmes had insisted from the beginning, was indeed a man of flesh and blood.

No sooner had introductions been completed and the two men settled in their seats than the doorbell rang once more. A few minutes passed before Mrs. Hudson announced Mr. Cedric Topham. Our client stepped into the room. As he caught sight of Inspector Lestrade's companion, he halted in mid-stride, expressions of confusion and outrage competing for dominance across his features.

"Who are you, sir?" he demanded of the stranger. "You aren't my father. You haven't so many years behind you but, by God, you resemble him greatly." He turned to my friend. "Do you have an explanation, Mr. Holmes?"

Holmes rose and approached him. "Calm yourself, Mr. Topham. Everything will be made clear to you presently. Allow me to introduce Inspector Lestrade of Scotland Yard. He has brought with him this gentleman who is so like your late father in appearance – Mr. Matthew Borwood."

Mr. Topham's puzzlement wasn't appeased. "But who – "

"You will recall your father's frequent absences from his home and his wife. This will come as something of a shock to you, but the fact is that he had a second family – and Mr. Borwood is your half-brother. His mother is deceased. She was a serving girl who raised him, mostly alone."

He paused to allow our client to absorb the shock. "Pray come and sit over here. The chairs are all taken, but the sofa is comfortable." He turned to address all three of our guests. "Before we begin, would anyone care for tea?"

Everyone declined, and after we were all seated, Holmes waited as a heavy cart rumbled along Baker Street. When the vibrations had ceased, he began:

"First, Mr. Topham, I should make it clear that Mr. Borwood impersonated your father under the threat of blackmail. Theatrical make-up was applied to cause him to appear older, and it was arranged that you should always become aware of him always at a distance. His only crime in this was in agreeing, although again under threat, to drive that cart last night with intent to injure you."

"That is not so!" Mr. Borwood cried. "I intended only to cause you to be afraid."

"That is something that has to be decided. Hence the presence of the inspector."

Our client glared angrily at Mr. Borwood.

Lestrade nodded and spoke harshly to his prisoner before Holmes continued.

"The perpetrator of this deception knew of your family circumstances and took measures to convince you that your father still lived. He had his body exhumed and disposed of secretly, anticipating that you would seek confirmation that such a resurrection had taken place." Holmes carefully didn't mention that Topham's actions had been without official sanction.

"Why?" asked our client when Holmes paused in his narrative. "What possible purpose lies behind all this?"

"The answer to that lies with your uncle, Mr. Albert Topham, who recently died in South Africa. I see from your shocked expression that you were unaware of his passing. You will perhaps be equally surprised to learn that he had amassed a considerable fortune to which your father was the heir." Holmes paused again, probably to allow our client to absorb his words. "All of which, upon *his* death, became yours."

"So someone who knew of this sought to substitute this man," he again glanced contemptuously at Mr. Borwood, "in place of my father to receive the inheritance? I see the reason for the cart now. It was feared that I would discover the scheme and raise objections, as I most certainly would have. Doubtless, it was intended that I should be murdered."

"No, no!" Mr. Borwood shouted. "The persecution was to be intensified until you were certified as mad, by a doctor who would be paid to do so. You were intended to be committed to an asylum until the legacy was settled. Then, when there was no chance of your interference, measures were to be taken to bring about your release." He looked frantically around him, searching for a sympathetic face. "That is the truth, I swear! It was meant that you should regain your freedom, never knowing what had been taken from you. You would have been unharmed. *He gave me his word.*"

"About whom are you speaking?" Lestrade enquired gruffly. "There is someone else behind this, I can see."

"Someone Mr. Topham knows well, as did his father," Holmes said quietly.

"But *who*?" our client asked in exasperation.

"None other than Mr. Bradwood Kitterly. It was he who told us of Mr. Borwood here, incorrectly believing that Borwood would hold his tongue.

Mr. Topham appeared more astounded than he had a few moments before, when he had learned of his uncle's death and his inheritance. "Kitterly? Our family solicitor? Surely not. The very idea is ridiculous. He and my father were friends for many years."

"Quite so. They shared an intimacy that gave Mr. Kitterly a position of power over your family, although they didn't realise it. It doesn't surprise me that he proved unworthy of their trust, since he has a long history of crime that Scotland Yard has been unable to prove – until now."

Lestrade affirmed this with a murmur, and Holmes turned his attention to Mr. Borwood.

"Mr. Kitterly has long been a great asset to the criminal classes, and will continue to use his position to be so – " My friend adopted the air of someone who has just received a revelation. " – unless, of course, you are prepared to give evidence that will convict him?"

Mr. Borwood stared at the carpet, saying nothing.

"You have stated that he was blackmailing you to secure your obedience," my friend persisted. "That is why he gave us your name and address. He believed that you would not reveal the truth. Pray be so kind as to explain how this was possible."

He raised his head and looked directly at Holmes, and for the first time I saw anger in his face.

"Mr. Kitterly *made* it possible. He said that I had murdered a man in a drunken brawl. He showed me the evidence that he'd manufactured and told me of the false witnesses he had arranged. Were it against someone else I, myself, would have been convinced."

"The scoundrel!" said I.

Holmes turned to the inspector. "What do you say, Lestrade? Has Mr. Borwood committed any crime, apart from driving the cart last night?"

"Pending verification, nothing I would call serious," the little detective replied.

"Then Mr. Borwood, will you assist us in bringing this man who is a disgrace to his profession to justice? You alone can do this."

Mr. Borwood looked at each of us in turn, his expression one of anxiety. Then he summoned some inner strength and smiled for the first time.

"Yes," he said. "Yes, I will do it."

"Capital!" Holmes sat back in his chair. "Watson, be a good fellow and ask Mrs. Hudson to bring us refreshments. There is no reason why we shouldn't fortify ourselves as we discuss this further."

Pit of Death
by Robert Stapleton

The day might have started out as a bright summer's morning, but this optimistic beginning was not reflected in the darkness shrouding the countenance of Mr. Sherlock Holmes. My friend wasn't pleased at having his peace disturbed by Scotland Yard's Inspector Lestrade so early in the day. The manner in which he held his smoking pipe, and the way he kept glancing between the open window and the morning newspaper he had hurriedly put aside at the arrival of the policeman all spoke volumes about his annoyance.

"Now, listen here, Lestrade," he snapped. "If you are asking me to take part in a search for a couple of men who have gone missing, then all I can say is that the police are much better equipped than I'm for finding these unfortunates. People go missing all the time. It is a sad fact of life, but it isn't a matter likely to engage my own professional interest."

Lestrade didn't appear to be deterred by this cold reception. From his facial expression and the way he held his body, I could tell that the inspector was also struggling to maintain his own composure. "I can assure you, Mr. Holmes, there is more to this business than simply a few men going missing. A body has now been found."

"Down the pit?"

"That's right."

"I'm sorry to have to admit the fact, Lestrade," continued Holmes, "but that isn't a particularly unusual tragedy in the coal mining industry, even today."

"Perhaps, but the Durham Constabulary have already been making inquiries into that man's death, and the more they investigate, the more they realize they are dealing with something extremely dark. For one thing, the corpse shows signs of having been crushed to death, but upon interviewing every single man on the shift during which the man died, they can find no satisfactory explanation for his demise. No machinery was being used in the locality that would account for the death, and no altercation had taken place which would satisfactorily explain human involvement in the tragedy."

Holmes shrugged. "But you hardly need my assistance with that."

"You aren't listening to me, Mr. Holmes," the policeman retorted. "I'm telling you that I *do* indeed need your assistance. There is something very strange about these disappearances. Extremely odd, and that's no exaggeration."

"Indeed, I have been listening to you, Inspector," replied Holmes. "You are telling me that these men went missing in County Durham, and that this mysterious death also took place there. That is nearly as far away from your customary haunts as anywhere in the entire country."

"I must concede the truth of that."

"Then why on earth can the Durham Constabulary not deal with the matter themselves?"

"That is something I'm trying to discover," continued the inspector in an exasperated tone of voice. "But all I can tell you at the moment is that the local constabulary are crying out for my help. And though I hesitate to admit the fact, they are crying out for your help as well."

"How have they heard of me?"

"Your reputation has spread far and wide – even to the slums and hovels of those poor working miners and their families."

"But why should this have anything to do with us down here?"

"Because the trail begins here in London."

Holmes steepled his fingers and thought deeply for a few minutes. "Very well, Lestrade," he concluded. "I shall give you the rest of this morning in which to convince me to travel with you up to Durham."

"I'm much obliged to you, Mr. Holmes."

"In that case, where do you wish to take us first?"

I could sense the inspector relax in a perceptible manner before he rose to his feet and retrieved his hat.

"To the home of Sir Archibald FitzMorris," he declared. "The owner of the County Durham mine at the center of our investigation."

Holmes and I exchanged glances of frustration. We both imagined that we were about to waste the rest of that glorious summer morning in pointless and mindless gossip – a wasted day in anybody's calendar.

We joined Lestrade outside, where he was waiting for us in one of Scotland Yard's four-wheelers, and together we trundled away along Baker Street and across town in the general direction of Chelsea.

The carriage drew to a halt outside an elegant Georgian townhouse, with a short flight of steps leading up to a solid front door, flanked by marble pillars.

"Coal mining is an extremely lucrative business," I opined as we stepped out of the carriage.

"For the bosses, perhaps," said Lestrade.

"But what about the ordinary working men?" asked Holmes. It was a long-discussed question which hung unanswered in the air as Lestrade rang the front doorbell, and we waited to be admitted into that glamorous building.

"We're here to see Sir Archibald," Lestrade told the maid as she opened the door. "He is expecting us."

After a hurried curtsey, the young woman led us into a cheerless side-room and left us there. She immediately turned and clattered away along the stone-paved corridor toward the rear of the building.

I looked around the room. I was surprised that I could identify very little which might connect the owner of the property with the coal-mining industry. Instead, it appeared evident that this man had spent some time in the Far East.

A man appeared in the doorway.

"Good morning, gentlemen," he began. "I am Sir Archibald FitzMorris. I know Inspector Lestrade, but you other gentlemen are new to me."

Holmes stepped forward. "I am Sherlock Holmes," he said, "and this is my associate, Dr. John Watson. I'm a consulting detective, and we're here at the behest of the inspector."

All eyes turned to the Scotland Yarder.

"May we talk with you in more congenial surroundings, Sir Archibald?" the policeman asked.

"Certainly, Inspector," said Sir Archibald, as he turned and led the way along the corridor and into a comfortable withdrawing room.

I now had time to observe the colliery owner himself – a habit I had picked up from so many years spent with Sherlock Holmes. Here was clearly in his middle years. His head, which was amazingly round in shape, was almost completely bald. This lack of hair on top was made up for by a neatly trimmed beard and sideburns, though any further facial hair had been carefully shaved away.

In attire, Sir Archibald was neatly dressed in a suit of dark gray cloth, evidently custom-made by a firm of bespoke tailors situated in the street of Savile Row in Mayfair.

Sir Archibald smiled and invited his three visitors to sit down.

"Now, gentlemen," he said, "how may I assist you?"

"You are the owner of a coal mine in County Durham," stated Lestrade.

"That is correct, Inspector," replied our host. "The Nanking Mine. It is a rather odd and somewhat exotic name, I must admit. My grandfather decided on it when he took over the working of a much-more ancient mine and sank the first new shaft. He thought the name would help to give the place a touch of class – a taste of the Orient. But that was more than fifty years ago now."

"And is the mine productive?"

"Very much so," said Sir Archibald. "Those old pit workings were abandoned long ago as worked out, but the new shaft was cut to a much lower level, where a far richer seam was discovered. That pit now supplies a good quality coal for household use, and it sells at a decent price."

"Providing you with a decent level of income, I see," added Holmes.

"That is true, Mr. Holmes. But of course that is nothing to be ashamed about, since I own the mine and its operations and, as a good capitalist, I believe I should be the one to enjoy the fruits of its success."

"Naturally," concluded Holmes, in a tone which made the mine owner purse his lips.

"I hope, Mr. Holmes," he said, "that you aren't one of these Socialists who believe the working man should share the profits of his labors."

"Perish the thought," replied Holmes, with a hint of sarcasm. "I merely feel that your workers should be paid a decent and fair wage for their toil."

"I pay as well as anyone else in the industry," replied Sir Archibald, clearly annoyed by the comment. "Now, may we please get down to the purpose of you visit here?"

"Certainly," said Lestrade, once more taking control of the discussion. "You will no doubt be aware that miners have gone missing in recent months."

Sir Archibald nodded slowly. "I'm of course aware of that fact," he said. "But I see nothing strange in it. After all, people do go missing from time to time, for their own particular and various reasons. Often they emerge again years later in some other part of the country. Sometimes even with another family." He laughed. "Having abandoned their former spouse, or after a falling out with their fellow workers."

"True," said Lestrade. "But you have lost five men in the last couple of years."

"I haven't been keeping count," admitted Sir Archibald, "but I see no reason for it to become the subject of a police investigation."

"But now a body has been discovered," added Lestrade.

"Again, I am aware of that fact," said Sir Archibald. "But coal mining is a dangerous occupation, Inspector. Tragically, men do die in the mines of our country. As in many other industries. We have attempted to introduce the latest safety measures for our miners, so once again, I see no reason for this to be a matter of concern for the police."

"It is merely that the coroner in Durham isn't satisfied with the *post mortem* examination, and has asked us to investigate the matter further."

318

"Well," said Sir Archibald, "I have told you all I know about the matter. Unless you imagine that I have been spiriting away these men and hiding them somewhere down here in London." He chuckled.

"Not at all, Sir Archibald."

"And as for the dead man, I'm confident that it will be shown to be an ordinary accident in a dangerous occupation."

Indicating that our interview was now at an end, Sir Archibald FitzMorris stood up and headed for the doorway.

"Wait a moment, Sir Archibald," said Holmes, sniffing the air. "I detect a slight musty scent in the atmosphere. Are you, by any chance, a collector of exotic animals?"

Our host brightened up at the mention of a subject which clearly was close to his heart.

"Oh, yes, Mr. Holmes. I have a collection of reptiles."

"May we see them?" asked Holmes.

"Why, of course," our host replied, and led the way through one of the connecting doors, into a room lined with glass vivarium tanks. These contained a selection of reptiles of various kinds.

"Lizards, skinks, and a number of small snakes," said Sir Archibald. "It is my obsession."

"Am I correct in thinking," said Holmes cautiously, "that all of these specimens originated in Southern Asia? French Indochina, perhaps?"

"You seem to know a great deal about reptiles."

"Not at all. Merely a passing interest."

"I began to acquire these animals during my travels in Southeast Asia, in the very area you mentioned. I was visiting there partly on business, organizing coaling depots for steamships across the Empire, and partly for pleasure. I spent a couple of years out there, and came back with a small collection of animals, which has expanded over the years."

"How long ago was that?"

"Oh, let me see now – it must be about twenty-five years ago."

Once more outside in the bright morning air, Holmes turned to confront the inspector.

"Well, Lestrade, you certainly seem to be in possession of a most intriguing mystery here. What do you intend to do now?"

"I intend to go up to Durham tomorrow, in order to help clear up this matter. It will allow them time to organize themselves in preparation for our visit. Will you come with me, Mr. Holmes? Dr. Watson?"

Holmes looked to me. "What do you say, Watson?" he asked me. "Will you be free to join us?"

"You know you can rely on me," I replied. "I'll certainly come along with you."

"If nothing else," continued Lestrade, "you might enjoy the Miners' Gala, which is due to take place in Durham City on this coming Saturday. The locals call it the Big Meeting because, for many people, it is the only time in the entire year when families are free to meet together. It's a day of games and competitions, along with speeches by Trades Union officials. Oh, and there's to be a service in the Cathedral as well, for the first time in the history of the event."

The following afternoon, we alighted at Durham's main-line station, courtesy of the North Eastern Railway. The view from the viaduct, which we crossed immediately before reaching the station, has always been for me, on the few occasions when I have traveled that way, one of the most spectacular of all railway views. The solid castle and the majestic cathedral are spectacular, particularly in the light of the afternoon sunshine. Inspector Lestrade also sat transfixed by the sight, although Holmes paid little or no attention to it.

On the platform, we were greeted by a small group of policemen.

The senior of the group introduced himself as Inspector Cragbrook, welcoming us to the City and the County of Durham.

We followed him outside the station to where an enclosed carriage was waiting for us.

"It's good of you all to come at such short notice," said the local man. "But this is also a particularly busy weekend. However, I have managed to arrange accommodation for you all – even though we could only find one hotel bedroom. That I have reserved for Mr. Sherlock Holmes."

Holmes nodded his thanks.

"Inspector Lestrade will be the guest of myself and my wife, whilst Dr. Watson has been invited to stay at the home of my sergeant."

I noticed one of the other policeman smile. He seemed affable enough.

"But first, Mr. Holmes, I imagine you will want to view the body of the victim."

"That is indeed my wish, Inspector," replied Holmes. "And without delay, if that is possible."

The carriage drove off. "In that case, we must travel to Police Headquarters at Aykley Heads."

We were soon there and ushered inside, to be taken down to the morgue, where the police surgeon was waiting for us.

"Ah, Mr. Holmes," said the police surgeon. "I have heard so much about you, and I'm sure that, if anyone can solve this strange conundrum, then it has to be yourself."

Without comment, Holmes turned to the slab in the middle of the room and indicated the white cloth covering it.

"Is this the body?"

The surgeon removed the covering with the utmost care.

"Here he is – Amos Williamson."

The body of a man, perhaps in his mid-thirties, lay before us. Apart from signs of the usual *post mortem* inspection, there seemed to be little wrong with the corpse.

"In every other respect," said the surgeon, "he is a fit and healthy man, even taking into account the nature of his employment. The mining industry is dangerous and life-shortening for many men."

"And what is your conclusion, Doctor?"

"He died of asphyxiation, Mr. Holmes. The air has been squeezed out of him. You can see some bruising to the upper abdomen. The man sustained a number of broken ribs, with one of them having pierced the right lung."

Holmes looked to me for comment.

"Yes, that is a most likely reason for his death," I said after examining the body. "I have seen it many times when I was on service in Afghanistan. Men crushed by a horse or a gun-carriage. If you can reach the man soon enough after the event, it is sometimes possible to breathe life back into him again."

The surgeon nodded.

"But how was the injury inflicted in this case?"

"It seems to me that there are three possibilities," said the police surgeon. "The first is that he was crushed by machinery. The mine authorities have looked into that possibility, and confirm that at the time, no such equipment was being used in the area where he had been working."

"And the second possibility?" asked Holmes.

"That the crush by a human stampede in the confines of the mine could have caused the death."

"And was such a stampede reported on the day of the accident?"

"None of those later interviewed remembered there being any such incident."

"And third possibility?"

"If it wasn't an accident," continued the police surgeon, "then we're left with the possibility that it was murder. That the man had been grasped from behind by somebody stronger than himself and had the air squeezed out of him."

"Is that possible?" asked Holmes.

321

"Theoretically," said the police surgeon, "but it would take a very strong individual to kill a man in that way."

"Even a physically active man like a coal-miner?"

"Even so."

"And which of these three possibilities do you consider the most likely?"

The surgeon gave us each a cold stare. "None."

"But what other possibilities are there?" I asked.

"That is what we're hoping Mr. Sherlock Holmes will be able to discover for us. That is the reason for you being here, is it not?"

"There is still the other matter," continued Holmes. "The business of the disappearing miners."

The police surgeon shrugged. "Without a body, that matter is outside my province. All I can tell you is that the coroner wishes to release this body as soon as possible for burial. As you can imagine, mid-summer isn't a good time to be keeping the dead from their final resting places."

"Then let us try to expedite the matter," said Holmes. He turned to Cragbrook. "I should like to see the place where the body was found, and then pay a visit to the dead man's family."

"Certainly, Mr. Holmes. But those matters will have to wait until tomorrow."

With thanks expressed to the police surgeon, we each made our way to our assigned overnight accommodation.

Holmes turned to the local police inspector. "I should be obliged," he began, "if you could let me see the statements made by the men who were working down the mine during that man's last shift."

"Certainly, Mr. Holmes. I'll have them delivered to your hotel room within the hour."

As far as I was concerned, Sergeant Allerwick and his wife were the best hosts I could have expected. Their two children – a boy aged seven years and a girl of ten – seemed well behaved and friendly enough.

I slept well and was awakened early, in time for breakfast and personal preparations for the day ahead.

A knock at the front door announced that a carriage was waiting for the sergeant and myself out in the street, with Sherlock Holmes already on board.

"I trust you had a good night's sleep," I said by way of greeting.

My friend appeared distracted. "Indeed. Thank you, Watson. My mind was much taken by this case. At first I had a handful of possible solutions, but they are gradually diminishing in number as I consider them each more closely."

"Then perhaps this morning will move matters along for you," I suggested.

"The colliery is inevitably the place where we must begin our quest for the truth."

The exotically-named Nanking Mine lay at the end of a half-hour's journey along rough roads. The closer we came to the place, the less I liked the look of it. The entire valley in which the colliery lay appeared grim, to say the very least. The pithead winding gear rose like some huge beast above the colliery yard, dwarfing the surrounding area. There I could discern dwelling places: Humble homes of a most depressing nature. Some lined the streets of the adjacent village, while others lay within the yard itself, cheek-by-jowl with the mining operations. Above all of this, even the winding gear, stood the huge spoil heap. This black mountain hung with a menacing presence above the lives of the people in that small community.

"What a dreadful place to bring up children," I said with a sigh.

"Indeed" returned Holmes. "But the backstreets of London possess their own horrors. Our concern at the moment is with the underground workings."

Suspicious glances glared at us from all around. Dirty faced children looked up from the cobbled streets. Raggedly dressed women paused in hanging out their clothes, as they turned to watch us drive by. I wondered how clean those clothes would be when once they had been dried by such a dust laden atmosphere.

Our carriage pulled to a halt in the colliery yard itself and we all climbed out. The place was full of noise. The coal dryer hummed and the grader rattled as it sorted the different sizes of coal, while the railway wagons waited in line while they were filled noisily from a hopper above.

A man in a brown suit approached us from the official office. His face presented us with the only smile we would find there all day.

"Good morning, gentlemen," said the friendly face. "My name is Giles Ravenstone. I'm the colliery manager here. I know Inspector Cragbrook and the sergeant, but not you other gentlemen."

Cragbrook stepped forward. "It is indeed good of you to agree to meet us here today, Mr. Ravenstone. These gentlemen with me are Mr. Sherlock Holmes, from London, and his associate, Dr. John Watson. They are here to assist us in solving the mystery here at the Nanking Mine."

"Mystery?" queried the manager. "We have no mystery here. Only a few missing men, and another who has died in a mining accident."

Holmes stepped forward. "In that case, Mr. Ravenstone, you will have no objection to showing where the body was discovered."

"If you feel it would help you in any way, Mr. Holmes," said the manager, "then I'm sure we can oblige. Have you been below ground before?"

"Not in a coal mine," replied Holmes. "Although I have been to some very unusual places during my career. So I'm sure I can endure and indeed value this new experience."

Mr. Ravenstone led us to a wooden building close beside the mine operations and the winding engine shed.

"Now, gentlemen," he began. "We have here a set of coveralls for each of you, together with a helmet and a Safety Davy Lamp for each. Its purpose is to give warning of bad air down there. Keep the lamp close to the ground. When it burns low, it will be a visual warning of the presence of the invisible choke-damp gas. It will certainly choke you if you pay no heed to the warning. You must come out as soon as you can when the flame burns low. But have no fear, gentlemen, I shall be with you at all times, and I shall be carrying the lamp to illuminate your way. You will be safe with me. Now, I suggest you prepare yourselves for the descent into the mine."

A few minutes later, each dressed in the somewhat unfamiliar attire of a coal-miner, Holmes, myself, and the two Durham policemen stood beneath the huge winding-gear.

Inspector Lestrade took a deep breath and joined the rest of us as we followed the pit panager into the metal cage suspended over the top of the shaft. The manager informed us that we would be descending a total of eight-hundred feet to the bottom.

"We each need to be issued with a tally," said Mr. Ravenstone. "A disc with a number on it. This will be checked off when you return to the surface. It allows us to make sure that everybody is accounted for."

"So there must be a few of these tallies which have never been returned," noted Holmes.

"That's right, Mr. Holmes. Over the last year or so, several tallies were never returned. Each time that happened, we made a thorough search of the mine workings."

"And found no trace of the missing men," said Holmes.

The manager coughed nervously. "We have no idea what happened to those men. They might have come up with the rest of their shift, and then have left the village."

"Or they might still be down there."

"There is no direct evidence for that. They simply vanished. Alive or dead, nobody knows."

As the cage descended, we passed through a realm of utter darkness, aware only of the presence of each other in the gloom.

"This is as black as Newgate's knocker," muttered Lestrade, referring to London's notorious prison – a Cockney phrase for "pitch black".

We kept going down.

Occasionally, we passed openings in the wall, which appeared even more intensely dark than the shaft down which we were now traveling.

"Those lead to the older workings of the mine," the manager explained. "Some of the earlier much-shallower seams were worked out many years ago. Then they were abandoned and blocked off when we extended the shaft deeper into the earth."

"So no one ever goes in there," noted Holmes.

"That's correct, Mr. Holmes. If they did, they would soon become lost in a warren of passages. Go in there, and you would never come out again."

After several minutes, during which it was impossible to say how fast we were descending, we finally reached the bottom of the shaft and the cage jerked to a clattering halt.

Mr. Ravenstone stepped out. "Now, gentlemen, kindly follow me, and I will show you where the dead man was discovered."

We followed him into the darkness, passing men and boys engaged in their various activities in the workings. Some of the boys held jobs which were merely to keep the air circulating through the mine – a humble but essential part of the operations.

I was glad to be wearing a stout pair of boots, as water was dripping from somewhere beyond our sight, and I had to avoid stumbling over the steel rails along which the mine's wagons, or tubs, were taken before being transferred to the surface.

The air was filled with the harsh noises of the working mine, and the atmosphere felt surprisingly hot and humid.

With nothing to guide us apart from the manager's lamp, I was completely lost when we came finally to a halt.

We gathered around a dark corner of the working area of the mine, into which Mr. Ravenstone shone his lamp. I could see nothing significant, but Holmes showed that he was intensely interested in this location.

"There," declared the manager. "That is the place where Mr. Williamson was discovered just a few days ago. There can surely be no mystery about his death. It was an accident, I tell you, like so many, caused by him being crushed against the rear wall by a passing tub on its way to the shaft. Those things can be extremely heavy when full of coal and can carry a considerable momentum when being pulled along by the ponies."

Without responding, Holmes began to explore the surrounding area, paying particular attention to a dark opening in the angle of the trackway.

"Where does that lead?"

"Lead? It doesn't lead anywhere. It least, not nowadays. It's one of the access shafts which were blocked off many years ago. I told you that there are ancient workings around here, and that shaft used to give access to the other levels above where we're now standing."

Holmes drew closer to the blocked-off shaft. And sniffed.

"What do you make of that smell?" he asked me.

The air was heavy with the odours of men, ponies, and industrial machinery. And yet, there was something familiar about it. Something that recalled another place and another time not so long before.

Holmes held his finger to his lips, so I remained quiet.

"I have seen all that I need to see down here, Mr. Ravenstone," he announced. "I think it's time for us to return to the surface. I would like now to pay a visit to the family of the dead man."

"Certainly, Mr. Holmes," said the manager.

The Durham policemen nodded that they could see no further reason to be down in the mine workings, so we headed back to the shaft, and to the cage that would take us back to the surface again.

The home which Amos Williamson had shared with his wife and family until his tragic death turned out to be a humble and yet well-cared-for property. We found his widow, Sarah, surrounded by her two children and her sister, Julia.

"I'm very sorry to hear about your loss, Mrs. Williamson," said Holmes. "I'm here to help the police to find out what really happened, and how your husband was died."

Sarah Williamson glared up at Holmes with her blue eyes, rimmed with red from so much crying. "His death was no accident!" she told him. "All his friends say that he was nowhere near the tubs at the time. That can mean only one thing: My husband was killed – *Murdered!*"

"But the police have interviewed everyone who was on that shift. I myself have read the statements, and they all seem to say the same thing: Nobody working that day was responsible for his death."

"That is nonsense!" declared the grief-stricken woman. "I know he was killed by somebody. And I want you to find out who that person was."

Holmes shook his head sadly. "The police have nothing to go on. No names. No suspects."

"But you are a clever man, Mr. Holmes," returned Sarah's sister, Julia. "I've heard about you. No matter how difficult, you are the man who can discover the truth."

"Even if the truth turns out to be something that neither you nor the police nor the mine officials have ever considered?"

The two women looked at each other for a moment.

Then Julia looked him in the eye. "Even so, Mr. Holmes. You have to find out for us."

With nothing further to discuss, it was clear that it was time for us to leave. I turned and followed Holmes out into the afternoon air. On the way out, I noticed Holmes, almost unobserved, leave a silver coin on the mantelshelf.

Saturday saw the Durham Miners' Gala, known as the Big Meeting, when mining families from across the coalfield descended upon the ancient city. It was a day for speeches, marches with banners, and a service at the Cathedral led by the Dean. Afterward, everybody returned to the Racecourse, where families and friends met together to share the food they had brought along with them.

"For many of these folk," said Sergeant Allerwick, "this is the one time in the year when they can get together. They all look forward to the Big Meeting eagerly."

Holmes and I wandered among the people, watching the children playing and the parents deep in conversation, until we heard somebody call our names.

"Mr. Holmes. Dr. Watson."

It was Julia. The sister of the dead man's wife.

We went across to join her and her own family.

"I have something for you, Mr. Holmes," said Julia, as she waved a piece of paper.

"What is it?"

"A list of the men we consider most likely to have killed Amos."

Holmes took the paper and looked down at it.

"Having read their statements, I see no reason why suspicion should be attached to any of these men," he told her. "Do the police know about your list?"

"I gave a copy to Sergeant Allerwick, but they're bound to have those men on their own list of suspects. Especially the one at the top: George Slimthorpe. He's a real character. Shady as well. And Mr. Holmes, he is a big man. Capable of crushing another to death with his own bare hands!"

"That's very interesting," replied Holmes. "Thank you for this."

"But you must act upon it, Mr. Holmes! Bring that beggar to justice."

As the day wore on, Holmes and I wandered through the streets of the old city and ended up in a small public house, filled with coalminers who were already halfway to intoxicated oblivion. Considering the harsh working conditions they had to endure almost daily, who could blame them?

327

We sat in a corner with a couple of glasses of ale in front of us, trying to remain unnoticed, but watching everything.

The door opened and another man came in. He was big, powerful, and sported a shaggy mane and brown beard. If anybody could ever be described as a bear, then it was surely him.

The bear scanned the tables, fixed his gaze upon the two of us, and advanced in our direction. His staggering gait showed that he had already drunk more than was good for him. Or perhaps for us as well.

He stood before our table and glared down at Holmes.

"So you are the famous Sherlock Holmes, are you?"

"I am Holmes."

"And you think I killed Amos Williamson."

"No."

"What do you mean by that? Am I not at the very top of the list of suspects?"

"If you are George Slimthorpe, then you are indeed at the top of *a* list. But not the list of my own suspects. Admittedly, you are probably strong enough to have killed the man by crushing the life out of him, but I don't think you did it."

Looking surprised, Slimthorpe sat down opposite us and accepted the offer of another drink.

When we were all settled, the miner rested his elbows on the table and stared at Holmes.

"Tell me, Mr. Holmes," he said. "Have you ever heard the legend of the Lambton Worm?"

"I have heard of it," said Holmes. "The Lambton Estate isn't far from here. But I should like to hear the legend told by yourself. There is obviously some reason for you to mention it, and I should like to hear what you have to tell me."

"Very well. Many years ago, John Lambton, heir of the Lambton estate, and a man with little respect for man or beast, one day went out to fish in the River Wear. He couldn't even do that right. Caught nothing all day. So he uttered a curse. Loud and long. Then he finally made a catch, but it turned out to be the ugliest and most vile worm you have ever seen or could imagine. It wasn't particularly big, but it was the most evil-looking creature anybody had ever seen."

"A worm?"

"So the legend tells us."

"Please carry on."

"In disgust, the young John Lambton threw the Worm down a nearby well, and paid it no further attention. But that worm grew, Mr. Holmes, and soon it emerged from its well and began to terrorize the entire

328

neighborhood. It slaughtered livestock. It killed people. It grew in size until the people called upon Lambton to do something about stopping it. Well, John realized he had done wrong in unleashing this monster upon the local community so, in order to atone for his sins, he left the country, and went as a knight on Crusade to fight the Saracen."

Slimthorpe sipped his ale thoughtfully for a moment.

"Almost given up for dead, after seven long years, Sir John returned home. There he found the matter far worse than he had left it. During the time he had been away, brave knights had tried to kill the great Worm, but each time, the creature had ended up either killing or maiming every one of them. It was now time for Sir John to risk his own life. He took counsel from a local witch, who explained to him how he could defeat the monster – but there was a price to pay. The price was that, on his return from killing the Worm, he must kill the very first thing that came out to meet him. So he set out and slew the monster, but the first person to come out and congratulate him was his own father. Sir John refused to kill the old man, and thus brought down a curse upon the family which lasted for seven generations. No head of the Lambtons would ever die in their beds."

"This is all very interesting," said Holmes. "But why are you telling me this today?"

"Because, Mr. Holmes, the Worm has returned. She is back again. A huge monster."

"How do you know this?"

"Because I have seen her with my own eyes!"

"You're drunk," I told him.

"That's right!" he cried, running a hand across his face. "I am drunk. If I was sober, I would never be able to tell you this story. The very memory of that hideous face would strike me dumb."

Holmes seemed much more sympathetic. "Where did this happen? Tell us exactly what you saw."

Slimthorpe again leaned forward and looked from one to the other of us.

"It was a few weeks ago. Down in the area not far from that mine, in the vicinity of the Old Grange. I have always been a small-time poacher. I have often taken rabbits for the pot, and pheasants for a special treat for my wife and family. Occasionally, I even ventured into that part of the countryside. I know the farmer there, and he has always been ready to look the other way whenever I've been out with my snares at night. But recently, even he has been nervous, sensing a terror among the local animals, and among his own livestock – as though something was wanting to kill them. And if the poor animals thought that, then they were right to be terrified. That farmer, along with others in that area, has lost livestock. Not to any wolf or big cat. No. They simply disappeared without trace."

"What exactly did you see on the night in question?" persisted Holmes.

"I'm telling you. It was the Worm. Lengthy. She was so long that I couldn't measure her. I was alerted at first by the sound of slithering among the undergrowth. I lay still and looked. The head appeared first. Evil, with big eyes and a huge mouth. I watched her for a while, but when that head turned in my direction, I knew that she had me in her sights. That was enough for me, I can tell you. I took to my heels and ran for my life. I didn't look back, in case the Worm took me. I haven't been back to those parts since that night. Even in the daylight."

Two other men now entered the bar-room and came to stand behind Slimthorpe.

"You haven't been boring people with that story of yours, have you, Geordie?" said one of them.

"We've come to take you home, you old fool!" said the other. "Your wife's worried about you."

As the two newcomers escorted away the man who had been telling us his tale, Slimthorpe turned with one final message for Holmes. "The men are all scared of going down that pit, Mr. Holmes. They're afraid they might not come up again. They go because they have no choice. That mine is known as 'The Pit of Death'."

When the three men had gone, Holmes turned to me. "The time has come for me to return the hotel. I have some thinking to do."

Within ten minutes, I had left Holmes sitting in his room, with the smoke of pipe tobacco swirling around his head.

The following morning, I returned to the hotel bedroom to find Holmes still asleep, and the room so thick with tobacco smoke that I would hardly see across the room. So I sat. And waited. Eventually, I heard him call my name.

"Watson."

"Yes?"

"Do you have your service revolver with you?"

"Indeed I do," I reassured him."

"Good. Because today we're going to either solve this mystery, or else die in the attempt."

"What do have in mind?"

"After luncheon, we must travel to the area of the Old Grange. But first I need to consult a plan of the old mine workings – the ones from before the present enterprise."

Later that morning, the manager shook his head. "We have no plans that go back that far, Mr. Holmes. All we know is that we need to keep well away from those old workings. Some of them came perilously close to ground level. Claims have been made against us for damage caused by subsidence, but we have always claimed that such liability has nothing to do with us."

"And the Old Grange?"

"The Old Grange is a large country house which belongs to the colliery owner, Sir Archibald FitzMorris. His grandfather built the place. Later, Sir Archibald's father lived there, and as soon as the old man died, the son moved away to London, left me in charge of the colliery, and leased out the old building."

"Who has the lease at the moment?" asked Holmes. "Who lives there?"

"A Scotsman has lived for many years – a man by the name of Rockall. I believe he used to be a Big Game Hunter somewhere in Southern Africa, but there's never been any big game around here for him to hunt."

"Until now." Holmes raised his eyebrows. "May we go and visit him?"

"Indeed. He prefers his own company, but he might be prepared to welcome you."

"But first, we need to examine the surrounding area."

The two local policemen grew bored of watching Holmes making his detailed exploration and went about their other duties. This left the pit manager, Inspector Lestrade, Holmes, and myself to continue our investigation of the area around the Old Grange. The countryside consisted of a wide but steep-sided valley, consisting of relatively rich pastureland.

Holmes spent much of the following hour examining the side of the valley nearest to the mining operations. "The original mining must have been not far from here."

"That has to be true, Mr. Holmes," said Ravenstone. "Behind that cliff-side. Somewhere."

"In fact," continued Holmes, "I can detect signs of the subsidence that you were telling us about. If I'm correct in my conclusions, there must be an opening from here giving access to those ancient workings."

We kept searching, until Holmes pulled aside a clump of shrubbery, stood erect, and pointed to a dark opening.

"I have never noticed that before," said the manager.

Holmes turned to me. "What do you make of this?"

I drew closer. "It certainly looks like the opening to a passageway."

"And the smell?"

331

"It's the same musty smell we came across inside the mine."

"Precisely. And where else have we come across it?"

I had to think carefully. "In London. At the Zoological gardens. The herpetological section."

"Come, come. You're evading the issue."

"We came across it at the home of Sir Archibald."

"I knew you would get to the point eventually."

"But what does it mean?"

The opening to the hole was large enough for a man to crawl into. And Holmes did just that, disappearing into the darkness for a couple of minutes, and returning with an expression of satisfaction on his face, and his lighted pipe in his mouth.

"Now, it's time for us to go and meet the Great Hunter. The man who lives at the Old Manor. Rockall."

The building was perhaps a hundred years old and somewhat poorly maintained, but the man himself was at home and answered Holmes's insistent knock at the front door.

"Good afternoon, gentlemen," said Rockall.

The hunter was a tall man with fair hair and a face of freckles, adorned by a rich red beard.

"Mr. Ravenstone, I know," continued Rockall. "And you must be the famous Sherlock Holmes and Doctor Watson."

"And Inspector Lestrade of Scotland Yard," added our accompanying policeman.

"I'm indeed pleased to meet you. Sir Archibald sent me a message telling me that you might be calling on me in the near future."

"And you are the hunter that people are telling us about."

Rockall nodded graciously. "Come inside," he said. "The afternoon is drawing on, and it must be nearly time for tea. As I live entirely by myself, I have to look to such things on my own."

Our host led us into a large living room. The walls were decorated with photographs of the man himself, standing over certain animals, mostly rhinoceros and elephant, which certainly looked to be dead. There were also the heads of various animals which had been expertly mounted and impressively displayed.

"This is quite a collection," Holmes said as Rockall returned to the room a few minutes later, carrying a tray of light refreshments.

"I'm retired now, Mr. Holmes," he replied as he laid out the small table in the middle of the room. "I exist mainly on the income from the books I write – relating the exploits of myself and my companions over many years in the wilds of Africa."

As we sat together, drinking tea, our host sat back and looked at my friend.

"Your arrival here suggests that you know something of my story, Mr. Holmes, although perhaps very little in the way of detail, so I shall now provide you with a little more in the way of explanation."

"Please carry on," said Holmes.

"A couple of years ago, after many years in Africa, I arrived back in England, determined to live out the rest of my life in quiet isolation. But at the time I had nowhere to live. It just so happened that, one day I was at a social gathering where I met Sir Archibald FitzMorris – the man you met in London."

Holmes nodded.

"He told me that he owned an old manor house in County Durham – this house. He told me that he no longer used the building, but that he would be happy if I would like to come and live here, at a peppercorn rent, for as long as I wished."

We remained silent, patiently waiting for something more to emerge.

"There was of course more to the matter than simply providing an impoverished hunter with a house. Sir Archibald told me that the people who lived in the area of the Old Manor were subject to an illogical superstition about a dragon being on the loose. They called it 'The Worm'. Apparently this Worm was in the habit of taking livestock, and occasionally people as well, but few people had ever seen this monster, and nobody had ever been able to capture or to kill the creature – if it really existed. He felt that the presence of a game hunter in the area might provide some measure of reassurance for the local people."

"And what makes you think that my presence here has anything to do with this mystery?" Holmes asked him.

"You are too modest, Mr. Holmes. It all began with the mysterious disappearances of men from the pit, and now the police have the body of a man who has been crushed to death. That is the sort of mystery that would inevitably intrigue you."

"Do you think that these scare stories are based upon some reality?"

"They are certainly based upon the existence of something real – something which perhaps emerges from time to time in order to kill livestock and feast upon the abundance of men in the mine."

"Well, you certainly seem to think that is true."

"I merely entertain the possibility."

"Such a creature, if it exists, must be cold-blooded," added Holmes. "And where else in this cold climate might be more suitable for such a creature to live as in the abandoned tunnels inside a coal mine – a place which maintains a steady temperature throughout the year."

Giles Ravenstone leaned forward, clearly paying close attention to the discussion.

"And what do you think this mystery might be, Mr. Rockall," asked the manager.

"The very same thing that has occurred to Mr. Holmes."

"My own opinion is that, having considered all the other possibilities, whatever is left, however improbable, has to be the truth."

Rockall nodded. "As a man who has spent many years hunting in the wild, I have in my possession a gun such as will deal death to any creature I may encounter. Large or small. I'm talking of an Elephant Gun." He pointed to a rife resting against the wall in the far corner of the room. "A real beast of a thing," he said. "Two barrels, all cleaned and oiled. I need only load the gun, and it will be ready to go hunting." A gleam entered the eye of the hunter. "But will the dragon emerge from her hole tonight?"

"I'm certain that she will," replied Holmes, calmly. "I have myself ventured into the creature's lair and left there my scent, along with a strong smell of the tobacco I use. If she is cold-blooded, then she will need to eat only rarely, but the creature must be hungry by now. She was deprived of her last meal, and was forced to leave her prey dead but uneaten in the mine workings. The discovery of that body is the reason I was invited to come here. I believe that the creature will emerge from her burrow after dark and come looking. For me. Tonight."

"Do you really think it will be tonight?" asked Ravenstone.

"We can only wait," said Holmes.

"In the high latitudes of this part of the world, the twilight comes on later than in places farther south," mused Rockall, "so as we have some time yet to wait, I would like to invite you gentlemen to join me in sharing my simple Sunday evening supper. Cheese and bread."

As the time drew near for us to set about our quest, Rockall stood up and looked Holmes over.

"Speaking as a man experienced in the art of hunting," he said, "I think you may need a little extra help to defeat the monster. Every knight needs his armour."

"Armour?" I asked. "Is this really going to be so dangerous?"

"Without doubt," he replied.

Rockall disappeared for a moment and returned carrying a thick leather jacket, reinforced with metal padding.

"You must wear this, Mr. Holmes," he said, holding it out. "It may save you from the teeth of whatever vicious creature is out there."

The garment made Holmes appear much more bulky than normal but, in view of the undoubted danger, he offered no objections. This turn of events made me wonder what kind of peril the hunter was envisioning for my friend.

Darkness was beginning to creep across the landscape and settle over the fields like a great cloak. The scents of night were hanging heavy on the still evening air as together we made our way to the opening we had discovered earlier in the side of the cliff.

"Is your service revolver loaded, Watson?" asked Holmes.

"Indeed it is," I replied. "All this talk of a giant Worm makes me feel I could well need it tonight."

We gathered at the opening in the cliff.

The pit manager was keeping his distance. I could hardly blame the man.

"It's quite clear now," said Holmes, as he turned to look around him at the undergrowth, "that the Worm has already left her lair. Look at the grass. It has been pressed down flat by something huge. Believe me, the monster is out here, somewhere. Looking for me."

"But what exactly is this creature?" I asked.

"I imagine we are going to find that out very soon," said Holmes. He wasn't going to enlighten me at that moment.

As my pulse began to race even faster, I struggled to remain calm. I fumbled nervously with my service revolver. This simple action took me back to my days in the Army serving in Afghanistan. Many a night I had kept watch out in the wilds of that faraway land, waiting for death or danger to descend upon myself and my companions.

For several minutes we stood and waited. Our senses were on high alert, and becoming ever more attentive to each sound and smell, straining to distinguish the unusual sounds from the more customary nocturnal noises. But a strange silence had gripped that entire area of countryside. Nothing was moving. Even the usual evening birdsong had been stilled. The usual rustle of small animals in the undergrowth was absent. A sense of impending doom hung over everything. By instinct, the wildlife sensed danger. Something was out there.

Holmes now stepped into the open, offering himself as bait for the monster. His pipe sent the familiar acrid smell of its tobacco curling about him in the light breeze. If the creature was hunting, she would soon make her appearance.

A rustling sound attracted my attention, but it was only Lestrade, moving closer to Holmes. Our friend from Scotland Yard appeared to be completely out of his depth in this unusual environment, but his courage was no less diminished. He had often been with us, or sometimes against us, during so many of our encounters with crime and evil, but here he joined us in facing something even darker than we had encountered before.

335

In the silence, each of us harbored his own thoughts, unable to share them, and that only increased the tension. I waited. Holmes waited. The manager waited. Lestrade and Rockall waited. And somewhere amongst that long grass, the monster waited.

The crisis, when it arrived, took us all by surprise as the creature made her move.

So many things happened at the same moment that I had little time to think.

The first thing I noticed in the half-light was a huge head with a vicious mouth, rising above the undergrowth. The olive-green skin was a perfect camouflage amidst the night-shaded shrubbery.

My blood froze.

Lestrade let out an oath.

The manager stood frozen to the spot.

Only Rockall remained calm.

Then, before I could even comprehend the speed in which it occurred, Sherlock Holmes was now gripped between the jaws of that monster, his body being quickly encircled by the crushing coils of a gigantic snake.

The creature had taken the bait.

But time was extremely short.

I knew what I had to do. I raised my revolver and, trying not to hit my friend, I fired at that monstrous head. My action distracted the Worm's attention for one vital moment. Or was it perhaps that she wasn't happy with her grip on the armored jacket? She loosened her teeth from their grip and turned those cold-blooded eyes upon me.

Perhaps the snake sensed danger.

The Universe held its breath.

Then Rockall, the Big Game Hunter, stepped forward, raised his elephant gun, and fired off both barrels at once.

The sound, exploded across the land, and echoed back to us like rolling thunder.

The devil-creature's head immediately disintegrated.

The hunter joined forces with myself and the pit manager to immediately tear Holmes away from the writhing clutches of the dead snake's coils. I examined him but, apart from some bruising to his ribs, he appeared to be unharmed by his close encounter with death.

Together we sat in the gathering darkness, all dazed and trying to make sense of what had just happened.

I felt physically sick at the memory of what I had been watching, the sight of snake's head, and now its gore, and the thought of what might have happened if Rockall had missed his mark.

336

All I could do was to breathe a word of thanks to the man with the elephant gun. Without him, my friend Sherlock Holmes would certainly have been crushed to death.

"It really is a great shame, you know," said Rockall, as he cradled his rifle.

"What is?" I asked him.

He indicated the dead snake. "No head to add to my collection. But the skin might yet be of some use."

"Perhaps it's edible," I told him.

Ravenstone shook his head vigorously. "I can't imagine anyone wanting to consume this animal after it has fed on the flesh of their loved ones."

"True," I conceded.

Then I turned to Holmes. "What have we here, then?"

"A python. Perhaps twenty-five to thirty feet in length."

"But how has it managed to live here almost entirely unnoticed?"

"Mr. Ravenstone tells us that the older workings of the mine are very ancient. Left to itself, such a monster would find plenty of room in there to live and grow. We have already discovered that underground tunnels maintain an even temperature, warm enough to allow her to live in relative comfort, and with a ready supply of food – both miners inside the workings, and animals in the fields around here. She had access to both."

"But where did she originally come from?" I persisted.

"Oh, that. You remember the smell we encountered at the home of Sir Archibald in London? The musty smell of reptiles in general, and of snakes in particular." Holmes relit his pipe. "I imagine that many years ago, when the family lived here at Old Grange, Sir Archibald's father, or perhaps even his grandfather, also kept reptiles as a pastime. Perhaps that is how Sir Archibald developed his own interest in the subject. It seems likely that one day, one of the snakes escaped and took up residence inside the mine. That must have been many years ago now – time enough for the python to have grown slowly but steadily to such a great length."

With our work in Durham completed, and with the monster having now been slain, Holmes and I joined Lestrade and headed south once more to London. And to home.

The sight of that huge python's head and mouth sometimes haunt my sleeping hours to this day.

Life in Durham returned to relative normality, and we have retained contact with many of the people we met there – not least the Big Game hunter, who emerged from his quiet life, becoming a famous local hero.

337

Rockall never again had to pay for his own drinks at any bar in the entire county.

Then, a few months later, Holmes received a parcel. It turned out to be a pair of snake-skin shoes.

Holmes was never likely to make use of such a gift, and instead he passed the shoes on to his brother. Mycroft Holmes proudly wore those shoes when he traveled to Balmoral in Scotland to attend an audience with Queen Victoria. Her Majesty was much amused at the idea that "Saint George" had finally slain the dragon, with an Elephant Gun.

The Adventure of
James Edward Phillimore
by Alan Dimes

Somewhere in the vaults of the bank of Cox and Co., at Charing Cross, there is a travel-worn and battered tin dispatch-box with my name, John H. Watson, MD, Late Indian Army, *painted upon the lid. It is crammed with papers, nearly all of which are records of cases to illustrate the curious problems which Mr. Sherlock Holmes had at various times to examine. Some, and not the least interesting, were complete failures, and as such will hardly bear narrating, since no final explanation is forthcoming. A problem without a solution may interest the student, but can hardly fail to annoy the casual reader. Among these unfinished tales is that of Mr. James Phillimore, who, stepping back into his own house to get his umbrella, was never more seen in this world.*

– "The Problem of Thor Bridge"

It had been raining heavily in London for more than a week. One morning after another, I awoke in semi-darkness with a chill in the air and water streaming down the panes. It was a pleasure, then, to rise from sleep that day in late April to see and feel the sun beaming through the windows of my bedroom in Baker Street. I had no doubt that the cessation of the daily downpours would also be welcome to my fellow-lodger, Mr. Sherlock Holmes. He was largely indifferent to the weather except when it affected his practice as London's first and only consulting detective, and, as he had remarked to me on more than one occasion, clients were less likely to call, and criminals to carry out their misdeeds, when there was heavy rain.

I shaved and dressed with a light heart and descended the stairs, eager to see what Mrs. Hudson had provided for our breakfast. When I entered our sitting room, I found Holmes already half-way through a plate of kedgeree, a dish for which I had acquired quite a taste during my time in India.

"Good morning, Watson," he said with a wide smile. "A pleasant morning, is it not? Perhaps when you have consumed Mrs. Hudson's excellent meal, you might like to come for a walk with me in this spring sunshine."

"By all means," I answered as I spooned a portion onto my plate.

I haven't spoken much in these chronicles of the frequent excursions that Holmes and I made from our lodgings into the wider world of the metropolis. He often claimed that he allowed his brain to retain nothing other than that which was strictly necessary to the pursuit of his profession, but in his more relaxed moments he was prepared to concede that this wasn't strictly true. A thorough knowledge of the layout of the city was, naturally, of great practical use to the detective, but this could not be said of the majority of the out-of-the-way facts he had accumulated over the years. Wherever we went, it seemed, he had an anecdote about the district's past inhabitants or the story of the origin of the name of a particular road or area.

When we had finished our coffee, and Holmes had smoked his first, malodorous pipe of the day, we went down into Baker Street and set off at a leisurely pace in a north-easterly direction.

After a pleasant stroll into lower Islington, during which Holmes informed me that the name of the borough had originally been "Giseldone", meaning "Gisla's Hill", after an early Saxon inhabitant, we returned to Baker Street some two hours later. On our entry, Mrs. Hudson handed Holmes a visiting card and informed us that a lady had called in our absence – young, about twenty-two or -three, and well-to-do.

We climbed the stairs to the sitting room and when I had sat in my accustomed armchair Holmes passed me the card, saying, "Let me hear what you can deduce from this."

On the printed side it said: *James and Viola Phillimore, The Poplars, 17 Oulton Rd, Bromley, Kent.*

I turned it over. On the other side was written, in a neat, feminine hand: *Will call again at half-past eleven. VP.*

"Well," I began, a little hesitantly, "the Phillimores are evidently well-off. The card is particularly thick and stiff, and the information is embossed, rather than merely printed on it."

"A reasonable inference."

"While it is clearly expensive, it is not ostentatious, which indicates modesty and good taste on their part."

"Sound enough. Anything more?"

"Not to my eyes."

"It isn't your eyes that are at fault, since they see no less than mine. You fail to deduce from what you see."

I passed the card back to him, sighed, and reached in my pocket for my pipe and tobacco pouch, saying as I filled the bowl with Ship's, "What do you deduce then?"

"We already know from Mrs. Hudson that Viola Phillimore is a young woman. I would add that she and her husband have probably not been married long, are childless, and have only recently moved into The Poplars, which is in all probability their first marital home. Mrs. Phillimore

340

is a sensible woman, not given to hysteria, so we may take it her visit to us has a serious purpose."

He handed me back the card.

"Observe," he continued. "Despite its stiffness, the card is slightly bent, and there are two small indentations on the lower edge."

"Why, yes. And what does that tell us?"

"That too many cards have been pressed into a card case. Which also tells us that the carrier of the case anticipated handing out many cards on the day the case was filled. When would one hand out more cards than at any other time? When one has just moved into an area and is calling on one's new neighbours."

"Very well, but your other deductions? Their childlessness, and the rest?"

"Both of the couple's names are on it. If the husband is, as we may infer from their address and the quality of the card, a member of the professional class, he doubtless has his own supply of cards with only his name upon them. His wife doesn't have her own cards, which indicates that she does not yet move comfortably in her new social circle unless accompanied by her husband. That is a characteristic of the early days of a marriage, especially among younger women. It is also her youth which persuades me that she has no children. It is among the lower orders, to which she clearly doesn't belong, that we must expect to see early marriage and young parenthood."

"How do you arrive at your conclusions about her personality?"

"Really, Watson! We have a sample of her handwriting, brief though it is! Women tend to write in a smaller hand than men and, allowing for that, her writing is of the middle size, which generally indicates a well-balanced personality. This inference is corroborated by the neatness of her script and the fact that the letters of her words are consistently connected."

"Well," I glanced up at the clock where it sat on the mantelpiece next to Holmes's jack-knife, "we don't have long to wait before we can test the accuracy of your conclusions."

Mrs. Viola Phillimore was a handsome young woman of the middle height, dressed in a modest outfit of dark blue taffeta, and with a small dark hat pinned to her hair, which was a deep chestnut in colour. Distress was visible on her pale, heart-shaped face.

"Good morning, Mrs. Phillimore. I am Sherlock Holmes, and this is my colleague, Dr. John Watson."

"Dr. Watson. I have, of course, heard your name in connection with that of your friend."

341

"Please take a seat, Mrs. Phillimore," said Holmes, "and tell us how we may be of service."

"Certainly, Mr. Holmes. My husband is James Edward Phillimore, a junior partner at the solicitors' firm of Killroy and Hay in the City, and we have recently moved into The Poplars, in the southern part of Bromley in Kent. Four days ago, on Saturday, we had just left the house at about half-past eight to visit my mother in Norwood, and were about to walk to the station when James realized that he had left his umbrella in the stand in the hall.

"'I'd better go and get it,' he said. 'It'll rain today, if the last few days are anything to go by. I'll just be a moment.'

"He turned his key in the lock once more and went in, closing the door behind him.

"Getting the umbrella should have been the work of a few seconds, so when a couple of minutes had gone by without his return, I took out my own key and opened the door, which had automatically relocked when James re-entered. The umbrella was still in the stand, but James was nowhere to be seen. I thought perhaps that he had forgotten something else, from another part of the house. I called out his name once or twice, but there was no reply. I went back to the door and looked down the street in either direction, but still he was nowhere to be seen. I stood for a while, dazed and baffled, then I went to the local police station to report his disappearance."

"Where, I would imagine, they were less than sympathetic," said Holmes.

"They seemed to think that either he was playing some absurd prank on me, or that he wanted to leave me and had chosen this particularly cruel method of doing so. They told me to wait a few days for his return. I have done so, with no result, so now I have come to you, Mr. Holmes."

The detective leaned forward, resting his elbows on his bony knees and pressing the tips of his fingers together.

"Before I take your case, let me warn you that should I discover the truth, it may not necessarily end your distress."

"I understand that, Mr. Holmes. Nevertheless, I wish to know it."

"Very well. Now, if you would be so good, I have some questions to ask you. Were there any servants in the house on that day?"

"No. We have a cook, and a maid, but neither of them lives in, and as we visit my mother every Saturday, we give them that morning and afternoon off."

"You said that you looked up and down the street without seeing your husband. Did you see anyone else?"

"It was quite early in the morning, and a Saturday. The street was empty except for a deformed man I had never seen before, about thirty yards from the front door. As I looked at him he turned and hobbled away. Since my husband has a straight back and a strong physique, it couldn't have been him, even if for some outrageous reason he had been disguised."

"Have you made inquiries at Killroy and Hay?"

"I have just returned from there. When I didn't find you in, I decided to use the time to call on them."

"And?"

"He hasn't been at their offices since last Friday."

"Now I must ask you some questions of a more delicate nature."

"Please proceed."

"How were the relations between your husband and yourself?"

"No marriage is ever perfect, Mr. Holmes, or utterly without conflict, but I believe that ours was as harmonious as one could reasonably expect. I am certainly happy, and James gives no indication that he is not."

"You have never had any doubts as to his fidelity?"

"Certainly not. James is a quiet man. He seldom goes out without me, and while he sometimes stays late at his chambers, he often brings any extra work home. I cannot see when he would have the time to be unfaithful, even if he had the inclination, which I can assure you he does not."

"Has there been any change in his habits of late?"

" He had been spending rather more time in his study over the last few days before his disappearance, but I gather that he has several important cases on at the moment."

"I see," said Holmes, standing up. "Dr. Watson and I will need to see your house. May we do that this afternoon?"

"Yes, of course."

"Then we bid you goodbye until then, Mrs. Phillimore."

After Mrs. Hudson had shown the lady out, Holmes asked, "So, my friend, what did you make of her story?"

"Well, people don't simply vanish into thin air."

"Don't they, now? What about Bathurst?"

"No doubt I am very slow, Holmes, but I fail to see what Australia has to do with this."

"I was referring to Benjamin Bathurst, not the gold centre of New South Wales. On 25 November, 1809, Bathurst, a British diplomatic envoy, and his German courier, a Herr Krause, travelled by chaise to the town of Perleberg, west of Berlin. After ordering fresh horses at the post house, Bathurst and his companion walked to a nearby inn, The White Swan. They ate an early dinner, and then Bathurst spent several hours

343

writing in a small room set aside for him at the inn. The travellers' departure was delayed and it wasn't until nine p.m. that they were told that the horses were about to be harnessed to their carriage. Bathurst immediately left his room, followed seconds later by Krause. Bathurst entered the chaise, but when Krause went in, he found it empty. He went around the horses to see if, for some reason, Bathurst had stepped out through the other door. But there was no sign of him anywhere."

"So what had happened?"

"No one knows. That's my point. Perhaps I am being a little vain in thinking that had I been in Perleberg at the time, I would have solved the conundrum. In this instance, I'm rather afraid that Mr. Phillimore, as the Bromley constabulary suggested, has left his wife, though at present I am at a loss to explain why he should have done so in such a bizarre manner. However, let us not speculate further until we have more data."

After a light lunch, we made our way to Liverpool Street and caught the two o'clock train to Bromley South. From there it was a short walk to Oulton Road. Mrs. Phillimore greeted us with a countenance suffused with hope. I had expected Holmes to make a thorough search of The Poplars, but instead he asked, "Is there any part of the house to which only your husband has access?"

"Yes, there is his study. He doesn't even allow the maid into it, which I grant is a little eccentric, but as I told you in Baker Street, he sometimes brings work home, and if he needs absolute privacy to concentrate on it, then so be it."

"May we see it?"

"I'm afraid that my husband has the only key, which he keeps on a ring that only he handles. It will have been in his pocket when he . . . when he . . . ."

Mrs. Phillimore's calm demeanour broke down and she burst into passionate sobbing. In that moment, she seemed like a desperate young girl rather than the composed married woman we had first met that morning. Clearly this business was putting her under considerable strain

"Put your faith in Mr. Holmes," I said soothingly. "If this mystery is capable of solution, then he is the man to solve it."

"And if we are to solve it," said Holmes, "then I am afraid that, with your permission of course, I must pick the lock of Mr. Phillimore's study."

"You have it," said Mrs. Phillimore, "but you will forgive me if I don't watch you at your work. I shall be in the parlour."

Once the lady had gone, Holmes took a little soft leather case from the pocket of his jacket and selected two metal tools from it.

"This will take but a moment. The lock isn't a sophisticated one." And within an instant, the door was open, and we stepped into James Edward Phillimore's private sanctum.

It was a square, spacious room with one small window, unremarkable at first glance except for a deal table covered with jars of chemicals and scientific equipment. It seemed that, like Holmes himself, Phillimore was an amateur chemist. The detective looked at the jars one by one, then turned to an examination of the rest of the room. Its walls were covered with a plain, conventional wallpaper, another indication of that modesty and lack of ostentation hinted at by the visiting card. The dark blue, unpatterned carpet, the brown mahogany desk, the white lampshade, the utilitarian furniture, all pointed to an occupant of simple, unaffected tastes.

On the wall behind the desk were two framed photographs, one of the couple together, clearly taken on their wedding day, and the other of Mrs. Phillimore by herself. Between the photographs was a set of shelves bending slightly under the weight of the books upon them.

"What a man chooses to read is among the best indicators of his character," said Holmes, and we began to scan their spines. As might be expected, given Phillimore's profession, there were many books on the law, but they were all crammed onto the top shelf. Those below were of more interest and, to judge from their condition, more frequently read:

The Zincali, Lavengro, and *The Romany Rye* by George Borrow, *Travels with a Donkey in the Cevennes* by R. L. Stevenson, *Confessions of an English Opium-Eater* by Thomas de Quincey, *The Gold Mines of Midian* and *The Lands of Cazembe* by Sir Richard Burton, *Tales of the Grotesque and Arabesque* by Edgar Allan Poe, and two volumes *of La Comedie Humaine* by Honore de Balzac.

"Are you beginning to discern a theme?"

"Travel. Escape."

"Certainly, but I think we can infer a little more. Let us consider the authors for a moment, rather than the content of their works. Stevenson rebelled against his Presbyterian background and the path laid out for him by his father. Borrow and Balzac both studied law, but found it stultifying, and rejected it in favour of literature. Poe was always at odds with his foster-father and failed at the military career planned for him. When Burton was at college, he deliberately tried to get rusticated by breaking every possible rule. De Quincey was sent to Manchester Grammar School, so that after three years' stay he might obtain a scholarship to Brasenose College, Oxford, but he ran away after only nineteen months."

"All rebels, " I said. "Defying what was expected of them."

"Indeed, and unless I am very much mistaken, if we look into Phillimore's background we shall probably find indications that he wished

345

for a different life, but hadn't the strength of character to go against his family's expectations."

"Holmes, both de Quincey and Poe were opium eaters. Do you think Phillimore emulated them?"

"One thing is clear: While part of him longed to escape from the prison of respectable conformity, he remained within it because he loves his wife. Here, in his private space, where no one else would ever see them, he has a wedding photograph and a portrait of her."

"What now?"

"A visit to Messrs Killroy and Hay, I think. But first, a word with Mrs. Phillimore."

Holmes locked the door once more with the aid of his metal picks and we made our way to the parlour.

"I require a little more data, Mrs. Phillimore," said Holmes, "Are any of your husband's clothes missing? Any personal effects, such as toiletries?"

"No, everything is just as he left it that morning."

"I see. May we have the address of Mr. Phillimore's law firm?"

"Of course. It is Killroy and Hay, 34 Austin Friars, EC."

"Thank you. And now, Mrs. Phillimore, we must bid you good day. Rest assured that your case has my entire attention.

"Now, Watson," said Holmes as we settled into a carriage on the Victoria-bound train from Bromley, "we can use the half-hour or so of travel we have before us to smoke a pipe or two and review the case of Mr. James Edward Phillimore. Let me have your thoughts."

"Well, your last question of Mrs. Phillimore tells against the idea that the whole thing was planned. Surely he would have taken some clothes with him if his aim was to leave her."

"No, I am afraid her answer doesn't prove that it was unplanned. He is a fairly wealthy man. He could, for example, have already rented himself a room somewhere, bought a fresh set of clothes, and established a new identity."

"Why did you ask the question, in that case?"

"Had she said, yes, there were clothes and toiletries missing, it would certainly have meant that it was planned. I was expecting a negative reply, but I had to ask. My belief is that his actions were a spontaneous response to something that must have happened to him in that brief span of moments. He saw something, or heard something, or possibly even felt something, that caused him to do what he did. But what?"

"Holmes! The deformed man in the street – that's what he saw! He must have known the fellow, and perhaps recognised him as someone who would use violence against him, and even against his wife. So he went back into the house and hid somewhere inside until his wife left for the police station. Then he came out and faced the man."

"Your idea isn't entirely without merit, but there are too many points which contradict it. If Phillimore had genuinely forgotten his umbrella, then seeing the man was a strange coincidence. He suddenly had both a motive for going back into his house and an excuse for doing so. You may recall that Mrs. Phillimore described her husband as being the possessor of a strong physique, bookish and sedentary as he was. A man of the kind she described would be unlikely to attack someone stronger and fitter. And how do you explain the fact that the fellow ran away – or, as Mrs. Phillimore put it, hobbled away – when she looked at him? And yet, there is a possibility that in some way he is a factor. Perhaps it would be better if we waited to see if our visit to Killroy and Hay can shed any light on this. You have your newspaper, I see, and I my Pocket Library edition of Marcus Aurelius' *Meditations*, so let us spend the remainder of the journey reading quietly."

Charles Dickens would have found the premises of Killroy and Hay, Solicitors, familiar. The room filled with copyists and clerks, the smell of ink and wood polish and the rustle of documents, the self-important head clerk keeping a close eye on his young underlings, the short flight of stairs that led to the partners' rooms, the clients coming in and out, their faces beaming, sullen, or downcast, depending on the nature of their dealings with the law and how they had turned out – all were there. Holmes and I were shown into the office of Benedict Hay, a senior partner and a descendant of one of the founders of the firm, which I later learned dated back to the sixteenth century. Hay was a tall, thin man with wiry grey hair and piercing blue eyes. He shook us both firmly by the hand.

"Pray be seated, gentlemen," he said. "It isn't every day that our office is graced by the presence of so famous a visitor as you, Mr. Holmes. Oh, and you too, of course, Dr. Watson. I assume you are here because of the disappearance of our Mr. Phillimore. James is a first-class solicitor and we feel his absence deeply. His wife came here earlier today and said that she was about to consult you, as she had been disappointed in the response of the police."

"You last saw him this past Friday."

"That is correct, sir."

"In the last few days before his disappearance, was there any decline in the quality of his work?"

"None whatsoever."

"Was there any change in his general demeanour? Did he seem worried, for example, or overly excited?"

"No, he was the same as ever."

347

"Mrs. Phillimore told us that he sometimes worked late at the office. Would he have been here alone on those occasions?"

Hay's eyebrows lifted.

"Worked late? He never did that. None of the partners do, junior or senior. It is a policy of the firm."

Holmes briefly turned his head and met my gaze. I instantly understood the meaning of that swift glance. For the first time, we had caught Phillimore in a lie to his wife. There must surely be something he had been hiding from her. A double life, perhaps.

"Who is handling Mr. Phillimore's cases in his absence?" asked Holmes.

"That would be Mr. Ockendon, another of the junior partners."

"May we speak with him?"

"Certainly."

Hay took us down the corridor to another office. He opened the door without knocking and we found it occupied by a fresh-faced young man in his early thirties, who was in the middle of giving instructions to one of his clerks.

"This is Mr. Sherlock Holmes," said Hay, "and his colleague Dr. Watson."

The young clerk's mouth fell open, and he was clearly disappointed when Ockendon sent him off to carry out the work they had been discussing.

Hay departed for his own office.

"I take it you're here about Jim," said Ockendon.

"I believe there might be a key to his disappearance in the cases he was dealing with at the time," said Holmes.

"It's all fairly workaday stuff. A contested inheritance – that's *Jarrowby v. Markham*. Pursuance of a debt, *Laker v. Collins* – breach of promise. *Arlen v, Coniston* – an inquiry for the relatives of Michael Enderby. The – "

"Did you say – *Michael Enderby*?"

"Yes, sir. Michael Enderby. You'd have thought, being a lawyer himself, that Enderby would at least have left his papers in order when he died, but everything's in a terrible mess. He died intestate, and we're making inquiries to see if he had any relatives. I suspect he may not have been of sound mind at the end."

Holmes stood up and, reaching across the desk, shook Ockendon by the hand.

"Thank you, your assistance has been invaluable," he said.

"But I – "

I followed Holmes through the door, bidding Ockendon a polite farewell.

A minute or two later we were seated in a hansom bound for Baker Street. My friend was silent, a grim expression on his face.

"Don't keep me in suspense," I said. "You have solved the case, have you not? Or at any rate, are in receipt of a vital clue. What is the significance of this Enderby?"

"My friend, I advise you to wait until you are sitting in a comfortable chair in our rooms, with a strong drink in your hand, before you ask that question."

"Just as you wish."

"As a literary man," said Holmes when we were back in Baker Street, "and also as a lover of sensational fiction, you have no doubt read *The Strange Case of Dr. Jekyll and Mr. Hyde*, by Robert Louis Stevenson."

"I would hardly describe the work as sensational. Stevenson may have begun his career as a writer of boys' adventure stories, but he has a good deal of psychological insight. The business with the potion is somewhat far-fetched, but the work overall is a metaphor for the human condition."

"I stand corrected, my dear doctor. Clearly, then, you have read it."

"Yes."

Holmes poured us both a brandy, then reached into the coal scuttle and took a cigar from his box.

"It may surprise you to learn, then," he said, holding a match to the end of his *Hoyo*, "that while the work is fiction, it is based on fact. You recall the death of Dr. Anthony Adamson?"

"Yes, I read about it in an English newspaper, sometime after it happened, as I was in the base hospital in Peshawur at the time. He was a respected and highly-placed member of the profession, and only about fifty when he died. Of a heart attack, I think it was."

"Yes, that is what was given out at the time. In fact, Adamson is still alive, and incarcerated in an asylum. Stevenson based the character of Henry Jekyll upon him."

"You surely aren't suggesting that Dr. Adamson invented a potion that could transform a man both physically and mentally?"

"A complete physical transformation as described in the novel is, of course, impossible. But while, as you said, the potion is pure fantasy, it conceals a truth which can be scientifically verified, though it is far outside the experience of the majority of Englishmen."

"Holmes, you have yet to connect all this to Michael Enderby, let alone James Phillimore."

"This is what I believe has happened: Enderby was Adamson's lawyer, an old friend and the executor of his will, though he had no role in drafting it. Enderby died intestate, and the task of finding his relatives, as we heard this afternoon, was given to Phillimore, who then had access to Enderby's papers. Among them must have been either a summary of Adamson's own papers, or the papers themselves."

"Something in those papers is the key to Adamson's incarceration, and to Phillimore's disappearance."

"Just so. I shall keep you in suspense no longer, and I apologise if I have tried your patience. Over the years, I have made a special study of the effects of various types of hallucinogens. Oh, don't look so worried. My experience has been confined to reading up on them. As a medical man, perhaps you should look into them yourself."

"I hardly think that, as a general practitioner, I am likely to encounter their use."

"As I've said before, education never ends, and you never know when such knowledge may prove valuable. However, let us return to the matter in hand. One of the key aspects of such drugs is that they can cause a feeling of liberation, of transcendence. The Masatec Indians of Oaxaca in Mexico have for centuries chewed a hallucinogenic mushroom called *psilocybe* to achieve those effects. The ancient Greek worshippers of Dionysus appear to have used something similar. The Masatecs and the Maenads used them infrequently, mainly at religious rites, so their systems were able to recover from the effects. Repeated doses at short intervals, particularly if the taker is unused to them, can cause mania, and an absence of conscience which may be accompanied by bursts of great physical strength. Another symptom of frequent use is that the drug's effects may reoccur even if the individual hasn't used it for several days."

I was beginning, in a vague and tentative manner, to see where Holmes's argument was taking us, but I kept silent as he continued his narrative.

"I knew none of this when I was called in to help investigate the murder of Sir Daniel Cremers. I was lodging in Montague Street at the time, and living a more or less hand-to-mouth existence. Lestrade asked for my assistance, which I took as an admission that he had some small faith in me, though he wouldn't have said as much to a third person.

"There had been one witness to the crime, a maid servant, who had seen the murder clearly from her window. The night was cloudless and there was a full moon. She saw a white-haired old gentleman coming down the lane. The old man was accosted by a second man, whose face she couldn't see. He took out a bludgeon and without warning, in a burst of inhuman strength and rage, showered blow after blow on the head and shoulders of Cremers until the aged man fell dead to the cobbles."

"That exactly mirrors the murder of Sir Danvers Carew in the novel."

"Yes, but unlike the detectives in the book, we didn't have so straightforward a clue as the broken half of a cane belonging to the murderer. I had one very slender thread, which by great good fortune turned out to be a key to the mystery. From the maid's evidence that the killer had suddenly appeared, I conjectured that he had been waiting for Cremers in the house next to the maid's, which was derelict and untenanted. On the floor of that house, I found an old newspaper with a distinct bootmark upon it. As well as its size, there was a pattern on the rubber sole which suggested that it came from one particular bootmaker and had possibly been specially made. I might have saved myself much time and effort if I had told Lestrade and let his men do the legwork, but I preferred to do it myself. If I succeeded, I would get the credit, and if I had made a false assumption, only I would know of it. It was weary, uphill work, and had none of those features of interest with which you delight your readers. To cut a long story short, the boot led me to Dr. Anthony Adamson. I informed Lestrade, and Adamson was taken to Bow Street Police Station.

"He claimed to have no memory of the evening in question and could provide no one who could vouch for his whereabouts. In the cells later that day, he experienced one of those reoccurrences of the drugged state I referred to before. This involved some powerful hallucination, as he screamed loudly, claiming that all the other inmates of the holding cells had been transformed into semi-human monsters who were planning his death. An alienist who was brought into Bow Street to examine him concluded that this was a deep-seated mania and recommended that he be transferred immediately to an asylum.

"The alienist reported the situation to the British Medical Association, who then petitioned the Metropolitan Police Commissioner to keep the matter from the public in the interests of the dignity and reputation of the medical profession. Word was given out that Adamson had died of heart failure. He was given a new name in the asylum, and I was likewise sworn to secrecy."

"How did Stevenson find out about it?"

"A good question. One of the policemen or one of the doctors involved must have outlined the bare bones of the case to him, which he then covered with fictional flesh, producing that fable on the duality of man you praised a few minutes ago. Some years later, while I was investigating the effects of these substances, it occurred to me that some of the symptoms described exactly fitted Adamson. I gained permission to

351

visit him in the asylum. He had accepted his responsibility for Cremers' death, but even after so long a period of abstinence from the drug he was still prone to those bouts of temporary mania. He confirmed that he had experimented with a cocktail of hallucinogens in an attempt, as he described it, to expand his consciousness beyond the confines and restraints imposed upon it by the strictures of society."

"But he became psychologically addicted, and continued to take the drugs even when the effect on him was deleterious."

"Indeed."

"I've seen other drugs have a similar effect. Opium, for example."

"So," asked Holmes, "are we now ready to apply our knowledge to the case of Mr. James Edward Phillimore?"

"I think so. Like Adamson, Phillimore longed for something beyond the bourgeois respectability of his life. Adamson's papers came into his hands, and he too saw a means of release in the use of these substances. Perhaps he was a little more cautious than Adamson, as Mr. Hay said that he could see no change in his demeanour or in his work. Phillimore may, as you suggested, have taken a room where he took small doses which had an effect, but didn't prevent him from going home to his wife the same night with his story of working late."

"Excellent, Watson! And what of his disappearance, the starting point of our labours?"

"No doubt you have reached a conclusion."

"Yes. Here is what I believe happened on that Saturday morning. As Phillimore and his wife prepared to leave the house, he began to feel the cumulative force of the effect of the drugs. He had, as you said, probably been taking them in small doses, but he had been doing so regularly. He must have felt that he was on the verge of some outbreak of madness, as he may well have been. He loved his wife and didn't wish her to see whatever it was that was about to happen to him. He deliberately left his umbrella behind so that he would have an excuse to go back into the house. He then made his exit through the back door, clambered over the wall and out into the street. That is when his wife saw him. He was the deformed man in the street."

"But you said there was no physical transformation."

"Not of the kind that Stevenson described, no. But one possible effect of these chemicals is muscular spasms, which can cause the victim to bend his back and lose full control of his limbs. He ran away as best he could to preserve his secret. Had Mrs. Phillimore been trained in my methods of observation, she might have noticed that the figure was clad in the clothes her husband had been wearing the last time she saw him."

"She did say that he was thirty yards away."

"True."

"This is all well and good, Holmes," I said, "but we are still left with the question: Where is James Phillimore? Is there any chance that he too has become a murderer? He must be apprehended, before, like Adamson, he commits some unspeakable outrage."

"Crimes of violence are common in the poorer parts of London, and the culprits seldom caught, so it is entirely possible that in the four days since he vanished, Phillimore has already committed some of those everyday atrocities which regularly go unsolved and unpunished."

James Phillimore was never seen again in this world, alive or dead, and his fate remains a mystery. Holmes was forced to swallow his pride and admit his failure, and his discomfort at being unable to provide any solace for the unfortunate Mrs. Viola Phillimore. Because this case is unsolved, and because of the unsettling nature of the revelations concerning Dr. Anthony Adamson's experiments, I am consigning this account to my old tin dispatch box in the vaults of Cox and Company, Charing Cross, where it will remain unread until seventy-five years after my death.

The Jade Swan
by Charles Veley and Anna Elliott

May 1896
From the notebooks of John H. Watson, M.D.

Chapter I

"Padma told us she was coming here," Marilee said. Her voice sounded tense with worry. "Why aren't there any footprints?"

She leaned forwards in the bow of our canoe. From my position in the stern, hefting my wooden paddle, I could see her small hands as she gripped the gunwales. Her knuckles were white with tension. The single long braid of her blonde hair swung from side to side as she scanned the riverbank.

We were we were only a few feet from an empty swan's nest, a huge and untidy affair nearly as big as a sleeping-mattress, near the banks of the River Cherwell, upstream from Oxford University. Spring had been wet that year. The water was high with a swift current, and I was grateful that Marilee had directed us to the relative calm of the little eddy by the nest.

"Why aren't there any footprints?" Marilee asked, her voice tense with worry.

"No sign of a boat landing? I asked. "Broken reeds, that sort of thing?"

"Nothing. Where in the world could she have gone?" A sob threatened to break into her words. "Why couldn't she tell us?"

Padma, one of Marilee's college roommates, had gone missing Saturday afternoon. It was Sunday morning now, and Padma still had not returned. Marilee had telephoned me an hour earlier, her voice worried and urgent. Could Holmes and I help with the search?

Holmes was busy with a matter for the Foreign Office, but I came to Oxford without hesitation, for I felt a familial obligation towards Marilee. She and her mother were distant relations of Mary, my late and dearly beloved wife of four wonderful years. We had met them after they returned from Bangalore, where Marilee's father, a major in the Princess of Wales's Own Regiment, had recently died of a wound sustained in the line of duty. Mary had welcomed their acquaintance with her characteristic sweetness and sympathetic disposition.

354

During the few years that remained to her, Mary grew even closer to her once-distant relatives. Perhaps with an intuition as to what was to come, she encouraged me to think of them as family and encouraged Marilee to call me "Uncle John". I was only too happy to help compensate in my small way for Marilee's loss of her father.

We kept in touch after Mary's passing. I watched with admiration as Marilee successfully completed her course of study at one of the London academies for young women, and then, with greater admiration still, as she applied for admission to St. Swithin's College in Oxford. We celebrated when Marilee was accepted. I immediately applied the lion's share of my modest savings to help defray the costs of her tuition. It was only a gesture, but it eased my heart. I felt Mary, looking down on us, would have applauded.

The morning of Marilee's telephoned appeal, she was waiting for me when my train arrived at Oxford Station. A confident young woman now, she reminded me of Mary. For a long moment, the sight of her, fair and blonde, blue eyes shining with anxious hope, filled my heart and kept me from speech.

Now, in the canoe, she sat hunched, her shoulders shaking.

"We'll find her," I said, trying to sound confident.

I paddled us round the small peninsula on which the nest rested. The swans had built it recently, for I saw some streaks of green grasses within the circular jumble of reeds and sticks, about five feet in diameter. The water lapped against the edges of the nest. I saw no eggs inside.

"I can't think where else she would have gone."

"And she said she was coming here."

"To the swan's nest. But it looks as if she hasn't been here at all."

"Maybe there is another nest. Upriver or downriver."

"No, it would be this one."

"How can you be sure?"

"I saw her right here, a week ago. We were coming downstream."

"We?"

"I was with my other two roommates. We were all in a punt, and we all saw her."

"A week ago."

"And yesterday she said would paddle here in her canoe, to visit the swan's nest."

A long pause. Then Marilee sighed. "We may as well go back. Besides, you haven't had breakfast, Uncle John."

"Quite right," I said. As long as I kept moving, my spirits remained high, but I knew that when I relaxed, I would not be at my best.

I maneuvered our canoe away from the peninsula and headed it downstream, merging with the current. Leaves of the riverbank trees and bushes, bright green in their new growth, brushed against my shoulder.

"Maybe there will be someone at the boathouse by now."

"Maybe someone saw her pick up her canoe yesterday."

The boathouse had been deserted this morning when we had come to pick up Marilee's canoe and found that Padma's was missing.

"What was she wearing?"

"A red-brown sari wrap-around affair. A green headscarf."

"Wasn't she cold?"

"She never complained. And the sari was wool. Specially woven for smoothness. Her mother had it made for her in Scotland, she said, especially so she – "

She stopped. "What was that? I thought I saw someone up ahead."

"A boat?" There were punters downstream, perhaps two-hundred yards off.

"No, on the land. On the right, close to the riverbank."

I saw only a wisp of fog. "Keep your eye on the spot and direct me," I said.

We stopped at the place Marilee indicated, but on closer inspection, we saw only undisturbed vegetation on the riverbank, and a narrow walking-path that ran parallel to the water's edge.

"To the boathouse, then," she said. "Then we'll go home. You can meet my roommates."

Chapter II

"Tell me about Padma," I said.

I was perched beside Marilee on her divan, inside the comfortable sitting room that she shared with three other students. Padma was not present, of course, but the other two, Barbara and Lucia, sat close by and their eyes were on me. Scones and hot coffee waited on the low tile-inlaid table. A small coal fire burned in the hearth. The chill of the fruitless morning search was wearing off.

"Will you tell Mr. Holmes?" asked Lucia, a dark-haired tall young Italian woman with a mischievous smile.

"I may, if it seems useful. And if I have the opportunity."

"But he will not tell the police or – " A surreptitious glance at the others. " – the Dean?"

I nearly laughed. "Why would Mr. Holmes do that?"

"We don't know," Marilee said.

356

"We just wanted to be sure," Lucia said. "You see, last week, Padma learned you knew Marilee."

"I told her," Marilee said. "It surprised her to learn that we have a family connection."

"What did she say?"

"That she was delighted to know it. But for a moment she looked a bit worried."

"Anything else?"

"She said she'd read your book about the treasure in India."

The Sign of Four."

"Yes, and she thought it would be a fine idea if the four of us formed a similar alliance."

"Not to steal a chest full of jewels, I hope," I said.

"To protect each other's secrets," said Lucia.

"To help each other with . . . things," said Marilee.

"Such as?" I couldn't imagine what things these young ladies would need help with.

She opened her purse and took out a packet of cigarettes. "Buying these, for example. We aren't supposed to have them in our rooms.

"Unladylike," Lucia said. "Bad for the college's reputation."

I smiled inwardly. "What else?" I asked. "About Padma?"

Barbara, a stolid-faced young lady with closely cropped flaxen curls, spoke up. "Well, she's frightfully rich. Her father's a maharajah or something. From India."

"He sends an allowance every week," said Marilee. "She really can afford to buy anything she wants. But she never spends much. She's never extravagant."

"And not at all snobbish either," Lucia said. "She always helps us braid each other's hair, and she makes tea whenever it is her turn."

"And she reads poetry aloud in that lovely sing-song Indian accent of hers," added Barbara.

"So you like her, and she reciprocates. But you haven't reported her missing. Why is that?"

A long, awkward silence.

"Perhaps you suspect that someone else was involved?"

"We hope not," Lucia said.

"Or, rather, we hope so," said Marilee, "as long as everything is all right."

"Please, let us stick to the facts. What is it that you're concealing?"

"Lohengrin," said Marilee.

Then they each chimed in, eager to help now that the secret had come out.

"The swan prince. From the opera."

"And the Russian ballet about the Lake."

"There's also a German legend – "

I held up my hand. "Please. Who is this Lohengrin?"

"Her young man. We saw them together a week ago."

"Where?"

"Where you and I were, Uncle John. On the river."

"They were punting," Barbara said, "she in her sari, lounging in the front part – "

"The bow," Lucia said.

" – The bow, like Cleopatra on the Nile, and he was standing tall and proud, with his great pole, pushing the punt along."

"Can you describe him?"

"Oh, that's easy. He's Indian. Like her. He might be her brother."

"Well, that's what she said he was – "

"But we saw through that, right away, didn't we?"

"I suppose we did."

I cleared my throat. "His description?"

"Yes, of course. Brown, light-brown skin."

"Tall, and slender."

"Like Padma."

"And he had wide brown eyes, imploring and excited and domineering, all at the same time."

"Like Padma's."

"Why don't you think they are brother and sister?"

"By the way he was looking at her, and she at him. Before they noticed we were watching."

"I think they're like Romeo and Juliet," said Barbara. "I bet his father's a maharajah too, and an enemy of her father."

No one seemed prepared to voice an opinion of Barbara's conjecture. She went on,

"Anyway, more description: Sleek black hair, heavy with pomade. Beautifully tailored suit. Starched white collar. Hardly what you'd expect to see on a person poling a punt."

"And this was a week ago," I said. "I assume you asked Padma about him?"

"Yes, we asked her when she came back to our room, of course," Marilee said. "She told us he was her brother. She showed us a little swan pendant she wore around her neck."

"This was the first time she'd shown it," Lucia said. "None of us can remember seeing it on her before."

I looked around. Nods came from the other two girls in confirmation.

358

"She said that her mother had given each of them an identical jade swan amulet," Barbara said.

"For their sixth birthday," Lucia said.

"She always talked about the swans and how serene they were," Marilee said. "That's why she wanted to come here to study – because of the swans – and her father being so wealthy, she could attend any university she pleased."

"So she came to Oxford because of the swans?"

"More than that. She selected St. Swithin's because of the swans. That's what she told us when she showed us her amulet."

"Because of St. Swithin's one miracle," Barbara said.

She looked at me as if I should know what the miracle was.

"You're having me on, aren't you?" I said.

"No, really. St. Swithin's one miracle was to mend an old woman's broken eggs. Some workmen in the church had smashed them by accident. He picked them up, the story goes, and made them whole again."

"That is what Padma said, Uncle John," Marilee said.

"Why do you call her young man 'Lohengrin'?"

"Oh, because in the opera, he enters on a chariot or a boat or something, pulled by a swan. Padma told us that too. That's what Padma said. I haven't seen the opera."

"Nor I," said Barbara.

"Is he enrolled at the university?"

"We didn't inquire. We didn't want to do anything other than wish her happiness. Brother-and-sister happiness, of course, was what we said, but we all thought they were a couple."

"Or would be."

"Eventually."

"So today is Sunday," I said. "She disappeared yesterday."

"One week after we'd seen them on the river."

"And she said she was going to the swan's nest."

"And taking her own canoe."

"And dressed in her sari," I said. "Did she normally dress in Indian garb?"

"No, mostly she dressed as we do."

"Why the sari, then?"

"Another reason we thought she was going to meet her young Indian prince."

"Do you know his name?"

"We didn't think to ask."

"But she did say he was a member of the new debate society. The one for Indian students. Not the Oxford one."

359

"Some Arab-sounding name."

"The Oxford Majlis. And she said he was debating tonight."

"So we were all going to go tonight and cheer him on."

"But she begged us not to."

"She said it would embarrass him."

"An Oxford debater, embarrassed by an admiring audience?"

"Yes, we thought that was a little odd. But then, perhaps she was just making excuses to keep us from meeting him. If they are sweethearts and her parents disapprove, she would want to keep him a secret, even from us."

"Would you recognise him again if you saw him?"

"Well, we three were on one punt and he was on the other, as I said."

"But I was poling us," said Barbara, with a note of pride in her voice, "and I came rather close. His eyes were very nearly at my level. Yes, I think I could recognise him."

"Then perhaps we four should attend the debate this evening," said Lucia, including me in her gaze.

Barbara nodded. "I can identify him, and if he is speaking, as Padma said he would be, then his name will be in the program. With that we can learn his residence."

"We might also follow him afterwards. Perhaps he has hidden Padma somewhere," Lucia said.

"Perhaps he will go to see her," Barbara said.

Chapter III

Away from Marilee and her two friends, I telephoned Holmes, using the telephone downstairs. Perhaps, I thought, he would offer me some insight and direction.

Mrs. Hudson answered. "Mr. Holmes should be here in a moment," she said. "If you will give me your number, I'll have him call you."

Within five minutes, the telephone rang. It was Holmes.

"Watson, where are you?"

I told him. At his invitation, I recounted the events of the morning and what Marilee and the other two students had said.

"Where is this debate to be held?" he asked.

I identified the location, one of the college chapels near the High Street.

"You may be late returning," he said. "I would recommend you take a room at The Chequers Inn, just off High Street on Logic Lane. From where you are now, Chequers is about a twenty-minute walk, if memory serves. Your debate will be just on the other side of the High Street from the Inn. You might fortify yourself for a long evening by taking supper there. The port is passable. You can meet Marilee and her friends at the debate. Now, I regret I must attend to another matter."

Holmes rang off.

I mounted the steps to Marilee's rooms again, to tell her of the plan.

"Fine with me," Marilee said, "but I'm going to the boathouse now. Padma may have returned her canoe. Come with me, Uncle John?"

I nodded. The boathouse was upriver, the opposite direction from The Chequers Inn, but I had the entire afternoon before me.

Her friends agreed to have supper on their own and meet us at the chapel for the debate.

"We're too off our feed to study, anyway," said Lucia.

"Besides, it's Sunday," said Barbara. "A day of rest."

Marilee and I set out. As the two of us walked to the boathouse, I reflected. On the telephone, Holmes had seemed somehow distant. He had listened, but hardly giving any opinion or direction, other than his advice that I should take a room at The Chequers. Perhaps his Foreign Office enterprise commanded his attention. Yet he had seemed to take my missing person case seriously. Normally, I thought, he would have scoffed, absent any definite evidence. After all, what did the case amount to? A young girl says she is going off on a canoe trip. She does not return, and her canoe is missing. But only one night has elapsed. Possibly she had not gone away in the canoe at all. Possibly she had a friend remove the canoe for her. But why?

I put that question to Marilee as we were walking to the boathouse.

"Out-and-out deception?" she asked. "That doesn't sound like Padma. But – "

"But what?"

"But since this young man is involved, whether he's a brother or a sweetheart, we can't really expect everything to proceed with Padma in the ordinary way."

"He might have influenced her."

"Yes, but to what end? What could she do for him? She's only a student."

"A wealthy one."

Marilee stopped. "Do you think they've eloped?"

"It would be consistent with her evasiveness. And her immediate assertion that he is her brother."

"Oh, dear," Marilee said. "I just had another thought. What if someone has kidnapped Padma? They might demand ransom money – "

"To transmit a ransom demand would be difficult," I said.

361

"Right. The parents are months away by ship. And telegraph messages are uncertain."

"Perhaps there is a guardian. A family friend. Did she ever mention one?"

"I seem to remember that last fall, after we'd first arrived, she said she was going to have supper with her uncle."

"Here in town?"

"I'm not sure."

We reached the boathouse. This time, an attendant was there. He had seen nothing of Padma and her canoe was still absent from the premises. "Number 42," he said, thumbing a gesture towards an empty rack along the bare-board wall. "Sometimes they stay out a week. Camping and so on."

We were leaving the boathouse when Marilee had another idea. "Let's walk along the river path," she said. "Near that spot where I thought I saw something move."

We did so. We found nothing.

"Does Mr. Holmes get discouraged during his cases?" Marilee asked.

"He does not show it," I said. "Yet I cannot help thinking that he does. He is, after all, a man with emotions – though he places his reasoning capabilities in the position of control."

"Like Plato said. Or was it Socrates? Anyway, I wish I could do that."

"Likewise," I said.

"The emotions do slow one down," she said. And we were both silent as we walked back to her college rooms.

I said goodbye to Marilee and made my way along the High Street, entering the great parklands which offer such tranquil shelter and so many beautiful views of the river.

I was observing one of these surpassingly lovely vantage points when I heard a man's voice call my name.

"Dr. Watson!"

The voice was deep and masculine, with a Slavic accent. Unfamiliar to me. About three feet away.

I turned to see. Just emerging from a grove of trees was a tall man in a dark suit. His features matched his accent, broad and Slavic. And he held a pistol, pointed at my midsection.

"Where is the woman, Dr. Watson? Where is the Indian woman?"

"I don't know what you're talking about."

The pistol moved closer, the barrel nearly touching my sternum. I thought of knocking it aside, but his finger was on the trigger and the gun was cocked.

362

"Come. It is useless to quibble or deny. We saw you just now with the English girl, one of the Indian woman's companions. We heard you make the inquiry at the boathouse."

"Then you would know that I am looking for her. If you are looking for her as well, we ought to be on the same side."

An enigmatic smile. "Perhaps we are. Then again, perhaps we are not. What are your plans to find her, this Indian woman?"

"First, tell me what you want with her."

"Why?"

"I believe someone may be holding her for ransom. At the moment, that is the only hypothesis I have."

He laughed. "We have no interest in obtaining ransom for her, I can assure you of that."

"Then why do you seek her?"

"She has aligned herself with some associates who are averse to our interests."

"You speak in riddles."

He studied me for a long moment. Then he gave a nod and put away his pistol.

"I believe you," he said. "For the moment."

"Then I shall say goodbye."

"We will follow you, of course. I take comfort in knowing that you continue to seek the Indian woman and may lead us to her."

I walked away, puzzled and somehow frustrated, though no harm had come to me. I had purposely held back any mention of the young Indian man who Marilee and her friends had called the swan prince. I had not mentioned the swan amulet, nor the supposed matching one carried by her young man, whom I expected to see at the debate later that evening.

Chapter IV

The sky had partially cleared and the sun was casting the long, golden rays of late afternoon when I reached The Chequers Inn. Fortunately, there was a room available. I went upstairs to it immediately. I felt the need for a moment's rest, and so took off my coat and stretched out on the bed.

I woke to a knock on the door of my room.

And the voice of a page boy. "Message for you, Dr. Watson."

"Slide it under the door," I said. I was unwilling to be confronted by a pistol twice in one afternoon.

The paper was on the Inn stationery. The message was in Holmes's neat, precise hand:

363

Reserve table for two, for six o'clock supper. SH

Holmes! My heart leaped. Holmes had reached out and all would be well. Or at least he would be at my side, and I would have a better understanding of what enemies to look for and when to take action.

I went downstairs immediately and reserved a table for two.

At six o'clock exactly, I took my seat. I scanned the crowded pub that adjoined the dining area. Would Holmes be in disguise? Would he appear as an aged bookseller, or a parson, or – though it might test his talents at makeup and impersonation – an Indian prince?

Then I spotted the Slavic man who had held me at gunpoint in the woods. He sat at a table across from mine.

He gave me a direct look.

I raised my hand in a momentary wave, hoping that if Holmes could see, he would be warned off.

Then, to my astonishment, a figure emerged from the crowd and came towards me.

It was a young Indian woman. Tall, thin, and quite beautiful.

"Dr. Watson?" she said.

I nodded.

She sat down across from me. Her voice was clear and smooth and unhurried.

"I am Parma Amritraj, daughter of the supreme ruler of Tamil Nadu province and ally of Her Majesty's government. Marilee has mentioned you, and I have read many of your accounts of your adventures with Mr. Holmes."

"*The Sign of Four*," I said.

"Yes, that one, and several others – including one about a young woman whose situation, I find, somewhat resembles my own. Only instead of being lied to by her stepfather, I must deal with a man who wishes to restrict my activities considerably."

"You mean the fellow behind you?"

Her eyes widened.

"At the table facing me. If you turned around, you would see him staring at you, quite openly."

"A Slavic man?"

I nodded.

"I have met him before. I shall speak with him."

"How can I help you?"

"By delivering a message."

"To the Slavic man?"

364

"No, to my three schoolmates. My three dear friends. You can tell them I showed you this."

Her hand went to her throat. Her fingers unclasped something from a chain of thin gold. She gave a little smile and opened her palm to reveal a green swan amulet, carved in jade. A small silver-painted tiara crowned the top of its head.

"What is the message?" I asked.

"That they should not seek to follow me. That I must go away for a long time. That I choose my path willingly."

"What else?"

"There is more, but you must not know it, for Marilee's sake. You must understand that such secrecy is in her best interest. Now, will you promise me to deliver the message?"

"But what of your brother?"

Her eyes clouded, but only for an instant. "Ah. The debate. You are here for the debate this evening."

"In the chapel," I said.

"Yes. He will be there. I asked my friends not to attend, but they will come all the same, I take it?"

"Indeed, they will. I am to meet them there."

"Then would you please deliver my message, and keep them from following if they should chance to see me? That would be ruinous, and the result, I assure you, would be not what any friends of mine would wish to have on their consciences. So please – at all costs, Dr. Watson, please keep the three young ladies with you and tell them I will write to them and explain. You may hint that I have a sweetheart. It will ease their minds. Say I will write when I can, but it may not be for some time. Several months, perhaps."

"You return to India?"

The same cloud darkened her gaze. "No more."

Then she stood. "Do not trouble yourself about the Slavic man. I shall go to him now, and then I shall leave, and he will not follow me."

"What will you tell him?"

"The truth. That I have asked you to convince my roommates not to interfere. That I am going to my future happiness with the man I love."

"That is the truth?" I scrutinized her face. Merilee and her friends might believe that Padma was having a love affair with the young man they had dubbed Lohengrin, but I sensed something deeper and perhaps more sinister afoot.

"Perhaps." Padma's smile was brief and tinged with something wry or even bitter. Then she turned away.

I watched as she walked directly to the Slavic man.

At his table, she bent low and said something into his ear.
He nodded.
Then, as she had promised, she walked out of the pub.

Chapter V

As I entered the chapel that evening, Marilee and her two friends were waiting in the small narthex. Perhaps fifty people were gathered there, mostly men, some in academic gowns, others in ordinary street dress. A few of those men wore turbans. All the Indian men appeared expectant and proud, which I surmised arose from their having created a debating society of their own here in Oxford. There were only a few women. Some wore sari robes and scarves, others dressed in ordinary British attire. I looked for Padma, of course, but did not see her. I had resolved to keep her message to myself for the moment. I would wait until we were all seated, when we were less likely to be overheard. Then I would explain. Surely, I thought, Marilee and her friends would want to do as Padma wished.

The four of us threaded our way through the crowd to the stairs that led up to the balcony seating. I stepped back from the stairwell to allow the ladies to precede me. As they did so, I felt a tug at my elbow.

It was Sherlock Holmes, wearing a gown and mortarboard.

He spoke in a low tone, directly into my ear. "Stay until the end of the event. Outside, a cab will be waiting for the young ladies, to take them to their rooms. See them into the cab and then come back to wait for me here. Do not disclose that you saw me."

Then, abruptly, he turned and vanished into the crowd.

I climbed the stairs and reached the balcony that ran on both sides of the nave. The three young ladies had found seats on my side, towards the front. I scanned the faces around me as I made my way to join them. I did not see Padma. I did not see the Slavic man.

I sat between Marilee and her friends. They leaned closer to hear me as I made my report.

Marilee's eyes widened in surprise, then in happiness. "Oh, Uncle John. What wonderful news! Of course we'll do as she wants, won't we, ladies?"

"She's going off with her Romeo," said Barbara.

"And he's here to debate tonight," said Lucia. "No wonder she didn't want us here."

"We might have told the Dean, and the Dean would tell her parents."

"That's why she told us about *The Sign of Four*," Marilee said. "So we would feel bound to keep her secret."

Lucia frowned. "I wish they had printed a program, so we could know his name. We'll have to stay alert."

Marilee was scanning the crowd below us. It was difficult to see faces, and many were wearing academic mortarboards. "Will he be down in front, I wonder?" she asked.

"We'll just have to wait and see."

A long table stood in the chancel area, jutting out from the altar in parallel to the central aisle. Four chairs sat empty on either side and one more at the head of the table.

Then a very dignified, clean-shaven Indian gentleman in a frock coat stepped up to the end of the table and turned around to face us. "May I have your attention, ladies and gentlemen?" he asked. "You are all welcome to the fifth monthly meeting of the Oxford Majlis. I shall proceed without further ado. The resolution before us is: 'This house shall, wherever possible, support Her Majesty's Government in its foreign policy, including, if necessary, direct participation of our members in Britain's military endeavours in South Africa.'"

He gestured towards the eight empty chairs behind him. "The four speakers on my right will present the affirmative position. The four on my left will oppose. Each speaker will have five minutes. After each round of affirmative and opposition speakers, there will be five minutes' debate from the floor. When all speakers have presented and the floor debates have concluded, there will be a five-minute interval for private reflection. Then the vote shall be taken. All remarks shall be directed to the chair. The evening's activity will be limited to ninety minutes, strictly observed. The chair will keep the time."

He took a very large watch from his waistcoat pocket and held it up, dangling it from its chain and eliciting a ripple of laughter from the audience. "The speakers will now take their positions."

Eight young Indian men stood and walked up to stand behind the empty chairs. Each carried a leather binder for, I assumed, their notes. They turned to face the audience and bowed. There were cheers.

Then seven of the young men took their seats, notebooks on the table before them, while the eighth, the one closest to the chair, remained standing.

"That's not him standing," Barbara whispered. "But I think he's the chair closest to us. On our left."

"The affirmative team," Marilee said. "So he's loyal to The Crown."

"At least for tonight," Lucia said.

"I just hope he's loyal to Padma," Barbara said.

The evening proceeded. The debaters made their presentations in turn, most holding their notebooks before them, like hymnals, as they

367

spoke. From time to time, those who were not speaking jotted entries in their own notebooks, no doubt points to be referred to later.

It was past eight o'clock when the final round commenced.

Padma's young man stood up behind his chair and introduced himself as Arun Banerjee. It was then that I saw a uniformed policeman appear at the front exit door, and another at the rear. Both remained impassive, stolid and silent. I wondered fleetingly at their presence. Then I saw young Banerjee lift his notebook from the table, raise it into the air, and then cast it aside in a marked manner, where it clattered against the surface of the table.

"Bit of a show-off," Barbara said. "Has to prove he doesn't need notes."

"As if he's better than the others," said Lucia. "Wouldn't have expected that."

"Youthful exuberance," said Marilee.

Banerjee cleared his throat and spoke in a deep, ringing voice. "We have a saying in my country: *What we possess is temporary. What we become is permanent.* Our homes, our worldly goods, even our lives, are as nothing more than blowing sand, here today and tomorrow gone. But we may choose to make our lives count for more than our individual petty concerns. We can choose loyalty, service, and sacrifice to a cause that is greater than ourselves."

Young Banerjee continued with the same theatrical flair with which he had begun, and I found myself swept up in the force and emotion of the young man's rhetoric. It reminded me of several speeches from Shakespeare, including the famous oration from Mark Antony to commemorate the death of Julius Caesar. There was applause when young Banerjee had concluded. He bowed to the audience.

He remained partially bent over, turning towards his opponents. He clamped his hands onto his knees in a marked manner. His head oscillated from side to side as though he were scrutinising the other debaters as they busily jotted down their notes. Then he picked up his own notebook from the table, extracted the sheaf of papers from the binding, and carried the papers over to the far corner of the room. He dropped the pages into a wastepaper bin. To a growing ripple of laughter, he tapped his forehead with one finger and then turned out his trousers pockets. "Nothing up my sleeve, either!" he said in a loud stage whisper, and with a broad smile.

The chairman half-rose from his position at the head of the table, lifting an admonitory finger.

Banerjee bowed deeply, and then quietly took his seat as his opponent stood up across the table.

"Still the show-off," Barbara said.

368

The remaining arguments and debates proceeded without any more colourful events. The vote was taken. Banerjee's side won. The two teams shook hands across the table. The chair announced the next meeting for the following month, at the same time and place.

We stood to file out. I kept my eyes on the crowd, looking for Padma, but she was nowhere to be seen. I felt a pang of melancholy as I glanced back at the barren table which moments ago had been the stage for such intellectual fire and zeal. It was empty, of course, and the eight young men were in the nave, accepting congratulations from their friends and colleagues.

"The tumult and the shouting dies," said Barbara.

An old grey-haired charwoman, bent almost double after years of hard labour, emerged slowly from the side entry door with her wheeled cart and push broom. Her black uniform dress and once-white apron appeared equally old and worn. Laboriously, she drew back the chairs, one by one, and bent awkwardly to reach her broom beneath the table.

"The captains and the kings depart." Barbara continued.

"And only the char remains," said Lucia.

"Dust to dust," said Marilee.

"I wonder if that poor woman ever dreamed of getting an education," Barbara said.

Then our queue moved forwards. As we reached the stairs to go down, I gave one last backward look, hoping to see Padma. I saw only the charwoman as she emptied the waste bin into her cart.

The young ladies and I reached the street without incident and found the cabman waiting. "I shall let you know if I hear anything," I told Marilee.

"And I likewise. Thank you, Uncle John."

I turned back to the chapel entrance to find Holmes. From within the nave came the sounds of a scuffle. I recognised the strident voice of young Banerjee. "You've no right, I tell you! No right at all!"

Then I saw a black police wagon draw up to the curb, its rear door already open. From the chapel doorway, a cluster of men burst forth. Two uniformed constables, with young Banerjee between them, broke away from the surrounding gaggle of students and hustled up to the police wagon. They shoved young Banerjee upwards and into the wagon and then slammed shut the door.

"Police business," said one of the constables, addressing the crowd.

"You all ought to go home now," said the other. They both stood on the side rail of the wagon, ready to prevent any onlookers from climbing aboard. The police wagon drove away.

I returned to the nearly deserted nave, as promised. Holmes was there, still cloaked in an academic robe. He held a finger to his lips.

"Walk with me," he said.

"Where are we going?"

"To catch the next train to London."

We purchased two first-class tickets to Paddington Station.

We boarded and entered the compartment of our carriage. I was happy to find it empty, for I hoped that would leave Holmes free to explain what had brought him to Oxford.

"I will need your help," he said. "I don't suppose you brought your service revolver."

I shook my head. "I could retrieve it from Baker Street," I said.

"Too late," he said.

"Where are we going after Paddington?"

"Not far."

My collar felt warm and my temples throbbed. He could be maddeningly reticent, and just at the times when I wanted explanations.

I pressed him. "What happened to young Banerjee?"

"His people will provide a solicitor. The police have no evidence against him. He will be freed soon."

"You might be more forthcoming," I said, "if you want my help – "

"All will be clear in time," he said. "We are bound for Chesham Place, and what I hope is the last act in a drama which you and your young friends entered inadvertently this morning. Now, it has been a long week, and I have had precious little rest. I pray you allow me to remain undisturbed for the next hour."

So saying, he leaned back against the seat cushion, sank his chin upon his chest, and shut his eyes.

Chapter VI

It was nearly midnight when Holmes awakened, just as we were arriving at Paddington Station. He opened his eyes, blinked, stretched his arms all the way to his fingertips, and stood up. From beneath the folds of his academic gown, he drew out a canvas hold-all. From this, he withdrew two ragged and filthy woollen army blankets, their colour nearly obscured by mud stains. He folded the gown and placed it into the hold-all.

The train stopped. The lights of the station illuminated the smoke from the engine. The sooty clouds that I knew to be black in the daytime now appeared grey.

Holmes handed me one of the blankets.

"When we reach our destination, drape this over yourself."

370

"Why?"

"For this evening, we are two vagrants, down on our luck."

At the left-luggage counter, Holmes handed in the hold-all and pocketed his receipt.

Outside the station it was raining.

"Already useful," Holmes said, pulling the blanket up over his shoulders.

"Where are we going?" I asked.

"A half-hour's walk, Watson. You will see."

We emerged from the station, crossed the rain-slicked street, and then plunged into the shadowy darkness of Hyde Park, working our way along a pathway only partially lit by a minimal number of gas lamps. Holmes strode ahead of me, swift and confident. Within thirty minutes we passed through the Albert Gate and emerged onto the darkened pavement of Knightsbridge. After three minutes' more walking, we approached another darkened park, far smaller, and Holmes slowed.

We made our way into the smaller park. The ground was sodden beneath my boots.

"Our destination," said Holmes.

I saw a huge, block-like building of grey stone, towering above the horizon. Lights burned within many of the windows.

"Behold, the Embassy of the Russian Imperial government," Holmes said. "They are working late."

The rain had slackened, fortunately for us. Holmes stopped beneath a tree. Across the street, an iron gate barred the way into the embassy entrance. The gate was apparently unattended.

"There is a bell-pull, and within the doorway two armed guards are waiting. Day and night."

"Why are we here?"

"We have a task to accomplish." He glanced back towards the nearly deserted entrance to the station, from which we had recently emerged. "Settle in and let us avoid the attentions of any passers-by."

He sank into a crouch and then sat. I followed his example. We each drew our blankets over our heads. For a moment, I held my breath against the overpowering scent of dried mud and mould. I saw a uniformed bobby pass along the pavement outside the embassy gate, swinging his baton. He glanced in our direction and then continued. To the patrolman, I realised, we might be part of the park shrubbery, merely two dark humps among many similar silhouettes of vegetation, not worth anyone's notice on a wet spring evening.

"We are here in the interests of Her Majesty's government," Holmes began. "I must emphasise that fact, for it may soon appear otherwise."

371

I waited.

"The conflict in which we find ourselves has its roots in the desires of the people in that building."

He gestured towards the fortress-like embassy. "The Russian Empire has long sought to gain an open-water seaport, preferably in India. Our government seeks to protect its own interests by denying them any opportunity for access."

"Via Afghanistan."

"As you know from direct experience, particularly in this damp weather."

"Indeed." At that very moment, my old war wound was acting up.

"Various Indian monarchs control the different provinces of Afghanistan. Both we and the Russians make secret alliances with those monarchs, to permit safe passage or to offer resistance, and to warn the other of military activity. Substantial sums change hands. Both sides eventually learn of such alliances, since each has been spying on the other for nearly a century. The spies come from all ranks and nationalities, but many are from India."

I understood at last. "And the young Mr. Banerjee is a Russian spy! That is why our police arrested him after his appearance at the debate."

"You are correct. Our government suspected Banerjee of stealing documents that describe an agreement with a certain Indian monarch. Publication of those details would be highly damaging to England."

"Did Banerjee really steal the documents?"

"We are quite certain that he is guilty."

"But you said the police would not hold him, since there was not sufficient evidence."

"Also correct. He did not have the stolen documents in his possession. In fact, he was released just after we boarded our train. The confirmation came to me via the receipt from the Paddington left-luggage clerk."

I felt a moment's admiration for Holmes, but then my spirits sank. "But what of Padma?" I asked. "I saw her at Chequers Inn. She may well be in love with Banerjee, which could prove disastrous."

"You would recognise the signs better than I, Watson. To me, the workings of a woman's heart are as inaccessible as the Afghan mountains."

He paused, turning his gaze towards the faint street lights behind us. "And deception is the most essential ability of a spy."

I turned as well.

I saw a man's figure striding boldly in our direction. I recognised the man's distinctive walk.

"That is Banerjee, surely," I said.

372

"I agree."

"Why is he here?"

"He is coming to the embassy."

"To deliver the stolen papers?"

Holmes shook his head. "From the moment he left the police station in Oxford until now, Banerjee has been watched. His very presence here shows that he still does not possess the stolen documents. He is here for diplomatic asylum."

"Is he being watched now?"

"Only by the two of us. That is one of our tasks this evening. To see that he enters the Russian embassy. There, he will be out of our reach."

My spirits rose. "And confined to the Embassy, he cannot endanger Padma by playing on her affections."

Holmes held a finger to his lips.

We watched. Banerjee did not see us. Apparently oblivious to the continuing light rain, he strode past our vantage point, stopped at the iron gate, rang the bell, and waited. A light came on inside the inner doorway. A man in military uniform came out to the gate with an umbrella. The two exchanged a few words between the bars, out of our hearing. The gate swung open and Banerjee was admitted. The gate swung shut. The two men walked to the door of the massive embassy building and were soon out of our sight.

"But what about the missing papers? What about Padma?" I asked.

"She is in Russian employ – "

"What?"

"But at the direction of the War Office."

I shook my head, baffled and feeling somewhat indignant. "Why would the daughter of a maharajah consent to employment with Russians? For that matter, why would she take direction from the War Office?"

"Because Padma is no more the daughter of a maharajah than you or I. You deserve to know the truth about her. She is a brave young woman recruited in India to play a significant part in the service of The Crown. Her target was the young man, Banerjee. She entered the college at Oxford specifically to influence him and discover his activities. Over the course of two terms, she gained his trust. She learned he had stolen British papers."

"Why didn't she report him? Why wasn't he arrested at that moment?"

Holmes shook his head. "I shall come to that. In any event, Banerjee trusted her. He knew he was being watched. He worried that he might fail in his mission to deliver the stolen papers. He shared his concern with her.

She volunteered to take the papers to London and deliver them to the Russians in this very building."

"Why would she aid in a treasonous act?"

"Because our government sanctioned her. She and Banerjee met to agree on the details last week."

"In a punt, on the River Cherwell," I said.

"But then Marilee and her two friends saw them."

"By the swan's nest."

"Precisely. So the three young ladies, quite naturally, questioned Padma about her 'young man'. She had to invent an explanation. She improvised brilliantly."

"Saying that Banerjee was her brother."

"And spinning a fanciful tale of two jade swans, held by her and her brother as family heirloom treasures. She even enlarged on the theme, by claiming to have chosen St. Swithin's for its association with a miraculous restoration of broken eggs."

"Marilee was convinced at that point."

"Yes, Padma's report to the War Office said as much."

"But Marilee's roommates did not believe Padma and Banerjee were sister and brother. They thought the two were lovers from warring maharajah families, like Juliet and Romeo."

"The very impression that Padma wished to convey. And she did it all on the spur of the moment, based on an amulet she had bought from a local jeweler, on a whim."

I drew in my breath. "Brilliant, indeed."

"For that reason, the War Office changed her code name. In their parlance, she is now known as the Jade Swan."

I recalled Padma's momentary smile as she showed me her jade amulet.

"And now you should know of a complication, since you inadvertently caused it."

"I caused it? How?"

"Banerjee was hiding in Padma's room at the time her roommates interviewed her."

"What?"

"He overheard them tell Padma that you were related to Marilee, and that you worked with Sherlock Holmes. Banerjee told his Russian masters. The Russians suspected Padma had betrayed them. They began watching Marilee. They saw you with her this morning. They thought Padma was working with you."

"The Slavic man," I said. "He was on the river pathway."

374

"But you convinced him otherwise when he held you at gunpoint this afternoon."

"Nonetheless, he followed me to The Chequers Inn. Padma spoke to him. I expect it was Padma who did the convincing."

"She is a very capable agent," Holmes replied.

"But where are the stolen papers now," I asked, "if Banerjee does not have them?"

"I think you know," he replied.

"You mean, Padma is still involved? That she will bring the papers? Will she be arrested?"

Holmes had turned his gaze back to the entrance of Paddington Station. "Let us hope not, for our mission tonight is to protect her. And I expect her to appear at any moment."

Chapter VII

Indeed, as I watched the mist that clouded the roadway behind us, a small, shadowy figure slowly emerged.

It shuffled towards us, cloaked and bent over, huddled against the rain. It grew larger.

I recognised the halting movement. I had seen it before, on the stage in the Oxford chapel after the debate.

"The charwoman," I whispered. "She picked up Banerjee's notes from the wastepaper bin."

"The Jade Swan," Holmes replied.

"But Holmes," I said, "if she goes inside the gate, she will be in the hands of the Russians."

"And if she remains outside, all her efforts will have been for naught, as will ours. It is a risk she has been aware of since we recruited her."

She was closer now, on the pavement before us, heading for the gate. I had a glimpse of her face beneath a ragged shawl, pale and wrinkled with what I knew must be stage cosmetics. She glanced in our direction, and I saw her eyes, dark and sparkling with excitement.

Then I heard a voice. "You, there – woman!"

I saw the uniformed patrolman, returning on his round.

Padma kept her head down and shuffled forward.

"Did you hear me?" The patrolman approached her.

She continued, moving step by laborious step. A yellowed knit string bag bulged at her side.

"Move only if absolutely necessary," Holmes whispered. "The Russians will be watching."

Indeed, the light of the ground floor embassy window revealed movement at the curtain.

"Madam?" asked the patrolman.

At this, she stopped and turned her head sideways towards the patrolman, her neck still craned forwards like a bird. Her voice came, cracked and hoarse. "Oh, it's that you scared me and I'm perishing late." She pointed with an elbow at the embassy gate. "Late for me cleanin' in there, y' see. They'll dock me wages, and those are pitiful small to begin with. Could you walk me over to the gate and help me reach the bell?"

I held my breath as the patrolman stood motionless. Then he offered her his arm. She took it, and the pair walked haltingly towards the gate. He rang the bell. The door opened and the uniformed guard came out, this time without his umbrella.

I recognised the guard. He had held me at gunpoint in the river park nearly twelve hours ago.

The gate opened.

"You're late," the guard said.

Padma turned to the patrolman. "Then I'd best be inside," she said. "Thankee, officer."

The patrolman touched his helmet and turned. Soon he was striding away into the mist and the rain.

The guard stepped aside for Padma to enter and then closed the gate behind her. She handed him her knit bag. They walked slowly together to the embassy door.

The door opened, and I saw another man silhouetted in the doorway's light.

Young Banerjee.

He came to Padma as though drawn by a magnet. She stood taller now.

The two of them embraced.

Then they were inside.

The guard followed.

He shut the door, and I never saw Padma again.

Chapter VIII

"Why did our government sanction the theft of documents that would damage our interests?" I asked. "And why would you help bring them to a foreign power?"

We were out of the rain, in a cab, on our way to Baker Street.

Holmes lit his pipe. "Think, Watson. You know my methods."

I considered. "Transmitting such documents would be a treasonous act. For you to commit treason, I believe, would be quite impossible."

He puffed at his pipe, filling the interior of the cab with smoke. "And therefore . . . ."

I understood.

"Therefore, you did not help transmit documents that would damage our nation's interests. Therefore, the documents that Padma delivered are false."

"You are correct."

"False, but they will somehow prove damaging to the Russians."

"We believe that will be the result."

"And to maintain the illusion that the documents are real, the police arrested Banerjee at the chapel in Oxford."

"Correct."

"And we were here to ensure the documents were delivered to the Russians," I finished, triumph in my voice.

"We were, indeed," Holmes said. "It was possible that the uniformed patrolman might have interfered with Padma. Fortunately, Padma was equal to the occasion and our intervention was not required."

A disturbing thought occurred to me, and I felt a wave of apprehension. "What will happen when the Russians learn they have been duped?" I asked.

"Padma understands the risk. We must hope she is equal to that occasion as well."

"Marilee and her friends would be proud of her," I said.

Holmes glanced at me.

"Of course, I shall not tell them."

He nodded, satisfied. "No doubt Padma will write them something about finding happiness with her Romeo."

We rode in silence for a time. I wondered. Did Padma really love young Banerjee? Or was her embrace just another competent deception, one in keeping with the legend of the Jade Swan?

But I knew those were not questions that Sherlock Holmes would answer.

Chapter IX

A week later I had a brief note from Marilee. I reproduce it below:

Dear Uncle John,

Padma wrote us yesterday. She is well and travelling with her young man. The police arrested him after the debate last Sunday, but it turned out they had made a mistake of some sort, so of course they let him go. The two are sailing to America. She says her father has a mansion with many servants ready for them in New York City. We're greatly relieved, of course. I thought you'd like to hear that she is safe and happy.

Love,
Marilee

P.S. There are now two large swans guarding the nest that you and I visited. They appear to be defending their family home with the utmost vigor, so apparently there will soon be little cygnets. Barbara hopes this is a good omen for Padma.

NOTES

1.   Sherlock Holmes and Watson stayed at The Chequers Inn during "The Adventure of the Creeping Man". The pub still exists, off High Street in Oxford.
2.   St. Swithin's College is entirely fictional, though it bears some resemblance to the several colleges available to women in Oxford at that time. The miracle of egg restoration has been attributed to St. Swithin himself.
3.   The British and the Imperial Russian Empires did indeed wage a clandestine battle with one another for control of the Afghan territories during most of the Nineteenth Century. Spy networks were active on both sides in "The Great Game", a phrase made famous in 1901 with the publication of Rudyard Kipling's novel *Kim*. Russia's drive for an open seawater port still creates controversy to this day.
4.   The Embassy of the Russian Empire (and later of the Soviet Union) was located at Chesham Place in Belgravia until 1927. The embassy then moved to Kensington Palace Gardens, where it remains in operation to the present.

The Devil Went Down to Surrey
by Naching T. Kassa

Over the years, various and sundry clients have visited the rooms of Sherlock Holmes at 221b Baker Street, all with problems for the great detective to solve. Some clients, such as Mr. Jabez Wilson, cut comical figures, while others were tragic ones.

Perhaps the oddest clients of all, both came to Holmes in the year 1896. The reader will remember the story of Mr. Robert Ferguson, but may be quite unfamiliar with the case of Signor Gianni Rossi. The events of his tale, the one I am about to relate, were among the strangest Sherlock Holmes has ever faced. For not only did he find himself protecting the life of a man – he found himself guardian of his very soul.

Holmes and I had spent that early October evening at St. James' Hall and, upon our return to Baker Street, found Mrs. Hudson waiting for us at the front door.

"There is a gentleman waiting for you, Mr. Holmes," she said. "I told him you'd gone out for the evening, but he insisted on staying. He's been here for more than an hour, pacing back and forth like a caged lion."

"His problem must be a desperate one, indeed," mused Holmes. "Come, Watson. Let us meet this fellow." We hurried up the stairs and soon entered our rooms.

A thin young man, clad in disheveled clothing, sat upon the settee wringing his hands. He rose as we entered and gazed at us with wide, frightened eyes.

"Mr. Holmes?" he said, "Thank Heavens you've come!"

He moved to take my friend's hand, but the effort appeared to be too much. His eyes rolled up in his head and he fell to the floor.

I rushed to the fellow's side and quickly loosened his collar. A few sips of brandy from my flask soon revived him, and Holmes and I helped him back to the settee.

"I must apologize," he said. "I have never fainted before. Not ever."

"It is no matter," Holmes said. "Rest yourself here, Signor Rossi."

"You know me?"

"What admirer of the violin does not? You are Gianni Rossi, a prodigy whose talent rivals that of Sarasate. I see you have recently returned from Camberly in Surrey, but the country air did little to improve

380

your health. You haven't been eating or sleeping well for the past week."

Rossi's eyes grew wider, his face pale. "How do you know of my visit? I told no one."

"The return ticket in your top pocket reveals you departed from Camberly this morning at eleven o'clock."

Rossi glanced down and then back up into my friend's face. "And what of my health? How did you know I haven't been sleeping or eating?"

"Your suit is new, but a trifle loose-fitting. Judging by the stitching, your sartor is an experienced one. The material is of an expensive weave, and no such person would have created such ill-fitting apparel. Therefore, you have lost weight. That fact, and your collapse, led me to the conclusion that you have not eaten as much as you should. As to your lack of sleep, your eyes tell all. There are shadows beneath them, and you can barely keep them from closing."

Something like relief passed over Rossi's face. "Ah, it is as simple as that. When you spoke before, it seemed as though you had somehow seen into my mind. I thought you were one of his minions sent to spy on me."

Holmes raised an eyebrow. "Minions?"

"My story is a fantastic one, that I will admit. You may not believe a word I have to say, but perhaps you will help me all the same?"

"You should eat first," I interjected. "And regain some of your strength."

"Watson is a doctor," Holmes said. "It would do you good to heed his advice."

"Dr. Watson? Ah, yes, the biographer of Mr. Holmes. Please, accept my apologies. I should have known you right away."

"Think nothing of it," I said, and hurried down to speak with Mrs. Hudson, who, as luck would have it, hadn't yet turned in. She prepared a cold supper of chicken, one which Rossi consumed with gusto. He was quite ravenous, and the saltshaker slipped from his fingers several times during his efforts to consume the fowl. Each time he dropped the shaker, he would toss a pinch of salt over his left shoulder. It was a rather amusing sight, but I didn't laugh, nor even smile. The young man seemed quite serious about this superstitious action, and I had no wish to annoy him.

When he had finished, I poured him a glass of brandy and he began his astounding tale.

"All of my life, I have striven for perfection. I suppose the trait is something handed down to me by my mother, a beautiful and uncompromising English woman. She drummed the idea into me day and night, night and day.

"My father, on the other hand, was a gentle fellow, and an Italian musician of some renown. He was also a friend of Sauzay. He convinced the great man to tutor me in Paris, and I found myself there at the age of six. At eleven, I performed at the Conservatoire. At sixteen, I toured the Continent. My parents often traveled with me, but during a concert in Venice, they were killed in a railway accident. I had taken an earlier train with my mother's solicitor, James Marston, or I would have shared their fate.

"After the death of my parents, I floundered. I lost all interest in my art and would, perhaps, have melted into obscurity had a legend of my childhood not reinvigorated me. As a boy, I had heard of a violin – a Stradivarius – of amazing and impeccable quality. It was considered an instrument without flaw, one which only the greatest musician could play. Performers had whispered and dreamed of it for years, and I resolved that I would have it.

"The bulk of my finances wasn't mine to do with as I pleased during this time. My parents had placed them in a trust, one which would become available to me upon my twenty-first birthday. I was, however, allowed a small stipend each month, administered to me by Mr. Marston. I used this money to fund my search, one which consumed my every waking hour. Mr. Marston didn't approve of my endeavors. He believed I should return to the art I had abandoned. Dear God! How I wish I had followed his advice! If I had, I wouldn't fear for my life, nor my salvation, and The Evil One would hold no sway over me."

Holmes had taken his chair before the fire while Rossi spoke, and had stretched his legs before him in that languid form he always adopted when listening to a case. He now leaned forward, an eager gleam in his eye.

"For months, I poured over manuscripts and letters, searching for the location of the treasured Stradivarius," Rossi continued. "I visited libraries in Paris, Venice, and Berlin before making my way here, to my mother's homeland. Here I stayed and, for the last two years, have searched. When my studies yielded nothing, I wrote to the greatest academics and musicians of the day. Last November, a professor *emeritus* from Durham College, one Jasper Hedgewick, replied to me and revealed that the violin did in fact exist. He said it belonged to an English gentleman in Surrey.

"I was ecstatic at this news and wrote him straight away, asking for the man's name. To my great disappointment, the professor refused my request. He said the man in question was one of dubious demeanor and eccentric habits, one I should stay well clear of.

"I went to see him after that, hoping that I might change his mind. The fellow was a kindly man with a bald head and graying hair at the sides. It took some doing to convince him. When his resolve weakened at last, he gave me the name of the gentleman in question. It was Mr. Lazarius Scratch of the Willows, Camberly.

382

"Mr. Marston believed my quest to be a foolish one. He counseled me against meeting this man, but I wouldn't be dissuaded. He was quite angry when I revealed my plans to him."

"And what did these plans involve?" Holmes inquired.

"After my meeting with the professor, I saved my allowance for three months and built up a tidy sum. This I intended to give Lazarius Scratch in return for the Stradivarius. Knowing how my guardian felt about the situation, I stole off early Monday morning so that he couldn't bar my departure. I took the train, expecting to hire a dogcart upon my arrival. To my great surprise, I found a carriage waiting for me.

"I arrived at Scratch's home around eight-thirty. The manor was a grand one with white walls, green shutters, and a flourishing rose trellis. Two large willow trees flanked the door. I don't mind telling you, my heart sank when I saw it. It seemed Mr. Scratch had far more resources than I had given him credit for. My meager savings couldn't buy the Stradivarius from him, I was sure of that. I would have to find a different way to acquire it.

"My first meeting with Mister Scratch was a strange one and unnerved me greatly. He was an imposing man with hair bleached by the sun. It hung about his face, giving him an almost angelic appearance. Like you, Mr. Holmes, it seemed he knew things about me he shouldn't know. I had told no one of my plans to visit Camberly, and yet, he expected me. A room, painted in my favorite colors, awaited me, and my favorite dish, *Pasta alla Norma*, was served for dinner. He knew my favorite wine, one I imbibe only on special occasions, and even had a suit made for me, the one I am now wearing. As you observed, Mr. Holmes, it was, at one time, tailored to my exact measurements. When I asked him how he knew these things, he grinned, revealing a row of pointed, white teeth.

"'I have my secrets, Gianni,' he replied. 'May I call you, Gianni? Or would *Gnocchi* serve you better?'

"The mention of my childhood name, the one used only by my father, chilled my blood. I didn't respond, but stared at him, speechless. He laughed then. The sound did little to warm me.

"'Dear boy,' he said, 'do not take on so. I have ears and eyes all over the world. That is how I have learned of you. It is also how I have learned of your obsession. Come, I will show her to you.'

"He led me from the dining room into a large room I can only describe as a library or study. Each shelf was filled with leather-bound tomes, jewels, cups fashioned from gold and many other treasures. A rich Persian carpet covered the floor, and heavy black drapes covered the windows. Oil lamps lit the room, creating a tasteful balance between light and shadow. On the wall, behind the African teakwood desk, hung the Stradivarius. The glow from the nearby oil lamp flickered over it. It was the most beautiful thing I'd ever seen.

"Mr. Scratch crossed to the wall and took it into his hands.

"'Beautiful, isn't she?' he crooned.

"I reached out for the Stradivarius, desperate to touch the wood, to feel the strings under my fingers, and to clutch it beneath my chin. He held it just outside of my reach, a smile playing about his lips.

"I am sorry, Gianni. I cannot allow you to hold her. She is my prized possession, the highlight of my collection. I have owned her since she entered the world, I cannot suffer another to touch her.'

"I nodded, the disappointment once again flooding my heart. I felt as though I were drowning in it.

"Mr. Scratch placed the violin beneath his chin and pulled the bow across the strings. The melodious sound filled me with a peace I had never known. When he finally ceased, I realized the midnight hour had come and gone.

"I licked my lips. My mouth had suddenly gone dry. Mr. Scratch turned and I took hold of his arm. 'You would never part with it? Not for any price?'

"He turned and grinned at me over his shoulder. There was something fiendish in that smile. If I had been in my right mind, I would have let him go, would have fled the house. Unfortunately, I had already been bewitched.

"'There is a trust in my name,' I said, 'one I shall have access to in but a few days. It is a substantial fortune. Not only does it contain monies earned by me, it also contains the fortunes of both my parents.'

"He shook his head. 'It isn't enough.'

"'Please . . . I will give you anything. I must have it. Name your price!'

"He cocked his head to one side and stared at me for a long while. 'I don't think you could pay it,' he said, at last, and ushered me from the room.

"For two days, I begged and cajoled Scratch for the Stradivarius, and for two days he rebuffed me. On the third day, he forbade me from speaking of it again. If I did, he would have me banished from the house.

"That night, as I sat brooding in my room, a terrible plan formed within my mind. I had observed the library for the past few nights and noticed that no guard had been set outside the door, nor in the room. What's more, the household consisting of a butler and three maids, often turned in at nine o'clock and didn't rouse until five. The Stradivarius was unwatched during these hours, and no one might notice its disappearance during the night.

"I see by your expression, Dr. Watson, that you are shocked by my behavior. I have no excuse for my actions, though I assure you, I have suffered mightily for it. There is no taking back what I have done. I can only tell you of how I crept from the room, my ears straining for any sound, and made my way down the passage to the library. I shielded the candle I carried with one hand, afraid that its glow might alert those whose doors I passed. The hall seemed to go on forever, and I was quite relieved when I reached the door to the library undiscovered.

"The door opened on quiet hinges when I slipped inside. The room was lit by a single oil lamp. It illuminated the Stradivarius and nothing else. I approached it, my heart in my throat.

"I set the candlestick on the desk and reached up to retrieve the instrument from the wall. Only seconds lay between me and it. And then, to my utter horror, a voice sounded behind me. I turned and found a shadow seated in a chair near the window. I knew at once to whom it belonged."

"'I am disappointed, Rossi,' Scratch said. 'I had such high hopes for you. It seems the temptation was too great.'

"You can imagine my shame, gentlemen. I couldn't speak a word. I simply stood there like a chastened child.

"Scratch rose from his chair and approached me. When he came into the lamplight, he wore a strange expression on his face, as though he thought the situation a humorous one.

"'In my time, I have seen a great many desperate men,' he said. 'Men who would give all for the love of a woman, for the taste of power, for unbridled wealth . . . I have never seen a man who would give everything for . . . *perfection.*'

"He circled me as he spoke. And though his voice held no anger, I couldn't look him in the eye.

"'What would you give for it, Gianni?' he asked in a low tone.

"'I glanced up and in a bold voice declared, '*Everything.*'

"He nodded. 'Suppose we were to have a contest? If you win, I shall give you the Stradivarius. What will you give me, should I win?'

"'Since you will not take my money, perhaps you will take my violin. I have it upstairs in my room.'

"Scratch shook his head. 'No, no. That will not do. That will not do at all. My Stradivarius is one of a kind, and I have no use for another instrument.'

"'What will you take as payment then? You have only to name it, and it shall be yours.'

"He nodded and that strange grin spread over his face once more. 'Very well, Signor Rossi. It shall be done. If I win, I take . . . *your soul.*'

385

"A chill stole over me then, as though someone, somewhere, had trodden over my grave. My mania, however, remained undiminished, and a question slipped from between my lips.

"'What sort of contest?'

"'A duel. Your skill against mine.'

"The proposition filled me with delight. I had heard Scratch play, and though he was quite accomplished, he was no virtuoso.

"'Very well,' I said.

"'I thought you might agree. The contract is over here.'

"'Contract?'

"He led me to the desk and withdrew the paper from it. I read it thrice before taking the quill he handed me.

"'Where is the ink?' I asked.

"'There is none.'

"'What am I to sign it with?'

"'Blood.'

"I stared at the man and the thought that he might be quite mad entered my head.

"'You do want the Stradivarius, do you not? Surely, a little blood will not deter you. Prick yourself just there – on the wrist – and dip the quill into it.'

"I did as he bade me and signed the document."

"What were the contents of the contract?" Holmes asked, speaking for the first time.

"It was very brief. There were no clauses, as such. Just what Mr. Scratch had said: Should I lose the contest, I was enjoined to surrender my soul to him upon my death."

"Was the document typewritten?"

"Yes."

"Did he sign it before you?"

"He did. The butler bore witness to it."

Holmes leaned back in his chair, seemingly deep in thought. At last, he waved his hand in our client's direction. "Pray, continue, Signor Rossi."

"It was agreed that we would each use our own violins. The butler went upstairs to fetch mine and when he returned, I tuned it carefully before beginning.

"Never in my life have I played so well, gentlemen. Perhaps you have heard of my performance at the Vatican, how it garnered an ovation from His Esteemed Holiness the Pope. This performance outdid even that. I put my heart and soul into my playing. When I finished, even Mr. Scratch couldn't help but applaud.

"'Amazing,' he said. 'Simply amazing. It appears I've my work cut

386

out for me.'

"He took up the Stradivarius then, and the moment he began Beethoven's *Violin Sonata No. 9*, I knew that I had made a grievous error. I had severely underestimated my opponent. Either the man was a virtuoso and had hidden the fact from me, or the Stradivarius was the most magical instrument there had ever been. I told him so, when he deposited the contract into the desk and returned the instrument to the wall.

"'You think yourself cheated, Gianni? Tell me, have you read all the legends surrounding the Stradivarius?'

"'I have.'

"'Then you must know who commissioned the Stradivarius, who it was created for.'

"The legend sprang to mind the moment he ceased to speak. I had discounted it as far too fanciful to be believed. Why it didn't come to mind when the bargain was made, I do not know. Perhaps, my overconfidence blinded me to everything and everyone.

"'It was said – ' My mouth grew drier. ' – that it was created for *Il Diavolo*, The Prince of Darkness. *The Evil One.*'

"He grinned then, displaying all of his pointed teeth. Then he raised his arms in the air and the room grew dark.

"When I awoke, I found that I was no longer at the Willows. Instead, I lay upon a bed in a local inn. The establishment was located at the center of Camberly, and when I questioned the innkeeper, I discovered that Scratch's carriage driver had brought me there the night before. He had also delivered my baggage and violin. When I asked him to hire a driver so that I might revisit The Willows, he refused.

"'No one goes to that place,' he said, his eyes as large as saucers. 'The Devil lives there. Be grateful you've escaped him and go back to London.'

"The innkeeper's words did much to erode my resolve. What happened moments later sent me back to London.

"I had left my coat in my room, and when I went back to retrieve it, I found a note on the chair it had been slung over. It wasn't there before – I am sure of it – and no one could've placed it in my room. I had been just outside speaking to the innkeeper. Such a person would not escape my notice."

He pulled a folded sheet of paper from his coat pocket and handed it to Holmes. My friend studied it for several seconds and then handed it to me. A chill filled me as I read the words:

Gianni,

You have three weeks to arrange your affairs. On the fourth Monday of the month, I shall collect my debt.

Scratch

"Needless to say, I returned to London on the very next train and made my way straight to Marston. I thought that in his profession as a solicitor, he might be able to help me break the contract. He vowed to look into things, and this gave me a modicum of hope. Alas, it was to be short-lived. We were in the midst of making our plans, when I realized The Evil One had followed me to Knightsbridge. He is here in London, Mr. Holmes, and I think he means to make good his threat. He will kill me and take my soul."

The young man fell onto the settee once more and cradled his head in his hands.

"Calm yourself, Signor Rossi," Holmes said. "How do you know he is here? Have you seen him?"

"Twice. First, outside Marston's home, through the sitting room window. Scratch was standing in the street, grinning at me through the glass. When I tried to call Marston's attention to him, I found that he had vanished. The incident unnerved me considerably, and I was in such a state that Marston could barely calm me. In my terror, I rushed from the house and into the street.

"When I regained my senses, I found myself here, in Baker Street. Upon sight of your address, a sudden thought came to me. I had read of your exploits, Mr. Holmes, and it seemed fortuitous that I had somehow come to the doorstep of the one man on earth who could save me. I came to your door and begged your landlady to allow me in. She did and while I waited, I noticed Scratch outside this very window. He disappeared shortly before you and Dr. Watson arrived."

Holmes rose to his feet. "Watson," he said, "would you be so good as to turn down the gas?"

I did as he asked and watched as he crossed the dimly lit room. He peered out the window into the street below.

"Signor Rossi, where did you see him?"

The young man joined him at the window. "Just there." He indicated a spot outside the empty house across the way.

Holmes nodded.

"What shall I do, Mr. Holmes?" Rossi asked.

"Do you trust me to aid you, Signor Rossi?"

"I am entirely in your hands."

"Then leave these rooms and make your way to the corner. When you reach it, wait there for a cab. Take the third and let the other two pass. When you have secured the hansom, return home."

The young man's eyes widened. "What if *he* finds me at the corner?"

"He will not. I promise you. Will you steel yourself and do as I ask?"

Rossi nodded.

"Good man. Go now and do exactly as I say."

The moment Rossi had gone, Holmes rushed from the room. I heard him rummaging about in his bedroom and within seconds, he emerged – not as Sherlock Holmes, but as a common loafer. Without a word, he sprinted for the door and down the stairs.

I moved to the window and watched as he left 221b and sauntered into the street.

Twenty minutes passed. Then thirty. Then thirty-five. At last, I heard steps upon the stairs. I threw the door open expecting to see Holmes and to my great surprise, found another man standing outside. His blond hair stood in stark contrast to his black overcoat and silk hat. He carried a stick in his hand.

"Good evening," he said. His handsome face seemed to hold no guile. That is, until he grinned. Then his entire demeanor changed, and the angel became a beast.

"Is Mr. Holmes at home?" he asked. "I know it is late, but I have urgent business with him."

"He isn't here," I replied. "But I expect him soon. Will you wait?"

I turned my back on him and approached the desk where my revolver waited.

"You will not need your service revolver, Dr. Watson," he called out behind me. "I assure you, I am unarmed."

I paused and turned to face him. He had entered the room and set his hat and stick on the table. My heart quickened in my chest.

"I would introduce myself, but I believe you already know me. At the moment, I am traveling under the moniker of – "

"Scratch," a voice said from the doorway.

Relief filled me as I looked into the face of my friend. He stood just outside the door, his left hand in his pocket, a cigarette in his right.

Scratch's grin grew broad. "Mr. Holmes! We've crossed paths on several occasions, but haven't actually met until now. You've been a thorn in my side for some time. A small, insignificant thorn, but one nonetheless."

"I am grateful for the compliment," Holmes replied. "You have come with a proposal?"

389

"I come with a warning. Keep out of my affairs."

"Ah, now that rings of familiarity. You sound less like The Evil One and more like the infamous Professor Moriarty."

Scratch's grin faded a little at these words. "Moriarty. An insufferable boor and the worst professor I have ever encountered. You dubbed him 'The Napoleon of Crime' as though he were the greatest criminal genius the world has ever produced. I assure you, Mr. Holmes, his deeds pale before mine."

"At last, you play your role correctly. The Evil One has always possessed an inflated view of self. You should have learned that pride goes before the fall."

"That is a lesson I hope to teach you, Mr. Holmes."

"Better men than you have tried." Holmes retorted. "Would you mind if we return to the matter at hand? I suppose you will not negotiate?"

"The contract between Signor Rossi and I has already guaranteed me what I want. He has nothing else to offer."

"If he has nothing to offer, perhaps there is someone else who does?"

The grin returned to Scratch's handsome face. "Are you speaking of yourself?"

Holmes gave a slight bow.

Scratch chuckled. "You challenge me to a test of skills? I have heard of your prowess as a musician, but you are no match for me."

"I think I would surprise you."

The scoundrel sneered. "That is something I highly doubt. No, I have no use for your soul. Those who thirst after justice are often the most tedious."

"Let us dispense with this charade," Holmes said. "You are not The Prince of Darkness."

"You do not believe in me?"

"I would rather believe the world threatened by oysters than by a false demon such as yourself."

Scratch shrugged. "It doesn't matter whether you believe. Rossi does. How long do you think it will take him to go mad? Or to die? He is already wasting away."

Holmes turned away as though deep in thought, and then spun round to face him once again. "What if I were to wager my career upon it? Suppose I were to test my skill against yours. My skill at detection versus the cunning of The Evil One. The winner claims the soul of Gianni Rossi."

Scratch's eyes gleamed with excitement. "And if you lose?"

"I will leave London and retire from the field of detection forever."

Scratch paced the floor, stroking his chin. He halted and pointed a finger at Holmes. "Done. But on one condition. I choose the test."

Holmes nodded. "Very well."

"I will give you three days to discover my true name. You must pronounce it to me on the third day."

"Done," Holmes said, taking up a notebook. "Will you draw up the agreement? I believe you are far more experienced at this than I."

Scratch took the notebook and quickly scribbled upon it. "I usually require signatures to be penned in blood," he said, handing the agreement back to Holmes. "But as souls aren't involved, we may forgo such dramatics."

Holmes studied the writing upon the page for several seconds and then signed it. He moved to pocket the notebook, but before he could do so, Scratch snatched it away. He waved a finger at Holmes, that same devilish grin upon his face.

"Very clever, Mr. Holmes, but not quite clever enough. You'll not discover my identity through my handwriting. I will keep this agreement." He collected his things and made for the door.

"Until then, gentlemen," he said, and laughed as he took his leave. I could still hear him as he descended the stairs and stepped out into the street.

"It was a valiant effort, Holmes," I said. "If only he hadn't known your intentions."

Holmes nodded. He crossed to the window and looked out. "Our Rumpelstiltskin has left us clues, Watson. Like breadcrumbs, he has strewn them about. All we need do is decipher them."

When I awoke the next morning, I found the commonplace books in a jumble on the floor. Of Holmes, there was no sign. I wouldn't see him until the sun had fled the October sky.

His mood was somewhat pensive when entered. He didn't speak and I, used to his ways, didn't engage him in conversation. He took his favorite chair near the fire and sat with his knees drawn up, his clay pipe clamped firmly between his teeth.

"I have spent an unprofitable morning at Scotland Yard," he said a half-hour later. "Six hours in the company of the ineffable Inspector Ambrose Burrows, searching through their rather dismal collection of criminal records, and I have found no sign of Scratch. If he is of the criminal classes, he has never been caught."

I motioned to the books on the floor, "You found nothing among them?"

"He may be there, but I haven't found him. There is no mention of a musician – or indeed a man – called 'Scratch'." He rose and paced the floor. "Our Rumpelstiltskin has too much information at his disposal. He

391

knows too much of Rossi."

"He is in contact with someone who knows Rossi?"

"Undoubtedly."

"Rossi's guardian, James Marston?"

"Perhaps. Marston is the only one who knows Rossi and his parents. According to 'M' volume of my commonplace books, he led a rather dull life before becoming Rossi's guardian. He attended Durham College and, upon graduation, joined the firm of Latham and Sands. The senior Rossi was his first client. When he and his wife were killed, Marston became the younger Rossi's guardian. They have resided at 342 Raphael Street in Knightsbridge ever since."

"You think him in league with Scratch?"

"It is possible. The trust contains a substantial fortune, and Marston has had unlimited access to it for several years. I doubt he would wish to relinquish it."

"If that is so, why would he discourage the lad from his pursuit of the Stradivarius? Would he not encourage the young man to seek Scratch out?"

"That is the question, Watson. One I hope will be answered on the morrow, when we visit our client. For now, I must concentrate my efforts on a different clue left us."

"And what is that?"

"Durham College. I don't believe in coincidence, Watson. And there are far too many here to suit me. Not only is it Marston's *alma mater*, but it's also the home of Jasper Hedgewick, the professor who directed Rossi to Scratch. According to Inspector Burrows, Hedgewick went missing. A certain Stradivarius bequeathed to the school disappeared with him. Oddly enough, it was the second time the instrument had been stolen."

"Could he be Scratch?"

"It's unlikely. Burrows revealed that Hedgewick was found murdered in Covent Garden two days after his disappearance. That was three months ago, and the Stradivarius wasn't in his possession." He curled up in his chair once more. "Perhaps the most interesting coincidence is that Durham was the last post of a certain infamous professor."

"Moriarty was dismissed from Durham?"

"Yes. And I'm certain his presence there is central to this case. Did you notice Scratch's reaction to the comparison I made between them?"

"He seemed displeased by it. It was almost as though he envied the villain."

"My impression exactly. He wishes to outdo Moriarty, to prove himself 'The Napoleon of Crime'. And what better way to accomplish that than to do the one thing Moriarty could not: Destroy the career of Sherlock

392

Holmes."

"You must find his name."

"I shall. There is a thread of logic connecting these coincidences, and I believe a journey to Durham may help to unravel the skein."

Neither Holmes nor I knew there would be no journey to Durham. A visit the next morning would preclude all that Holmes had planned and threaten his involvement in the case.

Just after dawn, I found Holmes at the breakfast table clad in his mouse-colored dressing gown. Crusts of toast lay upon the plate before him. A few coffee grounds lay within his empty cup.

"It appears we shall not be visiting Rossi this morning after all," Holmes said, as I approached the table. "Marston wired this morning to say that he wished to see me."

"He is coming here? Has he spoken with Scratch?"

"Patience, Watson. All shall be revealed. I believe that is his cab now."

The rumble of a hansom cab and horse's hooves sounded in the street outside and soon, the gentleman stood within our rooms. Marston was a tall man of sixty with a beard the color of newly fallen snow. His eyes were a cold blue and, like many military men of my acquaintance, he gave the air of one used to being obeyed.

"Mr. Marston, please be seated," Holmes said, motioning to the settee.

"I prefer to stand. My visit will not be a long one." He pulled a purse from the pocket of his dark coat. "I have come on the behalf of Gianni. Like most musicians, he is of a sensitive nature and prone to overreaction. I told him I would resolve the matter and I have. Your services will not be needed."

"You have found a way to break the contract?"

"In a manner of speaking. The charlatan had the temerity to approach me yesterday afternoon. We have made an agreement, and once certain monies have changed hands, he will destroy the contract. He is coming to my house tonight."

"That is odd. Mr. Scratch didn't seem interested in money. At least, he made that assertion when he called upon me."

"He called on you?" Marston cried, his expression one of great annoyance. "When?"

"The night Signor Rossi visited me. Scratch was very clear on the matter, stating that he preferred the young man's soul to any amount of money. May I ask how much he has agreed on?"

"You may not. As I said, the matter is no longer your concern." He tossed the purse upon the table. "I don't know what arrangement you've made with Gianni. I hope two-hundred pounds shall suffice."

"A generous sum for little work," Holmes replied. "Tell me, Mr. Marston, how much will you receive for the services you render? One-thousand pounds? Or perhaps ten-thousand would be a more accurate amount."

Marston turned and glared at my friend. He seemed accustomed to those who quailed before such a gaze. He found it had no effect on Sherlock Holmes.

"I don't find this amusing," said he.

"Nor do I," Holmes retorted.

"I am a man of some influence in this city. Such aspersions to my reputation are slanderous at best. I haven't robbed my ward, if that is what you imply."

"I imply nothing of the kind," Holmes said, spreading his hands before him. "Though should Rossi regain his life and lose his fortune, that evidence would be very telling indeed. Have you told Rossi of this meeting between yourself and Scratch? Never mind. I see by your face that you have not. Watson, I believe a journey to Knightsbridge is in order."

Marston took a step toward my friend, who stood unflinching before him. "If you so much as darken my door, I shall have you arrested." He turned on his heel and hurried to the door.

"You may take the purse," Holmes called to him. "I have never accepted a bribe and I shall not do so now."

Marston snatched the purse from off the table. The door slammed behind him as he rushed through it.

"I suppose that is the answer to our question," Holmes said with a chuckle.

"His attitude does suggest guilt," I replied. "We must follow him. He must know the blackguard's name. We should convince him to tell us."

"And what if he does not? Shall we accost him in the street and find ourselves before the magistrate?"

I threw my hands into the air. "You have accepted an impossible task. One which may very well end your career."

"Perhaps not. I have a few threads yet to follow, and though we've little time, all is not yet lost." He disappeared into his bedroom, then, and having changed his identity to that of a retired boxer – complete with facial scars and a pugilist's nose – headed out the door without a word as to his destination.

When he returned at five, I could see that whatever errand had taken him out had been unsuccessful. He seemed rather dejected as he entered his bedroom to remove his disguise.

"Scratch knows too much, Watson," he said five minutes later as he stood staring out the frosted windows, "It is as Rossi said: 'He has his eyes and ears everywhere.' Twice today he has thwarted my inquiries and closed the doors which have been open to me – first at a house of ill repute, and now at a certain den of iniquity, a place where a man's name may be sold for a few sovereigns. The mere mention of Scratch's name turned me into a pariah in both places." He thrust his hands into his pockets. "How does he know? And who is informing him?"

"Perhaps he too employs his own group of Irregulars," I suggested.

"It is possible, but not probable, if he is the man I think he is."

"You know his identity?"

"I suspect. But it is little use without proof." He crossed to the mantel and recharged his pipe using the shag from the Persian slipper. He had switched the oily clay for the cherry-wood, and a more fragrant scent wafted through our rooms.

"Perhaps he truly is The Prince of Darkness." My words were somber ones, but Holmes took them as a jest. He laughed for several moments.

"It would explain how he knows so much," I said a trifle indignantly. "When he came here before, he knew where I kept my revolver. He warned me against fetching it."

"He might have learned the location from your stories."

"I have never revealed it," I countered. "It wouldn't do to have your enemies know where the weapon is." *(The reader will note: The location disclosed in this tale has since been changed.)*

Holmes took a draw on his pipe. "Who would see it then? You wouldn't reveal your hiding place to a client." He glanced up at me, the keen glint in his eye once more. "You have found it! You have discovered who the eyes and ears of Scratch are."

For a moment, I didn't understand what I had found. At last, the thought dawned on me. "Good Heavens!" I cried. "It's a member of the police force! But who?"

"Someone who would be at Scratch's beck and call. A man who could hide Scratch's involvement and steer others away from his identity."

An expression of triumph stripped the cloud of gloom from my friend's face. "I have been a fool, Watson! A complete and utter dunderhead!"

Holmes took his coat and hat from the rack. Then, for the second time that day, he rushed from the room without a word.

A half-hour later, he returned. Cartwright, a messenger boy of our acquaintance, entered our rooms at his heels. Like most of the street Arabs, he appeared rather unkempt.

"Where is Wiggins now?" Holmes asked

395

"Waiting for you in Knightsbridge, sir," the boy replied. "'E's been watching the 'ouse, just like you said to. The gentleman arrived a few minutes after 'e did."

"At quarter-of-eight?"

"Thereabouts."

Holmes removed several coins from his purse and pressed them into the boy's hand. "Go at once and deliver the message I gave you."

The boy nodded and scampered away. Holmes turned to me.

"I have been to Scotland Yard and spent a most instructive time there. We must make for Knightsbridge. Will you accompany me?"

"Of course."

"You'd best retrieve your service revolver then. We may need it before the night is done."

Holmes seemed somewhat reticent as we trundled through the fog-shrouded streets of London, and though my mind burst with curiosity, I allowed him his thoughts. We arrived at the door of James Marston a few moments before eight.

Wiggins, who had concealed himself behind a great oak across the way, rushed out of his hiding place the moment we arrived. He conversed with Holmes in hushed tones for several minutes before accepting a coin and going about his way.

Holmes rubbed his hands together in anticipation. "All the players are assembled," he said. "Now, let us set the play in motion."

"Marston will not admit us," I said, as we neared the steps of the large Georgian home. "He may even have us arrested. How will you gain entrance?"

"We aren't here to see Marston. According to Wiggins, our quarry is here in the drawing room, and I am sure he will wish to hear what I have to say."

Holmes knocked on the door and, after conversing with the butler, convinced him to take a note inside to his master. A few moments later, we were shown into the sumptuous drawing room. Marston stood scowling near the large fireplace, a glass of sherry in his hand. Rossi sat at a table nearby, his pen hovering above a document lying upon it. Scratch stood beside him, his pointed teeth gleaming in the firelight. He held Holmes's note in one hand.

"You are just in time, Mr. Holmes," the young musician said. "Mr. Scratch has agreed to destroy the contract. I am to be freed."

"For what price?" Holmes asked his client. "The entirety of your trust?"

"No, not that. He wants all I may earn in futu – "

"This is none of your concern!" Marston interrupted.

"Signor Rossi," Holmes continued, raising his voice above that of Marston, "if that document seals the bargain between you, I pray you don't sign it until I have had my say. I fear you've been done a grave disservice by your guardian and his confederate."

A mask of fury covered Marston's face. "That is quite enough, Holmes! You are the one who has done a disservice. Did you not enter into a bargain with Scratch yourself? With Gianni's soul as the prize?"

"I did," Holmes said. "To win it back for him. And as our bargain precedes the one you have arranged, my claim takes precedence. I am prepared to pronounce your name, Mr. Scratch."

Scratch reached into his pocket. For a moment, I thought he might have a weapon concealed there, but I was mistaken. The object he produced was Holmes's notebook. He stared at it and the handwritten contract for several seconds.

"There will be no need, Mr. Holmes," Scratch said, at last. "My agreement with Signor Rossi has been satisfied and I release you from this agreement." So saying, he tossed the notebook into the fire.

"It makes little difference to me," Holmes said, with a dismissive wave of his hand. "I will pronounce your name, bargain or no: You are Jasper Hedgewick, Professor *Emeritus* of Durham College."

I stared at Holmes in some astonishment and would have spoken up, had the words not been stolen from me.

"How can that be, Mr. Holmes?" a voice called out. "Jasper Hedgewick is dead."

Inspector Ambrose Burrows stood in the doorway, hat in hand. A tall, stout man with a large, ginger mustache, he surveyed the room with an air of suspicion.

"Ah, Inspector. I take it you've received my message?"

"I did – though I must confess, it baffled me. As does the statement you've just made. Jasper Hedgewick is dead. I told you the news myself."

"So, you did," Holmes said. "And yet, there he stands."

Holmes took a step forward, and to my utter shock, snatched the blond hair from off Scratch's crown. A bald head fringed with sparse and graying hair lay beneath.

"You fool!" Marston said to Hedgewick. "You unmitigated fool. You have doomed us all. I had everything in hand, and you had to indulge your ego – had to bring Sherlock Holmes into it."

"Silence," Hedgewick barked. Marston grimaced but obeyed. Rossi had risen from the table, the pen still in his hand. "Sit, boy!" Hedgewick commanded. Rossi dropped back into his chair. Hedgewick turned to my friend.

397

"A most amazing feat, Mr. Holmes. Tell me, how did you know?"

"As one who himself dons disguises of varying types, I immediately recognized the subterfuge you employed. You didn't use the disguise just to suggest your similarity to The Evil One, but to hide your identity from those who might know you. The contract you had Rossi sign was typed and not handwritten. It suggested that he knew your handwriting and by it, might deduce your true identity.

"The fact that you and Marston are both connected to Durham College and that a Stradivarius of great value vanished from there along with you, narrowed the field considerably. However, when Inspector Burrows suggested you were dead, my investigation grew stale. It was only when I realized who your spy was that I understood you to be alive."

I had drawn my revolver during Holmes's revelation, and to my horror, felt something cold pressed against the nape of my neck.

"That will be enough, Doctor," the inspector said. "Drop the weapon."

"I wondered when you would show your duplicity, Burrows," Holmes said. "How long have you supplied information to Hedgewick?"

"Long enough to learn how to hold my tongue," the loathsome inspector replied.

Hedgewick leaned forward and retrieved my revolver. "You are shrewder than I thought, Mr. Holmes. It's a shame you and your friend must die."

"So this is your grand plan? To shoot us here, with Rossi as a witness? Or . . . is he to share our sad fate? Ah, I see you've gone quiet. I suppose he shall die as well, now that he knows you're a flesh-and-blood man and not a demon from the depths of Hell. Will Burrows attest to whatever story you create? He may find it difficult to prove. I am sure Stanley Hopkins will have something to say about this."

"Do not fear," Burrows said to his companions. "Hopkins will not come. I intercepted the message meant for him and came on my own accord."

Hedgewick's grin grew broader. "It is the end, at last, Mr. Holmes. I have done what no other could do. I have bested you." He raised the revolver, and I was forced to stare into the muzzle of my own weapon. "Now, you die."

"Your method of execution is considerably lacking," Holmes said without a trace of tremor in his voice. "Boring me to death with speeches and then shooting me is rather anticlimactic, don't you think? At least Moriarty possessed a sliver of imagination. He tried to throw me off the Falls at Reichenbach."

"Be done with it, Hedgewick!" Marston hissed.

Hedgewick stared at my friend for several seconds and then lowered the revolver. "As much as I dislike saying it, Mr. Holmes, you are correct. This is far too easy a fate for you. Let us come to an agreement."

"Another? You didn't keep the first."

"This one I shall keep. We will have another test of skills – a musical one. Should you win, I shall spare Dr. Watson and Signor Rossi. Should you lose, they both die. You, of course, will die no matter what the outcome. Do you agree?"

"It seems I have no choice."

"This is madness!" Marston cried.

"You have no sense of the dramatic, Marston," Hedgewick said. "Go upstairs and fetch Rossi's instrument."

"You will not use the Stradivarius you stole from Durham?" Holmes asked.

"You know of that? I had coveted it for a great while. Did you know, they accused me of stealing it the first time it went missing? That wasn't my doing, of course. It was Moriarty's. We had been rivals for some time and he thought he might send me packing with that little escapade. I proved myself innocent and then turned the tables on him. He was the one sent packing when I stole the school funds and hid them in his room. I never expected that he would become as famous as he did – not when I have the superior intellect.

"The Stradivarius is a souvenir of that time and so, when the time came for me to go, it seemed only fitting that it should accompany me when I left. Even now, it sits in a place of honor in my home. I consider it something of a good luck charm. Had Moriarty not taken it and blamed the theft on me, I might never have met my colleague, Inspector Burrows. He was the investigator at the time, and we struck up an acquaintance."

Marston returned at that moment with Rossi's violin. He deposited it rather unceremoniously into Hedgewick's hands.

Hedgewick tucked the violin beneath his chin. "This instrument is somewhat inferior, but I think it shall do well enough."

He began to play.

Young Rossi's description of the man's playing had been correct. It was amongst the finest I had ever heard. His interpretation of Brahms' *Violin Sonata No. 3* was nothing short of masterful. When he finished, a hushed silence filled the room.

He handed the instrument to Holmes.

My gaze strayed to Rossi's face. Never have I seen such a pale countenance. I thought he might faint again, as he had the night he'd come to see us. Tears trailed down his cheek and he lowered his face into his arms, his body quaking with silent torment. He did not, as I would have done, take up the revolver from the table where Hedgewick had laid it.

Holmes accepted the violin and, without hesitation, began.

The sweet strains of the Brahms once more flowed from the instrument. Holmes played it just as beautifully as Hedgewick, though his notes seemed to linger in the air. And then, the tune changed. and I recognized something I knew well. Paganini's *24 Caprices*.

Holmes played as he had never played, his fingers darting over the strings. On several occasions, I have seen my friend moved by music and this was one of those. His playing was more than masterful. I could call it nothing less than divine.

When he finished. Rossi rose to his feet and applauded.

Hedgewick took the instrument from Holmes's hands and lifted it once more to his chin. For the first time, I saw the arrogant mask fall away. Hedgewick's eyes reflected his fear and disbelief. He attempted the piece several times but could not continue. At last, he laid the violin down in defeat.

"Enough of this!" snarled Marston. He took the revolver from the table and pointed it at my friend. "We end it now."

A clamor arose outside then, and a rush of feet sounded in the hall. Someone pounded on the door. "In the name of Her Majesty, Queen Victoria!" the voice of Stanley Hopkins cried. "Open this door at once!"

Rossi leaped upon Marston at that moment, and the revolver went off. A bullet flew by my ear and hit the wall behind me. I scarce had time to react, for my attention had turned to the fleeing Inspector Burrows. He and Hedgewick made for the French doors, but Holmes and I fell upon them. Holmes caught the villainous professor with a right to the jaw, knocking something into the air as he did so, while my fist found Ambrose Burrows' middle. The odious inspector folded like a house of cards.

Marston had gone for the window, but Rossi had caught hold of him. He struggled with the man as Holmes rushed to his aid. I hurried to the door and admitted Hopkins and several uniformed police. They flooded the room.

"I see you received my message," Holmes said, as Hopkins clasped his hand.

"The boy came to me first and then to Burrows as you instructed," Hopkins said. "I only wish I had arrived sooner. It took a bit of doing to convince my superiors that Burrows was dishonest."

"No matter," Holmes said, clapping the young man on the shoulder. "You came when needed." He stooped to retrieve something from off the floor and I realized it was a set of false teeth. Every one had been filed to a point. Without them, Hedgewick resembled a harmless and rather wizened man.

400

Holmes dropped the teeth into Hedgewick's outstretched hand. "You are a decent enough musician, Professor Hedgewick, However, unlike Moriarty, you are lacking in panache and genius. I hope you have learned the lesson you intended to teach me."

Following the apprehension of Hedgewick and the revelation of his true identity, Gianni Rossi made a full and complete recovery. A week later, he stood in our rooms at Baker Street.

"I cannot understand it, Mr. Holmes," he said, shaking his head. "Why did Mr. Marston resort to such a strange method of securing my fortune? Why not just kill me and have done with it?"

"Marston revealed his plan to Hopkins and myself only this morning," Holmes replied. "It seems he was a gambler, a bad one at that, and he had been stealing from your trust in order to cover the debts he incurred. He had intended to return the funds, but as your twenty-first birthday approached, he knew the amount to be too much. He couldn't admit to you what he had done, and he couldn't stop the theft, so he lighted on a plan wherein he could continue to use the trust and take possession of whatever funds you earned in future. He took advantage of your superstitious nature to accomplish this. He never intended to kill you – at least, not until his means of controlling you had been destroyed."

"My superstitious nature," Rossi said with a frown. "He knew I would believe in the legend of the Stradivarius, that it belonged to Lucifer himself. I would have given anything for the instrument, but much more to secure my soul. That is why he created the agreement which guaranteed Hedgewick all of my future earnings. It would also keep me from discovering the plundering of my trust."

"Precisely. Hedgewick used information provided to him by Marston and Burrows to convince you that he knew everything there was to know of you and that he had procured such information through supernatural means. He rented a furnished house in Surrey as a place to meet, filled it with borrowed objects of wealth, paid the local innkeeper to slip the note into your room, and then to talk about the Devil to frighten you."

"I am a fool," Rossi lamented. "He was but a mere man."

"A man with an enormous capacity for evil and for envy," Holmes added. "When he learned that you had called me in on the case, he couldn't resist testing his mettle against mine. It would have been quite a feather in his cap if he had bested me when his rival, Moriarty, could not."

"He seemed to be a genius. His playing far outdid mine. And yours – Mr. Holmes! You are a *maestro*!"

Holmes smiled at the compliment. He did not answer, and I wondered if it had robbed him of his ability to speak.

"You have saved me, Mr. Holmes," Rossi continued. "Let me reward you for your efforts. Ask, and if it is in my power, you shall have it."

"Two tickets to your next concert," Holmes said. "And, if you could, I would enjoy a little Paganini."

The Dowager
Lady Isobel Frobisher
by Martin Daley

Chapter I

I have recorded elsewhere how young Doctor Verner purchased my Kensington practice upon Holmes's reappearance, and my subsequent return to join my friend in our old quarters in Baker Street. I was extremely proud of the practice that I had developed and part of me was loathe to let it go. However, the years prior to my decision had not been without pain – first my belief that I had lost Holmes, and then the all too real passing of my darling Mary. When the time came, therefore, it was with a sense of optimism that I agreed to the sale, believing a fresh start would do me good. And so it would prove over the years following, although I was delighted when Verner asked me to act as his *locum* on occasion when he was unavailable.

I recall one such instance when the young man spent a couple of weeks in France visiting some distant relatives of his. As I would be due to be back at my old desk for two weeks and, given that the surgery was almost three miles from our Baker Street lodgings, it made sense to stay in the living quarters which held such bitter-sweet memories for me. Both Verner and I agreed it was the sensible option, so I packed a bag and left Holmes to his latest chemical experiment.

It had been a relatively quiet few weeks for my friend and as I left, I couldn't help but glance at his desk drawer, hoping that it would remain firmly locked during my absence. Holmes was hunched over a microscope analysing some insect he had been telling me about the previous evening, while a test tube containing a strange non-descript coloured liquid bubbled and smoked beside him.

"With some of the aromas omitted from my experiments," said Holmes, apparently reading my mind, "I don't think there will be need for any artificial stimulants. Be on your way, Watson, and attend to your duties." He gestured towards the door without looking up from his work.

"You know where I am if you need me. Otherwise, I shall see you in a fortnight."

The following week proved to be an interesting, even enjoyable period, as I reacquainted myself with some of my old patients and took great satisfaction from engaging my professional skills once more. Little did I know that my final days as *locum tenens* would see my two worlds overlap.

It was the Thursday of the second week, with Verner due to return from France the following weekend. The maid wakened me and informed me that a telegram had been received from the home of Lady Isobel Frobisher, and I was being asked to attend urgently. I groggily looked at my watch on the bedside table. It was just after half-past-seven.

I wasn't familiar with the name of the patient so, after hurriedly washing, shaving, and dressing, I leafed through the patient files in Verner's surgery. There was no sign of any Isobel Frobisher. Rather than waste more time, I climbed into the hansom that the maid had waiting for me and set off. The address was one in the beautiful rows of stucco townhouses in the heart of Belgravia. I wasn't under the illusion that it would be an ordinary house call, but if I were, any such thoughts would have been dispelled as the cab pulled up. A small crowd had gathered and were being shepherded away from the white steps of the property by a uniformed policeman. Another of his colleagues appeared to be standing guard at the front door. There was a police wagon ominously parked along the street.

I identified myself to the officers and was shown into the house, "Just in there, sir, third room on the right," said the constable pointing down the hall.

From the doorway of the room indicated, I immediately saw the body of an elderly woman slumped over the dining table. There was another constable standing with his back to the window opposite and, with a nod, he consented to allow me forward to approach the body – it was clear that she was already dead.

"We are both too late, I'm afraid Doctor," said a familiar voice behind me.

I turned to see Holmes and Inspector Athelney Jones standing on the other side of the room.

"Holmes! What on earth – "

"Later, Watson," interrupted my friend. He wore an expression I seldom saw in all our years together – that of a defeated man. "Do your professional duties and I will explain later."

I turned my attention to the deceased. She was fully dressed and had fallen forward in her chair to the point where her head hung over the empty dinner plate in front of her. It appeared as though the large table hadn't been cleared from the previous evening, as dirty crockery and cutlery were still present around the five place settings. The fingernails and the lips of the corpse had a slight hint of blue while the skin felt clammy. The

404

advanced stage of *rigor mortis* had set in. I looked up from my preliminary examination at the sound of someone entering the room.

"Mr. Brotherton," said Inspector Jones upon the man's appearance. "The Dowager's butler, I believe?"

"Yes, sir," said the man without taking his eyes from the body, as though transfixed.

"We have met already," said Holmes to the policeman. "I would like to ask Mr. Brotherton some questions.

Brotherton was oblivious to the exchange and stared at his mistress. Holmes sought to ease his distress. "Come, Mr. Brotherton, let us move to the other room where we can speak a little easier – with your permission of course," he added to the inspector almost as an afterthought. Jones nodded. Holmes then turned to me, "Watson, if there is nothing more you can do right now, perhaps you would join us?"

"Certainly. Other than pronouncing the death and estimating the time of death around midnight, I can't confirm anything else until after the *post mortem.*" I certainly had my suspicions about the cause of death, but didn't feel it appropriate to speculate with Brotherton and some of the junior constables present.

I followed Holmes and the butler into an adjacent sitting room, while Jones commenced arrangements with his men to have the body removed.

"Now Mr. Brotherton," began Holmes after the butler had composed himself, "how long have you been in Lady Isobel's employ?"

"Martha, erm . . . Mrs. Brotherton and I have been in the service of the late Lord and his wife for more than twenty years now."

"Your wife is the cook?"

"That's right sir, and also lady's maid, I suppose. When Lord Frobisher died, some of the staff were let go because they weren't really needed anymore. Martha and I were retained as we had been with them for such a long a time."

"Are there any other staff here now?"

"No sir. There is a footman and groom back at the country residence in Berkshire, but it was only Martha and me who accompanied Lady Isobel into town."

Holmes looked round the room. "Does Lady Isobel own any other properties?"

"No sir, not anymore. Just this house and the family estate. The Earl used to have quite a few properties, but when he became ill, I think he made sure he had everything sorted for his wife. He sold most of his assets to make life as easy as possible for Her Ladyship."

"Who discovered the body?"

"I did, sir. My wife and I have rooms downstairs in the basement, so we don't really hear much once we are down there. It would have been unusual for Lady Isobel to be up so early," Brotherton paused as he tried to gather himself, "so when I came upstairs this morning, I didn't go into the dining room initially. As Martha prepared Her Ladyship's breakfast, I went to wake her. I knocked a few times, but received no reply. I announced that I would enter, but when I did, I found that it was empty and the bed hadn't been slept in. I then came back downstairs to find Lady Isobel slumped over the table, where she had been sitting the previous evening."

Brotherton put his head in his hands, clearly distressed by what he had found. His wife was equally so. Her sobs could be heard in an adjacent room where someone – a neighbour as it turned out – was comforting her. He continued by telling us that his wife had been alerted to the tragedy by her husband's cries. Rushing into the dining room, the housekeeper let out a shriek at the grim scene.

"And what time was this?" asked Holmes.

The butler inhaled deeply, "I would say about seven o'clock, sir. That's when I called for you, Mr. Holmes."

Holmes took out his watch and flipped open the lid. It was now a quarter-past-nine.

"Called for you?" I asked my friend and then turning to the butler, "Why did you call for Mr. Holmes and not myself or the police?"

"I – " Brotherton began, but Holmes interrupted and waved away my question.

"Tell me about last night." I was surprised by his question. It was if he had some prior knowledge as to the events of the previous evening.

"Lady Isobel hosted a dinner party for members of her family."

"And who was in attendance?"

"It was just a small gathering – Lady Isobel and the late Earl's niece. Miss Celia Frobisher. Lady Isobel's brother-in-law Mr. Noel Lytollis, her *own* cousin Reverend Laidlaw and the cousin of her late husband, Mr. Simon Frobisher." I thought I sensed a half-smile from Holmes, as though he could have listed the group himself. "They were all the family she had left, and now this. What a terrible way to go."

Brotherton continued, saying that the gathering had sat up quite late and Lady Isobel excused him and his wife from their duties, telling them that they could clear up in the morning.

"What time was this?"

The butler thrust out a lip as he pondered, "I would say around eleven o'clock sir. I had ordered a coach to take Her Ladyship's guests home around midnight." He nodded to himself, "Yes, so Martha and I must have left them to it around eleven."

"And you suggested the time of death somewhere between twelve and one," Holmes checked with me. I nodded my confirmation. "So the events between eleven o'clock and one o'clock are of interest," he added to himself.

I think it was only then that Brotherton realised that if there had been foul play, he – and his wife for that matter – must be considered as one of the handful of suspects.

"Yes," he said simply, almost to *him*self. And then, "As I said earlier, we don't hear that much from downstairs, but one thing I thought I heard at one point was the dining room door opening. I probably thought that was Lady Isobel going to bed."

"What time was this?"

"Well, I'm not sure. It would be sometime after her guests had left." Brotherton thought a little longer. "In fact, come to think of it, yes, I heard the dining room door open – the hinge has a distinctive creak that I should have attended to before now – but a couple of minutes later it opened and closed again. It struck me as a little unusual at the time, but I thought nothing more about until it just now came to mind. Probably nothing." As he spoke, the butler looked into the middle distance, clearly trying to recall the events of the previous evening and make some sense of them. "If only I had come upstairs to check. I didn't know anything until this morning – that's when I notified you, Mr. Holmes, knowing that you had been working for Her Ladyship. We also thought it best to summon the police and Doctor Verner, although I didn't realise he was away.

He looked at me when he made the last point, as if to answer the question I asked earlier. My instinct told me that it was unlikely he or his wife would be involved in any wrongdoing, but I understood that Holmes had to pursue the line of enquiry anyway, as gently as he could.

"Would you describe Lady Isobel as a good employer?"

"I would, sir," said Brotherton firmly, focussing back on the detective, "a real lady in every sense of the word. Never had a cross word with either of us. Nor did her husband before her. Lord Frobisher was a true gentleman. We've both been very happy working for them and they have always treated us well."

"Can you give me a few more details of the family members who attended last night?"

"Yes sir. There was the niece, Miss Celia. She only moved back to England last year after her father – Lord Frobisher's younger brother – committed suicide. Apparently, he had got into some financial difficulty and couldn't take it anymore. Had to sell his big house in Norbury at one point, but it didn't do any good. He kept losing money and it seemingly it all became too much for him. Left his widow virtually penniless, and she married some acquaintance of her husband. They planned to honeymoon in America, but tragically during the crossing, there was a fire in the engine room of the liner and it went down with all passengers and crew. Miss Celia then moved back here after she had been living on the Continent, as her aunt was then her only living relative."

"And the others?"

"Mr. Lytollis is Lady Isobel's brother-in-law. Poor chap was blinded in a house fire in which his wife, Her Ladyship's twin sister, perished. Apparently, he fought to save his wife, but to no avail. What a tragedy," Brotherton lamented, shaking his head, "She was such a handsome woman, just like her sister. They were like peas in a pod. What a shame – Lady Isobel took that really hard."

After a reflective pause, Brotherton continued. "Then there was the Reverend Laidlaw from St. Bartholomew's. He is Lady Isobel's cousin. And finally Mr. Frobisher, the Earl's cousin."

"What were their respective relationships like with your employer?"

"It's difficult to say, sir," answered Brotherton. "She didn't seem to see much of them, but in fairness, they have all rallied 'round since the Earl passed away. They have all been fairly regular visitors to Lady Isobel since then. I may be speaking out of turn, but Martha reckons young Celia can be a 'right little madam'! The others I only showed in at the door so I couldn't really judge." I was amused at Brotherton's last comment as he proceeded to do just that. "Mr. Lytollis was a bit of a sullen chap, although after losing his wife and his sight I'm not surprised. The Reverend was a bit of a cold fish, I suppose – difficult to read. And if I'm honest, I was surprised Her Ladyship welcomed Mr. Simon Frobisher, as I had never heard him spoken of before the Earl's death, let alone come to the house. But then it was none of our business, I suppose. We just looked after Lady Isobel."

"Thank you, Brotherton," concluded Holmes, "I will probably need to speak with you and your wife again, but I think that will do for now."

Once the butler left us, Holmes sat in silence for a few minutes before we made to leave. We met Inspector Jones again in the hallway and Holmes gave him the names and addresses of Lady Isobel's relatives. "I suggest you inform them of the Dowager's passing."

"Do you also suggest I bring them in for questioning?" asked the policeman.

"No, I don't think that will be necessary at this stage. Wait until the *post mortem* confirms the cause of death and tell them that the reading of Lady Isobel's Will will take place on the afternoon of her funeral – date still to be confirmed. I don't think any of them will be going anywhere in the meantime." He bid the inspector good morning and then turned to me. "Are you free later this afternoon, Watson?"

I knew it was irrelevant as whether I was free or not in Holmes's view. "Nothing I couldn't postpone," I said.

"Meet me back at Baker Street at four o'clock, where I shall tell you a little more about this strange case."

Chapter II

I met Holmes outside our lodgings at the appointed hour just as he was just stepping out of a hansom. Back in our sitting room, he lit a pipe and then used the match to bring the fire Mrs. Hudson had prepared for us to life before taking his favourite chair. Once I was positioned opposite in my usual station, he began to tell me of his investigations in my absence. On the very afternoon I had left, Holmes had received an extremely brief letter from Lady Isobel. He pointed to the envelope on the mantelpiece. It ran thus:

Eaton Square, SW 1

Dear Mr. Holmes,

I wish to commission your services in a delicate family matter. I fear that my life is in danger. I would be obliged if you would call at my residence tomorrow morning at ten o'clock.

Sincerely yours,
Isobel Frobisher

I looked up from the note and Holmes took up the story.

"As I had no current engagements, I was intrigued by the invitation and naturally went along. Brotherton met me at the door and showed me into the room where we interviewed him this morning. Lady Isobel was waiting and proceeded to tell me of her fears."

Holmes related how the Dowager had lost her husband two years earlier and she was now in the sole possession of their extremely wealthy estate. They hadn't had any children of their own, and their only living relatives were the people who Brotherton had informed us had been with Lady Isobel last night.

"'I have my concerns and suspicions about them all, Mr. Holmes,' Lady Isobel had said to me. 'My husband Geoffrey was a proud,

409

honourable man and I would hate to think his memory would be sullied in any way after I'm gone.'

"'You speak as though that is imminent, Madam.'"

"'No one is sure what the future holds,' said the Dowager cryptically. She referred to possible criminal behaviour perpetrated by her family members and asked me to investigate their various backgrounds. 'My husband's niece, for example. Celia Frobisher. I fear that she has done nothing but bring the family name into disrepute all of her adult life. Her father Richard was a good man – he worked hard to achieve a certain standing for him and his family. Yet it seems to me that his daughter repaid him by endlessly demanding funds to indulge her frivolous escapades in Monte Carlo, Venice, and Constantinople with her unscrupulous friends. Richard told Geoffrey that he believed she not only wasted his money, but she was also involved in embezzling some as well, and much of what she spent it on was illegal. The one thing that Richard was guilty of was his inability to refuse his daughter. The poor man couldn't take it anymore and ended up blowing his brains out.

"'Then there is the pathetic creature, Noel Lytollis . . . .' Lady Isobel proceeded to relate quite a bit about him, which I shall share with you in a minute. Then she stopped herself stating, 'No, this isn't fair. I should say no more. I want you to act with complete impartiality Mr. Holmes. If there is nothing to find and no wrong-doing, then so be it. If, however, my fears are confirmed, I want your complete candour in the matter.'

"The first person I visited was Lady Isobel's niece, Miss Celia Brotherton."

"And did she turn out to be a 'right little madam'?" I asked.

"Ha!" cried Holmes, recalling Brotherton's comment from earlier, "I'm afraid she was! I presented myself as Mr. Smike, a colleague of her late father's solicitor. With a wig, false nose – at the end of which balanced precariously a *pince-nez* – and a stoop, I enjoyed my visit immensely.

"'I don't know why you want to speak with *me!*' she announced haughtily, after I had finally tracked her down to a friend's house south of the river.

"'Because when your father died last year, there was some confusion,' I replied. 'We are trying to establish if some funds that have come to light were part of his estate.'

"Her eyes flashed and her attitude changed immediately, 'Oh, in that case you better sit down. Would you like some tea?'

"'That's very kind of you, thank you.'

"She disappeared momentarily and returned with a tray. Her hands were shaking with anticipation as she poured. 'Oh, I do love a nice cup of tea,' I said. 'It tends to reinvigorate one in the afternoon, don't you find?'

410

"'Yes. Now what is this business you spoke of regarding my father's estate?'

"'Ah, yes.' I interrupted myself as I peered out of the window into the garden. 'Is that a rose bush, Miss Frobisher?' I rose from my seat and walked over to get a better look.

"'What? Oh, yes . . . I suppose so . . . I don't know. Come and get your tea before it gets cold.'

"'What a beautiful thing. I'm somewhat of a rose fancier myself you know – it looks like *Rosa Damascena* if I'm not mistaken. My dear wife always encourages me to display them at those rather grand flower shows, but I don't think I have the confidence. They seem so very knowledgeable at these events, don't you find? I would hate to make a fool of myself.'"

I was amused by Holmes's narrative, picturing him playing the hapless buffoon – and referring to a wife! – much to the irritation of Celia Frobisher.

"'Mr. Smike, will you please come and sit down and tell me about my father's money!'

"'Well, that is just the thing Miss Frobisher,' I said retaking my seat, 'We aren't sure if it is proper to your late father or not. Apparently, there were some shares belonging to your grandfather that don't appear to have been allocated to your late uncle Lord Frobisher for some reason. As he passed away before your father – his younger brother – we are just informing all relevant parties of our investigations in trying to establish if they were bequeathed to anyone and if they were not, trying to establish if they are proper to your father and his descendants, or to Lord Frobisher's widow, the Dowager, Lady Isobel.'

"'How much are we talking about?'

"'Oh, I would say there will be several thousand pounds' worth.'

"At this point, she almost spilled her tea into her lap," recalled Holmes with a roar of laughter, "just managing to catch the spillage in her saucer."

"'Tell me Miss Frobisher, did you attend the reading of your grandfather's will when he passed away?'

"'No, I was just a child. He left me some money as his only grandchild, but that is all I know.'

"'I see. And the reading of your uncle's will, Lord Frobisher?'"

"'No, I think I was away in Monte Carlo at the time of his death.'

"'Did you not think to visit?'

"'Why should I want to visit?' she replied lighting a cigarette. 'There was nothing I could do.'

"'Perhaps show a little compassion for your uncle and his widow,' I ventured with a straight face.

"She didn't reply, but simply looked at me with distain."

I've witnessed Holmes enjoying the discomfort of many an interviewee in the past, and clearly this was one such encounter. He continued.

"'So you didn't actually return to England until your own father died last year?'

"'Yes, that is correct. Daddy was funding my stay in Venice, so I had to return. I must say, Mr. Smike, your questioning is more like that of a policeman than a solicitor.'

"'Heaven forbids, Miss Frobisher! I apologise if I'm giving the wrong impression. I am only trying to establish the chronology of the events so that any outstanding monies can be allocated to the correct individual.' Reverting to the subject of money appeared to refocus the young lady's mind.

"'Of course, of course.'

"From my deadpan expression, I don't think she could work out whether I was being sarcastic or genuine. Realising that she hadn't shown much sorrow at the loss of her parents or at her uncle's passing, she made no reply and turned her head away to look out into the garden at nothing in particular.

"'I will leave you to admire that beautiful rose bush, Miss Frobisher. Good afternoon.'"

"She was staying not too far from St. Bartholomew's in Greenwich, so I took the opportunity to visit the Reverend Christopher Laidlaw in the same guise. The vicar was a slightly built man with a sallow complexion. His facial expression upon my arrival had me puzzling over what word you might use to describe him in your flowery tales, Watson – I settled on, '*shifty*'."

"'I don't suppose anyone in the family ever mentioned the shares to you, Reverend?' I asked once I had explained the purpose of my visit.

"'No, I am not particularly close to my cousin Isobel," was the clergyman's curt reply. "I've never had the opportunity to visit."

"'Never? How long have you been back in the area?'

"The vicar's eyes flashed with concern at my apparent knowledge. He was wondering how I knew he had been *away* from the area. If I knew that, what else did I know? He decided not to pursue his own questions.

"'About twelve months, I suppose. I've been extremely busy, and we were never that close in our younger days. She had completely gone out of my mind, if I'm honest."

"'Yes, well honesty is always the best policy,' I said with a smile. 'Tell me, do you know of any other relatives of the Frobisher's in the area? Perhaps I could ask for their help too.'

"'I would hardly describe them as *relatives*, Mr. Smike. There is a niece of Isobel's husband – ' He thought for a while. 'Yes. *Celia* – that's her name. Absolute wastrel if I recall, always flitting around the country, and when she wasn't doing that, she was off gallivanting abroad. And then there is that poor wretch, Lytollis. I think I only ever met him once before, on his wedding day. He's the husband of Isobel's sister who died in a house fire. I think that's about it.'

"'Did I hear something about a cousin of the late Earl?'

"'Oh yes, now you mention it, I think there was. I'm afraid I couldn't tell you anything about him, however.'

"'Not to worry, Reverend Laidlaw. It has been kind of you to spare me some of your time. Our investigation will continue and if there is any news, I will be sure to pass it on.'"

When Holmes had finished his narrative, I asked, "How did you know Laidlaw had been out of the area?"

"As part of my preliminary investigation, it transpired that the Reverend Christopher Laidlaw wasn't quite as reverential after all. I now have evidence that this devious *clergyman* – " Holmes spat the word out. " – is guilty of stealing monies from charities connected to his former parish in Lancashire. What he got away with earlier in his career can only be imagined. The bishop was obliged to call the police in but, rather than risk the reputational damage to the parish and the diocese, he decided not to press charges against Laidlaw. Instead, and in agreement with the Archbishop of Canterbury himself, it was arranged to have him moved out of the Diocese and back to London where it was felt he could do less damage."

"Good Lord, it's almost so fanciful to be unimaginable!"

"You will always remain a kind soul, Watson," said my friend with a smile, "but money and power do strange things to people – even those in the most trusted of positions."

"How such a man can put his head on the pillow at night, having abused his position, is quite beyond me. Should have been defrocked if you ask me." After the shock of listening to Holmes's narrative regarding the Reverend Laidlaw, he them moved on to the tale regarding Noel Lytollis.

"Laidlaw had described Lytollis as a 'poor wretch'. I understood why when I met him. A seemingly once-handsome man had been reduced to a stooped cripple, shuffling along behind a tapping white stick that cleared his dark path.

"'You must forgive me, Mr. Smike. I'm not as light as I once was,' he said as he led me into a sitting room.

"'Don't worry about that, Mr. Lytollis, I will try not to fatigue you.'

"'I'm not sure I can be of any great help in the matter, as I'm technically the in-law of the family. But obviously if there is any light I can shed, I would be happy to do so.' Lytollis lowered himself into a wingback chair by the fire.

"'Well, Lady Isobel will need all the support she can get, no doubt, at this confusing time.'

"'Yes indeed, very confusing. I must make an effort to visit more often.'

"'How often do you visit the Dowager.?'

"'Not very often, I'm afraid. Isobel took the loss of her sister very badly and seemed to blame me. I not only lost my wife in the fire, but everything else I owned, as well as my sight. Whatever compensation I received has been virtually exhausted in the few years since.'

"'Yes, such a terrible tragedy. Please accept my belated condolences for your loss. I remember reading about the tragedy in the newspapers at the time, with their wicked rumours.'

"Lytollis shuffled uncomfortably in his seat. 'Yes, people can be so cruel.' He looked in my general direction with a pleading expression, 'I wasn't aware that my wife was in the house at the time of the accident. I simply knocked over an oil lamp after returning home late from a business trip. The flame skittered across the carpet and caught the hem of the curtain. From there the fire gradually got out of control and I had to get out of the house. It was only then that I heard my dear wife screaming – she had been asleep in bed the whole time. By the time I ran through the flames and into her bedroom, it was too late. I had to leap through the first-floor window to make my own escape. The creature you see before you is the result.'"

"A detailed account," I commented, as Holmes paused his narrative.

"Yes, and one which I never asked for. My Shakespeare is a trifle rusty, but I feel I am reminded of Hamlet."

"'*Me thinks he doth protest too much,*' to paraphrase."

"Exactly. As I mentioned, when I visited Lady Isobel for the first time, she shared with me her suspicions and relayed a very different version of events.

"'What my darling sister Evie saw in that gambling rake I will never know!' she told me. 'The day she died, she was due to come and spend a few days with me. Lytollis meanwhile was already away from home, no doubt at the track or in the bed of another man's wife. What he didn't know is that Evie took ill and didn't travel as scheduled. Instead, she decided to stay at home and travel the following day. She told me that Lytollis's gambling debts were mounting up and I suspect that, in order to raise some funds, he came up with the hair-brained scheme to defraud his insurance

414

company by perpetrating an arson attack on his own home. When he returned that night, he assumed the house was empty and it was only when he heard Evie screaming through the fire that he realised she had been asleep in her bed. His attempts to save her failed and he was left in the state you saw before you – poetic justice I suppose, but it will never bring my darling Evie back.'"

I was startled by Holmes's recollection of what Lady Isobel had told him. "A very serious allegation."

"Yes, but not without foundation," Holmes replied. "After I spoke with Lytollis, I made some further enquiries into his background and confirmed what Lady Isobel had told me. He had indeed accumulated considerable debts, and on the day of the fire, his 'business trip' had consisted of an afternoon spent in an East End brothel he was known to frequent regularly. The circumstances of the fire were also suspicious as the Dowager suggested. The report into the fire – which even made the newspapers – stated that there was a strong smell of coal oil around the perimeter of the house, suggesting that the fire had been started outside and not inside as Lytollis claimed. He may have been ultimately blinded by the fire, but Scotland Yard appear to have been blinded by the tragedy – and to the man's guilt, as established by additional evidence I have accumulated. The insurance company remained unconvinced and only issued a quarter of the policy total, something which Lytollis didn't challenge."

"Incredible." I sat shaking my head in disbelief. "Hang on! There was a fourth relative, wasn't there?"

"Ha! Of course – the feckless Simon Frobisher, cousin of the late Earl. A bigger imbecile never walked the streets of London! I shall be interested in the mutual reaction when we introduce him to our friends at Scotland Yard." We both roared with laughter at Holmes's mischief. "The sum of his contribution to his family's legacy was to attempt to impersonate his cousin on not one, but two occasions: Once to gain entry to the Tankerville Club, and another to gain entry to the Royal Enclosure at the Epsom Derby! On both occasions, the Earl had to rescue his cousin and his own reputation in the process – at great expense apparently – to keep the matter out of the courts. I also discovered a number of other illegal impersonations on his part.

"I visited Lady Isobel to present my findings."

"And what was her reaction?"

"She was disappointed, but not surprised. It seems my investigation had simply confirmed her own instincts about her family members."

We sat in silence for a while. "Holmes?" I hesitated, but had to ask anyway. "Do you think your investigation endangered her life?"

415

He sucked on his pipe, "I would be lying if I denied that it was the first thing that crossed my mind when I was summoned this morning. You probably picked up the strange vinegar smell from the Dowager's table?"

"Yes, I did. You suspect poison?"

"Unfortunately, I didn't have the opportunity of carrying out a thorough inspection of the scene, as Jones and his hoard of elephants arrived at almost the same time. I'm still considering the question following my enquiries this afternoon."

"This afternoon?"

"Yes. I retraced my steps and visited three of those present last night. Miss Frobisher looked at me with a hint of recognition, but obviously couldn't place me. I didn't waste time in referring to my previous visit. Instead, I was suitably vague about my identity and succeeded in giving her the impression that I was working with the official police force."

"How did she appear in light of the news of the Dowager's passing?"

"Ambivalent," replied Holmes. I asked about the evening

"'What time did you leave your aunt's house?'

"'It would be around about midnight I suppose. We all left together.'

"'And how did she seem when you left her?'

"'Absolutely fine,' she snapped, clearly bored with such meaningless questions, 'I hope you don't suspect me of doing anything.'

"'Why would I suspect you, Miss Frobisher? I'm simply trying to piece together what happened last night.'

"'Of course. It is quite shocking news, that's all.'

"'If you don't mind me saying, notwithstanding your family connection, you appear to be a slightly diverse group to be having dinner. What was the purpose of the gathering?'

"'Aunt Isobel said she had been looking into her affairs and she wanted to seek our views.'

"'Seek your views? In what way?'

"'Well, as we are – were – her only relatives, I thought she wanted to share with us what she intended to do with her estate.'

"'And did she?'

"'Not particularly. Every time I raised the subject, she would deflect my question and simply say how much she adored her family. I think the old girl was losing her mind, if you ask me.'

"'Well, sadly not anymore, Miss Frobisher. I will leave you to deal with your loss,' I said rising to leave.

"'Do you know when the reading of the will is due to take place?'

"'I'm sure you will be informed once the body is released for burial. Good afternoon.'

416

"No question where her main concerns are," I commented when Holmes paused. "Did you find out anything from the others?"

"The Reverend Laidlaw appeared as disinterested in the Dowager's passing as her niece had been. 'How did everything seem last night?' I asked.

"'Perfectly fine. Isobel appeared to be in perfect health when we left.'

"'Did you all leave together?'

"'Yes. It must have been around midnight, I suppose. Her butler had arranged for us to share a four-wheeler. I got back to the vicarage at about a quarter-to-one. I have the luxury of a telephone here, and it was this morning when I received a call from your police colleagues informing me of her death.' Naturally, I didn't bother correcting his assumption.

"'What did you talk about on the way home?'

'Nothing in particular. The usual inane chit-chat that one participates in during such circumstances. Much like the rest of the evening.'

"'You don't seem as though you were terribly enthusiastic about your cousin's invitation," I noted.

"'I wasn't particularly. I had to cancel choir practice.'

"Why didn't you just tell her you couldn't go?'

Reverend Laidlaw hesitated. "I . . . I just thought it would be the kind thing to do, given that she wanted some assistance with her affairs.'

"'Yes, very kind I'm sure," I said as I rose to leave. 'Thank you for your time, Reverend. No doubt I will be in touch.'

"Lytollis greeted my visit with the most enthusiasm. Unlike the previous two, he hadn't yet heard about his sister-in-law's death – not that prompted him to feign any form of loss. He launched straight into questions about the estate and the will. His enthusiasm was dampened a little when I informed him that I was there specifically to ask about the events of the previous evening.

"'What did you eat and drink at the dinner?'

"He was obviously taken aback by the question, 'I obviously couldn't swear to it, but I assume we all had the same thing: Isobel's cook produced a beautiful leg of lamb that was complemented by a fine claret. It was followed by a steam pudding. Why do you ask?'

"'Because Mr. Lytollis, your sister-in-law, appears to have been poisoned.'

"I could almost see his devious mind working overtime.

"'I didn't go anywhere near the kitchen – besides, in my case, I couldn't possibly have done such a thing.'

"'I'm not accusing you or anyone else of anything, Mr. Lytollis. I'm simply trying to establish the fact of what happened and when.'

417

"'Of course, of course,' he said, clearly relieved.

"What about the other person?" I asked. "This Simon Frobisher."

"He was missing, unfortunately, so I haven't had the chance to speak with him yet."

"They all seem a delightful group," I commented.

"You are getting very cynical these days, Watson," replied Holmes with a smile, "It really doesn't suit you. Nevertheless, there is more than an element of truth in what you state. I'm confident that they will all be available when the will is read."

We sat in silence for a moment and I checked my watch. It was just after five. I heard a foot on the stair and assumed it was Mrs. Hudson with some afternoon refreshment. Instead, there was a light knock on the door and Billy the page entered with his silver card tray.

"Letter for you Mr. Holmes," he said, standing to attention and offering the tray. "Came earlier, sir, when you were out."

"Thank you, Billy," Holmes suddenly looked unsure, as he slid the long cream envelope from the tray. It was as though he knew what the item was.

"What is it – were you expecting something?" I asked, as the page closed the door behind him. I sensed that all wasn't well, and noticed that the elegant cream stationery appeared to match the one I had handled earlier.

He stood up and very deliberately removed the jack-knife from the mantelpiece. Slitting open the envelope, he removed the contents and inspected the two items with his usual thoroughness before slumping back into his chair, almost letting the items drop to the floor as he held them delicately between the tips of his figures.

"Holmes, what is it?"

Without looking up from the fire, he gestured for me to take the papers from him. As he had taken the two items out of the envelope, I had observed that one was a cheque.

"Good Heavens!" I cried when I now saw the amount was for ten-thousand pounds. "Holmes, this is a king's ransom!" My friend snorted his derision.

The other item was a letter:

Eaton Square, SW1

Dear Mr. Holmes,

   I assume that we will not meet again. so I am writing to express my sincere thanks for your work and to apologise for deceiving you. You completed your commission with the utmost thoroughness and confirmed my worst fears about the people I am ashamed to call family members. What I failed to disclose to you, however, is that some months ago, after feeling a certain discomfort, my doctor, Verner, referred me to a specialist in Harley Street who diagnosed me with an aggressive cancer that couldn't be treated. I insisted that no one was to know about this – not even Doctor Verner, or my faithful and loyal staff, Mr. and Mrs. Brotherton.

Over the past few months, I have been self-administering morphine to ease the pain. As the pain has gradually increased, so has my dosage. It has now reached a point where I can't bear my condition, and fear of worse to come has brought me to the conclusion that now is the time to draw a curtain over the matter.

I should state categorically that I am ashamed to be associated with the people you investigated on my behalf. They are the epitome of avarice, profligacy, and duplicity. I would encourage the authorities to investigate their misdemeanours further and take whatever action is appropriate.

It is mischievous of me to intimate that one or all of them will also be responsible for my demise, but I must state in the interest of fairness that, to the best of my knowledge, they aren't murderers – not in my case at least. My death will be at my own hand. Whoever clears my home should find an empty vile in the top drawer of my dresser. This vile contained the morphine with which I contaminated – or should that be, will contaminate – my own wine. The purpose of your investigation was to confirm my worst fears before I commit what some may view as a crime against human decency. I can only hope anyone who judges me doesn't have to suffer the same illness themselves.

I would be obliged if you would carry out two further tasks as part of your commission: First, I have arranged for my solicitor to read my will seven days after my death. I would like you to attend on my behalf and subdue any disputes that may arise. Second, you have my permission to hand your findings regarding my family members' actions over to the police, where I hope they will take the appropriate action. I hope the enclosed cheque will suitably recompense you for your work any further inconvenience.

Once again Mr. Holmes, thank you for your marvellous work, and I again beg your forgiveness regarding my necessary subterfuge. Do not think too harshly of me, and believe me to be –

419

Very sincerely yours,

Isobel Frobisher

As I read, Holmes continued to stare into the fire that crackled and sparked – the only thing that broke the silence in the room. I sat back down and I looked at the postmark on the envelope – it was dated the previous day.

"What a remarkable woman. She must have posted this yesterday, knowing what events were to follow later that night." Holmes didn't respond. "Will you adhere to her final two wishes?"

He was clearly angry. "This is a new nadir, Watson. I have been reduced to police messenger and arbiter to squabbling families. I can promise her one of her wishes, but not the other."

Chapter III

Two days following the revelation, the results of the *post mortem* confirmed that the cause of death was excessive amounts of morphine in the body. I mused that Lady Isobel must have organised the dinner party as a final act of revenge against those who had wronged her, in order to mislead them into believing they were in line to inherit her fortune, whilst at the same time, casting suspicion on them regarding her pending death.

Holmes didn't disagree with any of my conclusions, but showed little interest in discussing the case further. Since receiving the Dowager's final letter which solved the mystery of her death and, despite the financial recompense received from his former client, he gradually sunk into one of his dark fits of depression as the week went on, clearly wanting nothing more to do with the matter.

On several occasions during our many years together, Holmes has asked me to represent him and carry out investigations on his behalf, as he claimed to be unavailable. On this occasion, he requested I go along to the solicitor's office of Lady Isobel and be present for the reading of her will.

I therefore acceded to his request and attended the offices of William James, who had apparently been Lord and Lady Frobisher's solicitor for years. It was on the seventh day following the Dowager's death that I joined a group of people in the anteroom of his chambers, waiting to be admitted. Looking around the room, it was obvious to me from the descriptions given by Holmes who those present were. Mr. and Mrs. Brotherton were also present at the instruction of Mr. James. Brotherton and I acknowledged each other when I arrived, much to the surprise and

420

confusion of the others who had never set eyes on me. Everyone sat in uncomfortable silence, alone with their thoughts.

I decided it was appropriate to speak and cleared my throat. "Good morning, everyone. I assume you are all here to hear the reading of Lady Isobel's Will. Perhaps I could introduce myself as a matter of courtesy. My name is Doctor John Watson. I'm the *locum* doctor who was called to the home of the Dowager on the morning she died."

"What are you doing here?" asked the haughty young woman, shamelessly smoking a cigarette – presumably Celia Frobisher.

"I was asked to attend."

"By whom?"

I was saved from further whittering by Mr. William James, who appeared at his office door. "Sorry to keep you all waiting. You can come through now."

I waited for the others to enter the spacious office and brought up the rear. As I did so – and naturally unseen by the others – Inspector Jones and four of his constables came through the main entrance and took their seats in the waiting room.

Holmes's last contribution to the case had been to hand his findings over to Scotland Yard the previous day. Jones and I nodded at one another before I entered Mr. James's office and closed the door behind me.

The solicitor took his seat. "Good morning, everyone. Just to confirm that my name is William James and I am Lady Isobel's solicitor and Executor of her will, which is the reason we are all here today.

"I don't know why *they* should be here," said the young woman I took to be Celia Frobisher, tossing an insulting head towards Brotherton and his wife. "Surely it should be family only."

"All those present are at the request of your aunt, Miss Frobisher," said the solicitor, calmly. "Now if you would all be seated, we will go over the contents of Lady Isobel's Will.

He proceeded to go over the peripheral and procedural points of the document before delivering the news that hit the room like a shell:

> I bequeath the whole of my estate in its entirety to Robert and Martha Brotherton.

There was an audible gasp. Before anyone could respond, Mr. James added:

> I wish to exclude from my Will the following people: My niece Celia Frobisher, my cousin Christopher Laidlaw, my brother-

421

in-law Noel Lytollis, and my late husband's cousin, Simon Frobisher.

"This is *outrageous!*" shrieked Celia Frobisher. "She must have been coerced into this nonsense. They obviously poisoned her!" She speared an accusing finger in the direction of the named beneficiaries.

Martha Brotherton began to sob into a handkerchief, while her husband sat there looking shocked at what had just happened.

"There, you see!" continued Miss Frobisher. "Proof of their guilt!"

"Your aunt changed her will only a fortnight ago, Miss Frobisher, and added a codicil, giving the reasons for her amendments."

This momentarily prompted silence in the room and allowed the solicitor to produce the document from the bottom of the pile of papers. He read:

> *The reason for my decision is that Mr. Robert Brotherton and his wife Martha have been faithful servants and friends (yes, friends) of both myself and my late husband for many years. I have found their loyalty and selflessness humbling and their behaviour should be held up as an example to all.*
>
> *Equally, I exclude the few family members I have remaining, as their behaviour is the opposite to that which is demonstrated by my deserving beneficiaries. I shall leave it to Scotland Yard to decide whether previous actions perpetrated by those excluded from my Will constitute criminal behaviour.*

After the shock of the announcement, there was a silence in the room that hung like a dead weight. It was the clearly nervous Reverend Christopher Laidlaw who broke it by asking, "What evidence does the Dowager have of *criminal behaviour?*"

"Perhaps you could help in that regard, Doctor Watson," said Mr. James.

With that, everyone turned to look at me. I had been sitting quietly to the side of William James's desk.

"Certainly, and perhaps I could invite Inspector Jones to join us." I called Jones into the office before continuing. His arrival seemed to cause an element of discomfort as those present shuffled in their seats. "I introduced myself earlier as Lady Isobel's *locum* doctor, which is perfectly true, but I'm also the associate of Mr. Sherlock Holmes, who is a private consulting detective. Lady Isobel commissioned Mr. Holmes two weeks ago to investigate the crimes that she suspected you of committing."

422

"I was aware of no investigation!" Celia Frobisher's tone had weakened somewhat signalling a diminishing of confidence.

"That is what you *can* be aware of when Mr. Holmes carries out his work." I must confess I did enjoy the statement. "You may remember being visited recently by Mr. Holmes under the guise of a 'Mr. Smike'." The sense of realisation in the room was palpable and Laidlaw actually bowed his head.

"What I can confirm is that all family members here present are perfectly innocent of any wrongdoing as far as the health of Lady Isobel is concerned, either before the night of the gathering, or on the night itself."

"There! That proves it! It must have been Brotherton that did it!"

"Be quiet you idiot!" It was Christopher Laidlaw who rebuked his cousin.

I continued, "What none of you knew was that Lady Isobel had been suffering with cancer for more than a year and had been taking morphine to alleviate the increasing pain. At a recent consultation, she was told that her condition was terminal and that she only had a few months left at most. Therefore, she got her affairs in order and changed her will, something that she hadn't done since the death of the Earl.

"She then knowingly self-administered an excessive draught of morphine after you all left the other night." Again, there was silence. "I am afraid that Lady Frobisher was ashamed of you all."

"Where is your proof of that?" Celia Frobisher's confidence was deserting her as she clutched at her final straw.

"Mr. Holmes reported his findings to the Dowager and with that, she ended his commission. Following her death, Holmes received a letter from her, revealing her illness and her feelings towards you all.

"Regarding yourself, Miss Frobisher: Your aunt told Mr. Holmes that you did nothing but bring the family name into disrepute, squandering your father's money and even using some of it as collateral in a conspiracy to embezzle funds from financial agents both here and abroad – which he confirmed.

"Then there is you, Reverend Laidlaw." All eyes moved from one to the other. "The bishop and archbishop may have forgiven your sins, but I'm not sure the authorities may be quite so understanding.

"As for Mr. Lytollis – " He must have felt the collective stare of those present boring into him. " – Mr. Holmes found evidence that the fire which took the life of the Dowager's sister could only have been started deliberately from *outside* the house and not by accident from inside as you claimed. You are therefore directly responsible for the death of your wife.

"Finally, Mr. Frobisher: Not only was it discovered that you tried to impersonate your cousin, the late Earl, on more than one occasion, you actually posed as Inspector Lestrade of Scotland Yard in an attempt to gain entry to the Christmas Ball at Windsor Castle last year." At this, Inspector Jones – who hitherto had had been unaware of this last revelation – managed to disguise a snorted laugh as an unexpected coughing fit. "Lady Isobel asked Mr. Holmes to turn over his findings to the police who will decide on the appropriate action, so I will now invite Inspector Jones to take over."

Jones called on his uniformed officers to enter before addressing his suspects, "I would like the four of you to accompany us to the Scotland Yard for questioning."

As they were being escorted out, Mr. Brotherton – who had been sitting quietly throughout – asked. "What about my wife and myself, Doctor Watson?"

"You, Mr. Brotherton? I suggest that you both enjoy your newfound wealth."

The Confounding
Confessional Confrontation
by Kevin P. Thornton

The seal of the confessional in the Roman Catholic Church prohibits a priest from disclosing the identity of a confessant – and the sin or sins the confessant has confessed – without exception.

Sherlock Holmes's life, or at least the parts of his life I have been witness to, has been one of adventure and also of secrets. As a result, there are many of his stories that will not be published until long after we are gone. Occasionally when I review the tales I have locked away until such time as they secrets can do no harm, one character looms large in them, as a catalyst anyway – a man who is only fleetingly referred to in those that I have already deemed fit for public consumption.

I had first met my friend's brother Mycroft during the tale I would eventually call "The Greek Interpreter". His was a shadowy existence, partly due to his reticence, but also because of his value to Her Majesty's Government. He is referred to only fleetingly in my initial tales because much of what he brought to 221b Baker Street was so sensitive that Kingdoms might have fallen and countries divided had news of the investigations leaked. Those that are *in pectore*, the ones that I cannot publish, refer to him much more. When Mycroft handed cases to his brother, they were often highly confidential, delicate and, sometimes even with a most secret status.

This wasn't one of those.

"I have been summonsed, Watson, on a matter of some small importance, by the Government of the day." Sherlock Holmes was standing at the window, looking down at the street. "Ah yes," he muttered, "my brother is as presumptuous as ever. He has even sent transport to speed up our travels." As he turned to face me, he handed me the telegram he had received.

S

Trivial matter St. Polycarp. See to it.

M

425

"That hardly seems urgent," I said.

"Is that not the way of English gentlemen?" said Holmes. "It is certainly Mycroft's way as a means of drawing me into his scheming. Yet he knows I will respond. Despite the message, he would never knowingly involve me in something trivial, and he has even sent transport to take us to Victoria Station, an expense Her Britannic Majesty's Government is normally loathe to spend. Do you have anything on today? If not, come with me to Brighton. I am sure it will be an interesting little adventure, and one day you may even be able to exaggerate it into your scribblings."

I didn't need a second invitation and, as my patients all seemed to be in rude health, I had no hesitation in following him down the stairs into the waiting cab.

The driver seemed to have been transported in time from the Circus Maximus, because he tore through the streets as if chased by rampaging Visigoths. His speed and recklessness were soon explained. The train had been held for us.

"I have never heard of such a thing before," I said as we rushed past the dirty-looks of passengers and the power-struck awe of the porters. "I didn't know it was even possible to delay a train. Their timetables are defined to the minute."

"I have only ever experienced this twice before," said Holmes. "On both occasions, Mycroft's hand was in play."

As we settled into the seats of our private compartment, I said, "There was no mention of a destination on the message. How did you know where we were headed? Brighton wasn't a surprise?

"If he had noted we were to go to Saint John's or Saint Mary's," said Holmes, "then I confess it would have been harder to deduce. There is only one church in the land that is named after Saint Polycarp of Smyrna, and for good reason: It is one of the few new Roman churches in the Arundel area not paid for by the Duke of Norfolk. There is a story that even the largesse of the Howard family had limits, and the Diocese went to the well one too many times. The thirteenth Duke tired of the pre-suppositions of the Bishop and asked his cousin, Father Howard, to deliver the message that they need best find another means to pay for the building – a cruel trick."

"Cruel in what way?" I asked.

"As the bearer of bad tidings," he continued, "Father Howard, instead of being posted to Rome, ended up as a missionary in Goa. The Bishop was so incensed at the Duke's refusal that he arranged for the early years of Father Howard's career to be in a colonial backwater. He then found someone else to pay for the building, provided it was named after a favoured servant of the church. Hence Saint Polycarp."

426

As usual, if Holmes actually answered one question he left two more unfulfilled,

"How do you know all of this?" I said.

"There was a time when I knew Father Howard," said Holmes. "A time when I was impressed by him. He was soldier once, before taking Holy Orders, and as a member of the Howard family who have supplied much of England's history, he wasn't a total waste of time. Indeed, the Howards are middling, I suppose, as noble families go. Fifteen Dukes – the most senior Dukedom in the land – as well as Earls Marshal and the most prominent recusants in the last four-hundred years. The Howards are descended from King Edward I and III and have two martyrs to their faith among their ranks, as well as two Cardinals and two of the wives of Henry VIII."

"Which two?"

"The two who were beheaded." Holmes permitted himself a tiny smile. "I think that answer fits both the wives and the martyrs. The Howards weren't always known for their tact."

"You rank them as middling nobility. I have heard you opine before about what a waste of time nobility and royalty are. Middling is almost a compliment."

"Indeed. If I was to attempt to codify the various chinless families of the realm, middling would be the highest rank."

"I would be interested to hear more of your pseudo-scientific system one day."

"I'm afraid your wish will remain unrequited. There aren't enough descriptors below the rank of dismal to do most of the noble families justice."

"You sound as if you know a lot about them," I said. "The Howards that is."

"I know too much to know that I know not enough about them, and wish for it to remain so. I have had dealings with members of the family before," he continued. "There are many of them, some as contemptible as the lowest scum of the docklands gutters. As a whole, they seem less annoying than most of their ilk, and Father Howard a lot less than that. It would have been easy for him to follow a well-trodden path and end up, like much of his family, as another cog in the Empire. But he gave it all up to become a priest."

"And you admired him?" I asked.

"I admired his gumption. I have never favoured any form of organized religion, as you well know. Occasionally someone will impress me, despite the shackles of their beliefs. Father Edward Howard, by his own example and the way he lived his life, came closer to changing my mind than any other."

I wanted to ask, "Change your mind about what?" but he closed his eyes and settled back into his seat.

We pulled into Brighton and were met by Inspector Honiball, who had transport waiting. He was a tall man, the apparent size of a labourer, although that was unclear as he wore a warm padded jacket against the elements. He extended his right hand in greeting even as he checked his pocket watch for the time. "Call me Peter," he said.

"During your service overseas," asked Holmes, "did you ever deal with either a high-profile or a politicised murder?"

"What? How did . . . ?" The inspector smiled. "I see the stories about you are true, Mister Holmes. Did my accent give me away? Can you tell where I served?"

"My first thought was New Zealand, but I am now inclined towards Africa. Not quite the southern Cape, nor Algoa. The Colony of Natal, perhaps?"

Honiball smiled in delight. "Wondrous, Mister Holmes, truly wondrous! And in answer: No, I haven't had much chance to hone my skills as a detective. My promotion is rather recent."

"Do you perhaps understand why you have been given charge of this case?" asked Holmes. "It's unusual, is it not, for the low-ranking inspector to be given a career-making case?

"Career-making cases can also be career-breaking," I said, and the inspector's face flinched a smidgen, as if in belated recognition.

"I was already on call about another case, but I should imagine I have been given this as well because I am Catholic," said Honiball, "the only one of higher rank in our town. I believe, due to the sensitive nature of the crime, the people in power are hoping this goes away quickly. If it does, credit will be claimed elsewhere. If it doesn't, I will make a suitable tethered goat for the scavengers of Fleet Street and Whitehall."

"Why is it so sensitive?" I asked.

"The murder took place in the confessional, on the confessant's side," said Honiball. I had my confessants and confessors in disarray. Honiball helped out with a stage whisper – "The sinner's side." – and I thanked him. "Ostensibly, it is just a murder case, but anything to do with the Catholic faith carries history, given how long the church was illegal. Also, they can hide behind their nation-state status, and Arundel and Brighton are seen to be Papist-enclaves, given who the largest employer in the area is. The Duke of Norfolk holds sway in all manner of matters, and the Howard family have been suspected of divided loyalties for hundreds of years."

428

"What do you think of your religion's ability to hide transgressions under the cloak of diplomacy?" said Holmes.

"I think the seventeenth verse of the twelfth chapter of Mark covers the topic concisely enough," said Honiball.

"Tactful," said Holmes, "but I would prefer your honest opinion."

"Well then, I believe I have been given charge of this investigation for two reasons: As a sergeant, my rate of clearance of investigations was unparalleled – hence my promotion, despite my beliefs."

"And the other reason," I asked.

"If this death has an untenable explanation, I will take the blame as part of the worldwide Papist conspiracy – hence my earlier tethered goat analogy." Honiball smile as he said this, as if to ameliorate his harsh words, but the smile didn't reach the eyes. "If you would be so kind, Mister Holmes, to find a tenable solution, it would be best for all."

We pulled up to the front door of St. Polycarp of Smyrna Catholic Church and followed Honiball inside.

"What can you tell me about the murder?" asked Holmes.

"Not much," said the inspector. "The constable is quite a bright young lad, and he feels he wasn't called right away. The story he was told is that there was a dead man in the church. He was shown to the body by, and I quote, 'an old fat man wearing a dress' who was quite unhelpful."

"Was the corpulent priest, for that is who your constable surely met, the witness to the murder, and is he the master of this domain?"

"He received no answers, but the constable thinks it unlikely. The large man in the dress is an unknown, a visitor to the parish. He also didn't think that the man was hearing confessions."

"And why would that be?" I asked.

"Because the inspector's constable is observant," said Holmes, "and doesn't think he would fit in the confessional."

"That's exactly right," said Honiball. He had led us across to the confessional boxes in an alcove off the nave of the church. There was a constable standing at ease near the entrance.

"Where is the body?" said Holmes.

"Despite my protestations, he has been taken away. I have notes that I took."

"Please," said Holmes, "give us the salient points."

I looked at the contraption in front of me. It was a large wooden apparatus, and looked like two medieval sedan chairs placed end to end, *sans* handles.

"The Confessional," began Honiball, "is this wooden boxlike piece of furniture weighing approximately thirty stone, slightly over four-hundred pounds. It is seven feet in height with a breadth of about the same, and a depth of four. As you can see, it has been moved from its normal place." Honiball pointed at the scratches on the floor as he said this. "In addition, the door on the penitent's side is damaged, half off the hinges, and the handle on the confessor's side looks marred in some manner. As to the body, there was a mark on the head behind the left ear. There are also a few hairs and a smattering of blood on the corner of the archway." He pointed at the spot then turned to look at Holmes. "I think that the priest was in his confessional. Someone came in and jammed him in so he couldn't interfere. Then the killer grabbed the victim, pulled him out and swung him in such a way that his head hit the stone corner, and he expired.

"Capital work, Honiball. You have deduced the easiest and most logical possibility of eight scenarios."

"Eight?" I said in astonishment.

"At the very least. The man who died – was he actually the man in the confessional or was he the third man, overpowered by the seeker of contrition, or the priest, or the two together? Is the priest even a priest? Were there only two people involved, in which case is the priest the killer, or were there three, or four, or seventeen? All of these questions might have been answered with the body *in situ*." Holmes glanced up at the astonished look on the inspector's face. "Calm yourself, Honiball. I don't mean to chide. Your thinking was stellar, if unimaginative, and you have reached the most likely outcome. Good work, man, good work. How did you estimate the weight of the confessional?"

"Ah," said Honiball. "I was one of the volunteers who helped to offload it when it arrived. The carpenter said it was more than four-hundred pounds as a warning to us so we would proceed with caution. That was some years back, before I went overseas, but I'll not forget that day, Mister Holmes. There were only three of us, and getting it up the steps outside nearly killed us all."

"Indeed," said Holmes, examining the handle. "Yet something was placed here to lock the priest in. The killer had no quarrel with him and wanted to make sure he didn't see anything."

"Begging your pardon, Mister Holmes," said Honiball. "I have just remembered. There is a trick with the candlestick from the side chapel." He pointed in the direction of the alcove and, before any of us could ask more, he fetched the single candlestick from the altar, removed the candle, and put the open end through the handle on the priest's side of the box where it was a perfect jam against the jamb.

"You were an altar server in this parish," said Holmes to the inspector. "Oh, don't look so surprised. Who else would know such a thing?

430

"I was," Honiball answered, "and I can tell you that every priest who heard confession here was caught out at least once."

"This tells us, said Holmes, "that someone had prior knowledge of the antics in this church. It means that the possibilities of how the murder was committed have been reduced by half." I must still have had my confused countenance apparent.

"There had to have been at least three involved," said Holmes "The priest couldn't lock himself into the confessional, and it is unlikely the victim did so before running himself into the stone corner."

Holmes opened the priest's side and looked inside the box, even going so far as to sit down and peer out. Then he invited me to do the same. There was a mesh panel between the two sides which allowed sounds to pass through easily, and visibility would normally be restricted. The inside of the cubicle would be dark with the door shut, but as it was, with the door on the penitent's side ripped open and the angle of the confessional altered by the violence of the altercation, it was possible to see outside the box – more specifically to see the part of the archway where the dead man had hit his head.

"The priest must have seen something," I said

"It is certainly possible," said Holmes, "and if the killer realizes this he will return to finish the job." He turned to Honiball, appraised him, and clapped him on the shoulder. "Good work." Then Holmes asked, "What manner of man was the victim? Tall, short, old, young? Would he have been easily overpowered?"

The inspector looked at his notes once more. "The body was that of an Oriental male, approximately two inches over five feet and possibly as much as eight-and-a-half stone. He presented as a Chinese, though he may very well have been from any one of many peoples. Japanese and Siamese also come to mind. Age was hard to estimate – older than twenty, maybe younger than forty."

"Inspector, could you direct your man to the likely spots in the vicinity to see if there are any men of such description missing? There can't be that many Oriental people in Brighton."

Honiball nodded to the constable. Before he could leave, Holmes added, "Constable, might I suggest you try the laundries. The inspector may be able to guide you as to where to go. By the look of the crispness of his shirt collar and right cuff, he is a customer of at least one of them. That is an exemplary starching."

Honiball seemed taken aback by Holmes's perspicacity. Nevertheless, he mentioned three likely places to the constable."

"What about Lonnie Chu's?" asked the constable. "The one where the girl was murdered last night. Shaken to death, she was," he said, "till

431

the blood came out her nose. It was horrible." The inspector's frown shut the constable up, and he stepped back as if chastened.

"I didn't know it had opened again," said Honiball. "I don't think it's necessary to go all the way there just yet. See to the others"

The constable had a look on his face as if he needed clarification, but he left at the dash. Meanwhile, Holmes was examining where the blood and hairs were on the stone.

"He was a small man then," said Holmes, "of slight weight, even given his size. He doesn't seem like someone who could move a solid confessional from its normal resting place. But was he someone who knew this parish, knew the trick with the candlestick. Inspector, do we know who found the priest and released him? Whoever it was knew enough to replace the candle in the stick and return it to the altar. I wonder what they wished to cover up. Let us question the confessor and the strange giant, and discover what mumbo-jumbo they wish to hide behind instead of presenting the truth."

"Oh, for Heaven's sake, Sherlock!" said a voice from behind. "There is no mumbo-jumbo, and no cover-up as much as a tidy-up. And you will only question Father Chiou in my presence."

The man behind us was nearly six-and-a-half feet tall and seemed almost as wide. He wore a shimmering black cassock, tailored in the finest silk. The quality of his robes and the black zucchetto on his head marked him as someone of importance, but I didn't know enough about the Roman hierarchy, and the differing reactions of my two companions didn't immediately answer my question. Who was he?

"Eminence," said Honiball and his body hovered between kneeling in obeisance and standing up for the long arm of the law. This resulted in him bobbing up and down like a boy on a buoy in the bay.

"Edward," said Holmes. "I suspected your hand in my involvement. I shall have to have a word with Mycroft about the company he keeps."

"Your brother bent to the winds of political expediency once the Nuncio invoked privilege," he replied. Turning to me he said, "You must be Doctor Watson. Mycroft speaks very highly of you." I was surprised and a little flattered, but before I could say so, Holmes interjected:

"Watson, allow me to introduce Father Edward Howard, one time conscience of the local nobility until he went to Rome and lost his way."

This seemed to amuse the priest, but less so Honiball, who looked as if he'd as soon run for the door. "Doctor Watson," he whispered in my ear, "that ain't no priest. That's a Cardinal."

His Eminence Edward Henry Cardinal Howard seemed to have had more titles than his relative the Duke of Norfolk. He was currently the

Cardinal-Bishop of Frascati, and formerly the Archpriest of St. Peter's Basilica, Titular Archbishop of Neocaesarea in Ponto, and Cardinal-Priest of the Basilica of Saints John and Paul on the Caelian Hill. In addition, he was once an officer in the Life Guards, and at various stages of his life he had been the nephew of the Twelfth Duke of Norfolk, cousin of the Thirteenth, uncle-once-removed of the Fourteenth, twice of the Fifteenth, and thrice of the Sixteenth. Despite the clear evidence that he ate unwisely and too well – my immediate estimate was the Cardinal was somewhere near thirty stone – he was a man who impressed easily, and as we moved through the church, he mentioned that he had retired and come home.

Holmes seemed indifferent. This was not unusual. I had seen him deal with princes as intellectual paupers, dukes as thugs, barons as robbers, and members of the Royal Family with barely controlled patience. Cardinals, it would seem, fell well within his poor views on societal self-perpetuating systems.

The Cardinal led us into the presbytery next door, stopped in the reception area, and said, "This time there are some ground rules, Sherlock."

"Ground rules?" said Holmes. "In a murder investigation. I think not." He turned to Inspector Honiball. "I wish you well, Inspector, but I cannot be part of this." He returned to the Cardinal and said, "I will inform my brother that this lunacy is over. I cannot begin to comprehend why he thought to send me here. Good day, sir."

"Sherlock," said the Cardinal, softly first, then more insistent. "Sherlock, please. You are here because I asked for you."

I don't think that Holmes expected that. "Then why did you not ask me yourself?" he said.

"I didn't know if you would come."

There was much left unsaid between the two, and so many questions that I wished to blurt out. I maintained my silence, though. Holmes, as always, would tell me what he wanted when he felt the time was ripe.

"You cannot question the priest," said Cardinal Howard. "If you try to, I will take him out of here and straight to Rome under diplomatic protection."

"Why?" said Holmes. "And why waste my time?"

"You cannot even look at him," said the Cardinal. "If you do, we will leave."

"One of these days, Edward, you will break these shackles that bind you, and you will again be the man I once knew. If you have created all these restrictions, what can I do that will be of any value?"

433

The Cardinal ignored Holmes and turned to the Honiball. "Inspector, I know you are of the Faith. For that reason, I have permission from your superiors to dismiss you for now. Believe me, it is for the best."

Honiball didn't look happy, and he left an angry man.

Holmes said, "Why all the games, Edward?"

"Once you have worked it out, you'll see why, and this time I will have done my duty by my priest. Think of it as an intellectual challenge. You may ask what you wish and I will answer what I can. Together, we will reach a satisfactory result. Please stay here until I prepare the room next door." He left us and I looked at my friend. His eyebrows were slightly raised in surprise, which was about as emotional as his features ever reached when he was working. I thought he would pace, or stare out the window. Instead he started to talk. It was for my benefit, but almost seemed to be telling the story to himself in reminder.

"Some years before I met you, I was in France, honing my fighting skills at a school of Savate. Edward was in the same village. He wasn't a Cardinal then. I'm not sure what he was. He has never delighted in the pomp of his roles, and even now, as you saw, he is dressed in the black of a priest only, albeit one with little concept of what a vow of poverty looks like.

"A church had been robbed while the priest was in his box forgiving sins. Edward told me that the priest couldn't answer me, as he could not break the seal of the confessional."

"And yet he must have done," I said.

"He did," said Holmes. "Inadvertently."

"I don't understand," I said.

"I asked him some questions anyway," said Holmes. "He didn't answer me vocally, but there are a whole range of mannerisms and tics that I knew would lead me to the truth. Just as I can look at a man and tell his profession, where he lives, and sometimes even what he is thinking, I could read this priest like a ha-penny dreadful. His reaction to my first question was fodder for my second, which led to the third, and then the fourth. Then I told him what had happened and he burst into tears."

"The burden must have been a heavy one to bear," I said.

"Not in the way you imagine. There was no seal of the confessional to break because there had been no other person – no thief save himself."

"The priest did it?" I said

"Indeed. He was a gambler who owed money to some bookmakers, and he was trying to get out from under his debt. He pretended they had been stolen by a penitent so he wouldn't have to say anything."

"Why then is the Cardinal so cautious?"

434

"He was disappointed at what he viewed as my trickery. We had become friends, and I think he felt betrayed at how easily I could have broken his silly confessional rules. He is taking precautions now." Holmes paused, as if wondering how to phrase what he wished to say. "There is a tale told of the Cree Tribe of Northern Canada. The missionary priests spent many years converting them all to the faith. With that came all the rules that such conversions require. 'Christians don't do this, they can't do that, and they definitely can't do that.' To a people born free, it was confusing. One of the elders one day asked the priest, 'There seem to be a lot of reasons why a Christian can go to Hell. What would have happened to me if I didn't know about God and sin? Would I still go there when I died?'

'No,' said the priest. 'Because you did not know. God would not have punished you.'

'Then why did you tell me?'"

I took a moment to understand what had just happened. "Holmes," I asked in astonishment, "did you just tell a joke?"

"Of course not. I merely used levity to make a point. The Cardinal is like the Cree Elder. The last time I questioned a priest under his charge, I would have been able to break their confessional walls, had there been any to break. Cardinal Howard would not have done anything wrong, as he couldn't have known of my skills, but he still felt guilty of negligence, I suppose. This time, knowing more of my particular talents, he has to try so much harder. He is unwilling to let me read anything from the priest."

"Then why did he ask for you?"

"That is a question still to be answered."

The Cardinal returned and for a moment his urbanity had deserted him. "Doctor Watson, could I please trouble you for your medical expertise." Puzzled, I followed him in to the other room. The priest lay on the armchair. Had he not had a cassock on, I could easily have seen Inspector Honiball's description of the murder victim in this man as well. Oriental, short, slight and between twenty and forty. The armchair seemed large enough to seat the Cardinal. The priest was curled up on it, shivering. I turned to the Cardinal. "Out," I said. "This man is now my patient." I had expected an argument, but instead he left, closing the door behind him.

The priest was scared, the beat of his heart was elevated, and his answers to my questions were short, as if he was duty-bound and would sooner have been anywhere else. He would be better after bed rest and a calming of his tensions.

I went out to see Holmes and Cardinal Howard some ten minutes later. "Physically there is nothing wrong with him that rest and peace will not cure," I said. "He appears to understand me well enough, but his spoken English is basic."

"He has come to England to learn the language," said the Cardinal. "Well, that's it I'm afraid. The priest is in a funk and cannot be questioned."

"That is not what he needs," I said. "And please don't re-interpret what I said for your own agenda. Your priest is scared and badly affected by what happened, but I believe his best cure is a resolution to the events of this morning. You may proceed if you wish. I will sit with Father Chiou and monitor his health while you two stare at each other and play mental chess.

"I cannot allow that," said the Cardinal.

"You have no more say in the matter. Father Chiou is now my patient. Whatever happened needs to be addressed, and in that, Holmes is likely his best chance. If you don't allow this to happen, then I will have no choice but to remove him into my care."

Holmes chimed in at the right moment. "Excellent. We'll find the answers then, once we are away from this turbulent priest."

"I must protect the seal of the confessional," said the Cardinal.

"Then proceed," I said. "I am bound by a higher oath, that of Hippocrates. I will do my job. Holmes will agree to your terms and do his. And you will be as helpful as you can be and do yours. Let us proceed."

And so the strangest interview of Holmes's career began. I sat at the back of the room tending to Father Chiou. Most of my treatment consisted of him holding my hand as tightly as he could, as if to draw strength from me. He was hesitant, as if he didn't quite know what was happening, and he was unhappy about it. I think he would have run if not for his sense of duty to his church.

Holmes sat in front of me, facing the Cardinal. I'm sure that there was a part of him that relished the challenge. In many ways it was his ultimate test: To solve a murder by an extraction of abstractions without questioning the witness. Truly I thought I saw him quiver in anticipation, though he would deny such a question.

Cardinal Howard faced him in such a way that he could watch me as well, as if making sure I gave no help to my friend.

"Let us review then," said Holmes. "The seal of the confessional prohibits a priest from disclosing the identity of a penitent – and the sin or sins the penitent has confessed – without exception. He can make no comment whatever about what he has heard."

"About what he has *learned*," said the Cardinal. "Not what he has *heard*. We changed that recently."

Holmes nodded modestly. "Then can you tell me what happened?"

"I cannot. But if you ask me questions, I will be able to answer, based on my experience as a priest, what *might* have happened."

Holmes, rather than getting annoyed, took to the challenge as a man born for the hunt.

"Is the victim the penitent himself, or is he the third party to the fracas?"

"He is likely one or the other, in a situation where, including the priest, there were only three people involved."

"Is that the case?" said Holmes.

"I don't know."

Holmes made a noise that sounded like a stifled laugh. "You enjoy this too much, Priest," he said. "If the murder victim was also the attacker, his aggression wouldn't have moved the confessional so. He is a small man. Watson!" he barked suddenly, startling me and putting the fear of God into Father Chiou. "Does the priest understand our conversation."

"Hardly," I said, answering quickly, lest Cardinal Howard try to prevent me. "He is barely reacting to anything you say."

The Cardinal stood up, his gravitas and anger unleashed in a display that would have breathed Hellfire from the pulpit. "This is over!" he thundered. "I warned you what would happen if you tried to break the solemn seal."

"Ha!" said Holmes, "This isn't about your secrets and lies. It's about not knowing who to trust. Once again there is no seal of the confessional to break, there is only fear. Father Chiou saw the man who murdered his penitent and he is scared – not of breaking the seal of the sacrament of confession, but of qualifying for whatever sacrament it is you reserve for the dead. Well, I, Sherlock Holmes, will not have that on my conscience."

And with that, he went to the door and jerked it open. Inspector Honiball fell into the room. This wasn't the calm and rational policeman of before, but a man enraged. He gathered himself and made a leap for my patient. As I turned in his defense, Holmes tried to scrabble past the Cardinal to stall the inspector. He was too late, but his effort was unnecessary. Cardinal Howard, lighter on his feet than I thought possible, charged into Honiball. It was like a bull crumpling a feather. Although Honiball was a tall man, near six feet and close to fourteen stone, the Cardinal knocked him into the wall so hard he fell to the ground with a sickening crunch of a sound, stunned and bent over at the ribcage. Holmes went back to the door. The constable was standing there, one hand raised as if in question.

"Give me your handcuffs," said Holmes, "and go and fetch more police, many more – and at least one of them needs to outrank your inspector."

It took a while. The police are loathe to arrest their own kind, especially on the say so of a civilian, but Cardinal Howard was who he was and they had also heard of Sherlock Holmes. They listened with respect, took Honiball away in chains, and promised to come back with even higher-ranking officers. "We will be gone by then," said Holmes quietly to me as one who loathed bureaucracy. I called a local doctor, and we gave Father Chiou a sedative and sent him to bed under the care of a nun from the convent next door. The poor priest's English was less-than-adequate, which made him perfect for hearing confessions, I suppose, but it was enough for him to thank Holmes and me, and to try and kiss the Cardinal's feet. Howard would have none of that.

Father Chiou hadn't been able to tell us much. He hadn't really understood. One minute he was hearing confession, the next he was watching his confessant get killed, all the while locked in his little room and unable to get out.

"Then the man he saw kill his cousin showed up at the presbytery carrying a Police Inspector's identification," said Holmes.

"Ah, you guessed that part as well," said Cardinal Howard. "I suspected it from the moment I saw Father Chiou's reaction, and I knew no one in the constabulary well enough to trust them. It was why I needed you."

"I do not guess anything," said Holmes. "I see all, I deduce all, and then I know all."

"We have someone like that as well," replied the Cardinal. "We call him God." There was a tinge of a hesitation before he chuckled into his snifter. Holmes let out a gentle snort, and I looked from one to the other as if I was seated in the middle stand at the All-England Lawn Tennis Club Championship match watching a volley rally.

"Why didn't you tell me what you suspected?" said Holmes.

"After our last *tête-à-tête*, I took time to study what you had shown me in France about reading actions of people and their body movement. Father Chiou was already jumpy, but at first I put that down to his origins in the East, where there is a legitimate distrust of authorities."

"Please," I said. "Eminence, Holmes – Can you assume, like most times, that I am lost, and explain to me how you blamed the police inspector for murder?"

"Two murders actually," said Holmes. "The penitent and girl who was killed near Lonnie Chu's laundry." He smiled at me in that way of his that made my blood boil. "Don't worry. This was an interesting and convoluted case made more so by the superstitious natures of the people involved. I'm not surprised you missed all the salient details."

"Mycroft said you had the patience of a saint," said the Cardinal to me. "Holmes is lucky to have you as a friend. Tell him, Sherlock, or I will."

"The murder at Lonnie Chu's laundry was seen by someone, likely our second victim. The circumstances do not matter. What does matter was he knew the killer, knew his name and rank, and knew he couldn't go to the police with what he had witnessed. Instead, he came to the one man who would understand his fears, the visiting Chinese priest. They may even have been of the same clan back in China."

"The spelling is different," I said taking out my notebook where I scribbled my notes. "Chu and Chiou."

"The family names," said Cardinal Howard, "derive from a written language which is logographic, pictures representing sounds. Chu, when translated to English, can have several spellings. There is another cousin in town, a cobbler, spelt Choo."

"No matter," said Holmes. "He may have felt safe coming to the church, but he was followed and killed."

"Inspector Honiball didn't behave like a man trying to hide his deeds," I said. "He almost seemed to lead you to himself as the killer."

"I have encountered such arrogance before, to my benefit. The police, as a rule, don't respect the amateur consultant. Honiball's hubris was part of his downfall. The rest was his faith in his Faith. The only time he faltered was when he realized he was in the presence of a Prince of the Church. He must have seen a picture of you, even though you don't dress in the frippery of your rank. Most church people rarely meet their ranking prelates, and the presence of a Cardinal discombobulated him. Why were you here, Edward?"

"I came to see how Father Chiou was doing," said the Cardinal. "We met in Rome when he was studying there. I stayed to help him. He is a gentle soul."

Holmes continued. "I realized the confidence was actually misplaced arrogance. He really believed no amateur detective could be smarter than a policeman, and he also thought the church and its secrets would protect him. He didn't kill the priest, because he trusted the hoopla of the confessional seal. At the same time, he was frustrated at not hearing what Father Chiou was saying to us in here. He also made silly mistakes. He didn't change his shirt, and when I noticed the stain on his left cuff, he remembered where it came from. It made him think how much more I might know."

439

"And where did the stain come from."

"I believe it happened when he killed the woman, and no, I don't know why he did so, nor is it germane to the case before us. He will tell the police that it was a lover's tiff, or she charged him too much, or he was drunk. There is always some reason. What mattered was he stained the cuff on his dominant hand, and he knew it, and he knew I knew it."

"He was left-handed?"

"He shook hands right-handed, as convention dictates, but a right-handed person would have shaken hands then taken out his pocket watch to check the time. Honiball did both at the same time, which suggested his left hand was dominant. It was one of two mistakes. The other was suggesting Lonnic Chu's laundry was too far for the constable's concern. It isn't. It's barely two minutes away. Honiball wanted to get there before the constable to make sure there were no more loose ends."

"But how did you know where it is?"

"I know all and see all," said Holmes.

"And you passed it on your way here," said the Cardinal. "It is two blocks away on the main road from the railway station."

Holmes shrugged and continued his tale. "When I pulled open the door, his rage overcame his reason and he would have reached the priest, had it not been for our ecclesiastical rugby forward here." Cardinal Howard inclined his head gracefully at the compliment.

"Yes, that was a capital move," I said. "Did you play in your younger days?"

"It was hard not to, given my schooling," said the Cardinal. "The most Christian establishments have the grimmest *curricula*: Rugby, boxing, marching, shooting.

As we parted, Holmes clapped the Cardinal on his shoulder and shook his hand, an action I had never seen from him before. Holmes was normally the stiffest and most formal of men. "It was good to see you, Edward."

"Likewise, my friend." Cardinal Howard leant in and hugged Holmes in the Italian way, as if Holmes's slight thawing of emotions had allowed the Cardinal's true affection shine through. The effect on my reticent friend delighted him. "Relax, Sherlock. Your humanity is one of your best features, if you set it free."

In the train on the way back, I looked at Holmes in such a way that he asked, "You are troubled. What is it?"

"Not troubled. Puzzled. I saw the affection you had for your old friend. Taking a man by his shoulder and shaking his hand so warmly would be an indicator at any level in our painfully reticent society. From you, it's almost as if your friendship has been revivified.

"Very poetic. Also very droll. Do you have a point to make? The Cardinal and I were once friends and seem to be so again. That is all."

"Then why did you reach out and do the same to Honiball. You even went so far as to tell him he had done good work."

"Subterfuge, Watson. If you recall, Honiball looked big, but he had on that large winter jacket and I needed to know if, underneath all that padding, he had the wherewithal to move a heavy confessional. I judged that he did." He waited for the next question, eventually leading me as patiently as he could. "What else, my friend?"

"Well," I said, "I don't know what to make of it. Everything wasn't as it seemed. It was a locked room mystery where the mystery was outside the locked room, an impossible crime that wasn't impossible at all, and a topsy-turvy interrogation through a third person to a man who couldn't tell you anything, and yet in the end told you everything. I don't know how to write it."

"That aspect of our partnership I leave to you," said Holmes.

I wasn't done with him.

"Did you ever think you might have had a vocation?" I asked

"Certainly not, but I did think about becoming a Jesuit. Unfettered room for self-education, a roof, food and clothing, and the challenge of living in a community of some of the finest minds of my generation. It was momentarily tempting."

"What dissuaded you?" I asked, although in truth I could have answered the question myself.

Holmes didn't disappoint. "Ha, where shall I start? The stricture of a strict monastic rule would have chafed more than the scholastic opportunities. Then there are the limits to one's freedom, as well as the inability to express true emotions such as rage or disgust – where appropriate, of course. Obeisance is another with which I would have difficulty. Catholics spend entirely too much time kneeling down. Then there are the vows. Poverty and chastity weren't insurmountable obstacles, but I have always struggled with obedience. Lastly, there is the whole difficulty with deities."

"God?"

"Who else?" asked Holmes. "They expect one to believe in one only, and I have always found that rather limiting."

There was a comfortable silence in which I did my best not to imagine Holmes in a robe and tonsure, only succeeding partly. In an effort not to snicker, I said "You never did explain how the church here in Brighton came to honour such an unknown saint."

441

"Saint Polycarp is well known, just not here," said Holmes. "I'm confident that in parts of Anatolia, Saint Polycarp churches are found with a similar frequency to the number of Saint Albans extant in England. However, the story is prettily petty. When the Thirteenth Duke refused to pay for the building, the Bishop found a local property owner to foot the bill. The story went that this benefactor, who shall remain unnamed as his descendants are litigious, had been a rival suitor of the Duke for the hand of the fair Lady Charlotte, the daughter of the Duke of Sutherland. She chose to marry Howard instead of some local who was unencumbered with a title or any social standing, and he never forgave either of them."

"He must have," I said, "if he paid for the church."

"He also paid for the naming rights, and he used that right to make a lasting comment on his view of the Thirteenth Duke and his wife. Saint Polycarp is the patron saint of two things. The first is ear maladies. It was presumed to be a comment on the Duchess, known to be a nag and a gossip."

"You said two?" I asked. "What is the other?"

"Ah," said Holmes, "Saint Polycarp is also the patron saint of all who suffer from dysentery. How that is related to his opinion of the Duke, I will leave up to you to fathom."

The Adventure of the
Long-Distance Bullet
by I.A. Watson

V ictor Trevor [1] was up in town for the first time since Holmes and I had returned from our wanderings, so as a "Welcome back" he invited us to join him for supper at the Criterion. [2] My old friend Lomax of the London Library made up a fourth for our party. We made a hearty feast of chops and mustard, and afterwards relaxed at table with wine and coffee and made good conversation.

Holmes diverted talk away from our prolonged absence [3] by describing some details of our recent visit to Sussex to investigate the "vampiric" behaviour of Mrs. Robert Ferguson (although of course we offered no names or identifying details). [4] "The matter was never much of a mystery." Holmes spoke lightly of a case that had deeply baffled me and many others. "We travelled to Lamberley only to verify certain points to my complete satisfaction, more from a professional desire for completeness than anything else."

"I blame Sheridan le Fanu," I told our host. "It was he who revived the word 'vampire' in his story 'Carmilla'. [5] Now every fellow who sneaked a peek at a 'Penny Dreadful' as a boy remembers *Varney the Vampire or the Feast of Blood* and so many grisly imitators." [6]

"You betray a delinquent childhood," Lomax chided me. Ever the librarian, he went on to cite earlier literary sources that had contributed to the popular idea that had possessed Mr. Ferguson to suspect his wife of sucking the blood of his ailing child. [7]

"It is hardly the only time that superstition has interfered with the actual facts of a case," Holmes mentioned. He alluded to several of our investigations that had initially seemed to be based upon supernatural forces, citing in detail the great hound that had so beset Sir Henry Baskerville. [8]

"You reduce every mystery in the mill of rational analysis," Trevor chided him. "Will you allow no frisson of the unknown to stir your blood on a cold winter's night?"

"I am quite content to encounter the unknown," Holmes owned. "Indeed, without it I am ill-content and morbid. However, it is the comprehension of such enigmas that engages me. Our human condition is to penetrate the darkness and bring what we discover into the light."

"There are many who seem happy in the darkness," snorted Lomax, who doubtless encountered many of them professionally.

Holmes folded his napkin and attended to his Turkish coffee. "In many remarkable adventures, I daresay that Watson and I have never encountered any circumstance that could not be properly explained by scientific method and an understanding of human nature."

I reviewed the strange adventures that we had experienced – and how uncanny some of them had seemed at the time! I was compelled to confess that Holmes had a knack for pulling aside the curtain and revealing the machinery of the trick.

Trevor was unwilling to give up his point, though. "I have every reason to know your acuity, Holmes, and much cause to be glad of it. [9] But *'there are more things in Heaven and Earth'*[10] and all of that. I have an example in mind, and had you not been absent for so long from your regular haunts, then you might well have been consulted on it yourself."

"I would be pleased to review your example," Holmes told him generously.

Trevor sipped his red and leaned back. "Very well. This involved a young man who rejoiced in the name of Captain Cador Godmanchester, of the Sussex Godmanchesters, not far from where your vampire wasn't. He was the second son of Sir Truman Godmanchester, the famous Temperancer who made his money in Virginian cotton and later in English textile mills. Young Cador took a lieutenant's commission with the Hussars and, showing some promise, found himself promoted to captain on the staff of Sir Francis Scott on the Gold Coast."

I knew of Major-General Scott. The papers last winter had reported much about "The Fourth Anglo-Ashante War", which had deposed the Ashante King Prempeh to "end slavery and human sacrifice". Scott was the officer who commanded the expedition and who achieved victory without a shot being fired. His triumph was afterwards marred by politicians and critics at home arguing over the cost and necessity of the action. [11]

"Well," Trevor went on, "although there were no combat fatalities, sickness hit the army very heavily. At one point, fully half the troops were down with disease and there were many deaths – eighteen of them were white men. And Cador Godmanchester was one of them."

"Poor fellow," I condoled. "It is one of the sad risks of adventuring for the Empire."

"But here's the queer part – the impossible part: Godmanchester sickened on the march to Kumasi. He was evacuated to the British Mission Hospital at Christiansborg on the coast, where he lay stricken over

Christmas. And yet on Christmas Day, he was seen by his mother, walking through the family gardens in Sussex!"

"Surely some mistaken identity?" I argued. "A fond mother, missing her absent boy . . . ."

"I'm not done," Trevor told me. "You hear these stories sometimes, of a wounded or dying man far away, appearing to his loved ones at the time of his passing. Well, Cador died in that hospital on the 18th of January this year, waiting the steamer to shuttle the invalid home. And that same day, he was seen again at Wokenstoke, his family's Sussex seat, moving through the house. And there's more."

"The murder of Sir Truman Godmanchester," Holmes supplied. Of course he had caught up with the crime news during our long absence. "The newspapers made no mention of a spectre's appearance, however."

"I had it from a member of the household," Trevor revealed. "They believe that not only did Cador's ghost-double appear that day to herald his father's death – *They believe that he killed Sir Truman!*"

"How did the old man die?" Lomax wondered. "Perhaps his heart, if he thought he saw a ghost . . . ?"

"It was a gunshot to the forehead," Holmes recalled without need of any directory or reference.

"A bullet that somehow passed three thousand miles from a dying man to kill his parent," Trevor concluded triumphantly. "Now there's a supernatural mystery no amount of deduction will untangle, Holmes!"

Holmes is a consultant, employed by the experts when they are baffled, or by some member of the public as a last resort when other recourse has failed, but he also has a lively and eclectic curiosity which is easily piqued. At those times he evinces a childlike enthusiasm, turning all his massive intellect to whatever matter has caught his fancy. How well I recall that week when Holmes was obsessed with the diminution rate of gobstoppers, [12] and the nightmarish time he determined to calculate the fluid volume flow of every one of Bazalgette's sewer channels. [13]

Something about the Godmanchester affair captured that vast attention, and after two sulky days where business confined Holmes to London and he was able to do no more than pore over newspaper accounts that made no mention of the "*long-distance bullet*", he almost dragged me to Victoria Station to venture back into the wilds of rural Sussex.

"I am offended by a bullet that can travel around the globe to claim its victim," Holmes told me as we travelled. The fertile patchwork fields and small hamlets scurried past outside our carriage window, and behind them the chalk hills of the South Downs, painted into watercolours by a light winter rain. "I have verified from the autopsy account presented at inquest that Sir Truman was shot by a .308 British cartridge, fired at sufficient distance as to leave no power burns."

"So more than six feet," I knew. "The British Army standard rifle these days is the Lee-Enfield, mostly the 1853 or 1858 models, which uses just such ammunition in ten-round box magazines. Very different from the Martini-Henrys our fellows had in Afghanistan. It has bolt action, smokeless powder, and cock-on-closing – significant improvements, I'd say, when chaps come under fire. That's the sort of rifle that the Gold Coast expedition would have had for their infantry."

"Such equipment is widespread across the British Army on five continents," Holmes pointed out. "Of more significance is the locked-room aspect of the killing. Sir Truman was alone in his second-floor study of his Wokenstoke country estate. All the doors to that upper floor were locked and bolted – a significant matter, Watson – and there were very few ways for an intruder to find his way to where Sir Truman worked late into the night."

"Sir Truman's cry roused his sleeping family," I remembered from Trevor's account. "He is believed to have cried out, 'Cador, no!' The noise roused Sir Rupert and Lady Justina Godmanchester, the elder son and his wife, along with the murdered man's wife, Lady Ophelia, and her companion maid. And then a shot was fired. Sir Rupert unbolted and unlocked the servants' stair door so that the staff might come to the family's assistance. The study door had to be broken down to gain access to Sir Truman's body. This was a case worthy of you, Holmes, had you only been available."

"Perhaps, Watson. There is something of a reluctance to have me poking my nose into this matter. My telegrams requesting a meeting on the topic of Sir Truman's demise have met with a cold response from Sir Rupert. He doesn't seem eager to have his father's death re-examined."

"The autopsy verdict was death by unlawful killing by person or persons unknown," I remembered. "No weapon was ever discovered. No arrest was ever made. The case remains open – unsolved."

"I have booked us in to the local hostelry," Holmes advised me as we pulled into our station. "We may be sure that our enquiries will continue at the sign of The Hare and Hounds."

"Be sure it was a judgement." Our hostess at the hostelry closest to Wokenstoke held strong views on the deaths of Sir Truman and Captain Cador. It was evidently a much-discussed local topic.

"A judgement how?" I dutifully asked, purchasing a round for the occupants of the saloon.

446

Our landlady leaned in closer. "Why sir, for the great quarrel what caused the lad to go into the army in the first place! Young Cador sent away to be a soldier, so far from 'ome. Be sure as he blotted his copybook, sirs, and no mistake. 'Be gone' the old man says, sour Temperancer as he was, and strict as any tyrant. The father purchased Cador a commission in a regiment that was bound overseas right away, and that was the lad off to Africa to die of diseases the likes of we has never suffered 'ere in a civilised country. No wonder as the dying lad took his revenge with his dying gasp! A judgement, I say!"

Holmes listened to this recitation, which had the smooth delivery of an oft-told account, with his usual precise discernment. "What was the exact cause of the estrangement?" he enquired of our witness.

We had heard from Trevor that the breach was due to Godmanchester senior's strict views on alcohol and tobacco. Sir Truman sponsored many Temperance causes, whilst his son was something of a toper in his London clubs. However, our hostess' answer was quite different.

"Well, sirs, I doesn't like to gossip, but it is common knowledge – that is, everyone says – there was a young lass involved. A common lass, I mean, not suited for the rich likes of them social-climbing Godmanchesters. Such airs that Lady Justina puts on, and them the best-part American. But I gathers as the girl wasn't welcomed, and 'specially since she was evidently in the – " Our landlady mouthed the words. " – *family way*."

That would explain the haste to have Cador out of the country, of course. He was hardly the first young sprig of a rich family sent aboard to do good works to reclaim some measure of honour.

"What of the girl?" Holmes wanted to know. "And the child?"

Our hostess frowned. "Dead," she confided in awful tones, delighted to offer such a grisly conclusion to her gossip. "When the family denied her, and her man sent away to never return, why she took and 'anged herself, baby and all."

Holmes wanted details, of course: Names and dates, order of events, and so on. I was more interested in what the locals might think of the phantom bullet.

It turned out that this story was also in common circulation at The Hare and Hounds. "They says as a soul passing over can sometimes go wandering," one of the old men in the nook told me sincerely. "That young Cador, so far from 'ome, so let down by 'is family, all a-fevered from that foreign sickness . . . It's no wonder 'e kept coming back in 'is final days."

"Kept coming back?" I echoed. "More than once?" We had heard that the dead soldier's mother had believed an encounter on Christmas Day, but there was apparently more.

447

There were plenty of patrons willing to illustrate the claim. It was well-known by now that Cador had perished at Christiansborg on the 18th of January. Holmes had acquired his death certificate and army paperwork. According to the locals, Cador had been seen walking his family home and grounds several times over almost a month before that.

The first sighting had been the lad's mother, Lady Ophelia, who had woken one night with a mild headache. Not wishing to trouble her companion-nurse who slept in the same room, she rose to find her nerve tonic and passed by the window. In the waxing gibbous moon, she saw a figure in a Hussar's uniform ghosting through the ornamental gardens below. Stricken, she watched the apparition that she believed to be Captain Godmanchester for several minutes before the soldier vanished from view. Only then had she awakened her companion and reported the strange experience.

Or at least such was the collective narrative at The Hare and Hounds.

Little of the supernatural had been reported during the police murder investigation. I expect that the family wished to avoid more scandal. The Coroner wasn't apprised of the various phantom sightings that Holmes and I easily discovered for one evening's worth of drink-buying.

The next discovery had been made by a footman, who had crept out one evening for a New Year "tryst with 'is true-love" and had observed a man in military garb walking the rose garden by night. The terrified servant was certain it was Cador because the apparition wore the same distinctive white scarf that he had affected during his residency at home.

Next had been Lady Ophelia's companion, Judy, a "sensible girl from London" who had encountered, one evening on the servants' stair to the second floor, what seemed like a solid man. As a new employee, Judy hadn't been able to recognise the intruder. When the soldier vanished right before her eyes, she determined not to tell anyone what she had seen, fearing the response of the strict and god-fearing Sir Truman. Not wishing to further upset Lady Ophelia, the girl didn't report her sighting to her mistress. Judy only came forward with her added confession when others at Wokenstoke reported seeing the spectre after her employer's murder.

Two other household staff had also seen Captain Godmanchester, one at some distance in the orchard and the other looking from the first floor balcony down into the main hall. Both incidents had been after nightfall. The servant seeing the ghost in the hall had fled and hidden in her bed until morning's light. After this there was some talk in the servant's hall about the apparition, and much morbid speculation about whether it meant that their master's exiled son had somehow perished on his Ashanti campaign.

"And they was proved right, wasn't they?" our nook-dwelling ancient insisted. "Dying young Mr. Godmanchester was, and coming to blame the old misery what condemned 'im to such an end!"

Word of the rumours had reached Rupert Godmanchester, who had dealt harshly with such gossipers. It was at his orders that the second floor was thereafter sealed each night, with connecting doors to the remainder of the house locked and bolted to deny access for "mischief-makers".

Holmes found one disreputable patron of the local bar who might have witnessed something first-hand. A shabby tap-room denizen admitted to some occasional "moonlighting" – that is *poaching* – on Wokenstoke grounds. He was checking his snares just before midnight two days before the murder. He observed at a distance outside the manor house "a cove wi' all gold braid across 'is chest," but he fled capture for trespassing rather than remain to see who had been stepping through the darkness. He refused to testify any more for fear of prosecution.

Cador's last appearance had been on the very night of the murder, when four curious thrill-seekers from amongst the staff had wagered to venture out to the rose garden "to spy the spirit" – and to share an illicit jug of beer that might have had them dismissed for such intemperate indulgence.

Though Cador didn't walk the gardens that night, the watchers observed a moving light on the sealed second floor. By chasing to a vantage by the main gate they could see the silhouette of a soldier – with a rifle – moving steadily between the vacant rooms towards Sir Truman's study.

The lamp was extinguished suddenly. An hour later, their employer was dead.

"What do you make of it?" I asked my friend as the company broke up for the night and the saloon prepared for closing.

"Enough time has passed for the facts of the affair to have accreted into legend," Holmes considered. "The commonality of the statements, the shared language and interpretation, are characteristic of a story much-repeated and probably embellished."

"Is everything that we have heard therefore to be discounted?"

"No. It is data, but it must be reviewed critically within its context. There is – "

The last few departures from the public bar were hastened on their way by the arrival of two burly fellows in dark jackets over high-collared shirts. Our landlady blanched as she saw the arrivals and found reason to carry a bowl of used glasses off to her pump-house for washing.

Holmes regarded the newcomers with delighted interest.

One of the men opened the door to admit a well-dressed woman of middle years. She was clad formally and well, with faded yellow hair pulled back into a severe bun. Her expression was unfriendly.

"Lady Justina," Holmes identified Sir Rupert's spouse. "What may we do for you?"

Our visitor frowned for a moment at Holmes's casual deduction, then glanced at her wedding ring, her retainers, and her apparel before replying, "You are the notorious Sherlock Holmes?"

"I am Holmes," the great detective replied, waiting.

"Your presence isn't welcome here. My husband is unwell. I have no wish to disturb his recovery with news of you rabble-rousing in the village."

"I am sorry to hear of Sir Rupert's infirmity. What is the nature of his malady?"

Lady Justina's jaw tightened. "I wish you to go. Indeed, I instruct you to depart."

"Madam," I interjected, "it might help to convince us if you would explain why you so object to our visit."

"I will pay you," she continued coldly. "That is why you have come to cause trouble, is it not? Well, I will give you what you came for – twenty pounds in banker's notes right now if you will only leave and trouble us no more."

"That is a handsome payment for avoiding a case," Holmes observed. "Unfortunately, our interest is not pecuniary. Indeed, your calling has only intensified my interest in fathoming the tragic events of last January. I ask you to consider allowing my colleague Dr. Watson and me the opportunity to review the facts of the matter and to seek a more satisfying conclusion than a village ghost story."

"If you will not see sense," Lady Justina pressed on, "these footmen will convince you on your way. Be warned." She gestured to the two large fellows who were looming by the door. They looked like the kind of tame ruffians that many well-off households retained for matters such as this.

Holmes smiled thinly. "If you wish to set on your staff for a breach of the peace, Dr. Watson and I will be pleased to defend ourselves," he assured her. "And to press charges thereafter."

"Holmes knows every police commissioner in the Home Counties," I cautioned. "His word is good in any court in the land. And he is a champion boxer."

The Wokenstoke footmen looked a little disconcerted. They had evidently limited their intimidations to forward locals until then. A pair of seasoned, confident, well-placed gentlemen who didn't fear their fists were another matter.

Lady Justina was evidently deafer to the nuances. She gestured them forward. Holmes and I knocked them to the floor. When mine strove to rise, Holmes downed him once more.

"You have captured my interest and guaranteed my investigation, your Ladyship," Holmes assured our suddenly-worried visitor. "You will not answer my questions and benefit our investigation? Then good night."

One unfortunate consequence of Lady Justina's visit was notice from the landlady at The Hare and Hounds that she wouldn't be able to put us up for another night. The Godmanchesters were a significant power in the village, and Wokenstoke had become a major customer for wines, spirits, and small-beer since Sir Truman's passing. It wouldn't do to offend them.

Consequently, Holmes and I were packing our things in preparation for seeking other accommodation when we had a post-breakfast visit from another member of the troubled family.

"Lady Ophelia," Holmes deduced as the white-haired and somewhat-frail dowager ventured to find us before we departed.

"Mr. Holmes," Sir Truman's widow answered him. "I apologise for my daughter-in-law. She lacks certain courtesies that one might wish for in an English lady."

I hastened to get our new visitor a chair. I could see that her health wasn't good and standing for any length of time would trouble her. It must have cost her considerable effort and no little discomfort to make her way down to the village, even with her companion-nurse assisting her.

"May we enquire the purpose of your call?" I ventured, wondering if we might now receive an appeal to sympathy and sentiment to refrain from the case.

"I am come to ask for your help in solving my husband's death," Lady Ophelia replied. "I wish to know if my son committed the murder."

"Your son was three-thousand miles distant – " I began to reply, but Holmes interrupted me to ask, "Which son?"

The lady shivered. I decided that she needed a small medicinal-only brandy and administered it. She gulped the drink gratefully before replying. "I have to know whether Rupert was responsible for his father's end."

Holmes steepled his fingers and set his elbows on the table. "You have reason to believe he might?"

"I hate to think so, but . . . there are very few people who could have got to Truman that night. The ways in were sealed. The only ones who slept on the second floor were my maid Judy and myself, in the same room where she could come at call if I was sick in the night, and Rupert and Justina in the bedroom opposite. Truman's room was beside mine, with an interconnecting door. His study was at the end of the corridor. There is no other way for anyone to enter, unless . . . it really was Cador's avenging spirit."

"You believed that you had apprehended your son on the 25th of December last," I mentioned. "You saw him in the garden."

Lady Ophelia conformed it. "I believe that my son was reaching out to me, trying to find me before passing beyond the spiritual plains that mortal eyes can see."

Holmes avoided the supernatural for the moment. Instead he asked some specific questions about the layout, from which he determined that there were three staircases up to the second floor, of which two continued to the servants' attics. It was the nearest to the study which Rupert had unbolted and unlocked to summon help after investigating the gunshot, since that was the servant's stair. He had later checked that the other two entrances remained locked and bolted.

Holmes was also interested in the sequence of events, though Lady Ophelia was a second-hand witness to much of it. Fortunately, she had brought her companion-nurse Judy with her to meet us, and from the neat, smart-looking retainer, we had a more comprehensive description.

"Lady Ophelia and I were asleep by nine-thirty, as is her custom," Judy reported. "Sir Truman generally stayed up later, working in his study with his books and papers. He was an avid correspondent, significantly involved in the Temperance Movement, and he sponsored several anti-alcohol campaigns. Since Sir Truman slept separately from Her Ladyship, in the adjoining bedroom, we often didn't hear him retire."

Judy and her mistress had been awakened by Sir Truman's cry, a shout loud enough to rouse everyone on the second floor. No more than a few seconds had passed before the report of a rifle was heard.

Judy placed the sound of a shot at eleven-fifty. "That was late for Sir Truman to be up, but lately he had complained of insomnia and had been known to potter about the house late into the night. I know that the servant's hall attributed it to growing guilt of his estrangement from his younger son and the measures he had taken for the young man's exile. Anyhow, when the noise awoke us, Lady Ophelia instructed me to go and see what had happened."

"Neither of us believed it was gunfire," Lady Ophelia clarified, "or I would never have sent Judy out."

"I quickly dressed in a gown and went to investigate. As I emerged from our chamber, Sir Rupert was coming from his and Lady Justina's room, pulling on a night-robe. He commanded me to stay where I was while he went to see what was going on."

"He turned immediately towards the study?" Holmes clarified.

"Yes. He strode down there very urgently, bearing an oil lamp. When he got to the study door he banged on it, calling to his father. Of course, there was no response."

Rupert had evidently searched the other rooms on that floor, first to discover if his father had wandered into any of them, and then to check for intruders. Only then had he gone and unbolted the servants' doorway and called in those same footmen that we had encountered earlier to force the study open.

It had been about ten minutes since the shot when the study door gave way, admitting Rupert and the staff to discover Sir Truman dead.

"I can't tell you what happened after that," Judy confessed. "I had gone back to Lady Ophelia, who had taken badly and required her medication. I know that the police were summoned, though it took over an hour for anyone to reach our isolated manor, other than the local constable. By that time, the staff who had been outside ghost-hunting that night had come forward with their extraordinary tale. I was the only one who believed it at first, because . . . ."

Holmes talked the companion-nurse through her encounter with a spirit on the stairs, seeking out details that had been absent from the popular account in the saloon bar. In particular he enquired about the uniform trim and whether the spectre in dress uniform had carried a rifle. It had not.

That made sense to me. A rifle isn't usually an officer's weapon. But it was the murder weapon.

Lady Ophelia whispered her gnawing fear. "Rupert and Truman clashed more and more when Cador was gone. It was mostly over money. Rupert was concerned at how much of our fortune his father was channelling into his Temperance politics."

"I suppose he was concerned over inheritance," I suggested.

"Rupert would have done well enough," the heir's mother answered defensively. "Especially with Cador disinherited. It all came to him."

I glanced at Holmes but couldn't read his reaction to the motive.

"What makes you concerned that Rupert may have killed his father, then?" my friend enquired clinically.

When her mistress hesitated, Judy supplied an answer. "You may have heard that Captain Godmanchester had an unfortunate liaison with a guttersnipe nobody, which ended badly," she suggested. "It was Sir Rupert who first informed his father of the scandal, and evidently goaded Sir Truman to demand that Cador put the woman aside. When Cador demurred, it was Rupert's persuasion that helped Sir Truman to decide that a military life overseas was the best way to avoid scandal and opprobrium."

"That is so," Lady Ophelia confirmed.

"You never met the girl?" Holmes asked the widow.

"No. I gather that she took her own life, poor deserted waif. She had no other family to rely upon, her only brother having predeceased her, and a young woman of that class in such circumstances does not . . . her future wouldn't have been a happy one."

Holmes would have liked to hear more about the girl, one Millie Eggler, but Cador's mother knew little about her.

"Truman could be very strict in his religious beliefs," Lady Ophelia reported. "Not a drop of alcohol and not an ounce of tobacco entered Wokenstoke while he was alive. He quarrelled with Cador often about the boy's 'wastrel ways' in London. He might have argued with Rupert too, except that Rupert was clever enough to conceal his occasional lapses while his father lived. I suppose it is no surprise that Cador, loosed in our capital with a healthy income, should encounter a young person who . . . Well, a mother doesn't like to think of such liaisons. Whatever her sins, the poor girl is dead now."

The lady was clearly upset, so I ventured an enquiry about the other rumours of Cador walking the family estate.

It didn't comfort Lady Ophelia as I had hoped. Her face grew paler and tighter. "I don't doubt that such sightings were made, much like my own, much like Judy's. Truman was sceptical, of course. The Spiritualists claim that such things might happen, but Cador and Rupert were brought up in a strict Primitive Christian household. Truman wouldn't countenance such talk."

"He suppressed discussion of the matter," I surmised.

"With threats of dismissal. And yet . . . my Cador was sent far from home, exiled from his family. Even his . . . *amour* and the fruit of their illicit passion were gone. In his final fevered illness, might Cador not have reached out for his mother, or yearned for reconciliation with his father? Or else was his appearance some warning of death at Wokenstoke, like the Irish fairy-woman who keens when a member of the household is to die, or the spirit-birds that attend certain ancient families when an ending draws near?" [14]

"I am sure that Cador would have wanted to be with you at his end," Judy assured her employer, "or give warning if there was danger."

"I know that, for all his strict views, Truman would have wanted to see Cador a last time. He often grieved at the choice he had made, even considered bringing our son home, but the rift was made. How many nights did my husband stay awake in his study, brooding over the son he had discarded? He may have been brooding at his desk at the very time that the unknown intruder came to end his life."

454

Lady Ophelia's voice quavered a little as she mentioned an "unknown intruder". Her doubts about her elder son's part in this – and his obvious gain by Cador's removal and Sir Truman's death – hadn't gone away.

Holmes also asked about Sir Rupert's present ill-health.

"It is a nervous disease," Lady Ophelia reported with concern. "The best specialists have been called in, but Rupert cannot sleep, cannot concentrate. He is listless all the time, far from his former robust self. I cannot wonder but that it is . . . a bad conscience."

"It would be a kind relief to my Lady if you could set her mind at rest on this," Judy told us. "It is true that only Sir Rupert had the means to get to the study by night. Yet to accomplish that task, which is surely abhorrent to any loyal son, he must also have had the collusion of Lady Justina, who has sworn that he was beside her until the noise of the shout and the gun awoke them both. She is a light sleeper and wouldn't fail to notice her husband rising in the night. If you could prove some other way by which Sir Truman's death might have been accomplished, you would be offering Her Ladyship an immense kindness."

Holmes made no such promise, but did secure an invitation to the Godmanchester estate, in spite of Lady Justina's objections. He promised to attend there at five p.m., after conducting other researches necessary to his investigation. After acquiring the details he required from the dowager and her companion, he bade them a farewell and we returned to our packing.

"Can we explain the mysterious double that haunts the Godmanchesters?" I asked Holmes earnestly.

"We must not disappoint Trevor and Lomax, Doctor," Holmes twitted me.

As we had warned Lady Justina, the name of Sherlock Holmes is not without cachet. If as part of those "other researches necessary" the "notorious" detective wishes to apply to a county judge for permission to examine a private bank account or two, if he seeks access to army records and memorabilia, if he wishes to consult the sales history of the exclusive tailors' shops on Savile Row and Old Burlington Street, or even if he wires off halfway around the world via subsea cable, [15] he is assured co-operation and swift response from those who understand his acuity.

He is also a ruthless assessor of good policing, well able to determine when a powerful and wealthy family's local influence have quietened a criminal investigation to avoid a complicated and difficult case. Such obfuscation becomes more difficult to maintain when senior Home Office administrators receive calls from high officials in the Metropolitan Police Force or sharp enquiries from Holmes's civil servant brother.

Most terrifying of all, though, is the relentless determination and boundless energy that Holmes tasks to accomplish his investigations, qualities which he now focussed entirely upon his enquiries about the strange world-hopping bullet that ended the life of Sir Truman Godmanchester.

Such was the welter of enquiries that Holmes set in hand that afternoon, prior to our engagement at Wokenstoke.

"Come, Watson, you know my methods," my friend chided me. "By now you must have followed my reasoning and know the nature of the hypothesis I am testing."

"I have learned, Holmes, that it is a futile exercise to second-guess your mental gymnastics. You will doubtless soon explain that nothing is what I thought it to be. The dead man was killed not by a bullet but by a rare South African venom, or the ghost was two dwarves in whiteface, or that it wasn't Sir Truman that died in the study but his gardener, and the old chap is alive and well in retirement at Cromer."

"Poor Watson! How I must try you! Well, you may set your mind at rest on those points, but for all that you aren't so far wrong about some of it. When we have conducted a search of the second floor of the Godmanchester house and I have checked certain sightlines and layout issues, and have received back the answers to several delicate enquiries, then I shall be pleased to relieve your torment."

I wanted to escape Holmes's pity, so I added, "I suppose you have been tracing the history of poor Millicent Eggler and the details of her demise, to ascertain the likelihood that her assumed suicide was indeed self-inflicted. You may have looked into Sir Rupert's financial history, and that of his ruthless wife. You have also sought out the London gentleman's outfitters that prepared Captain Godmanchester's uniforms for him before his departure for the Dark Continent."

Holmes chuckled. "You enjoy playing the baffled everyman, but you sometimes betray yourself. You are correct, of course, that I have elicited information on all of those topics. Bankers and tailors will be the key to unlocking our present puzzle."

I might have asked him more, but he turned aside for a discourse on the efficaciousness of hollyhock wine and the attraction which that brave little plant exerts over honey bees.

Wokenstoke was a house in the Georgian style, a long symmetrical four-storey brick rectangle under a hip roof with servants' dormers. I checked for ivy or other means by which an intruder might gain external access to the bedrooms of the second floor but saw none. Doubtless Holmes observed and eliminated many other possibilities.

456

The house was sparsely furnished inside with old, simple pieces, the home of a rich man of sober tastes and dour temperament, but there were signs of its new owner, Sir Rupert – or more likely his wife – making changes. Bright dimity curtains and modern tapestry rugs had been added to downstairs rooms and electrical lights were due to be fitted. Most telling of change, a tantalus of spirits sat on a side-table in the hall.

From Lady Justina's cold stares and the lack of the tantalus being unlocked, I deduced that our presence on the Godmanchester property was still unwelcome. Only her mother-in-law's staid presence prevented more incident. The attendant Judy remained silent throughout our chilly welcome. I inferred that she wasn't accustomed to speaking when Lady Justina maintained the room.

As Holmes completed his walkthrough of the second floor, including close inspection of the locks and bolts for signs of picking or tampering, and estimations of wall dimensions to discount hidden passageways, Sir Rupert emerged from his sick-room to encounter us.

"What the deuce d'you think you're doing?" he demanded with some choler.

"I am determining the actual events that occurred on the night of January 18th last," Holmes told him coolly. "I have inspected the room where your father perished, with special reference to the bullet-hole in the wainscoting above the mantelpiece, and have verified certain speculations regarding the intrusion. Of particular interest is the presence of a neglected flat-iron in a cupboard under the bookcase, along with a tin of brass polish. I now need only a moment with you to have all the evidence that I require."

Sir Rupert's red face, with its unsightly warts and pinkened eyes, was quite the opposite of his wife's pale mask of concealed fury. "Out and be d----d!" he shouted, only to clutch his chest and sway with nausea.

"Doctor," Holmes directed me, but I was already moving to attend the invalid.

"I'll get him his medicine," Judy offered, and vanished into Rupert's bedroom to collect a *cannabis indica* solution. [16]

"Just help him to a chair downstairs, Watson," Holmes told me. "We have visitors due and Sir Rupert should meet them."

"Visitors?" Lady Justina asked sharply. She looked around, either to repel more intruders or to re-summon her sheepish bruised footmen.

"I have asked the Sussex Deputy County Commissioner for Police to call upon us, with the Coroner who presided over Sir Truman's autopsy enquiry. They will bring with them the remaining elements I require to unfold the solution to your mystery."

"You mean you *know* how father was shot?" Sir Rupert gasped. "How?"

Holmes got the three Godmanchesters settled in the drawing room, with Judy in attendance beside the frail Lady Ophelia. At Holmes's suggestion, I set aside Sir Rupert's usual medication and administered him a stiff brandy.

Whilst we awaited Holmes's invited guests, he removed from his wallet a number of primitive photographs of the tintype and daguerreotype kinds. "We may as well begin with some identification," he suggested. "This is a school photograph of your son, Lady Ophelia?"

"Why yes," the grieving mother answered. "I always thought Cador looked handsome in his school uniform."

"And here we see him in his dress Hussar's uniform, posing with his horse. This was taken just prior to his departure for Africa."

"I have a similar picture in my dresser, taken at the same time," Lady Ophelia admitted.

Holmes nodded. "I have located the tailor who fitted the uniform. Your son chose not to go to his normal Savile Row man at Henry Poole and Company, but to a specialist in military officers' garb at Dege and Skinner, a few shops down. [17] Dr. Watson may be able to tell you if that additional expense was wise."

I could not. I had never been able to afford London prices for my uniforms with the Fifth Northumberland.

Holmes carried on. "You may be surprised to learn that Cador Godmanchester ordered two versions of his dress uniform, the fig that you see here and another with slightly different measurements. The tailor's records are quite detailed, down to the one inch difference in inside leg and a two-inch narrowing of the waistband."

"That makes no sense," Sir Rupert objected. "Why would Cador want clothes that don't fit?"

Holmes laid down the next of his photographs. "Here is a group image of Major-General Scott's newly-promoted staff officers arriving at the Gold Coast town of Accra. You may see the old trading fort in the background. Can you recognise Cador?"

None of the Godmanchesters could. "He isn't in the picture," Lady Justina objected.

Holmes placed one long finger on the rim of the image, where the photographer had scraped the names of those depicted therein. The pin-etched legend suggested that Captain Godmanchester was second from the left.

"That is not him," Sir Rupert insisted.

"No," Holmes agreed. "But by the measurements I can calculate this fellow would well fit the second set of gear that your brother ordered from his new tailor."

458

The Godmanchesters all took a breath. "How is that possible?" demanded Lady Ophelia.

Holmes laid down another photograph, printed on the back with the address of "*Chas. R. Vorbey Photographic Artist / Pierside Studio / Eastern Parade / Southsea.*" and stamped with the date of "*June 17th, 1893*". It much cheaper in quality than the others, and blurred by amateur handling, but it was clear enough to determine that the figure in the workmen's holiday best clothes was the same as the officer posing in Accra.

"Who is that?" I wondered.

"This, my dear Watson, is Joseph Eggler, only son of a disgraced officer from the L-------s. His father was drummed out as a card cheat and disowned by his family. Eggler senior lived in poverty in Portsmouth until he drank himself to death in '89. Still, before that, Joseph acquired a good education and could pass as an officer and a gentleman – if he only had a chance."

I saw it clear then. "Young Cador, forced overseas for his transgression, arranged instead for another to take his place. Wait . . . you said Eggler?"

"Joseph was Millicent Eggler's brother," Holmes revealed. "It was a natural connection to exploit. Eggler was supposed dead, and was therefore quite available to assume another man's life of exile. For him, it must have been his one great chance at distinction, for Godmanchester a last reprieve from his fate. I cannot yet say which of them proposed the exchange."

"Then it was Eggler who died at Christiansborg? Cador never went to Africa?"

"Oh!" gasped Lady Ophelia.

"What?" fumed Sir Rupert.

"Eggler didn't die either," Holmes suggested. He laid down a final image, one of those tiny black-bordered funerary portraits that desperate photographers in the colonies take in hopes that families back home might purchase a last picture of their loved ones. The reverse was marked with Cador's name, rank, and service number, and the date of his supposed passing.

Holmes indicated the sepia portrait. "This tintype was sent back with all the others, but was never offered since the details of family weren't included. Tracing it was a trifle, but examining it has been most instructive."

"This isn't Eggler," I observed. "Christiansborg must have been absolute chaos with half the army infected. The bounder must have

459

switched places with some other poor blighter that perished in the hospital and come back to England as a convalescent under another name!"

"Just so," Holmes approved. "I am having photographs forwarded of the various documents and registers that Eggler and his victim would have signed, but of course that will take time. Likewise, I have arranged for the late captain's brother officers to be shown Eggler's picture for certain identification. In the interim, I believe that these pictures support the idea of neither Cador nor Eggler having passed away."

"Cador alive?" Lady Ophelia gasped. "Then I *did* see him that night in the garden!"

"Not so," Holmes contradicted her. "Again, the tailors were most helpful. From the records of Cador's usual suit-maker, I can confirm that he has ordered and received *three* sets of civilian attire since his supposed emigration. His Poole and Company bill is sadly unpaid and significantly overdue. Moreover, from Dege and Skinner I know that in November of last year, yet another set of Hussar dress was ordered, but to different measurements again."

"Why?" Lady Justina puzzled, struggling between curiosity and outrage.

"This time the clothing would have fitted Sir Truman himself."

"Truman?" Lady Ophelia repeated, baffled.

"Of course!" I exploded. "The old fellow was wracked with remorse at having sent his son away to a distant shore, or so he supposed. He stayed up sleepless, brooding and yearning, and then one day he must have fixed on the sentimental idea of getting himself a uniform like Cador's, to wear when he is most despondent so that he could feel closer to his boy!" I took a breath. "That explains the iron and the button polish hidden in his study."

"That is who the servants saw? That my mother-in-law saw?" Lady Justina demanded. "It was my father-in-law playing dress-up by night?"

"Oh, Truman!" Lady Ophelia moaned.

Sir Rupert wasn't convinced. "If it *was* father, then why wasn't his fig found when he died? That room was thoroughly searched for the firearm that slew him, and all his other wardrobes and closets."

Holmes acknowledged the intelligent point. "It was removed at the time of the murder."

"Then," I reasoned, "the murderer knew of Sir Truman's masquerade."

"Indeed," Holmes agreed. "The absence of the dead man's costume was another way of confusing the story."

He perked up as he heard the rattle of carriages rolling over the gravel of the forecourt. "Ah, that will be the rest of our party."

460

All of us in the drawing room rose up to the entrance hall to see who had come. It was a larger group than Holmes had suggested, including not only the senior police representative and the Crown Coroner, but also four uniformed officers leading two manacled prisoners.

"Cador!" Sir Rupert bellowed, even more outraged and furious. His wife placed a cautioning hand on his chest. The elder brother was looking very seedy.

"Cador alive?" Lady Justina demanded in disbelieving – or disappointed – tones. "How could he have vanished for so long without money or shelter, only to be dragged in here now by the constabulary? Where has he been all this time? What is his game?"

Lady Ophelia just sat palely, one hand clutching Judy's, and mouthed her missing son's name.

"Hello, mother," said Cador Godmanchester bitterly. "I'm home." He pursed his lips and turned away from his family, unwilling to say more.

"Banker's records opened by police summons proved most illumining," Holmes assured us. "From such ledgers, I discovered the hidden account by which the absentee officer drew a meagre income, and therefore the address to which to direct the police to take Cador and his accomplice into custody."

"His army account and other investments would surely have been closed on his supposed demise," I objected.

"But not that secret account at another bank under a different name to which the fake Cador formerly sent monthly tithes of his military pay, and not the account of the other depositor that also paid into that hidden fund. That is the bank from which rent was paid upon the cottage where Cador and his housemate were hiding."

I looked more closely at the runaway heir's companion, a young man of similar age and build.

"That other one – that's Eggler," I recognised from the two images in Holmes's collection and his still-surviving remnants of tropical tan. "That's the hanged girl's brother."

Sir Rupert might have attempted more bluster at that revelation. Holmes prevented any further domestic discord by summarising again for the majesty of the law what he had revealed so far. He had evidently sketched some of this out before, since the Deputy Commissioner nodded at salient points but raised his brows at new proofs.

"They were just where you said they would be, Mr. Holmes," the senior policeman reported. "We also discovered there the sort of army rifle you described, same as the murder weapon. And not one but three Hussar dress uniforms."

461

"I am sad to say," Holmes revealed, "that one of these two men is Sir Truman's murderer. They are of similar height, despite the discrepancy in their measurements, so the angle of impact of the bullet in the wall-panelling is unable to determine the assailant. However, I believe that it is more likely that Sir Truman would recognise his son's voice and open his locked study door for him than for a stranger like Eggler. The victim did cry out his younger son's name before he died."

"No!" Cador protested. "It was Joe! It was him!"

"Shut up, you b----y fool!" Eggler told the prodigal. "They have nothing on either of us that can stick. How is either of us supposed to walk like a ghost into a sealed house, onto a locked landing, commit a murder, and then spirit away again leaving all the doors bolted behind us?"

Holmes answered, "In the same way that someone knew of the supposed ghost-sightings of Cador Godmanchester in the grounds of Wokenstoke, and realised that such a story might well cause superstitious servants to avoid a man so dressed if they happened to sight him entering the house."

"Both suspects owned such outfits," I recognized, "and Eggler could easily have returned to England with the Lee-Enfield rifle that fired the fatal shot."

"Bank accounts and tailors," Holmes emphasised to us. "We cannot overlook Sir Truman's sad uniform – the disappearing uniform. I'm sure that Sir Truman had many talents to amass such a fortune, but I doubt that seam-ironing was one of them."

"*Someone* had to press his uniform!" I recognised. "So someone knew of it!"

Holmes turned to Judy. "The only person who was alone in the corridor after the shot was fired was you," he told the companion-nurse. "You might have left the connecting doors unlocked and unbolted before retiring, to allow the killer entry, then sealed the way again after he had departed with the rifle and stolen uniform."

Judy displayed shock and innocent surprise. "Me? Why would I do that?"

"Because reports of your suicide have been grossly exaggerated. You are Millicent Eggler, another supposedly-deceased cast member."

"*You* are Millie?" Lady Ophelia asked, baffled and distressed. "And my grand-child?"

"Waiting his time," the supposed-Judy spat. "He was supposed to have all, the Godmanchester fortune and revenge for his forebears' wrongs."

"Cador, Joseph, and Millie set out to avenge the Godmanchesters' spurning of the pregnant Millicent," Holmes expounded. "Remember that it was only 'Judy' that supposedly witnessed the double actually vanish before her eyes. She alone encountered Cador's 'spirit' indoors before the fatal attack, save for one servant's brief glimpse at a distance in the main hall. Similarly, only Judy was left outside the study door when Sir Rupert hastened off to find footmen to help break into the crime scene. At that point, Judy could signal the murderer to depart the locked study and fasten it after himself. Judy then allowed him out through one of the other locked and bolted exits – acquiring those keys cannot have been difficult for an accomplished deceiver like her – and of course she could re-fasten the bolts when the killer was gone with the rifle and Sir Truman's uniform. All the fuss was at the servants' stair, where Sir Rupert brought his footmen to breach the study door that the murderer had fastened behind him."

Lady Ophelia stared at her younger son with horrified, devastated eyes.

"You b----y murderer!" Sir Rupert suddenly yelled and tried to leap at Cador. The constables were required to fend him off and separate the two brothers.

"We shall never outlive the scandal," Lady Justina moaned. "Never!"

"Then reports of Millie's supposed suicide were part of the ruse, to further divert suspicion from her new identity as the family nurse," I supposed. "This is a long-planned plot."

"Why?" Cador's mother at last found voice to ask her offspring. "Cador, why?"

The captured man made no reply. He wouldn't meet his mother's gaze.

Holmes supplied the solution. "Their eventual goal was to secure Sir Truman's fortune for the child – before Sir Truman spent too much of it financing his Temperance crusades. The Egglers are expert at pretending their demises and at assuming false identities. Is one such ruse how you first came to know Cador, Millie? In any case, you are all three complicit in murder and attempted murder."

"You can prove nothing!" Joseph Eggler insisted anew, struggling with his police guard.

"You will find your evidence in that bottle of *cannabis indica*," Holmes gestured, illustrating Sir Rupert's medicine. "It wasn't enough to eliminate the father. The elder brother must also diminish and die. Dr. Watson will attest to Sir Rupert demonstrating the appearance and symptoms of slow arsenical poisoning."

"Administered by the family nurse," I snarled. A fellow doesn't appreciate having his profession so misused.

Holmes summed it up: "With Rupert's death, and with Cador's assumed death, the entailed property reverts to Sir Truman's widow. If Cador then turned up alive and recovered his mother's good graces, then he could inherit if anything suddenly occurred to truncate Lady Ophelia's fragile health."

"Which leaves Cador, his trollop, and his crony with everything they wanted!" Sir Rupert snarled. "Officers! Arrest these murderers!"

"The grandchild is being cared for," I explained to Lomax and Trevor as we met to dine again on the subject of the Long-Distance Bullet. "With Cador and the Egglers all facing the long drop for their crimes, Sir Rupert and Lady Justina have consented to adopt and legitimise the boy."

"So my mystery was devoid of spectres after all," Victor Trevor lamented. "It is difficult to encounter the supernatural when one dines with Sherlock Holmes."

To which we all raised our glasses.

NOTES

1. Trevor, a university acquaintance of Holmes, became the detective's first client in "The Adventure of the *Gloria Scott*" (published in 1893), collected in *The Memoirs of Sherlock Holmes* (1893, dated 1894), and chronologically the first story in The Canon.
2. The Criterion Restaurant facing Piccadilly Circus, London, opened its bar and dining facilities in 1873 and became one of the oldest and most historic restaurants in the world. It is now a Grade II listed building.

    A plaque placed on the bar in 1953 reads:

    > HERE, NEW YEARS DAY 1881
    > AT THE CRITERION LONG BAR
    > STAMFORD, DRESSER AT BARTS
    > MET
    > DR JOHN H. WATSON
    > AND LED HIM TO IMMORTALITY
    > AND
    > SHERLOCK HOLMES

    with additional credit for erecting the sign given to The Sherlock Holmes Society of London and The Baker Street Irregulars. However, the present plaque also mentions "1981 by The Inverness Capers of Akron, Ohio". It can be viewed at:
    https://en.wikipedia.org/wiki/File:Plaque_criterion.jpg
3. The lack of any Canon account of Holmes and Watson's doings from the conclusion of "The Adventure of the Bruce-Partington Plans" on 24th November, 1895 until "The Adventure of the Veiled Lodger" in October, 1896 has led to this period being termed "The Missing Year" and is a favourite topic of Sherlockian speculation. Alas, Dr. Watson's present unearthed manuscript offers no more data on that particular debate except to reference a recent return. [Dating here and in later footnotes is from W.S. Baring-Gould's biography *Sherlock Holmes* (1962). Other chronologies exist.]
4. Watson recorded this case as "The Adventure of the Sussex Vampire" and it was published in the all-star January 1924 issue of *The Strand Magazine* alongside contributors Winston Churchill, P.G. Wodehouse, John Russell, E. Phillips Oppenheim, F. Britten Austin, and "Sapper" – a luminary contents list. The account was collected in *The Case-Book of Sherlock Holmes* (1927). Watson placed that case on November 19th, with subsequent Sherlockian scholars determining that the year was 1896.
5. Sheridan le Fanu's Gothic novella was published as a part-work in *The Dark Blue* (1871-1872) and first collected in *In a Glass Darkly* (1872). The story was inspiration for Roger Vadim's *Et mourir de plaisir* (1960), the Hammer horror film *The Vampire Lovers (*1970), and many other versions.

6. "Penny Dreadfuls" were cheap popular periodical pamphlets (initially costing 1d) featuring "shocking" part-work fiction. *Varney the Vampire* was serialised from 1845-1847, running to nearly 667,000 words in 876 double-columned pages. Varney was a major influence on the Victorian concept of the vampire, and much has been written about its influence on Bram Stoker's *Dracula* (published 1897, a year after our present story occurs).

7. Lomax might have begun with the poems "The Vampire" (1748) by Heinrich August Ossenfelder, "Lenore" (1773) by Gottfried August Bürger, and "Die Braut von Corinth" ("The Bride of Corinth") (1797) by Johann Wolfgang von Goethe, then alluded to Samuel Taylor Coleridge's unfinished *Christabel* (1797 and 1800), Lord Byron's *The Giaour* (1813), and John Polidori's *The Vampire* (1819), but Watson might not have had an interest in his friend's literary erudition.

8. Chronicled Holmes's investigation, *The Hound of the Baskervilles* (published in 1901-1902).

9. Holmes assisted his university friend Trevor in "The Adventure of the *Gloria Scott*". (See Note 1)

10. The much-quoted statement in full is "*There are more things in Heaven and Earth, Horatio, than are dreamt of in your philosophy,*" from *Hamlet* Act 1 Scene 5.

11. The conflict took place between 26th December, 1895 and 4th February, 1896, and ended with King Prempeh's abdication and exile, and his Gold Coast kingdom becoming a British protectorate. Major-General Sir Francis Cunningham Scott, KCB, KCMG (1834-1902) led with the main expeditionary force of British and West Indian troops, with a native levy commanded by Major Robert Baden-Powell (later the founder of the Boy Scout movement).

Baden-Powell later published a justification of the action, *The Downfall of Prempeh, A Diary of Life With the Native Levy in Ashanti 1895-96* (1896), which mentions abolishing human sacrifice and slave-taking amongst other colonial reasons, and begins with a splendid prologue as follows:

> *In the African bush one may see a lion making his meal on the beast which he unaided has hunted, and has slain by his mighty power, and round him, shrieking and snarling, snatching and tearing, there skips a craven pack of jackals.*
>
> *One need not go so far as Africa to seek a similar scene. Within a hundred miles of Westminster it may be found...*
>
> *But should he [the travelling Briton] feel a little too "uppish" in this elation and pride of birth, he can readily find an antidote. Let him obtain a ticket for the Strangers' Gallery in the House of Commons, and let him go and see for himself the working of what the nation is pleased to call its brain. There he will find – on both sides of the House (for I have no party predilections) – a few lions and a great many jackals behind them. The petty jabber and snarl of these as they*

snatch and worry at the subject under discussion well-nigh drowns the occasional, meaning "sough" of their betters.

A growl is enough to scatter them all like chaff, but only for a moment, and anon they are back again, blathering as before.

The whole book is available at:

https://archive.org/details/downfallofprempe00baderich

12. Americans might know these large sucking sweets as *jawbreakers*. Though only popularised in modern form by the Ferrara Pan Candy Company of Forest Park, Illinois from 1919, earlier versions of the confectionary are known back to the Middle Ages (where they were used medicinally). Some sources trace the gobstopper back to ancient Egypt and India.

13. Victorian detective mystery aficionados soon become aware of the extraordinary and comprehensive London sewer system overseen by engineer Sir Joseph William Bazalgette CB (1819 –1891), whose eighty-two miles of main sewers and 1,100 miles of street sewers still serve central London today and form the venue for many a murder story.

14. The legend of the Irish banshee (literally "Woman of the Fairy-Mound") dates back at least to *Cathreim Thoirdhealbhaigh* ("Triumphs of Torlough", 1380) by Sean mac Craith. She and her Celtic equivalents in Wales and Scotland were brought to wider literary attention by Sir Walter Scott in his *Letters on Demonology and Witchcraft* (1830) and *"family death omens"* became a part of fashionable upper-class British society, with many old families claiming long traditions of warnings about the death of clan head or kin. Such omens included phantom animals or birds, forewarning dreams, uncanny lights, tolling bells, ghost-carriages, spectral funeral processions, and spirit-doubles (in German: *Doppelgänger*.)

15. One little-recognised triumph of the Victorian age was the British domination of global communications via sunken oceanic telegraph cables, which led a French official in 1900 to say, *"England owes her influence in the world perhaps more to her cable communications than to her navy. She controls the news, and makes it serve her policy and commerce in a marvellous manner."* By the time of our present story, a cable message could be transmitted all the way to any colony in the world and a reply received within three days, except for the trans-Pacific section which was finally completed in 1902 (requiring the 1888 annexation of Fanning Island, now Tabuaeran in Kiribati as a relay station).

16. This was a legal and oft-prescribed remedy for colic, heart disease, and nausea up to the early days of the twentieth century.

17. From the latter half of the nineteenth century to the modern day, Savile Row in Mayfair, London has been the most prominent tailor's street in the world, specialising in bespoke (hand-made-to–measure) gentlemen's clothing. A suit from a Savile Row tailor today costs around £3,500 – £10,000.

Henry Poole and Company (founded by the creator of the dinner jacket – the American tuxedo) was the first to open a shop there in 1846. The company has held Warrants of Appointment from customers including

Emperor Napoleon III, Queen Victoria, Tsar Alexander II, Keiser Wilhelm I of Germany, and Queen Elizabeth II.

From 1865, Dege and Skinner originally specialised in army and navy uniforms, from whence comes their long-standing relationship with the British Royal Family and three present Royal Warrants of Appointment (to Queen Elizabeth II, the Sultan of Oman, and the King of Bahrain). Both of these shops still occupy Savile Row.

About the Contributors

The following contributors appear in this volume:
The MX Book of New Sherlock Holmes Stories
Part XXXV – "However Improbable . . . ." (1889-1896)

Donald Baxter has practiced medicine for over forty years. He resides in Erie, Pennsylvania with his wife and their dog. His family and his friends are for the most part lawyers who have given him the ability to make stuff up, just as they do.

Brian Belanger, PSI, is a publisher, illustrator, graphic designer, editor, and author. In 2015, he co-founded Belanger Books publishing company along with his brother, author Derrick Belanger. His illustrations have appeared in *The Essential Sherlock Holmes* and *Sherlock Holmes: A Three-Pipe Christmas*, and in children's books such as *The MacDougall Twins with Sherlock Holmes* series, *Dragonella*, and *Scones and Bones on Baker Street*. Brian has published a number of Sherlock Holmes anthologies and novels through Belanger Books, as well as new editions of August Derleth's classic Solar Pons mysteries. Brian continues to design all of the covers for Belanger Books, and since 2016 he has designed the majority of book covers for MX Publishing. In 2019, Brian received his investiture in the PSI as "Sir Ronald Duveen." More recently, he illustrated a comic book featuring the band The Moonlight Initiative, created the logo for the Arthur Conan Doyle Society and designed *The Great Game of Sherlock Holmes* card game. Find him online at:
www.belangerbooks.com and
www.redbubble.com/people/zhahadun and
zhahadun.wixsite.com/221b

Josh Cerefice has followed the exploits of a certain pipe-smoking sleuth ever since his grandmother bought him *The Complete Sherlock Holmes* collection for his twenty-first birthday, and he has devotedly accompanied the Great Detective on his adventures ever since. When he's not reading about spectral hellhounds haunting the Devonshire moors, or the Machiavellian machinations of Professor Moriarty, you can find him putting pen to paper and challenging Holmes with new mysteries to solve in his own stories.

Martin Daley was born in Carlisle, Cumbria in 1964. He cites Doyle's Holmes and Watson as his favourite literary characters, who continue to inspire his own detective writing. His fiction and non-fiction books include a Holmes pastiche set predominantly in his home city in 1903. In the adventure, he introduced his own detective, Inspector Cornelius Armstrong, who has subsequently had some of his own cases published by MX Publishing. For more information visit *www.martindaley.co.uk*

The Davies Brothers are Brett and Nicholas Davies, twin brothers who share a love of books, films, history, and the Wales football team. Brett lived in four different countries before settling in Japan, where he teaches English and Film Studies at a university in Tokyo. He also writes for screen and stage, as well as articles for a variety of publications on cinema, sports, and travel. Nicholas is a freelance writer and PhD researcher based in Cardiff. He previously worked for the Arts Council of Wales, focusing on theatre and drama. He now writes for stage and screen, as well as articles for arts and football magazines. They are the authors of the novels *Hudson James and the Baker Street Legacy* (based upon an ancient puzzle set by Sherlock Holmes himself!) and *The Phoenix Code*. They also serve as the "literary agents" for Dr Watson's newly uncovered adventures, *Sherlock Holmes: The Centurion Papers*.

Alan Dimes was born in North-West London and graduated from Sussex University with a BA in English Literature. He has spent most of his working life teaching English. Living in the Czech Republic since 2003, he is now semi-retired and divides his time between Prague and his country cottage. He has also written some fifty stories of horror and fantasy and thirty stories about his husband-and-wife detectives, Peter and Deirdre Creighton, set in the 1930's.

Sir Arthur Conan Doyle (1859-1930) *Holmes Chronicler Emeritus*. If not for him, this anthology would not exist. Author, physician, patriot, sportsman, spiritualist, husband and father, and advocate for the oppressed. He is remembered and honored for the purposes of this collection by being the man who introduced Sherlock Holmes to the world. Through fifty-six Holmes short stories, four novels, and additional Apocryphal entries, Doyle revolutionized mystery stories and also greatly influenced and improved police forensic methods and techniques for the betterment of all. *Steel True Blade Straight*.

Anna Elliott is an author of historical fiction and fantasy. Her first series, *The Twilight of Avalon* trilogy, is a retelling of the Trystan and Isolde legend. She wrote her second series, *The Pride and Prejudice Chronicles*, chiefly to satisfy her own curiosity about what might have happened to Elizabeth Bennet, Mr. Darcy, and all the other wonderful cast of characters after the official end of Jane Austen's classic work. She enjoys stories about strong women, and loves exploring the multitude of ways women can find their unique strengths. She was delighted to lend a hand with the "Sherlock and Lucy" series, and this story, firstly because she loves Sherlock Holmes as much as her father, co-author Charles Veley, does, and second because it almost never happens that someone with a dilemma shouts, "Quick, we need an author of historical fiction!" Anna lives in the Washington, D.C .area with her husband and three children.

Matthew J. Elliott is the author of *Big Trouble in Mother Russia* (2016), the official sequel to the cult movie *Big Trouble in Little China*, *Lost in Time and Space: An Unofficial Guide to the Uncharted Journeys of Doctor Who* (2014), *Sherlock Holmes on the Air* (2012), *Sherlock Holmes in Pursuit* (2013), *The Immortals: An Unauthorized Guide to* Sherlock *and* Elementary (2013), and *The Throne Eternal* (2014). His articles, fiction, and reviews have appeared in the magazines *Scarlet Street*, *Total DVD*, *SHERLOCK*, and *Sherlock Holmes Mystery Magazine*, and the collections *The Game's Afoot*, *Curious Incidents 2*, *Gaslight Grimoire*, *The Mammoth Book of Best British Crime 8*, and *The MX Book of New Sherlock Holmes Stories – Part III: 1896-1929*. He has scripted over 260 radio plays, including episodes of *Doctor Who*, *The Further Adventures of Sherlock Holmes*, *The Twilight Zone*, *The New Adventures of Mickey Spillane's Mike Hammer*, *Fangoria's Dreadtime Stories*, and award-winning adaptations of *The Hound of the Baskervilles* and *The War of the Worlds*. He is the only radio dramatist to adapt all sixty original stories from The Canon for the series *The Classic Adventures of Sherlock Holmes*. Matthew is a writer and performer on *RiffTrax.com*, the online comedy experience from the creators of cult sci-fi TV series *Mystery Science Theater 3000* (*MST3K* to the initiated). He's also written a few comic books.

Steve Emecz's main field is technology, in which he has been working for about twenty-five years. Steve is a regular speaker at trade shows and his tech career has taken him to more than fifty countries – so he's no stranger to planes and airports. In 2008, MX published its first Sherlock Holmes book, and MX has gone on to become the largest specialist Holmes publisher in the world with over 500 books. MX is a social enterprise and supports three main causes. The first is Happy Life, a children's rescue project in Nairobi, Kenya, where he and his wife, Sharon, spend every Christmas at the rescue centre in Kasarani. They have written two editions of a short book about the project, *The Happy Life Story*. The second is Undershaw, Sir Arthur Conan Doyle's former home, which is a school for children with learning disabilities for which Steve is a patron. Steve has been a mentor for the World Food Programme for several years, and was part of the Nobel Peace Prize winning team in 2020.

Mark A. Gagen BSI is co-founder of Wessex Press, sponsor of the popular *From Gillette to Brett* conferences, and publisher of *The Sherlock Holmes Reference Library* and many other fine Sherlockian titles. A life-long Holmes enthusiast, he is a member of *The Baker Street Irregulars* and *The Illustrious Clients of Indianapolis*. A graphic artist by profession, his work is often seen on the covers of *The Baker Street Journal* and various BSI books.

Paul D. Gilbert was born in 1954 and has lived in and around London all of his life. His wife Jackie is a Holmes expert who keeps him on the straight and narrow! He has two sons, one of whom now lives in Spain. His interests include literature, ancient history, all religions, most sports, and movies. He is currently employed full-time as a funeral director. His books so far include *The Lost Files of Sherlock Holmes* (2007), *The Chronicles of Sherlock Holmes* (2008), *Sherlock Holmes and the Giant Rat of Sumatra* (2010), *The Annals of Sherlock Holmes* (2012), *Sherlock Holmes and the Unholy Trinity* (2015), *Sherlock Holmes: The Four Handed Game* (2017), *The Illumination of Sherlock Holmes* (2019), and *The Treasure of the Poison King* (2021).

John Atkinson Grimshaw (1836-1893) was born in Leeds, England. His amazing paintings, usually featuring twilight or night scenes illuminated by gas-lamps or moonlight, are easily recognizable, and are often used on the covers of books about The Great Detective to set the mood, as shadowy figures move in the distance through misty mysterious settings and over rain-slicked streets.

Arthur Hall was born in Aston, Birmingham, UK, in 1944. He discovered his interest in writing during his schooldays, along with a love of fictional adventure and suspense. His first novel, *Sole Contact*, was an espionage story about an ultra-secret government department known as "Sector Three", and was followed, to date, by three sequels. Other works include seven Sherlock Holmes novels, *The Demon of the Dusk, The One Hundred Percent Society, The Secret Assassin, The Phantom Killer, In Pursuit of the Dead, The Justice Master*, and *The Experience Club* as well as three collections of Holmes *Further Little-Known Cases of Sherlock* Holmes, *Tales from the Annals of Sherlock* Holmes, and *The Additional Investigations of Sherlock Holmes*. He has also written other short stories and a modern detective novel. He lives in the West Midlands, United Kingdom.

Christopher James was born in 1975 in Paisley, Scotland. Educated at Newcastle and UEA, he was a winner of the UK's National Poetry Competition in 2008. He has written three full length Sherlock Holmes novels, *The Adventure of the Ruby* Elephant, *The Jeweller of Florence*, and *The Adventure of the Beer Barons*, all published by MX.

Roger Johnson, BSI, ASH, PSI, etc, is a member of more Holmesian societies than he can remember, thanks to his (so far) 16 years as editor of *The Sherlock Holmes Journal*, and thirty-two years as editor of *The District Messenger*. The latter, the newsletter of *The Sherlock Holmes Society of London*, is now in the safe hands of Jean Upton, with whom he collaborated on the well-received book, *The Sherlock Holmes Miscellany*. Roger is resigned to the fact that he will never match the Duke of Holdernesse, whose name was followed by "*half the alphabet*".

Naching T. Kassa is a wife, mother, and writer. She's created short stories, novellas, poems, and co-created three children. She resides in Eastern Washington State with her husband, Dan Kassa. Naching is a member of *The Horror Writers Association*, *Mystery Writers of America*, *The Sound of the Baskervilles*, *The ACD Society*, *The Crew of the Barque Lone Star*, and *The Sherlock Holmes Society of London*. She's also an assistant and staff writer for Still Water Bay at Crystal Lake Publishing. You can find her work on Amazon. *https://www.amazon.com/Naching-T-Kassa/e/B005ZGHTI0*

Susan Knight's newest novel, *Mrs. Hudson goes to Paris*, from MX publishing, is the latest in a series which began with her collection of stories, *Mrs. Hudson Investigates* (2019) and the novel *Mrs. Hudson goes to Ireland* (2020). She has contributed to several of the MX anthologies of new Sherlock Holmes short stories and enjoys writing as Dr. Watson as much as she does Mrs. Hudson. Susan is the author of two other non-Sherlockian story collections, as well as three novels, a book of non-fiction, and several plays, and has won several prizes for her writing. Mrs. Hudson's next adventure, still evolving, will take her to Kent, the Garden of England, where she is hoping for some peace and quiet. In vain, alas. Susan lives in Dublin.

David Marcum plays *The Game* with deadly seriousness. He first discovered Sherlock Holmes in 1975 at the age of ten, and since that time, he has collected, read, and chronologicized literally thousands of traditional Holmes pastiches in the form of novels, short stories, radio and television episodes, movies and scripts, comics, fan-fiction, and unpublished manuscripts. He is the author of over one-hundred Sherlockian pastiches, some published in anthologies and magazines such as *The Strand*, and others collected in his own books, *The Papers of Sherlock Holmes*, *Sherlock Holmes and A Quantity of Debt*, *Sherlock Holmes – Tangled Skeins*, *Sherlock Holmes and The Eye of Heka*, and *The Collected Papers of Sherlock Holmes*. He has edited over sixty books, including several dozen traditional Sherlockian anthologies, such as the ongoing series *The MX Book of New Sherlock Holmes Stories*, which he created in 2015. This collection is now at thirty-six volumes, with more in preparation. He was responsible for bringing back August Derleth's Solar Pons for a new generation with his collection of authorized Pons stories, *The Papers of Solar Pons*. His new collection, *The Further Papers of Solar Pons*, will be published in 2022. Pons's return was further assisted by his editing of the reissued authorized versions of the original Pons books, and then several volumes of new Pons adventures. He has done the same for the adventures of Dr. Thorndyke, and has plans for similar projects in the future. He has contributed numerous essays to various publications, and is a member of a number of Sherlockian groups and Scions, as well as The Mystery Writers of America. His irregular Sherlockian blog, *A Seventeen Step Program*, addresses various topics related to his favorite book friends (as his son used to call them when he was small), and can be found at *http://17stepprogram.blogspot.com/* He is a licensed Civil Engineer, living in Tennessee with his wife and son. Since the age of nineteen, he has worn a deerstalker as his regular-and-only hat. In 2013, he and his deerstalker were finally able make his first trip-of-a-lifetime Holmes Pilgrimage to England, with return Pilgrimages in 2015 and 2016, where you may have spotted him. If you ever run into him and his deerstalker out and about, feel free to say hello!

Mark Mower is a long-standing member of the *Crime Writers' Association, The Sherlock Holmes Society of London,* and *The Solar Pons Society of London.* To date, he has written 33 Sherlock Holmes stories, and his pastiche collections include *Sherlock Holmes: The Baker Street Case-Files, Sherlock Holmes: The Baker Street Legacy,* and *Sherlock Holmes: The Baker Street Archive* (all with MX Publishing). His non-fiction works include the best-selling book *Zeppelin Over Suffolk: The Final Raid of the L48* (Pen & Sword Books). Alongside his writing, Mark maintains a sizeable collection of pastiches, and never tires of discovering new stories about Sherlock Holmes and Dr. Watson.

Sidney Paget (1860-1908), a few of whose illustrations are used within this anthology, was born in London, and like his two older brothers, became a famed illustrator and painter. He completed over three-hundred-and-fifty drawings for the Sherlock Holmes stories that were first published in *The Strand* magazine, defining Holmes's image forever after in the public mind.

Tracy J. Revels, a Sherlockian from the age of eleven, is a professor of history at Wofford College in Spartanburg, South Carolina. She is a member of *The Survivors of the Gloria Scott* and *The Studious Scarlets Society,* and is a past recipient of the Beacon Society Award. Almost every semester, she teaches a class that covers The Canon, either to college students or to senior citizens. She is also the author of three supernatural Sherlockian pastiches with MX (*Shadowfall, Shadowblood,* and *Shadowwraith*), and a regular contributor to her scion's newsletter. She also has some notoriety as an author of very silly skits: For proof, see "The Adventure of the Adversarial Adventuress" and "Occupy Baker Street" on YouTube. When not studying Sherlock, she can be found researching the history of her native state, and has written books on Florida in the Civil War and on the development of Florida's tourism industry.

Nicholas Rowe was born in Edinburgh Scotland and attended Eton before receiving a Bachelor of Arts degree from the University of Bristol. He has performed in a many films, television shows, and theatrical productions. In 1985, he was Sherlock Holmes in *Young Sherlock Holmes,* and he also appeared as the "Matinee Holmes" in 2015's *Mr. Holmes.*

Dan Rowley practiced law for over forty years in private practice and with a large international corporation. He is retired and lives in Erie, Pennsylvania, with his wife Judy, who puts her artistic eye to his transcription of Watson's manuscripts. He inherited his writing ability and creativity from his children, Jim and Katy, and his love of mysteries from his parents, Jim and Ruth.

Jane Rubino is the author of *A Jersey Shore* mystery series, featuring a Jane Austen-loving amateur sleuth and a Sherlock Holmes-quoting detective, *Knight Errant, Lady Vernon and Her Daughter,* (a novel-length adaptation of Jane Austen's novella *Lady Susan,* co-authored with her daughter Caitlen Rubino-Bradway, *What Would Austen Do?,* also co-authored with her daughter, a short story in the anthology *Jane Austen Made Me Do It, The Rucastles' Pawn, The Copper Beeches from Violet Turner's POV,* and, of course, there's the Sherlockian novel in the drawer – who doesn't have one? Jane lives on a barrier island at the New Jersey shore.

Geri Schear is a novelist and short story writer. Her work has been published in literary journals in the U.S. and Ireland. Her first novel, *A Biased Judgement: The Diaries of Sherlock Holmes 1897* was released to critical acclaim in 2014. The sequel, *Sherlock*

Holmes and the Other Woman was published in 2015, and *Return to Reichenbach* in 2016. She lives in Kells, Ireland.

Robert V. Stapleton was born in Leeds, England, and served as a full-time Anglican clergyman for forty years, specialising in Rural Ministry. He is now retired, and lives with his wife in North Yorkshire. This is the area of the country made famous by the writings of James Herriot, and television's *The Yorkshire Vet*, to name just a few. Amongst other things, he is a member of the local creative writing group, Thirsk Write Now (TWN), and regularly produces material for them. He has had more than fifty stories published, of various lengths and in a number of different places. He has also written a number of stories for *The MX Book of New Sherlock Holmes Stories*, and several published by Belanger Books. Several of these Sherlock Holmes pastiches have now been brought together and published in a single volume by MX Publishing, under the title of *Sherlock Holmes: A Yorkshireman in Baker Street*. Many of these stories have been set during the Edwardian period, or more broadly between the years 1880 and 1920. His interest in this period of history began at school in the 1960's when he met people who had lived during those years and heard their stories. He also found echoes of those times in literature, architecture, music, and even the coins in his pocket. The Edwardian period was a time of exploration, invention, and high adventure – rich material for thriller writers.

Kevin P. Thornton was shortlisted six times for the Crime Writers of Canada best unpublished novel. He never won – they are all still unpublished, and now he writes short stories. He lives in Canada, north enough that ringing Santa Claus is a local call and winter is a way of life. This is his twelfth short story in *The MX Book of New Sherlock Holmes Stories*. By the time you next hear from him, he hopes to have written his thirteenth.

Charles Veley has loved Sherlock Holmes since boyhood. As a father, he read the entire Canon to his then-ten-year-old daughter at evening story time. Now, this very same daughter, grown up to become acclaimed historical novelist Anna Elliott, has worked with him to develop new adventures in the *Sherlock Holmes and Lucy James Mystery Series*. Charles is also a fan of Gilbert & Sullivan, and wrote *The Pirates of Finance*, a new musical in the G&S tradition that won an award at the New York Musical Theatre Festival in 2013. Other than the Sherlock and Lucy series, all of the books on his Amazon Author Page were written when he was a full-time author during the late Seventies and early Eighties. He currently works for United Technologies Corporation, where his main focus is on creating sustainability and value for the company's large real estate development projects.

Margaret Walsh was born Auckland, New Zealand and now lives in Melbourne, Australia. She is the author of *Sherlock Holmes and the Molly-Boy Murders*, *Sherlock Holmes and the Case of the Perplexed Politician*, and *Sherlock Holmes and the Case of the London Dock Deaths*, all published by MX Publishing. Margaret has been a devotee of Sherlock Holmes since childhood and has had several Holmesian related essays printed in anthologies, and is a member of the online society *Doyle's Rotary Coffin*. She has an ongoing love affair with the city of London. When she's not working or planning trips to London. Margaret can be found frequenting the many and varied bookshops of Melbourne.

I.A. Watson, great-grand-nephew of Dr. John H. Watson, has been intrigued by the notorious "black sheep" of the family since childhood, and was fascinated to inherit from his grandmother a number of unedited manuscripts removed circa 1956 from a rather larger collection reposing at Lloyds Bank Ltd (which acquired Cox & Co Bank in 1923). Upon discovering the published corpus of accounts regarding the detective Sherlock Holmes

476

from which a censorious upbringing had shielded him, he felt obliged to allow an interested public access to these additional memoranda, and is gradually undertaking the task of transcribing them for admirers of Mr. Holmes and Dr. Watson's works. In the meantime, I.A. Watson continues to pen other books, the latest of which is *The Incunabulum of Sherlock Holmes*. A full list of his seventy or so published works are available at: *http://www.chillwater.org.uk/writing/iawatsonhome.htm*

Emma West joined Undershaw in April 2021 as the Director of Education with a brief to ensure that qualifications formed the bedrock of our provision, whilst facilitating a positive balance between academia, pastoral care, and well-being. She quickly took on the role of Acting Headteacher from early summer 2021. Under her leadership, Undershaw has embraced its new name, new vision, and consequently we have seen an exponential increase in demand for places. There is a buzz in the air as we invite prospective students and families through the doors. Emma has overseen a strategic review, re-cemented relationships with Local Authorities, and positioned Undershaw at the helm of SEND education in Surrey and beyond. Undershaw has a wide appeal: Our students present to us with mild to moderate learning needs and therefore may have some very recent memories of poor experiences in their previous schools. Emma's background as a senior leader within the independent school sector has meant she is well-versed in brokering relationships between the key stakeholders, our many interdependences, local businesses, families, and staff, and all this whilst ensuring Undershaw remains relentlessly child-centric in its approach. Emma's energetic smile and boundless enthusiasm for Undershaw is inspiring.

DeForeest Wright III has a day job as a baker for Ralphs grocery stores. It helps support his love for books. A long-time lover of literature, especially of the Sherlock Holmes tales, he spends his time away from the oven hunched over novels, poetry, anthologies, or any tome on philosophy, mathematics, science, or martial arts he can find, sipping an espresso if one is to hand. He writes prose and poetry in his off hours and currently hosts "The Sunless Sea Open-Mic: Spoken Word and Poetry Show" at the Unurban Coffee House in Santa Monica. He was glad to team up writing with his father.

Sean Wright makes his home in Santa Clarita, a charming city at the entrance of the high desert in Southern California. For sixteen years, features and articles under his byline appeared in *The Tidings* – now *The Angelus News*, publications of the Roman Catholic Archdiocese of Los Angeles. Continuing his education in 2007, Mr. Wright graduated from Grand Canyon University, attaining a Bachelor of Arts degree in Christian Studies with a *summa cum laude*. He then attained a Master of Arts degree, also in Christian Studies. Once active in the entertainment industry, and in an abortive attempt to revive dramatic radio in 1976 with his beloved mentor, the late Daws Butler, directing, Mr. Wright co-produced and wrote the syndicated *New Radio Adventures of Sherlock Holmes*, starring the late Edward Mulhare as the Great Detective. Mr. Wright has written for several television quiz shows and remains proud of his work for *The Quiz Kid's Challenge* and the popular TV quiz show *Jeopardy!* for which the Academy of Television Arts and Sciences honored him in 1985 with an Emmy nomination in the field of writing. Honored with membership in The Baker Street Irregulars as "The Manor House Case" after founding The Non-Canonical Calabashes, the Sherlock Holmes Society of Los Angeles in 1970, Mr. Wright has written for *The Baker Street Journal* and *Mystery Magazine*. Since 1971, he has conducted lectures on Sherlock Holmes's influence on literature and cinema for libraries, colleges, and private organizations, including MENSA. Mr. Wright's whimsical *Sherlock Holmes Cookbook* (Drake), created with John Farrell, BSI, was published in 1976, and a mystery novel, *Enter the Lion: a Posthumous Memoir of Mycroft Holmes* (Hawthorne), "edited" with Michael Hodel, BSI, followed in 1979. As director general of The Plot Thickens Mystery Company, Mr .Wright originated hosting "mystery parties" in homes, restaurants, and offices, as well as producing and directing the very first "Mystery Train" tours on Amtrak, beginning in 1982.

Tim Newton Anderson is a former senior daily newspaper journalist and PR manager who has recently started writing fiction. In the past six months, he has placed fourteen stories in publications including *Parsec Magazine*, *Tales of the Shadowmen*, *SF Writers Guild*, *Zoetic Press*, *Dark Lane Books*, *Dark Horses Magazine*, *Emanations*, and *Planet Bizarro*.

Thomas A. Burns Jr. writes *The Natalie McMasters Mysteries* from the small town of Wendell, North Carolina, where he lives with his wife and son, four cats, and a Cardigan Welsh Corgi. He was born and grew up in New Jersey, attended Xavier High School in Manhattan, earned B.S degrees in Zoology and Microbiology at Michigan State University, and a M.S. in Microbiology at North Carolina State University. As a kid, Tom started reading mysteries with The Hardy Boys, Ken Holt, and Rick Brant, then graduated to the classic stories by authors such as A. Conan Doyle, Dorothy Sayers, John Dickson Carr, Erle Stanley Gardner, and Rex Stout, to name a few. Tom has written fiction as a hobby all of his life, starting with *The Man from U.N.C.L.E.* stories in marble-backed copybooks in grade school. He built a career as technical, science, and medical writer and editor for nearly thirty years in industry and government. Now that he's a full-time novelist, he's excited to publish his own mystery series, as well as to write stories about his second most favorite detective, Sherlock Holmes. His Holmes story, "The Camberwell Poisoner", appeared in the March-June 2021 issue of *The Strand Magazine*. Tom has also written a Lovecraftian horror novel, *The Legacy of the Unborn*, under the pen name of Silas K. Henderson – a sequel to H.P. Lovecraft's masterpiece *At the Mountains of Madness*. His Natalie McMasters novel *Killers!* won the Killer Nashville Silver Falchion Award for Best Book of 2021.

Josh Cerefice *also has a story in Part XXXVI.*

Chris Chan is a writer, educator, and historian. He works as a researcher and "International Goodwill Ambassador" for Agatha Christie Ltd. His true crime articles, reviews, and short fiction have appeared (or will soon appear) in *The Strand*, *The Wisconsin Magazine of History*, *Mystery Weekly*, *Gilbert!*, *Nerd HQ*, Akashic Books' *Mondays are Murder* web series, *The Baker Street Journal*, *The MX Book of New Sherlock Holmes Stories*, *Masthead: The Best New England Crime Stories*, *Sherlock Holmes Mystery Magazine*, and multiple Belanger Books anthologies. He is the creator of the Funderburke mysteries, a series featuring a private investigator who works for a school and helps students during times of crisis. The Funderburke short story "The Six-Year-Old Serial Killer" was nominated for a Derringer Award. His first book, *Sherlock & Irene: The Secret Truth Behind "A Scandal in Bohemia"*, was published in 2020 by MX Publishing. His second book, *Murder Most Grotesque: The Comedic Crime Fiction of Joyce Porter* will be released by Level Best Books in 2021, and his first novel, *Sherlock's Secretary*, was published by MX Publishing in 2021. *Murder Most Grotesque* was nominated for the Agatha and Silver Falchion

Awards for Nonfiction Writing, and *Sherlock's Secretary* was nominated for the Silver Falchion for Best Comedy. He is also the author of the anthology of Sherlock Holmes stories *Of Course He Pushed Him.*

Leslie Charteris was born in Singapore on May 12th, 1907. With his mother and brother, he moved to England in 1919 and attended Rossall School in Lancashire before moving on to Cambridge University to study law. His studies there came to a halt when a publisher accepted his first novel. His third one, entitled *Meet the Tiger*, was written when he was twenty years old and published in September 1928. It introduced the world to Simon Templar, *aka* The Saint. He continued to write about The Saint until 1983 when the last book, *Salvage for The Saint*, was published. The books, which have been translated into over thirty languages, number nearly a hundred and have sold over forty-million copies around the world. They've inspired, to date, fifteen feature films, three television series, ten radio series, and a comic strip that was written by Charteris and syndicated around the world for over a decade. He enjoyed travelling, but settled for long periods in Hollywood, Florida, and finally in Surrey, England. He was awarded the Cartier Diamond Dagger by the *Crime Writers' Association* in 1992, in recognition of a lifetime of achievement. He died the following year.

Ian Dickerson was just nine years old when he discovered The Saint. Shortly after that, he discovered Sherlock Holmes. The Saint won, for a while anyway. He struck up a friendship with The Saint's creator, Leslie Charteris, and his family. With their permission, he spent six weeks studying the Leslie Charteris collection at Boston University and went on to write, direct, and produce documentaries on the making of *The Saint* and *Return of The Saint,* which have been released on DVD. He oversaw the recent reprints of almost fifty of the original Saint books in both the US and UK, and was a co-producer on the 2017 TV movie of *The Saint.* When he discovered that Charteris had written Sherlock Holmes stories as well – well, there was the excuse he needed to revisit The Canon. He's consequently written and edited three books on Holmes' radio adventures. For the sake of what little sanity he has, Ian has also written about a wide range of subjects, none of which come with a halo, including talking mashed potatoes, Lord Grade, and satellite links. Ian lives in Hampshire with his wife and two children. And an awful lot of books by Leslie Charteris. Not quite so many by Conan Doyle, though.

John Farrell Jr. was born and raised in San Pedro, California. He became interested in Sherlock Holmes in the late 1960's. He joined *The Non-Canonical Calabashes* (A Sherlock Holmes scion Society) where he met and became friends with another Sherlockian, Sean Wright. He collaborated with Mr. Wright on *The Sherlock Holmes Cookbook*. Later he was a member of *The Goose Club of the Alpha Inn*. He submitted articles to *The Baker Street Journal*. *The Baker Street Irregulars* awarded him the title The Tiger of San Pedro in 1981. He was proud to include "*BSI*" after his name. John made his living as a classical music and play reviewer for multiple newspapers in the Los Angeles area. He passed away in 2015 while he was writing a review. He left behind his family and many friends. He has been accurately described by those that knew him as larger than life.

James Gelter is a director and playwright living in Brattleboro, VT. His produced written works for the stage include adaptations of *Frankenstein* and *A Christmas Carol*, several children's plays for the New England Youth Theatre, as well as seven outdoor plays co-written with his wife, Jessica, in their *Forest of Mystery* series. In 2018, he founded The Baker Street Readers, a group of performers that present dramatic readings of Arthur Conan Doyle's original Canon of Sherlock Holmes stories, featuring Gelter as Holmes, his

479

longtime collaborator Tony Grobe as Dr. Watson, and a rotating list of guests. When the COVID-19 pandemic stopped their live performances, Gelter transformed the show into The Baker Street Readers Podcast. Some episodes are available for free on Apple Podcasts and Stitcher, with many more available to patrons at *patreon.com/bakerstreetreaders*.

Hal Glatzer is the author of the Katy Green mystery series set in musical milieux just before World War II. He has written and produced audio/radio mystery plays, including the all-alliterative adventures of Mark Markheim, the Hollywood hawkshaw. He scripted and produced the Charlie Chan mystery *The House Without a Key* on stage, and he adapted "The Adventure of the Devil's Foot" into a stage and video play called *Sherlock Holmes and the Volcano Horror*. In 2022, after many years on the Big Island of Hawaii, he returned to live on his native island – Manhattan. See more at: *www.halglatzer.com*

Denis Green was born in London, England in April 1905. He grew up mostly in London's Savoy Theatre where his father, Richard Green, was a principal in many Gilbert and Sullivan productions, A Flying Officer with RAF until 1924, he then spent four years managing a tea estate in North India before making his stage debut in *Hamlet* with Leslie Howard in 1928. He made his first visit to America in 1931 and established a respectable stage career before appearing in films – including minor roles in the first two Rathbone and Bruce Holmes films – and developing a career in front of and behind the microphone during the golden age of radio. Green and Leslie Charteris met in 1938 and struck up a lifelong friendship. Always busy, be it on stage, radio, film or television, Green passed away at the age of fifty in New York.

Arthur Hall *also has stories in Parts XXXIV and XXXVI*

Stephen Herczeg is an IT Geek, writer, actor, and film-maker based in Canberra Australia. He has been writing for over twenty years and has completed a couple of dodgy novels, sixteen feature-length screenplays, and numerous short stories and scripts. Stephen was very successful in 2017's International Horror Hotel screenplay competition, with his scripts *TITAN* winning the Sci-Fi category and *Dark are the Woods* placing second in the horror category. His two-volume short story collection, *The Curious Cases of Sherlock Holmes*, was published in 2021. His work has featured in *Sproutlings – A Compendium of Little Fictions* from Hunter Anthologies, the *Hells Bells* Christmas horror anthology published by the Australasian Horror Writers Association, and the *Below the Stairs*, *Trickster's Treats*, *Shades of Santa*, *Behind the Mask*, and *Beyond the Infinite* anthologies from *OzHorror.Con*, *The Body Horror Book*, *Anemone Enemy*, and *Petrified Punks* from Oscillate Wildly Press, and *Sherlock Holmes In the Realms of H.G. Wells* and *Sherlock Holmes: Adventures Beyond the Canon* from Belanger Books.

Paul Hiscock is an author of crime, fantasy, horror, and science fiction tales. His short stories have appeared in a variety of anthologies, and include a seventeenth-century whodunnit, a science fiction western, a clockpunk fairytale, and numerous Sherlock Holmes pastiches. He lives with his family in Kent (England) and spends his days taking care of his two children. He mainly does his writing in coffee shops with members of the local NaNoWriMo group, or in the middle of the night when his family has gone to sleep. Consequently, his stories tend to be fuelled by large amounts of black coffee. You can find out more about Paul's writing at *www.detectivesanddragons.uk*.

Anisha Jagdeep is a 21-year-old senior at Rutgers University, currently pursuing a degree in Computer Engineering. With her twin sister, Ankita, a fellow Sherlock Holmes enthusiast, she enjoys watching classic films and writing short stories inspired by notable short story writers such as Dame Agatha Christie, John Kendrick Bangs, O. Henry, and Saki. They are also students of Indian classical music and dance. Anisha expresses her gratitude to Sir Arthur Conan Doyle for his unparalleled contributions to mystery literature with his exceptional characters, Sherlock Holmes and Dr. Watson.

In the year 1998 **Craig Janacek** took his degree of Doctor of Medicine at Vanderbilt University, and proceeded to Stanford to go through the training prescribed for pediatricians in practice. Having completed his studies there, he was duly attached to the University of California, San Francisco as Associate Professor. The author of over seventy medical monographs upon a variety of obscure lesions, his travel-worn and battered tin dispatch-box is crammed with papers, nearly all of which are records of his fictional works. To date, these have been published solely in electronic format, including two non-Holmes novels (*The Oxford Deception* and *The Anger of Achilles Peterson*), the trio of holiday adventures collected as *The Midwinter Mysteries of Sherlock Holmes*, the Holmes story collections *The First of Criminals*, *The Assassination of Sherlock Holmes*, *The Treasury of Sherlock Holmes*, *Light in the Darkness*, *The Gathering Gloom*, *The Travels of Sherlock Holmes*, and the Watsonian novels *The Isle of Devils* and *The Gate of Gold*. Craig Janacek is a *nom de plume*.

Amanda Knight was born and grew up in Sydney Australia. At the age of nineteen, she decided to travel and spent a wonderful time in the UK in the 1980's. Travelling through Scotland and Wales, as well as living and working in England for an extended period, and working in pubs, which is almost obligatory if you are an Australian in the UK. As a long-time fan of Sherlock Holmes, she spent many a pleasant hour investigating many of the places mentioned by Conan Doyle in the Sherlock Holmes stories. Amanda still lives in Australia and is enjoying the invigorating mountain air where she now resides. Amanda is the author of *The Unexpected Adventures of Sherlock Holmes* (2004)

David L. Leal PhD is Professor of Government and Mexican American Studies at the University of Texas at Austin. He is also an Associate Member of Nuffield College at the University of Oxford and a Senior Fellow of the Hoover Institution at Stanford University. His research interests include the political implications of demographic change in the United States, and he has published dozens of academic journal articles and edited nine books on these and other topics. He has taught classes on Immigration Politics, Latino Politics, Politics and Religion, Mexican American Public Policy Studies, and Introduction to American Government. In the spring of 2019, he taught British Politics and Government, which had the good fortune (if that is the right word) of taking place parallel with so many Brexit developments. He is also the author of three articles in *The Baker Street Journal* as well as letters to the editor of the *TLS: The Times Literary Supplement*, *Sherlock Holmes Journal*, and *The Baker Street Journal*. As a member of the British Studies Program at UT-Austin, he has given several talks on Sherlockian and Wodehousian topics. He most recently wrote a chapter, "Arthur Conan Doyle and Spiritualism," for the program's latest book in its *Adventures with Britannia* series (Harry Ransom Center/IB Tauris/Bloomsbury). He is the founder and Warden of "MA, PhD, Etc," the BSI professional scion society for higher education, and he is a member of *The Fourth Garrideb*, *The Sherlock Holmes Society of London*, *The Clients of Adrian Mulliner*, and *His Last Bow (Tie)*.

Gordon Linzner is founder and former editor of *Space and Time Magazine*, and author of three published novels and dozens of short stories in *F&SF*, *Twilight Zone*, *Sherlock*

Holmes Mystery Magazine, and numerous other magazines and anthologies, including *Baker Street Irregulars II*, *Across the Universe*, and *Strange Lands*. He is a member of *HWA* and a lifetime member of *SFWA*.

David Marcum *also has stories in Parts XXXIV and XXXVI*

John McNabb is a Welshman and an archaeologist, and a proud member of *The Sherlock Holmes Society of London*. He has published academic analysis of aspects of Conan Doyle's work, as well as its broader context. Mac also has a long-standing interest in Victorian and Edwardian scientific romances and the portrayal of human origins in early science fiction.

Will Murray has built a career on writing classic pulp characters, ranging from Tarzan of the Apes to Doc Savage. He has penned several milestone crossover novels in his acclaimed Wild Adventures series. *Skull Island* pitted Doc Savage against King Kong, which was followed by *King Kong Vs. Tarzan*. *Tarzan, Conqueror of Mars* costarred John Carter of Mars. His 2015 Doc Savage novel, *The Sinister Shadow*, revived the famous radio and pulp mystery man. Murray reunited them for *Empire of Doom*. His first Spider novel, *The Doom Legion*, revived that infamous crime buster, as well as James Christopher, AKA Operator 5, and the renowned G-8. His second *Spider, Fury in Steel*, guest-stars the FBI's Suicide Squad. Ten of his Sherlock Holmes short stories have been collected as *The Wild Adventures of Sherlock Holmes*. He is the author of the non-fiction book, *Master of Mystery: The Rise of The Shadow*. For Marvel Comics, Murray created the Unbeatable Squirrel Girl. Website: *www.adventuresinbronze.com*

Tracy J. Revels *also has stories in Parts XXXIV and XXXVI*

Roger Riccard's family history has Scottish roots, which trace his lineage back to Highland Scotland. This British Isles ancestry encouraged his interest in the writings of Sir Arthur Conan Doyle at an early age. He has authored the novels, *Sherlock Holmes & The Case of the Poisoned Lilly*, and *Sherlock Holmes & The Case of the Twain Papers*. In addition he has produced several short stories in *Sherlock Holmes Adventures for the Twelve Days of Christmas* and the series *A Sherlock Holmes Alphabet of Cases*. A new series will begin publishing in the Autumn of 2022, and his has another novel in the works. All of his books have been published by Baker Street Studios. His Bachelor of Arts Degrees in both Journalism and History from California State University, Northridge, have proven valuable to his writing historical fiction, as well as the encouragement of his wife/editor/inspiration and Sherlock Holmes fan, Rosilyn. She passed in 2021, and it is in her memory that he continues to contribute to the legacy of the "*man who never lived and will never die*".

Dan Rowley *also has stories in Parts XXXIV and XXXVI*

Alisha Shea has resided near Saint Louis, Missouri for over thirty years. The eldest of six children, she found reading to be a genuine escape from the chaotic drudgery of life. She grew to love not only Sherlock Holmes, but the time period from which he emerged. In her spare time, she indulges in creating music via piano, violin, and Native American flute. Sometimes she thinks she might even be getting good at it. She also produces a wide variety of fiber arts which are typically given away or auctioned off for various fundraisers.

Liese Sherwood-Fabre knew she was destined to write when she got an A+ in the second grade for her story about Dick, Jane, and Sally's ruined picnic. After obtaining her PhD, she joined the federal government and worked and lived internationally for more than fifteen years. Returning to the states, she seriously pursued her writing career, garnering such awards as a finalist in the Romance Writers of America's Golden Heart contest and a Pushcart Prize nomination. A recognized Sherlockian scholar, her essays have appeared in newsletters, *The Baker Street Journal*, and *Canadian Holmes*. She has recently turned to a childhood passion: Sherlock Holmes. *The Adventure of the Murdered Midwife*, the first book in *The Early Case Files of Sherlock Holmes* series, was the CIBA Mystery and Mayhem 2020 first-place winner. *Publishers Weekly* has described her fourth book in the series, *The Adventure of the Purloined Portrait*, as "*a truly unique, atmospheric tale that is Sherlockian through and through.*" More about her writing can be found at *www.liesesherwoodfabre.com.*

Award winning poet and author **Joseph W. Svec III** enjoys writing, poetry, and stories, and creating new adventures for Holmes and Watson that take them into the worlds of famous literary authors and scientists. His *Missing Authors* trilogy introduced Holmes to Lewis Carroll, Jules Verne, H.G. Wells, and Alfred Lord Tennyson, as well as many of their characters. His transitional story *Sherlock Holmes and the Mystery of the First Unicorn* involved several historical figures, besides a Unicorn or two. He has also written the rhymed and metered Sherlock Holmes Christmas adventure, *The Night Before Christmas in 221b*, sure to be a delight for Sherlock Holmes enthusiasts of all ages. Joseph won the Amador Arts Council 2021 Original Poetry Contest, with his Rhymed and metered story poem, "The Homecoming". Joseph has presented a literary paper on Sherlock Holmes/Alice in Wonderland crossover literature to the Lewis Carroll Society of North America, as well as given several presentations to the Amador County Holmes Hounds, Sherlockian Society. He is currently working on his first book in the *Missing Scientist Trilogy, Sherlock Holmes and the Adventure of the Demonstrative Dinosaur*, in which Sherlock meets Professor George Edward Challenger. Joseph has Masters Degrees in Systems Engineering and Human Organization Management, and has written numerous technical papers on Aerospace Testing. In addition to writing, Joseph enjoys creating miniature dioramas based on music, literature, and history from many different eras. His dioramas have been featured in magazine articles and many different blogs, including the North American Jules Verne society newsletter. He currently has 57 dioramas set up in his display area, and has written a reference book on toy castles and knights from around the world. An avid tea enthusiast, his tea cabinet contains over 500 different varieties, and he delights in sharing afternoon tea with his childhood sweetheart and wonderful wife, who has inspired and coauthored several books with him.

Tim Symonds was born in London. He grew up in the rural English counties of Somerset and Dorset, and the British Crown Dependency of Guernsey. After several years travelling widely, including farming on the slopes of Mt. Kenya in East Africa and working on the Zambezi River in Central Africa, he emigrated to Canada and the United States. He studied at the Georg-August University (Göttingen) in Germany, and the University of California, Los Angeles, graduating *cum laude* and Phi Beta Kappa. He is a Fellow of the Royal Geographical Society and a Member of The Society of Authors. His detective novels include *Sherlock Holmes And The Dead Boer At Scotney Castle, Sherlock Holmes And The Mystery Of Einstein's Daughter, Sherlock Holmes And The Case Of The Bulgarian Codex, Sherlock Holmes And The Sword Of Osman, Sherlock Holmes And The Nine-Dragon Sigil,* six Holmes and Watson short stories under the title *A Most Diabolical Plot*, and his novella *Sherlock Holmes and the Strange Death of Brigadier-General Delves.*

William Todd has been a Holmes fan his entire life, and credits *The Hound of the Baskervilles* as the impetus for his love of both reading and writing. He began to delve into fan fiction a few years ago when he decided to take a break from writing his usual Victorian/Gothic horror stories. He was surprised how well-received they were, and has tried to put out a couple of Holmes stories a year since then. When not writing, Mr. Todd is a pathology supervisor at a local hospital in Northwestern Pennsylvania. He is the husband of a terrific lady and father to two great kids, one with special needs, so the benefactor of these anthologies is close to his heart.

DJ Tyrer dwells on the northern shore of the Thames estuary, close to the world's longest pleasure pier in the decaying seaside resort of Southend-on-Sea, and is the person behind Atlantean Publishing. They studied history at the University of Wales at Aberystwyth and have worked in the fields of education and public relations. Their fiction featuring Sherlock Holmes has appeared in volumes from MX Publishing and Belanger Books, and in an issue of *Awesome Tales*, and they have a forthcoming story in *Sherlock Holmes Mystery Magazine*. DJ's non-Sherlockian mysteries have appeared in anthologies such as *Mardi Gras Mysteries* (Mystery and Horror LLC) and *The Trench Coat Chronicles* (Celestial Echo Press).
DJ Tyrer's website is at *https://djtyrer.blogspot.co.uk/*
DJ's Facebook page is at *https://www.facebook.com/DJTyrerwriter/*
The Atlantean Publishing website is at *https://atlanteanpublishing.wordpress.com/*

Margaret Walsh *also has stories in Part XXXVI.*

Marcia Wilson is a freelance researcher and illustrator who likes to work in a style compatible for the color blind and visually impaired. She is Canon-centric, and her first MX offering, *You Buy Bones*, uses the point-of-view of Scotland Yard to show the unique talents of Dr. Watson. This continued with the publication of *Test of the Professionals: The Adventure of the Flying Blue Pidgeon* and *The Peaceful Night Poisonings*. She can be contacted at: *gravelgirty.deviantart.com*

The MX Book of New Sherlock Holmes Stories
Edited by David Marcum
(MX Publishing, 2015-   )

"This is the finest volume of Sherlockian fiction I have ever read, and I have read, literally, thousands." – Philip K. Jones

"Beyond Impressive . . . This is a splendid venture for a great cause!
– Roger Johnson, Editor, *The Sherlock Holmes Journal,*
The Sherlock Holmes Society of London

Part I: 1881-1889
Part II: 1890-1895
Part III: 1896-1929
Part IV: 2016 Annual
Part V: Christmas Adventures
Part VI: 2017 Annual
Part VII: Eliminate the Impossible (1880-1891)
Part VIII – Eliminate the Impossible (1892-1905)
Part IX – 2018 Annual (1879-1895)
Part X – 2018 Annual (1896-1916)
Part XI – Some Untold Cases (1880-1891)
Part XII – Some Untold Cases (1894-1902)
Part XIII – 2019 Annual (1881-1890)
Part XIV – 2019 Annual (1891-1897)
Part XV – 2019 Annual (1898-1917)
Part XVI – Whatever Remains . . . Must be the Truth (1881-1890)
Part XVII – Whatever Remains . . . Must be the Truth (1891-1898)
Part XVIII – Whatever Remains . . . Must be the Truth (1898-1925)
Part XIX – 2020 Annual (1882-1890)
Part XX – 2020 Annual (1891-1897)
Part XXI – 2020 Annual (1898-1923)
Part XXII – Some More Untold Cases (1877-1887)
Part XXIII – Some More Untold Cases (1888-1894)
Part XXIV – Some More Untold Cases (1895-1903)
Part XXV – 2021 Annual (1881-1888)
Part XXVI – 2021 Annual (1889-1897)
Part XXVII – 2021 Annual (1898-1928)
Part XXVIII – More Christmas Adventures (1869-1888)
Part XXIX – More Christmas Adventures (1889-1896)
Part XXX – More Christmas Adventures (1897-1928)
Part XXXI – 2022 Annual Part (1875-1887)
XXXII – 2022 Annual (1888-1895)
Part XXXIII – 2022 Annual (1896-1919)
Part XXXIV "However Improbable . . . ." (1878-1888)
Part XXXV "However Improbable . . . ." (1889-1896)
Part XXXVI "However Improbable . . . ." (1897-1919)

In Preparation
Part XXXVI (and XXXVIII and XXXIX???) – 2023 Annual
. . . and more to come!

487

The MX Book of New Sherlock Holmes Stories
Edited by David Marcum
(MX Publishing, 2015-   )

Publishers Weekly says:

Part VI: *The traditional pastiche is alive and well . . . .*

Part VII: *Sherlockians eager for faithful-to-the-canon plots and characters will be delighted.*

Part VIII: *The imagination of the contributors in coming up with variations on the volume's theme is matched by their ingenious resolutions.*

Part IX: *The 18 stories . . . will satisfy fans of Conan Doyle's originals. Sherlockians will rejoice that more volumes are on the way.*

Part X: *. . . new Sherlock Holmes adventures of consistently high quality.*

Part XI: *. . . an essential volume for Sherlock Holmes fans.*

Part XII: *. . . continues to amaze with the number of high-quality pastiches.*

Part XIII: *. . . Amazingly, Marcum has found 22 superb pastiches . . . This is more catnip for fans of stories faithful to Conan Doyle's original*

Part XIV: *. . . this standout anthology of 21 short stories written in the spirit of Conan Doyle's originals.*

Part XV: *Stories pitting Sherlock Holmes against seemingly supernatural phenomena highlight Marcum's 15th anthology of superior short pastiches.*

Part XVI: *Marcum has once again done fans of Conan Doyle's originals a service.*

Part XVII: *This is yet another impressive array of new but traditional Holmes stories.*

Part XVIII: *Sherlockians will again be grateful to Marcum and MX for high-quality new Holmes tales.*

Part XIX: *Inventive plots and intriguing explorations of aspects of Dr. Watson's life and beliefs lift the 24 pastiches in Marcum's impressive 19th Sherlock Holmes anthology*

Part XX: *Marcum's reserve of high-quality new Holmes exploits seems endless.*

Part XXI: *This is another must-have for Sherlockians.*

Part XXII: *Marcum's superlative 22nd Sherlock Holmes pastiche anthology features 21 short stories that successfully emulate the spirit of Conan Doyle's originals while expanding on the canon's tantalizing references to mysteries Dr. Watson never got around to chronicling.*

Part XXIII: *Marcum's well of talented authors able to mimic the feel of The Canon seems bottomless.*

Part XXIV: *Marcum's expertise at selecting high-quality pastiches remains impressive.*

Part XXVIII: *All entries adhere to the spirit, language, and characterizations of Conan Doyle's originals, evincing the deep pool of talent Marcum has access to. Against the odds, this series remains strong, hundreds of stories in.*

Part XXXI: *. . . yet another stellar anthology of 21 short pastiches that effectively mimic the originals . . . Marcum's diligent searches for high-quality stories has again paid off for Sherlockians.*

The MX Book of New Sherlock Holmes Stories
Edited by David Marcum
(MX Publishing, 2015-   )

MX Publishing

MX Publishing is the world's largest specialist Sherlock Holmes publisher, with over five-hundred titles and over two-hundred authors creating the latest in Sherlock Holmes fiction and non-fiction

The catalogue includes several award winning books, and over two-hundred-and-fifty have been converted into audio.

MX Publishing also has one of the largest communities of Holmes fans on Facebook, with regular contributions from dozens of authors.

www.mxpublishing.com

@mxpublishing on Facebook, Twitter, and Instagram

Lightning Source UK Ltd.
Milton Keynes UK
UKHW040615111122
411925UK00003B/29/J